Mother's Day Collection 2026

MOTHER'S DAY COLLECTION 2026 © 2026 by Harlequin Books S.A.

Carol Marinelli is acknowledged as the author of this work
THEIR ONE NIGHT BABY
© 2017 by Harlequin Books S.A. First Published 2017
Australian Copyright 2017 Second Australian Paperback Edition 2026
New Zealand Copyright 2017 ISBN 978 1 038 97473 0

Teresa Southwick is acknowledged as the author of this work

THE COWBOY'S PROMISE
© 2020 by Harlequin Books S.A. First Published 2020
Australian Copyright 2020 Second Australian Paperback Edition 2026
New Zealand Copyright 2020 ISBN 978 1 038 97473 0

HER NOT-SO-LITTLE SECRET
© 2023 by Brenda Harlen First Published 2023
Australian Copyright 2023 First Australian Paperback Edition 2026
New Zealand Copyright 2023 ISBN 978 1 038 97473 0

RACHEL'S BUNDLE OF JOY
© 2004 by Christine Rimmer First Published 2004
Australian Copyright 2004 Third Australian Paperback Edition 2026
New Zealand Copyright 2004 ISBN 978 1 038 97473 0

Except for use in any review, the reproduction or utilisation of this work in whole or in part in any form by any electronic, mechanical or other means, now known or hereafter invented, including xerography, photocopying and recording, or in any information storage or retrieval system, is forbidden without the permission of the publisher.

This book is sold subject to the condition that it shall not, by way of trade or otherwise, be lent, resold, hired out or otherwise circulated without the prior consent of the publisher in any form of binding or cover other than that in which it is published and without a similar condition including this condition being imposed on the subsequent purchaser.

All rights reserved including the right of reproduction in whole or in part in any form. This edition is published in arrangement with Harlequin Books S.A. Cover art used by arrangement with Harlequin Books S.A. All rights reserved.

This is a work of fiction. Names, characters, places, and incidents are either the product of the author's imagination or are used fictitiously, and any resemblance to actual persons, living or dead, business establishments, events, or locales is entirely coincidental.

Published by
Mills & Boon
An imprint of Harlequin Enterprises (Australia) Pty Limited
(ABN 47 001 180 918), a subsidiary of HarperCollins
Publishers Australia Pty Limited (ABN 36 009 913 517)
Level 19, 201 Elizabeth Street
SYDNEY NSW 2000
AUSTRALIA

MIX
Paper | Supporting responsible forestry
FSC® C001695
www.fsc.org

® and ™ (apart from those relating to FSC®) are trademarks of Harlequin Enterprises (Australia) Pty Limited or its corporate affiliates. Trademarks indicated with ® are registered in Australia, New Zealand and in other countries.
Contact admin_legal@Harlequin.ca for details.

Printed and bound in Australia by McPherson's Printing Group

Mother's Day Collection 2026

Carol Marinelli   Teresa Southwick   Brenda Harlen   Christine Rimmer

MILLS & BOON

CONTENTS

THEIR ONE NIGHT BABY 7
Carol Marinelli

THE COWBOY'S PROMISE 159
Teresa Southwick

HER NOT-SO-LITTLE SECRET 347
Brenda Harlen

RACHEL'S BUNDLE OF JOY 577
Christine Rimmer

Their One Night Baby

Carol Marinelli

MEDICAL
Pulse-racing passion

Books by Carol Marinelli

Harlequin Medical

Desert Prince Docs
Seduced by the Sheikh Surgeon

The Hollywood Hills Clinic
Seduced by the Heart Surgeon

Playboy on Her Christmas List
Their Secret Royal Baby

Harlequin Modern

The Sheikh's Baby Scandal
The Innocent's Secret Baby

Visit the Author Profile page
at millsandboon.com.au
for more titles.

Dear Reader,

I thoroughly enjoyed writing the opening book for the Paddington Children's Hospital continuity series. The stories are set in a busy London hospital, and it was wonderful to work with other authors and to see all the characters come to life.

Though the book is set in London, my hero, Dominic, hails from Edinburgh, which happens to be one of my favorite places in the world. As well as its stunning architecture and history, the accent of its residents makes my toes curl. This summer I was lucky enough to spend some time in Scotland and made a little side trip to Edinburgh with my sister. She accused me of spending a lot of the time daydreaming, and of course I did—I didn't tell her that I was actually rather hoping to run into Dominic.

I hope he makes your toes curl, too!

Happy reading,

x

Praise for
Carol Marinelli

"It had me in tears at the beginning, and then again at the end, and I could hardly put it down. A brilliant emotional read by Carol Marinelli!"
—*Goodreads* on
The Baby of Their Dreams

CHAPTER ONE

'HELLO, BEAUTIFUL!'

Victoria's smile was friendly as she walked into the lounge ahead of Glen, to where little Penelope Craig, or Penny, as she liked to be known, lay on the sofa. Victoria had already had a conversation with Julia, Penny's mother, in the hallway.

Usually, two paramedics dressed in green overalls entering a home would be a somewhat nerve-racking sight for a six-year-old, but little Penny was more than used to it.

'Victoria!'

Even though she was unwell, little Penny sat up a touch on the sofa where she lay, and her huge grey eyes widened in delight. She was clearly pleased that it was her favourite paramedic who was here to take her to Paddington Children's Hospital, or the Castle as it was more generally known.

'She hoped that it would be you coming to take her,' Julia said.

Victoria gave a friendly smile to Julia and then went to sit on the edge of the sofa to chat to her patient. 'Yes, I was just thinking the other day that I haven't seen you in a while.'

'She's been doing really well,' Julia said.

There was a three-way conversation going on as Victoria gleaned some history from Julia and also checked Penny.

Penelope Craig had been born with a rare congenital heart

condition and had spent a lot of her life as a patient at the Castle, but for a while she had been doing well. Her dark hair was tied in braids and she was wearing pyjamas. Over the top of them was a little pink tutu that she wore all the time.

Penny was going to be a ballet dancer one day.

She told that to everyone.

'Your mum said that you've not been feeling very well today?' Victoria said as she checked Penny's pulse.

'I'm nauseous and febrile.'

Whereas most children would say that they felt sick and hot, Penny had spent so much time in medical settings that she knew more than a six-year-old should.

She was indeed febrile and her little heart was beating rapidly when Victoria checked her vital signs.

'She's being admitted straight to the cardiac unit,' Julia said as Victoria checked Penny over. It wasn't an urgent transfer but, given Penny's history, a Mobile Intensive Care Unit had been sent and Victoria was thorough in her assessment.

'Though,' Julia added, 'they want her to have a chest X-ray first in A&E.'

Which might prove a problem.

Accident and Emergency departments didn't like to be used as an admissions hub, though it was a problem Victoria dealt with regularly. In fact, just three days ago she had had an argument with Dominic MacBride, a paediatric trauma surgeon, about the very same thing.

Victoria just hoped he wasn't in A&E this evening, as they tended to clash whenever she brought a patient in.

Generally though, things were better at Paddington's than at most hospitals. The staff were very friendly and there was real communication between departments.

And also, Penny was a little bit of a star!

They'd just have to see how it went.

'I like your earrings,' Penny said when Victoria had finished taking her blood pressure.

'Thank you.'

Usually Victoria wore no jewellery at work. It was impractical, given that she never knew what her day might entail. Her long dark brown hair was tied up in its usual messy bun and, of course, she wore no make-up for work. So yes, her diamond studs stood out a touch.

The earrings had been a gift from her father and Victoria wore them for special occasions. She had been at a function yesterday and had forgotten to take them out.

Penny was ready to be transferred to the hospital. For such a little child, often Glen or Victoria would carry them out, the goal being not to upset them. Once though, Victoria had referred to the stretcher as a throne and Penny, who loved anything to do with fairytales, had decided that she rather liked it.

Penny insisted on moving onto the stretcher herself and Julia took a moment to check that she had all of Penny's favourite things to bring along. They were very used to a 'quick trip' to Paddington's turning into a longer stay.

'Ready for the off?' Victoria asked, and Penny gave her regular thumbs up.

Spring was a little way off just yet, and so even though it was only early in the evening, it was dark outside.

'Are you just starting or finishing?' Julia asked as Victoria took her seat in the back of the ambulance with them.

'Just finishing,' Victoria said.

'Have you got anything planned for tonight?'

'Not really,' Victoria answered, and turned her focus to Penny.

In fact, Victoria was going out on a date.

A second one.

And she was wondering why she'd agreed to it when the first hadn't been particularly great.

Oh, that's right, she and Glen had been chatting and he had suggested that she expected too much from a first date.

Not that she said any of this to Julia.

Victoria gave nothing away.

She was very discerning in her dealings with people. She was confident yet approachable, friendly but not too much.

The patients didn't mind; in fact, they liked her professionalism.

Socially, she did well, though tended to let others talk about themselves.

Victoria relied on no one.

She and Glen had worked together for two years and it had taken a long time for Victoria to discuss her private life even a little with him. Glen was a family man, with a big moon face that smiled rather than took offence at Victoria's sometimes brusque ways, and he loved to talk. He was happily married to Hayley and they had four hundred children.

Well, four.

But while Glen chatted away about his wife and children and the little details of his day, Victoria didn't. Certainly she wasn't going to open up to her patient's mother about her love-life.

Or lack of it.

Julia, as she often did, told Penny a story as the ambulance made its way through the Friday rush hour traffic. They weren't using lights and sirens; there was no need to, and Penny was too used to them to want the drama.

'I think it looks like a magical castle,' Penny said as Paddington Children's Hospital came into view.

The Victorian redbrick building was turreted and Victoria found herself smiling at Penny's description.

She had thought the same when she was growing up.

Victoria could remember sitting in the back seat of her father's car as he dashed to get to whatever urgent matter was waiting for him at work.

'That's because it *is* a magical castle,' Victoria said, and Penny smiled.

'It's her second home,' Julia said.

It had been Victoria's second home too.

She knew every corridor and nook. The turret that Penny was gazing at could be accessed from a door behind the patient files in Reception, and had once been Victoria's favourite space.

She would sneak in when no one was looking and climb up the spiral stairs and there she would dance, or dream, or simply play pretend.

On occasion she still did.

Well, no longer did she play pretend, but every now and then

Victoria would slip away unnoticed and look out to the view of London that she somehow felt was her own.

'Such a shame they're closing it down.' Julia sighed.

'It's not definite,' Victoria said, though not with conviction. It looked as if the plan to merge Paddington's with Riverside, a large modern hospital on the outskirts of the city, would be going ahead.

There was a quiet protest taking place outside, which had been going for a few days now, with protestors waving their placards to save the hospital.

Victoria's father now worked at Riverside. The only real conversations she had ever had with him were about work. The function she had attended yesterday had been for an award for him, and in a conversation afterwards Victoria had gleaned that it really did seem the merger was going to go ahead.

Of course, the beautiful old Paddington's building was prime real estate.

As always, it came down to money.

'I don't want it to close,' Penny said as they pulled up under the bright lights of the ambulance bay outside Accident and Emergency. 'I feel safe here.'

And Penny's words seemed to twist something inside Victoria.

That was how she had felt as a child whenever she was left here.

Yes, left.

Her father's quick check-in at work often turned into hours but, though alone, and though lonely, here Victoria had always felt safe.

'I don't want it to close,' Penny said again.

'I know that you don't.' Victoria nodded. 'But Riverside is a gorgeous hospital and the staff there are lovely too.'

'It's not the same.' Penny shook her head and there were tears in her grey eyes.

'You don't have to worry about all that now,' Victoria soothed. 'It might not happen.'

She wished she could say it probably wouldn't but it was looking more and more likely with each passing day.

And it mattered.

'Penny!' Karen, a charge nurse, recognised Penny straight away. 'You didn't come all this way just to see me, I hope!'

'No.' Penny gave a little laugh, but just as Victoria went to hand over, Karen was urgently summoned.

'It's fine—we can wait.' Victoria nodded.

They stood in the corridor and made sure that Penny was okay, while Glen chatted with her mother and Victoria started to fill out the required paperwork.

He was there.

She knew it.

And although they clashed, although she had told herself that she hoped he wouldn't be there this evening, Victoria had lied.

She wanted to see him.

Dominic MacBride had been working at Paddington's for a few months.

He was from Edinburgh and that low Scottish brogue had Victoria's toes curl in her heavy boots. Or was it his blue eyes and tousled black hair?

Or was it just him?

She couldn't quite place why she liked Dominic so much. He was crabby with the paramedics and he and Victoria tended to clash.

A lot!

And he was making his way over.

'Here we go,' Glen said under his breath, referring to the argument that Dominic and Victoria had had three days ago.

Victoria was very confident in all her dealings and her assertion seemed to rub Dominic up the wrong way.

He made his way straight over.

'Are you being seen to?' he checked.

'Yes, thanks,' Victoria said. 'Karen's taking care of us. She'll be back shortly.'

Victoria got back to filling in the patient report form but, just as she did, Julia chimed up.

'She's a direct admission but she's just going to have a quick chest X-ray before she goes to the ward.'

'I see.' Dominic nodded and then he came over to where

Victoria stood. She could feel him in her space and that he was requiring her attention but she carried on writing her notes, refusing to look up.

His scent was subtle, soapy, musky and male and the faint traces cut through the more familiar hospital scent.

And still she did not look up.

'Could I have a word, please?' he asked.

And now Victoria looked up, quite a long way, in fact, because he was very tall and broad.

He was wearing dark navy scrubs and he needed a shave. He looked as if he had either rolled out of bed or should be about to roll into one and she did her best to stop her thought process there.

'Sure,' Victoria said. She was about to be churlish and add, *In a moment*, and then take said moment to finish her report, but instead she moved away from the stretcher and followed him into a small annexe.

He leant against a sink and she stood in front of him, not quite to attention but she was very ready to walk off.

'Can you not see how busy we are?' Dominic said. 'We don't have time to do the wards' work as well.'

'I don't make the rules.'

'You know them though and your patient is a direct admission,' Dominic said. 'If she goes up to the ward she can wait in a comfortable bed.'

Victoria said nothing.

They both knew the unofficial consensus was that Penny would be pushed to the front of the X-ray list, just so she could quickly be moved up to the ward.

The annexe was very small.

Dominic was not.

He was tall and broad and his eyes demanded that she look at him; Victoria rose to the challenge and met his angry glare as he spoke.

'I've just come from explaining to a father that there's a three-hour wait for an X-ray. Your arrival has just added to that load.'

'So what would you like me to do?' Victoria asked.

She just threw it back at him because, despite the comfortable bed that Penny would have on the ward, once there she would be shuffled to the bottom of the X-ray pile. It could well be midnight before she was brought down to the Imaging Department.

'It's not just a matter of filling in an X-ray request,' Dominic said. 'She should be examined before she goes around. If anything happens to her without her being seen—'

'So,' Victoria calmly interrupted, 'what would you like me to do?'

She did not engage in small talk; she was confident and assertive and refused to row.

'There you are.' Karen came into the annexe. 'Cubicle four has opened up if you'd like to bring Penny through.'

She and Dominic stared at each other.

The choice was his.

'Fine,' he eventually said, and Karen nodded and went back to Penny.

'Next time...' Dominic warned, but Victoria just shrugged and walked off.

'Victoria!'

She halted.

There was an angry edge to his voice, but that wasn't what stopped her—she didn't think he even knew her name, so his use of it surprised her.

'Don't just shrug and walk off when I'm trying to have a conversation.'

'A pointless one,' Victoria said as she turned around. 'In fact, we had the same conversation three days ago.'

His mood had been just as bloody then and she watched as his eyes shuttered for a moment.

'As I said then, I just go where I'm told and deal with the inevitable angry consequence—I get your ire if I bring the patient here, or the ire of the ward if they arrive without the X-ray.'

She went to walk off, but this time it was Victoria who changed her mind and continued the conversation.

'Sometimes it's made easy though and the staff get that I'm just doing my job. That's generally the case at Paddington's, though I guess it just depends who's on. I have to go and move my patient and then I'm out of here. Which is just as well...'

And then she crossed the line.

For the first time she made it personal. 'Your misery is catching.'

Dominic watched as she swished out of the annexe and he let out a long breath.

They were both right.

There were limited resources and the staff all fought for the charges in their care.

She had rattled him though, not just with her little sign-off comment, but the reminder that they had had this conversation three days ago.

It was a difficult time for Dominic and he was self-aware enough to know he had been less than sunny on that day as well.

And he knew why.

Dominic had always been serious and a bit aloof but he loathed that, of late—Victoria was right—he was miserable.

Not to the patients though.

He shoved his messy personal life aside there.

And then from outside he heard laughter.

Victoria's.

He came out of the annexe and there she was making up the stretcher with her colleague.

'Victoria.'

She turned around. 'Yes.'

'Could I have a word?'

She rolled her eyes but came over. 'Are we really going to do this again?'

'No, I wanted to apologise for earlier.'

'It's fine.'

She didn't need it.

In Victoria's line of work, a small stand-off with a doctor barely merited a thought and she was trying to keep it at that.

But this was a genuine apology and he offered her a small explanation.

'Today's a tough one.'

He offered no more insight but Victoria knew she was hearing the truth.

'Then I hope it gets better,' Victoria said.

'It shan't.'

She gave him a smile and Dominic knew he had lied because it already had got a bit better.

Victoria was stunning.

She was wearing green overalls and heavy black boots and it should have been impossible to look stunning in those, yet she did. Her hair was worn on the top of her head but glossy waves tumbled over her face and her hazel eyes held his.

Yes, she was stunning.

And that was why she annoyed him.

Dominic was not looking to be stunned.

His personal life was very messy and, furthermore, Victoria was far from his type.

She was very direct and he usually liked subtle. He liked women who, well, stayed a bit in the background and didn't demand too much headspace.

And lately Victoria was starting to command a lot of his thoughts.

'I'm sorry too,' she said. 'That bit about you being a misery… well…' She couldn't resist a little play. 'I meant crabby.'

He got her little joke and smiled.

It was not the smile he gave to the patients, because they did not have to fight not to blush, as Victoria was doing. This smile felt as if it had been exclusively designed for her and he was holding her gaze as she completed her apology. 'I went a bit far.'

'That's okay.'

And suddenly things could not go far enough.

There was no way he was going to move things along.

Dominic had a hell of a lot to sort out before he should even consider that.

But…

'I'd offer to apologise properly over a drink but in my current mood I wouldn't foist myself on anyone.'

Foist.

That word made her smile.

First, for the way he said it—his accent was light but very appealing.

And second, because there would be no foisting required.

He was gorgeous, sexy, rugged and, yes, she fancied him like hell. He was older than she usually liked; but then again, Victoria liked few.

She guessed him to be late thirties and she was twenty-nine. He made her feel like a teenager though.

Dominic made her want to blush, but she steadfastly refused to.

And they kept staring.

'It's fine,' she said again, and then the communication radio on her shoulder started cracking and there was suddenly another voice in the room.

'Victoria!' Glen called, and he must have picked up on the tension as he walked by because he paused.

Thankfully Glen seemed to miss that the tension was of the sexual kind.

'Is everything okay?' he checked.

'Everything's fine,' Dominic said, and walked off.

And everything *was* fine now that he was out away from her gaze. Dominic had been very close to asking her out and now he wanted her gone.

It was that simple.

He did not want anyone closer.

But that did not mean he did not want.

CHAPTER TWO

DOMINIC PICKED UP the patient card and went to check on the new patient before she went down to X-ray.

He was a trauma surgeon and so he found himself working in Accident and Emergency a lot and often pitched in.

'Hey,' he said as he went into the cubicle where the little girl had been placed. 'Penelope, I'm Dominic.'

'Penny,' she confidently corrected him. 'And you're new here.'

'I've been here for nearly six months now.'

'Penny hasn't been an inpatient for ages,' Julia said. 'We've had a good run.'

'Well, that's good to hear.'

The little girl's medical notes were so extensive he could be there till midnight if he read them, but Dominic had caught up on the vitals and Julia was very well versed in her daughter's health.

Penelope Craig had hypoplastic left heart syndrome, or HLHS, a rare congenital defect. She had had surgery as a baby and all her life she had been either an inpatient or outpatient at Paddington's. She had presented a few times with infections and that was the concern now.

Examining Penny, Dominic saw that just from the minor exertion of sitting forward she became breathless and the slight blue tinge to her lips darkened.

And of course, as Victoria would have well known, it wasn't just a chest X-ray that was required.

Dominic took some bloods as a baseline. Penny would require a nurse escort if she went out of the department for her X-ray. But it wasn't to keep staff levels up that had Dominic call for a portable chest X-ray—he was concerned enough that she was really rather unwell.

And so he paged the on-call cardiologist and asked him to come down and see Penny here rather than waiting until she was on the ward.

It was a locum that he spoke to.

Again.

With the prospect of Paddington's closing down, a lot of the regular staff had gone elsewhere and it was proving difficult to attract new staff when no one really knew if the hospital would even be here next year.

Having spoken to the locum, Dominic went back into cubicle four to inform patient and parent of the new plan.

'Look what Penny just found,' Julia said as Penny lay there holding up an earring.

Dominic didn't need to be told whose it was; he had already noticed that Victoria had been wearing earrings this evening when usually she did not.

He noticed rather too many details about Victoria.

And even her earrings had intrigued him. They were large diamonds, and during their discussions he had been trying very hard not to picture Victoria dressed up to go out.

'It's Victoria's earring,' Penny said to Karen as she came in.

'There it is.' She smiled. 'I've just had a call from Victoria to ask me to look out for it. You've saved me a job. Good girl, Penny. I'll put it in the safe. Oh, and, Dominic, there's a phone call for you.'

'Take a message, please.'

'It's your father,' Karen said. 'And he says that it's important.'

'Thank you.'

Deliberately Dominic left his mobile phone in his locker at

the start of each shift. He did not want his private life intruding on work.

Yet it was about to.

This call was, in fact, three days overdue.

Yes, there was a reason he hadn't been sunny on that day.

The receiver had been left lying on the bench and Dominic hesitated. He let out the tense breath that he was holding on to. He had had months to prepare for this moment and had examined it from many angles, but even as he picked up the receiver, still he hadn't worked out what he would say.

'Hello.' His voice was as abrupt as it had been with Victoria.

'Dominic...' William MacBride cleared his throat before speaking on. 'I'm just calling to let you know that as of an hour ago you're an uncle.'

And still, even with the baby three days overdue, Dominic did not know what to say.

'Dominic?' William prompted.

'Are they well?'

'They're both doing fine.'

Dominic knew that he should ask what Lorna and Jamie had had and whether or not he had a niece or nephew.

He looked out to the busy Emergency Department, and given it was a children's hospital, of course there were children everywhere. There was Penny, being wheeled over to rhesus for her portable X-ray and in the background there was the sound of babies crying.

Dominic fought daily to save these precious little lives and so, naturally, he should be relieved to hear that mother and baby were well and doing fine.

And somewhere he was.

Yet it was buried deep in a mire of anger and grief, because for a while there he had thought that the baby born today was going to be his.

Dominic tried his best not to recall that first moment of truth—when he had realised the baby that his long-term girlfriend was carrying could not possibly be his.

But then his father spoke of the brother who had caused the second painful moment of truth.

'Jamie's thrilled.'

Dominic held in a derisive snort.

What had taken place wasn't his father's fault. Dominic knew that his parents simply did not know how to handle this.

Who would?

'Will you speak to your brother?'

'I've nothing to say to him.'

A year ago it would have been unfathomable that on the day Jamie became a father Dominic would have nothing to say.

They had always been close.

Dominic had been five when a much wanted second child had been born. Jamie was spoiled and cheeky and always getting himself into trouble, but the rather more serious Dominic had always looked out for him.

Or he had tried to.

Jamie had been run over when he was ten and Dominic was fifteen.

It hadn't been the driver's fault. Jamie simply hadn't looked and had stepped out onto the street and on that occasion Dominic had been too late to haul him back.

It had felt like for ever until the ambulance arrived, and then Dominic had watched the paramedics fight to save his brother's life. Later, at the hospital, as his parents cried and paced, Dominic had gone to try and find out some more. The doors to Resuscitation had opened to let some equipment in and he had seen the medical team in action, doing all that they could to save Jamie.

He had been steered away and sent back to the waiting area but on that terrible day Dominic had decided on his future career.

Jamie had survived and Dominic had really pushed himself to make the grades and get in to study medicine.

Family had been everything to Dominic—right up until the day he had found out that his girlfriend had been cheating on him with his brother, and that the baby Dominic had thought was his had been fathered by Jamie.

Jamie and Lorna had married a couple of months ago.

Dominic had declined his invitation.

Did they really think he was going to stand there dressed in a kilt, smiling for photographers and pretending to family and friends that things were just fine?

No way could he do that.

Not yet anyway.

'We have to move on from this, Dominic,' William said.

'That's why I'm in London,' Dominic responded. 'Because I have moved on.' He went to hang up, yet there was more he had to know. 'What did they have?'

'A wee boy. They've called him—'

'You don't need to tell me,' Dominic interrupted.

'You don't want to know?'

'I already do.'

Dominic was named after his paternal grandfather, as was the Scottish tradition for a firstborn son.

The new baby, if a boy, had always been destined to be called William—whatever brother Lorna happened to be sleeping with that month.

Hell, yes, he was bitter.

'Dominic...' William pushed. He wanted resolution for his family but it would not be happening today.

'I have to get on,' Dominic said.

He didn't.

Dominic's working day was over, but he headed up to the wards, then to ICU to check on a patient.

All was in order.

Only he was in no mood to go home.

That would mean collecting his phone and seeing all the missed messages, as well as spending the night avoiding going online. Oh, he'd blocked Jamie and Lorna ages ago, and his parents weren't on there. But there were cousins and mutual friends, and all would be celebrating.

A baby had been born after all.

'You're very quiet,' Glen commented as he drove them back to the station. 'Did MacBride upset you?'

'Please!' Victoria made a scoffing face and Glen grinned.

He knew firsthand just how tough Victoria was.

And she was.

Men.

She worked alongside them.

And, in her line of work, she saw a lot of them at their worst as the pubs and clubs emptied out at night.

Victoria had seen an awful lot.

She relied on no one and hid her feelings well.

But that tough persona had been formed long before she had chosen her profession.

There had been no choice but to be independent growing up, for there had been no one who had cared to hear her fears and thoughts.

She was outwardly calm and did not get upset about things others might. Even when she realised she had lost an expensive earring, she just checked the ambulance thoroughly and then called Paddington's and asked Karen if she could look out for it.

'You're taking it very well,' Glen commented. 'Hayley would be hysterical.'

'Well, I'm not Hayley.' Victoria shrugged.

Sometimes, she could make life easier playing sweeter, careful of a man's ego.

And sometimes she did.

Like now, as she went into the female changing room to get ready for her date.

She showered and then let down her hair and brushed it so that it shone. Wrapped in a towel she put on some mascara and lip gloss and then pulled on a gorgeous black dress and high shoes.

Sometimes it was nice to dress up, given that she wore overalls for most of her day. But even as she dressed, Victoria knew tonight wasn't going to work out.

He didn't want to hear about her work.

Which wasn't really a good sign, when Victoria worked an awful lot.

As for attraction?

Well, she had rather hoped that might develop.

And that wasn't a good sign, surely.

The condom in her purse would remain unused.

God, it had been ages, Victoria thought, and there was almost an ache for contact and to be close to another, even if just for a little while.

No, her date tonight could in no way deliver the zaps that Dominic's eyes had.

And so she cancelled it.

Right there and then, Victoria pulled her phone out of her purse and told him that she'd changed her mind about going out tonight.

'Another time...?' he went to suggest, but Victoria didn't play games.

'No.'

All dressed up and nowhere to go.

Or nowhere she wanted to be.

She had broken up with someone a few months ago when he had started to make noises about them living together.

No way!

There was no way on earth that Victoria would consider sharing her space with another.

And so she had ended it.

With the same lack of drama as she ended things tonight.

Victoria pulled on her coat and headed out.

'Goodnight,' she called out to her colleagues, but as she walked off Glen called her back.

'Paddington's just called. Your earring is in the A&E safe.'

'Oh.'

'Do you want me to drop you off?' he offered, but Victoria said no. The ambulance station was just a ten-minute walk from Paddington's and, though cold, it was a clear night and she wouldn't mind the walk.

Her heels clipped on the pavement as the familiar building came into view.

Outside were a couple of protestors holding placards with various messages to save the hospital from closure.

They might just as well go home, Victoria thought sadly.

From the way her father had spoken there would be a formal announcement soon.

She thought of little Penny's comment about feeling safe there, and that was exactly how Victoria felt as she stepped into the hospital.

There was a feeling that wrapped around her like a blanket, one of being taken care of. There was a sense of security when you were within these walls, Victoria thought as she walked into A&E and saw Karen.

'You're one lucky woman,' Karen said as she made her way over to her. 'Penny found your earring in the blanket. It's locked in the safe in Reception.'

'Thank you so much.' Victoria smiled.

Dominic wasn't here.

She could just tell.

And, Victoria conceded, she was disappointed. She knew that she looked good, and deep down she had hoped that maybe, just maybe, Dominic might revise his suggestion and take her for a drink.

But then what?

She didn't want a relationship. That was the simple truth, and the real reason why she always called things off.

Victoria didn't trust anyone and certainly she didn't want to get involved with a colleague who she would have to run into day after day.

They walked into Reception and Karen took out the keys and went into the safe, then handed Victoria the slim envelope that contained the earring. As Victoria put it on, Karen started chatting with the receptionist.

'See you!' Victoria called, and went to walk off but then she halted.

She checked that Karen and the receptionist were still talking and realised she could go behind the screen unnoticed.

It was something she had always done as a child and something she still occasionally did, though she always made sure that no one saw her.

Up the steps she went.

Remembering being little, and the hours that she had had to kill.

Growing up, Paddington's had been more of a home than the house where Victoria had lived and she could not stand the thought of it being sold.

She looked out to the night. The moon was huge and she could see the dark shadows of Regent's Park in the distance. There were taxis and buses below and she could see the protestors who, despite a shower of rain, still stood waving their placards.

They didn't want to lose their hospital.

That's what it was.

Theirs.

It was a place that belonged to the people, and now it was about to be sold off and possibly razed to the ground.

Victoria was tough.

She didn't get involved with the patients; she had made the decision when she started her training to be kind but professional.

But this place, this space, moved her.

The walls held so much history and the air itself tasted of hope. It seemed wrong, simply wrong, that it might go.

There was so much comfort here.

She thought of Penny and how un-scared she was to come to Paddington's.

Victoria had felt the same.

'I shan't be long,' her father would say.

Her mother had left when Victoria was almost one year old and her father had had little choice sometimes but to bring her into work. He would plonk her in a sitting room and one of the staff would always take time to get her a drink or sandwich.

Of course, then their break would end and she would be left alone.

Often Victoria would wander.

Sometimes she would sit in an old quadrangle and read. Other times she would play in the stairwells.

But here was the place she loved most and she had whiled away many hours in this lovely unused room.

Here Victoria would dance or sing or simply imagine.

And maybe she was doing that now, because the door creaked open and she heard his deep voice.

'Excuse me.'

CHAPTER THREE

DOMINIC HAD BEEN about to make his way home after visiting his patients on the wards but, not ready to face it yet, he had decided to spend some time in a place that was starting to become familiar.

He had never expected to see Victoria, yet here she was. Despite the heels and coat and that her hair was down, and despite that he could only see her back and that it was dark, still he recognised her.

But it seemed clear, not just from the location, but from the way her hand rested against the window, and Victoria's pensive stance, that she wanted to be alone.

'Excuse me,' Dominic said, and she turned at the sound of his voice. 'I didn't think anyone was up here.'

'It's fine.' Victoria gave him a thin smile.

'I'll leave you,' he offered, but Victoria shook her head.

'You don't have to do that.'

He walked across the wooden floor and came and joined her at the window.

He was still in scrubs and she could see that he was tired.

'I thought only I knew about this place,' Victoria said. 'It would seem not.'

'I don't think many people know about it,' he said. 'At least, I've never seen anyone up here and it looks pretty undisturbed.'

'How did you find it?'

Dominic didn't answer.

They stood in mutual silence, staring ahead, though not really taking in the view of London at night.

Unlike the thick modern glass in the main hospital, here the windows were thin and there were a couple of cracked ones. The shower had turned to rain and the air was cold but it was incredibly peaceful.

'Where did you work before here?' Victoria asked him.

'Edinburgh.'

'So you're used to wonderful views.'

He thought of the city he loved built around the castle, and of Arthur's Seat rising above the city, and he nodded and then turned his head and looked at something just as beautiful, though he could see that she was sad.

'Are you okay?' he asked, and Victoria was about to nod and say she was fine but changed her mind and gave a small shrug.

'I'm just a bit flat.'

She offered no more than that.

'Has a patient upset you?'

She frowned at the very suggestion and turned to look at him.

'Penny?' he checked, because he had found out this evening that the little girl had wormed her way into a lot of the staff's hearts here at Paddington's. But Victoria shook her head.

'I don't get upset over patients and certainly not over a routine transfer. If I did, then I'd really be in the wrong job!'

'And I doubt it was me that upset you,' he said, and she gave a little laugh.

'No, you I can handle.'

And then Victoria was glad that it was dark because she had started to blush at her own innuendo, even though she hadn't meant it in that way. And so, to swiftly move on from that, she offered more information as to her mood. 'If you must know it's this place that I'm upset about. I can't believe it might be knocked down or turned into apartments. I was practically raised here.'

'You were sick as a child?'

'No! My father worked here in A&E and he used to bring

me in with him. Sometimes I'd sneak up here.' She didn't add just how often it had happened. How her childhood had been spent being half-watched by whatever nurse, domestic, secretary, receptionist or whoever was available.

And she certainly didn't mention her mother.

Victoria did all she could never to think, let alone discuss, the woman who had simply upped and walked away.

'My father now works at Riverside—Professor Christie.'

She turned and saw the raise of his eyes.

It wasn't an impressed raise.

Dominic had spoken to him on occasion and knew that Professor Christie wasn't the most pleasant of people.

'He's crabby too,' Victoria said.

And Dominic decided to make one thing very clear. 'At the risk of causing offence, I might be crabby, Victoria, but I'm not cold to the bone.'

Dominic did not cause offence. It was, in fact, rather a relief to hear it voiced as, given her father's status, people tended to praise him rather than criticise, and that had been terribly confusing to a younger Victoria.

It still confused her even now.

She had stood at the award ceremony yesterday hearing all the marvellous things being said about him. Afterwards, at the reception, more praise had been heaped.

The emperor had really had on no clothes, though there was not a person brave enough to voice it.

Until now.

'Well,' Victoria said, 'I saw him yesterday and he seems to think the merge is going to go ahead.'

Dominic nodded; he had heard the same. 'It's a shame.'

'It's more than a *shame*,' Victoria said, and for the first time he heard the sound of her voice when upset—even when they had argued she had remained calm. 'This place is more than just a facility,' Victoria insisted. 'Families feel safe when they know their children are here. It can't just close.'

'Do something about it, then.'

'Me?'

She looked down at the protestors and wondered if she should join them. But in her heart, Victoria knew it wasn't enough and that more needed to be done.

'If you care so much,' Dominic said, 'then fight for what matters to you.'

It did matter to her, Victoria thought.

Paddington's really mattered.

And it was nice to be up here and not alone with her thoughts, but rather to be sharing them with him.

'How *did* you find this room?' Victoria asked again.

He still hadn't told her, and now when he did it came as a surprise.

'I saw you sneak behind the shelves a couple of months ago and I wondered where you'd gone. When I got a chance I went and had a look for myself.'

'You can't have seen me.' Victoria shook her head at the impossibility of his explanation. 'I always make sure that no one does. Anyway, I'd have known if you were around...' And she halted, because that was admitting that any time she was at this hospital she was aware of where he was.

'I was in the waiting room talking to a parent,' he said. 'I saw you through the glass...'

'I guess I stand out in those green overalls.'

'I don't think it's the green overalls, Victoria.'

She gave a soft laugh.

She was dressed in black now after all.

Yet he was confirming that he noticed her too.

'Did you see me come up tonight?' Victoria asked.

'No. I just wanted some space. I thought you were finished for the night.'

'I am. I was supposed to be going out,' Victoria said, explaining the reason for heels and things. 'But I cancelled.'

And now he thought he knew the real reason she was sad.

'Have you just broken up with someone?'

'I don't think you can really call it a break-up if you cancel a second date.'

No, she wasn't sad about that; Dominic could tell from her dismissive shrug. It would seem it really was just the building.

'Well,' he said. 'I'm sure he's very disappointed.'

And then he went to retract that because it came out wrong, as if he was alluding to how stunning she looked.

'What I meant was that—'

He stopped; whatever way he said it would sound like flirting, and he was avoiding all that.

'I think I've done us both a favour,' Victoria said. 'He didn't seem to understand the concept of shift work. So,' she asked, 'if it wasn't me, then what brought you up here?' She wanted to know more about those difficult days he had alluded to.

'I'm in the middle of something right now...' Dominic said. 'Well, not in the middle—I've taken myself out of the equation. I'm staying back from getting involved with anyone.'

'Good,' Victoria said, 'because I don't like to get involved with anyone at work.'

Yet here they were and the tension that had been in the annexe wrapped and slivered around them.

'Are you married?' she asked.

It was a very specific question and the answer was important to Victoria, because the cold air had turned warm.

'No.'

'Seeing someone?'

'Of course not,' Dominic said, or he would not be doing this—and his hand moved to her cheek. 'You got your earring back.'

'They were a gift from my father.'

'That's nice,' Dominic said.

'Not really, it was just a duty gift when I turned eighteen. Had he bothered to get to know me, then he'd have known that I don't like diamonds.'

'Why not?'

'I don't believe in fairytales and I don't believe in for ever.'

There was, to Victoria's mind, no such thing.

She held her breath as his fingers came to her cheek and lightly brushed the lobe as he examined the stone.

If it were anyone else she would have pushed his hand away.

Anyone else.

Yet she provoked.

'It was the other earring that I lost.'

And he turned her face and his hands went to the other.

This was foolish, both knew.

Neither wanted to get close to someone they had to work alongside but the attraction between them was intense.

Both knew the reason for their rows and terse exchanges; it was physical attraction at its most raw.

'Victoria, I'm in no position to get involved with anyone.'

They were standing looking at each other and his hands were on her cheeks and his fingers were warm on her ears. There was a thrum between them and she knew he was telling her they would go nowhere.

'That's okay.'

And that *was* okay.

'If you don't like diamonds, then what do you like?' he asked. His mouth was so close to hers and though it was cold she could feel the heat in the space between them.

'This.'

Their mouths met and she felt the warm, light pressure and it felt blissful. That musky, soapy scent of him had been imprinted and, this close, it made her dizzy. His tongue sliding in made her move closer and the fingers of one hand reached into her hair as the other hand slid around her waist.

It was almost like setting up to dance, as if the teacher had come in and said, *Place your hands here*.

But not.

Because then she hadn't felt a tremble, no matter how warm the palm.

They kissed softly at first as his hand bunched in her hair; he explored with his tongue and it met with hers and he tasted all that had been missing.

Passion coiled them tight; his palm took the weight of her head and pressed her in at the same time.

The pent-up rows and the terse exchanges had been many and could not be dispersed with a single kiss.

It was a deep slow kiss and it birthed impatience in both. He held her head very steady and kissed her hard, and the scratch of his unshaven jaw and the probe of his tongue was sublime. But then, unlike with most men, she tasted resistance.

There was resistance, because Dominic knew very well where they were leading. 'I don't have anything with me,' he said.

And she wanted to feel him unleashed.

'I do.'

And when most would kiss harder, instead Dominic made her burn with his stealth. He stepped back and moved her coat down her shoulders and did not drop it to the dusty floor. Instead he placed it on the window ledge and she went for her purse that was there.

He came up behind her as she rifled through her purse, praying that the condom was still there and trying to find it. One hand wrapped around her and rested on her stomach as his other hand slid up between her inner thighs to the damp in the middle. His fingers stroked her and she closed her eyes to the bliss.

'Here.' She had never been so pleased to find a condom as he peeled her knickers down and she straightened up and stepped out of them.

Still he stood behind her and he lifted her hair and kissed her low on her neck. His hand pressed into her stomach and she could feel him hard against her bottom. Victoria was shaking a little, wanting to turn to him, yet wanting to linger in this bliss.

'Come away from the window,' he said, and took her over to a wall in the shadows and he kissed her hard against it. His hands held her hips and now Victoria felt the delicious hardness of him against her stomach. She stretched up onto tiptoe and he moved his hips down so he met her heat.

It was nice, so nice, to be so raw and open with him.

He caressed her breast through the fabric and, since he could feel no zipper on her dress, with a moan of want he just slid his hand inside and it was the most thorough and deliberate grope of her life. Meanwhile, Victoria was doing the same to him; she was trying to hold on to the condom as she freed him from his scrubs and underwear.

Finally, she held him in her palm, and her hand was soft on skin that was so very firm to her touch.

'I want this dress off...' Dominic gasped, but it was impossible because they could not move their mouths for more than a second from each other.

They wanted nakedness and hours to explore, but their bodies would only give them minutes.

He took the condom and began sheathing himself, while she was pulling up her dress, and when he was done, he lifted her thigh and placed her leg around his hip.

And they were not dancing!

She balanced on one stiletto but his grip of her was firm and the wall behind her solid. Then her hips angled and both were just as urgent as the other as Dominic thrust and took her.

Victoria had never felt anything so powerful. He was rough and delicious and she felt matched for the first time in her life, because he held nothing back.

Everything he delivered.

Dominic's hand was behind her back and he could feel the scratch of stone on his knuckles but that was so far from his mind that it barely registered.

'There…' she said in a voice that was both demanding and urgent.

He met that demand and heightened it too.

She felt amazing. Dominic was rather more used to holding back, but Victoria invited intensity. It had been ages for Dominic, and he had wanted her for a very long time.

There was almost anger in him for how much she made him want her, so he thrust hard and fast and then harder still to the sound of her pleasurable moans, and then he lifted her.

Victoria had never had both feet off the ground like this; she had never been so consumed. His fingers were digging into her bottom as he took her hard against the wall.

Their faces were side by side and she wanted to find his mouth, but there was no time for that as she was starting to come. Never had she climaxed so deeply, and if she were not wrapped around him she would have folded in two at the pleasure.

He released to her deep shudder and together they hit high, and finally she found his mouth, tasted the cool of his tongue as she drank in his kiss. They rested their foreheads together, sharing those last beats of pleasure and breathing the same air until gently he lowered her down.

With long slow kisses he moved them away from the wall now. She pulled down her dress and then they broke contact and she moved out of the shadows.

Victoria picked up her discarded knickers but had to lean on the ledge, not just so she could put them on, but because her legs were shaky and she was still breathless.

She had never let herself go like that, she had never come so hard and she had certainly never been made love to so thoroughly.

When Dominic emerged from the shadows he, too, was dressed, though his hair was rumpled. It should have been really awkward between them, yet it was not.

'I look like I've been in a fight,' he said as he examined his hands in the moonlight. Victoria took his fingers and looked at them, and made him smile with what she said.

'You're going to have some trouble explaining those injuries, Doctor,' she teased, because it really did look, to her trained eyes, as if he had punched the walls.

Yes, it should have been really awkward but instead he came and sat beside her on the ledge.

'Victoria...' he started, but really he did not know what to say. Dominic was in no position to start anything. And what had just taken place was very far removed from his usual nature.

He felt amazing though, as if on the top of a high mountain.

And she saw him struggle with what to say, so she said it for him.

'You don't have to explain anything,' Victoria said. She was not referring to his knuckles, but still she smiled.

'You're sure?' he checked.

'Yes.'

What had happened was something she could never have imagined, something so far removed from her usual wary approach to intimacy, but he did not need to know all of that.

She felt liberated.

And feminine.

With him she felt she had found herself.

So, instead of an awkward parting they shared a kiss that was deep, long and slow, and ended by her.

'I'm going to go,' Victoria said, and stood.

And still she waited for awkwardness, even as she walked to the door.

So did he, yet awkward did not exist in this room.

'So, if you don't like diamonds,' Dominic called. 'What do you like?'

And she opened the door and laughed as he went back to the original question.

'Pearls.'

He sat in the room and looked around. The moon shone through the window and the air was still stirred and seductive from them; his knuckles were grazed and he was somewhat reeling.

Dominic had never really given pearls any thought before.

They were just something his mother or grandmother wore for weddings and such occasions.

Certainly he had never considered them sexy.

He did now.

CHAPTER FOUR

'PREGNANT?'

Victoria watched as her father took off his glasses and cleaned them. And, as he did so, she remembered the time she had got her first period and it had been almost an identical reaction—slight bemusement, mild irritation, though more at the intrusion of conversation rather than what was actually being said.

Victoria sat in her father's office at Riverside Hospital and waited. For what, she didn't know.

She had read somewhere that some terrible parents made the most wonderful grandparents. That without the responsibility of parenthood, they enjoyed the experience. And she had hoped, truly hoped, that it might be the case here. That this might breathe some life into her relationship with her father.

Apparently not, if his cool reaction was anything to go by.

And Victoria knew deep down that there had been no real relationship with her father. At least, not the sort she wanted. She hadn't seen or spoken to him since the function they had attended, despite Victoria having tried to call.

Her father was brilliant but completely self-absorbed.

Completely.

'How far along are you?' he asked.

It had been six weeks since her time with Dominic, and with the requisite two weeks added, Victoria knew her dates.

'Eight weeks,' she said.

'Do you want it?' Professor Christie asked.

He thought she was here to ask for a referral for an abortion, Victoria suddenly realised.

And he'd write her one, Victoria knew.

'Yes,' she said. 'I very much want my baby.'

She stared at him but he was reading through some notes that lay on his desk.

'What about the father?' he asked, and looked up.

'I haven't told him yet. We're not together or anything. He's in Scotland.' Victoria had heard that in passing. 'On annual leave,' she added to her father.

She was forewarned as to the response she might get from Dominic, when her father spoke next.

'Well, he's in for a pleasant surprise when he gets back.'

The sarcasm was evident in his voice and it told Victoria all she needed to know about her father's thoughts on parenthood.

'Victoria, you really need to give this some consideration. Being a single parent is hard work—I should know. It interferes in every aspect of your life. You're the one who always bangs on about your career—think what it will do to that...'

She hadn't seen him since the function and then it had been for an award for *his* career. Victoria didn't bang on, as her father described it. Given he was a professor and specialised in Accident and Emergency and she was a paramedic, she had, on occasion, tried to find some common ground.

But there was none and there never had been.

There was no room in this narcissist's world for anyone other than himself.

'I can't help you financially,' he said, for Professor Christie had amassed a small collection of ex-wives.

'I've never once asked you to.'

Victoria hadn't.

She had left home as soon as she had finished school and had never asked her father for anything.

But she was about to.

She looked at her father and knew that really there was no point even being here. He did not want to be a part of her life, and the occasional public showing of his daughter was only when he was between wives.

'Victoria, I need to get on.'

'There *is* something I want...' Victoria said, and he let out the little hiss of irritation that he always did when she asked for a moment more of his time. 'I was hoping to have the baby at Paddington's.'

Victoria had decided as she'd walked through the corridors of Riverside that she didn't want her baby to be born here. There was nothing wrong with the hospital—she often brought patients here—but it felt bland to Victoria, and her father worked here too.

She felt closer to a building than her own parents. It was sad but true, and that was why she asked the favour.

'They only take complicated cases,' Professor Christie said.

'Not always,' Victoria refuted. And she didn't point out that she'd been born there and that members of staff tended to choose, where possible, to have their child there, but she would not be fobbed off.

'It's closing.'

'Not necessarily,' Victoria said. 'And if it does close before the baby comes along, then I'll be referred elsewhere, but I'd really like to have my antenatal care there.'

As an adult she had never asked her father for anything, not one single thing. 'Can you get me in there?'

'I'll see what I can do.'

'Now,' Victoria said, because she knew this conversation would be forgotten the second she walked out of the door. 'I want to be seen before I tell work.'

And so, more to get rid of the inconvenience, her father made some calls and finally she was booked in to Paddington's maternity unit.

'You need an ultrasound before he sees you,' Professor Christie said, and he went through the details, telling her she had an appointment for tomorrow and that the referral form would be at Reception. Finally, he asked her to reconsider. 'I really suggest you have a long hard think about going ahead with this, Victoria.'

That hurt.

On so many levels it hurt.

Victoria knew he had never wanted her. She was certain that had her mother not left first, then he would have gone.

As she got to the door Victoria turned and could see that she was forgotten already—her father was straight back to work, though she still stood there.

Dominic was right—her father was cold to the bone.

'I can see why she left you,' Victoria said. 'My mother, I mean.'

Professor Christie looked up from his notes and he stared at his daughter for a long moment and then, just before resuming writing his notes, he, as always, had the last word.

'She left you too.'

His words shadowed and clung to her right through into the next day.

'You're quiet,' Glen observed as she was driven towards the children's hospital with Glen, for once not in an ambulance.

Glen had offered to come with her for her ultrasound appointment. Victoria had declined, though she was touched that her colleague had given her a lift. She had felt very sick on the underground but that was fading.

Glen knew that she was pregnant.

Of course he did.

He had no idea, though, who the father was.

They worked together, and when Victoria had started to turn as green as her overalls at the smallest thing, he had asked if everything was okay.

Victoria had said she was fine.

Then, a couple of days ago, he had asked outright.

'Hayley had terrible morning sickness, with Ryan,' Glen had told her.

It had been hard to deny a pregnancy when you were sitting holding a kidney dish in the back of an ambulance.

'You have to tell work,' Glen said.

'I know.' Victoria closed her eyes.

It was starting to be real.

For the last couple of weeks she had been in denial, but now she was facing up to things and telling work was something she knew she had to do.

She had this week to get through and then a weekend of nights before she went on two weeks' annual leave and she had decided that she would tell them at the end of her nights.

And now they sat in his car as Glen offered some further advice that she certainly didn't need.

'You have to tell the guy he's going to be a father.'

'Thanks, Glen,' she snapped.

'Listen to me, Victoria—'

'No.' She turned and looked at him. 'I accepted a lift, not a lecture.' And though she told Glen to stay back she knew he was right and that Dominic needed to be told.

When he came back from his leave she would tell him.

If he came back.

He might have decided that he missed home.

Victoria really didn't know him at all.

They had gone straight back to being strangers.

There was no flirting and certainly there had been no reference to what had taken place.

He was still moody and she was her usual confident self.

Really, if it hadn't been for the fact that she was pregnant, by now Victoria would be wondering if it had even taken place.

That night still felt like a dream.

Albeit her favourite one.

'Are you sure you don't want me to come with you?' Glen checked, but Victoria snorted at the suggestion of needing someone to hold her hand.

'For an ultrasound?'

'Hayley gets nervous whenever she has one...' Glen started, referring to his wife, as he always did.

'I'm not Hayley,' Victoria pointed out as she often did. 'I'll be fine on my own.'

She would be better on her own, in fact.

It was what she was used to after all.

Victoria walked through the familiar corridors of Paddington's and turned for the Imaging Department. There she handed over her referral slip to the receptionist.

'We're running a bit behind,' the receptionist explained.

'That's no problem,' Victoria said, even though she was desperate to go to the loo.

She had been told to have a lot to drink prior to the ultrasound so that they might get the best view of the baby.

Still, she had expected to have to wait and had plenty to do.

Apart from a baby, something else had been created that night.

Victoria was on the social committee and had decided to use her position there to start a campaign to save the hospital from the merger.

They met each week over at the Frog and Peach and there was a meeting being held tonight.

It was proving difficult to get things rolling though.

Most people seemed to think it was a foregone conclusion that Paddington's would close. Apart from the odd small write-up in the press, the campaign was not getting any real attention and Victoria was at a bit of a loss as to what to suggest next.

Rosie, a paediatric nurse, along with Robyn, who was Head of Surgery, were both a huge support and Victoria was hoping to catch up with them before the meeting kicked off.

Victoria sent a group text, reminding everyone of the meeting, and then she answered a few emails, but though she was passionate about doing all she could to save the hospital from closure, she could not give it her full attention right now.

She *was* nervous.

Oh, Victoria would never let on to Glen that she was, but she had butterflies fluttering in her chest. She was seated next to a heavily pregnant woman who, from the conversation taking place, was accompanied by her mother.

When Victoria was less than a year old, her mother had decided that motherhood and marriage were not for her and had walked out; Victoria hadn't seen her since.

Not once.

Growing up, she had asked about her, of course. She had craved information, but there had never been much. Her father refused to speak of his first wife and, apart from a couple of photos that Victoria kept to this day in a drawer in her bedside table, she knew very little about her, other than that she had worked at Paddington's.

As Victoria had got older, and she could more readily see her father's very difficult behaviour, Victoria had decided her mother had walked away because she was depressed. A few years ago, Victoria had decided that no mother could walk away like that and have nothing to do with her child.

And so she had to be dead!

It had been a shock and black disappointment to find out that no, her mother was alive and well.

Thriving, in fact, Victoria discovered when she found her on social media.

She lived in Italy with her second husband.

And was a proud mother of two grown-up sons.

Victoria didn't merit a mention.

She had contacted her but there had been no response.

That had been the final hurt and Victoria had decided she would never allow herself to hurt over her mother again.

Yet she was, and today, especially so.

Sitting in the ultrasound department, she was jealous of the stranger that sat beside her.

With her mother by her side.

She tried to focus on an email she was writing on her phone, rather than them. Hearing the doors swish open Victoria moved her legs to let a trolley carrying a patient past.

The child was crying and Victoria looked at him. She was just trying to guess what was wrong with him when she looked up into the eyes of Dominic walking alongside the trolley.

Usually they ignored each other, or spoke only about their patients. Eye contact was pretty much avoided, but today his met hers and she saw that he frowned.

And well he might.

She was sitting in a children's hospital ultrasound waiting room after all!

It hadn't once entered Victoria's head that it might be a problem to see him here today. It wasn't just that she'd thought he was on holiday, more the fact that Victoria was so used to Paddington's, so completely used to being here, that it simply hadn't entered her head that it might be an issue for her to see him.

Yet it had become one.

He couldn't come over—the child on the trolley was very ill—but he turned his head and gave her a questioning look as he walked past.

Victoria didn't quite know what to do.

Dominic was speaking with a nurse and they were about to be shown through to one of the imaging rooms; Victoria wondered if she should go down to Emergency after her ultrasound and speak with him then.

As he steered the trolley he turned and looked at her again but thankfully her phone buzzed and she could legitimately look away.

And, as she did, all thoughts of babies and fathers and ultrasounds rapidly faded.

Major Incident Alert
All available staff are to report to the station.

Sometimes there were mock-ups of major incidents and you were still supposed to attend, so that staff response times could be evaluated. Telephone lines and operators could not be clogged up with calls to check if this was real or not.

And something told Victoria that this was.

She looked up at the television on the wall but there were no breaking news stories yet.

Her phone bleeped again with another urgent alert and Victoria knew that the ultrasound would just have to wait.

Victoria was a terribly practical person and so the first thing she did was go to the ladies' room.

One problem solved.

As she came out, emergency chimes were starting to ring out as Paddington Children's Hospital's own major incident response was set into action.

'Victoria Christie,' she gave her name again to the receptionist. 'I'm a paramedic. I have to go.'

The receptionist nodded. She herself was already moving into action. If it was indeed a major incident then all non-urgent cases would have to be cancelled, and the department cleared for whatever it was that might be brought in.

'I'll call and reschedule,' Victoria said, and as she went to run off Glen called and said he would meet her at the front.

This was real, Victoria knew, for someone must have rushed to relieve Dominic from his patient because he was running out of the ultrasound department too.

'Do you know what's happening?' she said as he caught up with her.

'No.'

She was very fit but so, too, was he and he passed her.

By the time she reached Accident and Emergency, Dominic was wearing a hard hat and she realised that he was being sent out.

Hard cases were being loaded into the ambulance that would bring him to the scene and Karen was bringing out the precious O-negative blood that was kept in Accident and Emergency for days such as this.

The ambulance station wasn't far from the hospital but Glen, having received the same text as Victoria, had come to collect her.

As she got into the car Glen told her the little that he knew.

'There's a fire at Westbourne Grove,' he said, pulling off as soon as the door closed while Victoria put on her seatbelt. 'It sounds bad.'

Victoria said nothing—she never showed her true feelings, even in the most testing of times—but her heart started to beat fast.

Westbourne Grove was a primary school, and today was a weekday...

'Apparently there are children trapped in the building,' Glen said grimly.

CHAPTER FIVE

EVERY MOMENT MATTERED.

Victoria was well trained to respond to major incidents, and as soon as they were out of the car they ran to get changed.

The station was busy with many vehicles already out at the fire and off-duty staff arriving to provide backup and relief.

She went to the female changing room and took off her jeans and silky rust-coloured top that she had been wearing and then pulled on her overalls and boots. In the main station area she then collected her communication radio and ran out to the Rapid Response vehicle, which Glen was just boarding.

They hit a wall of traffic as soon as they left the station.

Already ambulances, perhaps the first vehicles at the scene, were making their way back to Paddington's with sirens blaring.

It felt as if it was taking for ever to get there.

They had their lights and sirens on but the streets of London were gridlocked. Drivers were moving their vehicles and mounting the kerbs in a bid to try and let the emergency services through.

As well as ambulances there were fire engines, police cars and emergency response workers on motorbikes heading there too, and there was the sound of many sirens as finally they approached the school.

They could hear the chatter over the airwaves. Children were being dragged out and there were reports of firefighters going back in over and over again in an effort to reach the ones that were trapped. Most had been evacuated and, as per protocol, were lined up on the playground, far from the burning building. The numbers had to be checked and constantly updated but panicked parents were also starting to arrive on the scene and the police were having trouble keeping some of them back as they desperately wanted to see for themselves if their own child had made it out.

'Your children don't go to Westbourne Grove?' Victoria checked.

'No,' Glen said. And then he added, 'Thank God!'

The stretch of silence between those words felt like the loudest part of his response and, Victoria knew, Glen was picturing just that—his children trapped in a fire.

A couple of months ago, when they had been called out to a particularly nasty motor vehicle accident, Glen had started relating everything back to his own family. He took it all so personally, and it was getting worse.

Victoria had, on several occasions, warned Glen that he would soon be on stress leave if he carried on like this and had suggested that he speak to someone.

Glen insisted that he was fine and that everyone had their Achilles' heel, and then he had turned it into a joke. 'Except for you, Victoria.'

That had given her pause, for while Glen's stress levels worried her, Victoria knew that she went the other way and stuffed down her feelings so that no one, not even her trusted colleague, could guess what went on inside her head.

Perhaps Glen was right and his responses were more normal, Victoria had reasoned, for there was a part of her that was perhaps a little jealous.

Not just of Glen and his ability to show emotion, but that he was part of a loving family and thought about them all the time, just as they all thought of him. Throughout the day Hayley would call and at night before the children went to bed, if able to, Glen would find the time to call and say goodnight.

'Let's just hope they're all out,' Victoria said as they got their first good look at the scene.

There was smoke billowing into the air, thick and black, as they were waved through the cordons. Some parents were being physically held back, not understanding the chaos they would create if let past.

They were guided to park behind the fire engines and they carried out their stretcher and equipment.

On a playground there were firefighters breathing in oxygen, and lines of children stood crying on a nearby playing field, clearly shocked and scared.

But they were alive and safe.

Some of the more seriously injured children were being treated on the playing field and it was then that she saw Dominic and two paramedics working on a child and draping the little body in saline sheets.

There were constant headcounts of the children taking place by the teachers but, Victoria and Glen were told, it was estimated that there were still two children in the building.

As the burnt child was being moved onto the stretcher a call went up for them to urgently move.

'Stay back.' A fire officer was pushing back the emergency personnel. 'One of the internal structures is about to collapse.'

They were told that the next casualty, be it child, staff member or firefighter, would be for Victoria and Glen to treat and that for now all they could do was watch and wait.

There was the violent sound of an explosion followed by a deadly silence. And Dominic, who was loading one of the burn victims into an ambulance, turned and looked at the building.

There weren't just children in there; there were firefighters too.

Dominic dealt with trauma daily.

He was trained to the hilt for this and, seeing the child into safe hands, he moved fast to get back to the changing situation.

But as he ran towards the line of emergency personnel, he saw a firefighter emerge, and then, too far to do anything to halt her, he watched as Victoria started to run.

Fury ripped through him at her blatant flaunting of the rules, for it was not only Dominic that called out to her to get back.

But no, she and Glen were moving towards the firefighter and child.

With good reason though.

Victoria took safety very seriously.

They were still being told to stay back, as another explosion could often follow the first, but as practical as she was, Victoria was in the business of saving lives and she could see that this little life was ebbing fast.

The firefighter was struggling, and as Victoria approached he dropped to his knees. She could see that he, too, was injured and had given all he had to get the child out. Victoria knew help was close for him but for now she was more concerned with the child.

It was a little boy and he was bleeding profusely from a neck wound and, as he was laid on the playground, Victoria knew that time was of the essence or he would soon bleed to death. She applied pressure to the wound with her gloved fingers as Glen, who had also ignored the orders to stay back, opened a pack. He passed her some swabs but, though she tried, Victoria could not stop the bleeding. But then she found the spot and Victoria let out a long breath of relief that the bleeding had stopped.

She looked up and saw that Dominic was running over and as he approached he let rip.

'What the hell are you guys doing running forward, when the order was to stay back?'

Victoria shot him a look that said she was a bit too busy to row right now. Dominic dropped down to his knees and his silence agreed to the same as he examined the child.

'It's venous blood,' Victoria said, not moving her fingers. If it had been an artery he would have been dead before the firefighter could get him out but, even so, he was practically exsanguinated.

Glen put oxygen onto the child and Dominic inserted an IV and took blood for cross-matching. He pushed through some IV fluids while calling to Karen to run through the O-negative blood that the Mobile Emergency Unit had brought with them.

It was the most precious commodity in a major incident; O negative is the universal donor and can be given to all without cross-matching. It was used sparingly and Dominic was now grateful for a couple of earlier decisions he had made to withhold some of this most precious resource, believing those patients could wait till they got to the hospital.

This child could not wait.

'We need to get him to Paddington's,' Dominic said. 'Now.'

They were working on him on the playground and Victoria looked up to a colleague. 'Can you bring the vehicle in closer?'

Just as she looked up, Victoria saw that another child was being carried out in the arms of a firefighter. The child had red hair. That was all she could make out—and that the child was limp in the firefighter's arms. Another crew was available to take care of them and so her focus went back to her own patient.

A teacher came over and identified the child that they were working on as Lewis Evans. 'His mother's here. She's frantic.'

'Get the police to take her to the hospital,' Dominic said. 'I'll speak with her there.'

Dominic could see the redheaded child receiving care from a Rapid Response team and a doctor, and his decision was made to leave the scene and escort this patient.

It was a very difficult manoeuvre into the vehicle. Even lifting little Lewis onto the stretcher caused Victoria to lose the pressure point for a few seconds.

It was enough to know that it could not happen again.

Through the streets the ambulance blue-lighted them towards the hospital. The police had the traffic under control now and streets had been closed off so that their return journey was thankfully far speedier.

Victoria's arms ached as she knelt on the floor, and Dominic was calling ahead to Paddington's and explaining he needed a theatre held and the head-and-neck surgeon to meet them in there, when she saw Lewis's eyes flicker.

The blood and oxygen were starting to work.

'Hey, Lewis, you need to stay very still,' Victoria said. 'You're in an ambulance and we're taking you to Paddington Children's Hospital.'

Lewis didn't answer but she spoke on as if he could hear her and her voice was calm and reassuring.

'I'm Victoria,' she told him. 'You're doing so well. I know you are scared and in pain but you're going to be okay. I just need you to stay very still.'

And then she looked up and arched her neck and Dominic offered her some water.

She nodded.

He held her head steady and she took a drink and then Victoria saw the familiar building come into view but she could not relax just yet. Lewis had already lost an awful lot of blood, his heart was beating rapidly and his blood pressure was barely recordable.

'Keep the pressure on,' Dominic told Victoria, and he saw her slight eye roll—she was hardly going to let go!

The stretcher was very carefully lowered so that Victoria could keep the vital pressure sustained.

'That's it...' Dominic said, and someone helped guide her out of the back. Victoria let out a sigh, not quite one of relief, but it was good to be on solid ground and have the patient at Paddington's where he would at least stand a chance.

It was chaos outside the hospital, and security and the police were working together to keep the foyer clear for patient arrivals.

Some parents had headed straight to the hospital in a bid to find out more, as had some reporters. As well as that, there were some people who loved to have a good look at others' misfortune.

It was a relief to step inside.

They didn't turn for A&E, instead they moved swiftly through the corridors, guided by a team leader, and with relief, Victoria saw that an elevator had been held for them.

Theatre was waiting and their efficiency was amazing, so much so, that Dominic raced back down to the Accident and Emergency unit as his skills were still in heavy demand.

It was so calm in the theatre and it was just a blessing to be there.

The head-and-neck surgeon had finished scrubbing and was

speaking with the anaesthetist about their approach to the neck wound.

Lewis was being given blood through both arms now and he had been given sedation before they went ahead with the intubation.

And Victoria felt dizzy.

Ignore it, Victoria told herself.

But she had been standing there for what felt like a very long time.

'How much longer?' she asked, because she was starting to see stars.

And whether it had anything to do with her complexion or voice, or just that they were ready now, the theatre nurse took over just in time.

'Come on,' Glen said.

Glen led her out of the theatre and down a corridor and Victoria bent over in the hallway with her hands on her thighs and took some deep breaths, but when that wasn't enough she sat on the floor and pulled her knees up and put her head between them.

'Do we have to go back to the school?' Victoria asked.

'No, we've been stood down,' Glen informed her. 'I'll go and find you some water.'

'Did they get them all out?' Victoria asked as Glen walked off, though she did not look up.

'I believe so,' Glen answered.

He returned a little while later and Victoria took a long, grateful drink as Glen spoke. 'Some have been taken to Riverside but most are here.'

She nodded and, having taken a drink, put her head back down. Victoria wasn't so much dizzy now but replaying the rescue in her head and questioning her decision to dash forward.

It had been instinct, she knew that, but now it was starting to hit home that it wasn't just her own life on the line.

And some time later, that was how Dominic found her.

Slumped against the wall, head between her knees, and Dominic was cross all over again with her for flouting the rules and crossing the line.

'How's the redheaded kid?' Glen asked Dominic as he approached.

'I've just brought him up for an urgent head CT and handed him over to Alistair, the neurosurgeon,' Dominic said.

He stood over her and she could feel him demand that she meet his eyes.

She looked up then and the look he gave her felt hostile, even if his voice was even.

'How bad is he?' Glen asked.

'GCS of six,' Dominic answered Glen while looking at Victoria. 'He was hiding in a cupboard.'

'Poor kid,' Glen said.

It was Glen who asked all the questions, Dominic noted, but he had one of his own, and though it was for the two of them he spoke directly to Victoria.

'Do you always ignore orders? You were told to stay back because a building had the potential to collapse.'

'I could see that the firefighter was struggling,' Victoria explained. 'And that the child was bleeding profusely.'

Victoria was starting to feel a bit better, but she was herself questioning the decision to run forward. She really didn't want to deal with Dominic right now and so she pulled herself to standing and spoke to Glen. 'Let's get back to the vehicle.'

'One moment...'

Victoria turned to the sound of Robyn's voice. Robyn Kelly was Head of Surgery and very much a part of the new drive to save Paddington's.

'Dominic, we need you to speak to the press.'

The hospital had been stretched today but the critically injured were now all in the right place and order was restoring. Speaking to the press after incidents like this was a part of the job and so Dominic nodded.

'And you too,' Robyn said, looking over to Victoria.

'Me?'

'They want a representative from all branches of the first responders,' Robyn explained, and then nodded her head towards a staff room. 'Come and see this.'

The news was on and the cameras were trained on the fire

that was still burning but had been brought a little more under control.

And there, in the top right hand of the screen, was an image of Dominic and Victoria bent over little Lewis and together fighting to save his life.

'Angela Marton, a reporter, just asked the viewers to consider how much more seriously things might have played out if Paddington's had been closed,' Robyn said. 'There are people talking about it all over talkback radio...' She looked over to Victoria. 'Finally there's some anger being generated about the merger.'

'Good,' Victoria said.

'This image is on all the channels...'

Both Dominic and Victoria did their best not to catch each other's responses as Robyn told them that they had just become the poster picture for the campaign to save Paddington's.

Robyn had to get on, and so it was Victoria and Dominic with Glen by their side who walked back through the hospital.

Glen was asking about all the injuries and Dominic was doing his best to reply, but of course his mind wasn't really on the conversation.

It was also moving on from the disaster and back to a few moments before the major incident alert had been put out.

He thought of Victoria sitting in the Imaging Department waiting room, and then he thought of her sitting slumped and pale on the floor outside the theatres.

Anyone would be feeling a bit faint, Dominic told himself. Victoria had been pushing on Lewis's neck for ages.

Then he looked over to her and he could see her staring fixedly ahead.

Once outside they walked over to the press area and Victoria spoke with her supervisor where she was given a brief.

The police would speak first, then the firefighters, followed by Dominic, and then Victoria was to speak briefly about the ambulance response.

'The last child pulled out was Ryan Walker,' she was informed. 'He's six years old.'

'Okay,' Victoria said, and she deliberately did not look over to Glen.

He had a son called Ryan and she knew he would get upset at the link.

She went and took her place in the line-up.

Yes, her mind was busy working out ways to get the angle she wanted included, but she was also acutely aware of the man who now stood next to her.

The cameras were on them as they stood side by side and she could feel his tension.

Though, this time, it was not of the sexual kind!

'We need to talk,' Victoria said as she looked straight ahead. 'Though not here.'

'Obviously,' came Dominic's rather scathing response.

She turned and looked at him, and wasn't sure if he was annoyed that they were going to be forced together as the poster image of Save Paddington's as Robyn had suggested.

Or if, somehow, he knew.

CHAPTER SIX

DOMINIC KNEW.

Or, at least, he was starting to!

He was trying very hard not to believe she might be pregnant by him, and was very determined that history would not repeat itself, and he would not be made a fool of twice.

The press conference went well. Dominic said that it had been a multifaceted effort. Victoria got in her little plug about the potential closure by pointing out that the most urgent cases had needed the proximity of Paddington's to have the best chance for a positive outcome and then they all went their separate ways.

The department was terribly busy and there was soot everywhere and the smell of smoke in the air. As well as injured children, there were staff and firefighters too but, by evening, the department was clearing and they were taken off bypass, which they had been placed on so that they could deal with the sudden influx of patients.

Dominic had been working since seven that morning, and after twelve eventful hours he should perhaps be heading for home.

Instead Dominic showered and changed into black jeans and a shirt and walked over to the Frog and Peach pub where the Save Paddington's meeting was being held tonight.

On arriving, he soon found out that the meeting had been

abandoned due to the Westbourne Grove crisis and would be held in a couple of days in a lecture theatre at the hospital.

Tonight, there was too much energy for sensible conversation.

The major incident meant that the staff all needed to unwind and debrief and so it was a very noisy pub that he found himself in.

There was Victoria.

She was wearing the jeans and rust-coloured top that he had seen her wearing at the Imaging Department, and he saw she was chatting with Rosie, one of the paediatric nurses.

And... Victoria was drinking soda water.

Not that that meant anything.

He had no idea if Victoria would normally be having a drink.

The fact was, he knew nothing about her except what had taken place that night.

'Hi, Dominic, how was your holiday?' Rosie asked as he came over.

'Fine,' Dominic said.

'Where did you go?'

'Scotland.'

'Visiting family?' Rosie asked.

Dominic gave a small nod. It was easier to do that than admit that while he had hoped to go and visit his family and let bygones be bygones, he hadn't felt ready.

Dominic didn't even want to attempt another relationship until he had dealt with the rather large items of baggage left over from the previous one. But the thought of asking Victoria out had spurred him on at least to try and so he had headed for home, but in the end he hadn't been able to see it through.

It wasn't that he was being stubborn, more that he was honest and could not simply walk in as if nothing had happened until he had dealt with it in his head.

Dominic wanted a real relationship with his brother and nephew—and yes, Lorna too—and he would not be pushed, for the sake of family peace, into a false one.

So, while he had hoped to visit family and the new baby, the hurt was still there. So he had stayed in a hotel and taken some time to drive around the land that he loved, and in that time he had done a whole lot of thinking.

A lot of his thinking had been about her.

Victoria.

And now she met his eyes.

'We decided not to hold the meeting tonight,' she started to explain. 'We're going to—'

'I already heard,' Dominic said, and when Rosie drifted off to join another conversation, it was just them.

'Do you want to get something to eat?' he offered.

'I've already had something. Do you?'

'No.'

No, he did not want to try and find them a table in a crowded pub. Already Robyn was making her way over, no doubt to discuss how the interviews with the press had gone.

'Come on,' Dominic said to Victoria, because there was no chance of having an uninterrupted conversation here in the pub.

They stepped out into the street but that wasn't the ideal location either.

'We could go to mine,' Victoria offered, but Dominic shook his head.

Given what had happened with Lorna he did not want to get closer to Victoria in the least. He did not want to see where she lived and sit and have a cosy chat. 'There's no need for that,' Dominic said. 'We can say everything we need to here.'

Victoria frowned. 'Are you sure?'

'Quite sure.'

So she went ahead and told him in her usual succinct way. 'I'm eight weeks pregnant.'

And what had taken place between them was six weeks ago, but she guessed, given his qualifications, that she didn't have to tell him that they added on two weeks.

Or maybe she did, because he was giving her a somewhat quizzical look, and so she clarified things in order that there could be no doubt.

'It's yours.'

Dominic said nothing.

What was there to say?

He hadn't even thought to have that discussion with Lorna.

Dominic had trusted his girlfriend completely and look how that had turned out.

How the hell could he even come close to believing someone with whom he'd had sex with on impulse, who carried condoms and who, by her own revelation that night, had just finished with someone else.

No, he would not be fooled twice.

'I've got to reschedule my ultrasound,' Victoria said. 'I wasn't sure if you might want to be present.'

He gave a snort as he recalled the last time he'd been at an ultrasound and all that had transpired then—listening as the doctor gave the dates and asking her to repeat them, then trying to catch Lorna's eyes as she turned away.

And Victoria saw the look he gave and interpreted it correctly. 'I don't need you to hold my hand, Dominic. I meant, I accept it might be hard to believe it is yours but the ultrasound will confirm the dates for you.'

'No, it won't—you say that you're eight weeks pregnant. Well, that means they can only give parameters between five to seven days...'

'Thanks for that.' Victoria sneered at the implication.

'We used protection,' Dominic pointed out.

'I'm not about to try and convince you,' Victoria said. 'I know it's yours but I accept that you might not believe that it is,' she said. 'Whatever way, I felt that you had a right to know and now you do.'

Dominic just stood there, for once unsure what to say. She was as factual and direct as always, but he had been let down so badly before that there was no way he would be letting down his guard again.

He would be keeping his distance until he was certain.

'When the baby is born, arrange for a DNA and, if it's confirmed as mine, then we'll speak about things.'

'That's it?' Victoria checked.

'What else do you want?'

'With that attitude I don't want anything from you,' Victoria said, and walked off.

He watched her hitch up her bag and cross the street, and she was about to disappear into the underground when Dominic found himself running after her.

'Wait!' he called out.

She didn't.

Victoria stepped onto one of the escalators but she didn't stand and let it carry her down. Instead she walked quickly but knew Dominic was fast and so he caught up with her at the bottom.

'Victoria, wait.'

'No.' It was just as busy here as it had been in the pub and so it was a hopeless place for conversation and, given his attitude, she would not be asking him again to come back to her flat. 'I'm tired, Dominic. It's been a helluva long day and right now I just want to get home and go to bed.'

He could see that she was tired and he thought of the day she had had. And he recalled the anger he had felt when she'd raced forward to grab that child.

No, not anger.

It had been fear that he had felt.

He moved her aside and she stood straight rather than lean against the wall; he put up an arm that buffeted them from the people that passed.

'Have you told work?' Dominic asked, already guessing the answer.

'Not yet,' Victoria said. 'My crewmate knows.'

'Work needs to know.' He thought of her today and the hell of that fire, and not just that—it was a dangerous job indeed. 'Victoria!'

'I'll make that choice,' Victoria said.

It wasn't really a choice; as soon as she knew she was pregnant she should tell them, but Victoria was still unable to get her head around things and had been putting it off.

'Look...' Dominic started, but she shook her head and made to leave.

'I'm not discussing this here. You were the one who chose to be told out on the street.'

He had been.

But to stop her from dashing off he told her some of his truth.

'Do you know how I know about date parameters?'

'Well, you're a doctor...'

'I know about them,' Dominic interrupted, 'because I'd been reading up on things in the baby books. A few months ago I sat in on an ultrasound with my ex and found out that the baby we were expecting couldn't possibly be mine, because I was in India at the time it was conceived. That's why I moved down to London.'

She looked at him, right at him, but instead of a sympathetic response Victoria told Dominic a truth. 'I'm not your ex.'

And then she ducked under his arm and was gone.

CHAPTER SEVEN

NO, SHE CERTAINLY wasn't his ex.

Two days later Dominic sat in the back of the lecture theatre and watched as a very efficient Victoria took to the stage.

She was wearing a grey linen dress with flat pumps and her hair was tied in a loose ponytail. She was petite, but her presence was commanding and despite stragglers arriving in the lecture theatre she started the meeting on time.

'Let's get started,' Victoria said. 'It's so good to see such an amazing turnout.'

She paused as someone's phone rang out and, Dominic noted, Victoria was far from shy—instead of putting the person at ease, she glared.

'Can everyone *please* silence their phones?'

'It might be kind of important, Victoria,' someone called out, and Dominic smiled at the smart response, given the people who were in the room.

'Then put it on vibrate,' Victoria said. 'We've got a lot to get through and if we have pagers and phones going off every two minutes we shan't get very far.'

There was a brief pause as a lot of people turned their phones onto silent.

Dominic's was already off.

He had started carrying it at work, though he kept it on silent. He still did not want his personal life intruding. But now, if his parents called, which they quite often did, he would let it go to message, then speak to them during a lull in his day rather than at the end of his shift.

There still wasn't much to talk about. They opted to discuss the weather rather than face the unpalatable topic as to what their youngest son had done.

And, Dominic knew, he had taken out his malaise and mistrust on Victoria.

That was the real reason he was here tonight; he hoped to speak with her afterwards.

For now though, he listened to what she had to say.

Victoria kicked off the meeting. 'The fire has really helped showcase to people how vital an institution the hospital is.'

Robyn's hunch had proven right, and now Victoria and Dominic were the face of the Save Paddington's campaign.

The image of them came up on the screen behind Victoria and she tried not to glance over at Dominic.

He hadn't been at the other meetings, though she now knew he had been on leave. But even if she was glad of the big show tonight and for any support that could be mustered, there was one exception—Victoria rather wished he would stay away, for Dominic was a distraction that she did not need.

Then again, that's what he had done since their night together—distracted her from her life.

Even before that, she had always found herself looking out for him whenever she and Glen brought a patient into the Castle.

'The travel time is a vital point we should make,' said Matthew McGrory, a burns specialist. He had been working around the clock with the patients from the school fire and looked as if he had barely slept in days. 'Due to the sheer volume of casualties there were some patients that were taken to Riverside, but the most severely injured children came here and were treated quickly. That first hour is vital and a lot of that time would have been lost had Paddington's not been here.'

'Indeed.' Victoria was up-front and well versed. 'And we do need to push travel time and the difference it will make to locals. However, patients come from far and wide for treatment at Paddington's. We need to promote both aspects and we need to start working out how best to do that.'

It was a call to arms meeting.

'The press is onside at the moment,' Robyn said, 'but we need to keep up that momentum.'

Rebecca, a cardiothoracic surgeon who headed the transplant team, spoke about the real issue with doctors leaving and the problems the cardiology department were facing. 'We're only able to recruit on very short-term contracts. Paddington's has always attracted world-class doctors and we can't let that change. The campaign needs to showcase the hospital in its best light.'

Ideas were building and they were starting to run with them; it was decided that the first major event to be held would be a fundraising ball.

The meeting ran for a couple of hours and Dominic watched and listened.

He could only admire Victoria.

From an initial very scattered effort, the drive to save PCH was now starting to come together.

Certainly, with the fire and its aftermath still prominent in the news, the public were starting to understand the real implications of Paddington's closing.

'Right,' Victoria said. 'I think that gives us enough to be going on with for now. Anyone who wants to carry on the discussion can—I think most of us who are not working will be heading over to the Frog and Peach.'

Phones went back on and people started heading out. Dominic made his way over to the stage.

'Well done,' he told her.

Victoria simply ignored him and packed up her computer and things in silence.

She had been on days off since the fire and hadn't seen him since the night she had told him about the baby. She certainly didn't want to see him now.

There was no getting out of it though. Dominic waited till everyone was gone and, when finally they were alone, she turned to face him and hear what he had to say.

'I want to apologise for my reaction the other night,' Dominic said.

She understood it though.

Victoria had sat bristling on the Tube but, even as she had let herself into her flat, she had been able to see where he was coming from. Dominic, especially given what he had been through with his ex, had every right to be suspicious as to whether or not the baby was his, Victoria had decided.

And she was right to hold back, but for reasons of her own that she could not think about right now.

'Dominic,' Victoria said. 'I'm pregnant from our one-night stand. Now, I accept, given what happened between us, you might assume that I drop my knickers like that...' She snapped her fingers. 'But actually I don't. I broke up with someone before Christmas and since then...'

'I don't need your history. Victoria, I'm thirty-eight. I'm sure we're both going to have had our share of past relationships.'

And that was perhaps the moment she fully realised just how very different they were.

Victoria was twenty-nine and as for relationships...

She hadn't really had any of note.

Oh, there had been a couple of boyfriends who had lasted a few months, but she had never lived with anyone and, in truth, had never really been in love.

'Well, you shouldn't be so sure,' Victoria responded. 'I don't do very well with relationships and so I tend to steer clear of them. As I said, I broke up with someone just before Christmas, and apart from a couple of first dates that went nowhere, there hasn't been anyone since then.' No wonder the condom hadn't been up to much, Victoria thought; it had been in her purse for months. 'This year, apart from one torrid tryst in a turret, there's been no one.' And she smiled at her little tongue twister. 'I believe you were the said torrid tryst.'

'Indeed I was.'

'And I'm sorry your ex cheated and that you're not over her, but that's your issue and—'

'It's not that,' Dominic interrupted.

She raised her eyebrows and Dominic had to concede a smile,

because yes, it probably sounded to her as if he wasn't over his ex. He guessed Victoria thought that he had run away to England because of a break-up, so knew he had to explain things a bit better than that. 'The person that Lorna was sleeping with was my brother.'

'Oh,' Victoria said.

And he waited for her to avert her eyes or to do what everyone else did and move to quickly change the subject, but instead she gave a small grimace.

'Well, that's awkward!'

And he smiled a little and admitted, 'Indeed it is.'

'Are you and your brother close?' Victoria asked.

'We were.'

'And had you been going out with her for long?'

'Yes,' Dominic said.

'Were you living together?'

'Yes.' He nodded but Dominic didn't want all these questions. He was just trying to explain, a little, why he had reacted to the news of her pregnancy in the way that he had. 'I really don't want to discuss it.'

Only that wasn't quite true.

Dominic had discussed it with no one.

Everyone in his family wanted to simply move on from the uncomfortable topic and to act as if nothing had happened. Not Victoria though—she actually made him smile when she spoke next.

'You're *very* good at torrid trysts.'

'It would seem that I am.'

'Were you both sleeping with her at the same time?'

'Victoria!' His voice held a warning. 'I don't want to talk about it.'

'Fair enough.' She shrugged. 'But if that's the case, then I'm going to go for a drink with my committee.'

'Don't we have rather a lot to discuss?'

'I'll be fine,' Victoria said. 'I cope with things. So really, at this stage there's nothing much to talk about. If you want a DNA test once the baby's here, then that's fine too.'

They started to walk down the corridor but as Dominic went straight she turned to the left.

'Where are you going?'

'It's a short cut.'

Dominic didn't want the short cut; he rather liked spending time with her and, though he didn't say that, of course, it was actually nice to be walking and talking.

The short cut was an old quadrangle that he hadn't seen before and there was a glimpse of a navy sky and the scent of fresh air; Dominic guessed it would be a very welcome space to know, if working over a long weekend.

'Maybe it's not such a short cut,' Victoria added as she looked up and felt the cool evening air on her cheeks. 'More, the scenic route.'

'You really do know this hospital like the back of your hand,' Dominic commented. 'Did your father bring you here a lot?'

'Yes, there were a lot of nanny changes and so I'd be brought along until a replacement was found.'

She had been close to a couple of the nannies but they all too soon found it unbearable to work for her father and left.

It had been the same with his girlfriends, who would attempt to win over the daughter to impress the father and then would drop her like a hot stone as soon as the relationship came to an end.

Even when she had been a bit older, Victoria would come here after school or on long weekends, rather than sit in an empty house. Here at the quadrangle, weather permitting, she had done an awful lot of homework!

'What about your mother?' Dominic asked as they started to walk.

'They broke up.' Victoria gave him no more information about her mother than that. She turned and looked at him. 'I shan't let you just drift in and out of my child's life. And I'm not having him or her dropped off here just because you have to work. My baby will be at home with me.'

Dominic said nothing. If Victoria thought he would be a hands-off father, then she was wrong, but Dominic wasn't going to argue about that now.

He had something to ask her. 'I would like to be at the ultrasound.'

But Victoria had been thinking about just that over the last couple of days and immediately she shook her head. 'I don't think so. That offer has been withdrawn.'

'Can I ask why?'

'It just has.'

Dominic knew he didn't have any right to be there and so he chose not to push the issue.

For now.

They were out of the hospital and walking over to the Frog and Peach but suddenly Victoria did not want to go in.

'Are you coming?'

'No.'

She offered no more explanation than that. Victoria didn't need to give him one and was annoyed when Dominic walked after her.

'What?' she asked.

'There's surely more to discuss.'

'I don't see that there is. I'll send you a copy of the images and you can...' She shrugged. 'You can do whatever you're going to do. Measure its little crown rump length and decide if it might possibly be yours.'

Yes, she had read the baby books too.

And she walked off with more purpose this time.

It was all starting to feel terribly real.

For weeks she'd been stuffing down the possibility that she might be pregnant; now she knew for certain that she was.

But it wasn't just the baby, or telling work that concerned Victoria.

It was Dominic MacBride himself.

She had heard his concern about her working the other night and now she could feel his slight push to be more present; she knew that it was only going to increase.

And she did not want to start relying on him.

She thought of her own mother, who had upped and left, and all the nannies and girlfriends and wives that her father had gone through.

There had been no constant in her life apart from her father and he had merely dragged her to work and palmed her off to others.

No, she did not want to start depending on a man who would no doubt soon lose interest and be gone.

She simply would not do that to her child.

CHAPTER EIGHT

DOMINIC AWOKE TO the sound of sirens in the street below.

In a decisive move, he had bought a three-bedroom apartment close to the hospital and, with the ambulance station nearby, he heard sirens often. Now, each time that he did, Dominic wondered if it might be Victoria's ambulance on its way to something.

She wouldn't even know that she had passed by his apartment, Dominic thought, as Victoria didn't even know where he lived.

They were so removed from each other's lives.

And yet they were not.

Because he thought about her all the time.

He liked her.

Or rather, he was attracted to her enormously and that didn't aide sensible thinking.

Since their liaison at Paddington's Dominic had found himself thinking about her an awful lot.

Prior to that even.

On finding out about Jamie and Lorna he had closed off from others and thrown himself into work.

Absolutely.

It had been his escape from hurt and anger, and the thought of starting again with anyone had been far from Dominic's mind.

But then she had stomped her way into his thoughts with her heavy boots and crisp handovers. Her confident smile had felt like an intrusion, yet he had found himself looking out for her.

Noticing her.

Victoria was a very different woman from any that he was used to liking.

She had intrigued him when Dominic had not wanted to be intrigued, so much so that, even while talking to a parent, he had been aware that she had been stood registering a patient in Reception. He had seen her duck behind the shelves and, later that same day, he himself had done the same and found the place to which she escaped.

And in his time at Paddington's he had escaped there a few times.

Once, when a young life had been lost, he had come from Theatre and told the parents that he had been unable to save their child.

In fact, Victoria and Glen had been the crew who had brought the patient in.

It had been the worst of nights.

His career meant that he was no stranger to death, but while all loss hurt, this one had been particularly painful.

Dominic had raced the little girl to Theatre but she had died on the operating table and telling the parents had been hell.

They had wanted her to be an organ donor and wanted her heart to go to another child.

It was their fervent wish, yet she was already dead.

Dominic had never been more grateful for the appearance of Rebecca in the interview room. She headed the transplant team and Dominic could only admire her empathy for the parents.

She had spoken with them at length and had gone through what *could* be done to give the gift of hope to another child.

Yes, she had empathy because, seeing Dominic, she had said that she would take it from here.

He had lain in the on-call room going over and over the surgery, wondering if there was anything more he could have done, while knowing that the child's fate had been sealed at the moment of impact.

Unable to sleep he had got up and it had been to the turret that he retreated, where he had looked out to a dark London night.

There, away from the constant background hospital noise, he had thought about the doctors who had fought so hard to save his brother, and accepted he had done the same for that child.

There was solace in that quiet space.

And together he and Victoria had found solace again on a very different night—the night that little William had been born.

Every sensible part of him screeched for caution and told Dominic that he could well be being taken for a ride.

Yet the sensible parts did not take into account the magic of that night, the mutual succour, for despite Victoria's denial, despite insisting her pensive mood was reserved only for the loss of the famed institution, Dominic was certain that she had been hurting for other reasons that night too.

He wanted to know Victoria some more.

Baby aside, caution aside, he wanted to know the woman behind the cool façade and it was time to do something about that.

'You've got an admirer, Victoria!'

She returned from a call-out with Glen to the light teasing of other staff. A large bouquet of gorgeous flowers was waiting for her at the station. There were freesias, which were her favourite, as well as hyacinths and other blooms. They filled the air with a rich sweet scent and all the gorgeous shades of spring were on display.

Though her heart was beating rapidly she did not show it in her expression. In fact, Victoria rolled her eyes as she opened the card, for she was quite certain who they were from.

If Dominic thought that a stunning array of flowers was going to give him a second hearing, and that she would let him in on the ultrasound, then he could not be more wrong.

But then she read the card and found out that no, she was not at the forefront of his thoughts.

'It's from Lewis's parents,' Victoria said, and she smiled as she read it. 'He was the neck injury from the fire at Westbourne Grove.'

'How is he doing?' her line manager asked.

'Apparently he's doing really well and they'll soon be taking him home.'

Victoria only knew that from the card. Unlike Glen, who checked on almost everyone, Victoria chose not to follow up on her patients.

It wasn't that she didn't care; it was more that bad news was unsettling and she had made a conscious choice not to get overly involved.

Lewis's parents had left a present for Glen too—a very nice bottle of wine that he decided would remain in his locker until they had finished nights next week, as on the Monday it would be his and Hayley's wedding anniversary.

Glen chatted about his plans for that night as they drove to their next job. 'Ten years,' Glen said. 'I can't believe it.'

Nor could Victoria envision it! 'So what are you getting her?'

'Hayley says that she doesn't want anything. She just wants...' Glen hesitated and then changed whatever he had been about to say. 'I'm getting her an eternity ring. Sapphire and diamonds.'

'That sounds gorgeous,' Victoria said. 'So what does she really want?' She looked over to Glen, who concentrated on the road ahead, but Victoria could guess exactly what Hayley wanted and Glen knew it.

'Leave it, Victoria.'

Victoria would not.

'How did you pull up after the school fire?' she asked.

'I'm fine. They got everyone out.'

Victoria knew that Glen was stressed. They had been crewmates for two years now. Though it had taken her a while to open up, even a little bit, Glen had been open right from the start.

He was friendly and laid-back and brilliant at his job, but recently things had changed.

They had been called out to a motor vehicle accident a couple of months ago and taken a very sick child to Paddington's, where she had subsequently died.

Some jobs were harder than others and Glen had taken this one very personally indeed. The little girl had been the same age as his daughter and the accident had occurred on a road that his wife often took.

It was a couple of weeks after that that Victoria had noticed the change in him. Instead of his usual laid-back self, he was tense at times and kept calling home to check with Hayley that everything was okay.

Despite Glen's insistence that he was fine, Victoria was sure that Hayley wanted Glen to speak to one of the counsellors made available to them, but Glen steadfastly refused to do so.

She would wait for her moment, Victoria decided, and, in the meantime, keep a bit of a closer eye on him.

'Your flowers were nice,' Glen said.

'Beautiful,' Victoria agreed.

Which they were, of course, but what was niggling her was that there *had* been a thud of disappointment that the flowers weren't from Dominic and this unsettled her.

It was a busy morning and just as they were starting to think about lunch they were called out to a woman who had collapsed in a shop.

'I haven't got time to go to hospital,' the woman protested as she lay there. Her daughter was with her and was upset, and as they were transferring her mother to the ambulance, they found out that it was her ninth birthday.

'No school today?' Glen asked the little girl.

'She's goes to Westbourne Grove,' her mother said.

Victoria looked over and gave the young girl a smile. 'You're having a bit of a time of it, aren't you?'

The girl nodded. 'My friend Ryan is very sick.'

'That must be so hard for you,' Victoria said.

They took her and her mother to Riverside but once they had settled them in, and just as they were making up the stretcher, Victoria saw her father walking into the department.

He gave her a very cool look. 'Victoria.'

She gave him a small nod back and let out a breath when he had passed.

'Who's that?' Glen asked, but Victoria just gave a noncommittal shrug as if she wasn't really sure who the man who had just passed was.

She wasn't going to tell Glen that it was her father.

Glen chatted about his family all the time and, though it drove Victoria bonkers on occasion, she liked the glimpses of family life and was embarrassed by the state of her own.

They were just starting to think about lunch again when Dispatch asked if they could transfer a patient from Riverside's children's ward to the burns unit at Paddington's.

The burns unit had been stretched to capacity by the fire but a bed had opened up and a very sweet little girl called Amber was, this morning, on her way to join the others at the Castle.

'Hello, Amber,' Victoria said when she met her.

She had a deep burn on her hand, arm and shoulder that was going to require grafting. Amber became teary when she saw the stretcher.

'It's no problem,' Glen said. 'We can take you to the ambulance in a wheelchair if you prefer.'

That seemed to cheer her up and so they fetched a wheelchair and the small problem was solved, but she became distressed again when she saw the ambulance. No doubt Amber was remembering the pain she had been in the last time, and remembered the fear of the lights and sirens.

'I'm going to make you a chicken to keep you company,' Glen said, and Victoria smiled as he pulled out a rubber glove and blew it up.

He was very good with the little children and knew how to amuse and distract them with antics, such as this one, and Victoria tended to leave that side of things to him.

Soon enough, Amber was holding her 'chicken' and seated in the ambulance, and the transfer went smoothly. As they made their way up to the burns ward she saw Dominic coming down the corridor and walking towards them.

He wasn't in scrubs; he was in a suit and tie and, to Victoria's mind, looked impossibly handsome.

Did she nod and say hi? Victoria wondered, but Dominic dealt with that—he nodded a greeting to them both and Victoria gave a brief smile back.

Glen was a bit cheeky. 'Direct Admission,' he said as they passed. 'We're taking her straight to the ward.'

'That's what I like to see,' Dominic called back.

It was just a little dig, a small exchange, but hearing his voice and dry response made Victoria smile and feel a bit hot in the face.

The burns unit was busy but they made Amber very welcome.

'Hello there.' Matthew, the burns specialist, smiled to Amber as she was wheeled in. 'I'm Matt.'

As Glen and Victoria wheeled Amber into her side room, Matthew had a brief chat with the girl's mother but she soon joined them.

'It's good to be at the Castle,' she admitted, clearly relieved and reassured to be at the famed hospital. 'Amber, you've got a couple of friends here already.'

'It's just like being back at school.' Victoria smiled.

Soon the little girl was settled and they could head off. It was incredibly warm on the burns unit as the temperature was kept high for the patients, but it made for hot work. Victoria would be very glad to get out of there, but first she had a small chat with Matt, who had spoken at the Save Paddington's meeting.

'Still being kept busy?' Victoria asked.

He nodded. 'I don't think that's going to change any time soon. I meant what I said about it being good that the fire happened so close to us. It made all the difference to some of these children. Did you bring in Simon?'

'Simon?' Victoria frowned and then shook her head.

'The little boy from the foster home?' Glen asked, because he knew about all the patients, and Matt nodded.

'No, that was another crew. How's he doing?' Glen asked while Victoria was overheating.

'I need a drink,' she said, and left them to it. Glen would stand chatting for ages and it really was terribly warm in there.

The drinks machine wasn't working but as they passed the canteen Glen nudged her.

'We'll get lunch,' he said.

And she couldn't really protest. There was no stretcher to take back to the vehicle and even if Dominic was in there Victoria knew that she couldn't avoid him all the time.

She just rather hoped that he wasn't there today.

'What do you want?' Glen asked, because they had their routine and usually Victoria would go and get a table while he went and got the food.

Except Dominic was there.

She had known the moment she stepped in, and though she deliberately didn't look over, she was aware that he was seated in the far corner chatting with a woman.

She really didn't want Dominic seeing her alone and coming over for another 'discussion,' or request to come to the scan.

'Victoria?' Glen checked, because she hadn't answered his question.

'I'm not sure what I want,' Victoria said. 'I'll come with you.'

She chose a salad sandwich and bought a mug of hot chocolate and a bottle of water, as Glen chose tomato soup and a couple of rolls. Together they found a table, thankfully one far away from Dominic.

She drank half her water and then opened up her salad sandwich and took an unenthusiastic bite as Glen slurped his tomato soup.

'Can I ask you something, Victoria?'

'What?' she snapped, awaiting the inevitable questions as to when she was going to tell work, or whether she had told the father.

Glen had asked both regularly since he'd found out.

'Do you put butter on your peanut butter sandwiches?'

Victoria smiled. She liked their often mundane conversations and it helped take her mind off Dominic. 'Of course I do.'

'Well, Hayley doesn't. And apparently Adam has asked that when it's my turn to make the sandwiches, for me not to put any butter on.'

'Adam's nine?' Victoria checked, and Glen nodded and took another slurp of his soup. 'Well, then, I'd suggest he makes it himself if he's going to be so choosy.'

'You haven't tried getting four children to school on time, have you?' Glen sighed. 'If they all made their own sandwiches, aside from the mess that they'd leave behind, they'd never get there.'

And she conceded, because no, she'd never had to get four little people to school before.

But hopefully in a few years she'd have one little person to get there.

The pregnancy was starting to take shape in Victoria's mind and she was beginning to get excited at the prospect of being a mother.

She liked the glimpses of family life that Glen gave her.

It helped her to picture things a bit.

Glen made sandwiches for everyone if he was on an early shift. It gave Hayley a break and it worked well.

Except he'd left his behind today.

Victoria could no more imagine her father making lunch for her than a flight to the moon.

It just hadn't happened.

And they hadn't taken meals together, unless they were out at some function.

'Have you told the guy he's going to be a father yet?' Glen asked, and Victoria sighed. She was just about to tell him to mind his own business when someone answered the question for her.

'Yes, Glen, she has.'

And she stared at her half-eaten sandwich rather than at Dominic, who very calmly took a seat at their table.

'Well, this *is* awkward,' Victoria said.

'Why is it awkward?' Dominic asked. 'All three of us already know you're pregnant.' He looked to Glen. 'Did you know that the father was me?'

'I had an idea that it might be,' Glen admitted, and Victoria threw him an angry look as she realised that he had deliberately steered her into the canteen. Glen picked up his rolls and then stood. 'I'll see you back at the vehicle, Victoria.'

As he walked off Victoria looked over to Dominic. 'I'll be having words with Glen.'

'I wouldn't bother. I was coming by the station tonight to leave a message for you to contact me,' Dominic said.

'Why?'

'Because we need to speak.'

'About what?'

'Well, Glen knows...' Dominic started.

'Glen guessed that I was pregnant,' Victoria interrupted, assuming he was annoyed that others knew.

'Victoria, I'm glad that he knows. It's good that you've got him looking out for you. Mind you, he should have stopped you when there was that fire.'

'Don't interfere with my work,' Victoria said. 'He's my partner, not my line manager. I make my own choices.'

'Fair enough,' Dominic said. He was trying and failing to treat her as he would a colleague. And trying to rationalise that he had every right to be concerned if she was carrying his child.

Only, it wasn't the baby he had been thinking about on that day of the fire, because he hadn't known she was pregnant then.

He had been loading a child into the ambulance and had turned at the sound of the explosion.

He had seen her rush forward towards the firefighter.

Glen had rushed forward too.

And he had seen the firefighters going into the burning building over and over, but it had been Victoria who he had wanted to go and haul back.

Dominic knew already that she wasn't anything like the women he was usually attracted to.

And his response to her was like nothing he had known.

He had just watched her arrive in the canteen a little pink and flustered, though he had soon worked out why when he had watched her gulp down half a bottle of water—they had just come from the burns unit and boots and overalls would not have been the most comfortable things to be wearing.

And he had seen her and Glen, casually chatting as they selected their meals.

He was actually very glad that Glen knew.

'I wasn't going to broadcast the fact you were the father,' Victoria added, 'until the paperwork came in.'

'Who else knows? What about family?' he asked, worried that she had been dealing with this on her own.

'I told my father.'

'And what did he say?'

'Not very much.'

'Is he cross?'

'Cross?' Victoria checked.

'Well, because you're single?'

'I don't think he gives me enough thought to be cross. He was irritated. I asked if he could pull a few strings so that I could have the baby here at Paddington's and he did.' She closed her eyes for a moment. 'Actually, I just ran into him at Riverside.' And she told him what she could not tell even to Glen.

'We hardly even said hello to each other. We had words the other day.'

'About the baby?'

'Sort of.' She gave an uncomfortable shrug.

'I've spoken with your father on occasion,' Dominic told her, and he watched as her eyelids briefly fluttered as he said without words that he got what an awful man he was. When she said nothing he moved the conversation on.

'And your mother?'

'She's not on the scene. I've already told you that.' Victoria took a long drink of her water but then chose to continue. 'That was what my father and I had words about.'

His patience was pleasant; he waited as her eyes scanned his and she wrestled with how much to say. 'He suggested that I think very carefully whether to go ahead with the pregnancy, and that he knew firsthand how difficult it was being a single parent.' Her lips were pale and they clamped for a moment and his eyes still waited. 'He didn't really parent though,' Victoria said.

'Did you say that?'

'No.'

'So what did you say?'

Victoria flicked her eyes away and she gave a tight shrug. 'Nothing.'

And at one-fifteen, in a busy hospital canteen, Dominic knew for certain that he was about to become a father. He knew that because Victoria had just lied.

Something far more had gone on when she'd had words with her father.

And if he could tell when she lied, then the rest was the truth.

'I think,' Victoria said, 'that I'd better get used to the idea that the only person with any enthusiasm for this baby is me.'

And she looked over to him with an angry gaze while her heart waited for him to refute, to say, *No, no, I'm thrilled, Victoria*, but he just looked back at her with an expression that she could not read.

And then she amended that request from her heart for Dominic to placate her because she wouldn't believe him anyway.

How could he be thrilled to find out that his one-night stand was expecting a baby?

Yet that was what he did—he thrilled.

There was such a pleasure to be had simply sitting here with him. There was such patience in his posture and a measured maturity to him.

Oh, what did he do to her? Victoria wondered, because she had forgotten to look away and still met his eyes.

There was an attraction between them that was so intense it was as if the rest of the people in the canteen had simply faded away.

'Would you like to go out for dinner tonight?' Dominic asked.

'Dinner?' She frowned. She had just stated that no one was very enthusiastic about the baby and he was asking her to bloody dinner. 'What sort of a response is that?'

'A very sensible one,' Dominic said.

He would not lie; he would not feign delight just to appease.

'A date,' Dominic said.

'No!'

'Just dinner,' he added, as if she hadn't turned him down. 'No talk of babies or DNA tests. We can see if we get on, see if we fancy each other.'

And she laughed.

It was such a moot point.

'That's the only thing we've got going for us,' Victoria said.

He liked her assertion.

'I think that's quite a lot to be going on with,' Dominic said. 'For a first date at least.'

CHAPTER NINE

IT WAS QUITE a lot to be going on with!

Victoria had never had this feeling while getting ready for a date.

As soon as her shift was over she raced out of the station and was then chased out by Glen because she'd forgotten to take her flowers.

From there Victoria made a mad dash to the shops where, shame on her, she bought some fresh linen for the bed.

In her defence, Victoria reasoned, she had been meaning to buy some for ages and it was on sale.

Yet, she was pushing it for time and there was one reason only that she was making sure that her bedroom was looking its best!

Yes, she hadn't felt like this in for ever. In fact, it was the first time she had been truly excited to welcome someone into her home.

There was anticipation and a flutter of lovely nerves as she made up the bed, put her flowers into a vase and carried them through to the lounge. She put them on the window ledge and then headed back to the bedroom to choose what to wear. She chose her underwear carefully and then made a dash for the shower.

Dominic pulled up at the flat and, when he buzzed and was let in, she was still in her dressing gown with wet hair.

'Sorry, we got another call-out just as we were heading back to the station...'

Which was true, but she omitted to mention the mad dash to pretty up her flat.

'It's fine.'

'I shan't be long,' Victoria said.

Her flat was tiny and really very lovely despite its very good view of trains.

It was, Dominic decided as he stood in the lounge, far more straightforward and homelier looking than its owner. There was a two-seater couch and a large chair, which was clearly her favourite, because there was a large ottoman and a pile of magazines beside it; the small shelf was crammed with paramedic procedure manuals.

It was neat but not as fastidiously so as he might have expected; it was very much a working girl's flat.

There was a gorgeous arrangement of flowers in the window and Victoria smiled to herself when she returned to the lounge to find him surreptitiously trying to read the card.

'They're from Lewis's parents,' she told him. 'The neck injury from Westbourne Grove.'

'Good.'

'I don't have a secret admirer.'

'No, you have a blatant one,' he said. 'You look beautiful.'

He made her feel just that.

Whether in boots and baggy green overalls with a messy bun, or dressed up, which tonight she was, he had always made her feel beautiful. This evening she had on a velvety, aubergine-coloured dress and black heels, and her hair was worn loose and down.

'Where are we going?' Victoria asked.

Bed, he wanted to say.

Bed, she hoped he would say.

Yet, there was so much that needed to be sorted first and it would possibly be easier to do that with a table between them.

'There's a nice French restaurant that I've heard about but have never been inclined to try,' Dominic said.

'That sounds lovely.'

Everything sounded lovely with his rich accent. He could have said they were going out for fish and chips and she'd have smiled.

She was putting in her diamond studs and she smiled as she saw him watching.

'They got us into this mess.'

'It's not a mess, Victoria. It's a baby and it will sort.'

But it still felt like a mess to her as she was so jumbled in her head. She wanted his kiss and his touch and to be just a couple going out to dinner, or deciding to hell with it and ringing for pizza later in bed. Yet they were so back to front, and he hadn't wanted to go out with her until he'd known she was pregnant.

It was a hurt that she knew, if they got closer, would only grow along with the baby.

Yes, there was an awful lot to sort out.

'Come on,' he said.

The restaurant was gorgeous and intimate and they were led to a lovely secluded table; it was so small that their knees touched, though neither minded that.

The menu was gorgeous and Victoria groaned when she saw all the lovely cheeses and raw egg sauces that she'd been told to avoid.

'When I'm not pregnant I'm coming here again and having everything on here that I can't have now!'

'Bad choice?' Dominic asked because he hadn't really given the menu a thought beforehand.

'Oh, I'm not complaining.'

She ordered coq au vin and he ordered steak béarnaise. Conversation was awkward at first, but then the food arrived.

'This is delicious,' Victoria said as she tasted her chicken. 'I make it sometimes but mine doesn't come close to this...'

'Well, it wouldn't, would it?'

She looked up. 'Why not?'

'You're not a French chef, Victoria.'

And he made her smile because he stood up to her; he challenged her. 'I could have been, had I put my mind to it—well, apart from the French bit.'

They chatted a little about the campaign to save the hospital and the fundraising ball and then she asked if he missed his old hospital in Scotland.

Dominic paused to think about it. He had been happy where he was, but working at Paddington's he was stretching his skills and really starting to settle in and enjoy it. 'More than I expected to,' he admitted. 'When I left Edinburgh, I wasn't planning on making a career move as such, yet I have. It's a great position and I doubt it would have opened up if there hadn't been the threat of closure.'

'A lot are leaving?'

Dominic nodded. 'They've just recruited a new cardiologist but I know a lot of departments are being held together with locums.'

'Was it hard to leave Edinburgh?'

'Of course,' Dominic said.

'Do you still miss it?'

He didn't really know the answer to that. Going back while on annual leave he had asked himself the same, but the fact was, he was enjoying work and had looked forward to returning to London.

He glanced over to Victoria, who had given up on her main and was waiting for his response. 'In part.'

She was scared to ask which part?

There was so much she wanted to know.

But some conversations were best had over chocolate crepes and vanilla ice cream.

Lorna and Jamie was one of them.

The food was delicious, the topic not so, but they chewed their way through both.

'Did you ever suspect there was something between them?' she asked.

'No, they only met the once...'

He swallowed and carried on.

'Every couple of years I go for a stint of working in India. I first went when I was in medical school and a few of us have kept it going. The week before I was due to go we had a get-together, and Jamie, my brother, came along. Until then he and

Lorna had never met. He'd been overseas and had just got back. Well, they got on really well...'

'Clearly!'

She had spent too long chatting on the road to be shocked, Dominic guessed. And it was actually refreshing just to let it out in the open with someone who wasn't shy or coy.

'Apparently they met a few days later by chance.'

'Do you believe that it was by chance?'

She was asking the same questions that Dominic had asked himself. 'No.'

'Does it matter?' Victoria asked.

'It did to me at the time, but no, not so much now.'

And instead of saying he didn't want to speak about it, this lone wolf shared.

Once upon a time, he had discussed things with family. Not everything, of course—Dominic did not readily share his emotions—but for the most part, he and his family would generally talk. About this they could not. His parents wanted to move on and put it aside, to simply act as if it had never happened.

Victoria was the first person he had felt able to explain to about how it had all unfolded.

'When I got back from India, Lorna was throwing up...'

'Tell me about it.' Victoria groaned.

'Do you have morning sickness?'

She nodded. 'It's fading now.'

But they were not here to discuss *their* baby; they were there to find out about each other, and so she was quiet. But Dominic wanted to know how she had been faring.

'Tell me.'

'It's pretty much gone now—I just get really tired. You're keeping me up—I'm usually in bed by eight.' She gave an eye roll. 'And I've got night duty next week.'

He looked at her and there was a twist of guilt that he hadn't been there for her, that Victoria was doing it all on her own.

'Can you change your shifts?'

'I don't roll like that,' Victoria said, and then changed the subject back to what had happened with him. 'So Lorna had it bad?'

'Yes.' He nodded. 'I told her that she was very probably pregnant and she said no, that she couldn't be. I went and got a test and, of course, she was.'

'Were you pleased?'

'I don't know,' he admitted. 'I think so, but it all felt a bit rushed...'

And together they smiled at the irony of *their* situation.

'Lorna wanted to wait before we told our families.'

'I'll bet she did.'

'I told Jamie though,' Dominic said. 'We were always that close.'

'What was he like when you told him?'

'He said congratulations, but not much else.' Dominic shrugged. 'He's always been a lot more the party type than I am. I thought his lukewarm reaction was because he didn't really see becoming a father as anything to get excited over.'

'So you found out at the ultrasound?' Victoria asked, bemused. 'Wouldn't she have known you might work it out there?' It seemed very cruel to have said nothing.

'In fairness to her, Lorna had a bit of spotting so we went to the hospital, and of course they did an ultrasound. For early pregnancy the dating is very accurate. I guessed she'd be nine weeks, but she was six.'

'So you realised then and there?' Victoria asked, understanding a bit better why he had been so opposed at first to attending her ultrasound.

'I did,' Dominic said. 'I asked the doctor to repeat the dates. I honestly thought at first that she must have them wrong, but of course she hadn't.'

'What did you do?'

'We had company at the time,' Dominic answered, referring to the doctor who had been present. 'So I said nothing. Lorna kept looking away when I tried to catch her eye. The doctor said that everything was fine with the baby and when she left we had a talk. Lorna admitted that while I was away she'd met someone. She said she'd been trying to work her way up to telling me, but then when she'd found out she was pregnant, she just didn't know how to, and she wasn't sure, at that stage, whose baby it was.'

'Did she tell you then who the father was?'
'When pressed.'
'Did you suspect?' Victoria asked.
'Not even for a moment,' Dominic said. 'Even when she said that it was Jamie, I was trying to think who we knew by that name. That it must be a colleague or a friend. Even when she said, "Jamie," I didn't straight away think of him. How stupid is that?'
'Not stupid,' Victoria said.
It showed the depth of the breach of trust.
'What did you do?'
'I told her she could take a taxi and I wished her the best—not very politely though. Then I went and met with Jamie. I'd like to say I did the macho thing and we had a fight, but...' He shook his head. 'My brother had a car accident when he was ten. I was there when he nearly died. I just couldn't bring myself...'
And Victoria could see the conflict on his face; she thought of all the bloody, testosterone-fuelled fights she'd seen in her line of work and admired that he'd held back.
'Jamie was crying and carrying on like an overgrown bairn. He said that he loved her, that as soon as they saw the other, they both knew and neither knew what to do.'
And she closed her eyes for a moment, because it wasn't such a torrid tryst after all. It was really rather sad.
'Do you still love her?'
'No.'
Did she believe him? Victoria didn't know.
Did it matter?
Yes.
It did to her. But though bold in her questions about his brother, Victoria wasn't so bold with her heart.
'I said that I'd leave it to him to tell our parents.' Dominic gave a resigned shrug. 'I basically walked out on my life.'
'You've been back though?' Victoria checked.
'No.'
'But you've just been in Scotland.'
'I didn't see my family though.'
And that unnerved her.

It truly did.

That he had walked out on his life, and that even all these months later, they were still estranged.

'What about your parents?' she asked.

'We've spoken on the phone but they just want it to be put to one side. They don't want to discuss it. They just want it forgotten and for things to go back to the way they were.'

'So what were you doing in Scotland?'

'Thinking.'

And so, too, was Victoria.

All she could see was a man who had walked away. 'Weren't you the one who told me to fight for what's important?'

'I'm doing so,' Dominic responded. 'It doesn't have to be with fists.'

'I'm not talking about physically fighting, but they're your family.'

'And I'm doing my best to sort it out, but I'm not a person who just rushes in. I believe that if you say all is forgiven, then you need to mean it. I can't say I'm there yet.'

As Victoria went quiet Dominic called for the bill.

Yet it wasn't just a lull in the conversation, or that the restaurant was near to closing—her silence ran deeper.

As they drove home all she could think of was her mother, turning her back on her own family. Oh, she knew Dominic had far better reasons, but to have completely walked away from everyone he loved, for Victoria it was deeply unsettling.

All the hope of a lovely evening had been left back at the restaurant and Victoria now just wanted to be alone.

'Thanks for a nice night.'

She didn't ask him up and it did not end in a kiss.

Victoria looked at him and all she could see was a man who had abandoned everything he had professed to love.

And so she ended things with her usual lack of flare.

'I'll see you at work.'

'Victoria—'

'Let's just keep it at that,' Victoria said, and when he reached for her arms, she pulled away. 'Please, Dominic, stay back. I want to focus on the pregnancy and I just don't have space right now for anything else.'

That was the longest speech she had ever given to a man when she broke off things, but she knew it wasn't really enough.

Still, he did not push for more explanation and she was grateful for that. A kiss, or attempts at persuasion, would only further confuse her.

Victoria let herself into her flat and the gorgeous scent of freesias greeted her.

She undressed and got into the cold, new sheets and just lay there.

He had loved Lorna, she was sure of that—they had been living together, having a baby together.

Victoria ached for that glimpse of him—she truly did—but knew it was not hers to see.

They were being forced together by default.

She knew he was an honourable man and might want to do the right thing, or at the very least give it a go.

And of course Dominic had said that he no longer loved Lorna, but what if he still did?

What if that was the real reason for leaving Edinburgh so completely?

Victoria had been honest when she'd told Dominic that she didn't know how to make relationships work.

How on earth could this one?

He had only asked her out in the first place because she was pregnant.

What if Lorna decided she had changed her mind? Victoria pondered.

Or what if Victoria gave them a go and then it was Dominic who decided things weren't working out?

Victoria could not stand to fall for him only to be hurt further down the line when later he left.

And he would.

Victoria had nothing in her life to indicate otherwise.

It was safer to face parenthood alone.

She trusted only in herself.

CHAPTER TEN

SHE WAS HER usual confident self at work and did not try to avoid him.

In fact, Victoria met his eyes when she handed over patients and didn't dash off.

Perhaps she actually wanted to be a single parent, Dominic pondered.

Some women did.

He knew that Victoria was incredibly independent and she had told him that she didn't really do well with relationships.

Yet, he wanted a chance for them, and more and more he was getting used to the idea of being a father.

Not in the rush-out-and-buy-the-books way this time.

He was starting to feel the fear.

He saw her leave the department and Dominic followed her out. He knew they would be making up the vehicle and sure enough there were Victoria and Glen.

She was sitting in the back drinking tea poured from a silver flask; it was the only hint that she might be avoiding him, because in months gone by she and Glen would have come into the department to grab a drink.

'How are you?' he asked.

'Fine.' She gave him a smile and Glen made some noise about calling his wife and left them to it.

'When are you on nights?' Dominic asked.

'We start tomorrow.'

'How do you think you'll go?'

'I'll be fine.'

'Well, if you need anything, I'm on call over the weekend, so just—'

'I shan't need anything, Dominic.'

'You do need to tell work,' he said.

Yes, the fear was real and he could not stand the thought of her out on the streets at night over the weekend.

'I know what I need to do.'

She tried to end the conversation but Dominic persisted.

'What happened the other night?' Dominic asked. He had been over and over it, and the night that had started with such promise had failed for reasons that he could not grasp.

'Nothing happened.'

Exactly.

'Just because I'm not talking to my family at the moment, it doesn't mean—'

'Dominic,' Victoria interrupted him. 'What happens between you and your family is your concern. I don't want to get involved with all the ins and outs. I've got enough going on in my own life. Aside from the pregnancy, the campaign for Paddington's is getting bigger by the day.' She gave a shrug.

'What about us?'

'There's no us,' she said, and she made herself look right at him as she did so. 'Dominic, you only asked me out when you knew I was pregnant...' He opened his mouth to speak but she overrode him. 'If I'd wanted anything more than that night, then I think I'm assertive enough that I'd have asked you for a date, but I didn't. We're adults—we'll work things out closer to the baby's due date.'

And still she made herself look at him, though it was almost her undoing because she wanted to lean on him; she wanted him to tell her again that it wasn't a mess.

That it would sort itself out.

She was scared how deep her feelings were for him and was terrified to let Dominic close.

'Have you rescheduled the ultrasound?' he asked.

Victoria nodded. 'It's on Monday at ten. I'll ask them to cc you in on the images.'

'Victoria,' Glen called her. 'We've got a collapsed infant...'

She tipped her drink into the bush and replaced the lid. 'See you.'

It was a call-out to a baby who was unresponsive and the location was a hotel.

Glen drove them right up to the entrance and they loaded their equipment onto the stretcher. A member of staff greeted them and told them what was happening as she showed them up to the hotel room.

'The father called down to Reception and said to get an ambulance straight away and that the baby was very sick,' she explained. 'That's all I really know.'

They took the lift and Victoria looked at Glen, who was very quiet, as had become usual for him when it was children or babies.

The woman who had guided them up knocked on the door and, as she opened it with a swipe card, Victoria stepped in. For the first time in her career, she faltered. A gentleman greeted them in a panicked voice.

'What the hell took so long?'

For an instant she had thought that the man was Dominic.

And in that instant, she told herself that Dominic was way too much on her mind if she was starting to think that complete strangers were him.

This man was younger. It was the accent that had sideswiped her.

And also, Victoria knew, Dominic didn't panic, which this man was clearly doing.

It was all just for an instant, so small that even Glen did not notice her pause.

Just a tiny slice of time, but it was enough for Victoria to realise that this was Dominic's brother.

And so this must be Lorna.

Dominic's ex.

A tearful Lorna was kneeling on the floor beside the bed and bending over her son.

'Why were you so long...?' Jamie persisted.

'Jamie,' Lorna shouted to him to stop. 'He's turned grey! At the hospital we were told he was fine,' Lorna said. 'But I knew though that something was wrong.'

Something was very wrong.

A very small baby was lying on the bed on his back with his limbs flaccid by his side. He wore only a nappy and Victoria could see even before she reached the bed that he was grunting and struggling to breathe.

'Come on, William,' his father cried. He was frantic. 'Come on, son!'

As Glen checked the baby's vitals, Victoria administered oxygen to the infant via a bag and mask. He was breathing, but it was with effort, and so she bagged him a few times, pushing oxygen into his little lungs to assist the little one with his breathing.

As Glen attached him to the cardiac monitor she could see from the trace and hear from the beeps that his heart was beating far too fast.

'We came down to London to bring him to Paddington's,' Jamie explained. 'My brother is a doctor there.'

And this was no coincidence, Victoria was starting to realise—they had come here to seek help for their baby.

'I know your brother,' Victoria said, and looked up briefly from the struggling infant. 'In fact,' she said to Jamie, though she was too busy to look at him, 'I thought that you were him for a second.'

She felt it better to say she knew Dominic now, rather than to say nothing. There was no time for small talk though; Victoria just felt it was better that she stated it up-front.

The baby had responded to the oxygen and was beginning to pick up; now his little hands were making fists and he was starting to kick at the air.

He went to cry and *that* was the best moment to bag him—Victoria actually saw him pink up before her eyes. In the background, she could hear them explain a little more of what had happened.

'I was feeding him and he just went all floppy,' Lorna explained.

'He's on the breast?' Victoria checked.

'For the most part.' Lorna nodded. 'He had formula yesterday while we were travelling. Sometimes he feeds well, other times it's a struggle, so I've been mixing them up.'

Little William had started to cry in earnest now and was looking a lot better than when they had first arrived.

Victoria and Glen discussed their options for a couple of moments. Inserting an IV would distress him and calling for backup wasn't required yet. Though stable now, he needed to be at the hospital if he deteriorated again, so the decision was made to transfer him as a babe in arms, the priority being to keep him from getting distressed.

They worked swiftly but calmly.

'He'll be more settled if he's held by you,' Victoria explained. As Glen watched the baby, Victoria helped Lorna onto the stretcher. Little William was placed in her arms and the monitor was laid by her legs, and soon they were in the ambulance and on their way to the Castle.

He was pinker now and looked so much better, but Victoria would relay to the staff at Paddington's just how very ill this baby had presented when they had first arrived.

'I've been so worried,' Lorna said. 'I've been saying that there was something wrong with him for weeks and everyone said I was just being neurotic.'

'You're not neurotic,' Victoria said.

Lorna started to cry, for, while it was nice to be believed, it was awful to have it confirmed that there was something very wrong with your child.

'There's been so much going on…' Lorna said.

'It's okay, Lorna,' Jamie said. 'None of this is your fault.' He looked over to Victoria. 'There's been a big family fallout. My wife's been through a lot of late.'

So they had married.

Victoria kept a very close eye on the baby and listened to

the couple trying to comfort each other while so very scared for their child.

'Should we ring your parents?' Jamie asked Lorna, and she nodded. 'They're in Greece,' he added to Victoria.

'Maybe we should wait and see what the doctors say?' Lorna suggested.

Little William was a picture of contentment now, pink and warm in his mother's arms, but Victoria's eyes never left him except to glance up and see how far away they still were.

Paddington's came into view, and when there was a very sick child in your care, it was such a sight to see.

That was why so many were fighting to save it.

There were many who knew from painful experience the value of this wonderful establishment.

Little William's arrival was seamlessly dealt with, though the department was clearly very busy.

Victoria knew that even before she stepped inside because there were several ambulances in the foyer when they arrived.

It did not affect the care that William received.

Even though he was pink and crying, Victoria swiftly conveyed that this was rather more urgent than it appeared, more with her eyes than anything else, and the triage was rapid.

They were taken through to the resuscitation area and that was busy too. There must have been a vehicular incident just brought in because most of the bays were full and there was a sense of urgency all around. It was then that she saw him.

Dominic.

He was standing talking to Alistair North, a paediatric neurosurgeon, but he glanced over as Victoria came in.

And then she watched as he looked down to the stretcher and she saw his forehead furrow and his jaw tense at the sight of Lorna holding her small baby.

'Dominic!' Jamie's voice was raw as he called out to his brother. 'He's not at all well.'

And she was right about him—Dominic wasn't one to panic.

He said something to Alistair and then he came straight over.

'William MacBride,' Glen said. 'He became unresponsive while his mother was feeding him...' He relayed some more details as Victoria lifted the baby from his mother's arms and placed William in an examination cot.

'I was going to call you today,' Jamie said to his older brother, 'and ask you to take a look at him.'

'You're in the right place now.' Dominic nodded. He called for assistance, but when there was none forthcoming, he knew that these next few moments were down to him and took command. 'What's been happening?'

'He's been struggling to feed and put on weight. The doctor didn't seem too concerned and the nurse said that Lorna, well...'

'She thinks that I'm overly anxious.' Lorna spoke for herself.

'How was the pregnancy?' Dominic asked.

'It went well.' Lorna just sat on the stretcher, helpless and wringing her hands as her son was transferred from the ambulance's monitor to the hospital's. 'It's just been these past two weeks. We've been getting nowhere. Finally, I got an appointment to see a paediatrician, but it's not for a couple more weeks. In the end Jamie suggested that we bring him down to be seen by you.'

Dominic nodded but did not comment on that—he was too busy taking care of the infant and, despite the pressure he must surely be under, he did not miss a beat. He was feeling the little boy's scalp and checking his fontanelle, which Victoria knew from her own examination was sunken, a sign that he was dehydrated, and Dominic asked for more information.

'So what happened today?' Dominic asked as Victoria helped Lorna from the stretcher.

'We were at the hotel.'

'How long have you been there?'

'We got there around midnight. The journey down was fine and he had a really good night. I was starting to think we were making a fuss to have come all this way. I was feeding him and saying the very same to Jamie when he started to make all these choking noises and he went floppy.' She started to cry and Dominic nodded when Karen suggested that she find someone to take the parents to get a detailed history.

Victoria had helped Lorna from the stretcher and the anxious couple were gently led away, but at the last moment Jamie turned and came back.

'Dominic, he looks fine now, but—'

'I get that he's unwell,' Dominic said. 'Jamie...' His voice was firm. 'You need to hold it together right now. You need to keep your head.'

'I know but—'

'Come on,' Karen said, and he was again led away.

Victoria guessed that it wasn't the first time Dominic had had to tell his brother that.

The baby was listless again—even crying seemed to exhaust him—and while he lay quietly, Dominic had a very long listen to his heart.

And still she stood there.

Glen made up the stretcher and replaced the used equipment, and still she watched as Dominic took blood. Victoria stood outside as a portable chest X-ray was taken.

But then, instead of heading for the ambulance, she went back in.

'Can we get the on-call cardiologist down here,' Dominic instructed.

'Victoria,' Glen called out to her. 'We've got another job to go to.'

She knew that they had to leave.

They were extremely busy, but Victoria found herself wanting to linger and to know more.

She admired how calm Dominic was. Oh, she knew it was his job to be, but no one could even guess what he was going through right now.

There was a sense of agency to him that Victoria liked.

And then he looked up and caught her eyes and she gave a thin smile, one of support, one that said she knew how hard this was.

And he gave back a grim smile of thanks.

'We'd better go,' Glen said.

Only she didn't want to go.

For the first time she wanted to linger—unfortunately, there was no choice but to leave.

It was a long day.

An incredibly long one, and there wasn't a patient aged under sixty in sight, which meant that they didn't get back to Paddington's once.

Oh, how badly Victoria wanted to go to the hospital to find out how William was, but instead they were in and out of Riverside and nursing homes. And in a quick coffee break, where Glen rang Hayley, Victoria thought not just about little William and how he was, and not just about Dominic and how he was coping.

But about Lorna.

Victoria had had neither the time nor the inclination to think about it when they had been dealing with the baby, but now, pausing for the first time since it had happened, she reflected on the woman that Dominic had once loved.

Perhaps he still did.

In her head Victoria had painted Lorna as some sort of vixen; in fact, she was softly spoken and pretty.

Dominic and Jamie were very similar in appearance.

Jamie, though, was expressive, not just with his emotions but with the information he shared. Oh, she knew the circumstances had been dire today and that people's reactions were often extreme when under pressure, but she just could not imagine Dominic opening up in front of someone else the way that Jamie had.

By Dominic's own admission, even when he had found out the baby wasn't his, he had stayed quiet as a doctor was present.

They were similar, yet different.

And it was the more stoic MacBride brother that Victoria very possibly loved.

It was a scary thought and one she did not want to pursue, but at the end of a very long shift she could take it no more.

'Could we stop by the Castle on the way back to the station?'

'Sure,' Glen said. He could see her tense face and was wise enough not to probe.

It had been a long day for Dominic too.

A new cardiologist had started at Paddington's and Dominic

had felt a wash of relief to hand little William over, especially as Dr Thomas Wolfe seemed very thorough, if rather stern.

'He's my nephew.' Dominic had given his findings and then started to explain the relationship he had with the patient but had immediately been interrupted.

'Then you need to step back,' Thomas had said. 'I'll be in to speak with the family shortly.'

Dominic relayed that information to Jamie and Lorna and though they had communicated throughout the day it had all been about the baby.

Lorna contacted her parents, who were holidaying in Greece, and Dominic was the one who rang his and Jamie's.

They had been very upset by the news and the call had been brief. They had soon rallied though and had called back to say that they were flying down to London and could Dominic meet them at the airport.

The underground would be far easier but their plane came in near the end of his workday and so Dominic agreed. Though he warned that he might be half an hour or so late, depending on traffic.

Then he rang his cleaner and asked her to stop by and give his apartment a quick once-over.

On top of that there were patients, of course, and near the end of a long and difficult day he looked up and there was Victoria walking towards him.

'Do you need me to come out?' he checked, assuming that she wanted him to come and assess a patient in the ambulance, as happened at times.

'No, no,' Victoria said. 'I just stopped by to see how William was doing.'

And he knew from experience that she chose not to get involved with patients, so it touched him that, for his nephew, she had made an exception.

'He's in the catheter lab at the moment. He's had a day of tests and they think he's going to need surgery.'

'Cardiac?' she asked.

'Yes.'

'How are his parents?'

'Exhausted. They're going to be staying with him overnight, of course.'

And tomorrow? she wanted to ask.

Would he be opening his home to them?

But it was not her place to ask such personal questions; Victoria had made very sure of that, so she was vague in her questioning.

'Do your parents know?'

'Of course. They'll be landing in an hour or so,' Dominic said. 'I'll be heading to the airport soon to pick them up.'

'I thought you weren't speaking.'

'We've always spoken,' Dominic said. 'We just didn't know what to talk about for a while.'

And she just looked at him as if he was speaking in a foreign language, and then she gave her smile.

'I've got to go,' Victoria said. 'Glen's waiting.'

'Okay.'

'I hope things go well.'

He watched her walk off, somehow elegant in boots and green overalls, and he did not want it left there. 'Victoria...' he called out, but she carried on walking.

She was, Dominic decided, a complicated lady.

And he wanted to understand her.

CHAPTER ELEVEN

DOMINIC RAN DEEP.

His thoughts he did not readily share and his emotions he kept under wraps.

And it took all that he had within him to keep it like that today.

He was on the phone when Jamie knocked on his office door.

'How is William doing?' Dominic asked.

'A lot better than he was this morning,' Jamie said. 'He's got a hole in his heart and he's going to be reviewed tomorrow by a cardiac surgeon to see if they'll repair it or wait.'

'Well, he's certainly in the right place,' Dominic said.

It was a phrase used often here but it was a heartfelt one and Dominic better understood it now. There was something very special about this place and he could see why Victoria and the others were fighting so hard to save it.

Little William really would get the very best care.

'Lorna can see that now. She didn't want to come down to London given...' Jamie gave a tense shrug. 'I insisted though. I wanted you to take a look at him rather than wait.'

'You did the right thing.' Dominic nodded.

'Look, about—' Jamie said, but Dominic interrupted him.

'Let's just leave it for now.'

'I don't want to leave it though!' Jamie said, his voice becoming distressed as he started to get upset. 'I'm beside myself, Dominic.'

'Listen,' Dominic said. 'For now, you're to focus on Lorna and William. That's it.'

'I need to know that you've got my back.'

'I've always had your back,' Dominic answered. 'You know that I do or you wouldn't have come down to London to have me take a look at William.'

Jamie nodded but he was impatient and wanted resolution. But Dominic would not discuss it today. 'All of that can wait,' Dominic said. 'You need to take care of your wife and son and let nothing else get in the way of that.'

'I know.'

He wanted to tell Jamie that it was time to grow up, but that took things too close to personal and it was everything Dominic knew they had to avoid for now.

'What time do they get in?' Jamie asked.

'Soon,' Dominic said. 'In fact, I need to get to the airport.'

He brought his parents back to the hospital where they fretted for a while, and then somehow the MacBrides did what families do in an emergency—they put differences aside and dealt as best they could with the new hand they had rapidly been dealt.

Most families.

He understood that look now from Victoria.

That brief look where she clearly hadn't understood what he was saying, but he wanted her to understand.

More than that, he wanted to see her.

It was late, he was tired and, yes, he had been told by her to stay back, but instead he found himself at her door.

Victoria opened it and she was wearing the same short white robe that she had been wearing the last time he was here.

She rolled her eyes when she saw him. 'It didn't go well, then?'

'What?' Dominic frowned.

'The family reunion.'

'It went very well, Victoria. I'm just here to see you.'

'Why?' she asked, and then she laughed. 'Stupid question.'

Sex was the last thing on his mind. Well, not quite, but with those three words he knew her a little bit more.

She didn't get relationships.

Not in the least.

'I'm actually here because I've had a crap day and I wanted to see you at the end of it. Are you going to let me in?'

Her flat was dark; clearly she had been about to go to bed but she let him in and turned on a side light.

He took a seat on the sofa and she sat on a chair as if they were in a waiting room.

'How are your parents?' she asked.

'Worried, but they feel better now that they've seen him. They're back at mine.'

'How's the baby?'

'He's on the cardiac unit and he's settled for the night. Lorna's staying with him.'

'Is Jamie back at the hotel?'

'No, he's staying at mine too.' He saw her eyes widen a fraction and chose to explain how it had come about. 'Jamie didn't know the way to the underground, nor about Oyster cards and things, so I offered to drop him off at the hotel. In the end I said to just check out and to come and stay at mine.'

'Are you two talking, then?'

'A bit,' he said, and then admitted more. 'Not really.'

'Then how come he's staying at yours?'

'Because he's my brother and his baby is sick, and right now the baby is the priority. The rest will have to wait.'

His voice was brusque, though he hadn't meant it to be. 'Sorry.'

'No, no...' Victoria said.

It really had been a difficult day.

'Thomas seems to think he might need surgery.'

'Thomas?' Victoria checked.

'Thomas Wolfe. He's a new cardiologist.'

'He's not new,' Victoria said, and shook her head.

'Yes, he is. He only just started at Paddington's the other day.'

'No, he used to work there years ago when I first started. He's a lovely guy.'

Dominic didn't comment; lovely wasn't how he'd describe any guy, but certainly it was not a word he'd expect to hear to describe Thomas, who he had found rather stand-offish.

Still, he didn't dwell on it.

He took in a breath and closed his eyes. It was the first time he had properly paused since he had looked up and seen Victoria walking towards him with Jamie by her side and Lorna and William on the stretcher.

'Jamie was going to call and ask me to take a look at him this afternoon...'

'I know that.'

And it was then she knew for certain that she loved him.

She didn't even have to ask what his response to that phone call would have been.

And yes, while she wanted happy reunions and for him to say that his family was fine, she was starting to understand that Dominic did not say what you wanted him to. He spoke the truth.

Having seen Lorna and Jamie for herself, she was starting to comprehend the magnitude of the betrayal.

It was a miracle, really, that Dominic had followed her into the underground that night when she had first told him she was pregnant, and that he kept coming back when so many men would have turned away.

She wanted to ask him about Lorna, how it had felt to see her today after all this time, but she knew that wasn't needed now.

'Jamie tried to talk about it,' Dominic admitted. 'But I told him that for now he has to focus on the baby. I am trying to work on things with my family, Victoria,' he said. 'But I need to do it at my own pace, not theirs.'

'I know that,' she said. 'But how can you sort it out living so far apart?'

'Because I couldn't work on it from there. Victoria, families fall out. You yourself said you've had words with your father...'

'Your family wants you to be in their lives though.'

'Doesn't he?'

'He wants me there to attend functions when he's between wives.'

'What was the row about between you?'

'I told you,' she said, but she knew she hadn't properly. 'I said I could see why my mother left him.'

'And what did he say to that?'

She shrugged.

Victoria simply wasn't ready to go there.

'Do you want a drink?' she offered.

'I do, but I have to drive.'

'I meant tea.'

'No thanks, then.'

She stood up to get him a Scotch or whatever she had to hand. 'Have a drink. I can drive you home.'

'No thanks,' he said. 'I need the car in case something happens overnight.'

She stood still. There were other solutions and both of them mentally explored them. Dominic wanted her to come back to his—he needed her tonight—but his family were all there and so he could not suggest that.

And though he wanted to stay here a while, both knew where that could lead.

Would lead.

He could see her nipples protruding through the dressing gown—life would be far less complicated if they did not so completely turn each other on.

But no, he could not stay here for the night.

'I really do need to get back home. I just wanted to stop by and tell you what was happening.'

It was nice that he had stopped by, Victoria thought, for she had been fretting about it all evening. It didn't really make sense to Victoria—after all, she had been to the hospital to see how the baby was, but she had just felt a bit sick about little William since the moment she had realised that the baby they had been called out to was Dominic's nephew.

'Will your parents worry if I keep you out late?' Victoria teased, and he rolled his eyes.

'My mother asked where I was going at this time of the night. They're driving me crazy already.'

And she smiled because it was said without malice. He put out his hand and when she took it he pulled her onto his lap.

'How are they driving you crazy?'

'Because in the twenty years that I haven't lived at home, nothing has changed. They hadn't had dinner and I suggested that we get a takeaway, as you do. But no, she wanted us all to sit down and have a proper dinner, as she calls it.'

Victoria found that her smile widened.

Oh, she loved glimpses of family life.

'Well,' Dominic continued, 'I don't really have the ingredients for a proper dinner in my kitchen, so I said I'd go shopping and of course that meant she had to come with me...'

And he was smiling now as he told her about the little shopping trip. 'Do you know how many different types of potatoes there are? Well, I do now. And for all the potatoes in the supermarket they didn't have the ones she preferred.'

'Of course they didn't.'

He let out a soft laugh and then looked to the woman on his lap and Victoria looked back at him.

She felt his hand around her waist and the warmth of his palm through the fabric. 'I'm sorry it's been such a bad day,' Victoria said.

'It's not now.'

The world and its problems were outside and waiting and he would give them all the attention that was needed. But right here, right now, the night felt kinder than the day.

'I do have to go...' he told her.

'I know that you do,' Victoria said, but she did not move from his lap and he made no move to stand.

He looked at her hair which tumbled down over her shoulders and he knew that she wore nothing beneath the robe. He looked at her mouth and then back to her eyes.

A train rattled past which told her the time. She actually liked the sound—it was like having an erratic cuckoo clock in her home but, Victoria knew, this train was the last of the night and she would not hear that sound again until just after five.

And what would her life be like then?

More complicated, Victoria was sure, because it was she who moved in for his mouth.

She tasted resistance—oh, yes, she did—for Dominic had not come here for that and did not want to muddy the waters… while, of course, also desperately wanting to.

For muddied waters became crystal clear as he tasted her kiss and it was all terribly simple after that. It had been a day of holding back and he could sustain it no more, for today *had* been hellish and now the night was not just kind, it was inviting.

Escape beckoned and he drew her in closer, hitching her up on his lap while his hands went into her hair. But Victoria pulled them down, for this was her kiss to him. And so she turned in his lap and straddled him so his hands were free to roam her.

And then he kissed her lazily as she rose on her knees to him, a kiss that simply let her lead and gladly she did. Victoria explored his mouth at her leisure as he ran his hands over her bottom and then released the tie on her robe so that it fell open.

Now his mouth was more urgent as they explored with their tongues and she knew she had never enjoyed kissing more than she did with him.

It was hungry and teasing and they shared moans of pleasure, and as his hands toyed with her breasts she was raw with need for him.

The kiss went deeper and he pulled her higher on his thighs so that she could feel him hard at her centre. She was holding his face in her hands as she kissed him and he ground her down on him.

Then she lifted higher so that he could taste her breast with warm licks, and when he pulled his mouth away, the sudden loss made her crave more.

Victoria had never wanted anyone as badly as she wanted him.

She had missed his touch and now, when there was so much to sort out, they sought the one thing that was already clear—a mutual and very deep want.

'Please…' she said while making room for his hands to free himself. Victoria could feel his breath on her breast as she held on to his shoulders. But when she could simply have lowered herself onto him, instead he ran his hand up her inner thigh and then played with her for a moment, sliding his fingers inside till she was quivering. But she did not have to ask twice for him to take her.

He eased himself inside her as she lowered herself down, and he swore with the bliss of her tight grip and told himself to hold on.

Victoria now wanted his skin pressed to hers. It seemed cruel that he was dressed, but she was so hot in his arms that all she could manage was a couple of buttons on his shirt before she gave up trying to open it.

He thrust upwards while pulling her down and the feel of him so deep inside her almost shot her into orbit.

It was raw and fast and there were hungry kisses in between, and then he turned his head to halt their kiss and slid his hips forward in the chair, taking her with him and allowing him to watch their union.

Victoria still held his shoulders and she, too, looked down. He lifted her hips and held her at his tip, then thrust just a little and the pleasure drove them both wild. She could not sustain it as she was starting to come so he pulled her hard down. She tightened and pulsed around him as Dominic came to her body's command. Relishing the heat of release, she rested on his shoulder, gathering her breath, while he moved her pliant body to extract every drop of pleasure.

Victoria closed her eyes at the bliss, while knowing she did not need to wait for morning to find out how she was feeling.

She wanted him to stay.

Victoria wanted to hole them up in her bedroom and never leave because it felt as if there were too many obstacles out there.

This love felt as though it might burst from her chest if she let it; it was just too vast to handle.

There were too many feelings that must be kept in check.

For how would he react to her barrage of questions?

Her feelings were in complete disarray.

'You need to go,' Victoria said.

She went to climb off but he did not let her. 'So you can say I got what I came for?'

He felt her short, reluctant laugh as he held her in his arms.

He was starting to know her a little too well and so she lifted her head up and looked at him.

'You do have to go.'

'I can call and tell them that if there's a problem...' And then he hesitated because family came first, especially at times such as this, yet she had edged her way up that list. 'Come back with me.'

It was possibly the most stupid thing to say, but he was still inside her and that allowed a person to say the occasional reckless thing.

'Isn't it a bit early to be meeting the family?' Victoria said, and got off him.

'Exceptional circumstances,' Dominic retorted as he sorted out his clothes. He was annoyed at himself for pushing things, and annoyed at the contrariness of her. 'Victoria, like it or not, we're going to be parents, and trying to sort things out from a distance isn't working out too well, is it?'

'I'm on nights tomorrow,' Victoria said. 'I just want to go to bed and have a long lie-in.'

'So when will I see you?'

'At work, I guess.'

'I meant away from work. I'm not going to have our relationship dictated by how often your ambulance is dispatched to the Castle, and you kicking me out isn't exactly helping us—'

'I'm hardly kicking you out,' Victoria interrupted. 'You have a family that you need to get back to and I need to get some sleep.'

She needed him gone because she was on the edge of telling him she was crazy about him.

On the edge of asking about Lorna and how it had felt to see her again.

If he knew her—the real, insecure her—Victoria was positive that he would not want her any more.

She had never cared about anyone else in the way she cared for him, and it terrified her. She did not want to add a failed relationship between them to the mix.

'You keep asking if there's anything you can do for me,' Victoria said. 'Well, there is. Just stay back.'

'You mean that?' he checked.

'I do.'

She even held the door open for him.

So much for wanting a long sleep, because Victoria was still awake when she heard the first train of the morning clack past.

Dominic, she decided, could be as involved in their baby's life as he chose to be but she would not allow him to get closer to her.

CHAPTER TWELVE

'WHAT TIME DID you get home last night?' Katie MacBride enquired as Dominic came into the kitchen the next morning.

Dominic, who hadn't had to answer that question for two decades, was certainly in no mood to answer it now.

'Did you hear what your mother said?' William prompted. He was sitting at the kitchen table, reading a newspaper. No doubt he had got up at six and gone out to get one, just as he did back home.

'I heard,' Dominic answered. 'I didn't make a note of the time when I got in.'

He had tea and toast all prepared by Katie, and Dominic laughed to himself at his own suggestion last night that Victoria should come here.

Dominic loved his parents very much but they were straight into his business and he could only imagine a very independent Victoria's response to his parents' fussing.

'What time will you be back?' his mother asked as Dominic went to leave at seven when he didn't really need to leave until half past.

'I'm not sure,' Dominic answered. 'And tomorrow I'm on call all weekend so I'll be staying at the hospital.'

'What about Jamie and Lorna?' William asked. 'Will you be in to visit your nephew?'

'I am going to be working!' Dominic pointed out.

'You should speak with your brother instead of avoiding him.'

'Jamie's here now.' Dominic pointed down the hall to the bedroom. 'How can I be avoiding him?'

Except deep down Dominic knew that he was.

Friday night was hell because little William had a run of atrial fibrillation and Dominic had to race Jamie back to be by Lorna's side.

Dominic sat in the waiting room on the cardiac unit and saw on the news that there was an incident at Piccadilly.

He had never felt fear watching the news until he had met Victoria.

It was hell watching flashing lights on the screen and brawls taking place and knowing she may well be in the thick of it.

And what was he supposed to do?

Did he send a text asking if she was okay and just irk her some more?

Or did he just sit there feeling ill while hoping to God she was safe?

She wasn't.

Victoria wasn't gung-ho but she could never be accused of holding back, yet as she climbed out of the vehicle to the sounds of a brawl, for the first time in her career she did hold back.

Victoria did not feel safe.

'Hey!' Glen warned the guy lying on the kerb as he lashed out with his boot. 'We're trying to help.' He looked over to Victoria. 'Can you bring the stretcher closer?' Glen said, and then he asked the police who were holding the man to get a better grip on him.

It was Victoria who drove the patient to hospital while Glen stayed in the back.

Nothing was actually said, but Victoria knew only too well that she wasn't carrying her share of the load.

Glen was lovely; he always was.

He sensed that she had lost her nerve and so he put his big body in between Victoria and the patients during a few of the trickier call-outs. But late on Sunday night, coming into the early hours of Monday morning, after attending a domestic dispute, Glen told her something.

'You need to tell work.'

'I know.'

She was on leave after this shift but she would tell her line manager about the baby this morning, when they returned to base.

And then the wheels would all be put into motion, and on her return from leave her duties would change and Victoria would no longer be operational.

'What time's your ultrasound at?' Glen asked.

'Ten.'

'You'll be wrecked,' he said because they finished at eight.

'I'll grab an hour of sleep at the station after we finish,' Victoria said.

'Is Dominic coming with you?'

'I don't want him to.'

'Let him be there.'

'Just leave it.'

She took a bite of her sandwich. She was not going to be discussing this with Glen, but also, she noted, he didn't offer to come with her this time.

Perhaps now that Glen knew who the father was, he felt that it wasn't his place to offer, but all the same, she felt terribly alone.

Victoria's job was her rock and a huge part of her identity.

She was excited to become a mother, yet it felt a little as if everything familiar was being stripped away.

How *was* she going to work and be a single mum?

Just who would be looking out for the baby on nights such as this?

Would Dominic really be there for them?

She tried to imagine him dropping over to her flat to look after their little one while she headed out, or taking the baby over to his.

How long would that last? How long till he tired of any arrangements they made or, like her father, suddenly got called into work and decided that his job was more important than hers?

Or what if he met someone else, which of course he would one day, and decide that his new family was his priority?

As her mother had done.

And then she tried not to think of the other possibility—the two of them together, knowing the odds were that they wouldn't work. He still hadn't sorted things out with his family. Even with a desperately ill baby the brothers were unable to be close.

And as for her?

Victoria had never been close to anyone.

That was her real fear—that, even with the best of intentions, he might give them a go for the sake of their baby, but that Dominic would one day tire of her and simply leave.

'How do you and Hayley make it work?' Victoria asked, but she didn't get her answer—a call-out came and as the address was given Victoria recognised it straight away.

'That's Penny.'

They put on the lights and Glen drove skilfully through the dark London streets and soon they were pulling up at her house.

The lights were on both upstairs and down and, as they made their way up the path, Victoria saw that the front door had been left open.

'Through here.' Penny's father was on the phone trying to find out how much longer the ambulance would be, which Victoria knew from experience meant things were bad. She took a breath and went through to the lounge.

'Hello, beautiful!'

Victoria's smile was bright and no one would ever guess that Victoria's heart sank when she saw Penny.

Julia was lying on the sofa with her daughter and holding her little girl's body in her arms.

Penny's hair was loose and it was damp with sweat; her eyes were sunken and she was struggling so hard simply to breathe. Glen put on oxygen as Victoria carefully checked the little girl over.

'I'm going to use the bag to help you breathe, Penny,' Glen said, and as Penny breathed in, Glen assisted her, pushing vital oxygen into her lungs.

She was terribly hot, though as Victoria peeled back the blanket she saw that she still had on her little tutu.

Victoria chatted to the little girl, but made sure she didn't ask too many questions so that Penny could save her energy.

Her lungs were full of fluid and as Victoria inserted an IV into Penny's arm she barely flinched.

'You are such a brave girl,' Victoria said. 'I'm going to give you some medicine now and that's going to get rid of all that horrible fluid that is making it so hard to breathe.'

Penny became a bit agitated but Julia knew why. 'She doesn't like the diuretics because they made her wet herself once, but that doesn't matter, Penny.'

It did to her though.

'I've got a bed pan in the ambulance,' Victoria said, 'and we'll put lots of pads on the stretcher, so if you do have a little accident we'll have you all cleaned up before you go into the Castle.'

Penny nodded and Victoria pushed through the vital medicine.

The oxygen was helping, and with the other medications she started to calm. Soon her breathing was a little deeper, and the horrible mottled tinge to Penny's skin was starting to recede.

They needed to get her to Paddington's.

This time there was no question that she could get onto the stretcher by herself so Glen gently picked Penny up. He placed her on the stretcher and made sure that she was safely secured, and then together he and Victoria raised it up.

'Ready for the off?' Victoria said as she always did.

And always Penny nodded and smiled, or if she wasn't well enough, as was the case today, would do a little thumbs-up sign.

Today though, she spoke. 'Not...' She gasped but she couldn't finish her sentence and Julia moved to reassure her.

'We've got everything with us, Penny,' Julia said, because she always made sure that she had Penny's favourite things.

But Victoria knew that that wasn't what Penny had been trying to say.

Victoria had seen it happen in many patients—they just wanted a moment more in their home, though usually they were much older than Penny when they felt that way.

'It's okay, Penny,' Victoria said. 'We can take a minute.'

Yes, she was time critical, but the priority, too, was to cause the little girl minimum distress, and rushing her out against her wishes would only cause her to get upset. And so she stood and waited as Penny's eyes moved around the room.

And Julia understood then what her daughter had meant when she had tried to say that she wasn't quite ready to leave.

Penny wanted to take a long look at her home.

And she did.

She looked over at the television, which had been paused in the middle of a cartoon, and all of her favourite characters were frozen on the screen. Then her eyes went to the chair and then over to the sofa where she had lain and she was imprinting it all.

Penny didn't know if she would be coming home.

Julia, who was very strong and used to seeing her daughter unwell, was choking up.

'Why don't you get a glass of water, Julia,' Victoria suggested, and as Julia wept in the other room, Penny sat just taking in the memories of her home.

Glen, of course, was tearing up and Penny gave him a stern look that warned him to stop then and there.

Julia bustled back in and saw Penny's eyes linger on a photo. It looked like a holiday snap of the family at the beach. 'Shall we bring that with us, darling?' Julia asked.

Penny nodded and then rested back on the pillows and now she gave her usual little thumbs up.

She was ready.

Peter, her father, gave his daughter a kiss and told her that he was going to lock up and would see her soon at the hospital.

Once in the vehicle they alerted Paddington's to let them know they were on their way along with the details and status of the patient that they were bringing in.

Glen drove and Victoria sat in the back with Julia and Penny. There was no need for sirens as the streets were empty, but the lights were on and if needed Glen would use the siren at traffic lights or if the situation changed.

The mood was sombre.

Usually Julia would read Penny a story on the way to the

hospital but she just sat there while the blue lights of the ambulance shadowed her face.

'Story...' Penny said.

'Well, let me see...' Victoria answered. And she let Julia sit quietly and gather herself for whatever lay ahead.

Victoria thought for a moment; she had told Dominic that she didn't believe in fairytales, but growing up she had loved them, just like any little girl.

She had just never had to make one up before.

Victoria thought for a moment and then she told Penny about a turret and a magic castle and a little girl who used to sneak behind the files and find her way up there. And she watched as Penny gave a faint smile so Victoria knew she must be telling the tale okay. 'There's a princess who lives there and she watches over all the babies and children.'

'Truly?' Penny gasped.

'Of course,' Victoria said. 'I told you, it's a magic castle.'

And she held the little girl's hand and told her some more and it really did seem to soothe Penny.

Her colour was terrible though and her heart was galloping, but then Penny looked up at the blacked-out windows and smiled.

Victoria glanced up too and relief flooded her as the familiar roofline came into sight.

The not-so-new Dr Thomas Wolfe was waiting for them. Victoria had been right—he had worked here. She recognised him from many years ago when she had just started to work on the ambulances, but this was no time to reminisce with him.

She was just relieved that someone so skilled was here to greet this very sick little girl.

Thomas listened to the handover as they moved her onto the resuscitation bed. He thanked the paramedics as he examined the patient and Victoria saw his expression was grim as he listened to her back and chest.

'You're doing very well, Penny,' he said to her, and he gently sat her back. She was upright in the bed as she was still struggling to breathe. The nurses worked deftly alongside him, attaching Penny to monitors and leads and pulling up the drugs and IV solutions that Thomas was calling for.

Victoria had done her job—she had delivered Penny safely to the Castle, and that had used to be enough for her. But so badly she wanted to stay and see how Penny was doing.

She actually had to prise herself away.

Maybe it was because she herself was going to be a mother that suddenly things were affecting her more.

Or maybe it was that since Dominic had come into her life she simply felt everything more acutely.

It was as if her emotions had been reset to a heightened level and Victoria felt on the edge of tears as she saw more staff running into the resuscitation room.

'I'm going to go and get a drink,' Glen said.

'Sure.' Victoria nodded and she set about making up the stretcher, telling herself to stop getting so upset, that it was just work.

Of course, Glen didn't really want a drink; his flask was in the ambulance and there was a coffee machine close by.

He walked through the department and stood in the kitchenette; he clung to the bench and told himself to take some deep breaths.

And that was where Dominic found him.

'Hi there,' Dominic said, but he got no response.

He knew that Glen's presence meant that Victoria was here somewhere, but he could see that Glen was struggling, and so, instead of heading out, he spoke with him for a while.

Dominic discovered that indeed Glen and Victoria had been at Piccadilly on Friday.

No, he didn't push for information but he guessed, and rightly so, that the weekend had taken a bit of a toll on both of them. Dominic was very grateful to this man for looking out for her.

And they spoke about the fire at Westbourne Grove and how there had been no choice really but to move forward when they had seen just how precarious Lewis's injuries were.

Then Dominic listened as Glen told him about Penny, about how bad it had been back at the house and how she had asked to stay for one lingering look.

'Poor little mite,' Glen said. 'You just can't help but compare them to your own sometimes.'

And then Glen asked him something.

'Do you remember a child we brought in...?'

And he spoke about a little girl that had been brought in a few months ago, one around the same age as Glen's daughter.

Yes, Dominic remembered it well—it was the same child that Dominic had lost on the operating table.

'I'd do anything for my children,' Glen said, 'and I just hope that for her I did the same, but I wonder if we'd just been a bit quicker extracting her from the vehicle and if we'd—'

'Glen,' Dominic interrupted.

Not unkindly.

He had gone over the very same questions about the same little girl himself, and so had the coroner.

'There was nothing that anyone could have done. Even if she had somehow been operated on at the scene, *still* there was nothing that could have been done.'

'I know that,' Glen admitted. He just needed to hear it again.

And again.

He really did need to talk it through.

'She really got to me.'

'I know,' Dominic said. 'It was awful.'

All losses hit hard, but some had the capacity for major destruction and that was what was happening with Glen.

'Victoria keeps on at me to go and speak to someone about it.'

Dominic was very glad that Victoria was on to things, and he was glad that this partnership looked out for each other.

'I think that would be very wise,' Dominic said. 'And if you do have any more questions, or talking it through raises some, then you can come and talk to me.'

Glen nodded. 'I'm just going to take a minute before I go back out.'

'Sure.'

Dominic walked out through to the department and he saw Victoria standing by the made-up stretcher, reading her phone. Dominic made his way over to her.

She felt him approach but Victoria didn't look up.

'Your colleague is crying in the kitchen,' Dominic told her, and though he kept it light he also let her know what was going on.

'I know.' Victoria looked up then and rolled her eyes. 'I'm going to politely pretend not to notice.'

But she *had* noticed, Dominic knew. Glen had just told him that Victoria had addressed this with him on many an occasion.

'Was it very grim at the house?' he asked.

'Not really,' Victoria said.

And Dominic frowned because Glen had just told him, in detail, that it had been awful—that Penny had asked for a moment to look around before they left and that Julia had become upset.

Then, as casually as anything, she told him that unless she got another call-out this morning, this would be the last time they ran into each other like this.

'I'm probably going to be working in the clinical hub—dispatch—from now on.'

'Is everything okay?'

'It's procedure,' Victoria said. 'I've got two weeks' leave, starting at the end of this shift, but when I come back I shan't be operational.'

'Good,' Dominic said. 'Well, I'll miss seeing you but I think it's better than the risk of being out there.'

'I'll still see you at the Save Paddington's meetings, I hope.' Victoria smiled.

'You shall.'

Dominic was doing his best to stay back and not crowd her. He was finding it hell.

Maybe he should take her at face value, Dominic reasoned. Maybe he should simply accept it when she said that things did not get to her, and that she really would prefer to go through this alone.

Yet it did not equate to the passionate side she revealed at times and, he was certain, she hurt just as deeply, even if she did not show it.

He should walk away, just treat her as coolly as she said she wanted, but instead he tried another tack.

'I'm expecting a transfer from Riverside,' Dominic said. 'I've actually just been speaking with your father.'

'Lucky you,' Victoria said, and got back to reading her phone.

'What did he say to you, Victoria?' He saw her rapid blink as she deliberately didn't look up. 'When you had that row, what did he say?'

She shook her head. 'I don't want to go over it again.'

'Please do,' Dominic said. 'Of course, if it's too upsetting…'

'It's not that.' She shrugged. 'It just paints me in a rather unflattering light. He pointed out that my mother didn't just leave him.'

She didn't say it verbatim, but he could almost hear Professor Christie saying that she had left her too.

'How does that paint you in an unflattering light?' Dominic asked.

'Well, I can't have been the cutest baby.' She tried to make a joke.

'How old were you when she left?'

'I think it was just before I turned one,' Victoria said with a shrug. 'She didn't even last a year.' And then Victoria pocketed her phone and she looked right at him. 'So you can see why I don't want you flitting in and out of my child's life.' Then she thought about it. 'Not that my mother did. When she decided to leave she left for good.'

'You don't see her at all?'

'No,' Victoria said. 'I found her on social media a couple of years ago. She's got two grown-up sons. I guess they're my half-brothers.'

'Did you make contact?'

'I tried to—they all blocked me.'

'Well, I shan't be doing the same.'

'Not straight away, but you might change your mind and decide to go and live in Scotland, once you've sorted things with your family…'

'Victoria, do you remember when I told you about Lorna and you pointed out that I wasn't your ex?'

She nodded.

'Well, it works both ways—I'm not one of your parents either. I shan't be turning my back on the baby. I shall *always* be there for my child.'

Victoria already knew that.

Deep down, she always had.

After Dominic's initial poor reaction on the night she had told him, he had run after her and had been trying to get *more* involved rather than *less*.

It wasn't the baby she was now trying to protect.

It was herself.

He would be agony to lose and her heart could not take further hurt.

'What about Lorna?' Victoria said, and she silently kicked below the belt. 'Did you say that you'd *always* be there for her too?'

He didn't baulk at her question; Dominic stared her right in the eyes. 'No.'

'I don't believe you.'

'Well, you should, because half Lorna's and my problem was that I'm not very effusive.'

'Did you say you'd always be there for your brother?' Victoria asked, and that kick delivered because this time he flinched.

Not much.

She just saw the slight tightening of his lips and then he righted himself.

'I thought as much.' She shook her head. 'Thanks but no thanks, Dominic. I really do want to do this on my own.'

Dominic looked at Victoria. He was not going to force himself on someone who clearly didn't want him too close in her life.

'Victoria,' Dominic said, 'I will stay back, if that is what helps you. But with one proviso.'

'What's that?'

'If you change your mind, you're to tell me.'

'I shan't be changing my mind,' Victoria said, and then she saw that Glen was making his way towards them. 'I'll see you around.'

CHAPTER THIRTEEN

SEE YOU AROUND!

Dominic had watched her walk out and had resisted yanking her back, but really—*see you around!*

Of course he could not force her to accept his presence at the appointment, nor could he demand anything from her.

He had loathed her working on the ambulance whilst pregnant but at least it had meant that they saw each other regularly.

Now it would just be Save Paddington's meetings and they were always busy. Though there were get-togethers afterwards, there would be no real chance for the two of them to speak.

He could hardly go around to her flat, given how it had ended the last time.

Yet, he could not regret what had taken place.

That night, it had not been just the sex that had soothed. It had been the conversation and just a glimpse of peace on a tumultuous day.

And a glimpse of another side to Victoria.

He was waiting for the transfer from Riverside to arrive but that could well be hours away. Still, rather than head off and get some rest, he hung around in case Victoria came back in, knowing that it might be their last chance to speak.

The nurses were stretched thin.

Karen was working in the resuscitation area and watching

Penny while also trying to take some observations on a wriggling two-year-old. When the buzzer went over Penny's bay, Dominic stood to answer it and Karen gave a nod of thanks to him.

'Hello.'

He smiled down to Penny.

'You're not a nurse,' Penny said. She was looking a bit better and could speak in short sentences, but even that seemed to deplete her.

'No,' he said. 'I'm not, but Karen is just giving a baby some medicine and doing its obs. Can I help you with anything?'

'I want some ice.'

'I think I can manage that.'

He went and filled a cup from the dispenser and then began feeding Penny a spoon of ice chips.

'Mum's speaking to the doctor,' Penny said.

'She shouldn't be too long,' Dominic reassured. 'How are you feeling now?'

'Better.'

'That's good.'

She was a little anxious and he guessed that tonight she must have had a fright, so he did not place the cup down but instead let her get her breath for a moment and waited until she spoke again.

'A princess lives in the tower,' Penny said, pointing to the roof. 'Victoria told me.'

'That's good to know.' He smiled because it would seem that even if Victoria didn't believe in fairytales she knew how to tell them. There were so many sides to Victoria.

And he wanted to know them all.

'A beautiful princess,' Penny added, and he waited for her to take a couple of breaths before she continued. 'She watches over all the children.'

'What about the handsome prince?' Dominic asked.

'Victoria didn't mention him.'

Of course she didn't! Dominic thought as he smiled.

He fed her a few more chips of ice. He guessed that, more than ice, Penny wanted some company and so he chatted about magic and fairies and wishes that came true and, because of his accent, she asked about the Loch Ness monster and if he believed it.

'Who, Nessie?' He made it sound as if the monster was a close friend. 'My brother and I saw her one holiday many years ago.' And because he was so serious it made it more believable somehow, so Penny lay there and smiled and told him one of her wishes.

'I wish I could have ballet lessons.'

'Well, I'm sure the princess is working on that as we speak,' Dominic said, and then turned as Julia came in.

'Oh, thank you, Doctor,' she said.

'No problem.'

'What did the doctor say?' Penny asked her mother.

'That they're going to keep you here for a few days. It's her second home...' Julia added to Dominic, taking the cup of ice chips and smiling as she did so.

He could see that Julia had put on some make-up and was doing everything in her power to hide her own terrified heart.

Children often amazed him, Dominic thought, but then adults did too.

Julia had just been delivered terrible news about Penny, Dominic knew.

This wasn't going to be just a couple of nights' stay.

He had heard Thomas speaking with Karen and the news wasn't good.

A viral infection was ravaging Penny's already damaged heart and had pushed her into a dangerous level of heart failure.

'Where's Dad?' Penny asked her mum.

'He's moving the car or he'll get clamped again!' Julia said, and then she turned it into a funny story, reminding Penny how Dad's car had got clamped a couple of times.

And either the guy was out there weeping, Dominic thought, or he really was trying to sort out a car that had been haphazardly parked in the race to get to his desperately sick child.

Julia chatted and fussed, and then in came Peter smiling and waving at Penny; he came over and gave his little girl a kiss.

And Dominic watched.

You wouldn't know that they were in agony.

Unless you knew.

And suddenly Dominic did.

Victoria was hurting.

Of course she was.

And probably she hurt a bit more with each and every passing day.

He thought of Glen, idly chatting, saying how you would do anything for your children.

And the firefighters who had run into a building to save children that weren't even theirs.

Every single day it must be rammed home to her just what her mother had done.

Victoria *was* hurting.

She and Glen sat in the vehicle and Victoria got out her flask so they could have a coffee as the sun was coming up over London.

'I'm going to miss this,' Victoria said.

'You'll be back.' Glen smiled.

'I shall be,' Victoria agreed. 'But even though I'll miss not being on the road, I am ready to give it away for a while.'

Since she had found out that she was going to be a mother, she knew it wasn't just her life she was risking at times.

It wasn't the heavy lifting, more the unpredictability of some patients, which meant that once she told work that she was pregnant, Victoria would probably be moved into dispatch.

Glen had looked out for her these couple of weeks and it was time now for her to look out for him.

Of course she wasn't going to politely ignore his tears; it had just been something she'd said to Dominic.

They looked out for each other and she didn't want to leave without knowing he was taking care of himself.

'Glen,' Victoria said, 'did you see about speaking to someone?'

He nodded. 'I've got an appointment in the morning. That's why I didn't offer to take you to the ultrasound.'

'Have you told Hayley?'

'Yep,' he said. 'She's relieved,' Glen told her. 'It's our anniversary now and she said it's the best present I could give her.'

'You've got that nice wine too,' Victoria reminded him.

'And a ring.'

'How *do* you make it work?' Victoria asked him again, and this time the radio didn't go off so he thought for a moment and then answered.

'You stop being too proud for your own good.'

She guessed he was referring to a recent conversation with Hayley, and that he had finally heeded the advice and was getting himself some help.

'So we're both getting ourselves sorted after this shift,' Victoria said.

'Starting to,' Glen corrected. 'Let him be there for the ultrasound, Victoria. Whatever happens between the two of you, whether you're a couple or not, you can parent together, surely?'

Could they? Victoria pondered.

Who was she to deny her child a wonderful parent?

It would have made all the difference to her.

CHAPTER FOURTEEN

THE TRANSFER FINALLY arrived and required surgery.

Dominic liked the quiet of theatre.

Some surgeons chatted or listened to music; Dominic liked quiet so he could concentrate, especially when he had been on call all weekend.

By seven in the morning his latest patient was settled on the ward. After he had done a ward round and checked on all his other patients and handed them over, Dominic was tired enough to want to go home.

But instead Dominic showered and then hung around.

He knew that Victoria's ultrasound was at ten.

But he wasn't just there for that reason; there was another thing that he needed to do.

Victoria was right to be cautious about getting involved with him.

She didn't need a man who came with baggage. He had been determined to get things sorted with his family before he approached Victoria. But then the baby had been sprung upon him and things had gone wayward for a while.

Dominic knew that the problems within his family needed to be dealt with, but more importantly, he finally felt ready.

He went to his locker and then Dominic walked through the hospital and made his way to the cardiac unit.

Some days were hard, when you were least expecting them to be.

Other days were unexpectedly not.

He walked onto the cardiac unit and there was Penny, hooked up to monitors and IVs but looking peaceful. She smiled and gave him a little wave.

Dominic waved back and then he went up to the nurses' station where Thomas stood.

'Morning,' he said.

'Good morning.' Thomas nodded.

Dominic was waiting for a nurse so he could explain that he was just here to visit, but for the moment they were all tied up so he stood at the desk.

Thomas didn't exactly invite conversation and he was back to busily writing up some notes.

'Hi, Rebecca,' Dominic said as she approached.

'Dr Scott,' Thomas greeted, and Dominic frowned at the rather formal address of her.

'Dr Wolfe,' Rebecca said, and her voice sounded strained but she pushed out her lovely smile for Dominic. 'What are you doing on the cardiac unit?' she asked him.

'My nephew's a patient here—William MacBride.'

'Oh,' Rebecca said in surprise. 'I thought the name was familiar. I'm actually here to see him.'

'I'll come back later, then,' Dominic offered. He didn't understand the tension between these two but he didn't want to make things worse. But then Rebecca declined his offer to leave.

'No, no, I need to speak with Dr Wolfe first and I have another couple of patients to see. Go ahead.'

A nurse came over then—it was Rosie—and Dominic explained why he was here and she waved him on.

Really, he could have just popped in, but he had wanted the separation, for this was not a doctor visiting.

It was a brother, a brother-in-law and an uncle that had come to visit this morning.

He looked through the glass as he approached and saw the little family.

Lorna was holding William, who was attached to monitors, but he looked rested and pink in his mother's arms.

And there was Jamie hovering over them.

Dominic could have waited until his parents arrived to drop in on them, but he had never needed the shield of his parents. He had just needed the ability to look his brother and Lorna in the eye.

Without hurt or malice.

'Hey.'

He knocked on the open door and Lorna looked up and he could see that she was startled.

Jamie stood up a touch straighter and was clearly nervous at Dominic's unexpected arrival.

'How is he doing?' Dominic asked.

'Better,' Jamie said. 'They've got him on something called beta...' He struggled with all the new terminology.

'Beta-blockers.' Dominic nodded. 'They slow the heart down and steady things.'

'I think I might need some,' Lorna said, and let out a nervous laugh as she made a feeble joke.

Oh, it seemed such a long time ago since they had been together and so much had happened since then.

'Well, you've had a very difficult time with William.'

Dominic chose his words carefully, refusing to allude to the situation between the three of them.

It was over with.

He gave her a smile and saw that she relaxed.

'I got this for William,' Dominic said, and handed over the wrapped present to Lorna.

She opened it while holding William, and with all his drips and things it took a while, but when Lorna saw what it was she smiled. It was a little Scottie dog, wearing a tartan bow.

'He's gorgeous,' she said. 'We didn't think to bring any toys with us. It will be nice to have something for his cot here.'

'Here,' Dominic said, and handed Jamie the card. Knowing how useless Jamie was with money Dominic had put in a generous cheque. It wasn't for the baby though. 'I thought you could get something for the nursery or a pusher or whatever.'

'Thank you.'

But it was the words on the card that mattered the most to Jamie and he read them again.

Dear Lorna and Jamie,
Congratulations on the birth of William.
  I am thrilled to be an uncle and looking forward to watching him grow up. I know you'll be amazing parents.
Love, Dominic

And Jamie knew that his brother always meant every word.

'Do you want a hold of him?' Jamie asked, and his voice was a bit choked. 'Or maybe...' He hesitated, worried that it might be too much for his brother, but Dominic *had* meant every word.

He was ready now to be in his nephew's life.

'I'd love to hold him.'

Dominic held many babies in a day's work but he hadn't held a baby outside of that parameter, ever.

And it was very different.

William really was a gorgeous baby and had the MacBride chin and long, long hands and feet. The change of arms woke him and he opened up his eyes and gave his uncle a smile.

'You don't remember me from last week, do you?' Dominic said to him. 'Because I was sticking needles in you then.'

'He's looking better though?' Lorna anxiously asked.

'He is. And I know you must be terrified but we're a tough lot and I'm sure that he's going to be fine.' Dominic held him for a couple of moments and, as he did, it occurred to him that in the not too distant future he would be holding a baby of his own.

How could you ever walk away from your own child?

Dominic wasn't one to let his emotions run away with him, but as he looked at the little baby, he felt a choke of emotion on behalf of Victoria.

He made a choice then to be patient, a choice that he would wait for however long it took for her to trust in him.

Not just as a father.

He had far greater plans for them than that.

Dominic handed the baby back to his mother and then he shook his brother's hand.

'Congratulations,' Dominic said, and he could finally look him in the eye and smile.

'Oh!'

He turned at the sound of his mother's voice and saw the concern in his father's expression.

'I was just dropping in to see how William was doing,' Dominic explained.

'Is everything okay?' William Senior asked as he came in.

'All's good,' Dominic said. 'I'll see you back at home. And, Lorna,' he added. 'If you want a *proper dinner* or to stay at my home, then you're very welcome.' He turned to his mother. 'But I've been working all night, remember, so can you please keep it down.'

And they were back to being a family.

Dominic made his way back to Accident and Emergency. He had a coffee and killed time, watching as a nurse rolled her eyes as she did her best to hold on to her temper as she spoke with someone on the phone.

'I am sorry about that but I wasn't working last night. I'll try and find out for you.' She pressed Mute and let out a hiss. 'That man!'

'Who?'

'Professor Christie over at Riverside.'

'What does he want?'

'A transfer last night...' She shook her head. 'Don't worry, I know you're not on.'

'It's fine.'

He picked up the phone and on the other end of the line he heard the great Professor Christie berate a member of staff.

'Hello,' Dominic said. 'Dominic MacBride speaking.'

'Oh!' Professor Christie said, and he switched to charming. 'Sorry about that, I'm working with clumsy imbeciles this morning.'

He had thought about it for a long time and examined it from many angles and, in this instance, Dominic *did* know what to say.

'Well—' Dominic's voice was curt '—that might have something to do with the fact that they're working alongside an arrogant git. So,' he asked, and adopted a more professional tone, 'how can I help you?'

He saw the nurse turn with eyes wide as he heard the professor splutter into the phone.

'*What* did you just say?' Professor Christie demanded.

'Do you want me to repeat it?' Dominic calmly replied. 'Or would you like me to come over now and say it to your face?'

'Now, listen here—'

'I do listen,' Dominic said. 'I listen very carefully and I also think before I speak.'

His voice held a warning and there was silence on the other end of the line.

'Now,' Dominic said, 'what did you want to know about the patient?'

CHAPTER FIFTEEN

VICTORIA SAT IN the waiting room of the Imaging Department.

There was a television up high on the wall but Victoria was too busy replying to some emails about the next Save Paddington's meeting to watch it.

Then her phone rang and Victoria grimaced when she saw that it was her father who was calling her.

He rarely called. In fact, it was always Victoria who called him.

Perhaps there had been a change of heart, Victoria thought.

'Hi, Dad,' she said.

'Who's the father of the baby?'

'Why?' Victoria asked.

'Just tell me.'

Victoria sat there.

Her father had shown absolutely no interest in this baby and from his very brusque tone she didn't think he sounded particularly interested now.

In fact, he sounded furious as he spoke on. 'You said that he was in Scotland…'

'Why do you want to know?'

'Well, I've just had some upstart insult me. Dominic Mac-Bride…'

Her heart was bumping against the wall of her chest.

'What did he say?'

She closed her eyes as her father repeated it.

What the hell was Dominic thinking to speak to her father like that? Dominic, who insisted his responses were measured, clearly hadn't thought this one through.

For it made a future impossible.

Any get-togethers would be fraught and tense.

And in that moment she felt as if she were about to cry, for she was mentally waving goodbye to Christmases and Easters and family celebrations and she had been trying so hard not to think of them.

'Well?' Professor Christie demanded. 'Is he the father?'

'Yes,' Victoria answered. She was cross with Dominic, even if she privately agreed with what had been said, but she did not tell her father that. Instead she told him a truth. 'And I'm very glad that he is.'

Dominic would be a wonderful father, she absolutely knew.

She was glimpsing Christmases and birthdays again, and even if she might not be in the picture, her baby would be taken care of during celebrations whenever it was in his care.

He deserved to be here.

She simply ended the call because there was another major incident occurring, but this time it was with her heart.

It wasn't just that he deserved to be there.

He would be the one she would call on if anything was wrong.

It would be Dominic's voice she would need if their baby was ill, or hot, or fussing.

Glen seemed to think it was possible but she didn't know how to let him into the baby's life without revealing how she really felt.

Yet, he did deserve to be there.

And so, before she could talk herself out of it she sent a hurried text.

Can you come to the ultrasound?

She hit Send and then panicked because that sounded too needy, and then started to write another.

You can come to the ultrasound if you still want to.

But that didn't read right and so she didn't hit Send but then she thought of him waking to the first, as he was probably asleep and would read it and think there was something wrong.

What if there was something wrong?

She needed him here.

And then suddenly he was there.

She knew, as she always did, whenever Dominic was close. He stood over her as she stared down at her phone and then she looked up. 'You got here fast.'

'I thought I'd hang around in case you changed your mind,' Dominic said as he took a seat by her side.

He would not rush in and scare her with his feelings. That text, asking him to be here, was enough for now.

'Have you been speaking to my father?' she accused.

'Aye.'

'What did you say?' she asked, wondering if he would be vague but Dominic told her exactly.

'He was talking down to a member of his staff and one of ours. I just said he was an arrogant git. That's all.'

'So how is it going to be when you see him?' She would not admit to the family get-togethers that she dreamed might happen one day. 'At the hospital and things.'

'I'll be civil.' He looked over to her angered face. 'Victoria, do you really think there are going to be many cosy get-togethers with me, him and the baby?'

'No,' she said, and she was struggling to keep her feelings in, because what he had said didn't bode well for any chance for them.

'But if they do happen,' Dominic said, 'then I will play the part and do the right thing, but he has to know that I know what he's like. I will not let him inflict his bloody nature on my child nor on the mother of my child. I just served him a warning today.'

His lips were taut and his words were clipped and Victoria nodded because deep down she knew that he was right.

It wasn't fear of confrontation that flooded her now; it was a wash of relief that came over her, though she tried not to show it. Finally there was someone in her corner where there never had been before, and even if he was there just to guard their child she was very glad that Dominic was on board.

'Are you nervous?' he asked.

'Are you?'

'Yes.'

And they smiled because given what had happened to Dominic, and given their short history, perhaps he should be, but Dominic nudged her and they looked up at the television.

'Look.'

It was that image of them from Westbourne Grove.

It seemed like ages ago, but it had been just a couple of weeks.

Yet so much had changed.

Images of the protestors outside the hospital came onto the screen.

The fire had been a terrible day.

It had changed so many lives, and the fight to save some of them was ongoing. Children were still desperately ill, and yet, from such a terrible event good had prevailed.

Angela Marton was now talking about the fight to save Paddington Children's Hospital and saying that Londoners did not want to lose the institution that brought hope to so many.

'I want my baby to be born here,' Victoria said.

'Our baby,' he corrected.

'So you believe me now,' she nudged.

'Victoria, the more I know you, the more I'm amazed at the speed with which you dropped your knickers.'

'Stop it!'

'It's true. That condom had probably expired.'

'So why are you nervous, then?'

'Because, like every other parent, I want our baby to be fine.'

He gave her a smile. 'You do believe in fairytales.'

'I don't.'

'Penny told me about the princess.'

'How is Penny?'

'Don't worry about that now.'

'I'm not worried,' she lied. 'Just tell me.'

'She's got a virus and she's in severe heart failure.'

She thought of Penny's beautiful eyes taking in the lounge and she prayed, so hard, that she would one day be back there.

'Do you think she'll be okay?'

'I don't know, Victoria. She's got a long road ahead of her.'

'Victoria Christie.'

She stood up for the radiographer when her name was called.

'Come through.'

She was shown to a little cubicle and asked to put on a gown.

'Then go in and lie down, and I'll be through shortly,' she said.

Victoria changed and went through to the little room and got up on the examination couch, putting a blanket over her legs.

And Dominic sat by her side.

The radiographer came in then and they chatted about dates and confirmed, when she had a feel of Victoria's stomach, that indeed she did have a full bladder.

They had a little laugh, then the radiographer's pager went off and she said that she'd be back soon.

They were both very quiet.

Dominic was probably feeling sick, Victoria thought, given what had happened the last time he was in this situation.

Dominic did not feel sick.

Not in the least.

He would not be demanding a DNA test.

He knew for a fact this baby was his.

Victoria didn't *need* anyone.

Except maybe she did.

'I'm nervous.' She just came out and said it. 'What if there's something wrong?'

'Then we shall deal with it together.'

He held her hand.

Oh, she did need a handhold because it felt like silk wrapping around not just her fingers but her heart.

She started to cry.

'It will be okay,' Dominic said, and he peeled off some tissues.

'I'm just tired,' she said. 'It was a busy shift and I'm worried about Penny.'

'I know,' he said.

But it wasn't just that.

'I'm sorry I was terse with your father.'

'It's not that.'

She was glad of it now.

It was her mother.

'I love this baby so much already. I don't get how she could just leave me like that.'

'Nor do I,' he told her. 'Victoria, I shan't be doing the same.'

And Glen was right; whatever happened between them, they would do what was best for the baby.

But it wasn't just that.

It was a huge comfort to know her baby would have such a wonderful father, yet the fears about Dominic were not for her child now. They were for her own heart.

The radiographer came in and he peeled off more tissues and she pressed them onto her eyes.

'I'm enthusiastic to see our baby,' Dominic said, and that made her smile. He hadn't rushed in and said it when her eyes had pleaded for him to in the canteen.

He said it now when he meant it.

'So am I.'

And there it was.

All that fuss for something so small.

Yet so beautiful and so vital and alive.

And they weren't really listening to dates and looking at crown rump length and things.

Just watching the baby with its tiny arms and legs and even fingers and toes. It was just a moment they shared.

He looked from the screen to Victoria, and there was the flash of fresh tears in her eyes. He would never leave her, yet she didn't even know. He didn't care if it took for ever; he would get right into that guarded heart. What had happened when their baby had been made was a rare magic; he bent over and gave her a light kiss. This man could not hold back any longer!

'I love you.'

He had sworn not to push her, but he couldn't not say it. He did not want her to go another moment in this life without love.

Though because he was all stoic and Scottish, and there was someone else in the room, that was all the romance she was going to get.

It meant everything and more to hear that, but she was certain it was just the emotion of the moment. The dates matched exactly and maybe Dominic had just gotten a bit carried away.

She lay there as his hand remained over hers but those fears in her head beat faster than the heart on the screen.

It was like the world was all in this room—his hand, their baby—and she was scared for the lights to go on, for she would surely wake up alone.

And then it was over.

The images would be looked at, they were told, but everything seemed perfect, and Victoria could now get dressed.

'Thank you,' Victoria said, but she was almost scared to move because the tears were threatening.

'I'll wait in Reception,' Dominic said, but as he turned to go she started to cry.

'What are you crying over?' he asked. 'Your mum?'

It would be so easy to nod and say yes and perhaps a whole lot safer too, because she was scared to reveal herself.

Then she thought about something else that Glen had said, about not being too proud for your own good and so *this* woman met his eyes in the ultrasound room and made her confession and told him her truth.

'You,' Victoria said. 'I'm crying over you.'

'Cry *on* me, then.'

He pulled her into his arms and held her as she wept, and she told him her fears; she had so many and he dealt with each in turn.

'You might change your mind.'

'Never.' Dominic knew that he would never change his mind.

And he sounded so sure, and here in his arms she was brave enough to voice her fears for them.

'You loved Lorna.'

'Not like this,' Dominic told her. 'I've never loved like this.'

She could hear the steady beat of his heart while hers was racing, and she could feel his quiet strength.

It wasn't the first time she had cried but it was the first time she had cried in someone's arms and so she voiced her deepest fear.

'If there wasn't the baby...'

'Then you'd still be here in my arms.'

And his deep voice was soft and it felt like the truth but she disputed it all the same. 'You stayed back.'

'You asked me to.'

'But before you knew about the baby you didn't make a move.'

'Neither did you,' he pointed out.

'I stayed back because I don't know how to make things work between us,' Victoria said.

'And I stayed back because I do.'

She frowned into his chest.

'Victoria, I told you at the start I was in the middle of something; I wasn't going to land it all on us and come into a relationship jaded and bitter. I needed to sort things out properly.'

She thought about that for a moment and then he spoke some more.

'Now I have sorted it out. I've taken the baby a present, I've had a hold and I've told Lorna she's very welcome in my home.'

'Do you still love her?' Victoria asked. 'You can't undo love.'

'Believe me, you can unravel it,' Dominic said. 'It pretty much came undone the day I found out. Victoria, I haven't been steering clear of Lorna because I have feelings for her. Not positive ones anyway. The last months have been hell, more over my family and brother, but I'll tell you this, since that night, I've thought about *you* every day.'

'Every day?'

'Every minute of every day.'

She looked up to him and she knew he was telling the truth. And that was what had been missing for ever, being thought of by another, every minute of every day.

She thought of her father and his money and occasional gifts.

And her mother who had simply walked away.

But she didn't just think about the bad things. Instead there were thoughts of Glen and how he carried his family in his heart throughout his working day.

And she was starting to believe that Dominic did the same.

'Go and get dressed,' Dominic told her, and he helped her from the examination couch. 'You need to get some sleep and so do I.'

And so she went to the ladies'.

Victoria was practical like that.

And got dressed.

Then she headed out to Reception where he was waiting and he gave her a smile as if he hadn't just rocked her world.

They took the scenic route and as they walked through the quadrangle it was as if the oxygen ratio in the air that she breathed was altered, a bit higher, the colours brighter, the air kinder.

'Thank you for being there today,' Victoria said as they came out to the ambulance foyer and she paused to say goodbye.

'Didn't you hear a word of what I said back in there?' Dominic lightly teased. 'Do you really think I'm going to let you disappear into the underground again? You're to come home with me and I'm not taking no for an answer this time.'

'What's wrong with mine?'

'I want you in my bed.'

CHAPTER SIXTEEN

AND VICTORIA WANTED to be in his bed too.

'I'm very tired,' she warned with a smile as they drove away from Paddington's.

'Victoria,' he said, 'I've been on call all weekend and you look like hell.'

She looked at him all unshaven and with dark circles under his eyes. 'So do you.'

'Good,' Dominic said, and glanced over to her, 'so you'll be able to keep your hands off me, then.'

God, but he turned her on.

His home was a large apartment, close to the hospital. They took the stairs up to his floor and, as he let them in, there were all the signs of a family in residence. Victoria was very used to coming home to her flat alone and finding it exactly as she had left it, but Dominic read a note that had been left on a table in the hall.

'I just saw them back at the hospital,' Dominic told her. 'But it says that they won't be back till this evening.'

She was too tired to look around but there was a nice feel to the place and, as she glanced in the living room, she saw two heavy-looking leather sofas with rugs over the back of them.

A stint of nights, then hanging around for the ultrasound and all the emotion of before, had left Victoria so tired that she felt cold despite the warm day.

They stepped into his bedroom and she looked at the large bed and wanted to sink into it.

'I am so going to enjoy sleeping with you,' Dominic said as he closed the drapes and turned on a bedside light, and she laughed.

'And I am so going to enjoy sleeping with you.'

She slipped off her clothes and got into bed. It had the wonderful, soapy, fragrant scent of him that was now familiar. Victoria suddenly realised that she had never seen him naked. But she was about to get that pleasure now, and she couldn't wait.

Dominic took off his shirt. She saw his pale skin and the dark hair of his chest and she just lazily watched. He undid his belt and as he undressed she saw strong thighs and then his tumescent male beauty.

'We *are* going to sleep,' he promised, yet Victoria wasn't so sure because she was starting to change her mind. There are moments so special that they have to be marked in some way, and this was one of them. So she stretched and sighed as he climbed into bed and turned off the light, and they lay there as a siren went past.

'Thank God it's not you out there,' Dominic said, and he pulled her closer into him. 'Every time I hear a siren I think of you, even before I found out that you were pregnant. I've been so worried about you out there.'

'I will be again,' she warned, because her career was incredibly important to her and she definitely would be going back.

'I know that you will,' Dominic said, 'but you shan't ever be out there again without knowing that I love you.'

And then she looked at Dominic and saw right down to his soul, and found out that she resided there and that she had ever since their first kiss.

She lifted her face towards him and he kissed not, at first, her mouth but her cheeks and eyes and then he kissed her lips long and slow.

A goodnight kiss, even though it was morning.

The kind of *I'm not going anywhere* kiss that she had never known, and then he held her tight in his arms as they drifted off to sleep together.

For the first time they lay together to the sounds floating up from the street and the bliss of being in each other's arms. They needed no more than this right now.

It was a sleep like no other.

The end of nights and their first together ensured that it was the sweetest, deepest sleep for them both.

Victoria rolled onto her side and he wrapped around her and peace was made.

It was Victoria who stirred first. Dominic was curved into her and she was disorientated as to place and time, for the room was dark and the direction she faced unfamiliar, but she was blissfully certain of the man in whose arms she lay.

Who knows how we awaken together? she thought.

That moment when you realise someone else is present and by your side.

When respite has been taken and you awake peaceful, and there is no need for a frantic examination for you to know it is a better world.

And it was.

His hand was on her stomach and she lay with eyes open to the darkened room, half asleep, half awake and completely content. Then Victoria closed her eyes as his hand roamed the curve of her hip and he moved in closer.

Dominic kissed her bare shoulder and his hand toyed with her breast. She felt the pinch of his finger and thumb on her nipple and the nudge of him between her legs. She turned her face to him and they shared a kiss that was slow, but then both wanted more and so she rolled in his arms for just that. As she did so Dominic moved too. He held himself over her and halted her on her back, resting his elbows by her head and pushing up on his arms. She had never felt so deliciously trapped, yet so safe in love.

On so many occasions Victoria had looked down when he silently demanded that her eyes meet his, but now she looked up to his gaze. Her hand came to the back of his head and she levered herself up to meet his mouth. But it was his kiss this time and so he pressed her back into the pillows and claimed her mouth as below she parted her legs for him.

The feel of him inside her made her shiver, though their bodies were warm and still loose from sleep. His kiss was deep and intense and they moved slowly at first, revelling in the feel of togetherness and the naked heat of their skin. They simply entwined into one as they forgot they were parents-to-be and found out the couple they had now become.

Each measured thrust he delivered brought her a little more undone.

And she was his.

For all the declarations Dominic had offered, when she had given none, with each building sob that she tried to hold in, she revealed herself to him some more.

He placed his hands on the bed, either side of her breasts, and he moved up onto outstretched arms. The separation between them allowed her to lean up on the pillows as he took her, in short rapid thrusts, as she clasped his face and took his lips in a deep kiss.

It was shockingly intimate for both of them—the kissing, the feeling, the watching each other so close to the edge.

Then she closed her eyes, not to him but because the feelings were intense. He moved faster despite the slow caress of his tongue and she searched for a headboard to cling to but settled instead for his solid arms. She couldn't resist the urge to tilt her hips and take him in more deeply.

Everything gathered tight within and Victoria wanted to twist or to lift her knees, almost to shield herself from the throes of frenzy, but instead her hands moved up his arms and her fingertips pressed into his shoulders and she came hard.

And there was nowhere for her heart to hide any more.

Dominic sunk down from his arms and she accepted the weight like a raft, and for a moment they lay breathless.

She waited, but this time regret did not arrive.

'Are you going to say you've made a mistake again?' Dominic asked in that familiar wry tone.

'Well, if it is a mistake, then I intend to keep on repeating it.'

She rolled to her side and they lay staring at each other for a while.

And the feeling remained.

So she told him something she never had said to anyone. 'I love you.'

'Good.'

'And I'm sorry that I asked about Lorna.'

'Don't be, the air needed to be cleared there. We're all going to be in each other's lives. But know this—I've never felt the way I do about you with anyone else. And I tell you now, I know he wouldn't but if my brother touched a hair on your head I would kill him.'

She smiled, because it would never happen, and his voice made her shiver with delight.

'You don't fight,' Victoria pointed out.

'My love for you is savage,' he said, and as he looked at Victoria he decided that she deserved a savage kind of love.

He made her entire skin tingle, just with the stroke of his finger on her arm.

She looked deep into his eyes, and yes, he could be crabby at times, but she liked that. She liked that he did not fight and that the man she loved could never hurt another. Even when they had fought over Penny that day, he had still put the patient first.

She liked his strength and how he fought, not with fists but by holding on to what was right.

'You've been sleeping on my side,' Dominic said, and she smiled, because he made her believe in fairytales after all. 'I mean it,' he said, and he knelt up and leant over her. First he turned on the bedside light and then he opened a drawer.

From there he took out a little, dark, velvet box and offered her a warning. 'This isn't a ring.'

'I would hope not, given that we've only had one date.'

'Victoria,' he said in that gorgeous brogue that had her toes curl beneath the sheets. 'We are going to have many, many more. You'll be getting a ring but, for now, I want you to have these. I really have been thinking of you all the time and I hope that these will show you how much.'

He opened the box as Victoria sat up in the bed and when she looked she saw a pair of beautiful earrings. Her heart squeezed and her fingers wanted to touch them but for now she simply looked at a gift from the heart.

'They're Scottish pearls,' he told her. 'I'm lousy at one-night stands and I wanted to get you something. When I was in Scotland I saw these and while I was talking to the jeweller I found out quite a bit about them—pearls are complex things,' Dominic said. 'The oyster tries to protect itself from intruders, and from that something very beautiful is formed.'

They were golden hued and the most beautiful pearls that she had ever seen, but more than that it was the care and thought with which they had been chosen that meant so much to her.

Yes, diamonds might be for ever, but they didn't count unless they were given with love.

Those long fingers were nimble and he carefully put them in for her and, as he did, he asked her a question. 'Do you know what daunts me when I think about a future with you?'

Victoria could think of many things that might.

An unplanned pregnancy from a one-night stand, her job, her independence, to name a few, but then he broke in.

'Nothing daunts me,' Dominic said. 'I had sworn off relationships until I met you. I know we agreed to no more than what happened that night but I was always going to ask you out. I made up my mind in Scotland. I decided that once I had properly sorted things out with my family I would see if we could give things a try. If you said no, then these earrings were still for you, because what happened between us was amazing. I never thought I could trust anyone again, but I do. And the thought of a future with you thrills me.'

She put her fingers to her ears and felt the gorgeous pearls, and then she looked over to Dominic.

This beautiful, rugged man had offered her his heart and she had never been this close to anyone before.

And what he had said applied both ways, for as she looked to a future with Dominic, there was nothing that daunted.

Yes, it thrilled her, in fact.

And then as they kissed, as they lay with the world at their feet, they heard a noise. Victoria, on hearing the front door opening, pulled away and grimaced.

The day had run away from them and there were voices from the hallway. This was so not how she wanted to meet his family.

'They won't come in,' he said.

'And I can't go out.' Victoria groaned, having visions of herself being trapped hiding in his room all night.

'Why ever not?' he asked.

'What will they think?' Victoria asked, aghast at the prospect. 'I can hardly just walk out of your bedroom and meet the family.'

'Well, if you were the type for a one-night stand with a man you barely knew, then I get that it might be awkward...'

He made her laugh and she knew then that they would tease each other about their torrid tryst for ever.

He made everything fine.

Better than fine.

'I'll tell them that I've been seeing you for months,' Dominic suggested, 'which I have been.'

It was no lie. They had noticed each other right from the day they had met.

It was actually now bliss to lie in bed with him and to hear the sounds of his family outside.

'Lorna's here.' It was Dominic who grimaced a bit when he heard her voice, because though he had meant it when he had said that she could come for dinner or stay here, he knew it might be a bit much for Victoria to deal with so soon. 'Do you have a problem with that?'

'None.' Victoria grinned; after all, she was in his bed. But then she thought about it more seriously for a moment and the answer was still the same, so she shook her head. 'None.'

'Good,' Dominic said, and he rolled out of bed and started to pull on some clothes. 'Though we might keep it to ourselves about the baby for now.'

'I know that it must all feel a bit rushed,' Victoria said, thinking of how he had said he felt when he found out that Lorna was pregnant.

'Hardly rushed,' he said. 'I'm thirty-eight.'

Dominic was pulling on his jeans and she would remember

that moment for ever. The moment she knew, completely, that they were meant to be.

And then he looked over and smiled as he realised the difference in his feelings between now and the last time that he had thought he was about to become a father. Still there was no need to dwell for they had moved past all that now. 'I'm just warning you,' he said, 'that when they find out they'll make an awful fuss.'

'I can't wait for the fuss,' Victoria said, and she thought of grandparents who would be thrilled at the news, and uncles and aunts and cousins and feuding brothers who had sorted things out. 'As soon as William is more stable we'll share the good news.'

She couldn't wait to get out there, but was actually quite nervous when they finally did.

The MacBrides were all in the kitchen. Jamie and Lorna and Dominic's father were sitting at the table, and his mother, a very small woman, was at the oven.

'Well, hello,' his mother said when together they walked in, and she looked a bit taken back when she saw that Dominic had company.

'This is Victoria,' Dominic introduced. 'She's been on nights too.'

'You never said that you were seeing anyone!' his mother scolded, though she smiled to Victoria.

'Well, we haven't exactly been speaking,' Dominic reminded her. 'But Victoria is very much in my life. Victoria, this is my mother, Katie.'

She met William and Katie, and Jamie and Lorna, who she had, of course, already met, but it was different this time because she was being introduced and integrated into all the main threads of this beautiful man's life.

'How is William doing now?' Victoria asked Lorna, and felt very glad that she had been up-front about knowing Dominic when they were at the hotel.

'He's doing well. Rebecca, the surgeon, doesn't seem to think surgery is necessary at this stage.'

As easily as that they chatted and Victoria understood what

Dominic had meant about needing to be properly free from baggage, for there were no dark feelings harboured, no grudges and absolutely no jealousy at all.

'He's getting excellent care,' Jamie said, and then looked over to his brother. 'I can see why you want to work there—it's a fantastic hospital.'

'Is it true that it's closing?' Lorna asked.

'Not if we can help it,' Dominic said, and from the conviction in his voice, Victoria knew that she had him fully on board now in the fight to save Paddington's.

And what were the best words in the world to hear when you've woken up having been on a stint working nights and just had really good sex?

Katie MacBride said them as Dominic put an arm around her and kissed the top of her head. 'Take a seat at the table, you two. You'll be wanting a proper dinner.'

And she was entered into his fold.

Victoria had found her family.

* * * * *

The Cowboy's Promise
Teresa Southwick

WESTERN
Small towns. Rugged ranchers. Big hearts.

Teresa Southwick lives with her husband in Las Vegas, the city that reinvents itself every day. An avid fan of romance novels, she is delighted to be living out her dream of writing for Harlequin.

Books by Teresa Southwick

An Unexpected Partnership
What Makes a Father
Daughter on His Doorstep

The Bachelors of Blackwater Lake

A Decent Proposal
The Widow's Bachelor Bargain
How to Land Her Lawman
A Word with the Bachelor
Just a Little Bit Married
The New Guy in Town
His by Christmas
Just What the Cowboy Needed

Montana Mavericks: Six Brides for Six Brothers

Maverick Holiday Magic

Montana Mavericks: The Lonelyhearts Ranch

Unmasking the Maverick

Montana Mavericks: The Baby Bonanza

Her Maverick M.D.

Visit the Author Profile page
at millsandboon.com.au for more titles.

Dear Reader,

From the time I was a little girl, babies have stolen my heart. Tiny humans fascinated and charmed me, which was a good thing as I grew up one of six children. Helping with the younger kids was expected and, for me, the only thing that didn't feel like a chore. In my opinion, infants are a pure blessing, although the timing of when they come into our lives can sometimes be less than ideal.

In *The Cowboy's Promise*, Erica Abernathy makes the decision to be a single mother after a long-term relationship goes south. She's thirty years old and having a baby is something she desperately wants. But losing her job forces her to return to Bronco, Montana, and her family is thrilled to have her home, but shocked that she's made such a momentous decision—and kept them in the dark! They're also hurt because she's visited home so infrequently in recent years. And then she meets a man who might be "the one"...except now she's a package deal. How will this cowboy feel about a baby that isn't his?

When Morgan Dalton meets Erica, the fact that she's *very* pregnant isn't the first thing he notices. It's the powerful attraction. Fighting it will be an uphill battle. But it's one he's determined to win because he doubts his ability to be a good father. Except every time he's in town, he finds himself running into her, even agreeing to be her childbirth coach! He's in over his head, but won't break that promise, no matter how big a price he'll pay when he has to walk away after she becomes a mom.

What they don't realize is that love will find a way and babies are magical and can bring stubborn, wounded people together. I hope you enjoy Erica and Morgan's story of finding their way to becoming the family each of them has always wanted.

Happy reading!

Teresa Southwick

To readers who adore happy endings as much as
I do. Without you I couldn't do the job I love.
Though it doesn't seem like enough,
this thank-you comes from the bottom of my heart.

CHAPTER ONE

THERE'S NO PLACE like home. And for Erica Abernathy home was Bronco Heights, Montana—where everyone had an opinion, and not always a positive one.

She was driving her loaded-to-the-roof SUV down the road to the big house on the Ambling A Ranch, where she'd grown up. The trip from Denver had been long, but now that she was so close, she wouldn't mind a couple thousand more miles between her and what was coming.

She loved her family, but wasn't looking forward to their reaction when they saw her. There would be so many questions.

Although that happened every time she came home for a visit. Usually some variation of "Do you like *city* life in Denver?" Or "Are you dating anyone? Getting serious about a special man?" And the ever popular, "Can we look forward to an engagement soon? We can't wait to be grandparents." Erica glanced down at her pregnant belly that was getting closer to the steering wheel every day.

"You're going to make them grandparents, little one. But they are not going to be happy with me."

Erica stopped her car in front of the large home constructed from Canadian red cedar and native Montana rock. The building materials were a salute to pioneers and the generations of Abernathys who came before and settled this land. Sturdy logs supported the second story roof over the front entrance. The sun had just set, and inside lights blazed through the tall windows.

There was a chimney sticking up over the pitched roofline and smoke drifted out of it. She could picture the fireplace in the great room, where flames would crackle and snap. That wasn't about providing atmosphere. Montana could get darn cold, and it wasn't unheard of to have a freak snowstorm the beginning of October. Shivering, she pulled her poncho up more snugly around her neck.

She'd missed this place. In spite of what her family thought about her choosing a career in Colorado over it, she did love the ranch, the land, the mountains. And after twelve years, she was back to stay, just like her parents always wanted. But when Angela and George Abernathy saw her, they were probably not going to ask about city life in Denver. They would have way too many other questions.

She sighed. Procrastination wasn't going to make this first step any easier. "Here goes nothing..."

She walked up to the front door and rang the bell. It was her childhood home, but she hadn't told them she was coming. It didn't feel right to simply walk in.

Suddenly the front porch light flashed on, the door was opened and Angela Abernathy stood there. She was in her early fifties with dark blond highlighted hair. Her blue eyes widened and she blinked once, then smiled with pleasure. "Erica! Sweetheart, what a surprise."

"Hi, Mama."

"This is wonderful. Don't stand out here in the cold. Come inside. Please tell me you're staying. And for more than a day this time."

"Big fat yes." She forced cheerfulness into her voice. "I definitely am."

"Is there a holiday I don't know about?"

Boom, there it was. First judgment. The subtext was that since her grandparents' funerals five years ago she only showed up on holidays and hadn't visited since last Christmas. And her mom hadn't yet noticed the main attraction.

"Why didn't you tell us you were coming?" She pulled her

daughter close for a hug, then backed away, looking shocked. "Erica?"

She walked farther into the brightly lit entryway and pulled her poncho off over her head. Her mother's eyes went wide and her jaw actually dropped. In her rebellious teens, there was a time when Erica might have taken pride in pulling off the miracle of rendering her unflappable mother speechless. Not so much now. Or like this.

"You're pregnant." Her mother stated the obvious. "*Very* pregnant. Why didn't you tell us you're going to have a baby?"

Her token teen mutinies were small potatoes compared to this, but every time Erica had disappointed her parents, it ripped her heart out. This was, pardon the pun, the mother of all rebellions and no matter how old she was, or how much career success she had, making them proud was always her intention.

"I was going to tell you—" No points for good intentions. She lifted her hands in a helpless gesture. "I couldn't figure out how to say it."

Angela's gaze dropped to the ring finger on her left hand. "Is there a marriage you couldn't figure out how to tell us about either?"

Erica flinched at the words. Not that her mother's tone was sharp, but because it wasn't. The hurt in her eyes and reproach in her voice were like pokes in the chest, jabbing her heart. This was why she'd put off the conversation. The problem was, the longer she had dragged her feet, the worse it got. That was her bad, just one on a very long list.

"No, Mama. I'm not married."

"Is it Peter's baby?"

Erica should have expected the question but hadn't. "No. I told you we broke up over a year ago."

Regret was stark in her mom's eyes. "You did but I just thought—" The breakup had stunned Erica because they'd dated for a long time. Peter Barron was handsome, smart, fun, successful and she'd really cared about him. They had a relationship that was the envy of all their friends. She'd been so sure he was The One. So, she brought up the subject of having children.

His answer was adamant and unequivocal: he didn't want any kids. Ever. And he wasn't going to change his mind.

She'd tried to tell herself it didn't matter. She could be content, fulfilled and live a happy life with Peter while having a successful career of her own. It could be enough. But every time she saw a pregnant woman or a baby in a stroller, she got a knot of emptiness and longing in her stomach. Like a protest from her uterus. The yearning for a baby, the ache to be a mother, just wouldn't go away.

"Erica, who is the father?"

The quiet question snapped her back to the present. "I don't want to talk about it."

The anxiety in her mother's blue eyes increased, and her face went pale. "Did something happen to you?"

"No." She reached out, took her mother's hand and Angela squeezed it hard. "I didn't mean to scare you."

She'd given her poor mother a lot of shocks since she walked through the front door. Maybe she should tell her the truth. It was possible that she would understand. Angela Abernathy had two babies in two years, a boy and a girl. She thought her family was complete. Then right around the time she turned thirty, she accidentally got pregnant and realized how very much she wanted another baby. But she miscarried and the loss was devastating. After several more tries and losses she was told she couldn't carry a baby. It nearly destroyed her.

When Erica was suddenly staring thirty in the face, she remembered her mother's difficulty with pregnancy. Erica had no potential husband material on her horizon and worried that the inability to carry a baby at a certain age was genetic. She wasn't willing to wait and hope for a man to come along. She wouldn't risk what might be her only chance and pulled the trigger on going the single mom route. A big part of her hadn't believed IUI—intrauterine insemination—would work, but it did, and she was thrilled.

If anyone would understand the primal longing to have a baby, it was this woman.

"Mama, I really want to talk to you about this—"

The sound of heavy footsteps coming closer stopped her. Before she saw him, Erica heard her father's voice.

"Angela? What's taking so long? Who was at the door?" And then George Abernathy walked into the entryway and saw her. Emotions swirled in his eyes from pleasure to shock.

"Surprise." She'd always been Daddy's little girl, but she'd never seen him look at her quite like this before.

He was fit and tan but the color drained from his face. "Good Lord, Erica. What in the world—"

"You're going to be a grandfather, Daddy." She tried to smile, but her mouth was trembling and her heart was beating way too fast.

"Did you come here alone?"

"You're asking if I'm married. The answer is no."

He waited for several moments, then rubbed a hand across the back of his neck. "Are you all right? You look well."

Erica was pretty sure telling him the details would make things worse. Her father was old-fashioned and set in his ways. She knew her brother, Gabe, had butted heads with him over trying progressive ranching techniques. *Stubborn* was her dad's middle name, and Gabe finally gave up. Now he was more involved with real estate wheeling and dealing than the ranch. No, admitting to her father that she'd gone to a sperm bank was the last thing she planned to do.

"I'm fine, Daddy."

He looked down for a moment as if gathering his thoughts. Then he met her gaze and his eyes churned with confusion and hurt. "We're your parents and we have concerns—"

"I know. And I love you both very much," she interrupted. "But please believe me when I say I'm fine. Obviously I'm going to be a mother and more happy about this pregnancy than I can even put into words. I will do my very best to do as spectacular a job with my child as you guys did with Gabe and me. When the shock wears off, I hope you'll be as excited about this baby as I am. I know how much you want to be grandparents."

Neither of them responded to her impassioned speech but simply stared at her. Then they looked at each other and seemed to exchange silent agreement not to say anything more.

Finally her mother asked, "How long are you staying?"

"Would it be all right if I lived here until I find a job?"

"Of course you can stay with us—" Then her father stopped as her words sank in. "Wait. You left Barron Enterprises?" George Abernathy didn't shock easily, but this was the second time in five minutes he'd looked completely bewildered.

Erica was on a roll apparently. "I was fired actually."

"I don't understand. Not long ago you got that big promotion," her mom protested.

"I did." To chief administrative officer. In the last few years, these two had been so busy quizzing her about her marriage prospects, she hadn't been sure the move up the corporate ladder had even registered with them. "But Mr. Barron Senior, called me into his office to tell me I was being transferred to the Miami office. I didn't want to go."

"Why would he do that?" her dad asked. "Doesn't the chief administrative officer work out of the corporate office in Denver?"

Wow, she thought. He really had been paying attention. She'd been hoping to gloss over this part. "Peter married one of the receptionists at work. And she's pregnant." Even though she didn't love him anymore, that news had come as a blow. The lying bastard. "His wife has been a little hostile to me, since everyone at the company knows he and I were together for a long time."

"You said he's not the baby's father," Angela reminded her.

"He's not. But the woman apparently had a problem seeing me every day."

"So, Peter's father fired you because the new wife is an insecure twit?" her mother scoffed.

Erica was glad they seemed to be annoyed with someone besides her. "Apparently."

"That's wrongful termination," her father chimed in. "You can't let them get away with that."

"Way ahead of you, Daddy. I already have an appointment with an attorney."

"Good for you," he said.

"The thing is, after I moved in with Peter I sold my condo

and banked a nice profit. When we split up, I rented an apartment while I figured out what I wanted to do." And how big a place she would need *if* she got pregnant. "I have savings, but no job means no income until I can find another one. There's no telling how long that will be, so my savings have to last."

Her father nodded his understanding. "And if you file a lawsuit against Barron Enterprises, it could be a long time until there's a financial settlement."

"Exactly. So, I was hoping you guys wouldn't mind if I stayed here until I get back on my feet," she said.

"Of course." He didn't hesitate. "You're back where you belong. Even if it means coming home with your tail between your legs."

Erica refused to flinch at the words. Her father was right. She'd thought she had everything figured out and was thrown a big curve. She refused to call it a mess because that reflected on the child she was carrying, and the choices had been hers. The way it had played out made her feel like crap, and now she needed help from the family she'd neglected.

"Thank you, Daddy."

Her dad nodded, held out his arms to her and she stepped into them for a much needed hug. "I love you, honey. I think I speak for your mother when I say we're glad you're home, but we aren't finished talking about this baby's father."

Erica was finished, but wisely chose not to say that. The line was drawn in the sand, and she knew which side of it she was on.

Her dad helped her unload the car and take some things upstairs to her old room. She appreciated that very much and knew all of this must be hard for him. After that, she felt an overwhelming need to see her big brother. Fortunately his house was on the ranch and was located not far from her parents, so Erica walked over.

For the second time that day, she knocked on a door and waited to shock the person who opened it. But she was the one who got a surprise when a pretty, petite woman with long, straight blond hair stood there instead of her big brother.

"Hi. I'm Melanie Driscoll."

"You're the woman who's going to marry my brother. I'm Erica." She couldn't believe they hadn't met. "Mom called me right after he proposed, and she said the ring is fabulous."

"I think so." Melanie held out her left hand with a platinum band supporting a spectacularly large diamond.

"Gorgeous." Erica smiled. "When's the wedding?"

"Next summer."

"I'm so glad to finally meet you."

"Same here." The other woman's gaze dropped to her belly. "And I hear congratulations are in order for you, too. Your mom called."

"I figured."

Melanie shrugged. "Gabe is still on the phone with her."

"My ears were burning," Erica said wryly, and slid off her poncho as she stepped into the warm house.

Melanie gave her the once-over. "I've known you all of a minute but I have to say, you're positively glowing. The baby bump is so cute and you're beautiful."

"You should probably get your eyes checked. I'm as big as a barn."

"Hardly. When is the baby due?"

"November."

"You look fantastic," Melanie said. "How do you feel?"

"The first three months were a little rough with morning sickness. But since then I've been great. Not too tired. I love being pregnant." She smiled at the other woman. "I've known you all of a minute, but I have to say this. I'm so glad my brother has the good sense to marry you."

"I'm the lucky one. I'd given up on finding someone and then, there he was." She turned an adoring gaze on the man in question when he came up beside her.

Gabriel Abernathy was a tall, broad-shouldered force of nature. When he looked at Melanie, his blue eyes were flirty. Then his gaze landed on Erica and turned serious.

"I just got off the phone with Mom."

"Hello to you, too," she said.

"Come here." He held out his arms.

She walked into them and sighed when he hugged her. "I'm so glad to see you."

"Same here. But I have to ask—what the hell are you doing, Erica?"

"I'm having a baby." She put her hands protectively on her belly. "And I want this child more than anything in the world."

"Mom told me you won't say who the father is." With his hands on his hips and looking all serious at her, Gabe looked a lot like their father.

It had been a long, emotional day, and Erica was just about at her limit. "Don't you start on me. I left for Colorado to go to college. I stayed to have a career. Every time I make a decision, I'm being judged in a bad way. And you all wonder why I don't come home more often."

"It's not judgment. It's just that—" he dragged his hand through his spiky dirty blond hair "we miss you. Me. Mom. Dad. Grandpa Alexander. Gramps."

Guilt zinged her hard. Gramps—her great-grandfather, Josiah Abernathy—was in his midnineties and had been diagnosed with dementia. The subtext of her brother's words was that no one knew how much time he had left and she'd been focused on career which didn't leave a lot of free time.

She pushed the guilt away. "I was entitled to a life that *I* chose. Not Mom and Dad. They wouldn't have been happy with anything but me marrying a local rancher. I wanted more. To travel. Broaden my horizons."

"And you did." Again he glanced at her belly. "But you've lost time with Gramps. Precious time. And he doesn't say much at all anymore."

"I'll go see him soon—" A lump in her throat cut off more words. She did love Gramps and felt badly that he was declining. There was no good excuse except that life happened. One day turned into the next and before she'd realized it, twelve years had gone by.

Erica didn't want to fight with her brother. She'd come here to get away from the tension at the big house. That thought pulled her up short. Wasn't that what they called prison? It was time to change the subject.

"So, tell me how you and Melanie met," she said enthusiastically.

"Mel moved to Bronco from Rust Creek Falls for a job. She ended up looking into the Abernathy family history. Gramps's history."

So much for a subject change, Erica thought. But Gabe was smiling lovingly at his fiancée. And this was the happiest she'd ever seen him look.

"How did that happen, Melanie?"

"It's Mel," she corrected, then her expression turned from tender to concerned. "I have a good friend in Rust Creek Falls named Winona Cobbs. It came to my attention that she and Josiah Abernathy were secretly in love when they were very young. She got pregnant. When she gave birth, she thought the little girl was stillborn and had a breakdown. But that's not what happened. The baby was alive."

Gabe jumped into the story. "It turned out that Gramps's parents forced him to leave town and put the baby up for adoption. We think somewhere in or around Bronco."

"Oh my God." Erica couldn't believe what she was hearing. "How did you find all this out?"

"When the Ambling A Ranch in Rust Creek Falls was sold, the new people found Josiah's journal in the house. There was a letter inside to Winona. Somehow he found out who adopted their daughter, Beatrix, and promised he'd find a way to bring her back to Winona."

Erica was holding her breath. Waiting for the happy reunion part of the story. When it didn't come, she said, "And?"

"Because of the dementia, he can't give us any information. A friend of mine who's really good with social media did an internet search with what information we have and got a hit." Melanie looked up at Gabe, and disappointment was all over their faces. "It turned out that was just someone looking for money."

"People like that make me so angry." Not only that, Erica was feeling even more guilty about neglecting her great-grandfather. "What now?"

"Good question," Mel said. "So far we've only turned up frauds and weirdos."

Erica looked at her and saw concern. "There's more, isn't there?"

"Winona was hospitalized recently. She's ninety-three and frail. I'm worried that if something doesn't break soon, we'll lose her before we can reunite her with her daughter."

"That would be awful. What are we going to do?" Erica demanded.

"What's this 'we' stuff?" he asked.

"I want to help."

"Really?" Gabe looked surprised.

"Yes, me. I'll do whatever I can."

"Why?"

"He's my great-grandfather." And that wasn't her only reason. Erica was definitely shocked that Josiah had a daughter out of wedlock that the family never knew about. But she felt a parallel to his story. Her own secret. She was having a baby, and no one was going to know how this child came to be.

"I love him," she said simply.

"I know that." But his tone and expression were skeptical, as if he didn't expect her to stick around.

And why would he? She didn't come home enough when her life was going great. Until it fell apart, she'd acted as if she didn't need any of them.

"I know I should have made more of an effort to visit. But I'm here now and I want to do whatever I can to help. I've certainly got time—"

Gabe's expression turned sympathetic. "Mom told me about Peter and his father."

Erica saw the blaze of fury in his eyes but knew that it wasn't directed at her. She loved him so much for that.

She let out a sigh. "It's been an emotional and eventful couple of weeks."

Mel put her arm around Erica. "You've been through a lot recently. Everyone needs a minute to get used to the new normal. It's all going to be fine."

"Listen to her, baby sister. She's a smart lady." He smiled tenderly at the woman he was going to marry. "And I'm taking her out to dinner tonight."

"Why don't you come with us?" Mel asked her.

"I don't want to intrude."

"You won't be. Right, Gabe?" She turned her big blue eyes on him.

He nodded. "Definitely, you should come. There's a new restaurant in town. Barbecue but better. DJ's Deluxe."

"I'm the CFO now and have connections," Mel said. "Come with us. A change of scene will be good for you. We could all use a distraction."

"I could sure use one."

"It's settled then," Mel declared.

Erica watched her brother hold his fiancée's jacket for her to slip on. He put his arm around her for a quick hug, then took her hand and laced their fingers together.

Oh man, he's got it bad, Erica thought. *The bigger they are, the harder they fall.*

She didn't for a moment regret that she was pregnant, but seeing Mel and Gabe together, loving each other, made her a little envious. On the upside, her baby was going to have the best aunt and uncle in the world.

CHAPTER TWO

MORGAN DALTON WALKED into DJ's Deluxe and went straight to the bar. He needed a beer, and if a woman came along after that, he wouldn't complain. A woman would sure take his mind off his problems.

The place was crowded tonight, but he found a spot at the bar. DJ Traub himself was tending it and delivering food. The man was in his forties, handsome, a friendly guy with a face you could trust. The restaurant owner, who looked like he could just as easily round up a herd of cattle, had dark hair, brown eyes. He put a plate of potato skins deluxe in front of the blond woman sitting beside Morgan.

"This looks fantastic," she said. "Even better than the supermessy wings I just ate. Everything you give me is better than the last."

"You keep eating, I'll keep the food coming. It's the least I can do for Bronco Heights' newest full-time resident and my CFO's future sister-in-law."

Morgan was eavesdropping, but it wasn't his fault. She was close enough that he could smell her supersexy perfume. And he liked her voice. There was something low and husky and sensuous about it that made him sit up and take notice of everything she said.

DJ noticed him and said hello. Morgan had been a regular since the place opened, and they'd struck up a friendship.

He angled his head toward the woman beside him, a signal that he'd like to be introduced. The other man nodded slightly, an indication that his message was received.

"Hey, Erica," DJ said. "Since you're new to town, I thought you'd like to meet my friend Morgan Dalton."

Still chewing a bite of potato, she full on looked at him for the first time. That face... *This is what it must feel like to get zapped with those paddle things when your heart stops.*

She was beautiful. He'd seen his share of beautiful women in his thirty-four years, some of them on a movie screen. But this one sitting so close to him was more than a wow. He liked women, they liked him and he did his share of dating, although it was never serious and never would be. But he was dead certain that he'd never had such a strong reaction to a female the very first time he laid eyes on her.

"Hello, Morgan," she said. "I'm Erica."

"Nice to meet you." He barely noticed when DJ put a glass of beer in front of him. He wanted to say *where have you been all my life* and was afraid the words had come out of his mouth. But she didn't look afraid, so he figured he hadn't made a fool of himself yet. "So, you're new to town?"

"Not exactly. But I haven't lived here for twelve years. What about you?"

"I've been here a year." Why did it feel so much longer? "My father bought Dalton's Grange. My four brothers and I work there with my dad."

"There are four more at home like you?" she teased.

Her smile was as spectacular as a Montana sunrise, and he swore his heart got zapped again. "Yes, ma'am."

"How do you like it here, so far?" She cut into the potato skin and ate a piece.

"Prettiest country I've ever seen. But a little on the chilly side." He took a sip from his beer glass. "Could just be me, but there are some folks who consider us new money, without deep roots or any legacy. A couple of families have been here for generations. The Taylors and Abernathys. If you're not one of them, you get some funny looks."

"Really? Thanks for the warning." She nodded her head, but there was a twinkle in her pretty hazel eyes.

"So where are you moving from?" he asked.

"Colorado. Denver. My parents have been wanting me to come back and I had a change of circumstances in my career."

"Oh?"

"I got fired."

Morgan wasn't sure how he knew, but some instinct told him it was not a just termination. "Whoever fired you was clearly an idiot."

"I think so. But that's very nice of you to say, considering that we just met."

"The length of our acquaintance doesn't make my comment any less sincere. I just know. Because… Where have you been all my life?" He couldn't believe the words actually came out of his mouth. "Wait. Forget I said that—"

"No way. I love it." Erica was laughing. "That was quite possibly cheesier than these potato skins."

"I take it back—"

"And without a doubt the sweetest thing a man's ever said to me," she added.

"So that didn't make you want to head for the exit?"

"I'm made of sterner stuff." She smiled her punch-to-the-gut smile again. "Besides, I happen to like cheese."

He met her gaze over the corner of the shiny teak bar that separated them as they sat at a right angle to each other. "That makes two of us."

"So tell me, Morgan, why don't you have a beautiful woman on your arm tonight?"

"I wouldn't say *you're* on my arm exactly," he answered, "but you're talking to me. And you're definitely beautiful."

Her smile was suddenly shy and a little sad for some reason. "But we're not together. A good-looking cowboy like you, in this place all by yourself, is a dozen kinds of wrong. So what gives?"

"I thought I made that clear. I've been waiting for you." He knew he was only half kidding.

"Are you flirting with me?" There was the cutest expression on her face, a look that said the flirt factor might be going both ways.

"Maybe a little," he admitted. "And that makes me want to ask for your phone number. It's not every day a man meets a woman like you."

"That statement is true in more ways than you realize," she said wryly. "And it's becoming clear to me you didn't notice that I'm—"

"What?"

She swiveled her bar stool sideways toward him. The good news was they sat close enough that her legs were touching his. The jaw-dropping news was that she was very much with child.

Morgan glanced from her round belly to her eyes a couple of times before blurting out, "You're pregnant."

"Really?" Her look was wry as she put her hands on her stomach. "I hadn't noticed. But that would explain why I've been eating my weight in food that DJ keeps bringing me, even after I ate dinner."

"I didn't mean it like that. It's just— I didn't mean to offend you." He automatically looked for a ring on her left hand.

"I'm not married or offended." There was laughter in her voice.

"Erica, you have to know that I've never hit on a pregnant woman in my life. I apologize."

"Well, Morgan Dalton, I'm thrilled to be your first. And speaking for pregnant women everywhere, it's quite flattering to be flirted with." She stopped and studied his face. "But maybe I should apologize to you."

"For what?"

"You're white as a ghost."

"And you're enjoying that quite a bit, aren't you?"

"Yes."

She pushed away the plate with food still on it. Either she was finally full or had suddenly lost her appetite. "But I should have said something sooner. It's been a long day and coming home is hard."

"Oh?"

"My great-grandfather has dementia. And my family is kind of upset that I haven't been back to visit him in a while."

"I'm sorry."

"Thank you. And today I found out that said great-grandfather, Josiah Abernathy, had a baby out of wedlock and no one in my family knew about it."

He wasn't sure about turning white when she pointed out her pregnancy, but he felt the color drain from his face now. This was a bad time to find out he never got her last name before bad-mouthing her family. "You're an Abernathy?"

"Guilty." She put her hand on his arm, a consoling gesture. "Don't feel bad. I didn't take it the wrong way. I understand where you're coming from. People in this town don't deal well with change. And my parents are no exception. They respect tradition, passing land down to their children."

"Like I said. We're new money."

"Yeah. It kind of makes you an outsider." She looked down at her stomach and sighed. "They also aren't thrilled that their daughter is pregnant and not married. It's been a long time since I lived here, and I feel a lot like an outsider, too."

"What about the baby's father?"

"Don't you start judging me." Her eyes flashed with anger. "It was bad enough coming from my parents and brother, but I barely know you."

"I wasn't judging," he assured her. "And we just met, but we've shared a lot of information over potato skins and beer."

"Technically, and for the record, I'm drinking club soda with lime."

"That doesn't change the fact that we've bonded over being outsiders."

She thought about that for a moment, then nodded. "Okay. You win. We've bonded."

It was nice to have a friendly conversation with someone. Morgan was just about to ask for her phone number when he saw her expression change. He hadn't known her long but would swear her guard went up. He glanced over his shoulder and saw Gabe Abernathy and Melanie Driscoll walking toward them.

Morgan had run into him in town, at events, and the man had been cordial but not overly friendly.

Looking wary, he stopped beside his sister. "Are you okay, Erica?"

"Of course. Why wouldn't I be?"

"Mel and I didn't mean to be gone so long. We ran into some friends and got to talking." He gave Morgan another careful look. "I'm sorry we left you alone."

"It's okay. Morgan kept me company." She looked back and forth between them. "Have you two met?"

"Yes," Gabe said in his best "don't get any ideas" tone.

Erica's eyes narrowed as she looked at her brother's fiancée. "Mel, you're pretty new in town, aren't you?"

"Yes. And I love it here," she said, as chipper as could be. "People have been so friendly and welcoming."

"I guess that happens when you're engaged to an Abernathy." Morgan maintained a friendly tone, but never looked away from the other man.

"It helps," Gabe said. Then he looked at his sister. "We're leaving. Are you ready to go?"

"Yeah. I'm tired. It's been a long day." From her perch on the high bar stool, she looked hesitantly at the floor. "I just have to get down from here first."

Instantly Morgan got up and took her arms to help her down. Touching her seemed to short-circuit his brain, because he couldn't stop looking at her mouth. With an effort he pulled himself together and said, "Gracefully done."

"Thanks to you." She gave him a grateful look. "It was really nice to meet you, Morgan."

"The pleasure was mine." And he sincerely meant that.

"Good night," Mel said. "I'll see you around, Morgan."

"You will."

Then he watched the three of them walk away. Mostly he watched Erica. From this view it was impossible to tell she was pregnant. She had on leggings and cowboy boots with a sweater covering her hips and butt. What he could see was damn shapely, and her face and smile would steal a man's heart and have him grateful for it.

That's when he remembered he hadn't gotten her phone number. Now that he could think straight again, he realized how idiotic the thought was. Why would he even consider it? But he knew the answer to that. He felt comfortable with her, and that hadn't happened to him in a long time. Clearly she wasn't looking for a relationship but that could be *why* he felt so comfortable with her. He wasn't looking for a relationship either. He'd fallen half in love with Erica Abernathy before realizing she was going to have a baby. And that complicated things in a way that would keep him from making a romantic fool of himself.

The next morning Erica was in the best mood. A man had flirted with her! Granted, when he started, he didn't know she was pregnant. What pleased and surprised her the most was that he didn't seem to lose interest when he found out.

Another surprise was how nice it felt waking up in her old room. Her mom kept it the way it was when Erica left for college. She slept in her queen-size bed with the brass headboard. Across from it was a cherrywood dresser and matching dressing table where she did her makeup. Lace curtains crisscrossed the window that had a spectacular view of the mountains. The walls were painted a pale lavender, with white doors and trim. And the room came with an en suite bathroom. The whole effect was soothing.

Except for the part where she couldn't get last night out of her mind. A man like that—those shoulders, that voice and face. His blue eyes twinkled with humor and he was tan, evidence of a rugged outdoor life. And he admitted flirting with her and wanting her phone number. In an alternate universe, where she wasn't pregnant and as big as the *Queen Mary*, she'd have seriously flirted back.

So it was probably a good thing she had her own personal speed bump. After being dumped by the man she'd thought was The One, then watching him take up with another woman so soon after, her self-esteem had been pretty battered. Last night made her feel better.

After showering, then doing her hair and makeup, she slipped on a dress she hoped projected confident professionalism. Then she went downstairs.

Erica heard voices, which was unusual at this hour. She'd only expected to see her mother, as her father was almost always busy with ranch work by now. Not today. And she got a bonus surprise. Her brother, Gabe, was there, too. And Grandpa Alexander. She kissed his cheek and gave him a hug.

"It's good to see you, Erica." The silver-haired man smiled, but there were questions in his eyes.

"How come you guys aren't out working?" She was practically positive the four of them had been talking about her, because they clammed up when she'd walked into the room. Now they all looked guilty. "What?"

"Good morning, sweetie." Her mother set the spatula she'd been holding on the granite countertop beside the stainless steel stove. "Did you sleep well?"

"As well as can be expected, what with being as big as a house." She made eye contact with each one of them. "Don't let me interrupt. Feel free to continue talking about me."

Gabe snorted. "What makes you think we were talking about you?"

"Oh please." She put a hand on her hip. "Since when are you and Daddy and Grandpa not doing ranch chores at this time of day? I grew up hearing that there's always something to be done around here. This looks very much like a family meeting. And it's not a leap to figure out that I'm the topic of discussion, since my presence on the Ambling A is the only variable."

"Why don't you let me make you a plate of food?" her mother suggested. "You need to keep up your strength."

"Thank you, Mama. Something smells wonderful. But first I'd like to know what's going on." She looked at her brother pointedly, and he squirmed under her gaze.

"You know I've always had your best interests at heart," he started.

"That's how you start when someone isn't going to like what you're about to say. Does this have anything to do with last night at DJ's?"

He pressed his lips together and wouldn't quite meet her

gaze, confirming the theory. "Do you always chat up strangers at a bar, sis?"

"Obviously you're talking about Morgan Dalton." Just saying his name brought to mind a very appealing image of the man, and it made her tummy flutter. This was something she hadn't felt in a long time. Or maybe ever. "He seemed to be a very nice man. I liked him a lot."

"Looks can be deceiving," her mother said.

"Do you have something against him?" Erica asked the question and looked at all of them for a response.

"The Daltons are new to Bronco Heights," Grandpa Alexander said.

"No one knows much about them." Her father planted his feet wide apart and folded his arms over his chest.

She remembered what Morgan had said about local folks being a little standoffish.

"Has anyone bothered to get to know them?" she demanded.

"There are rumors. You know how this town is." Her mother didn't actually answer the question. "Mel's friend Amanda is engaged to his brother. I heard something about the father cheating on his wife. No one knows how they got the money to buy the ranch."

"If it wasn't legal, I'm sure someone would be in jail." Erica wasn't sure why, but she felt strongly about defending Morgan. She met her brother's gaze. "Does Mel think her friend is making a mistake marrying Morgan's brother?"

Gabe shifted his feet before meeting her gaze. "She said he's a good man and a terrific father."

"Well, what do you know?" Erica looked at each of them in turn. "Amanda found out that one of the Daltons is a stand-up guy because she got to know him."

"People change," Erica continued. "They mature. Let them screw up first before you put their picture on a Most Wanted poster at the post office."

"But, sweetie, you're pregnant," her mother said.

"Not a news flash, Mama."

"He's after something," her father declared.

"Not my money." She was unemployed and her savings wouldn't last long. "I don't have any."

"But your family does." It seemed her father had already made up his mind.

"His ranch seems to be doing fine, no?" she asked them.

"No one knows for sure," Gabe said. "The smart move would be to stay away from him."

Erica looked from her brother to her father to her grandfather. "You know, I find this overprotective streak of yours equal parts adorable and annoying. You do realize that for the past twelve years I've been taking pretty good care of myself."

"Except for the part where you're having a baby without a husband." Her mother didn't pull any punches.

The zinger hit its mark, and Erica heard the message loud and clear. "Thank you all for your advice and I know it comes from a place of caring about me." It was also worth what she'd paid for it, no matter their good intentions. Wasn't the road to hell paved with them? "I'm not very hungry after all, Mama. And I have to run. I have an appointment in town with an attorney."

"Could you do me a favor since you're going into town?" her father asked. "I called in an order to the building supply store. It will fit in your SUV and you be sure to have one of the guys there load it up for you. That would save me a trip. Since I'm behind on work today…"

Because he'd felt an obligation to warn her away from Morgan. Defensiveness didn't trump her sense of obligation to do as he'd asked. "Not a problem, Daddy."

Erica walked away before anyone, including herself, could say another word. She'd grab something to eat before her appointment. More than one friend in Denver had suggested she might have a case to sue Barron Enterprises for wrongful termination, so she'd made the appointment before moving home.

After stopping for a fast-food breakfast sandwich, she was early for her ten o'clock slot at Randall & Randall, attorneys at law. It was a brother-sister firm located in the Bronco Heights business district. The receptionist was somewhere in her fifties, with stylishly cut short brown hair and brown eyes. The nameplate on her desk read Mrs. Frances Randall. *All in the family*, Erica thought.

She introduced herself and was politely asked to take a seat in the expensively furnished waiting area. Charlotte Randall would be with her shortly.

"Can I get you anything?" Mrs. Randall asked. "Water? Coffee?"

"Nothing, thanks."

A few minutes later a pretty young woman with red hair and brown eyes opened the door to the back offices. "You must be Erica Abernathy. I'm Charlotte Randall. It's nice to meet you."

"Likewise." Erica stood and shook hands.

"Let's go to my office and you can tell me why you're here."

They walked down a hall, then turned right into a large room with a desk full of files and a laptop buried in the middle of it. Floor-to-ceiling windows looked out on the gorgeous mountains while diplomas and certificates hanging on the wall proudly displayed her impressive credentials.

Charlotte sat behind the desk. "How can I help you?"

"I'm not sure you can, actually." She took a deep breath. "Until recently I worked for Barron Enterprises in Denver."

"I've heard of it. Big media company headquartered there. Powerful."

"Yeah." Erica fully expected to be told there was no point in wasting time because Barron had an army of lawyers. They would fight any settlement by every legal means necessary and drag out a lawsuit, making it too expensive to continue. "I was fired."

The young woman nodded thoughtfully. "Colorado is an at-will state. That means either an employer or employee can terminate an employment situation at any time without consequences."

"So, you're saying I have no recourse?" Though it was expected, her heart fell. She could practically hear the thud.

"Not necessarily. Were you given a reason for the dismissal?"

"No." She thought for a moment. "I was called in to see the company president. He told me I was being transferred to the Miami office."

Erica went on from there, explaining everything. Dating the boss's son. Their breakup. His relationship with another company employee. "I wanted to quit even before I was called on the carpet."

"Why is that?"

"Peter and that employee's sudden marriage and baby announcement. After that his wife became increasingly hostile as my pregnancy began to show."

"It's a good thing you toughed it out. If you'd quit, you would have lost any standing in the court to file a lawsuit."

"The transfer came out of the blue and I'm in my third trimester. The job I had was traditionally done from the home office in Denver. I pushed back. My boss got angry and said I was fired."

"I see." Charlotte's eyes narrowed a little dangerously. "So there was no misconduct on your part? No job performance issues like habitual tardiness?"

"No. I'd been with the company for eight years and had a spotless record. In fact, before the work environment turned hostile, I was promoted to chief administrative officer."

Charlotte nodded, her expression reflecting respect for that higher management job. "So you want to sue Barron for wrongful termination."

"I believe I was unfairly let go. And that I'm entitled to a severance package at the very least. But you should be aware that my resources are limited, especially because of my pregnancy."

The lawyer smiled. "Frankly, that's what gives you cause to bring suit."

"How so?"

"Even in an at-will state there are exceptions to the rule and legal remedies that could help keep your job, if you still want it. Or go for a settlement because you were wrongfully terminated. One of those exceptions is discrimination for a number of reasons, one of them being pregnancy."

"But I don't think he fired me because I'm having a baby. Everyone knows it's not his son's. It's all about the new wife not wanting to look at me every day and be reminded I dated her husband first." What she kept to herself was that he hadn't wanted to have a baby with Erica.

"It doesn't matter what the motivation for termination was. You're in a protected class and that gives you a very good chance of winning a settlement. No matter how many lawyers the company has. And I don't think they can drag it out. The optics for a powerful media company bullying a pregnant woman are really bad. They know it, and we can use that to pressure them."

"Does that mean you'll take my case?"

"Yes." Charlotte explained that she would take it on contingency and how the attorney-client contract worked. She seemed really eager to get started. "There are laws against what they did to you, Erica. I'll put the paperwork together and have them served as soon as possible."

"Thank you, Charlotte. You have no idea how relieved I am."

Erica left the lawyer's office feeling pretty darn positive. Kind of the way she'd left DJ's last night after Morgan had said *Where have you been all my life*. The memory made her smile, but she also felt a little wistful. In her car behind the steering wheel, she looked down at the belly that prevented her from seeing her feet. She was officially a package deal, and no man in his right mind would want her.

She'd been resigned to that when she decided to take the journey to motherhood alone. But that was before she met Morgan.

It was a short drive to the building supply store. She got out of the car and walked into the cavernous interior guaranteed to make men quiver with excitement. But she was the one doing the quivering when she practically ran into Morgan Dalton standing just inside the door.

CHAPTER THREE

MORGAN HAD BEEN thinking about Erica a lot since last night, but he hadn't expected to see her again. On top of that, the building supply store in town was probably the last place he would have expected to bump into her. Yet here she was. And when she smiled her beautiful smile at him, his day got a whole lot brighter. Possibly because he felt that lightning bolt to the heart even stronger than he had the first time he saw her.

"If it isn't the prettiest pregnant lady in town." Darned if she didn't blush, he thought. If she had at DJ's, the dim lighting in the restaurant prevented him from seeing. She was even more beautiful than she'd been last night, classy and stylish in her gray dress and black boots. Again his gaze was drawn to her full, sexy lips.

"I bet you say that to all the pregnant ladies."

"Nope. As a matter of fact, you're the only one I know." He steered her to the side of the doorway and out of the heavy foot traffic where she might get run into. Reluctantly, he removed his hand from her arm but couldn't stop the tingling in his fingers—or the urge to touch her and never stop. "To what do I owe the good fortune of seeing you again so soon?"

"Actually you can thank my father. I'm picking up an order for him." There was a wry expression on her face and more than a little satisfaction in her smile. "What brings you here?"

"Fencing materials. It's getting to be time to check them out and make repairs. Need to have all the supplies when that chore gets put on the schedule." When that happened, he was pretty sure his father would tag along and continue trying to "mend fences" with him. Morgan would have thought that pun was funny if it was anyone but his dad. He wasn't laughing.

"You turned very serious about something all of a sudden." That statement put a curious look on her face. "Does it have anything to do with family?"

"Why do you ask?"

"Because nine times out of ten a man looking like you do right now is having woman or family trouble. Since you flirted with me outrageously last night, I don't think it's about a lady. That leaves family. And I have to tell you, there are rumors spreading about yours."

Folks around here hadn't given him an especially warm welcome so he was a little surprised they'd waste their breath gossiping about his family. "I don't know whether to be pissed off or proud."

"Maybe both. But one of the things they're talking about is your brother."

"I've got four," he said. "Still, my guess would be that it's Holt."

Absently she tucked a silky blond strand of hair behind her ear. "Gabe mentioned he's a good man and father."

"Yeah. He is. Ten years ago he had a brush with the law. He did community service, but there's nothing permanent on his record."

"Then that's not a rumor. It's fact."

She wasn't judging, Morgan realized, and liked her even better for it. "Holt isn't proud of it and in a lot of ways that shaped the dad he's become."

"That would make you an uncle. Niece or nephew?" Interest sparked in her hazel eyes, cranking up the green, toning down the brown.

"Nephew. Robby. He's seven. As a matter of fact, somehow my brother talked me into looking after him this afternoon. I'm taking him to Happy Hearts after school."

"I'm sorry. Happy Hearts?"

He laughed at the puzzled expression on her face. "I forgot you just came back. It's an animal sanctuary run by Daphne Taylor. Robby picked out a dog and cat from there, both rescues."

"I know Daphne. She was a year ahead of me in high school." She tapped her lip thoughtfully. "As a matter of fact, I dated her older brother Jordan for a short time the summer after I graduated. He was an older man and I was flattered by the attention. At first."

"Oh?" Jealousy pricked him a little, and that was just plain stupid. Why the hell was it any skin off his nose that she went out with the son of the richest man in town a lot of years ago? And obviously she'd been with someone since then or she wouldn't be pregnant. If, and that was a very big if, there was any skin coming off his nose about anything, it would be that.

"Yeah. I haven't thought about him for a long time. Seems like a lifetime ago." She met his gaze. "My parents made no secret of the fact that they really wanted me to marry Jordan. Partly so I wouldn't go out of state to college."

"But you didn't do that."

"Nope. There was no spark with him." She shrugged.

Damn sparks were sure inconvenient. He was pretty sure he had some for her because he was unreasonably glad she hadn't felt them for Jordan Taylor. "So, are you and Daphne friends?"

"We used to be."

"Then you should come out to the sanctuary. This afternoon maybe. If you don't have something going on."

"I don't."

"You could meet Robby. See your friend." *I could see you.*

"Maybe." She nodded thoughtfully. "Now I better see about my father's order."

"Yeah. And I have to get those supplies."

It turned out the order for her father was wood cut into short pieces and a couple bags of hardware that were already loaded onto a cart. One of the store employees started to wheel it out to her SUV in the parking lot, but Morgan offered to help.

He followed her to the car and put her rear passenger seat

down flat, then slid the boards in one by one. That gave him the chance to spend a couple more minutes with her. Just in case he didn't see her later. On a one to ten stupid scale, that probably earned him a twenty.

Erica drove back to the Ambling A feeling as if she'd been on an emotional roller coaster all day. She woke up in a great mood but her family managed to bring her down with warnings to steer clear of Morgan Dalton. Then the lawyer said she had a strong case for a settlement and while doing her dad a favor she ran into Morgan.

When she saw him, she got that shivery feeling in the pit of her stomach again. The same thing she'd felt at DJ's, only stronger, especially because he kept looking at her mouth. He didn't have to mention the outing with his nephew, but he had. And, doggone it, she was curious to see him with a seven-year-old boy. Then she factored in her family's advice, the same family she was trying to make peace with.

It might be best to avoid Morgan. Not because she believed he wasn't a decent person, but because every instinct said he was. He seemed like an awfully nice man. And he was hot. In a world where she wasn't pregnant there was a good chance she'd have kissed him when he looked at her mouth. But she was pregnant, so that was that.

She drove down the long road to the ranch, turned toward the outbuildings and corral, then parked by the barn. Her father had said he would be there most of the day. She sniffed the air and savored the familiar, earthy scent of animals and hay. She'd forgotten how pleasant this all was. And inside the barn it was even stronger as she walked through. She located her dad in the tack room sitting on a stool in front of the workbench.

"Daddy, I've got the stuff you ordered from the building supply store."

"Thanks." He glanced over his shoulder. "I'll come unload it."

"Okay."

He slid off the wooden stool and walked toward her, a frown on his face. "Who loaded the car for you? Was it Jerry?"

She debated the pros and cons of telling him who had. In the end, she couldn't resist messing with him. After all, he'd warned her off Morgan, then sent her on an errand where he happened to be. Karma was funny that way. "No, I didn't lift a finger. Jerry offered, but Morgan Dalton happened to be there and he helped me out."

"Hmm." That was his only comment.

But Erica could feel the tension from him crank up. She didn't like this awkwardness and needed to try and lighten things up. She followed him out to her car, where he lifted the tailgate and pulled out a couple pieces of the wood.

"What are you going to do with this?" she asked.

"I'm building something."

"What?" she asked.

"A piece of furniture," he said vaguely.

"Something for Mama?"

"Sort of."

She walked after him back through the barn to the tack room but he didn't elaborate.

"I have a lot of good memories growing up here with Grandpa Alex and Gramps."

"Is that so?" Her dad set down the boards in an empty space on the far wall. He pulled his Stetson a little lower on his forehead. "Funny, you didn't have any trouble walking away."

It was on the tip of her tongue to explain her reasons again. How she wanted independence. And didn't want to be pressured into marrying Jordan. Or settling down in Bronco, Montana without ever experiencing another way of life. But she kept that to herself because this man had heard it all before and none of what she'd said changed his attitude.

"Do you remember that litter of kittens the barn cat had?"

"Yup." He walked past her back outside.

Erica followed behind him, just like when she was a little girl and shadowed him everywhere. "They were so cute."

"Took us forever to get rid of 'em."

"You mean find them good homes."

"Whatever," he said.

"Morgan told me about Happy Hearts, the animal sanctuary. His nephew adopted a dog and cat. If that place had been around, we wouldn't have had such a hard time getting people to take the kittens."

"Hmm." He set a few more boards down with the others, then turned to make another trip.

"I'll never forget that time we went fishing in the creek. You were trying to teach me how to cast a line."

"And you fell in." He half smiled. "Your mama wasn't too happy with us."

"No, she wasn't." As they walked through the barn, she saw the stall where her first horse had lived. "Do you remember Belle?"

"Of course. You learned to ride on her."

"Yeah." She fell off and broke her arm, too. But she was trying to lighten his mood, not remind him how he blamed himself for that accident. "She was a sweetheart."

"Gramps knew she would be. He picked her out for you."

Erica had forgotten that. Again she felt bad about not seeing him more while she could still talk to him about these memories.

"Gabe told me about the baby girl Gramps gave up for adoption. Beatrix."

"Yeah." Her father put the last piece of wood on the stack.

"He and Mel are trying to find her. Do you think they will?"

"Long shot, I figure."

"She would be your—" Erica did the family connection in her head "—aunt. How do you feel about all this?"

"Family is family. It's good to know your folks, I guess. For us and for her."

"Yes." Erica sat on the stool while he went to get the bags of hardware. When he came back she said, "It's weird to think about Gramps having a baby and not telling anyone."

Her father's gaze snapped to hers, and irony glittered in his hazel eyes. "You didn't tell any of us you were going to have a baby until yesterday. And only because you had to."

"I would have said something. Eventually," she mumbled. This was not going at all as she'd hoped. Instead of easing the tension between them, she was making it worse.

"I don't understand this world anymore," he said. "Times are changing. I can't keep up. And not sure I want to."

"Talk to me, Daddy." That was the most he'd said. Maybe he was ready to get it out in the open. "What's bugging you?"

His gaze settled on her belly for several moments, so she braced herself for more third degree about the baby's father. When he finally spoke, she was surprised by what he said.

"You really want to know what's got me twisted up?" He set the bag down. "That damn animal sanctuary of Daphne Taylor's."

"What?" Her eyes opened wider. "Why?"

"This is cattle country. It's always been survival of the fittest. That's nature's way. What doesn't kill you makes you stronger. That's a cliché now, but it's always been the way of it on a ranch. Whether it's horses or cows, the ones that make it against the odds ensure the strength of the bloodlines to produce hardy offspring able to withstand adverse conditions. Like cold, heat, drought and anything else Mother Nature throws at us."

Erica could understand his point of view, but science made advances to benefit animals and humans. Without artificial insemination she wouldn't be having this baby. Those words would not come out of her mouth, however. Her father would never understand how very much she wanted this child. How deeply she'd longed to be a mother.

"Look at it this way, Daddy. As I understand it, Daphne takes in animals and hooks them up with someone to love them. Like an adoption agency." Or a sperm bank. "She provides a service to the community."

"If you ask me, that girl has too much time on her hands if she can take care of animals that have no practical function."

"You have dogs," she pointed out. "And you love them."

"I do. But they serve a purpose on this ranch. They herd cattle."

"Okay." Time to exit this conversation. "Just so I'm clear. Does this mean you're a no vote on Happy Hearts?"

For half a second he grinned, as if forgetting to be mad at her. As if she was the smart-ass kid he'd always called her. Then the amusement disappeared and serious dad was back.

"Have you ever seen this animal place?" he asked. "After all, you've been gone for twelve years."

She refused to engage on something she couldn't change. "No, I haven't been there yet."

"Okay, then." That meant *don't argue something you know nothing about*. He pointed to the bench where the tack was laid out. "I've got work to do."

"Right." She slid off the stool and moved toward the doorway.

"Erica?"

"Hmm?" She turned back toward him.

"How did your appointment go? With the lawyer?"

"Oh." She'd almost forgotten. "She said I have a strong case and will draw up the paperwork to file the lawsuit."

"Good. Thanks for getting my order." He nodded and picked up a bridle, effectively turning his back on her and any more conversation.

"You're welcome. See you later."

She headed outside, mulling over their talk. One positive thing had come out of it, and her dad wouldn't like the result. He was right that she was advocating for something she knew nothing about. So, she made up her mind to go to the animal sanctuary. She smiled when she realized the trip came with a bonus. Morgan would be there with his nephew.

Morgan finished feeding the horses, then jumped in his truck for the short drive to his house on Dalton's Grange. It was one of three, the other two going to the second- and third-oldest Dalton brothers—Holt and Boone.

His place had three bedrooms, two baths, living and dining rooms and a kitchen. A little more space than a single cowboy needed and this was the second largest. They'd agreed Holt should have the most square footage since he had a boy he was raising.

That boy was the reason he was in such a hurry. He was going to pick up Robby from school, then take him to Happy Hearts. While Holt was attending a cattlemen's association meeting, his fiancée, Amanda, had promised the kid an outing. Morgan was going along to provide another pair of eyes, or possibly some muscle. Robby loved to roam and roughhouse. And if Erica showed up while they were there, well, he sure as heck wouldn't turn down another chance to hang out with her.

Fifteen minutes later he was showered, changed into clean clothes and smelled pretty good, too. There was a knock on his door, and when he opened it, Holt and Amanda were there. She was a pretty little thing with long brown hair and eyes the color of warm chocolate.

He hugged her. "Hey. When are you going to get smart and leave this guy to run away with me?"

She laughed. "As tempting as that offer is, I love him."

"Hands off my woman, big brother." Holt didn't look the least bit worried. He'd loved her for a long time, and they were eager to be a family for his son.

Morgan was teasing, but if he did have a thing for her, he'd fight it into submission. No way he'd be like his father and cross the boundaries of fidelity. But he had to ask, "How come you don't think I could take her away from you?"

"Because with women you're all hat and no saddle. As soon as one gets seriously sweet on you, that's it. You're outta there." Holt grinned. "You're only interested when there's no serious danger of making a commitment."

Morgan admitted, if only to himself, that his brother had a point. But he was a little envious of Holt's happiness. "How did you guys know you were it for each other?"

"That's hard to put into words." Holt thought for a moment. "The first time I laid eyes on Amanda, I knew she was something special." He smiled down at her. "That was ten years ago. It didn't work out then, but I never forgot her. And now she's never getting rid of me."

"As if." She moved closer and slid her arm around his waist. "To answer your question, Morgan, love is when you light up in the presence of one certain person. That someone you can't wait to be with and never want to leave. It can sneak up on you gradually or hit you like a bolt of lightning. And you just *know*."

He doubted he'd find that, but out loud he teased, "That's the best you can do?"

She shook her head, exasperated. "You're impossible."

"Thank you. I try."

"And succeed nicely," Holt joked. "Seriously, Morgan, thanks for helping out with Robby today. He's always pretty active but after being cooped up in school all day he'll have a lot of energy to work off."

"Happy to help." Morgan had a deep respect for his brother, raising his son alone for the last four years. The boy's mother hadn't wanted to be a mom but Holt handled fatherhood like a pro, better than anyone could have imagined. "How did you get to be such a good dad? God knows ours left a lot to be desired in the role model department."

"Neal isn't as bad as you make him out. He's made mistakes, but he loves our mom. When she was in the hospital after the heart attack, I overheard him talking to the chaplain, promising to be a better husband. I believe he was sincere," Holt said. "And don't sell yourself short, big brother. You're really good with my kid. Just saying."

"Glad you think so."

"I know so. You are and always were a great big brother, looking out for the rest of us. And, except for Amanda, I trust you with my son more than anyone."

"Stop," Morgan teased. "You'll make me blush, or cry. Or both."

Holt grinned. "Robby will cry if you guys are late and he's waiting in front of the school all alone."

"Let's go get him, then."

Holt kissed Amanda, then said, "I'm off to my meeting. Be home as soon as I can."

They walked outside, and before getting in his truck, Holt kissed Amanda one more time as if he didn't want to let her go. After he drove away, she and Morgan got into his truck and headed out to pick up his nephew.

When the boy was successfully retrieved from school and in the truck, Morgan thanked the good Lord for booster seats and seat belts that kept an active boy contained. It did not, however, put any limitations on the chatter. All the way there the kid talked about Bentley and Oliver, the dog and cat he'd brought home from the sanctuary.

He made the turn onto the road leading to the facility. There were two buildings—a barn and a squat structure for the smaller animals. In an enclosure, he could see goats, pigs and a variety of creatures milling around.

When Morgan parked the truck in the dirt lot, Amanda said so only he could hear, "I'm under strict orders *not* to let him get attached to an animal or under any circumstances bring another one home."

"Okay." Morgan scanned the open area and was disappointed when he spotted a few trucks and cars but no SUV with Colorado license plates.

"Is something wrong?" she asked.

"Hmm? What?" He met her gaze. "No. All good."

"Yay, we're here," Robby shouted. "I'm going to see Tiny Tim."

"That potbellied pig is his favorite," Amanda said.

"No kidding. If we brought it home, do you think Holt would ever trust me with his son again?" he teased. Then he gave the area one more look for the familiar car.

"In a word? No." She laughed, but it faded when she studied him. "Are you looking for someone?"

"No." Yes, he thought. Until he didn't see Erica, he realized just how very much he'd been looking forward to it. "Why do you ask?"

"You look like that potbellied pig just two-stepped all over your favorite Stetson."

"No. I'm good." The rear passenger door slammed shut, a clue Robby had freed himself and was off. "And we're up."

"Right."

Morgan slid out of the truck and called after his nephew. "Stay where we can see you."

"Okay, Uncle Morgan." But he continued to race toward the animal enclosure as fast as those seven-year-old legs could go.

Amanda came around the truck and stood beside him, shading her eyes from the sun with her hand. "He'll be fine. Daphne is out there with the animals. She'll look out for him."

Behind them there was the sound of a car driving up the road. Dust trailed behind it, but the SUV looked familiar. It was the same color as Erica's, and he smiled. Although he didn't realize he was until Amanda pointed it out.

"Someone you know?" It was the tone a woman used when she knew the answer to her own question and planned to make something of it.

"Yeah. Erica Abernathy."

"And you know her—how?"

"Ran into her last night at DJ's then again today at the building supply store." With everything he had, he was trying to look indifferent.

"Well, you're lighting up, Morgan." She was definitely making this into something. "Did she know you were coming out here?"

"I might have mentioned we'd be here this afternoon."

"Hmm."

Morgan had no idea what that meant. Could be anything from "she's way out of your league" to "I can tell you're sweet on her." Oddly, he wanted both of those things to be true.

The SUV parked next to them and two women exited. Erica had brought Melanie with her.

"Mel!" Amanda squealed with delight when she saw her friend and gave her a hug.

"Hi." Erica walked around the front of her car and smiled at him, then the other two women. "I found her wandering around the Ambling A, and she had the day off. She volunteered to show me where she adopted her cat."

"Where are my manners?" Mel said. "Erica, this is my friend Amanda Jenkins. We met when I rented an apartment in the same complex as Amanda and her roommate Brittany." She looked at her friend. "This is Gabe's sister. She just came in from Colorado."

"Nice to meet you, Erica." Amanda said to both women, "I guess you know Morgan Dalton."

"Yes. He helped me out today," Erica said. "Loaded some stuff in my car."

"Aren't you the gallant one." Amanda had a shrewd expression on her face that implied she could read his mind and thought he was an idiot for trying to pretend indifference.

"Speaking of Brittany, I sure haven't seen much of her lately," Mel said. "I get short phone calls and texts. Reading between the lines, she couldn't be happier." She turned to Erica and explained, "Brittany's married to Daniel Dubois, a local rancher who's raising his orphaned niece." Then she turned her attention back to Mel. "I hear she's up to her ears in alligators what with handling Denim and Diamonds."

"What's Denim and Diamonds?" Erica asked.

"It's a black tie fundraiser," Amanda explained, then mentioned the early November date. "It's going to be a real swanky affair at the Taylor Ranch. Everyone is going to be there. You should come, Erica."

"Oh, I don't know—"

"Your folks are probably going. Gabe is too, right, Mel?"

"We wouldn't miss it," she agreed.

Erica looked down at her gently rounded belly. "Only two problems. It's the week before my due date. So..."

"I don't see that as an issue if you haven't had the baby yet." Amanda shrugged.

"You said two problems," Morgan reminded her. "What's the second one?"

She looked up at him and tucked a strand of blond hair behind her ear when it blew across her lips. After hesitating a fraction of a second, she said, "Remember I told you I dated Jordan Taylor a long time ago?"

"Yeah." How could he forget? His reaction to it was way out of proportion. But the other two women looked pretty surprised at her revelation.

"Well," Erica continued, "I met his father. Cornelius. Just a couple of times but he was always bossy and domineering. Going to any event on his ranch makes me a little uncomfortable."

"There will be so many people there he probably won't even see you," Melanie said.

"I'll be even bigger by then. No one will be able to miss me."

"You are not that big," Amanda assured her. "And we just met, so if this is out of line, don't judge. But it looks as if pregnancy agrees with you. You're radiant."

Morgan couldn't agree more, but kept that to himself. No way a guy should insert himself into this conversation. Although he could see a vulnerability in Erica that made him feel protective.

"Thanks." Erica smiled a little shyly, a lot self-consciously. "I appreciate that. And just so you know, I wasn't fishing for compliments."

"I didn't think you were." Amanda waved it off. "And you really should think about coming. It will be the biggest social event of the year. From what Brittany says, the guest list is pretty extensive. You're going, right, Morgan?"

His father mentioned an invitation and Neal Dalton had said it was a good chance to expand their ties to the community. He wanted the whole family to show up and their mother agreed with him. Morgan and his brothers would do anything for her, so that pretty much made it a command appearance.

"I wish I could say no, but…"

"So you'll see some friendly faces, Erica," Amanda persisted.

"Still," she said hesitantly, "Jordan's father can be intimidating. Facing him alone—"

"I'll go with you." Morgan was just as surprised as the three women when the words came out of his mouth.

CHAPTER FOUR

ERICA HELD HER BREATH, expecting any second for Morgan to grin at her and say *Gotcha*. Or *Just kidding*. She couldn't believe he'd just volunteered to escort her to the biggest social event of the year. But he looked completely serious and possibly a little embarrassed. Mel and Amanda were staring at both of them, and she couldn't imagine what they must be thinking. Actually she could see that her brother's fiancée was a little shocked—maybe even a little skeptical.

"That's awfully brave of you to offer," Erica finally said.

"Why?" He shrugged. "I don't mind running interference for you. And you'd be doing me a favor. If I have to go, the least you could do is go with me so I have someone to talk to."

"But I'm pregnant." *Nothing like stating the obvious, but... Seriously?*

"Really? I didn't notice," he teased.

"I'm not even sure I'll go." Erica looked at the two women who'd been glancing back and forth between them, like watching a tennis match.

"It's over a month away," Amanda said. "There's time to decide."

"That's true," Mel agreed a little too quickly. "Talk about it later. We came here to see the farm animals. I was going to show you around, remember?"

"And I have to go make sure Robby isn't driving Daphne crazy." Amanda headed for the farm buildings. "Mel, why don't you come with me and say hi to Daphne. There might be another cat adoption in your future."

"No more for me. But I love looking at the kittens." She glanced over her shoulder. "Coming, Erica?"

"I'm right behind you. Moving a little slowly these days."

"Okay." Mel nodded and hurried after her friend.

When they were alone, Erica turned to Morgan. "Seriously? You asked me on a date?"

"I wasn't thinking about that so much as offering moral support. And I wasn't kidding about having someone to talk to."

"I'm not all that sure I *want* to talk to anyone at a big posh party."

They started slowly walking toward the two buildings. Robby had disappeared inside the smaller one, and she saw Mel and Amanda go in there, too. Chickens wandered everywhere, pecking at the dirt, while ducks waddled aimlessly. Goats moved around the enclosure and made bleating sounds.

"Why wouldn't you? Want to talk to anyone, I mean?" Morgan asked. "You grew up around here. Aren't there people you want to reconnect with?"

"Not right now. There's no way to hide my belly, and everyone will be curious and it's none of their business." She looked up at the tall man strolling beside her. "I don't feel like I belong here anymore. That's why I'm not sure if I even want to go."

"Okay, then. To be continued."

His black Stetson shaded his eyes, hiding his expression so she couldn't tell what he was thinking. But he must have questions. To his credit, he didn't ask, and that added to his likability points.

As they strolled, their arms bumped and brushed together. He was wearing a fleece-lined jacket against the chill in the air. But every time their bodies connected, even in the slightest way, Erica swore she could see sparks. And there was a definite fluttering in her stomach, an I-really-like-this-guy feeling. And it didn't hurt that he was helping look after his nephew and had brought him to see the animals.

"So, this is quite a place Daphne has here." Erica felt the need to change the subject to something not about a date.

Morgan told her about the glassed-off cat room inside with hay bales where the animals could frolic freely. Across from it, he explained, there was an area for the dogs that had an outside door to a fenced-in area with runs where they could roam at will.

"Before Daphne opened the sanctuary, this property sat empty for a lot of years. There are rumors it's haunted."

"Really?" She felt a shiver, but it had nothing to do with awareness of him and everything to do with being just a little freaked out.

"You never heard that? You used to live here."

"Maybe." Funny how much a woman could forget in the twelve years she'd been away. "Wasn't there a fire here?"

"That's what I've been told." Their shoulders bumped, and he looked down at her, hesitated a moment, then stuck his hands in the pockets of his jacket. As if he needed to do something safe with them. "The story is that when the barn burned down, a cowboy died along with his girlfriend and some horses." They strolled around the enclosure, and goats moved up to the fence, bleating piteously. "Story has it that the ghosts of the cowboy and the woman show up here and sometimes horses are neighing when none are around."

"Nothing creepy about that." She moved a little closer to him. "If your offer about running interference for me still stands, feel free to go for it if the ghosts show up."

"You don't believe in that kind of thing, do you?" He grinned and tipped his head enough to show the amusement in his eyes.

"I'm reserving judgment." Although not on his smile. It rocked her world as surely as if she'd seen a ghost. She felt tingles in places that never tingled before. "Speaking of judgment, my father is not a fan of a farm animal sanctuary."

"Oh?"

"Nope. He thinks farm animals should be able to pull their own weight. Work. Earn their keep and if they can't... well, let nature take its course."

"I'm a rancher, too. I can see his point."

Maybe her father's attitude about Morgan would be more favorable if he knew they shared an opinion. For some reason it mattered whether or not her dad liked the Daltons.

"So you think Daphne has too much time on her hands and should abandon the animals?" Erica asked him.

"I didn't say that. This place is important to Daphne and a lot of other folks, too. She's making it work. Live and let live, I say. But your father and mine are ranchers from a different generation."

"True." She hadn't thought about it like that. And mentioning his father opened the door on their conversation just that morning. "Remember those rumors about your family I mentioned? There were more."

"Such as?"

She wasn't sure but thought he might be trying too hard to cover irritation with nonchalance. She stopped walking and looked at the animals in a cluster close by trying to get their attention. "It was something about your dad cheating on your mom."

His mouth pulled tight for a moment as he stared at the mountains in the distance. "Although I have no clue how that became public knowledge, it's a fact."

"Are your parents still together?"

"Mom forgave him." His tone said he didn't approve. He shook his head. "He swears the women meant nothing. Just slipups when he was drinking and stressed about money."

Erica was a little surprised he admitted that. But maybe he was in the mood to share. "Speaking of money... Where did your dad get the money to buy the ranch? Please tell me you're not a reincarnation of the Dalton Gang from the Old West. They were brothers who specialized in train and bank robberies."

His mouth curved up in a reluctant smile. "Nothing illegal. He won it in Vegas. A three-buck bet on a million-dollar slot machine. On one pull he won a bundle. He sold his ranch and came here for a fresh start."

"Wow." She could feel her eyes widen. "Now you and your brothers are all here."

"For our mom. We were scattered, working ranches all over. She wanted the family together."

"I guess it's a mom thing." Without conscious thought, she put her hands on her baby bump. "It won't be long until I know what that feels like. I have an appointment with a doctor the day after tomorrow."

"Already?"

"Yeah. Because of being fired and having to move home, I had to find a new doctor."

"A lot of change in a short period of time." His rugged face was suddenly creased with concern.

"It is. I really liked my obstetrician. And to start with someone new so close to the end of this pregnancy is a little scary." Erica didn't know why she was confiding all this to Morgan. She liked him and was comfortable with him, had been from the moment they met. On top of that, she didn't feel there was anyone else she could confide in. Lately, she blamed her hormones for everything, so why not blame them for spilling her guts to this man? "The thing is, I have no choice."

"Are you going alone?"

"Yes." She was doing this whole adventure alone. Nothing had changed just because she came home.

"I thought maybe your mom would go with you. Or Mel."

She shrugged. "I don't want to bother my mom. And Mel is busy working."

He stared at her for a long moment and seemed as if he had another question. But what he said instead was a surprise. "I'll go with you to the doctor, if you want."

"Wow." Her heart fluttered a little. "Why? More running interference for me? That's getting to be a thing with you."

"Just moral support." He shrugged. "Doesn't seem right for you to go alone."

Her eyes suddenly grew moist at his sweet offer, proving her hormones were at it again. "That's awfully considerate of you, but I'll be fine by myself."

"Okay."

He opened his mouth, then shut it again. There must be a million questions in his mind but he didn't ask. That made her like him even more than she already did. And she already liked him quite a bit.

Childish laughter floated to them on a light breeze, and Morgan looked at the small animal building. "I better go make sure Amanda doesn't need help with Robby."

"I'm so sorry. I've talked your ear off," she said.

"Can't say you're not a distraction."

A good or bad one, she wondered but couldn't tell from his expression. Now they walked quickly and were just opening the door when, without warning, Robby came running outside, straight into Erica.

She was a little clumsy these days what with her body being out of proportion, and the unexpected bump knocked her back a couple of steps.

Morgan instantly caught her arm to steady her. At the same time he said, "Robby, remember what your dad says about watching where you're going."

"Yes, sir." He looked up and pushed the brown, shaggy hair out of his blue eyes. "Sorry."

"That's okay, kiddo. No harm done." Erica smiled. "You're a very handsome young man."

"Thank you," he said courteously.

"I'm Erica Abernathy."

"Nice to meet you." Apparently that was all the polite a seven-year-old who was quivering with excitement could manage. "I'm gonna look at the horses and cows now."

Morgan followed him and called out over his shoulder, "I'm on it."

Amanda and Melanie emerged from the building with another woman. Erica recognized Daphne Taylor's strawberry blond hair and doe-shaped blue eyes. The recognition was mutual and then those blue eyes took in her pregnancy.

"Oh my God, Erica! Look at you." Her friend moved closer and hugged her. "You're back."

"I am." She glanced around. "And you've got this place."

"I do. It's my pride and joy. And not without controversy." Her eyes narrowed. "My father doesn't approve."

"Neither does mine." Erica put her hands on her pregnant belly.

They smiled over shared paternal disapproval just as Morgan walked out of the barn carrying Robby and scolding.

"You'll get hurt climbing on the stalls like that, buddy. The animals spook and could hurt you without meaning to."

The boy did look remorseful as he rubbed a finger beneath his nose leaving a dirty streak. "I didn't mean to scare 'em."

"I know you didn't."

"If I promise not to scare 'em, can I go see the goats, Uncle Morgan?"

"Yes. But be careful and watch where you are." Morgan easily lowered the boy and his feet were moving before they even touched the ground.

"I've got it this time, Morgan." Amanda followed the boy, and the other two women tagged along.

"He's a cutie," Erica said. "Pretty active boy."

"That kid just took ten years off my life when he fell into the horse's stall." Exasperation laced with fear tightened Morgan's features as he shook his head. "I don't know how my brother does it. Kids. It's one thing to watch him for an afternoon, but I don't know if I'd want to be responsible for one all the time."

Erica's warm feeling instantly cooled. For reasons she couldn't understand, she suddenly felt lonelier than at any other point on this solo journey to motherhood. When Morgan had offered to accompany her to the doctor, hope must have taken root. The idea of someone to share the experience.

But based on his reaction just now, this man didn't particularly like kids. Her disappointment about that was way out of line. She had no right to be disappointed because that smacked of having expectations of more. Because of the baby, friendship was it for them.

Two days later Erica drove to the Women's Health Center where her new OB was located in the Bronco Heights medical district. The minute she was fired and realized her only option was to move home, she worked on securing a new doctor. With the help of her Denver OB she'd found this new physician, made an appointment and had all her records forwarded even before packing up her apartment.

She pulled up to the parking structure entrance, took a ticket and the gate lifted, allowing her to drive in and look for a space. Nerves tied her stomach in knots because she was so sure she had everything figured out when she'd made her decision to use insemination to have a baby. Changing doctors during this pregnancy hadn't been part of her strategy.

She'd established a bond and trusted her Denver doctor and would barely get to know this one before her baby was born.

She found a parking space on the fifth level, then walked to the elevator. After riding it down to the first floor lobby, she checked the building directory and found Grace Turner, Obstetrics and Gynecology, Suite 100. Right around the corner.

Pressing a hand to her belly, she whispered, "Here we go, little one."

Sliding the strap of her purse more firmly on her shoulder, Erica took a deep breath and walked into the office. She checked in at the reception desk, and after filling out the forms, she looked around the waiting room. A quick glance told her she was the only expectant mother without a partner. She wished she'd accepted Morgan's offer to accompany her and would welcome his way of making her laugh.

The families around her were in different stages of development. The couple by themselves seemed to be expecting their first child and were clearly nervous. A father and mother had a brand-new tiny, adorable baby in a car seat and looked tired. The last couple had a little one running around as they prepared to add another to their growing brood. One by one the expectant moms were called back to see the doctor.

Erica was wistful but would rather do it alone than not at all. Her first choice was the traditional way but that hadn't worked out. Her next thought was a flashback of Morgan the other day, sounding as if he didn't want any part of fatherhood. Later she'd observed him protecting Robby from overeager baby goats. Tossing the laughing child in the air. Affectionately ruffling the boy's hair. Sure looked as if he was at least a favorite uncle and enjoying the heck out of it.

The door to the back office opened and a woman in pink scrubs stood there. "Erica?"

Immediately she stood and walked over. "That's me."

"Come on back. I'm Scarlett, Dr. Turner's nurse." She closed the door and indicated the scale behind her. "I guess you probably know the drill."

"Yup." She set her purse on the chair beside it and stepped on.

Scarlett made a note, then led the way down a hall and stopped outside the ladies' room. "I guess you know the drill for this, too."

"My favorite thing," Erica joked.

After getting a sample and leaving it where instructed, she met the nurse in the hall and followed her to a room. She sat at the end of a paper-covered exam table and had her blood pressure taken.

"Good." Scarlet recorded the result, then smiled. "The doctor will be in to see you shortly."

"Thank you."

In Denver, Erica had felt just fine waiting by herself in the exam room. What was it about being back home that made her feel more alone? Probably the sad disappointment and regret in her mother's eyes every time she looked at her pregnant belly. Her happy childhood home now wasn't a happy or accepting place to talk about her baby. It always felt as if she was the elephant in the room.

Not long after the nurse left, the door opened and a thirtyish woman walked into the room. Holding out her hand she said, "I'm Dr. Turner. It's nice to meet you, Erica."

"Thank you for fitting me in. I had a change in work status and moved home. It's so late in my pregnancy, and I wasn't sure how that would all fall into place."

"Believe it or not, women change doctors in the third trimester for a lot of reasons." She was a very pretty blue-eyed brunette. "I received your medical records from your previous OB and reviewed them. I saw the early ultrasound and there's a note in your chart that you don't want to know the baby's sex?"

"That's right."

"So you want to be surprised. No gender reveal party?"

"No."

Her close friends were all in Denver. She'd been gone for so long there wasn't anyone here in Bronco she'd want to invite. Maybe Morgan. But she couldn't picture him amid a cloud of pink or blue balloons.

"And this baby was conceived with IUI using donor sperm."

"Yes."

"Okay. Is the baby moving a lot?"

"I think this child is going to be a kickboxer."

Dr. Turner grinned. "That's what I like to hear."

"It's reassuring. Although at two in the morning…"

"That's Mother Nature's way of preparing you for those night feedings." There was a sympathetic look on the doctor's face. "Go ahead and lie back on the table. I want to do a Doppler and measure your abdomen."

After Erica did as instructed, the doctor moved the instrument over her belly. She nodded. "This baby's heartbeat is strong. Everything looks good. And I think pregnancy agrees with you."

"I've never felt better," she said truthfully. "I experienced some morning sickness and was a little tired in the beginning. But now I feel great."

"It shows. I know it's a cliché, but you really are glowing."

"Thank you."

"Do you have any questions for me?" Dr. Turner asked.

"Yes, actually. I was enrolled in a childbirth class but had to withdraw when I moved. Is it too late now to do that?"

"You've got a little over a month. And it's never too late. The more you know, the better. I can give you some information on a class that's just starting at the Health Center and arrange enrollment if you'd like."

"That would be great."

"Do you have a birthing coach?" The doctor must have seen something in her face because she quickly added, "It can be anyone—a relative or friend."

"What if I don't have one? Can I still take the class?"

"Of course. There's a lot of good information for first-time moms or even a refresher course for women who already have babies. Methods of delivery. How to know when you're in labor.

What to do if your water breaks. Relaxation techniques. Pain management options. Breastfeeding. Caring for a newborn."

"Sounds like—pun intended—just what the doctor ordered."

The woman smiled. "Okay. I'll have Scarlett put together the information, and she'll give it to you when you check out."

"I was nervous about this appointment but you've really put me at ease, Doctor."

"Then I've done my job. Just relax and enjoy the rest of your pregnancy," she advised.

That was easy for her to say, Erica thought. The woman didn't have to find a job and a labor coach, not necessarily in that order.

CHAPTER FIVE

THE AMBLING A had a herd bull for sale and Dalton's Grange needed one to improve the calf crop, so Morgan was sitting across a desk from Gabe Abernathy. The main house was pretty impressive and this office kept that theme going. It was filled with rich leather chairs, wood beams overhead and a stone fireplace. The environment smelled of old money and reminded Morgan that until recently his family hadn't had much to spare.

The Abernathys' operation produced superior stock and they'd quickly agreed on a price, making the negotiation smoother than he expected.

"So, we have a deal?" he asked.

"Yes."

"Good." Morgan leaned forward and put out his hand, the way gentlemen did to finalize a negotiation. The other man took it.

"Okay, then."

The leather chair creaked as Morgan stood on the other side of the desk. "I guess we're finished."

"One more thing." Gabe stood up, too, and met his gaze.

"And that is?"

"My fiancée said you were at Happy Hearts the other day when she was there with Erica."

"That's right. My nephew loves going to see the animals."

"So it was a coincidence? You being there at the same time?"

Morgan sensed the other man's disapproval but he wasn't going to lie. "Actually, I ran into Erica in town. I mentioned that I'd be at the animal sanctuary with Robby."

Gabe nodded. "Mel said you and my sister were talking for a long time."

"Yeah." They'd laughed a lot, too. And Erica was the opposite of hard on the eyes. He'd enjoyed spending time with her more than anything he'd done in a long time. "She's easy to talk to."

"She's also pregnant, Dalton." There was a warning tone in his voice.

"And your point is?"

"She doesn't need someone like you complicating her life."

"Someone like me?" Morgan felt his temper flare but stopped short of telling this guy to go to hell. Mostly because he was Erica's brother. Why that should matter, he wasn't sure. But it did. He blew out a frustrated breath. "Not that I owe you an explanation, but we're friends."

"And that's all?"

"What more would I want?" Morgan's tone gave the man some of his warning back.

"You tell me." Gabe's eyes narrowed.

On some level Morgan was aware that this man was a big brother looking out for a younger sibling. He got that.

"I'm the oldest of five. I understand about keeping an eye on the younger ones. I only have brothers so I'm going to cut you some slack for being protective of your sister. I'm guessing that responsibility weighs a little heavier. So, I'll say this one more time. We're friends. Nothing more."

Gabe's look said he was going to hold Morgan to that. "Okay."

"I'll see myself out."

Morgan turned and headed out of the office, then back through the house to where he'd come in. He was frustrated and angry. How long would he have to live in Bronco Heights before he was good enough to be accepted by these people? It was a lesson, if he needed one, that money didn't buy everything. And then he saw Erica in the entryway by the front door and his irritation disappeared.

She looked fresh and pretty and made his heart skip and slide sideways in his chest. In her black leggings, long cream-colored sweater and cowboy boots, she looked beautiful. And when she saw him, she smiled with genuine warmth, which was just what he needed. Except that every time she smiled, he wondered how her lips would feel against his own.

"Morgan. What are you doing here?"

"I had some business with your brother."

She tipped her head to the side, studying him. "Did something happen?"

Other than Gabe declaring him off-limits to her? That still rubbed him the wrong way and irritated his sense of fairness. "Yes. I bought a herd bull from him."

"You don't look happy about it."

"No. It was a good deal," he said. Changing the subject, he asked, "What are you up to?"

"Just going for a walk. I've got to keep up my exercise. I used to ride horses but I can't now. It's a big no-no because of the risk of falling. That could harm the baby."

"Yeah. I can see that." He was oddly reluctant to say his goodbyes and leave. Glancing over his shoulder toward her brother's office, he frowned. Also, being warned off really bugged him, made him want to push back. "Would you like some company on your walk?"

"You don't need the exercise." She gave him a once-over and didn't seem to mind what she saw.

"A stroll with a pretty lady sounds like a healthy thing to do."

She flushed with pleasure at the compliment. "If you're sure, I wouldn't mind someone to talk to."

"Let's go." He took her jacket out of her hand and held it while she slid her arms into the sleeves. Then he opened the front door and let her precede him outside.

"Thanks."

"My pleasure." And that was the truth. She smelled really good. The scent of her hair and a certain fragrance that was uniquely her stirred in the air and burrowed inside him. *Nice* didn't even begin to describe what he was feeling. "Which way are we going?"

She pointed to a path that went behind the barn and corrals to a grass area and beyond. "Try and keep up."

"Someone's feeling pretty sassy today." He grinned.

"Yeah." Her smile faded as they headed out.

"Are you sure you're up for this? After all, you're walking for two."

"Funny. And I'm fine." She breathed deeply. "It's a beautiful day. The sun is out. It's all good."

"Okay."

They walked in silence for a while, surrounded by the sounds of nature. The birds singing, the whinny of a horse somewhere out of sight and a breeze that made tree leaves rustle.

"How's Robby?" she asked.

"Good. Rowdy. Healthy. Happy."

"Can't ask for more than that. Where's his mom? It seems like your brother was raising him alone before Amanda came into his life." She shrugged. "Women talk."

"His mother is in Colorado." But Morgan had a feeling that's not what she was asking. "She wasn't keen on being a mom. She sends presents for Christmas and birthdays but that's about it. Not hiding but not involved either."

"I see." With the toe of her boot she kicked a rock off the path and into the grass to the side. "He's a great kid."

"You'll get no argument from me about that."

"Can I ask you something?" she said hesitantly.

"Sure." But he braced himself.

"You're so good with Robby and clearly he loves you."

"I love him, too," Morgan said easily.

"But you don't want kids."

"Why do you say that?" he asked.

She looked up and the breeze blew a strand of hair across her face, into her eyes. She brushed it away and met his gaze. "The other day you seemed a little exasperated and said you don't know how your brother does it. That didn't sound like you were in favor of having the experience yourself."

"The truth is, I don't know if I'd be a very good father."

"I guess it would be hard to go for it if you have doubts." She slid her hands into the pockets of her jacket. "It was easy for me. There was no question in my mind about wanting to be a mom."

And she made it look good, he thought. But she was right. With his brother, the pregnancy happened and Holt manned up. He was all in when Robby was born, and Morgan would have done the same. But if he had a choice, it would be a tough call for him to make.

But that reminded him. "You had a doctor's appointment. How did that go?"

"Good."

Morgan hadn't known her long, but he felt as if he knew her well enough to see when something was bothering her. And that was now. He was certain of it.

"Did you like the doctor?"

"Yes. Very much." That might have been a little too enthusiastic. Compensating for something?

"Did someone give you a hard time? Was the office a dirty, windowless shack without running water and electricity?"

"It was fine."

He'd been going for the absurd to make her laugh. That was an epic fail and convinced him not to let up until she came clean about what was going on. "Tell me what's wrong, Erica. Please don't say *nothing*, because I can see different."

"Everything is good."

"I'm not buying that. Come on, this is me. Give it up." He met her gaze and saw in hers when she stopped pretending.

She left the dirt path and leaned against a tree. "I want to take a childbirth class. The doctor says it's not too late to do it."

"That's a good thing. No?"

"Yes and no." Her frown deepened. "I could use someone to go with me. A coach."

"Okay. So who's it going to be?" The baby's father? This wasn't the first time he'd wondered where the guy was. He was still curious, but it wasn't his place to push for information.

"That's just it. I don't know." She caught her top lip between her teeth.

"What about your mom?" he suggested.

She shook her head. "I can't ask her. As much as my parents nagged me about making them grandparents, their plan included marriage before motherhood. I need someone who is one hundred percent in my corner without making a judgment."

"You grew up here." From his perspective, that was the family background someone needed to be accepted in Bronco Heights. "How about a friend?"

"I was gone so long I've lost touch with my friends. Or they've moved away." Her shoulders slumped and the sunshine in her face was all clouded over.

"What about Daphne Taylor?"

She shook her head. "We didn't stay in touch, and it seems presumptuous to ask. And Mel travels for her job. Even if that's only once or twice a month it could be inconvenient to rearrange her schedule, not to mention when I go into labor."

"There must be someone," he said.

"I don't know anyone I'd feel comfortable asking."

"You know me." Morgan couldn't hold back the words. Seeing her like this made him want to put the sparkle back in her eyes.

"You?" It wasn't quite a sparkle, but something jumped into her expression. "You do know this is a childbirth class?"

"Yeah."

"This inclination of yours to volunteer to help me out is getting to be a habit. It's very sweet, but I won't hold you to it."

Morgan wasn't sure why he felt so strongly about this. He was willing to admit that it was more than bonding over being outsiders. Mostly he just really liked her and couldn't help wanting to fix her problems.

"It's all right," he said. "You can hold me to it."

"Surely you're joking." She was incredulous.

"Nope. Dead serious."

"Why would you do it?"

"We're friends." And thrown into the mix was just a little bit of in-your-face to her brother for warning him off. "It's what friends do."

"But kids aren't your thing," she protested.

"You're doing the work. I'm being the support." He shrugged.

"But what if this baby is born in the middle of the night?" she challenged.

"It happens all the time with cows. I'm always on call."

"You didn't really just compare me to a cow," she teased. "Maybe I'm starting to look like one—"

"No way." He thought she was beautiful. "I didn't—I mean, I was just saying—"

"It's okay. I know what you meant. And I wouldn't ask you to be there for the labor—"

"What kind of friend would I be to abandon you? A coach doesn't train his players, then not show up for the game." Morgan shook his head.

"I'm completely blown away that you'd offer to do this for me. I just can't believe you would—"

"Well, believe it," he said firmly.

"I don't know what to say."

"For Pete's sake, just say yes and thank you."

"Okay. If you're absolutely sure... Yes." She laughed and looked as if a great weight was lifted from her shoulders. "I don't know why you would do this. And I'm not sure why it feels right, but it does. I'm very grateful to you. Thank you, Morgan."

When she looked at him the way she was now, as if he'd hung the moon, he would do anything for her. And it's not like this was forever. In a matter of weeks the baby would be here and his job would be done and their paths would take them in different directions. Probably he wouldn't see her and would miss that beautiful smile more than he wanted to admit.

A few days later Erica insisted on picking Morgan up for the birthing class. She knew where Dalton's Grange was and easily found his house on the property. She was early, which was a chronic thing with her because it had been drilled into her growing up that being late was rude. Now punctuality was a habit. As big as the baby was getting, she hoped this child would take after her and at least arrive on time.

Still, she wouldn't turn down the chance to check out his house. And she couldn't help being curious, especially when she noticed smoke curling out of the rock chimney and light pouring out of the windows making his home seem really warm and cozy and inviting.

She walked up to the wooden porch with the railing that spanned the front. The style was the same as the main house she'd passed, with a rock and log facade and peaked roof.

Her boots sounded on the porch as she walked up to the door and knocked. Moments later an older woman answered it. She had a blond bob hairdo, blue eyes and a welcoming smile.

"You must be Erica Abernathy. I'm Deborah, Morgan's mom."

Erica shook the hand she held out. "Nice to meet you."

It was. And it wasn't. Since he lived in his own house on the ranch, it hadn't occurred to her that she'd meet any of his relatives and have to explain her reason for being here. Especially when she hadn't told her own family about Morgan being her birthing coach.

"You are just the most adorable pregnant lady I've ever seen." The other woman beamed at her. It was the sort of look she'd hoped for from her own mother.

"I feel just the opposite of adorable," she said ruefully.

"Some women are lucky enough to barely look pregnant right up until giving birth. I have a feeling you're going to be like that." She shook her head. "This is the honest truth. I've had five babies and never looked as radiant as you."

"I'm not going to try and talk you out of that impression."

Deborah laughed. "Just to set the record straight, no matter what it looks like, my son does not live with his mother."

"What a relief. That would be weird," she teased back.

"He was working on a project with his father and got back late, then had to feed and water the animals." She angled her head toward the hallway off the great room. "I brought him some dinner, which he wolfed down. He just went to shower and clean up."

Erica glanced around the room with a cheerful fire crackling in the hearth. Braided rugs were scattered over the wooden floor. A leather sofa and chairs were arranged on one big enough to accommodate the overstuffed furniture.

"I hope it's not a problem that I'm early." Another habit of hers was to prattle on and say too much when she was nervous. Like now. She made herself stop talking.

"Not at all. Morgan told me he's going to be your labor coach."

She felt the woman was only being chatty and nice, not fishing for gossip. To not give her a little information felt impolite. "Yes, he is. Your son is a kind, sympathetic and thoughtful man. It was the first thing I noticed about him when we met." Right after she'd rated him a solid fifteen on a one to ten hotness scale.

"He's always been that way. A sweet and sensitive little boy and a good man."

"I'll be a single mom, and I'm grateful he'll be my coach."

"He'll be a good one." The next obvious comment or question would be about the baby's father, but Deborah didn't bring it up.

Erica felt compelled to. "The baby's father isn't involved. Just so you know, there's no bad breakup or hard feelings in any way."

"Good to know." Deborah slid her hands into the pockets of her jeans.

This wasn't awkward at all. "Morgan tells me that you and your family have lived here for a year. How do you like it?"

"It's great." There was a little too much enthusiasm in her voice. "We came from a pretty small town in northern Montana. This is bigger. More civilization, I guess. Shopping, if you know what I mean."

"I do." She nodded, also with too much enthusiasm.

"My son said that you just returned to Bronco Heights."

"That's right. I went to college in Colorado and I ended up with a job there. But now I'm back home. My parents would be thrilled if I wasn't…" She looked down at her belly.

"Why do I get the feeling this homecoming wasn't planned?" Deborah asked. Then she waved her hand and said, "Never mind. It was rude of me to ask."

"No, actually, I think you're psychic."

The woman laughed. "It's a mom thing. Gives a woman a sixth sense."

"Well, you're right. My company let me go. Coming home was plan B." Erica didn't want Morgan's mother to believe her a screwup, and gave her an abbreviated version of what happened. She wasn't exactly sure why she spilled her guts to this woman. The best thing she could come up with was that her son got his kindness and empathy genes from his mother. "In the end, my only option was to come back home."

"So your parents aren't thrilled about having their daughter back?"

"If they are, they're hiding it pretty well. They're old-fashioned."

"I'm sorry to hear that, Erica." She made an understanding sound.

"My family has expectations and I keep not meeting them."

"I'm sure they love you and just want what's best. For you to be happy."

"They absolutely do. I know that. And I want to make them proud, but I keep letting them down." Erica smiled sheepishly. "I'm sorry to dump all that on you. You're just easy to talk to."

"Your parents will come around, honey. Don't give up."

Just then Morgan walked into the room bringing with him the wonderful, masculine scents of soap and some spicy cologne. His hair was still damp from the shower and he was freshly shaved. In his plaid, snap-front shirt, jeans and boots he looked every inch the sexy cowboy he was. Erica felt that familiar flutter in her stomach, but this time her heartbeat kicked up, too.

"Sorry I'm running late," he said.

"No. I'm early." She hoped her voice wasn't as breathless as it sounded to her. And if it was, she prayed neither of the Daltons noticed. "Your mom and I have been talking. She assured me you aren't one of those men in his thirties who still lives with his mother. Although, she brings you food and that makes one wonder."

He simply grinned at the teasing. Erica got a little weak-kneed but chalked it up to simple appreciation for a good-looking man. Who was also being an exceptional friend.

"My mom is a good cook," he said. "It would be stupid to turn down a meal from her and she didn't raise any fools. It's one of her many talents. And it should be said that my brothers and I are all a little afraid of her."

Deborah laughed. "I always knew how to keep five unruly boys in line. Still do."

"I'd love to know your secret," Erica said.

She wasn't kidding. Obviously Morgan had a great relationship with his mother, and it was heartwarming to see. She wanted that with her child. It was also revealing to see him with the woman who'd raised him. She'd heard you could tell a lot about a man by the way he treated his mother. From what she could see, Morgan treated his mom with love and respect. He wasn't just a pretty face. He was a very good man.

"Please don't get her started on stories of the Dalton boys," he warned. "The naked baby pictures won't be far behind."

"I so want to make a pun out of what you just said." Erica laughed when he groaned.

"I think it's time for us to go. Now," he told her.

"Okay." She looked at his mom. "Can I drop you at the main house?"

"No, honey. I could use the walk. But thank you. I'll just gather up the dishes I brought." Deborah smiled and waved before walking into the kitchen.

Erica shivered when they went outside, and she told herself it was the chilly October evening not the nearness of Morgan. Inside her car, he was even closer, because he was tall and broad and built for a truck. Her heart did that bumping inside her chest thing again.

That made her hands shake a little and fumble as she inserted her key into the ignition. Eventually she managed and off they went, headed back the way she'd come. Past the main house with its log walls and big windows all lit up. Maybe the silence wasn't awkward, but it felt that way to her.

"Your mom is nice. Easy to talk to." Not nosy, Erica thought to herself. A good listener.

"Yeah, she's pretty great."

"I can't imagine raising five boys."

"Me either, but she made it look easy. She probably had the hang of it by the time my youngest brother came along."

"So, you told her about being my childbirth coach," Erica said casually.

"Yeah. When work ran late, she pitched in because I mentioned being late to the first class wasn't an option. Should I not have said anything?" There was a frown in his voice.

"No. Not at all. She was great about it. And didn't once share that you birth baby cows all the time."

He laughed. "Yeah. She's pretty cool about things. Always been there for me even when—"

His tone had turned sort of introspective, almost as if he'd forgotten she was there. Then he suddenly clammed up. There was a story, a personal one. Erica tried to be like his mom and not ask questions, but she was too darn curious.

"When what?" she prodded. "Something happened. Just so you know, I don't plan on letting this go. Friends talk to each other."

He was quiet for so long it appeared he wasn't going to answer. But finally he said, "I fell in love once. When I'd just turned twenty-one. I met a girl and felt the lightning strike."

That actually wasn't exactly what Erica had expected to hear. "Okay. And? There must be more."

"Unfortunately." He looked out the car window at the darkness going by. "I bought a ring, proposed, and she accepted. We set a date."

"But? I can hear one coming." She wished very much that there wasn't.

"About a week before the wedding I found out she was pregnant with another guy's baby. And she wasn't the one who told me."

"She was going to pass it off as yours?"

"She denied it, but I didn't believe her, what with not telling me and all." There was a trace of bitterness still in his voice.

That took her breath away. She shouldn't feel a parallel, because he wasn't in love with her, hadn't proposed, given her a ring or set a date. But, even though she hadn't slept with her baby's father, it surely was another man's child.

She managed to keep emotion out of her voice when she said, "So I guess you called off the wedding."

"Good guess." There was irony in his tone. "She made a fool out of me."

"Oh, Morgan, you were young and she was the fool." To do that to a great guy like him was just really and truly stupid. "I gather from your tone that it put you off the whole notion of marriage."

"It's not high on my list," he agreed. "And that's not the only reason. My father is not anyone's example of the perfect husband."

"But your parents have overcome obstacles in their relationship and your mom seems happy. No regrets. She's given your dad a chance. Maybe you should, too."

"And maybe you should give your family a chance," he shot back.

Touché. She didn't say anything more but her mind was spinning. Such a personal and profound betrayal could explain why he was still not some lucky girl's husband and a father. That was a shame because he would be so good at both. As chances went, she would give him one in a heartbeat.

CHAPTER SIX

MORGAN HADN'T PLANNED to talk about his romantic crash and burn. A long time ago he put that unfortunate incident behind him, at least he thought he had. But suddenly the words were coming out of his mouth. One minute he was talking about how cool his mother was, and the next, he was confessing his past and explaining why marriage wasn't in his plans. All of this on the way to a childbirth class. What was wrong with this picture?

Too many things, but the only one that mattered was Erica. She was going through a tough time without a lot of support and he wouldn't turn his back on her, too.

"We're here." She turned the SUV into the parking lot of the Women's Health Center and found a space close to the entrance. "It's not too late to back out, Morgan. Speak now or forever hold your peace."

He opened the passenger door and the overhead light went on, illuminating the uncertainty in her expression. Every time he looked at her, all he could think about was fixing whatever problem she had. Tonight was no different.

"You can't get rid of me that easily," he assured her.

"Okay then." She retrieved a rolled up mat and pillow from the rear of the SUV. "Let's go learn something about birthing babies."

She smiled, and Morgan felt the power of it deep down inside.

Fortunately there was no time to analyze his response because he had a feeling he wasn't going to like the results.

They made their way inside and up to a conference room at the far end of the top floor. When they walked in, the floor-to-ceiling windows revealed a beautiful view of Bronco, lights stretching to the base of the mountains.

The clock on the wall said five minutes to seven and not being late was a relief. Fixing fences had taken longer than anticipated today when he and his father had found more than one calf caught up. Freeing them without injury had taken time, and he didn't want to let Erica down, especially the first night of class. It was important to prove that she could count on him.

The rectangular room had a large open area at one end and three tables arranged in a U-shape with a lectern set up at the other. A woman in her late twenties stood there flipping through her notes. Three couples were already there, and Erica was looking around, eyes wide.

Morgan put his hand to the small of her back and fought the urge to pull her close. Only for reassurance. As a friend. "We should probably sit."

She glanced around one last time and nodded. "Right."

They found chairs at a right angle to a very young couple. The man smiled at him, the kind of look that implied sharing the ups, downs, joys and fears of this adventure, the one called fatherhood. The other two men nodded in his direction with similar expressions. Morgan noticed they were all wearing wedding rings, which made him the odd man out.

He didn't feel awkward or out of his element as much as he was relieved Erica wasn't facing this alone. But she wouldn't be if her baby's father was here. Up until now Morgan hadn't been all that curious, but this class highlighted the absence. What was the story?

That question would have to wait, because he had things to deal with now. The other people in this class probably thought he was going to be a father. There was no good reason he could think of to disabuse them of that impression. If it came up, he would let Erica take the lead. This was all about her.

The brunette standing behind the lectern glanced at the clock, then cleared her throat. "Everyone is here so let's get started. There's a lot of information to get through and you're on a deadline." There was chuckling and she waited a few moments before continuing. "My name is Carla McNicol. I'm a registered nurse and work in Labor and Delivery at the hospital. I'm also a certified childbirth educator. Why don't we start by quickly introducing ourselves."

The couple on the far side of the table started with first and last names, adding that this was their second baby. Married, as he'd suspected. The other two couples did the same. Then it was their turn.

"I'm Erica and this is Morgan. First baby," she said, "and I'm getting nervous."

"You've come to the right place," Carla assured her. "Knowledge is power. The more you know, the more in control you feel. This may be repetitious for second timers, but reminders never hurt. So, tonight I'm going to talk about things you can do to prevent preterm labor. You're all within weeks of delivery, but it's best for baby to stay put until nature takes its course."

She started with basics and Morgan was a little surprised at how very basic the things were. The importance of prenatal care. No alcohol or smoking. Prevent infections. Maybe use a condom during sex. He couldn't resist looking at Erica, and her cheeks were bright pink. The RN got as basic as taking care of teeth, keeping gums healthy. Although Carla teased that she was sure couples conscientious enough to take this class already brushed and flossed.

"Believe it or not, stress and avoiding it as much as possible is a very big factor in preventing labor too early," she pointed out. "If there's job tension, do what you can to minimize it. People who make your blood pressure spike—and we all have them in our lives—politely but firmly distance yourself as much as possible. Grandparents mean well but they can add to your tension. Do what you need to do to put yourselves first, Moms."

Carla talked about family-centered maternity care in the hospital, methods for pain management and birth options. She said there would be more information on that presented in upcoming classes.

"And the last thing we're going to do is go over relaxation techniques. I'll demonstrate tonight, but I can't emphasize this enough. Practice makes perfect. The goal is to relax your entire body while one muscle contracts. Your uterus needs to push down and retract the cervix. If other muscles are tight during contractions, you're wasting energy and oxygen. This technique also helps with stress."

She directed them to spread their mats on the floor. Erica sat with her legs crisscrossed, knees out, while Morgan knelt behind her. Carla demonstrated deep breaths to fill the lungs, then exhaling while concentrating on relaxing other parts of the body. Doing it daily would help moms-to-be master conditioned responses to a labor coach's commands.

"I recommend practicing these techniques every night in bed," Carla said. "And that's it for tonight. I look forward to seeing everyone next week."

Erica was thoughtful and quiet as they rolled up the mat, collected the pillow and were the first ones to walk outside to the parking lot. No chatting after class. No awkward questions to be answered. He could feel her tension and remembered what the RN had said about avoiding it. She hit a button on her key fob and the rear hatch of the SUV slowly lifted.

Morgan put the mat and pillow in the car, then held out his hand. "Give me the keys."

"What?"

"Your keys," he said again.

"Why? Is this a carjacking?"

"If I was going to rip off a pregnant lady, she'd need to be driving one heck of a fine truck." They were standing under a light and he met her gaze, bracing for her stubborn streak to kick in and push back. "I'm driving. Take some stress off you."

She hesitated a moment, then nodded and set the keys in his open palm. "Okay."

Obviously she was lost in her own thoughts, because there was no conversation until he pulled the SUV into the parking lot of The Daily Grind, a coffee shop at the edge of town.

"Why are we stopping here?" she asked.

"I just thought before going home you might need to talk."

"Why would you think that?" She didn't deny it.

"Because you're not talking at all, and it's kind of freaking me out."

She sighed. "Coffee is a nice idea but I've already had my ration of caffeine for the day."

"I think this place has tea, without the kicker. Or water. Until tonight I had no idea you were supposed to drink that much." He looked over at her. "And I bet you wouldn't say no to dessert. Coach is buying."

She shook her head. "I should treat you. I had no idea—"

He put a finger to her lips to stop her words. The jolt he got from touching her nearly stopped his heart. "Arguing is stressful. My treat. End of discussion."

"Okay."

At the counter she ordered a caffeine-free herbal tea and a pumpkin scone. He got black coffee and paid for everything. They carried their stuff to a table in a far corner and sat.

He blew on his steaming cup. "So, what's on your mind?"

"I wouldn't hold it against you if you want to back out." Her tone said that's what she expected. "I had no idea this class would be so..." She didn't finish the thought, but added, "If this experience is too weird for you, I completely understand."

"If you're okay, I'm okay."

"I am more than okay," she said. "I was very glad you were there. As long as you're sure—"

"Yes, I'm sure. We're friends. I feel as if I've known you for years." But he saw that she was still anxious. "What else is bothering you?"

She looked up, her hazel eyes more brown than green and very uneasy. "This class made it all real. There's only one way out of this. I don't know if I can do it."

"You can."

"Just like that?" she asked.

"Yeah. And there's the fact that there's no way out except birth." He shrugged. "We'll practice the breathing, go to the classes and you'll feel prepared."

"I desperately want to believe you so I'm going to." She smiled at him. "Thank you."

"Anytime."

But he was standing in for another man. That made him curious and a little bothered by the lack of information about her baby's father. The guy had to be a jerk to not be around for her.

Was she still in love with him? Morgan hoped not and the intensity of that feeling surprised—and worried—him.

When Morgan stopped at his house, Erica thanked him again for going with her, then headed home to the Ambling A. All the way she kept seeing the questions in his eyes. In class tonight he'd looked perfectly comfortable with all the information, even when she'd blushed to the roots of her hair at the mention of condoms during sex.

But when they stopped for coffee, after he'd reassured her he was her friend and would help her get through this, his expression grew more thoughtful. She knew he was wondering why he was there instead of the baby's father. Should she tell him?

That rolled around in her mind as she parked her car near the main house. No one had been around earlier when she went to pick up Morgan, so she'd left a note. The front porch light was on but she hoped no one was waiting up for her. Partly because her parents had to get up early to do ranch work. And partly because she knew there would be questions about where she'd been. Talking about anything to do with the baby seemed to create more tension.

Carefully opening the front door, she slipped inside as quietly as possible, then turned to close it. When footsteps sounded behind her, she knew stealth had been futile.

She whirled around. "Mama. I thought you'd be in bed."

"Your father is. I was watching TV in the other room. Waiting up for you."

"I'm sorry." It was sweet but sort of made her feel like a teenager sneaking in after curfew. "You didn't have to do that."

"I know." Angela stifled a yawn and pulled her long sweater more snugly around her. "But it's a funny thing. When you lived in Denver, I didn't actively worry about you coming in at night. Now that you're here, I can't relax until I know you're home safe and sound."

"But I'm a grown woman," she protested.

"Doesn't matter. You'll always be my baby." Her gaze dropped to Erica's pregnant belly. "You'll understand one of these days."

"I didn't mean to keep you up."

"It's okay." Her mom smiled. "Are you hungry? How about a cup of tea to warm you up? It's chilly outside."

"I'd love one." This was nice. It reminded Erica of the closeness they'd shared before she'd gone away to college.

They walked into the kitchen together, and her mom filled a teakettle with water and put it on the stove, lighting the burner beneath it. Erica pulled two mugs out of the cupboard and found her mom's stash of tea bags. Her father and Gabe had no use for anything but coffee, so this ritual was something only she and her mother shared.

Erica chose something decaffeinated that promised peaceful rest. She showed her mother and laughed. "I won't hold my breath about that since I'll probably be up peeing half the night."

"That's my nightly go-to tea." Her mom grinned. "But I'll be racing you to the bathroom."

Erica laughed. "It's like old times."

"I've missed this." Angela's expression was wistful. "You used to come home at night and tell me about what happened with you and your friends. Your dates. I remember the first time you went out with Jordan Taylor."

"Yeah. I was pretty stoked that a former high school big man on campus and local legend like him would even notice me, let alone ask me on a date."

"Do you think you gave him a fair shot?" her mom wondered.

"Mama, we've been over this." A few dates with the son of the wealthiest rancher in town had been part of the parental push to get her to stay home and attend a local college. "He was like a brother. There was no chemistry at all, no lightning strike."

Not like with Morgan Dalton, she thought. They had declared themselves friends tonight, but her strong feelings for him didn't fit neatly into that box. Under different circumstances she would be hoping for more, but with the baby coming, a friendship was all they'd ever have.

"Too bad." The kettle whistled and her mom filled the two mugs. They carried them over to the table and sat, just like in the old days.

Angela blew on the steamy tea. "Your note only said that you were going out. Where were you tonight?"

Suddenly the warm, fuzzy, nostalgic feeling was replaced by wariness. Being able to go home again was an illusion. You could physically be there but emotionally it would never be the same.

The walls went up. "Oh, nowhere special."

Her mother's eyes said she didn't miss the evasive tactic. "What did you do?"

"Oh, you know—" Erica wasn't prepared to talk about this. She wanted mother-daughter warm and fuzzy, not tension and judgment.

"Actually I don't know. That's why I'm asking." Her tone hinted at hurt feelings. "Did it have something to do with Morgan Dalton?"

"Why would you ask that?"

"Gabe said he was here recently on ranch business and then you took a long walk with him." She dunked her tea bag with more force than seemed necessary. "And Mel said he offered to take you to the Denim and Diamonds fundraiser next month."

"That's true."

"Which part?" Her mother frowned. "The walk or the asking out?"

"Both, actually." Erica was not going to say more but decided to add one last thing. "I like him. He's a good man."

"You haven't known him very long."

"Sometimes you don't have to know someone a long time. You can just tell."

"You were with him tonight, weren't you?"

She had to give the woman something. "I was at a childbirth class tonight."

"Oh." That seemed to appease her mother. "How was it?"

"Interesting. I'm a little nervous about the birth." This woman had been through it twice in addition to emotionally painful miscarriages. She knew how it felt. "Does it hurt, Mama?"

Angela's expression turned soft, a combination of sympathy and concern. "I want badly to lie and tell you it doesn't. But I can't. Yes, honey, it does hurt. But it's nothing you can't handle. And when you see your baby... There's just no feeling in the world like it. It's worth everything you go through."

That's what Morgan had said. The part where she could handle it. That helped some. "I'm still a little nervous."

"That's completely normal. Trust me, by the time this baby comes you'll be so ready to do whatever it takes to bring him or her into the world. The childbirth class will help with those nerves—" She stopped and her bonding-mom expression was replaced by something more skeptical. "I thought you needed someone to go to those classes with you. A coach."

"It's recommended." *Please don't ask more*, she silently begged.

"Do you have one?"

She hesitated and thought about a lie, but this was her *mother*. And dishonesty never ended well. "Yes, I do."

"Who?"

Erica sighed. "Morgan."

Surprise and disappointment battled for dominance in her mother's eyes. There was no sympathy or concern now. Just more hurt feelings. "Why him?"

"You and Dad and Gabe have made your negative opinion clear. I didn't feel I could ask you. Mel is a sweetheart, but I don't want to compromise her relationship with my brother. I don't know anyone else. Morgan has been there for me since I came home. There was no judgment." She shrugged. "And he offered."

"Oh, Erica—" She shook her head. Her mother sighed. "I'm concerned about you and how difficult it will be for you being a single mother."

"I gave it a lot of thought, believe me. But more than anything I want to be a mother. If I have to do it alone, then so be it. If I'd had anywhere else to go, I would have. As soon as I find a job I'll move out."

"Erica, no one is asking you to leave."

"I know. But I think it would be better if I did."

"You are more than welcome to stay. This is your home, and we love having you here. But I completely support your decision, whatever that is." Her mother stared at her, eyes suspiciously bright. She stood, leaving her now-cold tea untouched. "I'm going up to bed. Sleep well, sweetie."

"Good night, Mama." She watched the woman she loved so much walk away.

Just then the back door opened and Malone walked in. This man with the craggy face and bushy mustache was no one's idea of what a cook looked like. And he was the walking, talking explanation of why it wasn't wise to judge a book by its cover. He had a way with food. And not just meat and potatoes. His sauces were to die for and he made biscuits from scratch that melted in your mouth.

"Hi, Malone." She settled her elbow on the table and rested her cheek in her palm.

"Hey, Erica. Missed you at dinner tonight." It was dark outside, but the man still wore his tattered old hat and a bandanna tied around his neck. But the look worked with his old jeans, boots and faded plaid cotton shirt. "There's leftover chicken if you're hungry."

"I'm not." A pumpkin scone had taken care of that. "Why are you here?"

"Gonna get a head start on breakfast. Omelets tomorrow. If everything is cut up and ready I can whip them up in a jiffy." He angled his head toward her obvious condition. "If there's anything you're craving, just let me know."

"I will."

"Once knew a pregnant lady who had to have her avocados." He grinned. "And melons—cantaloupe, honeydew, watermelon—didn't matter which."

"Right now I can't say I have any cravings." At least nothing that food would fix.

"You feelin' all right? That baby giving you trouble?"

Yes, but not the way he meant. "No, I'm fine."

"Don't look like it," he observed.

"There's still some tension between Mama and I."

He sat his six-foot frame into the chair her mother had recently vacated. This man was a talker and he was settling in. "It was awful hard on your mama and daddy when you went away."

"I know. But it's my life. Shouldn't I be able to live it my way?"

"Yup. And they know that." His eyes were piercing. "It may not be my place to say but look at the view from their front porch. You come home without telling them there's gonna be a baby. Now here you are, and that little one is going to be here real soon. And their feelings were hurt. They might just need a minute or two to adjust."

She sighed. As much as she wanted to argue with him, she couldn't. When she lived here Malone had more than once put in his two cents and she'd missed his plain-spoken wisdom. "You're right. I should have said something right away. I just couldn't face what I knew I'd hear in their voices and see in their eyes. I only ever want them to be proud of me."

"They are, honey. But what with you working and living somewhere else, they didn't get much chance to fiddle with their feelings about you being all grown-up. It's hard for parents to figure out how not to butt in and try to keep their kids from making mistakes."

"This baby isn't a mistake. I've wanted to be a mother for a long time now."

He smiled and patted her hand. "And you'll be a good one, too. Just like your mama."

"Thanks, Malone." She smiled sadly. "For just a little while tonight Mama and I were having such a nice talk. Just like we used to. Then it went bad. They say you can't go home again, and I probably shouldn't have."

"Well, you did, though. And things have changed. My advice is remember the old while you're making the now new. And it doesn't happen overnight."

"That sounds like good advice."

"It is. But worth what you paid for it." He grinned, then stood up. "Gotta get going on my chores. Breakfast comes awful early around here."

"Can I give you a hand?"

"That's okay, honey. You should get some rest. The baby needs it."

She stood, too, then went up on tiptoe to kiss his cheek. "Thanks for the talk. I'll do my best to make the now new."

And until this baby was born, the new included Morgan. He was a new she could easily get used to.

CHAPTER SEVEN

ALONG WITH LAWYER and doctor appointments and birthing class, Erica was busy sending out résumés. She was encouraged by quick responses to them asking for interviews. But after the second one without an offer of employment, she was forced to admit two things. Because she'd been hired at Barron Enterprises as a college intern, she didn't realize what a challenge job hunting could be. The second thing was that being very pregnant didn't make the search any easier.

This was her third interview, one she'd actually scheduled before moving back. She was sitting across the desk from Sandra Allen, the Human Resources director of an energy company in downtown Bronco Heights. This was a face-to-face meeting for their accounting/marketing position, following a phone interview during which this same woman had seemed very enthusiastic. Probably Erica should have mentioned being pregnant, but she just wanted a foot in the door, an opportunity to display her personality and business knowledge. One look at Erica's well-developed baby bump had cooled off any interest.

She knew what the woman was thinking because she'd had to deal with personnel issues like this at her last job. She needed to get ahead of it, so to speak, then highlight the skills she could bring to the table in the long term.

She smiled. "You probably noticed that I'm pregnant. My due

date is next month and I already have child care arranged." That was a lie but she would make it true. "If you decide to hire me, I'll get to know the company, and when I return from maternity leave, I can hit the ground running." She was going to throw everything at the wall and hope something stuck. "In my previous job, I was in charge of day-to-day operations. I oversaw Human Resources, accounting, marketing and IT."

Sandra folded her hands and rested them on her desk. "You have an impressive résumé, Erica."

"Thank you." She was pretty sure she heard a "but" in the woman's voice but hoped she was wrong.

"The thing is," she continued, "you're overqualified for the job we have. Upper management would be a better fit and we just don't have an opening right now."

"You're concerned that I'll leave if something better comes along." It was about more than that, but she was determined to leave it all on the table. "As you can see from my work history, I was hired during my college internship and stayed with the company for eight years. That shows a high degree of loyalty. If you give me a chance, I won't let you down."

"I have no doubt." The woman nodded. "But you should know that I have more people to interview. So, when that process is complete, I'll make a decision. I will call you one way or the other. Thanks for coming in."

Erica knew that was a "don't let the door hit you in the backside on the way out." She stood and shook the other woman's hand. "I appreciate your time."

She walked out of the office and left the building. It was hard not to be discouraged, even though she understood why hiring someone in her condition was a risk. On top of being discouraged, she was starving. And needing someone to listen to her bitch and moan. She knew just the place where both needs could be met and a short time later she walked into DJ's Deluxe looking for Mel. The restaurant's new manager directed her to a large office upstairs.

She found it and stood in the doorway, taking in the cushy conversation area and large desk with a computer. Mel sat behind it and was so engrossed, she didn't even know she had a visitor.

"Knock, knock."

Mel looked up and it took two beats for her to register recognition. "Hey. Sorry. I was so focused. What are you doing here?"

"I'm hungry. And I need a friendly face and sympathetic ear."

"Well, you've come to the right place. Am I wrong that you want privacy for this conversation?"

"You are not wrong."

The other woman stood and walked around her desk. "I'll get you some food. Anything you're craving? Cheesecake? Death by chocolate?"

"Call me a peasant, but a burger and fries would be just about the best thing ever," Erica said.

"Coming right up." She indicated one of the chairs in front of her desk. "Have a seat."

"Thanks."

Erica sat and closed her eyes for a moment, breathing in and out. Trying to relax the way Carla, the childbirth educator, had instructed. This scenario was not what she planned for her baby and the least she could do was try to neutralize her stress. She knew her family wouldn't put her and the baby on the street, but the judgment would always be in their eyes.

The one unexpected positive was Morgan. Literally without any questions asked, he was there for her and the baby. He calmed her when they were together. And she was happy around him. He was a friendly port in a storm of tension and hormones. A bright spot in an otherwise challenging chapter of her life. Once upon a time she'd naively believed she could pull off perfect for this baby, but now she knew better. The best she could do would have to be good enough and at least she had Morgan.

It wasn't long before Mel returned with a plate. She set it on the edge of the desk. "Dig in and feed that baby."

"You don't have to tell me twice."

Erica ate a couple of the fries and closed her eyes in ecstasy. "Best thing I have ever tasted."

"That happens when you're starving. Although DJ's Deluxe sets a high bar in all its restaurants."

"I only care about this one. Right here, right now." She cut the burger in half to make it manageable.

For a few moments there was only silence in the room, if one excluded her appreciative moans. After the first half was gone, she took a break and sat back in her chair.

Erica looked at the lovely woman who was going to marry her brother. "You're a lifesaver. Almost literally. I thank you, and my unborn baby, your future nephew or niece, thanks you."

"Don't mention it. Happy to help." She was sitting behind the desk again, frowning at all the paperwork in front of her. "With great power comes great responsibility. I'm grateful to you for giving me an excuse to take a break."

"It's the least I can do for family."

"That means a lot." Mel's smile was sweet and soft. "You know, before you came back home, I was a little nervous about meeting Gabe's sister."

"Me? Why?" She wiped her hands on her napkin and crumpled it in her hand.

"You're important to him. And he's important to me. I'm an only child and I lost my parents six years ago. So, I feel as if I'm not just getting the best guy in the world, but a family, too."

"Aww..." Erica felt an emotional lump in her throat. That happened a lot lately.

"You and I have hit it off even better than I'd hoped. I've never had a sister and always wanted one."

"Me, too." She reached a hand across the desk and Mel took it, squeezed affectionately. "You're going to make me cry."

"I would take that as a compliment, except I'm guessing pregnancy hormones might make you emotional if I said *the sky is blue*."

Erica laughed. "You're not completely wrong."

"Speaking of family..." Mel folded her hands and put them on top of her desk. "Have you seen Josiah since you've been home?"

Erica knew the other woman wasn't trying to make her feel guilty, but she did anyway. Gabe had told her Gramps was in Snowy Mountain, a facility north of Bronco Heights that offered a full range of services, from independent living to caring for patients with dementia or Alzheimer's. "Not yet. I've had a lot to deal with since I got home, and it hasn't been that long. I had to see a lawyer. And had a doctor's appointment. A couple of job interviews."

"I understand," Mel said. Clearly she meant that. "It's just that I'm so frustrated. We've hit a wall finding his daughter Beatrix and aren't sure what to do next. More than anything I'd like to give Winona some peace about her child, the comfort of knowing she's all right. Josiah has occasional lucid moments. Gabe and I are wondering if seeing you might just jolt him out of wherever he is and get him to give us something."

Erica sighed. "I feel so bad that I haven't visited yet."

"I know. But try to see him soon if you can." Mel nodded sympathetically. "And I'll stop now. How's the job search going?"

"Not so good."

"Is that what you wanted to talk about?" the other woman asked.

"Yes." Now it was Erica's turn to be frustrated. "I understand what's going through their mind when they look at me so pregnant. I used to deal with this situation, but on the other side of the desk, so to speak. If hired, I would work my butt off for just a few weeks, then have a baby and leave them shorthanded again. I could be back to work in six weeks, if all goes as planned. But what if it doesn't? If I was making the decision and had two equal candidates for one position, but one was very pregnant, the best business decision would be to hire the other one."

"I hear you." Mel sighed. "For women, work and motherhood is always going to be a balancing act."

"That's the best you've got?" Erica was only half kidding.

"Yeah. So let's talk about something more pleasant."

"I'm open to suggestions."

"You've met Amanda, but not our friend Brittany yet. She's the one organizing the Denim and Diamonds fundraiser. Apparently it's all coming together really well."

"Great."

"Are you planning to go? If the baby hasn't come yet? I know you said Jordan Taylor's father isn't your favorite person."

"True. But I wouldn't mind seeing Jordan. He and I managed to stay friends even after dating a short time."

Mel nodded. "I can see why your folks got their hopes up. His father and uncles own Taylor Beef. Not only is he good-looking, he'll never have to worry about money."

"I should hope not. It's a big company." And suddenly flashes went off in her brain. There might be a job opening for her in that big company.

"And his father is putting on this big charity shindig to raise money for programs to help lower income families in Bronco Valley. I'm going to need a shindig kind of dress," Mel said.

Erica looked ruefully at her belly. "I'm going to need a tent."

"Oh please. You hardly look pregnant and you're beautiful." Mel toyed with a pen. "At least Morgan thinks so."

"How do you know?"

"I saw the way he looked at you that day at the animal sanctuary."

"You're imagining things."

"Am I? Because right after I noticed that, he asked you for a date."

"No. It's more like he offered to be my bodyguard."

Mel looked skeptical. "How do you explain him volunteering to be your labor coach?"

"Mom told you."

"Yeah." The other woman looked concerned. "And it makes one wonder why."

"Because he's a really nice guy."

"Your family is nice, too."

"I couldn't agree more. But they don't approve of my decision to have this baby alone. I couldn't ask my father. Which would be really weird anyway. My mother is concerned about me being a single mom so I guess I'm trying to prove I can handle the challenges that come up. And you're engaged to Gabe, who thinks I've lost my mind. So I didn't want you in the middle of it," she explained. "Morgan is my good friend. I don't feel like I fit in here anymore, and he feels as if he hasn't been welcomed into the community with open arms." She shrugged. "We get each other."

"Okay."

Erica could see the other woman still had something on her mind. "Go ahead. Sisters can tell each other things that no one else could get away with. Spit it out."

"It's just..." Mel sighed. "Things between you and Morgan seem to be moving pretty fast. I'm afraid you're vulnerable and you'll get hurt."

"He wouldn't hurt me. You'd think a man that good-looking would be a jerk, but he's not. I met his mom and can see why." She thought for a moment. "And your friend Amanda is engaged to his brother. Do you approve of him?"

"Well, yes, but—"

"No buts." Erica held up her hands. "Morgan won't hurt me. It's not like that between us. He doesn't want me that way. I'm pregnant. In fact, no one wants me."

"That's not true."

"Feels true."

After Peter, she'd given up on dating, but being with Morgan gave her a glimpse of possibilities and she had to remember that none of the possibilities included forever with him. She was almost sorry that all of it would change when the baby was born and she wouldn't have a reason to see him anymore.

When Morgan pulled his truck to a stop in front of the main house on the Ambling A, the front door opened immediately and Erica walked out. She must have been waiting for him. That could only mean tension with her family, quite possibly because of him, and she was trying to head it off. He was all in favor of steering clear of stress for her and the baby, but facing the Abernathys didn't bother him.

He'd been surprised but really stoked when she called and suggested going to the Bronco Harvest Festival, so here he was to pick her up. He got out of the truck and went around to the passenger door to open it for her.

"Hi," he said.

She smiled up at him. "You're very punctual."

"So are you." He watched her put a foot on the running board, then handed her into the truck. When she was settled in the seat, her face was very close to his. Her breath was soft on his cheek and her slightly parted lips were a whisper away.

Leaning in to see if they were as soft and sweet as he imagined would be so easy, and he really wanted to. It wasn't the first time the thought crossed his mind. But—no.

He met her gaze. "I would have come up to the door, like the gentleman my mother taught me to be."

"I was ready and waiting. Wanted to save you the trouble."

It was late in the afternoon, and the sun was setting behind the big house, putting them in shadow. Still, Morgan was almost sure her cheeks turned pink and her voice was a little too perky, even by Erica standards. "You didn't want me to come inside, say hi to the family."

She stared at him for a couple of beats, then sighed. "I'm protecting you. They've got some stupid idea that you're pretending to be interested in me because you want to take advantage of me somehow."

That burned because it was so off the mark. But showing anger wouldn't help, so he deflected with a smart-ass comment. "They're right."

"Really?"

"Yes. I'm using you. Before you, I was just a misfit outsider. Now I'm a misfit outsider who's taking the prettiest lady in Bronco Heights to the Harvest Festival."

"I'm taking you to the Harvest Festival, remember?" Her wariness slipped away and she grinned. "You, sir, are a sweet talker."

"And don't you forget it."

"Well, I'm using you right back. It's way past time my family gets the message that I'm a grown woman. Strong and independent. They can't tell me who I can or cannot see socially." She caught herself and added, "Or who my friends are."

"So I'm your rebellion guy?" He couldn't help smiling.

"I know I'm a little old for that, but now that I'm back, ground rules need to be set," she said firmly.

"Hey, I'm just glad you called."

"It's not much," she said, "but I really want to thank you. I'm very grateful not to be the only woman in that birthing class without a coach."

"Happy to help." He closed the door and went around to the driver's side, then got in. "So, how are you?" he asked as he drove away.

"Still unemployed and guilt ridden."

"You might want to give me some context for that statement."

"Yeah." She sighed. "I had three interviews and got zero job offers. They take one look at me and it's game over."

"I'm sorry to hear that." And he wanted badly to fix her situation but kept that to himself. "And the guilt?"

"Mel reminded me I haven't been to see Gramps yet. It's no excuse, but I've had a lot to do since I moved back."

"That's the truth."

"Mel thinks seeing me might shake him up, provoke a lucid moment so he'll give up something that will help us find his daughter."

Morgan shook his head. "I can't imagine having a child and not knowing where they are, or anything about them."

"That child would be in her seventies now," Erica said. "Mel wants to find her and bring her to her mother so that Winona can see her daughter and know she's all right. But Mel is getting discouraged about finding a lead."

He happened to glance over and saw her put her hands protectively on her belly. Erica was already shielding her child. No way she'd give it up, and he deeply respected her commitment.

"I'd sure like to help find her," he said. "If there's anything I can do, let me know."

"Thanks, Morgan. I wish there was. But aren't you getting tired of doing me favors?" she teased.

"No." It'd be another reason to be with Erica, and he relished that. In fact, it was getting harder to think the time would come when she wasn't in his life anymore.

A short time later they arrived at the Bronco Fairgrounds. Local law enforcement was directing traffic, and Morgan followed the line of cars to an unpaved field where vehicles lined up in rows.

He parked the truck and looked over at her. "You ready to do this?"

"Yes. I haven't been to one of these since before I went away to college. I used to love it."

The sun had gone down, but large spotlights were strategically placed around the big, open field. The parking area was on a rise, and as they walked toward the festival entrance, the expanse of activities was spread out before them. There were carnival rides, booths with games and a bouncy house for the kids. Strings of white lights were hung around the whole area.

"This is bigger than I remember," she said, eyes wide.

"It's my first time, so I have nothing to compare it to."

Just inside the entrance there was a temporary enclosure holding animals. Daphne Taylor was in the middle of it surrounded by a sheep, a baby goat, a pony and the pig—Tiny Tim. She was supervising children as they petted the docile creatures. In the line of kids awaiting their turn, he recognized his brother, Holt, with Amanda and Robby.

"Hey, you guys." Morgan squatted down to eye level with his nephew. "Hi, dude. Haven't you had enough of the animals yet?"

"No." The little guy vigorously shook his head. "There are dogs and cats here, too. For adoption." His blue eyes were big, bright and eager.

Erica said hello and looked up at his brother. "We haven't met. I'm Erica Abernathy."

"Nice to meet you." If Holt was surprised about the pregnancy or the fact that Morgan was with her, it didn't show.

"Daddy, I want to adopt another dog," Robby said. "They need a good home. It says so on the sign."

"Whoa, kid." His father held up his hands. "We're here to pet the animals. That's all. Remember?"

"Yes." But the boy pointed to the separate enclosure, where several pudgy puppies were running around and tumbling over each other. "There's a black-and-white one over there, and he keeps lookin' at me."

Erica laughed. "You're in trouble now, Dad. If you can figure out how to say no to that eager little face, I'd appreciate you sharing the secret."

"Start practicing now." Holt grinned. "So, what are you two going to do?"

"Not sure yet." Morgan looked down at her. "We just got here. I figured we'd just browse and then see what grabs us." And then he couldn't resist saying, "Hey, Robby, that black-and-white pup is really cute. I think he's smiling at you again."

Holt gave him a look that could laser paint off the barn. "There will be retaliation. You won't know when or where, but it will happen."

Morgan laughed. "Bring it, brother. See you later, guys."

He put his hand to Erica's back, guiding her through the crowd. But with all the people moving every which way, they kept getting separated. So he took her hand in his. "I don't want to lose you."

"And I don't want to be lost." She squeezed his fingers and smiled up at him.

They meandered up and down the rows of booths containing food and games. She stopped by a giant ring toss game and admired the stuffed bears it had for prizes.

"Let's win one for the baby," he said.

She eyed him skeptically. "It might be less expensive to just buy one at the store."

"You doubt my skill?"

"I didn't say that."

"Not in so many words." He walked over to the woman taking money and bought five rings. Three out of five would win a prize. "I never back down from a challenge."

"You could light that money on fire and have just as much fun," she teased.

"Oh, ye of little faith…"

He turned back and tuned out distractions as he lined up his shot. With a flick of his wrist the first ring landed successfully around the neck of a bottle. Erica gasped in surprise. But his second and third ring missed their mark.

"Come on, Morgan. Just two more and the baby gets a bear. Baby needs a bear. No pressure."

He grinned, then cranked up his concentration. The shot was successful. One more and he'd have it made. Taking his time, he did a couple of flicks of his wrist, testing. Then he let the ring go. It wobbled and nearly slid off before firmly settling around the bottle's neck.

"You did it!" In her excitement Erica threw herself into his arms and hugged him.

He pulled her close and breathed in the fresh scent of her hair. Nothing had felt so good in a very long time as this woman did in his arms. He could have held her all night, but too soon she moved away.

"I was wrong about you and not too proud to admit it." She picked out a fluffy brown bear with Harvest Festival embroidered on his paws. Hugging it close she said, "I love this. The baby will, too."

"Maybe mama needs one."

"You're pushing your luck, cowboy."

"Another challenge." And it was a gamble he couldn't back down from. Maybe there was more of his father in him than he wanted to admit. "One more time," he said to the woman, handing over his money.

Five tosses later, Erica was picking out another bear. He carried it as they walked away. "What do you have to say now?"

"You are the king of the carnival games."

"Okay, then."

At the end of the row of booths he stopped and pointed to a sign. "Hayrides. What do you say?"

"I think that sounds like fun."

Her happy smile hit him squarely in the gut and nearly dropped him to his knees. What was it about this particular woman that made him want to be her hero? She'd said more than once that he was making a habit of bailing her out. He couldn't seem to stop himself. He should be bothered by that and probably would be in the middle of the night when thoughts of her made him toss and turn.

But right now, he was going to sit close to her in a wagon with the moon shining down on them. Playing with fire was dangerous but he couldn't find the will to resist. And if he had the chance to kiss her he wasn't sure he could stop himself.

CHAPTER EIGHT

ERICA WAITED A short distance from the hayride while Morgan took the bears he'd won back to his truck. He didn't want them to get mangled or dirty, which was incredibly sweet. And that level of sweetness after a fairly impressive ring toss performance made her realize, not for the first time, that he was a pretty impressive man in so many ways. If things were different maybe...

Nope. Not going there. Wondering "what if" was a waste of time and energy. She was going to be a mother. All the responsibility of taking care of this child would be on her, and she'd reconciled herself to that. Until Morgan, she'd never felt wistful about taking this road alone. She needed to focus on being grateful to be traveling this road at all, because it was impossible to imagine her life without children in it.

"You're still here." Morgan walked up beside her.

Erica had been so lost in thought, she hadn't heard him coming. "I told you I would be."

"One never knows. You hear those stories of an evening gone wrong when a woman heads to the ladies' room and never comes back." His look was wry. "Poor schmuck just sits there until he finally gets it that he's been ditched. And hopes no one noticed."

"First of all, you were the one who left me," she retorted.

"Second, I can't wrap my head around any scenario where that has actually happened to you."

"Nope, never has." His expression was casually innocent. Maybe a little too casual?

She put her hand on his arm. "This will either reassure you or feed your ego. But what woman in her right mind would ditch the Harvest Festival ring toss legend?"

"Legend, huh?"

"And ego wins." She tsked. "Don't let it go to your head, cowboy. Your Stetson won't fit."

"Can't a guy just enjoy the moment?" he teased.

"I don't think that's going to be a problem. You're enjoying it quite a lot." She grinned. "But, seriously, that was a pretty awesome accomplishment. My little Ichabod or Ingrid will be very impressed when he or she is old enough to hear this story."

"Shucks, it was nothing, little lady."

"Not so little, actually. And enough with the B Western cowboy imitation." He was the real deal, not an actor and way more exciting than any of them, she thought. "I was under the impression that we were going on a hayride. But here we are, standing around and talking about you."

"But that's my favorite subject—" He laughed when she playfully slugged him in the arm. "Okay. Let's go. Are you warm enough?"

She had on fur-lined boots, black leggings, a big sweater and a tightly knit fringed poncho over that. "I'm good."

Morgan offered his arm and she slid her hand into the crook of his elbow, liking the feel of him. He was tall and muscular and made her feel feminine and protected, even if it was just for tonight.

Her heart tilted a little and she didn't mind. For right now she wasn't going to question her attraction to him. Or the fact that she wasn't ready to stop touching him when they arrived at the hayride. Over her protest, Morgan paid the man for two tickets.

"A group went out a little while ago," the old guy said. "Should be back any minute. So if you'll just wait over there, I'd be obliged."

"Sure thing." Morgan took her arm and gently steered her to the side. "Don't want to get run over."

"That could ruin a perfectly wonderful evening," she agreed.

"So you're having a good time?"

"Yes." She couldn't remember the last time she'd felt so carefree and content. And just plain happy.

Just then the sound of an approaching tractor drifted to them. The machine rumbled to a stop. It pulled a big wagon with hay bales for seating. The old guy put out a step stool, and once the riders disembarked, he waved the waiting group on.

Morgan jumped up first, then held a hand down to help her. They took their seats and squeezed closer to make more room as others joined them. When the tractor slowly moved forward, it lurched enough to knock Erica into Morgan. He put his arm around her, holding her securely. It felt good, right somehow, and she sighed a little when he didn't let her go.

Smiling up at him, she said, "This is it."

"Ready or not."

She took out her cell phone to snap some pictures of the pumpkin patch they passed. Then the road curved to the right, taking them past Pine Lake, where a nearly full moon left a trail of silver light on the water. It was so beautiful, and she couldn't help thinking romantic, too.

She lifted her phone and snapped another series of pictures, trying to take a selfie of her and Morgan. Since his reach was longer, he managed to get one.

"Let's see if we broke my camera," she said laughing.

She opened her pictures on the phone. The first one was of the lake, which came out pretty well considering the circumstances. Then she noticed something strange.

"What's this ball of light?"

"Probably just photographic artifact from the flash." Morgan took her phone and looked closely. Then he scrolled to the next picture and said, "Whoa."

Erica gasped. "Now there are three of them. I think they're called orbs. If it's from the flash, why did they multiply?"

"Good question." He scrolled to the next picture and there

was just one again. "There's no reason for the change. We're not moving that fast so everything should be about the same."

"I've heard that unexplained lights can be orbs from the spirit world. Light energy. And they often collect around water."

"It's weird for sure. Could just be a coincidence, but—"

"What?" In the moonlight she could see the uneasiness on his face. "Morgan?"

"Daphne Taylor's place is just across the lake."

"The animal sanctuary with resident ghosts?" she clarified.

"Yes," he agreed. "Cue the spooky music. Evan Cruise would love this."

"Who's he?"

"A guy in town who runs ghost tours."

"He should talk to Daphne about her haunted barn." She stared at the pictures. "Maybe these orbs should zip over there, too, and keep her ghost lovers company."

"Are you creeped out?" he asked.

"Yes." She shivered and leaned into him a little more.

His arm tightened around her reassuringly. She looked up and saw an intensity in his eyes that she sensed wasn't about spirit orbs or unexplained phenomena. It had everything to do with her, and their eyes locked in a moment of acute awareness. Everyone around them faded away. It was just him and her.

Slowly he lowered his head and kissed her. The touch was sweet and almost tentative at first, until she moaned softly so that only he could hear. Then it turned into something more, an explosion of attraction that burned away rational thought. She strained for more and he was eager to oblige.

Erica had no idea how long the kiss lasted but suddenly became aware of the steady movement slowing and people around them in the wagon starting to stir.

Morgan lifted his head and glanced around. "I think we're back."

"Yeah—" Erica was in sort of a haze as the tractor slowed even more and came to a stop right where they'd started. "I guess they'll want us to get off."

The other passengers stood there waiting patiently to disembark. In front of her, a woman about her mom's age turned and smiled indulgently at them.

When she noticed Erica looking, she said, "I'm sorry. Don't mean to stare, but you two are just the cutest couple."

"Oh—" She shook her head. "We're very good friends—"

"Even better. Marrying your best friend is a solid foundation for life together. And now you're starting a family." Her gaze dropped to Erica's belly. "And look at you so pregnant and cute. Beautiful expectant mama. Doting dad. And both of you so good-looking. That baby is going to be beautiful." It was her turn to get down from the wagon, and she apologized for holding them up. "Have a good night."

Erica and Morgan were the last to get off, and he helped her down, as carefully as if she were a piece of delicate crystal. His protective attitude hadn't changed, but something else had. She could feel it.

They walked around some more, got something to eat. She chatted about the weather and any other shallow subject that came to mind. He responded in monosyllables. But they carefully avoided discussing the elephant in the room, so to speak.

After seeing all there was to see, they walked back to his truck, and Erica felt an air of tension between them, most of it coming from Morgan. Her teasing friend had disappeared and left a quiet, preoccupied man in his place. She wanted the other guy back, but that would require a conversation. Something told her he wasn't going to raise the subject, so it was up to her.

After he merged the truck into the line of cars exiting the fairgrounds, he turned onto the road leading back to the Ambling A. It was now or never.

"So—" She took a deep breath. "That was awkward. Do you want to talk about it?"

"The kiss?" He gave her a quick glance, then returned his gaze to the road. "Or the woman who assumed I'm the father of your baby?"

She'd been sort of hoping he would grin and say there was nothing to discuss. But she'd given him an opening and he made it bigger. Only a coward would slam it shut now. He'd given her two choices and she picked the latter.

"Does it bother you that people might think you're the baby's father?" She folded her hands in her lap and squeezed them tight.

"If I cared what people thought, I wouldn't have gone to childbirth class with you. People will think what they think. It's a logical conclusion and I don't blame them."

She waited for a "but." It didn't come, and yet his response hadn't relieved the tension. "Who do you blame?"

Instead of answering he asked, "Why isn't the baby's father going with you to the class? Where is he? Shouldn't he be involved?"

In a perfect world, yes, she thought. But this was so far from perfect. She'd decided on a course of action to get what she wanted and would never be sorry for that. No one was going to make her feel like she wasn't enough or that she'd done something she should be ashamed of.

"No," she said. "He shouldn't be involved. I don't need him to be."

"That's a bunch of BS." In the lights from the dash his expression was harsh. "A man takes care of his own if he's any kind of a man."

The words were confirmation that for Morgan being a father was a duty. An obligation. Cleaning up a mess he'd made. And the realization hurt her heart more than it should have.

"Look, Morgan, it's all right if you don't want to be my coach. I understand if it makes you uncomfortable."

"That's not what I'm saying." He didn't raise his voice, which made the words all the more electric. "I said I'd be there and I will. I want to be. I'd just like to know who the father of this baby is. A deadbeat or a jerk?"

For reasons she didn't understand, that made her dig in and pull stubborn around her like a blanket. "That information is on a need-to-know basis, and no one needs to know."

"That kiss says otherwise." Morgan's tone said he had his own brand of stubborn going on.

"I don't think so. Blame it on ghosts and orbs and spirit energy. And that's all I'm going to say about that."

"You're the one who asked if I wanted to talk about it." He

turned onto the road leading to the main house on the ranch. "But the truth is *you* don't want to."

"I guess not."

He pulled to a stop at the front door and turned off the engine. "Erica—"

"I had a good time," she said. "Thanks. Good night."

Before he could say more, she got out of the truck and walked inside the house. She leaned her back against the door and held her tears in check. Why was he pushing this? What did it matter? She had walked through fire to have this baby, and he wasn't sure he wanted kids. That was a deal breaker. She had no business even letting it cross her mind that she liked him very much and even less business wishing this thing with them could be more.

It was too bad, really, because she had a feeling they could be good together, that he would be an exceptional husband and father. But he got burned and almost married a woman having another man's baby. Erica's baby would always be another man's. All of that took him out of the need-to-know column about how this baby was conceived.

She didn't think he would take it well and didn't want to find out she was right.

Erica pulled herself together but didn't feel up to putting on a perky face for anyone who might be awake. Still, while living under her parents' roof, she owed them the courtesy of letting them know she was home.

She walked into the great room and found her mother there alone, reading.

"Hi, Mama. I just wanted to let you know I'm home."

Her mother looked up from the book. "Thank you, sweetie."

"Is Daddy in bed?"

"Yes. He was tired." She took off her reading glasses. "How was the Harvest Festival this year?"

"That implies I can compare it to last year, but the truth is that I haven't been there in so long I can't compare it to anything recent."

Her mother closed the book, put it on the table beside her

and set her glasses on top of it. "Let me rephrase. Did you have a good time?"

"Yes." Right up until that stranger mistook Morgan for her husband and the father of her baby.

"Did you see anyone there?"

"Of course. The place was packed." But that's not what her mom was asking. All she'd told her folks was her destination. Not the details. Especially that she'd asked Morgan to go. What a brazen hussy, a pregnant brazen hussy. Still, it was one thing to politely follow house rules, quite another to let anyone dictate who she could and couldn't see at thirty years old.

"I went with Morgan Dalton. He picked me up." She glanced down at the stuffed animals in her arms. "He won these playing the ring toss. One for me and one for the baby."

"So, he has skills—"

"Please don't start, Mama."

"That was a joke."

"I'm sorry." She sighed and walked over to sit on the sofa beside her mother, setting the stuffed animals between them. "I guess pregnancy hormones are making me supersensitive."

"I remember. That part is a bitch," her mother said ruefully.

"Language, Mama." She smiled. "But body chemistry does seem to have turned me into one."

Her mother picked up one of the bears and touched the plastic eyes. "These will have to come off. The baby could swallow them."

Erica had already thought of that. Since the pregnancy had been confirmed, she'd been reading everything she could find on child care.

"I'll take care of it," she assured her mother.

"I'm sure you will." Angela put the bear on her lap. "How is everything? Have you heard from the lawyer? Your father said she was going to file suit against Barron Enterprises."

"Yes, she did, but she warned me they can delay the process practically indefinitely and force me to give up."

"But you're made of sterner stuff," her mother said emphatically.

"To a point. But I need a revenue source because the money

I have won't last indefinitely." She set the bear down. "I really need a job."

"How's the search going?"

"Nothing so far. I've had some interviews but…" She shrugged. "No one will say it straight out that they don't want to hire me because I'm pregnant. That would be discrimination. But… It's discouraging. I feel as if I'm stuck until after the baby is born. And it's a catch 22. I want to settle in a place of my own for the baby. But I don't feel comfortable doing that until I have cash flow again. I'm sorry that I'm putting you and Daddy out."

"Are you kidding?" Her mother glanced around the large room. "This place is huge. And we love you. You're welcome to stay here as long as you want." She caught the corner of her lip between her teeth. "But I can't help thinking—"

"What?" Apparently sensitivity hormones were just waiting to pounce, because they kicked up again. "If only I had a husband?"

"No, sweetie. I wasn't going to say that. If only someone could see past the pregnancy. Someone who knows how smart and determined you are. You'd be an asset anywhere you worked if they could see their way clear to give you an opportunity. Those bozos are thinking short-term and that's their loss."

"Thanks, Mama." The words were encouraging and made her want to explain why she was in this situation. "I'd hoped to find a husband. That perfect someone. Get married, then have a baby right away before my eggs get old and dry up like raisins." She shook her head. "It just never happened. You were lucky with Daddy."

"I know it. He's a keeper."

Erica thought she'd found that with Peter, until she mentioned having children and they broke up. The thing was, there'd been no hole in her life when he was gone. In a lot of ways it had been a relief. She'd put in so much energy, and maybe that was just about trying to make it work because her biological clock was ticking.

Shouldn't caring about someone be effortless? The feelings just there? Like with Morgan. The thought popped into her mind and stuck. She wondered if they might have had a chance if it wasn't for the baby. But there was still the question of having kids at all. If she fell for him, it would land her in the same boat as she'd been with Peter.

"I need you to know something, Mama."

"What, sweetie?"

"Do you remember how much I loved my dolls when I was a little girl?"

"Of course." She smiled and looked as if she was pulling up those long-ago memories. "Your daddy built you that dollhouse and little furniture for your babies."

"Is it still in that storage shed in the barn?"

"As far as I know."

"Good." She pressed her palms to her belly. "I'll want to get it out if this baby is a girl."

"Absolutely." There was a soft expression in her mother's eyes. "I know there are all kinds of urban myths about how to tell the sex of a baby, and you'll think I'm being silly, but—"

"I'd never think that."

"You're carrying this baby a lot like I did you. With Gabe I was all out front. Daddy teased that it looked like I had a basketball under my shirt. From the back you couldn't tell I was pregnant."

Erica laughed. "And with me?"

"I seemed to spread out."

"Pretty soon I'll need a warning sign that says Wide Load."

"Hardly. You look healthy and beautiful."

"You're just prejudiced, Mama."

"Of course I am. You're my baby. I love being your mother. And I wanted more babies." Something flashed in her eyes. Something distant, sad and painful.

"I remember how much you did. And the miscarriages."

Angela linked her fingers around the teddy bear she still held and pressed it close to her body. "I had you and Gabe two years apart and it was hard, emotionally and physically. When you were a little older, a bit more independent, I realized I wanted more children."

"I've never forgotten the heartbreak you went through trying to have another baby," Erica said. "And now I understand, because I feel the same way. How you'd move heaven and earth just to feel that sweet warm body in your arms. And because of what happened, you should appreciate better than anyone why my life would not feel complete without a child. And why it's so important for me to do it now. Because I'm the same age you were when—"

"I get it." Still, there was a question in her mother's eyes although she didn't say more.

"I promised myself that if I was fortunate enough to get pregnant, I was having the baby. No matter what. Because later could be too late."

Angela sighed and nodded, but didn't say more or ask any questions. Talking about that painful time was hard for her, but opening up even just a little made Erica feel closer to her mother than she had in a very long time. The mother-daughter bond had suffered in the past twelve years. She took responsibility for that, and tonight was another small step toward fixing it.

She could feel how much her mom wanted her to talk about the baby's father, but now even more than before she was afraid to go there. If she confessed that she'd gone to a sperm bank, it could set their fragile bond back, even make it irreparable. And she couldn't do that. Wouldn't do that.

Neither of them broke the silence. But her mother still held that bear.

Finally she smiled. "So, you had a good time with Morgan?"

"Yes. He's fun."

"I'm glad. You've had a lot to deal with lately, and there's nothing wrong with having some fun." She glanced up. "And it's important that you're comfortable with the person who's going to coach you through labor."

The truth was she did feel comfortable with him, and he was the only one she felt that way about since coming back. She wasn't sure why she'd refused to explain to him how the baby was conceived. Maybe it was because she hadn't been ready for the question. Or she was afraid of how he would react.

That's what happened when your feelings became more than they should be.

Whatever the reason, she needed to tell him the truth. As soon as possible.

CHAPTER NINE

A FEW DAYS after the Harvest Festival, Morgan was mucking out stalls in the barn. As the oldest brother he probably could have delegated to one of the others, but the crappy job suited his crappy mood. He hadn't talked to Erica since dropping her off that night and didn't much like the way they'd left things. It didn't make him happy, but he missed her. And he was ticked off. Mad at himself for pushing. Mad at her for stonewalling him. He chucked a pitchfork full of hay and muck into the wheelbarrow beside him with more force than was necessary.

He was also mad that the evening had been ruined. He'd been having a really good time, the best since moving to Bronco. Kissing Erica was a particularly memorable highlight. Her lips were soft and eager. Her sexy, throaty sounds said she liked it, too. Then it all went sideways with that lady's comments.

Truth was, Erica was carrying another man's child. Yet all she would say was that the father wasn't an issue and Morgan didn't need to know more.

That kiss said he did and was the reason he couldn't let go of the questions. Did the father know about the baby? Did he not care? What if he had a change of heart and came after her? What if she had a change of heart and wanted to make it work with him?

Another pile of muck went in the wheelbarrow. That was

followed by a string of language that made him glad he wasn't a kid anymore with his mother standing there holding a bar of soap to wash out his mouth.

He really liked Erica. It was why he'd offered to help her. But things were changing; feelings were shifting. Getting complicated. He was confused and didn't know what he wanted. But he was crystal clear that he didn't want to keep stumbling around in the dark and get blindsided by another man. He intended to see Erica through the birth of that baby, but before the next class they needed to have a chat.

Morgan heard voices and one of them was a woman's. He looked up and saw Erica coming into the barn with his father. That man being around her tweaked his already bad attitude. He rested the pitchfork against the stall's fence and stepped into the opening, watching the two of them walk down the center aisle toward him. She was smiling at something Neal Dalton said and Morgan felt the knot in his gut pull tighter.

His father noticed him there. "Hey, son."

He wanted to say he didn't need the reminder about their shared DNA. But he didn't, not in front of Erica.

"Look who's here," Neal said.

Erica smiled a little tentatively, not her usual, bright wattage cheerful expression. "Hi, Morgan."

"Hey."

"Watch your step," his father said, putting a protective hand under her elbow. "Don't want you falling, or stepping in something."

She laughed. "I'm a ranch kid. Grew up in the barn. I used to ride all the time, but that's on hold for now."

"Deb, my wife, loves to ride. After her heart attack, I got a little overprotective about her on a horse." His expression was teasing, but there was worry around the edges. "She wasn't a happy camper. And that's an understatement. Right, Morgan?"

"Yeah." His curt answer got a raised eyebrow from Erica.

Neal noticed but overlooked it and kept up the charm crusade in front of a pretty woman. "She followed doctor's orders to exercise and change her diet. Dinner isn't as exciting these days, but she's more important to me than carbs and cream sauce."

"So, she's all right now?" Erica asked.

"She is. Me and the boys are making sure of it. She put a scare into all of us." His amiable, easygoing grin disappeared. "I honestly don't know what I'd do without that woman."

"Hopefully you won't have to find out. And she's lucky to have you," Erica said.

Morgan's scoffing sound earned him another sharp look from her, but his father ignored it. After a year of working together, the man had apparently gotten used to his attitude and met it with gruffness. Morgan made no secret of how he felt and let the man deal with it however he wanted.

"No. I'm the lucky one." Neal met her gaze with a remarkably sincere look, then said, "Okay. I'll let you two talk."

"It was nice to see you, Mr. Dalton."

"Neal. Please." He politely touched the brim of his Stetson. "The pleasure is mine, Erica."

In silence they watched him walk away. Morgan knew there was a fine line between charm, flirting and just plain friendliness. He wasn't sure which side of that line his father had just walked, but women usually had a sense of those things and Erica seemed fine. He, Morgan, was the one she apparently had an issue with.

When they were alone, she said, "I know you're working. I hope I'm not interrupting."

He gave her an "oh please" look. "Yeah, because shoveling dirty hay takes a lot of concentration."

"I'll take that as a no." She twisted her fingers together. "So, your dad is nice."

"That's a matter of opinion."

"I know you told me your parents had problems, but I just saw them together. They were like newlyweds."

"Yeah." He took off his work gloves and shoved them in the back pocket of his jeans.

"How long ago was your mother's heart attack?"

"Before we moved here."

"You came for her, but why do you stay?" Her eyes narrowed. "Clearly you resent your father. I know ranch work. It's not like you can avoid him. My father and brother have a really good relationship. But Daddy is set in his ways. He and Gabe get into it when my brother comes up with some 'newfangled' ideas. My brother rebelled in his own way by backing off and getting into real estate."

Morgan thought about his recent negotiations with the man. "I don't know about real estate, but he can wheel and deal pretty well when stock is involved."

"My point is that he distanced himself from conflict and you put yourself into the middle of it. Why don't you go?"

"I stay for my mom. She wanted her family back together, and I won't be the one to break it up. We all want to take care of her."

"That's sweet." Erica's eyes grew soft. "You're probably not going to like this, but you remind me a lot of your father. In a good way. I can see where you get your charming streak."

"I'm nothing like him." Morgan did his best to push back against the bad. But her words gave him an opening. "You're probably not going to like this. But we all have DNA. From our mothers and fathers. The baby you're carrying is no different. You know what I'm asking, and I'd appreciate it if you didn't tell me again that I don't need to know."

"I don't plan to," she said. "That's actually why I'm here. To tell you about the baby's father."

"Are you in love with him?" Morgan surprised himself with the question. He hadn't planned to ask, but the words were just right there and he couldn't stop them.

Erica blinked at him, then started laughing.

He'd expected anger or indignation, not this. "What's so damn funny?"

Her amusement faded slowly and she got serious. "There is no father—well, not like *that*. I went to a sperm bank."

He moved closer and badly wanted to touch her, but he'd been doing a dirty job and kept his hands to himself. He also wouldn't stop this flow of information. "That's not an easy thing to do on your own, Erica. If you want to talk about it, I'm happy to listen."

She nodded. "It would be a relief actually."

He angled his head toward the other side of the barn. "There's a bench over there. Something tells me this isn't going to be fast."

"Probably not—" Then she stopped and looked unsure. "But you're working. I don't want to bother you."

"Trust me—the stalls will still be there after I take a break."

"Okay." She fell into step beside him, and they stopped at the wooden bench, then sat side by side.

He met her gaze. "I'm listening."

"I dated someone in Denver. Peter. He's the son of the owner of the media company where I worked." She looked down for a moment at the clasped hands in her lap. "Things were getting serious and I thought marriage was the next step. It seemed as if we wanted all the same things—until I brought up kids."

"I take it he was a no vote?"

"Yup. And that was a roadblock for me. So we broke up."

Morgan studied her and decided she didn't seem too upset about it. So he stayed quiet and let her go on.

She told him how loud her biological clock was ticking, how she was pushing thirty and fearing the fertility issues her mother had faced at that age. How she felt it was now or never.

"Never, for me, wasn't an option. So, I went the sperm bank route. Got lucky on my first round of insemination."

Morgan saw a look on her face, part anger, part disillusionment. "There's more, isn't there?"

"Yeah. Peter started dating a receptionist at the company not long after we split. I wasn't at all hurt. Figured I dodged a bullet. But they got married and she was pregnant."

"That had to have hit a nerve," he said.

"I'm not going to lie. It did, but even that was okay. I didn't love him, and I was over the moon about having a baby." But not everything went well, she told him, when Peter's father gave her the ultimatum: transfer to Miami or get fired. She shrugged. "And here I am."

"That sucks." He heard how that sounded. "Not that you're here, but the way it happened," he clarified.

"I knew what you meant." When she looked at him, there was uncertainty in her expression. "This experience of becoming a mother isn't going at all as I planned."

"I'm really sorry you went through that. But I can't say I'm sorry to hear that some guy isn't going to turn up and arm-wrestle me to be your labor coach."

"Nope, that's not going to happen." She grinned, but wariness erased it. "But this is why I can't say anything to my folks. Daddy can't even embrace new and improved ranching techniques. I don't think the idea of a sperm bank grandbaby would go over well."

"I can see why you're hesitant. But you were the one who said we should give our families a chance."

"You first," she said.

"Touché." He laughed, then turned serious. "So you weren't in love with Peter."

"No." She caught the corner of her lip between her teeth, and uncertainly met his gaze. "Are you still in love with the girl you bought the ring for?"

"I thought I was at the time. Looking back, I don't think I ever really loved her."

And speaking of love... Morgan was awfully damn glad Erica wasn't in love with her baby's father. But that meant his feelings were turning into more than he wanted them to be. If it was anyone else, he'd walk away, but after giving his word to see her through the birth, he wouldn't back out. It would be okay, though, he reasoned. It wouldn't be long until the baby was born. He'd keep his promise, then that would be that.

The morning after clearing the air with Morgan, Erica was both relieved and full of purpose. He didn't resign as her coach. That made her unreasonably happy. Also, crying on Mel's shoulder about her job search turned out to be not all bad. She'd come up with an idea and was energized.

She'd interviewed with perfect strangers who could only see her pregnancy. They knew that shortly after starting she would be absent for six weeks. So, she needed to talk to someone who *did* know her.

It was barely nine o'clock, and she was in her room because privacy was required for the call she was about to make. And she had a strategy. She wanted to catch Jordan Taylor just as the workday started, before he was up to his neck in Taylor Beef business. After tapping in the number on her cell phone, she waited.

But she didn't get further than the receptionist.

"I'm sorry. Mr. Taylor's busy today and asked me to hold his calls. But I'll make sure and give him a message."

The woman was friendly but firm. Erica knew assertiveness was almost certainly not going to work in her favor. So, she could leave the darn message, then go camp out at his office and be the proverbial squeaky wheel. It was incredibly irritating, but the woman was simply doing her job.

Erica would admit to the tiniest bit of prejudice toward anyone in that position. Based on the fact that a receptionist at Barron Enterprises was responsible for putting her in need of a job, she had a right to the feeling.

"A message would be great." She repeated her name, recited her phone number and said to tell him that she was back in town and would like to say hello.

She ended the call and thought about her next move to contact the man she'd gone out with all those years ago. She'd never felt they'd clicked romantically and apparently neither had Jordan. One night he'd told her he liked her, but she felt more like his little sister than his girlfriend and he hoped they could still be friends. Then they'd had a nice dinner together. It was the best brush-off she'd ever had.

Since then she'd run into him on visits home over the years, and Jordan had always been friendly. At least that's how she saw it. Hopefully he did, too, and would give her a chance to prove she had a lot to offer his company if he could see his way past the pregnancy.

Her stomach rumbled, reminding her that she hadn't eaten yet this morning. She needed fuel for this job-hunting campaign and went downstairs to the kitchen. Malone was the only one in the room.

"Mornin'," he said.

"Same to you." She looked around. "Where's Mama?"

"She left early. Said she had shopping to do. Something about a new dress for that Denim and Diamonds shindig."

"Right."

A wave of mixed feelings washed over Erica. On the one hand, with all the tension in the house right now it was kind of a relief not to see her mom. Their one talk after the Harvest Festival had made things better but hadn't completely resolved the strain. On the other hand, she missed the time when they would have made a day of buying a special occasion dress, then gone to lunch. She missed that so much.

"Are you hungry?" Malone looked at her baby bump. "Gotta feed that little one. And before you say anything, I know you're not eating for two. You don't have to double your rations."

It surprised her that he knew about not doubling up on calories when you were pregnant. "I am starving, actually."

"Okay. I can whip up some pancakes and eggs. Got some fruit cut up. Now sit. I'll have breakfast ready in a jiffy."

"And I can have one cup of coffee."

Caffeine wasn't strictly forbidden during pregnancy, but limiting it was recommended.

She did as he instructed, and he put a mug of steaming coffee in front of her. Then he proceeded to mix the pancake batter. While she watched, her cell phone rang and the ID said Private. She hoped this was who she thought it was.

As soon as she heard his voice, she knew it was.

"Hi, Jordan. You got my message." And he was returning her call a lot faster than she'd expected. Hopefully that was a good sign.

"Yes, you caught my receptionist when she was actually working." Oddly, there was a smile in his voice. "So, you're back. Are you home to stay?"

"Yes. And that's kind of what I wanted to talk to you about."

"Okay. I have a meeting now but I'd really like to catch up. Could you meet me for lunch?"

"That would be great, Jordan. Tell me where and when." After he gave her the information, she said, "Okay. See you then."

She ended the call and saw Malone looking at her. "What?"

"That's what I'd like to know." He poured batter on the griddle and scrambled eggs into a skillet.

"I'm just meeting an old friend for lunch. I have to feed the baby, right?"

"And this old friend just happens to be the one your folks were hoping you'd end up at the altar with." That wasn't disapproval in his voice. Not exactly.

"Yes. Why?"

"He's got a reputation with women. Quantity, not quality, or so I've heard."

"It's not like that with us," she assured him. "Besides, look at me." She glanced down at her very rounded belly. "I'm so not his type."

"Still—" He finished cooking, then slid pancakes and eggs onto a plate and carried it to her at the table, along with a bowl of fruit.

"You're sweet to worry about me, but there's no need." She was the one who wanted something from Jordan.

Which was why a few hours later she got to DJ's Deluxe and told the hostess she was meeting someone. The woman pointed him out and Erica walked over to the table where he was already seated. He stood as she approached and his eyes widened, evidence that he noticed her condition.

He gave her a hug and kissed her cheek, then held her at arm's length. "Look at you."

"Yup." She smiled. "Gonna be a mom."

"I didn't know you were married."

"I'm not."

He studied her for several moments, then simply said, "Congratulations."

"Thank you." She sat down across from him. "It's been a while. How are you, Jordan?"

"Good."

"And your dad?"

He shook his head slightly. "Same as always."

She saw a look in his eyes and said no more. The man who intimidated her also had a reputation for being difficult, and she couldn't imagine being his son. But not everything was his cross to bear. He was very tall and very handsome, with short dark hair and brown eyes that were incredibly compelling. A man that women noticed. He was also the son of the richest man in town, and women noticed that, too.

"What's new?" she asked.

"Not much." He shrugged those broad shoulders. "But you've got a lot going on. A baby on the way. Miss Independent moving back to Bronco Heights. Why?"

"Because I got fired from my job in Denver." There was no point in evading. They'd always been honest with each other, and she wasn't about to be anything less now. She told him the whole humiliating story, except for the part about how she got pregnant. Then she explained about filing a lawsuit against her previous employer.

"I think your attorney is right that you've got a good case."

Their server walked over then, and they ordered.

When he was gone, Jordan met her gaze. "How can I help, Erica?"

"I was hoping you'd ask." She leaned forward. "I need a job. The money I've saved won't last forever, and this lawsuit could take a long time to resolve."

"I see."

"I realize this is presuming on our friendship, but no one in their right mind will hire a woman in the third trimester of pregnancy."

"It's touchy," he admitted.

"I have upper management experience and a lot to offer. If you give me an opportunity, I promise you won't regret it."

"Of course I can help." He didn't even hesitate. "We're always looking for good people."

"Really? Just like that," she said.

"It's the least I can do for a friend. But I have a feeling you'll be doing me a favor in the long run." He took out his cell phone and started tapping into it. "I'm texting my assistant now to check my schedule and then she'll contact you to make an appointment to come by."

Her eyes got a little blurry with grateful tears, but she blinked several times, determined not to get emotional. "I don't know how to thank you."

"Name the baby after me. Jordan works for a girl or a boy."

His teasing smile brought women to their knees, but she was immune. Why was that? Because she had that reaction to another man. Every time she saw Morgan, her heart skipped a beat and her legs wobbled a little. It made her wonder about what combination of factors attracted a certain woman to a certain man.

Before she could decide, their food arrived and she couldn't believe she was hungry again after the big breakfast she'd eaten. Now that the reason for this meeting had been settled, she could relax and enjoy catching up. They reminisced about the short time they'd dated and decided it wasn't a total waste, what with the friendship that came out of it.

She speared a piece of chicken and lettuce. "You know my parents were hoping I'd fall for you and not go away to college."

"Really?" He took a sip of his beer. "I don't think you ever told me that."

"It's true. They wanted me to marry you. Hometown boy."

"Sorry to disappoint," he teased.

"Unless I miss my guess, I think they're still holding on just a little bit to some kind of fantasy that we'll see the error of our ways and get married." She laughed, then looked up from her salad, expecting that he would be laughing, too.

He wasn't. And his expression was a little dark and brooding. "You deserve someone better than me, Erica."

"Don't be ridiculous."

"I don't think I am. I'm not good enough for you." He looked thoughtful. "And you're going to have a baby. That's a special responsibility."

"The fact that you recognize it as such is proof that you're so much better than you think you are."

He shook his head. "You're wrong."

Erica disagreed, but trying to convince him of that would be a waste of time. There was no question that he was flawed, but who wasn't? She considered him a good friend. And she was confident he was a good man.

As good as Morgan?

Since when was he the bar by which she judged other men? Maybe it was talking about the responsibility of a baby that made her think of him now. It was a darn shame that he didn't want kids and doubted his suitability as a father.

She liked him very much and that kiss at the Harvest Festival said he liked her, too. But this baby had to be her first priority. Sometimes liking someone a lot just wasn't enough.

CHAPTER TEN

TALKING TO JORDAN the day before had eased Erica's stress level by a lot. As promised, his assistant had called to make an appointment for the following week. He'd assured her there would be a job after the baby was born, and in all the years she'd known him, he'd never lied to her. There was no reason to believe he was now. That morning she'd visited Gramps and tried to coax him to talk. Sadly he didn't say anything. After lunch she was at loose ends and the waiting without anything to fill her time was driving her nuts. She was used to being busy.

Between Malone cooking and hired help with the housekeeping, her mother didn't need any assistance. So, Erica wandered down to the barn to see what her father was up to. She walked inside and found him cleaning out stalls. The last time she'd seen Morgan, he was doing the same thing. Not too proud to handle a dirty job. Just like her father.

"Hi, Daddy. Don't you pay people to do this?"

He looked up from shoveling horse manure into a wheelbarrow. "It's relaxing. Keeps me from thinking too much." She was probably a big part of what he didn't want to think about. But burying his head in the sand wasn't going to change anything, and she wanted to do what she could to repair their relationship. "I'm looking for something to do to earn my keep. Can I give you a hand with this?"

He frowned at her. "Don't you need to take it easy? With the baby?"

"The doctor says to do whatever I've been doing. Except riding horses. Can't risk a fall."

"Yeah. I remember that from when your mama was pregnant with Gabe and you." He smiled, remembering something. "She's pretty stubborn and missed riding. It was awfully tempting to get on a horse. Lucky she had me to keep her honest."

The subtext of that was Erica had no one. Well, she had herself and was doing all the right things for her health and the baby's. And she had Morgan to help her through the birth. Just thinking about him brought a blush to her face. It was involuntary because if she had any control, it wouldn't happen.

She refused to think about what their relationship would be after the baby was born. Day-to-day survival was her priority now and she didn't have to worry about a job. Everything was falling into place, so she refused to let her father's comment bother her.

"How about you let me sweep up when you finish that part. And I can spread out clean hay. If you lift the bale, I'll just walk back and forth with the pitchfork. Think of it as getting my daily exercise."

"Sounds okay to me." He smiled at her. It was almost the way he used to before she decided to have a baby by herself.

They worked in silence for a while and then Erica asked, "Do you think about retiring, Daddy?"

"Why would I?"

"Running a ranch is a lot of work."

"And if I don't do it, who will?" He shoveled more muck, then met her gaze through the fence dividing the stalls.

"Gabe will."

"I suppose." He leaned on the shovel. "If he doesn't have me to contend with, he can do it his way. We don't see eye to eye on how to run things these days. I don't see any good reason to change. This land has been in the family for generations and we're doing just fine. Your brother is into his real estate deals. That's *his* way of pushing back."

If Erica was the sensitive type, she would have bristled at

that remark. As if her having a baby without marriage and a husband was her preferred rebellion strategy. But, again, she made a conscious effort to let that roll off her back.

"What did Gabe want to do that was so revolutionary?"

Her father stopped working and pushed his Stetson off his forehead a little as he thought about the question and looked down at the wheelbarrow. "Well, take this for instance."

"Horse poop?"

"Yeah." He grinned. "He had me read an article and the title was 'What to do with poo.'"

"Catchy." She laughed. "You compost this, right? And spread it in the pasture?"

"We do. But there's something called manure share."

"Do I even want to know about this?" she asked.

"Probably safer than talking about other things," he said, looking down at her belly. "It's a program that connects livestock owners who have excess manure with gardeners, landscapers and large scale composters. According to your brother, it benefits the environment and the economy of local communities."

"Call me crazy, Daddy, but that sounds like a good program."

"Maybe." He didn't look convinced. "But I've got better things to do than coordinate poo pickups."

"I think you're just being stubborn."

"Takes one to know one," he said pointedly.

She ignored that and pitched more hay on the stall floor. "We're talking about you now."

"Okay. I think the terms old-fashioned and set in my ways have been thrown out more than once to describe me." He met her gaze. "There's probably some truth in it."

"They say recognizing a problem is halfway to solving it."

"I never said I had a problem. If it's not broke, don't fix it, I always say. When I'm not running things, this operation will change. And someday this land will belong to Gabe and you and my grandchildren—" He didn't finish the thought, and the silence was—well—pregnant.

She walked over to the opening of the stall next to hers where he was working. "What is it, Daddy? Something other than the obvious is bothering you. Please talk to me."

He looked at her. "The baby you're carrying is my grandchild. Mine and your mother's. It's something we've looked forward to and prayed would happen for a long time now. We've worked hard for all these years to know that everything will pass on to another generation of Abernathys. Whether you want to talk about him or not, that baby has a father. What if he turns up demanding visitation and more? Some cockamamie claim on the Ambling A?"

"That won't happen," she assured him. "I guarantee it."

"How can you? There are stories on the news all the time about courts granting property and all kinds of demands to someone with flimsy paternity claims."

Her father had just admitted he was set in his ways and had no use for new techniques. Her pregnancy via anonymous sperm donation would, in his mind, fall in that category. This was the absolute wrong time to explain how she could be so certain that no one was going to show up and demand anything.

"You're just going to have to trust me, Daddy."

She went back to the stall where she'd been working and finished spreading the hay. Her father didn't say much more, and the awkward silence persisted. More than once it crossed her mind to leave him alone, but there was a lot of truth to that stubborn Abernathy streak. She stuck it out until the job was finished.

Afterward, Erica want back to the main house, left her dirty boots on the back porch then went up to her room to shower away barn dust. She'd thought the spray of warm water would relax her after the conversation with her father, but it didn't. She was still feeling a little raw.

On her way to the stairs she passed her parents' room and noticed her mother was there, looking at something on the bed. "Mama?"

"Erica. Come on in."

She walked inside the large room and went directly to the king-size, cherrywood sleigh bed.

"Is that your dress?" She looked down at a fancy gown laid out on the duvet. "This is for Denim and Diamonds?"

"Yes." Her mother picked up the hanger and held the dress up in front of her. It was a long-sleeved black sheath with gorgeous beading. "What do you think?"

"It's just beautiful, Mama." She smiled. "That's going to look fabulous on you."

"You don't think it's too young for me?"

"No way. It's classic. Elegant. And besides, you aren't old. Unless it's a miniskirt and boots, you can pull off anything."

"Okay. Good." Her mother sighed. "I just love it, too. So, what about jewelry?"

"It is Denim and Diamonds after all. Don't you have some big, honkin' diamond earrings that Daddy bought you for a significant birthday?"

"Yes. They'd be perfect." Her mother walked to the mirror over the dresser, held the gown up in front of her and assessed the look. She beamed a satisfied smile.

"You're going to be the belle of the ball, Mama." It felt really good to just talk girl stuff. No undercurrents. Just enjoying feminine conversation.

"It should be something," her mother agreed. She walked over to Erica and started to say something, then pressed her lips tightly together. "So, Malone tells me you had a call from Jordan. Unless you know another one, I assume that's Jordan Taylor?"

"Yes. I had lunch with him yesterday."

"Oh?" Her mother's eyes gleamed with interest. "And?"

"He looks good."

"Of course he does. They don't call him Bronco's most eligible bachelor for nothing." She waited a moment, then prodded a little. "So you just stared at a nice-looking man over a table at lunch?"

"Funny." Erica grinned. "We did some catching up."

"Is he seeing anyone?"

"He didn't say, so the answer to that question is either no or nothing serious."

The gleam in her mother's eyes intensified. It was a spark of hope. "I guess he noticed that you're pregnant."

"Yes. He congratulated me." And didn't ask any questions, which she appreciated.

"Did you make plans to see each other again?" Angela asked.

"As a matter of fact, we did." She was going to hell, but Erica couldn't resist leading her mother on a bit. Served her right for not letting this go.

"Lunch again? Or maybe dinner?"

"I have an appointment to talk to him about a job."

"And?"

"That's it. He said they're always looking for talented people at Taylor Beef, and he was sure there was something for me."

Her mother looked a little startled. "But you're going to have a baby."

"That's not a news flash, Mama. And that's why I really need a job."

"There's no need to rush into anything, Erica. This is your home."

"I appreciate that. More than I can say. But—"

"But nothing. What will you do with the baby after it's born?"

"I'll find child care."

"Babies need their mothers."

"And I will take care of him or her," Erica protested. "Part of that is earning a living so I can support us."

"Like I said, you have a home. Your father and I can take care of you both—"

"Mama, please don't take this wrong. But I only moved in here temporarily. To get on my feet. I appreciate you and Daddy letting me come home so I can do that. Once the baby's born and I'm back at work, I'll find a place for us to live."

"I suppose I can't talk you out of that."

"If I hadn't been fired, that's what I'd be doing in Denver. It was always my plan, Mama."

"I see." Her mother walked past her to the closet. Without turning, she said, "I need to hang this up, then I've got some things to do."

Erica had seen tears in her eyes and heard the break of emotion in her voice. She started to say something, then stopped. It wouldn't do any good. Angela Abernathy had never come to terms with her daughter going away to school, then having a career somewhere so far from home. Being a ranch wife and mother was her career, and she didn't understand Erica's choices any more than her father accepted new ranching ideas. This wasn't the time to point out that at least she would be living close by this time.

Still she felt awful. She didn't want to hurt her parents, but she had to live life on her own terms. She'd kept intending to tell them about the baby but put it off. Maybe in the back of her mind she believed if they held their newborn grandchild and bonded, the circumstances wouldn't be a big deal.

Women plan, God laughs. But she didn't think this was funny. The only thing getting her through was Morgan. They had childbirth class tonight and she would see him. She was looking forward to that very much.

"So, Erica is picking you up again this evening?" Deborah Dalton toyed with the mug of coffee in front of her.

"Yeah." Morgan sat at the round, oak table in his kitchen, eating the stew his mother had brought over. Her excuse was that she always fixed too much, and that was probably partly true. The other part was, feeding him was a way to stay connected. Better known as pumping him for information.

He figured her question was just the beginning of an inquisition. The innocent expression on her still-beautiful face was a dead giveaway.

"Erica insists on it," he said.

"Usually a gentleman picks up a lady for a date."

"It's not a date, Mom. She says I'm doing her a favor. The least she can do is drive."

His mother looked down for a second, then met his gaze again. "Why *did* you agree to be her labor coach?"

"Actually I offered. She's going through a lot and I can help. That's it." He shrugged.

"But having a baby is an intimate and emotional experience."

One that should be shared with the father of said baby. His

mother didn't say that straight out, but it was there all the same. He wished the woman would get off this subject, and he planned to make that happen. "Cops and firefighters and regular civilians deliver babies for perfect strangers all the time. Not that I'm delivering it, but... She's my friend. It's the least I can do."

"You really like her." That wasn't a question.

It was a different subject and he was even less comfortable talking about this one. "As a friend."

"Erica told me that your kindness and sensitivity are the first things she noticed about you."

"I'm a hell of a guy."

"Just like your father." Her unwavering look was a dare for him to convince her she was wrong about the man's character.

Morgan tried to resist the challenge, but just couldn't. "I'm not like him."

She shot an exasperated look in his direction. "There's no getting around the science. He's your father. You have his DNA—the good, bad and handsome. It's been thirty-five years and he still makes my heart flutter and my knees weak."

"I don't want to know that, Mom." He did not like where this conversation was going.

"Tough. If I can forgive him, so can you."

"That's where you're wrong." He loved his mother a lot. He'd do anything for her and proved that when he moved to Dalton's Grange because she'd explained how important it was to her. None of that meant his attitude toward his father had or ever would change.

"Morgan, we're all only human. We have flaws. You. Me. And your father. People don't always make the best choices when they're under stress. That doesn't mean we should disregard the positive parts of them."

"You made your choice. You have to live with him," he allowed. "I just have to work with him." He buttered one of the biscuits she baked and took a bite. It melted in his mouth. "These are really good."

"Your father said the same thing." Again the challenge was in her eyes for him to deny the connection.

"There isn't anyone on the planet who wouldn't like these. Don't give me that look," he said.

"Okay. Suit yourself. But don't expect me to stop trying."

"Suit yourself. It's your time to waste." He would do almost anything for this woman, but letting his father off the hook wasn't one of them. "I love you, Mom."

"I know. And I love you, too. Even though you're stubborn like your father. Although, in all fairness, you get it from both sides. Truthfully, I'm not sure whether or not that's a flaw."

"I'm not stubborn," he said. "It's just that I'm always right."

She rolled her eyes. "When did you say Erica is coming?"

"About a half hour." Morgan was keeping a close watch on the time and planned to be outside waiting, so she didn't have to come up to the door and knock.

"I'll get out of here before that. Otherwise she'll think I lied about you living with your mother."

"Maybe I should hire you to cook," he teased.

"You couldn't afford me." Her grin was equal parts confidence and self-satisfaction.

She got up and washed the casserole dish she'd brought the food in. Then she said goodbye and headed to the door. Just before she opened it, there was a knock.

"She's really early," Morgan said.

"Hmm." His mother opened it. "Erica. Hi."

"Hello." If she was surprised, it didn't show. "Nice to see you, Mrs. Dalton."

"Oh please. Call me Deborah. Better yet Deb."

"Okay. Thanks. Is Morgan—"

"I'm here." He moved beside his mom. "Come in. It's cold outside."

"Thanks."

"You're really early. I was going to wait for you outside so you didn't have to get out of the car."

"Oh—" She looked first at his mom, then him. "Sorry. I was ready and didn't want to wait around."

He saw tension in her eyes and the set of her mouth. "Is something wrong?"

"No. At least nothing new."

"Come and sit down," his mom said. "And tell us what's bothering you."

"There's plenty of time before the class," he assured her.

She hesitated for several moments, then sighed and nodded. After walking over to the leather sofa, she sat and he settled beside her. Not as close as he wanted to be.

His mother took one of the chairs and set the empty casserole dish on the matching ottoman. "Okay. How can we help?"

Erica's smile was rueful and sad. "Just don't click your heels three times and say 'there's no place like home.' Or 'you can't go home again.' I found that out."

"That would mean there's no positive movement with your family," he guessed.

She shook her head. "I tried. I was hanging out with my dad in the barn. Helping him. Earning my keep. But he's stubborn."

"There's a lot of that going around." Morgan met his mom's gaze and saw sympathy in her eyes.

"Right." She twisted her fingers together in her lap. "And my mother—" She looked at Deborah. "We were so close before I went to Colorado."

"Letting go of her children is hard on a mother. Especially when they go far away."

Morgan didn't miss the message in his mother's eyes. She wasn't above using her not so long ago health crisis to bring her sons together.

"Well, now I'm back," Erica said. "With a baby on board. But I'm not married, and that's not the way they wanted to be grandparents."

"Oh, honey—" His mother made a sympathetic sound. "They'll come around."

"I don't think so. Apparently I made another mistake." She looked down for a second. "I had the audacity to look for a job. I contacted Jordan Taylor." She told them about Jordan's promise to find her a position at Taylor Beef.

Morgan had heard about the guy. A newcomer picked up a lot of information hanging out at DJ's Deluxe bar. He'd heard about Jordan Taylor's reputation with the ladies. "Isn't that the guy your folks wanted you to marry?"

"Yes. Even today Mama was hoping and hinting there might still be a chance with him. The thing is, she said I don't need a job because they can take care of me and the baby." She clasped her hands so tightly her knuckles turned white. "I don't want that. It's my responsibility to support us. My mother's always been a ranch wife. She doesn't understand that I want to do it on my own. And I can."

His mother's expression was kind and concerned. "Women have hard decisions to make when it comes to family and career. I know all about that."

"Really?" Erica's eyes widened.

She nodded. "Before I met my husband, I was a career woman. On my way to top-tier management. Or possibly the first female president of the company."

"Wow. What happened?"

"Neal Dalton happened." She got a soft look on her face and shrugged. "I was a city girl and met him at a rodeo, of all things. He was kind and caring. One look at him, his smile, and I fell in love. I knew he had a ranch and that was his life, in his blood. It wasn't as if he could relocate to the city and find a job with his skill set. Ultimately I couldn't live without him."

"That's so romantic," Erica said.

"My parents and family were professional people and less than thrilled with my decision. But I love him, and love is worth every sacrifice. If you're not willing to do what it takes to be with that person for the rest of your life, it's probably not love. I chose to be a ranch wife and never regretted it." She met Morgan's gaze. "Not once."

"Mama never understood my passion for a career. But I also want very much to be a mother."

"Every mother is a working mother. It's just that some women have jobs outside the home, too." His mother's tone was firm and supportive. "But attitudes have changed, and women have more options and support than ever before."

Erica nodded. "I know they'd like for me to be married with a baby coming because they're concerned about the difficulties of being a single mom."

"They love you, that's all. They just want what's best for you."

"I know that. But—" She hesitated a moment, then waved a hand in front of her face. "I'm sorry to talk about my problems."

"I don't mind listening. But trust me on this. Things will be fine. You wait and see." His mother smiled. "Now I have to go. And so do you two. Go learn something." She stood, grabbed her casserole dish, then let herself out the door.

Morgan was alone with Erica. "You feeling better?"

"Yes, actually." She smiled. "It really was nice talking to someone who understands what I'm dealing with. I've probably said this before, but you're lucky to have her, Morgan."

"I won't argue that. But we have our blind spots, too."

She was staring at the door where his mom had just left. "She sure does love your dad."

"Yeah."

Morgan was well aware that the part of her motivational speech about never regretting her choice had been for his benefit. He thought about the woman he'd proposed to and finding out she was pregnant with another man's baby. Oddly, he realized that he hadn't been that shocked. He felt betrayed and angry about the lie, but he wasn't really hurt. In hindsight, letting her go was the easiest thing he'd ever done. And he never regretted it.

He'd met his fair share of women since then. They were sweet, pretty, bold and sassy. Blondes, brunettes and redheads. Shy, forward, fun and serious. But not a single one of them stuck in his mind or heart when he looked in his rearview mirror.

Not until Erica.

He stared at her now. The tension in her eyes and around her mouth was gone. She was glowing, and no, that wasn't the sun shining through the window. She got to his heart in a way he'd never been gotten to before. She was becoming awfully important to him, but...

Why did there always have to be a *but*?

She had moved heaven and earth to be a mother, have a baby.

He had doubts. Not only whether or not he wanted kids, but also about being a good father. Unless he could be sure about both, he had no business saying anything to Erica about his feelings.

CHAPTER ELEVEN

"Mama, thank you so much for taking me shopping."

"You are so welcome, sweetie."

Her mother's suggestion had come out of the blue that morning. The olive branch gave her hope that this was the beginning of better times.

Erica burrowed into the butter-soft leather passenger seat of her mother's luxury SUV. They were finally on their way back to the ranch in the late afternoon. More than once after buying a dress for Denim and Diamonds, Erica had suggested it was time to head home but her mother insisted they browse just one more store—a baby store. How could she resist?

"And the thing is," her mother said, chattering on, "Denim and Diamonds isn't that far off. We had to find you a dress."

"A tent, you mean. Just because it has sequins doesn't make that much material less than a parachute," Erica teased. "Seriously, Mom, it's gorgeous. And I can't believe you whipped out your credit card faster than me."

"I wanted to. So I did."

"And the sleepers you got for the baby are—" Emotion cut off the words. But the tiny outfits were too sweet for words anyway. This surprise shopping spree was her mother's way of mending fences, and Erica was happy that Morgan's mother was right about her coming around. "Thank you again, Mama, for everything."

"You're very welcome. It was fun." Angela drove down the road toward the main house. "I don't know about you, but I can't wait to sit and have a tall glass of iced tea."

"Sounds like heaven."

Her mother parked by the front door and they exited the car. Erica grabbed her dress and the bags of baby things out of the back.

"I'll open the front door for you." Her mother hurried to it, then stood back to let her go in first.

Erica had barely crossed the threshold when she heard, "Surprise!"

"What—" She looked around the entryway decorated with blue and pink balloons that said Baby. Streamers were hanging from the ceiling, and fresh flower arrangements graced the tables. "What is this?"

"A baby shower," her mom said. "Mel's idea."

"My friend Brittany did all the work," Melanie explained. "She's an event planner and very good at it."

Erica looked at her mother. "You knew about this and kept it a secret?"

"Of course. My job was to get you out of the house while everything was being set up." Her mother took the dress and bags from her.

"You played the part perfectly. And I quote, 'just one more store.'" She was completely surprised. "I can't believe this is for me."

"You're the only one here who's pregnant." Mel grinned at her.

Erica glanced at the women gathered there and smiling at her. She recognized Amanda, who was engaged to Morgan's brother Holt.

Deborah Dalton stood beside her. "I love baby showers."

"I'm glad you're here." Erica smiled at her just before her gaze landed on Daphne Taylor, Jordan's sister. "Thank you all for coming."

"Now that our mother-to-be is here, it's my job to make sure everyone has a good time." Mel's friend Brittany was a statuesque woman with light brown skin and beautiful, long dark curls. She wore a formfitting red dress with a shiny black belt and matching patent leather four-inch heels with a red suede insert. "We haven't officially met yet. I'm Brittany Brandt Dubois, BFF to Amanda and Mel, so I feel as if I know you."

"It's nice to meet you," Erica said. "I never expected to have a shower."

Brittany grinned. "My husband Daniel and I are raising his niece, Hailey. I love her to pieces. She's nine months old and so adorable, but babies are a responsibility. This party is a chance for you to be carefree and have fun before your bundle of joy arrives."

"I don't know what to say. Thank you all." Erica looked ruefully at her outfit, trying not to compare her large sweater, black leggings and cowboy boots to the chicly dressed Brittany. "If I'd known, I'd have dressed up."

"It's not called a surprise for nothing."

She looked up and saw Malone standing at the back of the group. He was the only man there and looked completely fearless. "The food is all set out on the dining room table. So if you ladies will move this party into the other room, I'll start taking drink orders."

There was a rousing sound of agreement, then Mel escorted her to the seat of honor in the great room. Brightly wrapped packages decorated with rattles and pacifiers were stacked around the wing chair. The women settled on the leather sofa and temporary chairs set up for the occasion.

Brittany took charge in a firm but charming way. They played games and then it was time for food. Malone was on duty to serve.

"We'll have cake soon," Brittany said afterward, "but now it's time for presents."

Erica opened a seemingly endless line of boxes of disposable diapers, baby lotions, tiny sleepers, receiving blankets, a baby monitor, even a thermometer.

She looked around at this incredibly generous group of women who'd come together for her. Even though she'd only known them a short time. "This is so wonderful. I don't know how to thank you all. I'm speechless—"

"Wait. There's one more." Her mother brought over an unwrapped white box and handed it to her.

"What's this?"

"Open it and see."

Erica lifted the lid and pushed aside the protective tissue paper to reveal a small, white dress, delicate lace-covered booties and a stretchy headband with floral appliqués. "Mama? This is gorgeous."

"That was your christening gown. I saved it for you. For your baby."

Erica couldn't count how many times today she'd been overwhelmed, but this was right at the top. She hugged her mom. "Thank you."

"You're welcome." Her mother gently tucked a strand of hair behind her ear and looked at her with love shining in her eyes. "Now, enjoy the rest of your party."

"That's excellent advice because pretty soon it will be all baby, all the time," Amanda said.

"It's a good thing they're cute, adorable and cuddly when they're born," Deborah chimed in. "Because for the first few weeks it's all about changing diapers, trying to interpret the different cries and getting up in the middle of the night to feed them."

"That's true." Her mother sat next to Morgan's mom on the sofa and smiled at the other woman. "You can't even get a smile out of them for the first few weeks. And don't even get me started on teething."

"Oh goodness." Deb rolled her eyes. "The first time Morgan got sick he was about three months old. There's nothing scarier than a sick baby—" She must have seen something in Erica's face because she added, "But babies are incredibly resilient. A little runny nose barely slows them down."

Erica looked at the open packages piled on the floor beside her and fixated on the thermometer. The baby chose that moment to move and stretch. Something, probably a foot, lodged up against her ribs and made her sit up a little straighter.

Suddenly the enormity of the challenge she was facing became all too real. Whatever had possessed her to think it was a good idea to have a baby all by herself? She alone would be responsible for raising this tiny human. Oh dear God...

Somehow she managed to keep the panic at bay through cutting the cake and the random girl talk that followed until the shower was over. She said all the right things, thanked everyone again for coming.

Since Deborah had been dropped off and had to wait for a ride home, she insisted on helping Malone put away leftover food in the kitchen. Amanda and Brittany were pitching in, too. Erica was alone with her mother and just couldn't hold back the anxiety any longer. She burst into tears and almost instantly was wrapped in a familiar, warm embrace.

"What's the matter, sweetie?"

"Oh, Mama, I don't think I can do this."

"I'm pretty sure this is your hormones talking, but let's sit down and you can tell me what's wrong." Her mother led her back to the sofa, where she sat and held her hand. "Now, talk to me."

Erica met her mother's gaze through a blur of tears and was glad she couldn't see the disappointment that was no doubt there. "I'm scared."

"About the birth?" She squeezed the hand still in her own. "You're preparing for that with your class. When the time comes, you'll be ready with all the tools you'll need to make it a positive experience."

Including Morgan, she thought. But after the baby was born he'd be gone. She looked at the infant thermometer again.

"No, Mama, it's not the birth I'm worried about. It's when I have to take care of a newborn. I'm so afraid I'll do it all wrong and mess this child up. I'm scared that I'll disappoint my baby the way I have you and Daddy."

"Oh, Erica—" Her mother looked astonished. "Is that really what you think?"

"That's how it felt every time I picked my own path instead of yours."

"I didn't realize—" Angela pressed her lips together for a

moment. "It never occurred to me that we didn't tell you often enough how proud we are of you. We constantly tell other people how wonderful you are."

"Really?"

She nodded. "We could not be prouder of you. And I can't stress this enough. You are not alone. Your brother and Mel. Your dad and me. Grandpa Alex. Malone. We're all here for you. I'm truly sorry you feel judged. Although, in all fairness, when you came home it was a shock to see you so pregnant when we had no idea about the baby. It was an adjustment and that takes time."

"I'm sorry, Mama. I knew there would be questions about the baby's father, but I should have told you. I just didn't know how."

"Tell us what?"

Erica just had to get this off her chest and hope she had the words to explain in a way that her mother would understand. "Promise me you won't tell Daddy. I know you tell him everything, but you have to swear you won't say anything about this."

There was a wary expression on her mother's face, and she was silent for several moments, obviously conflicted. Finally, and reluctantly, she nodded. "I won't say anything."

"Okay. The thing is, I went to a sperm bank and was inseminated. I've never met the father of this baby, but I have a medical history and a lot of information." Erica took a breath and blew it out. "Daddy's worried about him showing up to try to get something out of us. That will never happen."

"I see. And you felt you couldn't tell us?" Angela asked.

"I was afraid you guys would think I was crazy or foolish, or both. But I felt it was my only choice. My relationship with Peter ended. There was no one in my life and I was pushing thirty. I couldn't help feeling it was now or never, after what you went through…"

"The miscarriages. My bout with depression after."

"Yes."

Her mother sighed and it was a sad sound. "After the miscarriages, my heart broke when the doctor finally told me that I just couldn't carry a baby. First I felt as if I had done something wrong. Then it felt wrong to not be content with the two beautiful, healthy children I already had. I was only a little older than you are now."

"I was so scared, Mama. I remember that you didn't even want to eat. You weren't sleeping and didn't want to get out of bed. I was afraid you were going to die."

"I'm so sorry you were afraid for me." Angela's eyes teared up. "You brought me peanut butter sandwiches and read to me. You tried so hard to help. I think the only reason I snapped out of it was you, Erica. You made me push myself to put one foot in front of the other."

"You couldn't help it, Mama. And I understand a little better how you felt now that I'm going to be a mother, too."

"And I made you afraid you might never be one." Angela sighed. "That's why you moved heaven and earth to get pregnant."

"Yes." Erica smiled, knowing her mother understood. "But I'm not sure Daddy will get it. Please, don't say anything to him."

"There's something you need to understand, sweetie."

"What?"

"Your father and I want so very much to be grandparents. You know we have for a very long time."

"Yes. You guys aren't subtle." Erica was glad when her mother smiled at that.

"It doesn't matter how this baby came to be, he or she will be loved to the moon and back. Fair warning, though, if you let us be grandparents, I can't promise we won't spoil our grandbaby."

"Oh, Mama—" Erica put a hand over her mouth and nodded. "Yes, please. I would like that very much."

They cried and hugged and laughed. It was cleansing and so very freeing to get all of the hurt out in the open.

"You know—" Her mother brushed a tear from her cheek. "You're going to find out all the joys and challenges of raising a child. And it is joyous."

"I'm glad you'll have my back."

"I absolutely will. In that spirit, here's a piece of motherly advice, just something to tuck away. You may not always understand or approve of your child's choices, but that doesn't mean you won't support and love them unconditionally. Always."

"Like you do me?"

"Yes. And your brother, too." Her mother nodded. "The hardest part is letting go. Standing back without being able to make things better when your children get hurt. In good times and bad, you'll be there for them. No matter what."

"I'll remember that from now on, Mama."

"And one more thing. You took care of me when you were just a little girl and managed to help me out of that downward spiral. Even then your maternal instincts were working overtime. Never doubt that you're going to be a fantastic mother."

Tears blurred Erica's eyes and she sniffled. "That means so much to me coming from you. Thank you."

It was a relief to finally unburden herself. Her mother would somehow make her father understand there was nothing to worry about from the baby's father. She remembered Morgan had asked if she was in love with the guy. Maybe he was a little jealous?

Wishful thinking. All she knew was that if Morgan hadn't been there for her from the moment they met, she would have been so completely lost. Counting on him had come fast and easy. But she still couldn't decide whether that was a good thing.

Morgan parked his truck outside of Erica's house and waited for his mother. His dad had dropped her off because her car was in the shop and Morgan had volunteered to pick her up when his father got sucked into a spirited game of Go Fish with Robby. Morgan told himself it was about helping out his parents and that was true. But there was another reason. Getting even a glimpse of Erica wouldn't bother him a bit. His mom texted that she'd be a few minutes, so he got out of the truck and leaned against the front of it.

The house lights were on making it almost as bright as day out here. And he focused all his attention on the front door. That's why he didn't see Gabe Abernathy approaching and wasn't braced for the usual confrontation.

"Morgan Dalton. Just the man I wanted to see."

"Oh?" He straightened away from the truck.

"What do you want with my sister? Why are you going out of your way for her? She's having a baby soon. Most guys would be running away as if her hair was on fire. You must have an angle. What is it?"

"You think I'm after something just because my family doesn't go back generations like yours? Because we bought the land instead of inheriting it? That doesn't make us bad people."

"You should see someone about that chip on your shoulder. I never said you were bad people."

"You didn't have to say it." But Morgan wondered if the guy had a point about him being overly critical.

Gabe shook his head. "My sister has enough to deal with. She doesn't need some guy taking advantage of her."

"You're dead wrong and way out of line. Erica is my friend. That's it." Friend fell far short of what he felt for her, but Morgan didn't understand it completely himself. He wasn't going to try to put it into words to appease her overprotective brother.

"I don't believe that's all there is to it."

"Not my problem to convince you otherwise." Morgan shrugged and slid his hands into the pockets of his sheepskin jacket.

Gabe looked more concerned than hostile. "I just don't understand. What do you want with my sister?"

Her. I just want her.

The truth was that he really couldn't blame Gabe for asking. If he had a pregnant sister and some guy who wasn't the father was hanging around her, he would want to know why. On the other hand, what would Gabe say if Morgan confessed that he had feelings for Erica that were more than friendly? He was having trouble wrapping his own head around that.

Just then the front door opened and he saw Amanda and her best friend Brittany. But Morgan only had eyes for Erica, who was walking out with them, looking radiant and happy. His heart seemed to skid sideways in his chest in the most unsettling and extraordinary kind of way.

"Hi, Gabe," Amanda said. "How are you? What are you doing here?"

He smiled and the protective expression disappeared. "I was hoping to catch you. I was wondering if your internet search has turned up anything new on my great-grandfather's daughter."

She shook her head. "I'd have called right away if it had. Without more information, something to go on, I'm stuck. Wish I had better news."

"I'm going to see Gramps again tomorrow," Erica said. "Maybe this time he'll say something to me."

"Would you like me to go with you?" Gabe asked.

Morgan didn't miss the look the other man slid in his direction. As if he'd expected Morgan to offer and beat him to it. The fact was he'd been about to. She told him seeing her grandfather unresponsive wasn't easy, and he wanted to be there for her. He had no idea why, but helping Erica seemed to be hardwired into him.

"Thanks, Gabe," she said. "I'd really appreciate that."

"Of course."

"Mel will be out momentarily. Are you ready to go?" Brittany asked Amanda. "We came together."

"I am. But since Morgan is here I can hitch a ride back with him and Deborah," Amanda answered. "Come to think of it, why are you here? I thought Neal was going to pick her up."

"I volunteered because he and Robby were playing a game, and I wasn't doing anything important."

"Hmm," Erica said wryly, "Could one surmise that you think an adult spending time with a child is important?"

"Yes." Morgan suspected she was trying to make a point, but he wasn't going there. "That and my dad has a cold. Best if he stays in where it's warm."

"Okay, then. I'll ride back with you, Morgan." Amanda hugged her friends one last time. "I'll get Deborah."

"And I'll go inside with you to get Mel," Gabe said.

"And I'll say good night." Brittany waggled her fingers at everyone and walked to her car.

Suddenly it was just Morgan and Erica. He resisted the urge to say "alone at last."

"So, how was the shower?"

"I was completely surprised," she admitted. "My mom was

actually in on it. She even took me shopping and bought some adorable little clothes for the baby. And she gave me my christening outfit. I was just blown away."

"I'm glad it went well." And he got to see her, although he could have skipped the confrontation with her brother.

She must have heard something in his voice because her eyebrows drew together. "What were you and Gabe discussing a few minutes ago? When I walked outside?"

"Just small talk."

"Really? Because I'd swear you were looking at him as if he was a cattle thief and horse rustler all rolled into one."

"I didn't know I was," he hedged.

"Come on, Morgan. This is me. I've gotten to know you pretty well. My brother said something to make you angry. I'm betting it was about me."

So much for bluffing. She was way too smart and observant for that. "He asked me what I wanted from you."

"What did you tell him?"

"That we're friends."

"Hmm." She frowned. "From the look on his face, I'm guessing he didn't buy that."

"Not even a little bit."

She sighed. "Just give it time. He'll come around."

"I won't hold my breath."

"I didn't think my mother would come around either," she said.

"Even though you preached hope and giving people a chance?"

"Even though." Her expression was sheepish. "The thing is, I didn't really believe what I was saying. And I was wrong. Today all the little infant things made me freak out about raising this baby by myself. My mother gave me a great pep talk and I ended up telling her about going to the sperm bank."

"Really?" That surprised him.

She nodded. "She understood why I did it. If she can do that, my brother will eventually understand that you're a good man. You'll see."

He was skeptical. Her brother had already made up his mind

that Morgan was using Erica for some underhanded reason. Truthfully Morgan couldn't wrap his own mind around what was going on with him. Why he would do anything for her and couldn't seem to help himself. If he had this under control, he wouldn't have kissed her. That touch of his mouth to hers had opened the dam and he wasn't sure how to stop wanting her.

CHAPTER TWELVE

IT HAD BEEN a hard day. Erica had gone to see her great-grandfather again and he still didn't know her at all. Feelings of helplessness and disappointment gave way to recurring guilt for having lived far away and not making an effort to see him while he was still responsive. The family dinner that followed with Gabe, Mel and her folks had been a little sad, but the food was fantastic.

Maybe sensing that the Abernathys needed comfort, Malone had outdone himself with a roast and all the trimmings. As they ate, they told stories of Gramps during healthier, happier times that made them laugh. And if all that wasn't enough for big-time comfort, there was cheesecake for dessert.

Now she was sitting beside Gabe at the kitchen table while Malone finished putting away leftovers and washing pots and pans. Mel had excused herself because she had work to do. The folks were watching TV in another room. She and her brother stayed put for some reason. Maybe he felt the need to bond. She sure did.

"Thanks for going with me today." Erica wrapped her hands around the mug of tea Malone had insisted on giving her. "It's hard to see him, but I'm glad I wasn't alone. Having you there made the whole thing so much easier."

He took a sip of his coffee, then smiled. "What kind of a big brother would I be if I didn't support my little sister?"

"Well, it's much appreciated." She reached over and touched his forearm for a moment. "And speaking of the whole big brother thing, you can stand down with Morgan Dalton. He's not a threat to me."

"Do you know that for sure?" Her brother's eyes narrowed. "Have you asked yourself why he's around? Always there for you?"

"Maybe because he's a nice person. What other reason could there be?"

"He wants something."

"What could he possibly want?" She laughed. "I don't have much money and even if I did, his family is pretty wealthy."

"The rumor is that his father won it gambling."

The rumor was true. "So what does it matter where the money came from? It's not ill-gotten gain. And doesn't change the fact that Morgan is a wealthy man."

"What about the baby?"

"Oh please. My life is a soap opera but not to the point where he'd kidnap my child and sell it to a desperate couple who couldn't have one of their own." She laughed again, and it was a welcome relief from the sad day. "Look, he's a really good guy. Trust me. You'll see."

"I don't know." There was doubt in his voice.

"Seriously, Gabe, it's not about the baby. And—"

"What?" he asked when she stopped.

Erica looked at him. "He's not sure he wants children. So what could he possibly want from me except to be my friend?"

Gabe studied her and a gleam stole into his eyes. "Are you in love with him?"

"Of course not," she said. The response was automatic, but the question made her think.

She liked everything about Morgan, from his sense of humor to his loyalty and friendship. It didn't hurt either that he was awfully good-looking. And she couldn't deny that every time she saw him, her heart just swelled with something wonderful that she refused to name. When she wasn't with him, she longed to be. At the Harvest Festival, when he kissed her, it was the most magical kiss ever.

But was she in love? She sure hoped not. When the baby was born, his promise would be fulfilled. She would be immersed in raising her baby, and he would still be an eligible bachelor. Their relationship would be nothing but a memory, and that made her sad.

Malone finished drying the big pot he'd used for the mashed potatoes and set it on the stove. "More coffee, Gabe?"

"Yes. Thanks, Malone."

"Sure thing." The cook brought over the pot and refilled the mug. "How about you, Erica? More tea?"

"No. Thanks." She smiled at him before he nodded and walked back to scour the roasting pan. She was glad he'd interrupted the conversation because she had no answers for her brother. "Gramps sure didn't say much," she commented, deliberately turning the conversation away from herself.

"I really hoped he would." Gabe shook his head. "You did your best, chattering away about all kinds of things. I was hoping that the two of us there together might jar him out of wherever he is. But he was the same."

"It's hard to picture Gramps as a young man," Erica said. "And to have the responsibility of a baby when he was hardly more than a boy himself."

"Yeah."

"It must have been agonizing for him to give up his baby girl."

Gabe nodded. "He didn't have any family support. In fact just the opposite. Grandpa Alex hardly remembers his grandparents except that they were not the warm and fuzzy type."

"That must have been awful for Gramps. I know you and Mama and Daddy aren't doing the dance of joy about my baby, but no one is pressuring me to give him or her up for adoption."

"We would never do that," he protested.

"Well, I wouldn't—I couldn't give up my child even if there was pressure to. I love this baby so much already. I can't imagine not being there for the first smile, first steps, first word. The thought of it makes me so angry that Gramps was forced to give up his baby girl." Her brother was suddenly staring at her as if she had fire coming out of her eyes. "What?"

"I'm such an idiot."

"Well, I've always suspected as much," she teased. "But what makes you so sure?"

"It just hit me." There was wonder in his expression. "I'm going to be an uncle."

"Really?" she said wryly. "Imagine that. It's what happens when your sister has a baby. You just now figured that out?"

"Of course I knew. I just—" He shrugged. "I just didn't think about it that way. Too busy resenting you for living so far away. Blowing through on holidays."

"I truly regret that."

"You had your reasons, I guess. And it really doesn't matter now. You're having a baby. Bringing a new life into the world." He looked at her pregnant belly and a warmth stole into his eyes. "I'm going to be an uncle."

"You are."

"I'm going to be the best uncle you've ever seen," Gabe said grinning.

"I know you will because you've always been the best big brother a girl could ask for." She swallowed the lump of emotion in her throat. "I've missed you. Been so busy proving my independence that I didn't realize how much I missed you until I got home. I love you."

"I love you back. And I'm going to love this baby so much. In case you aren't aware, you should prepare for the reality that our parents are going to spoil this kid rotten."

"I'm not so sure. Mama maybe. She's come around. But Daddy—" She shook her head, wishing things could be different.

"Give him time. A boy will be hard enough for him to resist. But a girl? Forget about it." Gabe grinned. "If you have a daughter, she'll wrap him around her little finger."

"You think?"

"I know so. If you have a girl who looks like you, she'll be the prettiest little girl in the world."

"Oh, Gabe—" Her eyes got misty at his compliment.

"What did you say?" Malone shut off the faucet and came over, still holding a saucepan. There was an odd expression on his rugged face.

Gabe gave him a puzzled look. "I said, if Erica has a daughter who looks like her, the baby will be the prettiest little girl in the world."

Erica had forgotten he was there. She'd known this man since she was a kid and had never seen him quite so intense. "Why, Malone? What is it?"

"It just reminded me of something your Gramps said a while back..." There was a strange and thoughtful expression in his eyes, as if he was trying to remember something.

"What did he say?" Gabe prodded.

Malone hesitated for a moment. "It was something like you just said. And I think it was about five years ago. I remember that because it was when his memory was starting to go. A lot of the time he seemed stuck in the past."

"What was it?" Gabe said again.

"I remember him going on and on about 'the prettiest little girl in the world.'" He looked from Erica to Gabe. "And he said a name. It wasn't his wife, Cora. So I thought it might be an old girlfriend."

"Was the name Winona?" Erica asked.

"Nope." Malone shook his head.

"But it was someone from his past." There was excitement in Gabe's voice. "What if he wasn't talking about a woman? What if it was about his daughter? Beatrix?"

Malone thought for a moment. "Nope. That wasn't the name he said."

"Are you sure?" Gabe pushed.

"Yeah." Malone looked apologetic and frustrated with himself. "I just can't recollect what the name was." He tapped his forehead. "It's right there, but I can't grab onto it. I'm sorry, Gabe."

"Don't beat yourself up over it," her brother said. "Sometimes trying too hard just pushes things even more out of reach. It'll come to you."

"Hope so. Sure would like to help find her."

"I know you would."

Although Gabe did his best to hide it, Erica could hear the disappointment in her brother's voice. Like Amanda said, without another clue of some kind, the search for their great-grandfather's daughter was going nowhere. An Abernathy was out there and they all wanted to find her. For just a moment, Malone's comment stirred hope that things would break their way. A name from the past that would unlock a mystery.

Then, just as fast, that hope was gone because there was no way to force a memory. Gramps too had some memories of his lost baby girl buried so deep in his mind they couldn't be reached, and it was frustrating.

Memories were funny and precious and bittersweet. Pretty soon Morgan would be only a memory. When she was as old as Gramps, would she remember him? After she gave birth, the time she spent with him would become the past. That was tearing her apart. She couldn't wait to say hello to her baby, but her heart didn't want to say goodbye to Morgan.

Morgan sat in the passenger seat of his father's old truck. They'd been mending fences at the outermost boundary of Dalton's Grange, and it was a big piece of land. That meant a long ride back with Neal Dalton, the last man on earth he wanted to spend time with. No matter how he grudgingly respected the man's work ethic and his dedication to a physically demanding job, Morgan couldn't forgive the hurt to his mother. And the longer the ride went on, the more awkward the silence became. He was determined not to break it.

But apparently his father had no problem doing it. "Sure is a pretty day. There's nothing like a clear Montana sky. A little cold, though. Winter is coming, so it's a good thing we got this job done while the weather is holding."

Morgan thought about not responding, then changed his mind. But one word was all the man would get. "Yeah."

Neal glanced over, then back to the road in front of him. "Your mom said Erica's baby shower was really nice. She had a good time. Thanks for picking her up."

"No problem." Unless you counted Gabe Abernathy and his

suspicious attitude. The guy was way off base. Morgan didn't want anything from her. Not really. Nothing except to spend time with her. Picking up his mom from the baby shower was one way to make that happen.

His father's even-tempered disposition was starting to make Morgan feel like a complete jerk. He could throw the man a bone. "How's your cold? Any better?"

"Yeah. Your mother insisted I take it easy and filled me with liquids and chicken soup. Cold and flu don't stand a chance against her soup. And her, for that matter."

Morgan didn't want to smile but he couldn't help it. "That's Mom."

"Yeah." The man looked over again, just for a moment. "Appreciate you and your brothers picking up the slack for me around the ranch."

"No big deal. Like you said—no one argues with Mom."

After that, neither of them seemed to have anything to say. Morgan just wished this ride would be over.

"How's Erica?" Neal finally said. "Baby's due pretty soon, right?"

"A couple weeks." Morgan smiled to himself just thinking about her. She grumbled about growing big as a house, but he thought she got more beautiful every day.

"She sure is a pretty young woman," his dad said. It was like the man could read minds. "Your mom sure likes her. Said Erica's mom is real nice, too."

"Yeah."

His father waited for more, and when it didn't come he finally said, "Sure is nice of you to support her and be her labor coach. It would be hard to go through that alone."

"I suppose."

"No supposing about it. Bringing a baby into this world is pretty scary." His father maneuvered the truck around a big rut in the unpaved road, then they continued to bounce along. "I remember when your mom was first pregnant. You weren't planned. And I have a confession to make."

"Another one?" Morgan said sarcastically.

Neal ignored that. "I wasn't sure I wanted to be a father. Didn't really know whether I wanted kids."

Wasn't that just great? Morgan took after his unfaithful father. "So why'd you have four more then?"

"Because of you." His dad looked over, then back to the road.

"What about me?"

"You were the first and I worried about everything. Not your mother. She had a knack for knowing when to worry and when to let it go." He laughed and shook his head. "And she loved being pregnant. Was never healthier or more beautiful, but that didn't stop me from being anxious about her. Anything could happen. And she was…"

In spite of himself, Morgan was pulled into this walk down memory lane now. "Mom was what?"

"Everything," Neal said reverently. "She's my whole world and she gave up a successful career and a different kind of life because she loved me. The isolation of ranch life was a lot to ask of her."

"But she did it."

"And I always felt the pressure to give her whatever she wanted so she didn't feel like she made the wrong choice and wasted her life on me."

"And she wanted a baby," Morgan prompted.

"Yeah."

"And you didn't?" he challenged.

"I won't lie. I wasn't fully on board." He suddenly grinned at a memory. "Not until I saw you for the first time." He glanced over, probably to see how Morgan reacted to that statement. "Don't take this the wrong way, but you were not all that good-looking right after you were born. Neither were your brothers. All red and scrunchy. But I had a son. And from that day on the feelings were, are—"

"What?" Morgan asked.

"Bigger than anything I'd ever felt in my life. I loved your mom, but the son we made was—" Hands on the steering wheel, he shrugged. "I can't even describe the love. Maybe as big as this Montana sky."

Morgan looked out the truck window at the blue that seemed

to go on forever. That was a lot of love. One of his earliest memories was this man putting him on a horse, patiently teaching him to ride it. Letting Morgan follow him around the ranch. He never raised his voice, even when his brothers came along one by one and the chaos multiplied.

Morgan had a clear memory of resenting Holt for stealing his own time with their father. As the oldest he was expected to share his mother, but he wasn't in the mood to graciously share his father, the man he hero-worshiped.

"If you love mom so much, how could you cheat on her?"

His father pressed his lips together and shook his head slightly. "I messed up big-time. It wasn't a pattern, but happened more than once."

"Slipups," Morgan said angrily.

"Too much liquor was always involved."

"That's just an excuse. The least you can do is be honest and take responsibility."

"Maybe you can't understand, but I have to say this. I was always stressed about money. Ranch operations depended on cash flow. I had doctor bills for my family. The price of beef went up and down. Too much rain or snow could affect the cost of hay, loss of livestock. It was all about keeping the ranch going for you boys and your mom. Sometimes the strain got to be too much. Drink took the edge off."

Morgan remembered several times when his mom had tried to hide that she'd been crying. The man he'd looked up to above all others had broken his mother's heart. Morgan had been hurt and angry the first time. A couple of slipups later and his anger had boiled over.

He'd been the first to leave the family ranch and hire on with another outfit. One by one his brothers all followed him. And for the same reason. They couldn't stand to see their mother with the man who treated her that way.

"Tell me one thing," he snapped.

"Okay." There was no hesitation in his father's voice.

"Why did she forgive you? Why in hell did she take you back?"

"You'll have to ask her that, son. But I thank God every day that she did." Neal let out a long breath. "The money I won to buy this ranch was the second-luckiest thing that ever happened to me."

"What was the first?"

"The day the minister asked your mother if she would honor and cherish me and she said, 'I will.'" He looked over for a moment. "The day I won that money I vowed it would be a new beginning for Deborah and me and our boys. I could finally give the family I love the lifestyle they deserve."

Morgan stared at the man's profile. "You do know that my brothers and I are only here to work the ranch because Mom asked us to, right? That, and we needed to make sure she'd be okay."

"I'm aware." There was sadness and acknowledgment of the fault in his tone. "I know none of you trust me."

"How can we?"

He made the turn onto the road that led to the barn. "I don't expect you to believe this after what I've done, but I love her, too. I'd give my life for hers. I'm going to make it up to her."

"You're right. I don't believe you." He huffed out a breath. "I used to look up to you and you let me down. Tell me why in the name of God I should believe what you're saying now."

"I don't drink anymore, Morgan. Not at all." He glanced over and the resolve in his eyes was unmistakable. "Marriage has its ups and downs, but if a man and woman really love each other, they can work through tough times and make it to the other side. Stronger than before. I swear on everything I hold dear that I only have eyes for your mother. I'm so grateful that she loves me enough to give me another chance. And, son, I hope you and your brothers will follow her lead and do the same."

His father drove up to the barn and parked. "I'm just asking you to keep an open mind."

When he got out of the truck Morgan's mind wasn't necessarily open but it was sure spinning. As he helped unload the tools, he thought back to the day he'd come to Dalton's Grange. From that day on he couldn't recall seeing his father consume alcohol. Because of his anger and resentment, he'd never noticed before.

He'd never seen his mother happier, and more than once she'd told them this was the best time of her life. Having her sons nearby was such a blessing. And his parents were like newlyweds, always touching, exchanging secret looks, kissing like teenagers when they thought no one was watching. And now this. His dad had come out and asked for another chance.

Morgan remembered Erica saying more than once that they both should give their families an opportunity to patch up relationships. The night of the baby shower, she'd told him she and her mom were on the mend.

It occurred to him that everyone made mistakes, but attempting to right those wrongs was the foundation of character. Maybe Erica was right about second chances.

When the truck bed was empty, Morgan lifted the tailgate and made sure the thing was securely latched. His father stood beside him and their gazes met. There was no mistaking the sincerity in the other man's eyes.

Morgan stuck out his hand. "I believe you, Dad."

Neal's mouth trembled just for a second, and there was a suspicious moisture in his eyes. Then he shook hands and pulled Morgan in for a hug. "Thank you, son."

Morgan nodded and felt his own throat tighten as a weight lifted from him. Holt seemed at peace with their father, but the rest of his brothers would have to figure out where they stood with him. Morgan wouldn't interfere or influence them one way or the other. But ending hostilities was the right decision for him.

And he had Erica to thank for putting cracks in his attitude in order to give understanding and common sense a way in.

It was a relief to know the man loved being a dad and was a good one. That meant there was hope for Morgan. If—

He pulled up short. For such a small word, *if* had awfully big consequences. Did he want complications? A baby? All he knew for sure was that he couldn't shake the feeling of wanting Erica, and he had no idea what he was going to do about it.

CHAPTER THIRTEEN

Erica checked her appearance in the mirror over the bathroom sink and nodded with satisfaction. Her hair was in a ponytail for tonight's childbirth class in which they would be practicing breathing and relaxation techniques. She hadn't seen Morgan since that brief, unsatisfying encounter after her baby shower. There had been barely enough time to say hello, and she wanted more.

She was very aware of the time limit on their involvement and wasn't trying to fight it anymore. Trying to turn off her feelings to avoid emotional messiness was pointless. After the baby was born, she would have Morgan withdrawal and would fall back on her memories, but for now she was going to enjoy the time she had left with him.

After applying lipstick, she headed downstairs and found her mom in the great room reading. It was cozy with a fire crackling, and she had a few minutes to visit before leaving to pick up Morgan. "Hey, Mama. Is that a good book?"

"Yes." She marked her place, then set the book aside. "You're going to class?"

"Pretty soon." It was such a relief to be on good terms again. Up front and honest about her situation. If only she could talk to her dad, too. "I'm picking up Morgan."

Angela nodded. "I invited his mother to join the Bronco Valley Assistance League and she seemed eager to be a part of it. I liked her very much."

"I do, too. And I like Mel, too. I talk to her almost every day. She's becoming the sister I never had. My brother chose wisely."

"I feel the same way. And they're meant to be together, although when they first met there was tension, not all of it the good kind." Her mom smiled. "But they worked it out."

"I'm glad." Erica was so happy for her brother, but also wistful for herself. It was possible that she and Morgan were meant to be together, but her pregnancy made that too big a hurdle.

"You and Morgan seem to get along pretty well. And you have from the very beginning, I hear." Her mother didn't look upset.

"We definitely clicked," Erica admitted. "As friends. We're not like Mel and Gabe. Not romantic."

"Really?" There was a gleam of speculation in her mother's eyes. "You're sure?"

"Yes. Completely." Because he had doubts about being a father. Her family had doubts about him. "And you don't trust him. Why would you think there's anything serious between us?"

"Because of Deborah Dalton. I got a sense about her that she's a good person who raised her boys to be good men. She and I were talking. She knows her son and I know my daughter." Angela shrugged. "We were just playing 'what if.'"

"You know Morgan had words with Gabe that night," Erica said.

"He's protective. And if I hadn't met Deborah, I might agree with your brother's doubts. She's good people. I'd be really surprised if Morgan isn't, too."

"Well, he's certainly been a good friend to me." She looked at her watch. "I have to go or I'll be late for class."

"Can't have that."

"See you later." She leaned over to kiss her mother's cheek, then straightened and headed for the door.

After driving to Dalton's Grange, she saw Morgan waiting for her outside his house. He walked over to the driver's side of the SUV and she opened the window.

"I know you insisted on picking me up, but at least let me drive from here."

"What? You don't trust me?"

"That's not it at all." He leaned over and rested his arms on the doorframe, his face not far from hers. "It seems to me that my job in all this is to take care of you. Driving you there checks that box."

"Okay." She turned off the engine and stepped out. "I'm not too stubborn to accept a generous offer of assistance."

Especially when the man offering it tugged at her heart in a way no man ever had. Telling him no just might not be possible. She took his outstretched hand and walked to the passenger side of her car. He held the door open for her to get in.

"Thank you," she said.

"Don't mention it." He closed her door and walked around the front of the vehicle, then got in behind the wheel. "And we're off."

Erica had to admit it was nice to sit back and be driven. She could get used to this. As soon as that thought popped into her head, she pushed it away. She couldn't let herself think about getting used to anything with Morgan.

"So, what's new?" he asked.

"You mean since my brother practically took your head off?" She looked over at him, and the dashboard lights revealed the humor on his face.

"Yeah, since then," he said.

"Well, my mom said she really liked your mom. And I quote, 'she's good people.' And she invited your mother to join the Bronco Valley Assistance League."

"What do you know? It's only been a year. And all it took to be accepted by the old guard was you having a baby." He grinned.

"It's a miracle, all right. Along with the fact that my mother and I are still getting along. And you should know that she doesn't seem to object anymore to you being my coach." In fact, Erica strongly suspected her mother of going in the opposite direction. She'd been doing a little matchmaking tonight. It was a sweet thought but doomed to failure.

"Speaking of getting along..." He glanced over at her for a second. "I had a talk with my dad."

"An actual conversation that consisted of more than yup, nope and livestock feed?"

He laughed. "This will shock you. But we discussed our feelings."

"Gasp." She pressed a hand to her chest in mock surprise. "I thought I felt a ripple in the fabric of the cosmos."

"I know."

Erica listened as he told her about his father taking responsibility for his actions, his vow to make it up to his wife and family and especially his promise to Deborah to love her and make her happy.

"So, you and your dad are really speaking to each other?"

"Thanks to you, yes."

"I don't understand," she said. "I didn't do anything."

"You were the one preaching second chances," he reminded her. "Although I don't think your brother is willing to give me even a first chance."

"Gabe is a good man and normally fair, too." She sighed. "But something about you pushes his buttons."

"Yeah, something. Your brother wants to rip my head off, and I've never even touched you."

Except for that kiss. He hadn't done it again, but every innocent touch—helping her into the car. When their arms brushed or he took her hand—it felt like more. And, right or wrong, she wanted this to be more.

She didn't quite trust her voice not to give away her yearning and didn't talk for several moments. After a deep breath she finally said, "Be patient, Morgan. Gabe will come around. I can see you two becoming good friends."

"That's just crazy talk."

She laughed. "You'll see I'm right about this."

"Agree to disagree," he said. "Change of subject. Did you get lots of good stuff at the shower?"

"I did. All I need now is a crib. And a car seat. Can't bring the baby home from the hospital without one."

"I guess so."

He turned the car into the lot at the Women's Health Center and parked. As they walked to the building, Erica had an almost overwhelming urge to slide her hand into his, but managed to hold back. That's not what a friend would do.

When they reached the conference room, only Carla was there. They were the first ones to arrive.

"Hey, you two." The nurse/educator smiled. "How are you?"

"Good." Erica looked up at Morgan as he nodded.

"Your due date isn't too far away," Carla said. "You both must be getting excited."

"I can't wait to hold this little one." She rested her hands on her belly, then she glanced up and saw the expression on Morgan's face, something that looked a lot like longing. Was it possible that he might not want to say good-bye after she had the baby?

By anyone's measure, what he was doing fell into going above and beyond the call of duty. She'd been drawn to him the first time they met at DJ's Deluxe and the feelings had escalated since then. She'd never met anyone like him and had never felt about a man the way she did about Morgan. Before she could take that thought further the other three couples walked into the room.

"Hi, everyone," Carla said. "We're in the pregnancy home stretch now. I hope you've all been practicing your breathing at home, but let's go over it again. So, if you'll all settle on the floor, we'll get started."

Morgan unrolled the mat and she sat on it with him behind her. She could feel the heat of his body all around her and barely resisted the urge to curl into him. He had her back. He'd always had her back and she loved that he did. Before she could think too much about that, Carla explained what they were doing.

"Okay. First stage of labor. Organizing breath. Take in a deep breath as the contraction starts, then slowly breathe out releasing tension from your head to your toes. Slowly inhale through your nose. Exhale slowly through your mouth. Every time you do this, focus on relaxing a different body part."

Morgan spoke quietly into her ear, reminding her of what the instructor had said. "Okay, now you're in active labor. Keep breathing as slowly as possible, speeding it up as the intensity of the contraction increases."

"Okay."

Moments later he gently rubbed her arms. "You're tensing up. Concentrate on your right leg, relaxing your toes, your foot and ankle, up your calf and thigh."

Erica tried her best to follow his directions but the feel of his breath on her cheek and the sound of his deep voice in her ear made her feel as if he was actually touching her everywhere. And she wanted that so much.

Carla looked at each of them, nodding enthusiastically. "Okay, you're all doing great. Now transition breathing."

"Okay," Morgan said, "Focus on that picture on the wall. You're having a contraction. Breathe in and out through your mouth, Carla said it should be at a rate of one to ten breaths every five seconds. Every fourth or fifth breath blow out a longer one."

"This is really complicated," she said. "I'm really glad you're here."

"Nowhere else I'd rather be."

Morgan put his big hand at the small of her back and began to gently caress. "Okay. Deep breath."

Erica nodded, even though she wasn't certain she could breathe at all with him touching her. The feel of his warm fingers shorted out her brain and made her want to melt into him. Somehow his deep, steady voice penetrated her mental slide, and she followed his instructions.

"Doing great," he said.

His breath was warm on her cheek and her breathing escalated, but not in any kind of controlled way.

"Good job, everyone." Carla smiled at the group. "You're all here to prepare for a positive birth experience. Relaxation is important. If you tense up, discomfort is magnified. Dads, this is where you can step in. If you feel her tensing, give her a big bear hug."

Without hesitation, Morgan wrapped his muscular arms around her and squeezed gently. The embrace was sure and strong and made her feel so safe she could have stayed there forever. His lips were so near her cheek and she felt him hesitate, as if he was going to kiss her but he didn't. Then Carla started giving them more pointers.

As instructed, Morgan gently stroked her forehead, jaw and hands. Rhythmically, he kneaded her shoulders and neck, and she thought she'd died and gone to heaven. He used firm pressure with the palm of his hand to rub her from shoulder to hip, then from thigh to knee.

Erica was fairly certain nothing she'd ever experienced had felt quite so perfect as Morgan's touch. And she didn't think there was a breathing technique in the world that could control her reaction to the exquisite sensation of his hands on her body.

She glanced up at his face and recognized the intensity that turned his eyes a darker shade of blue than normal. At first she thought it was only concentration. Then she saw the pulse throbbing in his neck and knew. He was feeling something for her, too, and it was more than just being her support partner. It was the scariest, most exciting feeling she'd ever had. But where did they go from here?

Holy crap! Morgan couldn't believe how close he'd come to kissing Erica in that class. Her skin was so soft and she was so beautiful. Time after time, he caught himself and stopped, but there was something in her eyes. Something he'd never seen before. But he couldn't identify it, and she didn't help. She hadn't said a word since he started driving them back to Dalton's Grange.

It was time to break the silence. "Do you want to stop for something to eat? Are you hungry?"

"No, thanks." Her voice was soft and the tone a little unsure, as if she had something on her mind.

"Okay."

He was thinking hard about what to say but could only come up with an apology for wanting her. But he wasn't really sorry at all. God help him.

She was pregnant and he most likely was crazy. But she was the most beautiful, sexiest woman he'd ever met. And if he was being honest with himself, it was more than that. She was sweet, caring, friendly, kind and funny. He'd never met a woman who had it all. Not until Erica.

And now he'd made it weird.

He turned onto the road where Dalton land started, and Erica still hadn't said anything besides no thanks. If he didn't fix this, she was going to let him off, then drive home, and there would be this unspoken, awkward thing between them.

He pulled up in front of his house, but didn't turn off the car's ignition. "You're awfully quiet. Everything okay?"

"Yes—" She sighed. "No."

"I knew it." He shook his head. "It's me, isn't it? I did something—"

"Morgan, no." She released her seat belt and put her hand on his arm. "It's me. I—"

"What?" he asked when she hesitated.

"I haven't been practicing my breathing, and tonight I guess Carla really got through to me how important it will be."

"So, we'll practice," he said.

He nodded toward his house with the light shining in the front window. "In fact, why not now while the class is still fresh in our minds?"

"Really? Are you sure? I know you get up early—"

"It's fine." He put his hand over hers and tried not to notice the heat that shot through him. "I can see that you're stressed about this. That's not good. The best way to deal with it is to practice. What do you say?"

"Okay."

Morgan turned the key and shut off the car. He got out and went around to open Erica's door, then offered his hand to help her out. When her fingers touched his palm, his whole body went tight with need, and fire licked through him. The heat threatened to consume him.

Get a grip, Dalton. Don't be a jerk.

They walked into the house and she looked around. "This is awfully tidy for a single guy."

"If you don't look in the kitchen, my halo will stay all shiny and bright." Teasing cut the tension and that was a relief. "Can

I get you anything? Water? Iced tea? Beer?" He held up a hand. "Just kidding."

"I knew that. Water would be great."

"Coming right up." But he was having a beer. It might take the edge off his wanting her more than his next breath. That thought was ironic considering they were here to practice breathing.

On his way to the kitchen he said over his shoulder, "Make yourself comfortable."

"I guess we should sit on the floor like we do in class," she called back.

"Whatever you want."

Morgan grabbed the drinks, brought them into the living room and set them on a table beside the leather sofa. Erica was sitting on the floor.

She glanced over her shoulder and smiled. "Whenever you're ready."

He was so ready. And, damn it, why couldn't he stop thinking in double entendres? *Focus*, he ordered himself. It would be hard to do that since he had to sit behind her. So close. Touching her. Breathing in the scent of her. But this wasn't about him. For her, he would be the best coach on the planet or die trying.

He assumed his position and couldn't help thinking for the hundredth time how good she smelled. How soft and delicate and graceful her neck looked. How much he wanted to see for himself if her skin tasted as sexy as he thought it would.

"Okay—" He braced himself. "Organizing breath. Slow and deep as the contraction starts, then let it out, releasing all the tension from your shoulders, legs and all the way to your toes."

She did as instructed, but he could feel that she wasn't responding to the technique. He wasn't sure what to do except continue instructing and counting. So, that's what they did and went through all the different stages of breathing.

"Do you want to start over again?" he asked.

"No." She said that a little too quickly. Oddly enough, after all that breathing she'd just done, there was a sexy, breathless quality to her voice. "That went okay. I think we work pretty well together."

"Yes, we do." And he could really get used to the nearness of her. The warmth of her burrowing deep inside him, thawing out a place that had been frozen for a long time.

She glanced over her shoulder and said, "How can I ever thank you?"

"By not hating me for how much I still want to kiss you." Morgan wasn't sure he'd actually said that out loud.

Her eyes widened and she blinked up at him. A couple of seconds passed before she said, "Does that mean you wanted to kiss me before now?"

There was no way to dodge this, so he didn't try. "In class tonight. So many times I came very close to kissing you. It's official. I'm a jerk. I know it. Right there in front of everyone I wanted to just—"

"I wasn't completely sure I didn't imagine that." She turned around to face him and smiled softly. "There's no one here now except you and me."

"What?"

"If you're a jerk, then so am I. It was so hard to concentrate when all I could think about was you touching me and how good it felt." Definitely that was a breathless whisper.

"Erica—"

Morgan saw that his hand was shaking a little as he traced the curve of her cheek with one finger, then kissed where he'd touched. Her eyes closed, and she shuddered just before the sound of her throaty moan burned through him. She leaned toward him, and this time he didn't hesitate, but took her mouth with his own. The touch sparked a bone-melting fire that spread through his blood.

Not here, he thought. Not on the floor.

Without a word, he stood and held out his hand, helping her to her feet before leading her to his bedroom. Both of them were breathing hard when they sat side by side on the bed.

He kissed her again and let his mouth wander over her cheekbones, her eyes, her chin. He nuzzled her ear and nipped her neck. Settling his hand on her thigh, he moaned with satisfaction as he remembered how badly he'd been wanting to do this.

He slid his fingers underneath her sweater, over her soft

skin and found her breast, cupping it in his palm. She was perfect, the most beautiful, most sensuous woman he'd ever held in his arms. He brushed his thumb over the tip and heard her gasp of pleasure.

She leaned her head against his shoulder. "Oh, Morgan. That feels so good."

"I want you, Erica."

"Yes, please," she whispered.

Mindless with desire, he wanted to touch her everywhere and slid his hand over her belly. There was a rippling movement beneath his palm and he froze. As he hesitated, he felt it again, a rolling motion across her abdomen. If ever there was a cold shower moment, this was it. He pulled his hand away as if he'd touched a hot coal. And maybe he had.

Erica was having a baby. That made her a package deal and sleeping with her was not a step to be taken lightly.

"Morgan?" She was frowning at him.

"I felt the baby move."

"I know." She stared at him and not in a good way. "What's wrong?"

In her eyes he saw the exact moment when she shut down emotionally. "It's not what you think."

"And what do I think?" She slid sideways, a bruised look on her face.

"It's just—" He dragged his fingers through his hair, searching for the words to explain. "I don't want you to think I—"

"I don't think anything except—" She stood up and headed for the door. "I need to go."

"Erica, wait. Let me explain."

She'd stopped in the living room and was looking around. "Where did you put my keys?"

"Just wait a damn minute. We need to talk about this," he said.

"There's nothing to talk about. You've made your feelings crystal clear. So it's better to stop this before either one of us gets hurt." She picked up her purse and looked around the room, anywhere but at him. "I'll go."

Morgan wasn't so sure they weren't already in territory where one of them could get hurt. And, for crying out loud, he needed to take fifteen seconds to process everything. She was bringing a life into the world and that was huge. If he was going to be a part of that, he needed to be sure. He never wanted her to think he'd used her.

He'd thought they had a special connection. Was this just an overreaction to his hesitation? Or something else? Maybe he really was just a friend. A rebound guy from Peter and she was still in love with her ex.

"I need my keys, Morgan."

Damn it, were those tears in her eyes? He didn't think he could take it if she cried. Then he remembered he'd put her keys in his jeans pocket and fished them out. He dropped them into the hand she was holding out and managed to do it without touching her.

She walked to the door and opened it. "Good night, Morgan."

"Erica?"

She brushed a hand across her cheek before looking at him. "What?"

"I'm sorry."

She nodded and without another word walked out the door.

Morgan really felt like putting his fist through a wall. Before she came inside things were weird, but he could have worked with that. If he'd just kept his hands to himself, everything would have been fine, but he hadn't. Now he didn't think there was any coming back from this.

CHAPTER FOURTEEN

Erica was hurt and disappointed, but she couldn't be mad at Morgan, and that was super annoying. From the beginning he'd been honest about his doubts, but she'd fallen in love with him anyway. *Love.* Four letters italicized. Capital *L*. In a very short time she'd realized he was a forever-after kind of guy and he cared about her, too. She could tell in everything he did. Especially his kisses. She'd hoped he would change his mind about having kids. Being a father. Being a father to her kid. But last night hope died.

When he felt her baby move, the look on his face had told her everything she needed to know. The man wanted no part in her child's life. That meant Morgan could have no part in hers either.

The tears started again and she was exasperated with herself. She couldn't believe that, after crying most of the night, there could still be any left.

Unable to sleep, she'd gotten up early this morning and showered. Did her hair and put on a little makeup. It was her plan to act as if nothing was wrong. Her family had warned her about Morgan. Her mother, father and Gabe had been afraid he wanted something from her. Ha! It was just the opposite. He wanted nothing to do with her. Only Mel had worried about her getting hurt.

And hurt she was. When she and Peter broke up, she'd been

frustrated that her plans for marriage and family had fallen apart. In the end, though, the split felt right. With Morgan there was an ache, an emptiness and a feeling that no other man could ever fill up her heart the way he did.

A tear trickled down her cheek, and impatiently she brushed it away. "Oh, for crying out loud…" Not funny.

She slid off the bed she'd made before the sun came up. If she sat there much longer, she was in real danger of dehydrating. Sooner or later she was going to have to go downstairs and put on a brave face for everyone. Best get it over with.

She took one more look in the mirror and winced at her reflection—the red, puffy eyes. Probably there wasn't enough concealer in the world to hide the evidence of her broken heart, but she applied it anyway. Maybe no one would notice. And it was always possible no one would be there.

Apparently luck abandoned her, because only her father and Malone were missing. Her mother and Gabe were sitting at the kitchen table having coffee. The smell of cooked sausage and eggs filled the air. Not even that made her hungry.

Since her brother was here, that probably meant Mel was out of town for work. Gabe did a double take when he saw her. "You look terrible."

"Thank you." She glared at him, then poured herself half a cup of coffee and sat down at the table.

"Aren't you going to have some breakfast? Malone fixed a plate for you and is keeping it warm in the oven," her mother said.

"I'm not hungry."

"You have to eat something, sweetie. Think about the baby."

Everything she did was for this baby. After making the decision to use a sperm bank, she'd reconciled herself to doing the parent thing alone. But that was before Morgan. Couldn't she feel just a little sorry for herself that things hadn't worked out?

"I don't feel like eating breakfast, Mama. I think the baby will be just fine."

Gabe's eyebrows rose as he sipped his coffee. "Someone is grumpy this morning."

"I'm not," she said, "But keep it up and I'm happy to show you just what grumpy looks like."

"I had cravings when I was pregnant," her mother said. "With Gabe it was candy and chips. Junk."

Erica gave him a smirk. "You are what Mama ate."

Their mother held up a hand to cut off his retort. "He's fine, in spite of what I ate. And with you," she said to Erica, "I wanted avocados and fresh melon."

"Nothing sounds good."

"How was your childbirth class last night?" Her mother met her gaze over the mug of coffee as she took a sip.

"It was good. Lots of information." Afterward sucked. Well, not the kissing Morgan part. That was pretty perfect. So was the touching. Right up until the baby moved.

"I'm surprised the guy hasn't backed out of this labor coach thing yet."

Erica slowly looked up at her brother as the reality hit her. She'd been so caught up in Morgan pulling away when the baby moved, she'd forgotten about everything else. After the way she left his house last night, she wasn't sure if he'd back out. Why wouldn't he? And then what would she do for a coach?

Gabe's expression went from easygoing to concerned as he studied her. "Is something wrong?"

"I don't want to talk about it."

"What happened?" her brother demanded. "Did he come on to you?"

If only.

She tamped down that reaction and speared her brother with a hard look. "He's a good man, and someday you're going to realize that. I predict that you two will be good friends."

Her brother snorted. "Fat chance."

"Ask anyone about him. You won't hear a bad word."

"Uh-huh." Gabe shook his head.

"I don't even know what to say to you right now. If I was ten, I'd call you a butthead. And Mama would scold me and tell me not to call you names."

"Okay, then. That's my cue." He pushed back his chair and

stood. "You're crabby. That's not calling her names, Mama. It's an adjective. And I have to go."

"Have a good day, Gabe." Angela smiled at him as he walked out the door, then looked at Erica. "Your brother is right. You are in a mood. What's going on?"

"I'm pregnant, Mama." *And the man I love can't handle it. That's what's wrong.*

"You know, honey, it's completely natural for a pregnant woman to feel uncomfortable. Your body is supporting life. Your ankles are retaining enough water to float a cruise ship. Sleeping is hard because there's no comfortable position and bedtime is usually when your little unborn angel decides to do the backstroke."

Erica couldn't help smiling at the exaggerated but all too accurate description. "And your point is?"

"It's no secret we haven't been as supportive of your pregnancy as we could have been. I wonder if you feel that if you complain about being uncomfortable, we'll think you regret your decision. Or that we'll think this is what you get for making your choice. We don't."

"But, Mama—"

Her mother held up a hand to stop her words. "I'm not finished." She took a deep breath. "It also doesn't mean that we'll think you don't love your baby. Or that we won't love your baby. This is our first grandchild."

A tear rolled down Erica's cheek. "Damn hormones."

"I remember it well." A smile teased Angela's lips.

"The thing is, Mama, I know you understand. But you're a mother. I'm afraid Daddy will never be able to forgive me for doing the motherhood thing the way I have."

"Don't sell your father short. He understands more than you give him credit for."

"But more than once I've heard him criticize technology, newfangled contraptions. If it wasn't for science and a little bit of a miracle, I wouldn't be having a baby. Women do it all the time and that choice is widely accepted. But I don't know if he can get over his daughter taking that path."

Her mother didn't respond to that for several moments. She

looked thoughtful, then seemed to come to a decision and stood. "Come with me."

"What? Where?" Erica questioned, but stood anyway.

"There's something you need to see. Get your jacket. It's cold outside."

Erica grabbed her poncho from the hook by the back door, then put it on and followed her mother outside. "Where are we going?"

"To the barn."

"Why?"

"Because one picture is worth a thousand words." That cryptic statement was all she would say.

They walked to the ranch outbuildings and into the barn. Erica kept pace with her mother past the hay-filled stalls and to the tack room in a far corner of the structure where her father was working. He was down on one knee and his back was to them as he dragged a paintbrush across something. The smell of wood sealer was faint in the air.

"George," her mother said. "I think it's time you show Erica what you're doing."

He stood and turned toward them. "Angela, it's supposed to be a surprise. I asked you to keep her away while I finish this."

"What's going on, Daddy? What are you doing?" She moved closer until she was standing right beside him. When she saw it, her heart melted and she pressed a hand to her chest. "Oh my gosh. You made a cradle."

"Yeah." He set the brush on the open can beside him, then looked at her. His gaze narrowed and concern replaced his tender expression. "Are you all right? Is there something wrong with the baby?"

She laughed, although the sound came out a little like a sob, what with hormones and emotions clogging her throat. "I'm fine. So is the baby. Gabe told me flat out that I look terrible. I guess it's unanimous."

"I didn't say that," her father protested.

She moved closer to the sweet little bed suspended between two supports that allowed it to rock. "I can't believe you made this. It's completely wonderful."

She recognized the grain of the wood as what she'd picked up for him that day she'd run into Morgan at the building supply store. Her father had planned this very soon after he'd learned she was pregnant.

She burst into tears and covered her face with her hands. A moment later she felt strong arms come around her.

"Don't cry, honey. Your mama told me about how the baby came to be," he said gently.

"I guess I knew she couldn't keep a secret from you," she blubbered.

"No," he confirmed. "And I don't keep things from her. It's just how we are."

"It's a good way." She looked up at him. "Please try to understand why I had to have a baby this way, Daddy. I know it's not what you pictured for me, but in time I hope you'll be okay with my decision and with me."

"What?" He took her arms and held her away as he stared at her. There was shock on his face as he met her gaze. "How could you even think that? You're my daughter. My flesh and blood. And your child is, too. I love you. Nothing can change that. And I will love him—"

"Or her." His wife smiled at him.

"Right." He grinned. "I'm looking forward to holding this child. Being a grandfather. Don't you ever doubt that for a second."

"I won't. And thank you. For the cradle, too. I love it. And I love you."

She was sad that Morgan would never see this sweet little bed. When she put the baby down to sleep, she would remember her own father's love and be sorry that Morgan would never know what a good father he'd be. She would think of him and regret that he wasn't with her when they could have made a family together, something real and satisfying and wonderful.

Then she looked at her own amazing father and her mother. "Because of how I chose to conceive my child, there's no father in the picture. But he or she will have you guys. And Uncle Gabe and Aunt Mel. We're family. The baby will always be a part of my life and yours. Not like Gramps's daughter. I can't even imagine how he felt not just without support, but pressured to give his child away. This baby is loved and wanted."

Erica held out her arms and drew her mother and father into a group hug. She really did have so much to be grateful for and felt selfish for wishing she could have Morgan, too.

Erica had spent the morning with her brother and the two of them went to see Gramps. It was becoming their habit to go together. And her secret was out. The whole family knew how the baby had been conceived and assured her of their support. That was a great weight lifted from her. She needed that, because what happened with Morgan still hurt a lot.

He kept calling her cell, but she let it go to voice mail. She didn't think there was anything left to say. She would never forget the expression on his face when the baby moved, and it made her sad. The outing this morning helped a little to take her mind off what might have been.

She'd had lunch with her brother, and now she was taking her afternoon walk. Exercise was important, even near the end of her pregnancy when all she wanted to do was sit and feel like a slug. Gabe insisted on keeping her company, and now they were moving past the barn, heading for the corral and the path beyond it.

"How did you think Gramps was today?" she asked.

"Seemed about the same to me. Why?" He slid his hands into the pockets of his down vest.

"I don't know. It just seemed like there was a spark of something in his eyes. And when I put his hand on my belly and the baby moved, I think he might have smiled."

Gabe's expression was sad as he shook his head. "That's just wishful thinking, Erica. It would be great if he was still in there somewhere, but I'm not hopeful."

"Maybe if we could find his daughter..."

"To do that we need a break. Some piece of information that would send us in the right direction." He met her gaze for a moment. "If Malone could just remember the name Gramps said when he was talking about the prettiest little girl in the world..."

"I know," she agreed. "It's human nature to gloss over things.

If we knew how important a piece of information would be later, we'd pay more attention."

"Yeah." They strolled along the white fence where a couple of the horses were hanging around. "I've been meaning to ask. Have you heard anything from your attorney about the Barron Enterprises lawsuit?"

"She called the other day to let me know she'd heard from their legal department. They received the paperwork and were reviewing it. She warned me again that the process could drag on indefinitely. So, I'm glad Jordan Taylor is going to give me a job."

"Hmm."

Erica glanced up at him. "What?"

"He doesn't exactly have a reputation as a guy with a soft heart."

"I've been gone for a lot of years so I don't know much about him lately. But he's always been straight with me."

"Okay." Gabe's tone had a healthy dose of skepticism. "Then I hope he keeps his word and hires you."

"I've already filled out the employee paperwork. And I have a tentative start date." Before she could say more, her cell phone vibrated in her pocket. She fished it out and looked at the caller ID. Speaking of the devil, she thought, and she didn't mean Jordan. She stopped walking and said to her brother, "I have to take this." When Gabe nodded, she hit the green Accept button on the screen. "Peter. Why are you calling me?"

"How are you, Erica?"

The familiar deep voice used to be one that made her happy when she heard it. Not now. "I'm fine. What do you want? My attorney advised me not to speak to anyone from Barron."

"I'm just asking for a few minutes of your time," he said.

Erica noted that her brother's frown deepened. He shook his head slightly but she was curious enough not to hang up. "Okay."

"First of all I want to apologize for my father. He's not used to employees pushing back, and he lost his temper. Firing you was a knee-jerk reaction."

"Your father is a jackass." She saw Gabe grin and give her a thumb-up. "Feel free to tell him I said that."

"He has his moments." Peter cleared his throat. "The thing is, when someone's employment is terminated, there's a procedure and legal is involved. He didn't consult with the company attorneys when he took that action with you."

"So, you're saying that I have grounds for a lawsuit? Since pregnant women are part of a protected class." She wasn't really asking.

And Peter didn't directly respond to the question. "Barron Enterprises is putting together a generous severance package for you."

"A severance package," she repeated for Gabe's benefit. His eyes widened.

"Yes. I would consider it a favor if you would seriously contemplate accepting it."

"And dropping the lawsuit would be a condition." Again she wasn't asking.

"I won't deny that we would like to avoid any negative publicity." That was his lawyer voice.

"I'm sure you would." That was her "you're not going to push me around" voice.

"It's not just that, Erica." There was a sigh on the other end of the line. "I personally want to make sure you're taken care of."

"Really?" The sarcasm in that single word was laced with a good deal of anger. "Funny how it took filing a lawsuit to bring out your sensitive and caring side."

"You're not going to make this easy, are you?"

"Is there some reason I should?"

If he responded, she didn't hear, what with the blood pounding in her ears. She was shaking with anger. No matter how much she told herself it wasn't good for the baby, she couldn't suppress the feeling. In his father's office that day, her life had been thrown into chaos.

It was all about this man's new, pregnant wife, who didn't want to see Erica every day and be reminded that she'd dated her husband first. No one seemed to care that Erica was pregnant, too. She'd had a viable plan and it would have worked. But his father's power trip put her in a position of extreme stress wondering how she was going to support not just herself, but the baby she was carrying.

Finally she calmed down enough to say, "There's no way in hell I'm going to make this easy for you."

"Okay. We deserve that." There was silence for a moment. "Erica, I don't expect you to believe this, but I'm sorry things didn't work out between the two of us. That's my fault," he added quickly. "But I do care about you. And I truly do want to make sure you're going to be okay."

"You're right, Peter. I don't believe you."

"Erica, please—"

"Send the severance package to my attorney. You have her contact information."

"Seriously, Erica, I'm sincerely sorry about everything. It would mean a lot to me if you'd accept my apology."

There was a retort on the tip of her tongue, but she held it back. It occurred to her that she didn't care about this man. In fact, marrying him would have been a very big mistake. She should, in fact, be grateful to him for breaking things off. For being honest about not wanting children, although that turned out to be a lie, since he was expecting with the new wife. So, he just didn't want children with her. But feeling gratitude for his actions was a work in progress.

What she realized was that being angry over her termination was about fairness in business and a yearning for justice. But being angry on a personal level would mean she still had feelings for Peter, and that just wasn't the case.

This was a time for neutrality and generosity of spirit. "I accept your apology, Peter."

"Thank you. And I'll contact your attorney as soon as we hang up."

"Okay. Goodbye, Peter." She ended the call.

She looked at Gabe, who was grinning from ear to ear. "I guess you got the general picture of what's going on."

"The Barrons blinked. They want to pay you off. If you go to court, they're going to take a beating financially and in the media."

"That's the way I see it, too," she said.

Gabe hugged her. "You did great, sis. Way to keep your cool and tell him to go to hell, without actually saying it. Class act."

"Thank you."

She should have felt triumphant as her brother obviously did. But in reality, she felt deflated. Because there was only one person she wanted to share the news with. And she'd walked away from him. Ever since that night with Morgan she'd been wondering if she should have stayed to hear him out. Now it was too late.

That thought made her burst into tears. She looked helplessly at her brother. "I'm sorry. Hormones."

"Is it?" Gabe gave her a challenging look. "You've been in a mood. Ever since the last time you saw Morgan."

"How do you know?" Before he could answer she said, "Mom."

"Something happened with him."

"I don't want to discuss it."

"I don't need a blow-by-blow," Gabe said. "But there's something I do know."

"What?"

"You care about him. And he cares about you. Before you ask how I know that, it's obvious. Why else would he volunteer to be your labor coach?" Gabe shrugged as if it was a no-brainer. "I could see it that first night you met him at DJ's Deluxe. It's why I got so ticked off. You had stars in your eyes, and he had that look a guy gets when he's met a special woman. I don't know him so I didn't like it."

"Really?" She brushed the moisture from her cheeks. "But it wasn't—"

"Don't try to rationalize. It's a big brother thing. Plus, I wasn't subtle," he admitted. "But I *was* wrong. You two care about each other, and you need to talk to him."

That startled her. "Who are you and what have you done with my brother?"

"I deserve that." He looked sheepish. "Shouldn't a person be allowed to change his mind?"

"Of course. I'm just wondering what changed yours."

"I talked to Morgan after the baby shower. I'm a pretty good judge of people and I believed him, that he cares about you," he said. "And I trust your judgment." He leaned over and kissed her forehead. "You know your own mind and you're smart. I love you, sis. And I just want you to be happy."

"Okay—" Emotion choked off her words.

He pointed at her. "Don't you dare cry. It drives guys crazy because we can't fix it. So, just stop."

"I love you, too. And I'll try—" Who was she trying to kid? There was no way that was going to happen. She burst into tears again, and he pulled her in for a hug.

"It's okay. Just talk to Morgan. Do as your big brother says, and everything will be all right."

She wanted to believe that. The problem was, she didn't think Morgan would give her another chance. And she couldn't blame him.

CHAPTER FIFTEEN

MORGAN GLANCED INTO the office in the big house where Neal Dalton was sitting at his desk, scrutinizing the ranch spreadsheets on his computer.

The door was open but he knocked on it and said, "Dad, can I talk to you?"

His father looked up, then removed his reading glasses and set them down on some file folders. "Have a seat."

Morgan closed the door, then walked over and sat in one of the chairs. After taking a big breath he said, "I screwed up with Erica."

"And you're here because out of everyone you know I've had the most experience screwing up?"

"Look, I'm not here to bust you about that—"

"It was a joke. Guess I'll have to work on my delivery." The man sighed. "What did you do?"

Morgan told him about kissing Erica. "Everything was fine and then I felt the baby move. It was awesome, Dad. But it hit me. There's a real baby in there. That sounds so dumb, but it's the honest to God truth."

"I get it. Believe me."

"That changed everything. It wasn't just about the two of us. There's another life involved, and I needed to take that into consideration before moving forward, before, you know—"

"Yeah. So what did you do then?" his dad asked. "After you felt the baby?"

"Nothing. I froze."

Neal looked puzzled. "I'm not seeing the problem, son."

"Erica jumped to a conclusion. She took my reaction to mean that I didn't want her because of the baby. But I just needed a minute to process." He met his father's gaze. "She walked out without giving me a chance to explain why I was hesitating."

"Okay." The other man nodded thoughtfully. "I don't think this is a screw-up. More a misunderstanding. When did it happen?"

"A couple of days ago. I've tried calling her, but it goes straight to voice mail." He lifted his hands, a gesture of pure frustration. "I don't know what to do."

"You have two choices, son. You can let her go—"

"No," Morgan said firmly. That response came straight from the gut, by way of his heart. "That's not an option."

"You're sure?" His dad studied him. "You haven't known her very long."

"I'm absolutely sure. Don't ask me why—"

"Never crossed my mind," the other man said. "With your mom I knew pretty much from the moment I met her that she was the one. Holt proposed to Amanda pretty fast. It might take us Dalton men a while to find the right woman, but when we do, we move to seal the deal right away. But—"

"What?" Morgan asked sharply.

"That means you'll be a father right away. I know that gave you pause not so long ago. And you're right. It's not just you and her to consider. There's another life involved. If you can't accept that fully, best back off now. Otherwise there's a lot of heartache down the road."

"I hear you, Dad. I can't let her go." He shrugged as if to say he just knew. "So, how do I get her back?"

"You need to find a way to show her you're all in. For her *and* the baby. A big gesture. When you figure that out, you drive over there and show her you really mean it."

A gesture. All in for her and the baby. Morgan's mind was racing, then suddenly he had an idea and it was perfect.

He met his father's gaze, then stood and headed for the door. "Can you spare me for the rest of the day? I've got some stuff to do."

"Of course. And Morgan?"

He stopped with his hand on the doorknob and turned to look at his father. "Yeah?"

"Good luck. If there's anything else I can do, you only have to ask."

"No offense, Dad, but I hope I won't need you." Morgan smiled. If there was one positive thing to come out of this, it was getting back a relationship with his father. "Thanks, Dad."

After the talk, Morgan jumped in his truck and headed downtown. He needed to purchase two things, and the first one was easy, what with just buying the highest consumer rated and most expensive one on the market. The second item took longer. Part of the reason was him calling Erica's cell every half hour to let her know he was picking her up for childbirth class later. And every half hour he got her voice mail. His guts were in a knot, and the uncertainty was killing him.

It was early, but he couldn't wait any longer to see her. He drove to the Ambling A and went up to the brightly lighted porch. He rang the bell, then nervously waited for someone to answer.

When the door was opened, he was surprised to see Gabe Abernathy. In his mind he'd been running possible speeches to Erica and was unprepared to see anyone else. "What are you doing here?"

"The better question is why are *you* here?"

"I came to pick up Erica." Morgan braced for hostilities. He planned to stand his ground even though he knew the Abernathys didn't trust him. They were just going to have to suck it up and get used to him being around. Oddly enough, her brother didn't look hostile.

"Did she know you were coming to get her?" Gabe's amusement disappeared.

"We have class tonight. And I left messages that I'd be here." Morgan glanced down for a moment. "Would you please let her know?"

"I would be happy to except she left already."

The words felt like a punch to the gut, and Morgan hadn't braced himself for that. "Where did she go?"

"I heard her tell my mom that she was going to her class. Doesn't she usually pick you up?"

"Yeah." But that was before.

"Maybe there's a miscommunication and she thought you were meeting her at the class."

"No. But we will be meeting." Morgan touched his fingers to the brim of his Stetson. "Thanks, Gabe. Sorry to bother you."

"No problem. And, Morgan?"

He stopped and looked over his shoulder. "Yeah?"

"For what it's worth, I'm rooting for you, Coach."

"Thanks."

Morgan wouldn't have thought anything could make him smile, but that did. It helped knowing her brother was on his side, and right this minute he was in no mood to question what had happened to make him change his mind. His focus was on making his case to the person who mattered most to him.

He drove the now familiar route to the Women's Health Center and realized this was the first time he'd come alone. He didn't much like that and hoped it wasn't a bad omen for the rest of his life. When he arrived at his destination, he went up and down the rows of cars until he found Erica's. For a desperate man in need of some hope, he took the empty space beside her SUV as a good sign.

He exited his vehicle, then opened the rear passenger door of his truck, removed the brand-new infant car seat and headed for the building's lobby and the elevator.

His heart was racing as he walked down the carpeted hallway and into the conference room. Carla was there at the lectern. The other three expectant couples sat at the U-shaped tables. When he walked in, all conversation ceased and everyone stared at him. He only had eyes for Erica.

He walked over to her. "Hi. I'd have been here sooner but I stopped at your place to pick you up. Gabe said you'd already left."

Eyes wide as saucers, she nodded. "I didn't think you wanted to do this with me anymore."

"You thought wrong." He set the carrier on the table in front of her. "We're going to need one of these for the baby."

She stared at it for several seconds, then ran a finger over the small harness. "I don't know what to say."

"It's easy to hook up," he said. "Just takes seconds. An indicator goes from red to green when it's installed correctly." He couldn't tell whether she liked it. "Unlike me, it's idiot proof. But if you want something else, we can return it."

"No," she said quickly. "It's fantastic. The one I wanted. But I don't understand. What does this mean? You keep saying 'we,' but—"

It was time for part two of his screw-up redemption plan. "Erica, I have a million questions about how to be a good father, but zero doubts about you and me."

"But I thought the other night— You made it clear you didn't want this."

He shook his head. "You assumed that and then walked out before we could talk about it."

"You're not wrong." Her hazel eyes were huge as she looked at him, then glanced at the others in the room who were watching this conversation unfold with undisguised curiosity. "But you want to talk about this *now*?"

"Yes. I've waited too long already." He sat in the chair beside hers. "I'm not bailing on you. Not walking away from you. Not now, not ever. I want to be a father to this baby."

"Really?" Her expression was hopeful, but she didn't seem convinced he was all in.

"Yes, really. I've had feelings for you since the first moment I saw you. I was falling for you before I even realized you were pregnant. Love at first sight." He couldn't believe he hadn't put his feelings into words before now. And it was way past time. "I love you, Erica. I love the baby you're carrying. And that makes it my baby, too. I want to be your husband, and I very much want to be his or her father."

"Morgan—" Her voice caught and she swallowed. "I don't know what to say."

"That's because I haven't asked you anything yet." He took the velvet jeweler's box from the front pocket of his jeans. He opened it to reveal the ring he'd picked out at the jewelry store. Angelique, the jewelry designer, had assured him this was the one that would dazzle any woman. He needed the dazzle and a little razzle to convince Erica he was worth taking a chance on.

So, he went down on one knee and said, "Will you make me the happiest man on the planet and marry me? Make a family with me? In case there's any question, the only correct answer is yes."

"Oh, Morgan—"

He waited for her to finish that statement, then couldn't stand it. "Is that an 'Oh, Morgan, I wish you hadn't asked'? Or, 'Oh, Morgan, that's a big fat yes'?"

"It's an 'Oh, Morgan, I love you so much' followed by a heartfelt and unqualified 'absolutely yes.' Nothing would make me happier than to marry you and be a family."

"Thank you, God." He stood and pulled her up and into his arms. The baby kicked just then, and the miracle of it took his breath away. This time there was no doubt or hesitation when he put his hand on her belly. He smiled into her eyes. "I believe our daughter approves."

"Oh? You think we're having a girl?"

"There are five boys in my family. Six with Robby. We're definitely having a girl."

She smiled tenderly. "You are a remarkable man, Morgan Dalton. And I am the luckiest woman in the world. I love you so much."

"I love you more."

And he kissed her, trying to prove just how deeply he meant those words. When they finally came up for air, the expectant dads shook his hand and their wives were sniffling. All of them blamed hormones, but Carla was brushing tears off her cheeks, too, and she wasn't pregnant. The fact of the matter was that everyone loved a happily ever after.

EPILOGUE

THE FIRST SATURDAY in November, Erica was in her childhood bedroom getting ready for her wedding. She and Morgan wanted to be married before the baby came. Her dream of marriage then baby was coming true after all, though not in the most traditional sense.

Her dress was ivory silk with a lace bodice and long sleeves. The skirt was empire and fell over her tummy and gracefully to the floor. A simple lace veil trailed down her back, secured by a comb in her hair.

Mel, her maid of honor, was fussing with it, making sure the material lay perfectly. She was wearing a lacy, tea-length royal blue dress with a flirty, flared skirt. When she straightened, they stood side by side and looked in the mirror together. And grinned.

"You look beautiful," her almost sister-in-law said.

"Being completely happy does that to a girl."

"This whole bridal thing really suits you."

"When it's right, it's right." She sighed. "With Morgan it was love at first sight. Somehow I knew I would love him forever and beyond."

Mel nodded. "I mean, how can you not be crazy about a guy who proposes with a very impressive diamond ring in one hand and an infant carrier in the other?"

Erica laughed. "He's very special and I'm a lucky girl."

Mel took her hands and squeezed them. "You so deserve the best, and Morgan is that for you."

There was a knock on the door just before her mother opened it. When she saw her daughter, her expression turned achingly tender as her eyes glistened with tears. "Oh, sweetie, you look so beautiful."

"Thank you, Mama."

"And you're not the least bit nervous."

"No room for nerves. Not when I'm so full of happiness. I can't wait to be Mrs. Morgan Dalton."

"Okay, then. Let's get this show on the road. I came up here to let you know the car just arrived to take us to the church." Her mother headed to the door. "Your father and Gabe are already there waiting for us."

"Mama, just real quick before we go—"

"What, sweetie?"

Erica moved close and pulled her into a hug. "I just want to thank you for making today happen. For putting up with me through good and bad. And for being the best mom in the world." She pressed a hand to her belly. "If I'm half as good as you are, I'll do right by this little one."

"You're going to be a wonderful mother. I love you." Angela smiled but her mouth trembled for just a moment. "You're going to make me cry and ruin my makeup."

"I'm sorry, but I needed to say it."

Over the years there'd been ups and downs in their relationship. But the bonds between them were stronger now than ever.

"Okay, ladies," her mom said, "let's get moving."

Erica followed the other two women down the stairs. The house was decorated with flowers for a small reception following the ceremony. Her mother had hired Brittany to handle the event, and Erica already knew that woman could make a feast out of bread and water.

She picked up her bouquet from the box on the entryway table. It was made up of greens and white roses with several orange ones to add a pop of fall color. Mel took her own bouquet, a smaller version of Erica's and they left the house, then stepped into the waiting town car.

A short time later the three of them arrived at the small white church with its graceful, elegant spire. It was charming and traditional and completely perfect. In the vestibule Brittany was waiting for them, looking tall and chic in a pale pink sheath dress with her hair smoothly pulled back into a side bun. Robby was by her side, dapper in his little dark suit and tie, and holding a pillow with two rings. They were symbolic since Morgan's best man had the real ones. And then she saw her father, so handsome in his black suit and tie.

"Hi, Daddy."

"Baby girl—" He stopped and swallowed. "I'm not sure I can give you away."

She moved closer, then stood on tiptoe and kissed his cheek. "You're not. You're just relieved of duty. I have a good man who will be there for me every day, every step of the way."

"I know. Otherwise I wouldn't be able to part with you."

"Okay," Brittany said, taking charge as she gave them all a critical once-over. "Believe it or not, so far everything has gone off without a hitch."

"Of course," Erica said. "You wouldn't accept anything less."

"Darn right." She gave Erica a final approving look. "You ready?"

"Absolutely." She grinned at the boy who would very soon be her nephew. "Robby Dalton, you look awfully handsome."

"Grandma says it runs in the family." The boy gave Brittany a wary look. "My dad and Uncle Morgan told me I have to do everything *she* says."

"They're right." But Brittany smiled at him. "You're going to do great."

Just then the vestibule doors opened, and Gabe walked in. When he saw Erica, a tender look of approval slid into his eyes. But when his gaze settled on his fiancée, he was speechless. Finally he said to her, "Next summer this will be us."

Mel blew him a kiss. "I can't wait."

"Hold that thought, you two. It's time to do *this* wedding,"

Brittany said. "The groom's mother is already seated. Gabe, escort your mother down the aisle."

He held out his arm and Angela took it. The doors remained open when he walked her down to the front row.

"You ready, Robby?"

The boy looked up at Brittany. "Yes, ma'am."

The organist in the choir loft started playing the traditional "Wedding March," and Robby confidently walked down the aisle, followed by Mel.

"You're up, bride." Brittany hugged her quickly, then brushed away a tear. "You look radiant. Go be happy."

"Thank you. For everything."

Erica took her father's arm, and he put his hand over hers as they matched their steps to the music. She smiled at people as she passed them on her way to the altar. Her groom stood there with his father by his side. Morgan had asked him to be best man, and his mother had cried more than a few happy tears over that.

Then she looked only at Morgan, and he was looking back at her as if she was the most beautiful woman in the world. He sure made her feel that way. In his dark suit and royal blue silk tie, the man defined the word *handsome*, but he was and always would be her cowboy. Eagerly they said their vows and made forever promises that felt so very right.

After pictures, everyone came back to the Ambling A for the reception. Furniture had been moved out of the living and great rooms and tables set up. There were white tablecloths and flowers and a cocktail hour before dinner.

At the family table Malone looked a little uncomfortable being a guest instead of doing the cooking. But Erica had insisted he enjoy her wedding, too. And he'd pronounced the catered food not bad.

There was a dance area on the patio where they shared their first dance as husband and wife. Morgan held out his hand, and she put hers in his palm, knowing somehow that this would never get old.

Afterward he led her back to the family table, where Gabe and Mel were sitting with her parents and Grandpa Alex. She took the seat beside Malone, who she swore was trying to hide that he was brushing away a tear.

"Sure do wish Josiah could be here to see how pretty his great-granddaughter is."

"I believe he's here in spirit." She leaned her head against his shoulder for a moment.

Then the DJ started talking. "The bride requested a song, a real oldie. It's a tradition at Abernathy weddings. Her great-grandfather, Josiah Abernathy, had it played at his wedding to Cora. Her grandfather did the same as did her parents, George and Angela. So, without further ado, here we go."

The strains of the music began and when the lyrics kicked in, all the guests began to sing along.

"Daisy, Daisy, give me your answer do—" They finished with a rousing, "But you'll look sweet upon the seat of a bicycle built for two."

"Holy cow." Malone sat up straight and sounded very excited. "Holy cow, that's it!"

Erica had never heard that tone from the normally reserved, unflappable man. "What's it?"

"The name I couldn't remember. The name Josiah said when he was talking about the prettiest little girl in the world. It was Daisy."

Erica let that sink in for a moment, then she quivered with excitement. She looked at Gabe and Mel, whose expressions mirrored her own. "Call me crazy, but I don't think he was talking about a girlfriend."

Her brother nodded. "Unless I miss my guess, that's his daughter's name. Her adoptive name."

Erica gripped her new husband's hand. "And I bet Gramps had that song at his wedding as a way to keep his daughter a part of him and his family in any way he could."

"This may be the piece of information we needed," Gabe said. "I'll clue Amanda in right away and we can continue the search." He and Melanie went to find her.

"Way to go, Malone," Erica said.

"Glad I could help. Finally. I need a drink." He got up and went to the bar, and the rest of her family followed.

So, Erica was alone with her new husband and grinned at him. "Do I know how to clear a table, or what?"

"It's your superpower." He smiled, then kissed her.

She was breathless when he stopped. "I aim to please."

"So that song is a family tradition?"

"It is. And I wanted all the Abernathy customs today, because we didn't start out in the most traditional way."

"That song worked in more ways than one." Then he put his hand on her abdomen and smiled at the baby's movement. "And you'd look sweet anywhere, but we need something more family friendly than a bicycle built for two."

"I like the way you think."

It took a very special man to so completely embrace raising a child he didn't make, and her heart was full of emotion. "I love the man you are. You have a heart as big as the Montana sky, Morgan Dalton, and you really stepped up. You'll be an incredible daddy."

"I had no choice," he said. "I made a promise to you. And then I fell in love." He kissed her softly, then met her gaze. "And this cowboy always keeps his promises."

* * * * *

Her Not-So-Little Secret

Brenda Harlen

HEART

Home is where the heart is.

Brenda Harlen is a former attorney who once had the privilege of appearing before the Supreme Court of Canada. The practice of law taught her a lot about the world and reinforced her determination to become a writer—because in fiction, she could promise a happy ending! Now she is an award-winning, RITA® Award–nominated, nationally bestselling author of more than fifty titles for Harlequin. You can keep up-to-date with Brenda on Facebook and Twitter, or through her website, brendaharlen.com.

Books by Brenda Harlen

Match Made in Haven
Captivated by the Cowgirl
Countdown to Christmas

Montana Mavericks: Brothers & Broncos
The Maverick's Christmas Secret

Montana Mavericks: The Real Cowboys of Bronco Heights
Dreaming of a Christmas Cowboy

Montana Mavericks: What Happened to Beatrix?
A Cowboy's Christmas Carol

Montana Mavericks: Six Brides for Six Brothers
Maverick Christmas Surprise

Montana Mavericks: The Lonelyhearts Ranch
Bring Me a Maverick for Christmas!

Visit the Author Profile page
at millsandboon.com.au for more titles.

Dear Reader,

It's the worst possible time for Sierra Hart to meet the man of her dreams, so it's a good thing that local attorney Deacon Parrish *isn't* the man of her dreams. To the contrary, he's arrogant and exasperating, incessantly flirtatious, annoyingly charming, and his smiles make her knees weak.

Okay, so maybe he could be the man of her dreams if she'd met him at a different place and time. But here and now, he's simply a complication she doesn't need—no matter how much she might want him.

Deacon Parrish isn't looking for happily-ever-after. Marriage and kids? No, thank you. No way. But flirting with the sexy new ADA? That's a plan he can get on board with. And the fact that she's going to be in town for only a limited time guarantees neither of them will get too attached.

So why, when he learns that Sierra is pregnant, doesn't he run far and fast in the opposite direction? Why does he, instead, suddenly find himself imagining a future with this woman?

As a former attorney, I occasionally find myself itching to get back into the courtroom—if only in my stories—which is one of the reasons I had so much fun writing Sierra and Deacon's story. I hope you have just as much fun reading it.

All the best,

Brenda

PS: Please check out my website, brendaharlen.com, for a complete list of Match Made in Haven titles and upcoming releases.

For Lauren,
who has always marched to the beat of her own drum
and has always made me proud.

CHAPTER ONE

THERE WAS ONE box of Frosted Flakes on the shelf.

Which shouldn't have mattered in the least to Sierra Hart, because she already had cereal in her cart.

The spoon-size shredded wheat (tucked between the loaf of twelve-grain bread and a package of low-fat, low-sodium crackers) was undoubtedly a healthier choice, and she was trying to make healthier choices. Over the past few weeks, she'd willingly reduced her intake of sodium and fat (*goodbye* convenient microwavable meals) and completely cut out alcohol (*au revoir* cabernet sauvignon), but her sweet tooth continued to protest the lack of brownies and cookies and ice cream.

And now, apparently sugary cereals that reminded her of her childhood, too.

Frosted Flakes had been her breakfast of choice while she was growing up in Summerlin South, a suburb of Las Vegas—or at least after her fourteenth birthday. Prior to that, her favorite morning meal had been homemade breakfast burritos: scrambled eggs and crumbled bacon wrapped up with shredded cheese and tangy salsa inside a warm tortilla. Whenever Sierra had a test at school or a basketball game after, her mom insisted that she start her day with a home-cooked breakfast to fuel her brain and her body.

She shrugged off the memories. It wasn't so easy to shrug

off the ache in her heart that, sixteen years later, had faded but not disappeared.

It was when her brother had come home that she'd started eating cold cereal in the mornings before rushing out of the house to catch the bus for school. Weekends usually meant toaster waffles, and sometimes Nick sat at the table with her, always with a textbook of some kind at his elbow despite having taken a hiatus from college.

He'd grumbled only a little about buying the sugary cereal for her when she was a teen, but she imagined he'd have a lot more to say if he knew she still craved it now.

But why should she feel guilty about the occasional indulgence when the other items in her cart were healthy?

When she'd lived in Las Vegas—and been on a partnership track at Bane & Associates—she hadn't had the time to cook. And with countless takeout options available, there had been little incentive to bother. But her new job in the Haven District Attorney's Office had, so far, afforded her a more regular schedule, and so she'd started to prepare her own meals.

At first, she'd been more resigned than enthused about tackling that particular chore, but she didn't really have much of a choice as dining options in town were severely limited. There was the Sunnyside Diner, famous for its all-day breakfast and not much else; Jo's Pizza, which offered wings and some simple pasta dishes alongside its namesake specialty; Diggers' Bar & Grill, a popular choice for those wanting standard roadhouse fare; and The Home Station, whose menu boasted creative and upscale cuisine.

Of course, even in Vegas there had been times when she wasn't in the mood for takeout and opted to pour herself a bowl of cereal instead. And quite often it was Frosted Flakes.

She started to reach for the box—

"Never go shopping on an empty stomach."

She drew her hand back and turned to the shopper who'd drawn her cart up alongside Sierra's. The other woman had long dark hair tied in a ponytail, pretty blue-gray eyes and a warm smile.

"That's what my sister tells me, anyway," the stranger confided. "But since I got pregnant, I'm constantly hungry, which makes it impossible to follow her advice."

"Um...congratulations?" Sierra finally ventured.

The expectant mother laughed. "And now you're wondering why you ever decided to move to this town where people overshare personal information in the breakfast foods aisle at the local grocery store," she guessed.

"I don't think it's just the breakfast foods aisle," Sierra said. "The guy working behind the deli counter told me all about his upcoming knee replacement surgery while he was slicing my oven-roasted turkey."

"That would've been Dustin Hobbs," the other woman said, reaching for a container of steel-cut oats and dropping it into her cart. "He's been grumbling about his bad knee for years."

"Since 2010—the year he carried three passes over the goal line for the state champion football team?" Sierra guessed.

"Sounds about right." A box of Corn Pops joined the oats. "You're Sierra Hart, aren't you?"

"Have we met?" Sierra was certain they hadn't, though the other woman did look vaguely familiar to her.

"Not formally, but our paths sort of crossed at April's House last weekend. I'm Sky Gilmore—Sky *Kelly*," she quickly amended, offering a smile along with her hand.

Though Sierra had only been in town two weeks, that was long enough to have heard about the Gilmores. In addition to being one of the founding families of Haven, they were owners and operators of the Circle G, one of the most successful cattle ranches in all of Nevada.

She'd also heard about the historic feud between the Gilmores and the Blakes, the gist of which was that both families had come to Nevada to settle the same parcel of land more than a hundred and fifty years earlier. Rather than admit that they'd been duped, they agreed to split the property. Everett Gilmore, having arrived first, took the prime grazing land for his cattle, leaving Samuel Blake with the less hospitable terrain. As a result, Crooked Creek Ranch—and the Blakes—struggled for a lot of years before gold and silver were discovered in their hills.

Although both families had ended up ridiculously wealthy,

the animosity between them had remained for a long time. It was only in recent years—and as a result of a handful of reunions and romances—that the Gilmores and Blakes had finally managed to bury the hatchet.

"Do you work at April's House?" Sierra asked, shaking the woman's proffered hand.

"I'm a volunteer counselor," Sky responded.

"Tough job," she noted. And because Sierra had some experience of her own working with abused women and their children, she felt an immediate kinship with—and a lot of respect for—the other woman.

"I'm sure being an ADA isn't a walk in the park."

"It's just a temporary gig," Sierra told her.

"And your stay in Haven?"

"Also temporary."

Sky's smile was knowing. "That's what my husband said, too, when he came to Haven. Three years ago."

"What did I say?" a masculine voice asked from behind her.

Sky's smile was quick and warm as she turned her head. "That your stay in Haven was only temporary."

Obviously this was the aforementioned husband, and Sierra couldn't help but think that the counselor had lucked out when she fell in love with the six-foot-tall, dark-haired, hazel-eyed man standing beside her now.

"How was I to know that I would fall in love—with Haven almost as much as you?" he said.

Spoken by another guy, the response might have made Sierra want to gag, but not only did Sky's husband sound absolutely sincere, the way he looked at his wife when he said the words made her heart sigh.

"Well, I have no intention of falling in love with the town—or with you," Sierra said lightly.

Sky laughed. "Jake, this is Sierra Hart—the new ADA. Sierra, my husband—Jake Kelly."

"*Temporary* ADA," Sierra clarified.

Now Jake grinned. "And what do you think of Haven so far?"

"It has its charms," she noted.

"But being able to make a quick stop at the grocery store isn't one of them," he warned.

"So I've discovered."

"For the first few months that Jake was in town, he went to Battle Mountain to buy his groceries so that he wouldn't have to make small talk with the locals," Sky told her.

"Something to consider," Sierra said, only half joking.

"Which completely backfired on him," the other woman continued. "Because that's how he happened upon me, stranded on the side of the road one day."

"And while I don't mind strolling down memory lane now and again, I'm sure the ADA is more interested in finishing her grocery shopping," Jake said.

"You're right," his wife acknowledged. Then to Sierra she said, "I'll bore you with the story over coffee sometime."

"I'll look forward to it," Sierra said, a little surprised to realize that she meant it.

"It was nice to meet you," Jake said, nudging his wife along.

"And both of you."

Sierra watched them make their way down the aisle, walking side by side, so close that their shoulders were almost touching. They seemed completely in sync with one another, like her brother and sister-in-law, and Sierra's heart sighed again, more than a little wistfully, as they disappeared from sight.

Maybe one day she'd be lucky enough to meet someone who looked at her the way Jake looked at Sky and Nick looked at Whitney, but that was a dream she'd put on the back burner for at least the next seven and a half months. The move, the job and swearing off romantic entanglements had all been her choices, and while she didn't have any regrets, she couldn't deny that she yearned for something more.

"Excuse me," a deep voice said, at the same time an arm reached past Sierra to pluck a box of cereal from the shelf.

Not just *any* box but the *last* box of Frosted Flakes.

The very same one that she'd been eyeing.

"Hey," she protested.

The cereal-stealer turned his head. His dark blue gaze locked with hers, and Sierra felt a frisson of awareness shiver down her spine.

Well, *damn*. She certainly hadn't expected *that*.

"Is there a problem?" he asked, sounding completely unconcerned about the possibility there might be.

She swallowed and tightened her grip on the handle of her cart. "Yes, there's a problem," she told him. "You took my Frosted Flakes."

Of course, the bigger problem was that Sierra seemed to be attracted to men who inevitably ended up trampling her heart, and she already knew that this was one she should walk away from—as far and as fast as her legs could carry her.

Unfortunately, her feet seemed glued to the floor and her brain stubbornly determined to battle over a box of breakfast cereal, even as her eyes enjoyed a leisurely perusal of the hottest guy she'd crossed paths with in the fourteen days she'd been in Haven. He had slightly tousled dark blond hair and a squarish jaw covered with golden stubble that, on another man, might have looked scruffy, but definitely worked for this one. He wore a dark brown bomber-style leather jacket, unzipped, over a blue sweatshirt, faded Levi's and brown cowboy boots. His shoulders were broad, his hips narrow, his legs long.

"*Your* Frosted Flakes?" he echoed, clearly amused by her declaration.

She yanked her errant gaze back to his mouthwateringly handsome face. "I was just about to reach for that box of cereal."

"Were you really?" he challenged. "Because you stood in front of it for at least three minutes without making a move to pick it up."

"I doubt it was three minutes," she said indignantly.

"*At least* three minutes," he said again.

"Which still doesn't give you the right to elbow your way past me to take it."

"I said *excuse me*," he reminded her.

As if being polite justified his actions.

"A gentleman would give up the box of cereal," she said, her tone both piqued and prim.

He grinned, and her knees turned to jelly. *Dammit*.

"You're definitely new in town," he decided. "No one from around here would mistake me for a gentleman."

She could see it now, in the devilish glint in those blue eyes. He was a bad boy. The kind a mother warned her daughters about. Not just dangerous but dangerously tempting.

Sierra knew that she should walk away—it was just a box of cereal!—but she decided to give it one last shot.

"You're really not going to give me the cereal?"

"I can't," he said, sounding almost regretful as he shook his head. "But I can give you some advice—add a couple tablespoons of sugar to a bowl of cornflakes."

"Why can't *you* add sugar to a bowl of cornflakes?" she challenged.

"I don't have to." He grinned and held up the box in his hand. "I've got Frosted Flakes."

She scowled, annoyed that his smug arrogance somehow added to his appeal. "I hope your milk is sour."

"That's harsh," he chided. "But the truth is, the cereal isn't for me. I've got company coming tonight and they have very specific breakfast demands."

"They?"

She didn't realize she'd spoken aloud until she saw his lips twitch, as if he was fighting against a smile.

"Twins," he said, with a wink.

She shouldn't have been surprised. Men like this one always had women clamoring for their attention, and he was obviously willing to give it—and to more than one at a time.

Rather than continue this pointless conversation, she decided to relinquish her claim to the cereal and move on.

He deliberately stepped into her path as she started to push her cart past him.

"I'd be happy to share the cereal, if you wanted to come over for breakfast. Better yet," he said, with another wink, "you could *stay* for breakfast."

Her gaze narrowed in response to the blatant innuendo even as her hormones stirred with interest. "Aren't you going to be busy with the twins?"

"Tonight and tomorrow, yes," he agreed. "But my schedule's wide open next weekend."

A not-at-all tempting offer, because as much as she had a weakness for bad boys, she had more important things to focus on while she was in Haven. "In your dreams, cowboy."

"I'm not a cowboy," he said, refusing to take the hint. "I'm a lawyer."

"Let me guess—" she zeroed in on the logo emblazoned on the front of his sweatshirt "—Columbia Law?"

"That's right." He pulled a business card out of his pocket and offered it to her.

Deacon Parrish
Attorney at Law
Katelyn Davidson & Associates
355 Page Street
Haven, NV

"In case you ever need a lawyer—" he flashed that devastating smile again "—or breakfast."

"That's not going to happen," she said, ignoring the card in his outstretched hand and steering around him.

"Legal troubles or breakfast?"

He called out the question as she walked away.

Sierra forced herself not to look back.

"Neither."

CHAPTER TWO

DEACON PARRISH WAS a man on a mission—and a very tight schedule. He didn't have time to waste flirting with an attractive stranger in The Trading Post, but there had been something about the stunning brunette in the cereal aisle that had piqued his immediate interest and encouraged him to linger.

Haven wasn't such a small town that everyone knew everyone else, but it was a safe bet that he'd crossed paths with all the other residents at one point or another in his almost twenty-eight years. Which meant that this woman was either a visitor or newcomer, because he'd never seen her before. Maybe it was cliché, but he was certain he would have remembered.

He guessed that she was average height for a woman—but that was the only ordinary thing about her. In deference to the frigid January weather, she'd been wearing a long coat—black wool—and black knee-high boots with a modest heel. Beneath the coat, she wore a slim-fitting skirt the color of ripe cranberries and a matching jacket buttoned over a snowy-white blouse with a deep V neckline.

She was overdressed for grocery shopping, which suggested to Deacon that she'd come from work and led him to speculate as to what profession would require her to work on a Saturday. Real estate was the first thing that came to mind, and he'd heard that The Ruby Realty Team had recently hired a new agent. Perhaps she'd had an open house earlier that afternoon and was now picking up a few essentials on her way home. Or maybe she had a list of ingredients to cook a meal for someone special.

His gaze had automatically gone to the fingers curled around the handle of her shopping cart then. She wore what looked like a college ring on her right hand, but her left hand was bare. There was no sparkling diamond to herald an engagement and no wedding band to indicate a more permanent commitment.

He'd exhaled a grateful sigh of relief. Because Deacon didn't have any particular type when it came to the women he dated—blondes, brunettes, redheads, short, tall, skinny, curvy—but he did have two hard and fast rules when it came to dating. The first was to never make a move on another man's woman.

Once that concern had been alleviated, he'd shifted his attention back to her face, admiring the flawless skin, dark eyes fringed by darker lashes, high cheekbones and glossy pink lips. She was focused on the shelves as if choosing a breakfast cereal was a matter of great internal debate.

Deacon experienced no such indecision. He'd gone into The Trading Post knowing exactly what he was after, but when he reached past her for the familiar blue box with the tiger mascot on the front, he'd somehow started an unexpectedly provocative conversation that seemed to be about a lot more than Frosted Flakes.

Until she'd abruptly shut him down.

Perhaps she would have been more amenable to his flirtation if he'd relinquished the cereal, but that wasn't an option.

Not if he wanted peace in the morning.

And while he knew why *he* needed the cereal, as he made his way toward home, he found himself wondering why *she'd* been after the perennial kids' favorite and acknowledging that the absence of a ring didn't mean the absence of a family. Maybe she had kids at home who would kick and scream when she returned home empty-handed.

And if she had kids, she was off-limits to him. Because that was his second dating rule: no women with children.

It wasn't that he didn't like kids. In fact, he was crazy about his brother's two little girls. But aside from the fact that kids were an inevitable complication in any relationship—and potential collateral damage when a romance didn't work out—he simply wasn't dad material.

Maybe he sometimes wished it wasn't true, but there was simply too much of his own father in him to ever let himself believe otherwise. And yeah, it sucked that he still carried some emotional scars from the man who'd walked out on his family two decades earlier, but he couldn't deny that he did. And he knew that the only way to ensure that his kid never hated him the way he'd hated Dwayne Parrish was to never have a kid—or pretend to be a dad to someone else's.

Because Deacon wasn't the only one who'd been scarred by his dad's "parenting." His half brother Connor had suffered even more, being the preferred target of Dwayne's drunken fury—and deliberately putting himself in front of Deacon on the rare occasions that the man lashed out at his own son.

It was a testament to his brother's character that Connor had managed to turn his life around and not only let go of the past but embrace his future. Or maybe it was a testament to his feelings for the woman he'd married. Whatever the reason, Connor had been able to fall in love and have a family, and perhaps that example should have given Deacon hope that he might someday do the same. But while the brothers had both suffered at the hands of Dwayne Parrish, there was one crucial difference between them—only Deacon carried the man's blood in his veins.

It was a fact he tried not to think about too often, and he pushed it out of his mind now as he turned onto Sherwood Park Drive. As he drew closer to home, he saw the deputy sheriff's personal vehicle parked in his driveway.

Damn, he was late.

He'd no sooner pulled up alongside the curb and shifted his Jeep into Park when the back door of his brother's truck flew open and two little girls spilled out.

"Unca Dunca! Unca Dunca!" They raced toward him, blue eyes sparkling and wide smiles on their faces.

He set the bag from the grocery store on the hood of his SUV and crouched to catch the twins in his arms.

"Can we build a snowman?" Piper asked.

"Can we have hot choc'ate?" Poppy wanted to know.

"Can we watch a movie?"

"Can we have p'za?"

"Can we—"

"Can you give Uncle Deacon a minute to catch his breath?" the girls' dad interjected to suggest dryly.

"I'm good," Deacon said, rising to his feet with a smile on his face and a child propped on each hip—a more cumbersome task than usual as both girls were bundled up in snowsuits and winter boots.

"You're late," his brother admonished.

"Three minutes," he guesstimated.

The same amount of time he'd stood watching the stranger contemplate her cereal options.

Piper and Poppy lavished him with hugs and kisses then wriggled to be set down again. Deacon obliged, and they immediately threw themselves onto the snow-covered ground and began making snow angels.

"Two more minutes and I might not have had time to come in for a cup of the hot chocolate that you're going to make for the girls," Connor remarked.

"I don't know that Regan would approve of them having hot chocolate before dinner," Deacon said, picking up the grocery bag again and fishing his keys out of his jacket pocket.

"Which is why they love coming to Uncle Deacon's house—because he doesn't follow Mommy's rules."

"I follow some of them," he protested. "But not so many that I risk losing my 'Fun Uncle' title."

"It's not as if you've got a lot of competition," Connor noted. "Both of Regan's brothers have kids of their own, so they understand the importance of rules."

Deacon unlocked the door and called for Piper and Poppy to come inside as he exchanged keys with his brother. He helped out with the girls often enough that he and Connor had long ago discovered it was easier to swap vehicles than transfer car seats.

"But we're makin' snow angels, Unca Dunca," Piper said.

"Well, I'm going to be making hot chocolate," he said.

Apparently those were the magic words, because both girls jumped to their feet and hurried—as much as they could hurry in their heavy boots and bulky outerwear—toward the door.

"With whipped cweam?"

"An' spwin-kohs?"

"Snowsuits and boots off right here," Connor reminded his daughters as they pushed into the foyer.

They dutifully started yanking on zippers and tugging at Velcro fastenings to reveal fuzzy sweaters and printed leggings.

"Then can we watch *Fwozen*?" Piper asked, kicking off her boots.

"I wanna watch *'canto*," Poppy said.

"How about *Frozen* today and *Encanto* tomorrow?" Deacon suggested as a compromise.

"Okay," Piper said.

"'Kay," Poppy agreed.

"That's a lot of screen time," Connor noted, as the girls scampered off to the living room.

"Don't worry," Deacon said. "I've also got sharp knives and matches to keep them busy."

His brother slid him a look.

"Okay, we'll stick with coloring pages, building blocks and modeling clay."

"They've got some toys and books in their backpacks, too," Connor said, as he followed Deacon to the kitchen. "Which reminds me—Regan asked me to remind you to make sure they brush their teeth *before* story time, in case they fall asleep while you're reading."

"I know the drill," he assured his brother.

"And bedtime is eight o'clock. Actually, it's seven o'clock at home, but eight o'clock is okay for a sleepover. But no later than eight," Connor cautioned, "or they'll be cranky all day tomorrow."

Deacon set a pot on the stove, filled it with milk. "This isn't my first sleepover—or theirs."

"I know, but Regan likes to remind me to remind you."

"And what are your plans for tonight?" he asked.

"I've got a table booked at The Home Station for dinner and dessert at home from Sweet Caroline's for after."

"What's the occasion?" Deacon asked curiously.

"Does there need to be an occasion for me to take my wife out for a romantic meal?" his brother challenged.

"Maybe not," he allowed. "But I'm getting the feeling there's something you're not telling me."

"Regan and I are thinking about having another baby," Connor finally confided.

"Because Piper and Poppy don't keep you busy enough?"

"Because we love our life with the girls and we've got a lot more love to go around."

"Do you really work in law enforcement?" Deacon wondered aloud. "Because it should be illegal for someone who carries a gun in his job to say something so sappy."

Connor shrugged, clearly unoffended by his remark. "Talk to me after you've had a child with the woman you love."

"That will be...never," Deacon said, reaching into the cupboard above the stove for the hot chocolate mix.

"Never say never," his brother warned.

Then Connor's gaze zeroed in on the old-fashioned glass canister, with the hand-printed label that identified it as *Hot Chocolate* in a decidedly feminine script, as if it was evidence at a crime scene.

"What kind of hot chocolate is that?"

Deacon measured out the mix in accordance with the (also hand-printed) directions on the back of the container and whisked it into the milk. "The same kind you get at Sweet Caroline's."

His brother's jaw dropped. "Who gave you the recipe?"

"No one gave me the recipe. According to Annalise, it's a proprietary mixture. But I did sweet-talk her into letting me buy some of it."

"You mean you slept with the Sweet Caroline's barista?" Connor guessed.

Deacon couldn't prevent the smile that curved his lips. "Not for the hot chocolate."

"How long has this been going on?"

"It's not going on," he said. "We went out for a few weeks and then things fizzled out."

"Have you ever gone out with a woman longer than a few weeks?" his brother wondered.

"Sure." He poured cold milk into two plastic mugs, filling them halfway, then topped them off with the hot chocolate.

"Have you ever thought that any of those women was the one?"

"Every one of them was the one—at least in the moment," he said easily.

"Are you trying to be an ass or does it come naturally?" Connor wondered aloud.

"It comes naturally," Deacon said, with a grin. "But if you're asking if I ever thought one of them might be someone with whom I want to spend the rest of my life, I'd have to say *no*, because I don't see my future following the same path as yours."

"You don't want to get married and have a family?"

"I don't see it happening," Deacon said again.

"Which isn't actually what I asked," his brother noted.

Deacon popped his head into the living room. "Who wants whipped cream on their hot cocoa?"

"I do!"

"I do!"

Two pairs of feet pounded as his excited nieces dashed into the kitchen, clamoring for their treat.

"I'm glad you're going to be dealing with the sugar rush and not me," Connor muttered.

"Is that your way of saying you don't want whipped cream?"

"Of course I want whipped cream."

He grinned and filled two ceramic mugs with the steaming liquid, then topped all four drinks with a generous heap of whipped cream and a sprinkle of chocolate shavings.

"You make the best hot choc'ate, Unca Dunca."

His heart melted like the cream on top of his hot drink.

Still, he felt compelled to remind her, "It's Deacon, Pop. Uncle *Deacon*."

She wrinkled her nose. "But that does'n rhyme."

Connor chuckled.

Deacon sighed. "I'm going to be Unca Dunca forever, aren't I?"

"Probably not forever," his brother said. "But at least another few years."

CHAPTER THREE

LIVING IN NORTHERN Nevada was taking some getting used to, Sierra acknowledged, as she tugged the fleece-lined hat over her ears and stuffed her hands into matching gloves. Then she opened the door to step outside and sucked in a shocked breath.

When she'd told her brother that she was taking a job in Haven for six months—starting in January—he'd warned her that it would be cold. Sierra hadn't been concerned. No one had ever accused her of being a shrinking violet.

But right now, she felt like a frozen violet—and she'd only been outside for fifteen seconds.

A quiet whimper escaped her as she thought longingly of the twenty-four-hour gym in the basement of her apartment building in Las Vegas.

Former apartment building, she reminded herself.

She'd vacated the premises at the same time she'd walked away from her eighteen-month relationship with Eric Stikeman. She still missed the spacious two bedroom with the floor-to-ceiling windows and mountain view. Eric...not so much.

In any event, when she'd agreed to take the job in the Haven DA's office, she'd been hopeful that she might find similar accommodations here. Those hopes had quickly been dashed.

The good news was that she'd found a fully furnished townhouse in a newer development. Unfortunately, the furnishings hadn't included a treadmill.

The real estate agent had told her that there was a gym at the community center, but Sierra was reluctant to commit to a membership, not knowing how often she'd use it when her only goal was "moderate" daily physical activity. But the gym also offered yoga classes, and her friend Aubrey had frequently remarked that Sierra should take up yoga to help her relax.

Former friend, she amended.

And a reason for some of her current tension, as well as more evidence that she was a lousy judge of character—at least when it came to her personal interactions.

So for now, Sierra had decided that morning walks would provide not only exercise but also the opportunity to explore the area and maybe even meet some of her neighbors.

Apparently the locals were a hearty breed, as she crossed paths with more than a few residents out walking their dogs, spotted a couple others up on ladders taking down holiday decorations and observed several children playing in the snow.

But if she was going to continue walking in frigid weather, she was going to need a warmer pair of boots. And a thicker coat. And probably some thermal underwear, too.

On second thought, a gym membership might be cheaper.

She exchanged greetings with a man holding a leash attached to an Old English sheepdog and considered the benefits of a canine companion. It would be nice to have company, she mused, not only on her daily walks but at home.

But as appealing as the idea was for now, she was only going to be in Haven for six months. After her contract with the DA's office was finished, she'd be going back to Las Vegas, where she no longer had an apartment. Which meant that she'd be staying with her brother and sister-in-law until she could find a place of her own—which she wouldn't be able to do until she found a new job—and Whitney was allergic to dogs.

She paused on the sidewalk near where two little girls were building a snowman—or trying to with the limited amount of snow on the ground. Because the air might be frigid, but it was still desert, and snow was as scarce in the winter as rain was in the summer. Still, they'd managed to put one modest-sized ball of snow on top of a slightly bigger ball of snow.

Sierra didn't have a lot of experience with kids, but one of the partners at Bane had a four-year-old grandson who sometimes came into the office and these girls looked to be a similar age. One was dressed in a pink snowsuit with blue boots, the other wore a purple snowsuit and orange boots.

Twins, she guessed, and shuddered at the possibility of heightened nausea and vomiting, which she'd read could be experienced by women carrying multiple babies.

The girl in pink took the knitted hat off her own head to set it on the snowman.

"Now your scarf," she said to her sister.

The girl in purple dutifully began to tug at the knot by her throat.

"That's a nice snowman you've got there," Sierra said.

Both girls beamed with pleasure.

"He needs a scarf," Pink said.

"Can you help me wif it?" Purple asked, still tugging on her scarf.

"I don't know that your mom would want you dressing up your snowman in your accessories," Sierra said.

"It's okay," Pink told her. "Mommy's not here."

Sierra wasn't sure how to respond to that and was relieved when the front door opened and a man walked out.

Relieved, that was, until she recognized him as the thief of her Frosted Flakes.

"Here we are," Deacon said, his attention on the two girls. "Mini Oreos for the eyes and mouth and a baby carrot for the nose."

Then he spotted Sierra on the sidewalk. Their gazes locked.

"Oh," he said, obviously as surprised to see her as she was to see him. "Hi."

"Hi," she said back.

"She wikes our snowman," Pink chimed in.

"Well, of course she likes your snowman," Deacon agreed. "He's very handsome. Or he will be when you give him a face."

The girls took the proffered items and returned to their snowman-in-progress.

"Did you change your mind about needing a lawyer?" he asked Sierra.

She shook her head. "I was just out for a walk."

"You live around here?" he asked.

"A couple blocks over."

"I guess that makes us neighbors, sort of."

"Sort of," she agreed, before shifting her attention back to the little girls who were now stuffing mini Oreos in their mouths. "Your daughters are adorable."

"They're not mine," he said, shaking his head to emphasize the point. "They're my brother's kids."

"So...your nieces?"

Now he nodded.

She looked from one child to the other, noting their similar heights and features.

"Twins?" she guessed.

He nodded again. "Double Trouble, I call them."

The girls giggled at the obviously familiar nickname.

"We need mo' cookies," Purple said.

He glanced over, sighed. "You were supposed to use them to make the snowman's mouth, not put them in *your* mouths."

That remark earned another round of giggles.

"You know where the cookies are," Deacon told them. "You can go get one more package, but that's all."

They raced toward the door.

"I get the carrot," she said. "But why mini Oreos?"

"Because I'm all out of lumps of coal."

"None left in your Christmas stocking?"

His lips twitched at the corners. "Is it so hard to believe that I might have been on Santa's 'nice' list?"

"Were you?"

"I can be naughty or nice, depending on the situation," he told her.

And suddenly their conversation was inching toward potentially dangerous territory again, the air between them charged with electricity.

Deciding that a change of topic was in order, she asked, "Did your nieces enjoy their Frosted Flakes for breakfast?"

"They always do," he said.

She should have left it at that, but she felt the teensiest bit uneasy thinking that she might have judged him not only too quickly but also unfairly.

"So why did you let me think that you would be spending the night with two women?" she asked him.

"Is that what you were thinking?"

She narrowed her gaze. "You know it was. You *winked*."

"And somehow you interpreted that as code for a threesome?"

She huffed out a breath. "I don't even know why we're having this conversation. It doesn't matter."

"Maybe it does," he countered. "Maybe I want to know why you'd assume a casual mention of breakfast with twins meant a night with two women."

"It was the wink," she said again.

"Or was it the fact that you looked at me and wanted me and guessed that most other women do, too?"

"What I guessed is that you'd be as obnoxious as you are arrogant—and I was right."

"Here's an idea," he said, seemingly unfazed by her retort. "Why don't we talk about my character flaws over dinner?"

"Because I don't date players."

"And, after two very brief conversations, you think you've got me all figured out, don't you?" he challenged.

She shrugged. "Some people aren't very complicated."

"Are you always so quick to rush to judgment?"

No, she wasn't. But she was apparently quick to judge *him*, and that was something she'd have to give some consideration to on her own time.

For now, she simply said, "Goodbye, Mr. Columbia Law."

"It's Deacon," he reminded her. "And you haven't given me your number. Or even your name."

"Not an oversight," she told him.

She was right.

He'd acted like a dick, and she'd called him on it.

Well, she'd accused him of being arrogant and obnoxious, which was essentially the same thing. And not a completely inaccurate characterization of his behavior, Deacon acknowledged, if only to himself.

He was usually much smoother in his interactions with the opposite sex. But there was something about the cool reserve of the woman—who still hadn't even told him her name—that made him want to elicit a reaction.

He'd at least succeeded in that, even if the reaction wasn't quite what he'd hoped for. But as his high school baseball coach used to say, if you're going to go down, go down swinging.

"We got the cookies," Piper announced, running toward him, her sister close on her heels.

He imagined the snow they'd tracked inside melting on his hardwood floors but decided that he'd wipe it up later. Now he helped the girls put the finishing touches on their creation, took some pictures of them posing beside it and sent the photos to his brother and sister-in-law.

They both immediately responded to his text with heart emojis, then Regan sent another message:

We'll be there to pick them up in about an hour.

Make it 2 hours, he suggested. We haven't watched Encanto yet.

2 hours, she confirmed. And thank you again. xo.

"Okay, girls—take your hat and scarf off the snowman now so we don't forget them out here," he instructed.

"But he'll get cold," Poppy protested.

"He's a snowman," Deacon said. "If he wasn't cold, he'd melt."

"Like Fwosty," Piper said, nodding sagely.

"I don't want him to melt," Poppy said worriedly.

"I don't think you have to worry about him melting anytime soon," Deacon said.

It was far more likely that the snowman would meet his end courtesy of the seven-year-old bully who lived three doors down and already had a reputation for kicking over and stomping on the neighborhood snow people. Not that he was going to tell his nieces that.

"And even when he does eventually melt, it just means that you can look forward to building him again when the snow comes back," he said instead.

"Can we watch *'canto* now?" Poppy asked.

"First, we need to pack up your stuff, so you're ready to go when your mom and dad come to get you, then we can watch *Encanto*."

"Can we have popco'n with the movie?" Piper wanted to know.

"An' Wed Vines?"

"You ate all my Red Vines last night," he reminded them. "But yes, we can have popcorn."

While the girls hung up their snowsuits, he wiped up the melted snow on the floor, then together they gathered up pj's, toothbrushes, books and toys before carrying their backpacks downstairs and settling in front of the television to watch the movie.

He adored the two little girls and was always happy to spend time with him. Of course, he would have been even happier if his brother hadn't confided that his babysitting services were being utilized so that the twins' parents could focus on making another baby.

Not that Deacon objected to his brother having an intimate relationship with his wife—because wasn't that supposed to be one of the benefits of marriage?—he just didn't want to hear about it. Especially when he was achingly aware that it had been far too long since he'd enjoyed any action between the sheets.

His own fault, Deacon knew. He'd had a good thing going with Mariah Traynor for almost six months—or they'd had some pretty good chemistry, anyway. But it turned out that they didn't have much in common beyond that. He was a Dodgers fan; she couldn't stand baseball. He cheered for the 49ers; she abhorred football. He enjoyed watching the Golden Knights; she didn't even know that Vegas had a hockey team.

Now, of course, he was kicking himself for ruining a good

thing—or at least a sure thing. Because since then, he'd discovered that one really was the loneliest number.

And if Mariah wasn't the type of woman that he could envision spending the rest of his life with, maybe that was because he couldn't envision spending the rest of his life with any one woman.

Never say never.

The problem was, Haven wasn't exactly overflowing with single women.

Or maybe the real problem was that he'd already dated most of them—way back in high school when he'd been looking for love (or at least sex) in all the wrong places. And if he hadn't found love, he'd at least discovered the pleasures of physical intimacy. There had been plenty of girls willing to share those pleasures with him—and others who'd looked at him with obvious disdain, who'd snickered in the hallways when he walked by and whispered (not very quietly) about Faithless Faith Parrish's youngest son.

With his brother's words still echoing in his head, and Piper and Poppy singing about not talking about Bruno, Deacon went into the kitchen to make the kids' snack.

He tossed some mini marshmallows and M&M's in with the hot corn when it was popped, and Piper and Poppy immediately declared it was "the best popco'n ev-uh."

Of course, they weren't quite four, so he didn't put much stock in their use of the superlative. Case in point, they also claimed that he read "the best sto-wees," gave "the best hugs" and was, overall, "the best unca."

While he appreciated their enthusiastic endorsement, he was painfully aware of his own shortcomings. And he was definitely not looking forward to the day that they learned the truth about him.

Because he wasn't the best anything—he'd found that out long ago. But he was determined to be better than his beginnings.

CHAPTER FOUR

SIERRA BOUGHT A pair of waterproof boots with a minus-forty-degree cold rating and a down-filled hooded coat so that she could continue to walk every morning, no matter the weather. She continued to explore the neighborhood in various directions, and if she avoided Sherwood Park Drive—where she now knew Deacon Parrish lived—that was simply because she wanted to discover new paths.

Unfortunately, not seeing him didn't stop her from thinking about him—and then she ended up annoyed with herself for thinking about him.

Damn hormones.

At least at work her mind was too busy to wander in his direction. And by the end of her third week on the job, Sierra felt more and more confident that the move to Haven—albeit temporary—had the right move for her. Even if her brother and sister-in-law remained unconvinced.

Of course, they didn't know all the reasons that she'd chosen to leave Bane & Associates, and she had no intention of telling them. As a result, Nick worried that she was being impulsive, and while Whitney tried to be supportive, her sister-in-law wasn't happy that Sierra had decided to move so far away, especially now.

She understood why they wanted to keep her close, but she'd

needed some distance from the mistakes she'd made. And while she knew she'd miss her family—and she did—Haven wasn't so far from Vegas that she couldn't go back to visit during the six months of her contract. She was also hopeful that Nick and Whitney would come to see her, when their schedules allowed, as her townhouse had plenty of room for guests.

For now though, she refocused her attention on proofreading the pretrial memo she'd drafted for her boss, then clicked the print icon on the screen and leaned back in her chair.

Her lips curved a little as she glanced around at the four walls that comprised her office. It was a small thing, the fact that she had an office—and it was a small office—but it was a big step up from the cubicle that she'd spent sixty hours a week in for the past three years. Not only four walls but also a door that closed, to afford her privacy for confidential phone calls or meetings with colleagues, and even a trio of windows with a view of the courthouse across the street.

A sharp rap of knuckles on the open door drew her attention back to the present as her boss stepped into the room carrying a file box.

She retrieved the pages she'd printed and stapled them together as Brett dropped the box on her desk. "What's that?"

"The Dornan file."

Sierra had taken careful notes when he'd briefed his staff on upcoming cases, so she immediately recognized the name. "The fraud case?"

He nodded.

"You want me to write up a sentencing memo?" she guessed, recalling that he'd mentioned he was working on a plea deal with Rhonda Dornan's defense attorney.

Now he shook his head. "She turned down the deal her counsel negotiated and got a new lawyer. She wants to go to trial."

"So what is it that you want me to do?" Sierra wondered aloud.

"Prep for the trial."

She felt a frisson of excitement shimmer through her. She'd been one of the most junior associates at Bane, hired right out of law school, so she wasn't surprised that she had to start out researching case law and drafting arguments for other lawyers to present in court. But almost three years later, she'd been inside a courtroom only a handful of times, and most often only to deliver documents to one of the partners.

"You want me to assist?" she asked cautiously, unwilling to get her hopes up.

"No," Brett said. "I want you to take the lead on this one."

She swallowed. "The lead?"

"Trial starts on Monday," he told her. "And I'm on vacation next week."

She remembered him mentioning that, too, but she hadn't expected the vacation to actually happen. At Bane, she'd known several colleagues who'd booked holidays only to cancel them when something came up at the office that required their attention. Because the work always came first, and any associate who wanted to move up the ranks had to demonstrate that nothing was more important than the job.

Sierra had never had to cancel a trip, because she hadn't been foolish enough to make plans to go away. But she'd bailed on outings with her friends more times than she liked to admit and had even stood up the occasional date when one of the partners dropped something on her desk at the eleventh hour.

"Disneyland," Brett said now, returning to the topic of his vacation with a shake of his head. "What was I thinking?"

Sierra smiled. "You were probably thinking that your kids will love it."

He had three sons, ages ten, seven and five, with his wife of almost fifteen years. A photo taken at their wedding was prominently displayed on his desk alongside another of Jenny and the boys, and he wore a chunky band on the third finger of his left hand. Brett Ryckell was a man devoted to his family and proud to let everyone know it.

"Have you been to Disneyland?" he asked her now.

"Once," she said. "A long time ago."

Before her parents had died and her life had been turned completely upside down.

"Any words of advice?" he asked.

"Take lots of pictures."

"I can do that," he said, as he started for the door.

She lifted the lid of the box, eager to dig into the files.

He turned and gave her a gently admonishing look. "It's almost six o'clock, Sierra."

"Yes, sir," she said, not sure what point her boss was trying to make in mentioning the time.

"Go home," he said.

"But...it's not even six o'clock."

"The contents of the box aren't going to change overnight," he pointed out. "You'll have plenty of time to familiarize yourself with the case before Monday."

"Yes, sir," she said again, reluctantly replacing the lid.

"Don't misunderstand me," Brett said. "I appreciate your enthusiasm, but I don't want you to burn yourself out before you've been on the job a month."

"I don't think there's any danger of that."

"Still, you should take some time for yourself, go out with friends."

"I haven't been here long enough to make friends," she said, even as she thought fleetingly of the woman she'd met in the grocery store the previous weekend. But despite Sky's suggestion that they should get together for coffee sometime, Sierra had yet to hear from her.

"Then you should go out and make some."

She managed a smile. "I'll work on it."

Truthfully, though, she didn't see the point in making friends when she was only going to be in town for six months. That was the length of the contract she'd been offered, temporarily filling in for ADA Jade Scott who was on maternity leave for the same period of time. And even if Jade decided that she wasn't ready to come back at the end of six months, Sierra wasn't in any position to stay in Haven beyond that.

She left the office with the file box and made her way to Jo's Pizza.

She'd heard nothing but good things about the place since her arrival in town, and she figured it was time to try the infamous pie for herself.

Jo's had a front entrance with a sign over the door that said

Restaurant and a side entrance designated as Takeout. Sierra opened the Takeout door and stepped inside, her stomach growling hungrily as she breathed in the scents of garlic, oregano and tomato sauce. If the pizza tasted half as good as the restaurant smelled, then Jo's would undoubtedly live up to its lofty reputation.

She turned toward the takeout counter and stopped midstride, because wasn't it just her luck that Deacon Parrish was there, flirting with a pretty blonde working on the other side of the counter?

Deacon needed to get a life.

Instead, it was six thirty on a Friday night and he was picking up pizza.

A single medium pizza that he would take home to eat by himself.

Even Lucy, daughter of the infamous Jo, had teased him about his lack of plans as she'd taken his order.

And she was right—he was an old man at twenty-eight.

Well, almost twenty-eight, but that clarification didn't make him feel much better about the fact that it was a Friday night and he had no plans.

Worse, he didn't want any plans.

He sincerely wanted nothing more than to go home, put his feet up on the coffee table—because it was his house and his coffee table, and there was no one to tell him to get his feet off the table—and eat his dinner while watching the hockey game on TV.

Well, there was maybe one thing that he wanted more—and wasn't it a happy coincidence that she'd walked through the door just as his pizza came out from the kitchen?

"Who's that?" Lucy asked curiously, having followed the direction of his gaze.

"I was hoping you could tell me."

She shook her head. "I can't say that I've ever seen her before."

"But you're about to get her name and number," he mused.

"And if you happened to leave her order slip right here on the counter for your ninth-grade lab partner to take a peek at—"

"No," Lucy said bluntly. "You want someone to help you get a date? Join match-dot-com."

"Come on, Luce."

"No," she said again.

The phone rang just as his not-quite-neighbor approached the counter.

"I'll be right with you," Lucy told her, before snatching up the receiver.

"Hello, again," Deacon said, grinning.

"Hi," she replied, with a distinct lack of enthusiasm.

"Long day for you?" he asked.

She shrugged. "No longer than usual."

"I thought winter was generally slow season in the real estate market," he said, determined to engage her in conversation and at least learn her name.

"Sorry," she said, sounding more dismissive than regretful. "I don't know anything about the real estate market."

"You don't work at Ruby Realty?"

She seemed taken aback by the question. "What made you think that I did?"

He gestured to her attire. "The red jacket is part of their signature outfit."

"My jacket isn't red, it's cranberry."

Which was exactly what he'd thought the first time he saw her wearing it. "Isn't cranberry just a more specific shade of red?"

"I have a question for you," she said, declining to answer his. "If I was wearing a green jacket, would you assume I'd won it at the Masters?"

"Probably not, as women don't currently compete at the Masters."

"Touché."

"So you don't work in real estate, but you are new in town," he mused.

"Is that a statement or a question?"

"A statement."

"Because you know everyone in town?" she guessed.

"Maybe not by name," he acknowledged. "But I'm sure if I'd ever met you and known yours, I would have remembered."

She narrowed her gaze on him. "Are you capable of having a conversation with a woman without flirting with her?"

"I am," he assured her with a wink. "But flirting is so much more fun than regular conversation."

"Can I give you a word of advice?"

"I'm all ears."

"Save your flirtatious charm for someone who might be interested, because I'm not."

"Ouch," he said.

"You don't look particularly wounded," she noted.

"Because I know you're lying."

"I'm not lying," she said.

"You don't want to be interested," he said. "But the flush of color in your cheeks suggests that you are."

"Which can also be a physiological response to irritation."

"Can be," he agreed. "But in this case, I'd bet that it's indicative of attraction."

She rolled her eyes. "Apparently you're someone who likes throwing his money away."

"Okay, let's forget any kind of wager and instead grab a table so that we can share our pizzas and conversation," he suggested as an alternative.

"No, thanks."

"You've got that down to a fine art, don't you?"

"What?" she asked, with obvious reluctance.

"The affected disinterest and casual brush-off."

"I'm not trying to hurt your feelings," she said. "But I'm really not looking for any kind of romantic entanglement."

"What kind of entanglement are you looking for?"

"None," she told him.

But there had been a slight hesitation before her response—as if she regretted turning down the offer.

Interesting.

Lucy finally finished on the phone and returned to the counter. "Sorry about that," she said to his neighbor. "Are you here to order or pick up?"

Deacon effected a casual pose against the counter, as if he wasn't listening for her to give her name.

"Pick up," she said. "Medium pizza for—"

"Deacon Parrish!"

The excited squeal drowned out the rest of what she said, and he barely had a chance to turn his head to identify the source before a woman threw herself at him—so hard she nearly cracked his ribs. Soft breasts pressed against his chest and teased blond hair tickled his nose, but it was the cloud of Viva La Juicy perfume that took him back to tenth grade, which was, coincidentally, when he'd lost his virginity with Liberty Mosley.

"Oh. My. God." Liberty drew back a little to smile at him. "I can't believe it's you." She pressed her red-painted lips to his. "I haven't seen you in...forever."

"It's been a few years," he acknowledged, sliding a cautious glance at his neighbor.

"Last time I saw you, you were just heading off to law school," Liberty recalled, oblivious to the fact—or maybe not caring—that she might have interrupted something. "And now you're a big-shot lawyer."

"Well, the lawyer part is right, anyway," he acknowledged.

"Where was it you went? Somewhere in New York, right? Harvard?"

"Harvard's in Massachusetts," he told her.

Her brows drew together. "I was sure your brother said you'd gone to New York City."

"I did," he confirmed. "Columbia."

"Wouldn't want to miss an opportunity to slip *that* into the conversation," he heard his neighbor mutter under her breath.

Before Deacon could respond, Liberty linked her arm through his and tipped her head against his shoulder. "Obviously we've got a lot to catch up on—why don't we order a pizza and take it up to Lookout Point?"

"For starters, because it's about ten degrees outside."

"I'm sure we can figure out a way to stay warm." The statement was accompanied by a smile that promised a lot more than conversation.

"Also, because your husband would likely object to that plan."

"I'm not married yet," she pointed out. "And anyway, Travis is out of town this weekend with his buddies—his last weekend of freedom, he called it, so I figure it should be my last weekend of freedom, too."

"And finally, because I've already got a pizza—" Deacon continued, gesturing to the box on the counter "—and other plans for tonight."

And while Deacon had some very fond memories of Liberty, he wasn't interested in revisiting their history—and even less interested in hooking up with a woman who would be exchanging vows with another man in the near future.

She pouted prettily, but Deacon's attention was on the sexy brunette who was staring at the screen of her phone, pretending not to eavesdrop on his conversation.

Or maybe she really wasn't.

"How about tomorrow, then?" Liberty suggested hopefully, toying with the zipper of his jacket.

Out of the corner of his eye, Deacon saw Lucy return from the back with another pizza box. She set it on the counter and rang up the order. His neighbor paid for her food, picked up the box and headed for the door.

"No." His tone was firm and final. "It was nice to see you, Liberty. And congrats on your upcoming wedding, but I have to run."

"Deacon—wait!"

It was Lucy who called to him this time, and he turned with his hand on the door.

She gestured to the box on the counter. "Don't you want your pizza?"

Of course he wanted his pizza.

And by the time he raced back to the counter to grab the box and rush out the door again, his neighbor was already gone.

CHAPTER FIVE

SIERRA'S HEART WAS beating a little too hard and a little too fast—though she didn't think it was an unusual physiological response for someone about to enter a lion's den.

Or at least knock on the door of the lion's den.

She paused to draw a deep breath (that stabbed at her lungs like icy needles!) before tapping her knuckles against the wood, then waited, the pizza box clutched in her hands.

"This is a surprise," Deacon said when he opened the door. "Did you change your mind about wanting to have dinner together?"

The smile that accompanied the question was warm and sincere and far too tempting.

"No," Sierra said quickly, refusing to let herself be tempted. "But I do want my dinner."

His brows lifted. "Isn't that what's in your hands?"

"No," she said again, lifting the lid of the box to show him the pie. "I didn't order pepperoni, bacon and sausage."

In fact, just the smell of the bacon—usually one of her favorite foods—was churning her stomach, so she quickly closed the lid again.

"I haven't looked at mine yet. Why don't you come on in out of the cold and I'll see what I got?" he invited.

Enter the lion's den?

No, thank you.

Except that it was cold outside—*really* cold—and it seemed kind of rude to stand there, holding the door open and letting his heat escape, when he'd invited her in.

She stepped into the tiled foyer and closed the door at her back. She was both surprised and relieved there was no indication that the blonde from the restaurant had come home with him.

Or maybe she'd gone straight to the bedroom.

But Sierra didn't imagine that Deacon would have responded to her knock if he had a willing woman waiting for him.

So she pushed the idea aside and surveyed her surroundings. His house was a detached two story and obviously bigger than the townhouse she was renting, but the ground floor layout was a similar open-concept design, with the foyer leading into a family room that connected to a dining room. She suspected the kitchen was at the back of the house, facing the dining room, though she couldn't see past the stairs to the upper level to be sure.

Instead, she focused on the nearby living space. The walls were painted a warm cream color with a trio of abstract prints in neutral shades on the longest wall. The dark hardwood floors were covered with an oatmeal-colored rug, on top of which sat an oversize sectional of chocolate brown leather and mission-style tables in some kind of dark wood. Facing the sectional was an enormous flat-screen TV.

It was very much a masculine space—the proverbial bachelor pad—absent any decorative pillows or whimsical knickknacks.

But there was a photo of his nieces, mugging for the camera, in a frame on one of the end tables—a reminder to Sierra that, whatever his faults, Deacon obviously doted on the girls and, therefore, couldn't be all bad. And in the brief interaction that she'd witnessed between Deacon and the twins, it had been just as evident that they adored their uncle.

As her gaze shifted away from the photo, she spotted a lump of what looked like modeling clay beside it. No, not a lump, she realized, but a figure, with googly eyes and four strands of yellow yarn on the top of its head.

"Is that a self-portrait?" she asked, gesturing to the clay figure.

"I only wish I was that talented," he said. "The true artists in the family are Piper and Poppy."

And he was proud enough of their efforts to display them in his living space. Obviously there was a lot more to this man than she'd assumed, aspects of his character that she couldn't help but like, but none that affected her determination not to get involved.

"Who's winning?" she asked, hearing the play-by-play of a hockey game in the background.

"There's no score yet." He lifted the lid of the pizza box on the coffee table, made a face. "Tomatoes, green peppers and black olives?"

"That's mine," she confirmed.

"Are you a vegetarian?"

"Only when I'm selling real estate," she said dryly.

He chuckled at that—and *damn*, if the low, sensual sound didn't turn her knees to jelly.

The sound of a cheer emanating from the television thankfully diverted her attention, and she inched a little closer to peer at the screen.

"Are you a hockey fan?" Deacon asked, as they exchanged boxes.

"I enjoy watching the game, especially when the Golden Knights are playing."

"I'd get down on one knee and propose right now if I actually knew your name."

"It's Sierra," she said, because it seemed silly to continue to withhold such a basic piece of information.

He started to drop to one knee.

"I didn't tell you because I wanted a proposal," she was quick to assure him.

He straightened up again. "So why did you tell me?"

"Because we're neighbors, sort of," she said, borrowing his description. "And since we seem destined to run into one another around town, we should probably be able to exchange pleasantries on a first-name basis."

"Destined, huh?" He seemed to ponder that for a minute before he asked, "Do you believe in destiny?"

Though his tone was casual, there was something in his gaze that told her he was genuinely interested in her answer to the question.

"No," she said. "I think destiny is just an excuse for people to avoid responsibility for their actions."

"So you don't think it was destiny that there was only one box of Frosted Flakes on the shelf that day and we both wanted it?" he pressed.

"No," she said again. "I think it was a delay in the shipment from the supplier."

"And you stopping to talk to my nieces, not knowing they were my nieces?"

"Geographical proximity."

"And crossing paths at Jo's?"

"A statistical probability," she decided. "In a small town with only one pizza place, it's almost inevitable that we'd run into each other."

"Haven isn't all *that* small," he protested.

"Compared to Vegas, it is."

"So that's where you're from," he mused.

"And where I'm going back to, when my contract here is finished. But right now, I'm taking this—" she held up her pizza box "—home to have my dinner."

"Are you sure you don't want to stay and watch the game?"

She hesitated, because the truth was, she did want to stay. Not because she was wildly attracted to him—although she was—but because she'd spent every night of the past three weeks alone and it might be nice to hang out with and talk to another person for a while.

Except that Deacon wasn't simply another person—he was a man who made her all too aware of the fact that she was a woman, and that made her wary.

It was the sound of cheers emanating from the television that tipped the balance.

"Actually, I think I will stay." She shrugged out of her coat. "Just for the first period."

Deacon grinned. "I've got beer and wine and soda. What can I get for you?"

"Water?" she suggested, unzipping her boots.

"You're a cheap date," he remarked, as he headed into the kitchen to get her drink.

"This isn't a date," she said firmly, because even though she knew he was only teasing, she needed to be clear about that fact.

He returned with a glass of water and a couple of plates. "Okay, you're a cheap hockey-watching and pizza-eating companion."

"I can live with that," she decided, taking a seat on the opposite end of the sofa. Not only to reinforce the point that this wasn't a date, but also to ensure her stomach wouldn't rebel against the scent of the bacon on his pizza.

"Is it that you don't date or that you don't want to date *me*?" Deacon asked, transferring a slice from his box to his plate.

She plucked an olive off her own slice, popped it into her mouth. "I'm on a dating hiatus," she confided.

"Recent breakup?" he guessed.

"Not so recent."

"Broken heart?"

"Only bruised." She nibbled on a slice of green pepper.

"Are you going to eat that pizza or dissect it?"

She responded to his question by lifting the slice to her mouth and taking a bite, then moaned.

Deacon grinned. "Is this your first experience with Jo's Pizza?"

She nodded, still chewing. Savoring.

"It totally lives up to its reputation, doesn't it?"

She nodded again, swallowed. "I didn't think it was possible, but—" she couldn't wait to take another bite, continued with her mouth full "—ohmygod—this is..." She closed her eyes to better focus on the perfectly harmonized flavors and complimentary textures of crust and sauce and cheese and veggies as she searched for the right word. "Orgasmic."

"Should I leave you alone with your pizza?"

Her eyes popped open in response to his amused question. She felt heat rise in her cheeks again.

"No," she said. "I'm good now."

"And I'm very intrigued," he told her. "How long do you plan for this dating hiatus to last?"

"Another seven months, at least. Maybe more."

His brows lifted. "That's a fair length of time. Is it random or specific?"

"I think it's my turn to ask the questions now," she told him.

"So ask me a question," Deacon said, happy that his sexy new neighbor was finally willing to get to know him—and let him know her.

Sierra reached for another slice of pizza. "Who was the woman you were talking to at Jo's?"

"Lucy Delgado—Jo's daughter. She and her husband mostly run the pizzeria now."

"I wasn't asking about the woman behind the counter but the one in your arms."

"That was Liberty Mosley," he told her, because after inviting her to ask questions, he could hardly balk at answering them.

"High school girlfriend?" she guessed.

"Off and on. Probably more off than on."

"And yet she seems to have some very fond memories of you."

He shrugged. "Aren't we all a little nostalgic when it comes to the past? Or at least select parts of it."

She acknowledged that with a nod before following up with another question. "What's Lookout Point?"

"A nearby golf course...and popular..." Now he did balk, for a brief moment, as he scrambled for an appropriate description. "Uh, dating destination."

Sierra considered his response as she chewed another bite of pizza.

"You mean make-out spot," she finally said.

"Yeah," he admitted.

"So why did you turn down Liberty's invitation?"

"For all the reasons I told her—and one reason that I didn't."

"What's that?"

"I have a new neighbor who's piqued my interest."

Sierra's expression immediately shuttered. "Deacon—"

"I know," he interjected. "Dating hiatus, bruised heart, not-so-recent breakup. I heard everything you said—but I wanted to be as honest with you as you were with me."

Her gaze skittered away.

Because she was uncomfortable with his confession?

Or because she hadn't been as honest with him as he believed?

Before he could decide if he wanted to further pursue either of those possibilities, the buzzer sounded to end the first period.

Sierra leaned forward to close the lid of her pizza box, then she got up to carry her empty plate and glass to the kitchen.

Deacon wanted to invite her to stay to watch the rest of the game, but he didn't because it was evident what her answer would be. Truthfully, he was surprised that she'd stayed at all, but he was grateful that she had because he'd enjoyed her company.

He followed her to the door, waiting for her to put on her boots and coat before handing her the box of leftover pizza.

"Is that the right one this time?" she asked.

"You better hope so," he said. "Because I ate all of mine."

She smiled at that, and his heart bumped against his ribs before he remembered that she was on a lengthy dating hiatus.

But the reminder didn't discourage him so much as it motivated him to change her mind.

"You know, one of these days you're going to chase after me, and it's not going to be because you want my pizza," he told her.

"It was *my* pizza," she reminded him. "And don't hold your breath."

He didn't hold his breath, but he was smiling as he watched her make her way to the green Kia Soul parked in his driveway. Because he might have struck out, but he'd gone down swinging.

Even more important—he knew the game had only just begun.

When Sierra got home, she sat at the dining room table with the Dornan case file in front of her and the hockey game in the background. But after thirty minutes, she realized her mind was flitting around so much that she might as well have stayed and watched the last two periods with Deacon.

Still, she felt confident that she'd done the right thing in coming home, because she'd been trying to make it clear to him that she wasn't interested in any kind of relationship, and hanging out together for several hours on a Friday night would definitely send a mixed signal.

It wasn't just that she wasn't interested in a relationship, it was that the circumstances of her life right now made it impossible for her to get involved. At least for the next seven and a half months—and that's why the smart thing to do was to keep her distance from Mr. Columbia Law.

Which shouldn't be so difficult, she reasoned. After all, she was only going to be in town for six months.

Though it did seem an odd coincidence that their paths kept crossing. First at the grocery store on Saturday, the next day in front of his house and again at the local pizzeria only five days later.

But it wasn't destiny.

Maybe it wasn't even so odd but, as she'd pointed out to Deacon earlier, inevitable.

Though she didn't know what kind of law he practiced—she'd resisted the urge to google him—she knew that Katelyn Davidson ran a full-service law firm (and Sierra's new colleagues spoke highly of all the attorneys who worked there), so it seemed likely that she'd encounter him at the courthouse.

But likely wasn't destiny, either.

In any event, she was in Haven to do a job and, in the process, reassess her own career goals. Obviously her track to a partnership at Bane & Associates had been derailed by her abrupt resignation, but there was no way she could have stayed. Not after what happened in San Francisco.

Of course, there were plenty of other firms in Vegas, and she had a decent enough résumé that she felt confident she could get another job elsewhere in the city. But she didn't want another job where she'd be constantly on edge, wondering every day if she'd cross paths with Eric or Aubrey.

And so far, she was truly happy with the choice she'd made. She was enjoying the challenge of her work at the DA's office and excited about the opportunities her boss had given her.

But she did miss her brother and sister-in-law.

As if on cue, her phone chimed. She picked it up and smiled when she saw a message from Nick on the screen.

Just checking in to see how you're doing.

I'm good. Prepping for a trial next week.

Her phone rang. She swiped to connect the call.

"I hate texting," Nick said, in lieu of a more traditional greeting.

"I know," she agreed. "It's your chubby thumbs."

"I don't have chubby thumbs," he protested. "They're just big. Manly."

She chuckled.

"So are you still at the office?" her brother asked.

"No. My boss kicked me out before six."

"Wow. Your boss is a lot nicer than mine."

"Yours isn't so bad," she said, because Nick was his own boss now. After a decade of working at another firm, he'd decided to hang out his own shingle. Two years after that, he had three associates working with him.

"Well, I'm probably going to be stuck here for another couple of hours, anyway."

"Are you still tied up with the Chekhov trial?" she asked, referring to the insurance case that he'd been working on for the better part of six months.

"Yeah."

"Isn't this week three of what was supposed to be a two-week trial?"

"Yeah," he said again, and she could hear a world of frustration in that single syllable. "The insurance company has been delaying at every stage of the proceeding."

"Because they want to hold off having to make the big payout they know is coming," she guessed.

"Let's hope so," he said. "Anyway, closing arguments are on Monday, but we're heading to San Bernardino to see Whitney's parents this weekend, so I want to get this nailed down before we go."

"You'll knock it out of the park," she told him. "You always do."

"I appreciate your faith in me. And my wife would probably appreciate it if I made it home tonight, so I'm going to sign off now."

"Before you do," she interjected hastily, to prevent him from disconnecting the call, "I wanted to let you know that I got in to see the doctor in Battle Mountain that Dr. Shah referred me to."

"When was that?" Nick asked, and she knew she had his full attention now.

"Wednesday," she admitted, feeling just a little bit guilty that she'd waited more than forty-eight hours to tell him.

"I assume I would have heard about the appointment before now if there was any cause for concern."

"There's no cause for concern—I'm good," she assured him. Then she laid a hand on her still mostly-flat belly. "And the baby's good, too."

Deacon grunted in response to the elbow that slammed into his ribs.

"Who said this would be fun?" he grumbled.

"Early exercise helps you start the day with energy, focus and optimism," Claudio Delgado—Lucy's husband—told him.

"That might be true." He jumped up to intercept a pass. "If the form of exercise is sex."

"You getting too old for basketball?" Luke Ross—a childhood friend of the same age—taunted.

"No." And he proved it by sinking a basket. "But I'd rather be getting physical with a woman in the bedroom than sweating with you guys in a gym."

JJ Green—a local real estate agent—caught the ball and started toward the other end of the court.

"That was twenty-one," Claudio announced. "Game's over."

"Twenty-one to twenty," JJ called back. "The game has to be won by two."

Ben Powell—another childhood friend—swore as he started to chase the play.

JJ's toss kissed the backboard before dropping through the hoop.

"Now we're tied again," he said smugly.

"Since when do you have to win by two?" Luke demanded, as Ben snagged the ball and sent it through the air to Gerard Flaherty—the (very tall) husband of one of the lawyers who worked with Deacon.

"Since always," JJ said.

Gerard dribbled the ball around the defender, deliberately moving away from the net rather than toward it.

Deacon ran into the key, as if anticipating a pass. Claudio chased him.

Gerard set up outside the three-point line and took his shot.

Everyone stopped to watch the ball arc in the air before dropping through the net.

Swish.

"Twenty-three to twenty-one," Ben said smugly.

JJ muttered a string of curses beneath his breath as he made his way to the bench to grab his water bottle.

The other five men on the court followed suit.

"I thought Harvey was going to be here today," Gerard said, naming the courthouse security guard who was a usual Saturday morning pickup participant.

"He said he was," Deacon confirmed.

"But that was before I saw him getting cozy with Melanie Noble at Diggers' last night," Ben said.

"Which means he was likely enjoying Dekes's preferred form of physical exercise this morning," Claudio chimed in.

"Actually, I half-expected Dekes to bail on us today," Luke said.

"Why would I bail?" he wondered aloud.

"Because there was a bright green Kia parked in your driveway last night."

Ben's brows lifted. "Overnight?"

Luke shrugged. "How would I know? I just happened to notice the car as I was driving by."

Ben turned to Deacon. "Overnight?" he asked again.

"No."

"He said regretfully," JJ added with a smirk.

Deacon scowled at him as he lifted his water bottle to his lips.

"So...who is she?" Ben pressed.

"No one you know."

"How do you know?" his friend challenged.

"Because she's new in town."

"Sierra Hart?" Claudio guessed. "Lucy said you were flirting with her last night."

Sierra Hart. Deacon wondered why the name struck a chord with him now when he'd experienced no similar sense of recognition when Sierra introduced herself to him, using only her given name, the previous evening.

"Is it possible The Daily Grind rumor mill is failing?" Ben wondered aloud. "Because I stopped in to grab a coffee this morning and didn't detect a whisper of this."

"He was flirting with her at Jo's."

"Is she hot?" Luke wanted to know.

Claudio shrugged. "I wasn't there."

"Don't you have security cameras in the restaurant?"

"Sure," the restauranteur agreed. "But I don't review the footage looking for hot women."

"Because Lucy would kick your ass," Ben said.

"Because I'm lucky to be married to the hottest woman in town," Claudio said, managing to sound just a little smug.

"Lucy *is* hot," JJ acknowledged. "But Sierra is hot *and single*."

"How do you know?" Deacon wondered aloud.

"I listed the house she's renting."

"Hot and single," Ben echoed, sounding intrigued.

"I saw her first," Deacon reminded his friend, an unmistakable warning in his tone.

"Actually, it sounds like JJ saw her first," Gerard noted.

"I guess I did," the real estate agent mused. "But I also just booked a trip to take Veronica to Aruba for Valentine's Day."

"Are you finally going to pop the question?" Claudio asked.

JJ nodded.

"And another one bites the dust," Deacon remarked, shaking his head.

"Your time will come," Gerard said.

The words sounded to Deacon more like a warning than a promise.

He shook his head. "I don't think so."

"Dekes doesn't believe in happy-ever-after," Luke said, not without sympathy.

"Maybe Ms. Hart will be the woman to change his mind," JJ suggested.

Deacon was skeptical that anyone could do that—but, to his surprise, realized that he was more than willing to let Sierra try.

CHAPTER SIX

SIERRA WAS EXCITED (and admittedly a little nervous) about her upcoming trial. Aside from one appearance in traffic court for the purpose of reducing a speeding ticket given to Harold Bane's seventeen-year-old grandson, she'd never had the opportunity to argue a case on her own.

But the Dornan case wasn't a complicated one, and a quick review of the file confirmed that all of the evidence required for a conviction was there. And by Sunday night, she'd pretty much memorized the police reports, drafted her opening arguments and made detailed notes for the examination and cross-examination of all the witnesses.

She set out Monday morning, confident that she was prepared to handle anything that might happen in court.

And she was—anything except discovering that the opposing counsel was Mr. Columbia Law himself.

Deacon was already seated at the defense table when she walked in. And it was a good thing he was sitting down, because the realization that Sierra—his not-quite-neighbor, not-a-vegetarian, not-a-real-estate-agent—was the new assistant district attorney would have knocked him off his feet.

At least now he knew why Claudio's use of her full name had tripped something in his brain, because of course he'd heard mention of "Ms. Hart," the new ADA.

And apparently she'd been right about the fact that they were destined to run into one another around town—and who was he to fight against destiny? Instead, he pushed his chair back and rose to his feet to cross the divide, an easy smile on his face.

"You didn't tell me you were a lawyer," he said by way of greeting.

She shrugged. "I'm not one of those people who feels compelled to mention my job in every passing conversation."

"I mentioned it *once*," he said. "And only after you called me a cowboy."

"Being a lawyer doesn't mean you're not a cowboy," she noted.

Though a lot of people had romantic notions about cowboys, he knew that her remark hadn't been intended as a compliment. And maybe it should have bothered him that this woman had already formed an unfavorable opinion of him, but it didn't. Because the fact that she obviously had an opinion suggested that she'd been thinking about him—as he'd been thinking about her. And for now, he was going to count that as a win.

"There's a note in the file that Rhonda Dornan fired her previous attorney and hired Nolan Hollister to represent her," Sierra said, obviously eager to move on with business. "Where do you fit in to the picture?"

"At seven o'clock last night, Rhonda was informed by Nolan Hollister that he couldn't represent her at trial. At eight o'clock, she contacted Katelyn Davidson's office. Katelyn passed the case to me."

"I wonder if her retainer check to Nolan Hollister bounced," Sierra mused.

Deacon had wondered the same thing when he discovered the nature of the charges against his client. And perhaps it had, because Rhonda had promised to bring a certified check to court this morning for his representation.

Of course, it would be unprofessional to share any of that information with the ADA, so he remained silent.

"And I'm guessing, since you were assigned this case just about twelve hours ago, that you're not here to start the trial but to ask for a postponement."

"Just a short one," he said, adding a smile that more than a few women had described as irresistibly charming.

She glanced at her watch. "Thirty minutes?"

Apparently the new ADA wasn't easily charmed.

"A little longer than that."

Thirty minutes later, he walked out of the courtroom with his client's certified check in his briefcase and a forty-eight-hour postponement. It wasn't a lot of time, but he didn't think he needed a lot to get up to speed on the case.

"Do you have time for coffee?" Deacon asked Sierra. "And before you say *no*, remember that I know you were scheduled to be in court all day."

"And now that my schedule has been cleared, I can catch up on some of the other work that's waiting for me at the office," she said.

"What if I wanted to talk about the case?"

"I'd think you need some time to familiarize yourself with the details first," she pointed out.

"Or you could summarize those details for me," he suggested. "Over coffee."

"I don't drink coffee."

"You don't drink coffee?" he echoed incredulously.

"I don't drink coffee," she confirmed.

"I don't know anyone who doesn't drink coffee. Well, aside from Double Trouble," he clarified.

Before she had a chance to respond to that, Skylar Gilmore—now Skylar Kelly, he reminded himself—fell into step beside them.

"Well, if it isn't my sister's favorite junior associate and the new ADA," she said. "Were you guys battling in court this morning? And, more important, who won?"

Despite the fact that he'd grown up on the wrong side of the tracks that her ancestors had laid through town, Deacon had always liked Sky. Right now, though, he'd like her a lot more if she went away.

"The battle was adjourned," Sierra said.

"Does that mean you have time for coffee?" Sky asked.

"She doesn't drink coffee," Deacon interjected.

"You don't drink coffee?" Sky echoed, just as he'd done.

"But I do drink tea," Sierra said.

"I could do tea," Sky agreed, before turning to him to say, "Do you want to join us?"

"Thanks, but I'm going to head back to the office," he decided. Then he shifted his attention to Sierra, noting her obvious surprise—and relief—at his reply. "I'll touch base with you later, Ms. Hart, after I've familiarized myself with the case."

"I'll look forward to hearing from you," she said politely.

And though it was maybe no more than the expected response to his comment, he walked away with a smile on his face, pleased that this time he'd been the one to throw the curveball.

Oh yes, the game had definitely begun.

"The Daily Grind has the best coffee in town—and usually the hottest gossip," Sky said to Sierra, as they made their way down Main Street, away from the courthouse. "But if you're looking for something other than coffee—and/or you want a bit of indulgence—then Sweet Caroline's is where you want to go."

"I've walked by it," Sierra admitted. "But so far, I've managed to avoid the temptation."

"You won't be able to avoid it after today," Sky warned, opening the door to the bakery. "Because once you've tasted the deliciousness of Sweet Caroline's, resistance will be futile."

"I hope you're exaggerating," Sierra said. But as she followed the other woman inside and breathed in the mouth-wateringly decadent scent that permeated the bakery, she suspected she wasn't.

"Have you heard of Quinn Ellison?" Sky asked.

"The *New York Times* bestselling author?"

"That's the one," Sky confirmed. "She comes in here twice a week for the chocolate peanut butter banana croissant."

"Quinn Ellison lives in Haven?"

"Cooper's Corners actually, which is about fifteen miles from here."

"She drives fifteen miles to get a croissant?"

"No, she drives fifteen miles to get a *chocolate peanut but-*

ter banana croissant," Sky said. "And to stock her Bookmobile at the library."

"Apparently Quinn Ellison is every bit as interesting as the characters she writes," Sierra mused.

"She is, indeed."

"So...what days did you say she comes into town?"

Sky chuckled. "I didn't say. But it's Mondays and Wednesdays. Usually."

"It's Monday today," Sierra noted.

"And she's already been and gone," the woman behind the counter told them. "Took half a dozen croissants with her."

"This is Caroline," Sky said to Sierra. "The bakery's namesake."

"My mother started the bakery," Caroline explained. "I took over when she moved to Arizona a few years back."

"Caroline, this is Sierra Hart, the new ADA."

"Temporary ADA," Sierra clarified.

"You're filling in while Jade's on mat leave?" Caroline guessed.

Sierra nodded.

"Well, welcome to Haven. And to Sweet Caroline's."

"Thank you."

"What can I get for you ladies today?" Caroline asked.

"I'll have a hot chocolate and a chocolate peanut butter banana croissant," Sky said, as Sierra perused the herbal teas on display.

"Whipped cream on your hot chocolate?" Caroline asked.

"Of course."

"And do you want the croissant heated?"

"Yes, please."

"And for you?" Caroline asked, as her assistant got busy filling Sky's order.

"I'll try a cup of the raspberry bliss tea," Sierra decided. "Black."

"And?" Sky prompted.

She wanted to say "just the tea," but her mouth was watering as her gaze skimmed over the various offerings on display in the pastry case. "And a raspberry crumble bar."

Sky grinned.

"Good choice," Caroline said. "Do you want it heated with whipped cream?"

"Um." She looked to Sky for guidance.

"You have to go for the whipped cream if we're going to be friends."

"Yes, please."

Sky told Caroline to ring up their orders together and insisted on paying, promising to let Sierra pick up the tab next time.

"In case you were wondering, that's my way of saying that we're going to do this again."

"I'd like that," Sierra said, as they carried their mugs to a nearby table.

"Me, too. My best friend since high school moved to North Carolina in the fall, and I really miss having a female friend to talk to.

"I do have a sister—actually two sisters," she amended. "But Kate is busy with her career and her husband and kids—not necessarily in that order—and Ashley is only sixteen."

"Wow—that's quite an age gap," Sierra noted.

Sky shrugged. "Since everyone in this town knows everyone else's business and it's not exactly a secret, I'll tell you that Ashley is my half sister from a drunken encounter my dad had on the fifth anniversary of my mom's death."

She sniffled a little then and blinked away the moisture that covered her eyes. "I'm sorry. I'm not usually so emotional. But even though my mom's been gone a long time, I seem to miss her even more now that I'm going to be a mom."

"I know how you feel," Sierra said, fighting against her own tears. "About missing your mom, I mean," she hastened to clarify. Because despite having felt an immediate kinship with the other woman, she wasn't ready to share any more than that.

"You lost your mom, too?" Sky guessed.

"Both my parents, actually," she said. "They were killed in a car accident when I was fourteen."

"I'm so sorry," the other woman said. "And you definitely win the 'Most Tragic Childhood' round."

Sierra managed to smile, appreciating the attempt at humor. "Life does like to throw curveballs, it seems."

"Are you a baseball fan?"

"A Dodgers fan," she clarified.

"You can definitely be my new best friend," Sky decided. "And you're right about those curveballs." She touched a hand to the slight swell beneath her sweater. "Though sometimes they're exactly what we need, even if we don't realize it at the time."

Conversation paused for a moment while their desserts were delivered to the table.

"And now that we're best friends, do you want to tell me about the vibe between you and Deacon Parrish?"

Sierra's fork slipped from her fingers to clatter against the plate. "What? There was no vibe."

"There was definitely a vibe," Sky insisted. "And why wouldn't you embrace having a vibe with a very sexy man?"

"There was no vibe," she said again.

"I know a little about denial," Sky said. "But since I want to be your friend and not your therapist, I'll defer to you on this."

Sierra wasn't quite sure how to respond to that, so instead she asked, "What were you doing at the courthouse today?"

"Offering emotional support to a woman swearing out a statement for a restraining order."

"Not a fun way to start the week," Sierra noted sympathetically.

"But a lot better than the way hers ended, with a visit to the emergency room."

"No doubt."

"Now, back to Deacon," Sky said.

"I thought you were deferring to me."

"And I did—in the moment. But now I want to know why you're trying so hard to deny your attraction to him. Is there someone special in Las Vegas?"

"No," she admitted. "But even if I was attracted to him—and I'm not saying that I am—I'm only in town for six months."

"Your contract at the DA's office is for six months," her friend acknowledged. "But there's no reason you couldn't decide to stay in Haven after that."

"Not having a job would be one reason."

"And another reason?"

Sierra looked at her blankly.

"The way you said *one reason* implied that there might be another," Sky said.

"Isn't a lack of gainful employment reason enough?"

"Which isn't a direct answer to my question."

"My family is in Vegas."

"And yet, you obviously had reasons for leaving Vegas."

"A romance gone bad," she said lightly.

Skylar considered this as she sipped her hot chocolate.

"You don't strike me as the type of woman to run away just because her heart was broken," she finally remarked.

"Okay, so it was a little bit more than that," Sierra acknowledged. "The breakup coincided with a…work incident…that made me realize I didn't want to stay at the firm where I'd been working."

"I'm sorry," her new friend said.

"It was a tough decision to make, but I have no doubt that it was the right one."

"Are you talking about your ex or the job?" Sky wondered.

"Both."

"So you're not still nursing a broken heart?"

She shook her head.

"In that case, let's circle back to our original topic of conversation—Deacon Parrish."

"You can circle as many times as you want," Sierra told her. "I have no interest in a romance with Deacon Parrish or anyone else."

"How about sex?" Sky asked with a grin. "Because I can assure you, there isn't any better way to combat the chill of a long, cold Nevada winter than hot sex."

"I don't know," Sierra said. "My new boots are apparently rated to minus forty degrees."

Sky laughed. "Spoken like somebody who has cold feet when it comes to relationships."

"Well, right now, these feet need to get me back to the office."

"I've got things to do, too. But we definitely need to do this again," Sky said, then she frowned. "Or maybe we shouldn't."

Sierra was a little surprised—and disappointed—by the other woman's abrupt reversal. "Why not?"

"Because I have no doubt that we'd be great friends, but I already said goodbye to one of those and it was really hard, so I don't want to get too attached if you're really planning to leave at the end of your six-month contract."

"I *am* leaving at the end of my contract," Sierra told her, needing to be very clear about that.

"Of course, Jake didn't plan on staying, either," Sky said with just a hint of smugness in her smile. "And I've still got more than five months to change your mind."

CHAPTER SEVEN

RHONDA DORNAN WAS GUILTY.

She knew it, Deacon knew it, and he had no doubt that the ADA was going to prove it at trial. Which was why he'd spent the past three hours going over every piece of evidence with his client, to illustrate for her the strength of the prosecutor's case, though so far his efforts to convince her to change her plea had been futile.

"But there are mitigating circumstances," she kept insisting.

"And I will make sure those are taken into consideration at sentencing," Deacon assured the crying widow. "But they don't mean you're not guilty."

"I wasn't thinking clearly when I wrote those checks."

"But you did write the checks."

She didn't—couldn't—deny it. Not when anyone comparing her usual signature to the signatures on the checks could see that they were identical—even without the testimony of the handwriting expert on the district attorney's witness list.

"But I took the flowers to Twilight Valley, for the long-term care residents there to enjoy."

"Which was a thoughtful gesture," he acknowledged. "Or would have been if you'd actually paid for the flowers."

"But I made retribution."

"Restitution," he clarified. "And the fact that you paid back the people who were defrauded is another mitigating factor, but mitigating factors don't come into play until sentencing."

When he finally said goodbye to Rhonda, he had a much better understanding of the case that was going to trial—and absolutely no doubt that his client was going to be convicted.

Instead of immediately returning to his desk, he detoured to knock on the partially open door of his boss's office.

"Come in," Katelyn invited.

He pushed the door open wider and stepped inside.

She gestured to the chairs opposite her desk, inviting him to sit.

"How did it go with Mrs. Dornan?" she asked when he was settled.

"She's guilty."

"I had no doubt."

He frowned at that.

"Rhonda Dornan has been writing bad checks for longer than I've been practicing law," Katelyn told him. "It was her way of getting her husband's attention—and it usually worked, at least for a while. He'd repay whoever was wronged, adding a little extra to ensure they didn't grumble loudly enough to get the sheriff's attention, and take his wife out of town on a vacation.

"A year or so later, it would start all over again. The difference now is that Leopold isn't around to clean up her messes anymore."

"You're saying that her husband had money? That she wrote bad checks on purpose?"

"That's exactly what I'm saying," Katelyn said. "And now his money is hers, so don't feel guilty about billing her for every minute of your time."

"The trial—if she insists on going through with the trial—will likely take a few days, and I've got a couple of matters scheduled for small claims court Thursday afternoon."

"Are you okay letting Brenna handle them?" she asked, referring to another of the firm's junior associates. "Or should we ask the court to reschedule?"

"Brenna can handle them, if she doesn't mind."

"Why don't you get the files together for her before the end of the day?"

"I'll do that right now," Deacon said, rising to his feet. "But I have to admit, I hate going into court knowing that my client's guilty."

His boss smiled. "Welcome to the world of a defense attorney."

The rest of the week proceeded much as Deacon had anticipated.

Wednesday morning, the ADA gave opening arguments and called her first witness, then he went through the motions of cross-examination, though he made little progress in discrediting the testimony. Throughout the afternoon and all the next day, it was more of the same, with the ADA hammering more nails in his client's proverbial coffin through the precise and methodical presentation of her case.

Before court adjourned on Thursday, the judge informed both attorneys that the trial needed to be put over to Monday, as he had to go out of town to deal with a family emergency. He advised them to use the time to attempt to resolve the case, noting—with a pointed look at the defense attorney—that there didn't seem to be any doubt what the outcome would be.

Sierra didn't get many visitors.

In fact, aside from Ayesha Dhawan, who'd stopped by with a loaf of banana bread to welcome her to the neighborhood—and then stayed to chat for more than an hour—she hadn't had any visitors since she'd moved in. But if she was surprised by the knock on her door Saturday morning, she was even more surprised to find Deacon Parrish standing on her doorstep.

"Good morning, Sierra," he said politely.

"Good morning," she echoed, immediately following that up with the questions that sprang to the forefront of her mind. "But what are you doing here? And how did you know where I live?"

"Can't one neighbor visit another without there being ulterior motives?" he countered mildly. "Also, it was easy to figure out where you live because you drive a distinctive car."

And she loved every inch of the acid-green Kia Soul parked

in her driveway, but she was still a little wary. "So you drove around the neighborhood looking for my car?"

"You said you lived a couple blocks over," he reminded her. "It wasn't a far drive. Which is a good thing, because I brought tea—and treats—from Sweet Caroline's."

"Magic words," she admitted.

He grinned.

"I suppose you expect me to invite you to come in now?"

"I brought tea and treats," he said again.

She stepped away from the door.

He followed her down the hall and into the kitchen. "Nice place."

"I can't take any credit," she said. "I rented it furnished."

And though it hadn't really mattered to her what the place looked like, Sierra had been pleased to discover that she liked her temporary home. The rooms were spacious and bright and mostly decorated in subtle earthy tones, but the kitchen was her favorite room in the house—with steel blue cabinets, white quartz countertops, stainless steel appliances and a set of French doors that opened onto the back deck. (She hoped to get some use out of the deck in the spring and summer, but right now, those doors remained tightly closed, keeping the frigid air out while letting in lots of natural light.)

"Do you have a dog?" he asked, eyeing the flap in the wall adjacent to the doors.

"No," she said. "But I'm guessing the previous tenant—or more likely the owner—did."

"That's too bad," he said, removing the cups from the paper tray. "I like dogs—and they like me. And if you had a dog who liked me, maybe you'd realize I'm not such a bad guy."

"I don't think you're a bad guy," she denied.

"Raspberry bliss tea, black," he said, setting one of the cups on the counter in front of her.

"Although now I'm wondering if you're a stalker," she said, only half joking.

He smiled. "Would it reassure you to know that Sky was at Sweet Caroline's and suggested it?"

"Maybe," she allowed. Except that now she had another reason to be concerned. "So Sky knows that you were coming over here?"

"Is that a problem?"

Yes.

"No," she denied.

He peeled the lid off his own cup, and she inhaled deeply, filling her lungs with the fragrant scent.

His brows lifted. "I thought you didn't like coffee."

"I didn't say I didn't like it. I said I didn't drink it."

"I'm not even going to pretend to understand that," he said. "So I'll tell you that Sky also mentioned that you were partial to Sweet Caroline's raspberry crumble bar."

"It's the only thing I've had from the bakery," Sierra said. "But it was pretty darn good."

"Well, I got you one of those and a couple other things to try."

"What other things?" she asked, her curiosity definitely piqued.

"An almond croissant, a lemon tart, a chocolate éclair, a mille-feuille and a salted caramel brownie."

"Now I *know* you want something from me," she decided.

He held her gaze for a long moment—a hint of amusement along with something deeper in his eyes. "Maybe. But why don't we take it one brownie at a time?"

She lifted her cup to her lips and nearly choked on the hot liquid.

"Are you okay?"

She nodded, not sure that her scorched vocal cords were operational.

Deacon sipped his coffee, did not choke.

"But for today," he said, continuing with their conversation as if she hadn't just been coughing and sputtering, "I was hoping we could maybe chat about Rhonda Dornan before the trial resumes on Monday."

"Is your client planning to change her plea?"

"Give her an incentive to do so," he suggested.

"The incentive is that she could start serving her sentence right away and be out by spring, pending good behavior."

"That's not much of an incentive," he protested, lifting the lid of the bakery box.

Of course Sierra couldn't resist peering inside, and then she couldn't hold back the sound of pleasure that hummed in her throat when she saw the exquisite offerings contained within.

Deacon grinned, obviously satisfied by her reaction.

"Are you trying to bribe an officer of the court?" she asked, making her way to the cupboard to retrieve two plates.

"Of course not," he immediately denied. "I'm just enjoying a chat with a professional colleague."

"A professional colleague who has all the evidence she needs to prove every element of the crime," she said, taking a knife from the utensil drawer.

He eyed the sharp instrument warily. "My client wrote a few bad checks—she didn't commit capital murder."

Sierra cut through the middle of the chocolate éclair, then put half on each plate and slid one of the plates toward him. "She willfully defrauded more than a dozen people."

"She was grieving the loss of her husband and not thinking straight."

"It isn't the first time she's written bad checks," Sierra told him.

He dropped his gaze to study the pastry in front of him.

"But I'm guessing you knew that, didn't you?"

"She's made full restitution to all of the victims," he said, ignoring her question.

"Is there any point in us even having this conversation?" she asked wearily. "Mrs. Dornan's first attorney worked out a plea deal with my boss, and then she decided to toss it aside."

"Her grief has interfered with her ability to make smart choices," Deacon acknowledged. "But she didn't protest too vehemently when I told her that I wanted to talk to you about a resolution of the charges."

Sierra sighed. "If your client agrees to plead guilty to the charges first thing Monday morning, I will agree to honor the terms of the original deal."

"Thank you."

"But if she hesitates at all, the deal is off the table."

"Got it," he said, swiveling on his stool so that he was facing her. "And now that we've taken care of business..."

"You can go, but you're not taking the pastries," she told him.

"The pastries are for you," he assured her.

"Well, you can take half," she relented. "I definitely don't need all that sugar."

Now he smiled. "Don't you know that the best things in life aren't what we need but what we desire?"

It was suddenly very warm in the kitchen, and Sierra knew it had nothing to do with the thermostat control on her furnace and everything to do with the heat emanating from the very hot body of the man sitting far too close.

"What do you want right now, Sierra?"

You.

She swallowed the answer that immediately sprang to her lips. There was no way she could admit that truth to him, because nothing could ever come of her foolish desire.

She didn't even know the man, really, so she definitely shouldn't be lusting for his body.

Darn pregnancy hormones.

"The lemon tart," she said instead.

His lips curved in a slow smile as he lifted the tart out of the box and set it on her plate. "You don't want to like me, do you?"

"Why would you think that?"

"Because every time you start to warm up to me, even just a little, you deliberately pull yourself back."

Apparently the man was much more observant than she'd given him credit for—or maybe she was more obvious than she wanted to believe.

"I work for the DA's office. You're a defense attorney. It's inevitable that our jobs are going to create conflict between us."

"My boss has represented plenty of defendants put in cuffs by her husband, but they don't let that interfere with their relationship," he told her.

"Your point?"

"I don't think your hesitation is professional. I think it's personal."

"You want me to be honest? Okay, you're right—I don't

want to like you. You're a little too good-looking, too effortlessly sexy, too annoyingly charming, and you remind me, a little too much, of my ex-boyfriend."

"Ouch. I mean, the good-looking, sexy and charming parts were okay," he said. "But being compared to an ex is rarely a good thing."

"You asked for honesty," she reminded him.

"I did," he agreed. "And now I'm going to be honest and tell you that, notwithstanding your attempted evisceration of my character, I like you."

"Why? You barely know me."

He shrugged. "Apparently I have a thing for contrary women."

"Or you just like a challenge."

"That might be part of it, too," he acknowledged. "But the truth is, from the first moment I saw you, I knew that you were someone who was going to matter to me."

"But I'm not," she protested. "I can't be."

He just smiled again. "I'll see you in court Monday morning."

Then he walked out, leaving Sierra alone with a whole lot of desire that she knew would never be satisfied by a box of pastries.

CHAPTER EIGHT

AS A KID, Deacon loved Mondays. Especially during the school year. Because Mondays meant getting up early and getting out of the hellhole he'd called home. Then, for seven blissful hours, he could pretend that his life wasn't any different from that of Nathan Pineda or Chase Hampton or Travis Bell. And when he got home again, he could usually hide out in his room with the excuse that he had homework.

But dinner was a family affair, and he was expected to be at the table to eat with the family and then help with the cleanup afterward. He didn't mind the mealtime routine so much when his mom was home to cook and supervise the tidying. But his mom wasn't always home and his dad could be a mean sonofabitch, especially when he was drunk. And he was quite often drunk.

So after dinner, Deacon would go back to his homework, then he'd go to bed and get up and do it all over again the next day. And the day after that. And so on. It wasn't until the final bell went on a Friday afternoon that he'd get knots in his stomach. While his friends celebrated the end of the week and made plans for the weekend as the bus took them closer to home, the knots in Deacon's stomach tightened, because he knew that his dad was probably already drunk and angry and everything would only go downhill from there.

That had been his life until Dwayne Parrish went a little too far in disciplining his stepson one day. It was Deacon's fault—he'd knocked over his dad's beer, his dad had responded by knocking him over and Connor had immediately inserted himself between them. Because even at fifteen, his brother had the makings of a hero.

But he'd been no match for his stepfather, who was bigger and meaner and likely more than half drunk. Thankfully one of the neighbors heard the ruckus and called the sheriff.

It was Jed Traynor who'd worn the badge back then, and he'd shown up right about the same time that Faith arrived home from work. During all the commotion, Connor escaped out the back door, so the sheriff never saw how badly he'd been beaten, and Jed gave Dwayne a choice—leave the house voluntarily or be taken into custody to spend the night, or maybe a few years, in lockup.

Dwayne left voluntarily—and never came back.

Deacon's life settled down after that. And when he finally accepted that he no longer needed to tiptoe around the house, he started to enjoy weekends and the freedom they afforded from his Monday through Friday routines. The two-day break became even more important when he went away to school, not so much as a reprieve from classes as an opportunity to complete reading and assignments, to work hard and study harder. Because college wasn't just his escape from Haven—it was his chance to make something of his life, to prove that he was something more than the useless offspring of Faith Neal and Dwayne Parrish.

After two years as an associate in Katelyn Davidson's law office, he was finally starting to feel as if he'd done that. He'd also learned to fully appreciate weekends, especially when the time away from the office was spent with family or friends.

But as he drifted off to sleep Sunday night, he wasn't disappointed that the weekend was over, because he knew that he'd see Sierra in court the next morning, and he couldn't wait.

Late Friday afternoon, Sierra began to gather up the files on her desk to transfer them to her briefcase. After only a few weeks, she was starting to get used to packing up at five o'clock and suspected it would be a lot harder to readjust to the twelve-hour days that were the norm when she was living and working in Vegas.

As she zipped up the case, the blue box tucked in the outside pocket caught her eye, making her smile.

Rhonda Dornan had pleaded to the charges on Monday, per the terms of the original agreement, and the judge had signed off on her sentence of community service. The widow had seemed genuinely remorseful—and grateful—at sentencing, and she'd promised the judge that he wouldn't see her in court again. Sierra wasn't convinced, but that was a worry for another day.

After they'd finished in court, she'd surprised Deacon by offering to buy him coffee. Because he'd been right when he accused her of not wanting to like him, and she knew that wasn't fair. After all, it wasn't his fault that she was wildly attracted to him, and as long as she kept that fact to herself, she figured there was no reason they couldn't be friends—or at least friendly.

She'd suggested The Daily Grind rather than Sweet Caroline's, because the former was closer to the courthouse—and also, she told him, because she didn't want to be tempted by the offerings in Sweet Caroline's display case when she still had some in her fridge at home. But that wasn't actually true. After he'd gone Saturday morning, Sierra had taken the bakery box over to her neighbor, pawning the sweets off on Ayesha's family so that she wouldn't overindulge any more than she'd already done. (Of course, she'd almost immediately regretted doing so, and since then had been trying to alleviate her sweet tooth cravings with various "healthy cookie" recipes she'd googled. So far, none had quite hit the mark.)

Anyway, they'd had coffee together—or rather he'd had coffee and she'd had cranberry apple tea (not as flavorful as Sweet Caroline's raspberry bliss, but not bad)—and shared some conversation before going off in different directions. Though Sierra had been at the courthouse every day after that, she hadn't seen Deacon again until today, when he tracked her down to give her the box of cereal.

"Not a bribe but an apology," he'd told her.

"Apology accepted," she'd replied. "But contrary to what you apparently believe, I don't usually eat sugary cereal."

"And yet, you were ready to arm wrestle me for the last box of Frosted Flakes at The Trading Post the first day we met."

"A moment of weakness," she acknowledged.

"Do you have many of those?" he asked curiously.

"More than I'd like," she confessed.

He tipped his head toward her, a hint of a smile curving his lips. "Anything other than sugary cereal that makes you weak?"

Yes. You.

Even now, her heart was beating a little too fast and her knees were trembling, just because he was standing close to her.

She racked her brain for a more appropriate response. "Pastries from Sweet Caroline's."

"I probably could have guessed that one," he said.

"Then you know all my weaknesses."

"Not yet," he'd denied. "But I'm going to."

Then he'd given her a full, bone-melting smile before turning and walking away, and she'd stood there watching him go, a tiny part of her wishing that she might have met him at a different time, under different circumstances.

But she knew it was futile to wish for things that could never be, so she pushed the box deeper into the bag and pushed all thoughts of Deacon Parrish out of her mind.

"Four weeks down, only twenty more to go," Sierra said, as she slung the strap of her bag over her shoulder.

"Are you really hating the job so much that you're counting down the days?"

She felt heat rise into her cheeks as she glanced up to see investigative analyst Julie Keswick standing in her office doorway.

"I thought everyone else had gone," she admitted.

"Which doesn't answer my question," her colleague noted.

"I don't hate the job at all," Sierra said. "But I didn't anticipate that I'd miss my family so much."

"So why'd you take a job so far away from Las Vegas?" Julie wondered.

"Because I needed to get away from my family."

Her colleague chuckled at that. "What you need is a distraction," she decided. "I'm getting together with some friends tonight and heading to Sparkle—a new dance club in Elko. You should join us."

"I appreciate the invitation," Sierra said. "But I've actually got plans tonight."

"Hanging out with case files doesn't count as plans," her colleague protested.

"That's not what I was planning. Or not exclusively what I was planning," she amended, in response to the other woman's openly skeptical look.

Julie laughed. "Okay. But if you change your mind, you've got my number."

Sierra thought about the offer throughout the drive home. While she was pleased that the other woman had thought to include her, she was certain the invitation wouldn't have been issued if Julie had known of her condition.

Of course she was going to have to tell her colleagues about her pregnancy eventually—and probably sooner than she'd anticipated, considering that her pants and skirts were already starting to feel snug around her waist—but she wasn't in a hurry to make herself the hot topic of gossip at The Daily Grind. Not only because she was pregnant and unmarried—which shouldn't be at all scandalous in this day and age—but also because the circumstances of her pregnancy were a little unusual.

Then she pulled into her driveway, where a silver SUV was already parked, and the only thought on her mind was of her family, and her heart overflowed with joy that they were here.

Her brother stepped out of his vehicle at the same time she did hers, and she rushed into his arms.

"It's so good to see you," she said, somehow managing to push out the words around the lump in her throat. "But why didn't you tell me you were coming?" She turned her head then, looking for her sister-in-law, but the passenger-side door remained closed and the seat, she could see now, was empty. "And where's Whitney?"

"It's good to see you, too." His words were muffled in her hair as he held her tight. "And I didn't tell you I was coming because I was afraid that you'd tell me not to—especially as Whitney's stuck at home waiting for her jury to come back with a verdict."

"I would never tell you not to come," she assured him. "Though I might have pointed out that I've barely been gone a month."

"Can we continue this conversation inside?" he asked, shivering. "It's freezing out here!"

She chuckled. "Yeah, you were definitely right about the weather." She gave him one last squeeze before releasing him.

"I see you got a new coat."

"And new boots," she added.

She returned to her car to grab her briefcase while he retrieved his duffel bag from the backseat of his vehicle.

"How long has Whitney been waiting for her jury?" Sierra asked, as she unlocked the door and led her brother inside.

"Three days. She's trying to remain optimistic that they're deliberating the award rather than the verdict, but juries are unpredictable."

"Isn't that the truth?" Sierra agreed, hanging her coat. "You're probably thirsty after that long drive—what can I get for you?"

He set his boots on the mat beside hers. "Any chance you've got coffee?"

"Decaf."

"So long as it's hot, it'll do."

She set her briefcase on one of the stools at the island, then found a pod for her single-serve coffee maker, dropping it into place and setting a mug under the spout. While Nick's coffee was brewing, Sierra filled a glass of water for herself from the dispenser in the fridge, then put some cookies on a plate and set it on the counter.

Nick selected a cookie, took a bite. "Did you make these?"

"Yes, and they're good."

"No," he said, setting the cookie aside. "They're not."

"Well, they're at least good for you," she said. "Made with all natural ingredients and carob chips instead of chocolate."

"Why?"

"Because I'm trying to eat healthy—for the baby."

"Trust me," he said. "The baby doesn't want those any more than I do."

She returned the other cookies to the container. Most likely, she'd toss them in the garbage later, but she wasn't going to give her brother the satisfaction of doing so now.

"And if you're on such a health kick, what's with the box of Frosted Flakes in your bag?"

"What?" She followed his gaze, felt her cheeks heat. "Oh. That was a gift from a colleague."

"A rather strange gift," he noted.

"Yeah," she agreed.

"But it's a good sign that you're making friends already."

"I said a colleague, not a friend."

"But you had a little smile on your face when you were thinking about…him?"

She sighed. "Stop."

"Stop what?"

"Prying into my life."

"I'm not prying," Nick denied. "I'm interested. And happy that your broken heart seems to finally be on the mend."

"Okay, it's true that I've rediscovered my love for Frosted Flakes," she acknowledged.

Now her brother sighed. "Are you ever going to tell me what went wrong with Eric?"

"No, because you and Eric were friends long before he and I started dating, and I don't want what happened between us to cause a rift between the two of you."

"You're my sister," Nick said gently. "And even without knowing the details, I know he hurt you, so the rift is already there."

"I'm sorry for that," she said.

"So if you were seeing someone new, I'd take it as a sign

that you're moving on and be happy for you." He paused. "But I'd still be pissed at Eric."

"I appreciate the thought, but I can assure you that I don't have any plans to get involved with a new man—certainly not anytime in the next seven months."

Nick looked troubled by this assertion. "Because of the baby."

"Not only because of the baby, although I can't imagine any man wanting to get involved with a woman carrying someone else's baby—"

"Any man who truly cared about you wouldn't let a pregnancy get in the way," he interjected.

"—but also," she continued, "because I'm only going to be in town for another five months, so any relationship would automatically have an expiration date."

"That could be a bigger obstacle," her brother admitted. "And while some couples seem to make long-distance relationships work, the distance between here and Las Vegas is a little daunting."

"And yet, you drove all that way just to see me."

"I needed to see for myself that you were doing okay."

"I told you that I was."

"Are you suffering from any nausea?" he pressed.

"Occasionally," she admitted.

"It might be the cookies."

She balled up her napkin and threw it at him.

He caught it easily.

"And now," she said, pushing her stool away from the counter, "I'm going to cook dinner."

"Please, don't."

She narrowed her gaze.

"I just meant that I want to take you out for a meal," he said, eager to dig out of the hole he'd put himself into.

"You can take me out tomorrow," she said. "And you're going to pay—big-time—for disparaging my cookies, because I'm making a reservation at The Home Station, the fanciest place in town."

CHAPTER NINE

DEACON WASN'T IN the habit of getting tied up in knots over a woman, but there was no denying that he was all twisted up over the new ADA.

There were plenty of women in Haven, so why did he keep going back to the one who was always brushing him off?

And why did she keep brushing him off?

He'd considered the possibility that she had a boyfriend back in Vegas and discarded it for two reasons: one, he was certain that she would have told him if she did; and two, she'd mentioned that he reminded her of an ex-boyfriend. Which forced him to consider the possibility that she honestly wasn't interested, though he didn't want to believe that could be true. Because it didn't seem fair that he could be so tangled up while she was completely unaffected.

So when Ben had mentioned, at their morning pickup game, that a bunch of guys were getting together to enjoy some wings and watch the game at Diggers' that night, Deacon immediately agreed to join them.

A Saturday night with the guys was just what he needed to get his mind off a certain sexy brunette with dark eyes and kissable lips. And if the opportunity arose to flirt with other pretty girls, well, that would be even better.

Puck drop was scheduled for eight o'clock, but he pulled

into the parking lot behind Diggers' at seven forty-five, giving him just enough time to stop by the reception desk at The Stagecoach Inn and chat with Mariah for a few minutes before heading over to the bar.

"Hey, stranger." Mariah greeted him with a warm smile. "What brings you around here on a Saturday night?"

He held up a silver hoop earring.

She laughed. "Ohmygod—I was starting to think it was lost forever."

"Me, too," he admitted.

The earrings had been a gift from her grandmother—their value more sentimental than monetary, but Deacon and Mariah had combed every inch of his bedroom when she realized she'd lost it, to no avail.

"Where did you find it?" she asked.

"Lodged under the corner of the cabinet in the bathroom."

She smiled again. "We had some good times in there, too, didn't we?"

"We did," he agreed.

"Well, I'm glad to have this back." She tucked the silver hoop into the pocket of her jacket. "Thank you."

"You're welcome."

It struck him suddenly that the whole interaction between them was civil and bland, proving that whatever chemistry had once drawn them together had fizzled out long ago.

"I'm seeing someone."

The way she blurted out the information made Deacon realize that she thought he was lingering, perhaps in the hope of picking up where they'd left off.

The truth was, he'd been about to say "see you around" and head over to the bar when Sierra walked into the lobby of the hotel.

With a man.

"It's been a few months now," Mariah elaborated, when he failed to respond.

"That's great," he said, his attention focused on the ADA and her companion.

Were they headed to the desk to check in?

Or did her companion already have a room key in his pocket?

They turned toward the hotel restaurant, and he exhaled a sigh of relief.

They were here for dinner, not a hookup.

But who knew what might happen after a romantic meal and a couple glasses of wine?

Deacon certainly didn't—and he didn't want to speculate.

The coat check was located outside of the dining room, and he watched as Sierra's date helped her remove her coat before handing it to the attendant. She wore a lot of suits in court—pants and matching jackets or sometimes skirts and jackets—but Deacon had never before seen her in a dress before and... *wow*!

The dress was a wrap style with long sleeves, a short skirt and a deep V neckline. The color was somewhere between gold and brown (maybe bronze?) and the fabric hugged her curves in a way that he'd only dreamed of doing.

There was a comfortable familiarity between her and her date that suggested affection more than attraction. A theory that was given further credence when she hugged the man and he dropped a kiss on the top of her head before they disappeared into the restaurant together.

Old friends, perhaps?

Or was that just wishful thinking on his part?

He vaguely registered the sound of Mariah's voice and realized she was still talking about the new guy she was seeing, about how great he was, how happy they were together.

"Then I'm happy for you, too," he said.

The vibration of the phone in his pocket finally dragged his attention away from the door through which Sierra had disappeared. He pulled it out and glanced at the screen.

Wings R on the table.

That was followed, almost immediately, by another message:

FN Penguins just scored!

He quickly tapped out a reply:

Be there in 2 min.

"It was great to see you, Mariah, but I have to run," he said, lifting a hand in a wave as he headed toward the exit.

He was no longer in a sociable mood, but he took solace in the fact that he could bang his fist on the table and his buddies would think he was reacting to the game.

Sierra said goodbye to her brother Sunday morning and stood at the front window to watch him drive away. His SUV had barely disappeared from sight when another vehicle pulled into the recently vacated spot on her driveway.

She immediately recognized Deacon's truck from his visit the previous weekend.

"This is getting to be a habit," she said, when she responded to his knock on the door.

"Can I come in?"

"You seem to be empty-handed."

"Should I go to Sweet Caroline's and come back?"

"No," she said, stepping away from the door so that he could enter. "I've got a cup of tea in the kitchen already."

"Any chance you've got coffee?" he asked.

"Decaf."

He made a face as he pulled his boots off and left them by the door.

"Is that a *no* on the coffee?"

"That's a no," he confirmed.

"Hot chocolate?"

That seemed to pique his interest. "What kind?"

"The kind that comes in a little pod labeled Hot Chocolate."

"Well, it can't be worse than decaf coffee," he decided.

She popped a pod into the machine and positioned a mug beneath the spout. When the hot chocolate was ready, she set the drink on the island in front of him.

"Now are you going to tell me why you're here?"

"I was at Diggers' last night with some friends—one of whom is the drummer for the Cowboy Poets."

"Who?"

He frowned. "You really haven't heard of them?"

She shook her head.

"Well, they're a pretty big deal around here, and tickets to their shows can be hard to come by, but Gavin hooked me up with a pair of tickets for their show Tuesday night.

"It's at The Vicar's Vice in Battle Mountain, and I thought you might want to go with me. I know having a first date on Valentine's Day puts a lot of pressure on the date, but I promise it will be a good show."

He was asking her to go out with him. On Valentine's Day.

Her fickle heart fluttered.

She ignored it.

"I appreciate the invitation, but I'm going to have to decline."

"You already have plans for Valentine's Day?"

"No," she admitted. "And I don't want any, to be honest."

"How about Friday night, then?" he suggested as an alternative. "Maybe dinner and a movie?"

Another flutter.

"No, thank you," she said, polite but firm.

He studied her over the rim as he lifted his mug to his lips. "Is your answer going to be the same if I suggest another activity on another day?"

"It is," she confirmed.

"Because of the guy you were with at The Home Station last night?"

She was startled by the question. "Because I'm not in a place right now to consider any kind of romantic involvement," she told him. "And, FYI, the guy I was with last night was my brother, who hasn't had any say about who I date since I went away to college."

"I didn't know you had a brother."

"Probably because we don't really know anything about the other."

He smiled. "A problem that could be easily remedied if you'd only agree to go out with me."

Damn, he really was sexy and charming—and far too tempting. Which was why she needed to shut him down right now, before he proved to be a greater temptation than she could resist.

"Except that I don't see it as a problem," she said.

He finished his hot chocolate and carried the empty mug to the sink. "I'll get out of your way, then."

She had to bite her tongue to hold back the urge to apologize as she walked him to the door.

Because she was sorry that she'd had to say *no* when she really wanted to say *yes*.

Sierra had gotten in the habit of stopping at The Daily Grind on her way to the office in the mornings. Now that her stomach was no longer rebelling against the scent of coffee, she opted for the local café over the bakery because she was less tempted by the muffins and donuts in their display case than she was by the decadent offerings at Sweet Caroline's.

It was also closer to the courthouse, and that proximity meant it wasn't unusual for Sierra to see familiar faces there—another lawyer or a judge's secretary or an administrative assistant and, several times, Deacon. So she wasn't surprised to see that he was ahead of her in line when she entered the coffee shop Wednesday morning but, unlike the other times their paths had crossed, today he wasn't alone.

The woman he was with had blond hair cut in long layers that framed a heart-shaped face with porcelain skin, sharp cheekbones, a slightly pointed chin, green-gray eyes with dark lashes and a Cupid's bow mouth slicked with pink gloss. She was absolutely stunning, and though Sierra felt a stir of something in her gut that might have been envy, she couldn't deny that they made a gorgeous couple.

Deacon lowered his head to say something to his companion, and she tipped her head back against his shoulder and smiled up at him.

There was an easy affection between them that told Sierra they were close—two people who'd shared more than a single night together. And while she knew it shouldn't bother her— no doubt he had history with a lot of women in this town—it annoyed her to realize that after she'd turned down his invitation to go out on Valentine's Day, he'd immediately penciled another name into his calendar.

A completely irrational response, she acknowledged.

She'd told him she wasn't interested, and he'd taken her at her word. She should be relieved—even happy—that he'd found someone else to smile at, flirt with and deliver boxes of pastries to. Instead, she felt...annoyed. (She settled on that word again because she was unwilling to admit that her feelings might be a little deeper and a little more complicated than that.)

He ordered an extra-large coffee, black; the blonde asked for a decaffeinated, non-fat, sugar-free vanilla latte.

Deacon passed some money across the counter, then dropped his change into the tip jar, and they moved down the line to wait for their drinks to be prepared.

The next customer—a brunette with a ponytail and a weary smile—ordered two extra-large coffees, one black, one with double cream and sugar.

"How's MG doing?" the woman behind the counter asked cautiously, as she punched in the order.

"He has good days and bad—though more bad than good, it seems these days."

"It's gotta be tough for him, to be laid up. And for you, too, Paige."

The brunette—Paige—nodded and offered her debit card for payment.

The other woman waved it away. "This one's on me."

"Thanks, Felicia." Paige managed a wobbly smile as she moved down the line.

The two women behind Sierra, obviously having heard the same exchange, started whispering to one another. And though she wasn't trying to eavesdrop, Sierra managed to put together enough pieces to figure out that there had been some kind of accident at the ranch (which ranch? she had no idea, except that it was apparently MG's ranch) and that he was lucky to be alive.

"Cranberry apple tea, black," Sierra said, when it was her turn to order.

She paid for her drink and followed Paige to the other end of the counter just as Deacon and his companion got their drinks.

The blonde picked up her to-go cup and kissed his cheek. "Thanks again for last night."

His smile was warm and sincere. "Anytime."

It was only when his companion had gone—and Paige was getting her drinks—that he seemed to realize Sierra was standing there, waiting for her beverage.

"Good morning," he said.

She echoed his greeting coolly.

"Are you in court today?" Deacon asked.

"Not until this afternoon."

"Can we sit for a few minutes, then?"

Sierra murmured her thanks to the barista as she accepted her tea before turning her attention back to Deacon. "Was there something in particular you wanted to discuss?"

"No," he admitted. "I just thought it would be nice to have some company with my coffee instead of gulping it down on the run like I do most mornings. And a muffin," he decided. "Do you want a muffin?"

"No, thank you."

He went back to the counter, returning a minute later with a banana nut muffin on a plate.

"I didn't hear you offer to buy your...friend...a muffin," she noted.

"My friend?" he echoed, uncomprehending.

"The blonde whose lip gloss you're currently wearing."

"Oh." His lips curved as he rubbed a hand over his cheek. "Regan doesn't eat breakfast. And she's a lot more than a friend."

"Yeah, I got that impression," she acknowledged.

He eyed her speculatively. "Why are you mad at me?"

"I'm not," she denied.

"You sure sound mad," he noted. "And your tone is chillier than the weather this morning."

"I'm mad at myself."

"Because..." he prompted, tearing off a piece of muffin.

"Because I was actually starting to think that you were a decent guy."

"And now, because I didn't offer to buy Regan a muffin, you think I'm not?"

"And because, only three days ago, you invited *me* to go see the Poet Cowboys with you."

"Cowboy Poets," he corrected automatically. "And you turned me down."

"You're right," she acknowledged.

"And you think that I took Regan to the show," he realized.

"Or maybe you skipped the show," she allowed.

"But spent the night together."

"She thanked you for last night."

"You could have been the one thanking me for last night," he pointed out, a spark of what she was certain was amusement dancing in his eyes. "After all, I did ask you first."

"I told you that I wasn't looking for any romantic entanglements and I meant it."

He shrugged. "I'm not averse to skipping the romance and going straight to the sex, if that's your preference."

"Wouldn't I have to take a number—like at the deli counter in the grocery store?"

"Not necessary," he said. "We both seem to have a couple hours free right now."

"A not-at-all-tempting offer," she told him.

"I think you are tempted," he said. "And that's the real reason that you're annoyed."

He wasn't just arrogant—he was right.

She wasn't looking to get involved, and certainly not with another man who clearly had no understanding of loyalty or fidelity, and still there was something about Deacon that stirred her up.

Or maybe it was simply an overabundance of hormones running rampant through her system that was responsible for the inexplicable feelings churning in her blood.

"I'm on a dating hiatus," she reminded him.

"So you said," he acknowledged. "But seven months seems

like an excessive amount of time to get over a not-so-recent breakup that supposedly only bruised your heart."

"It's closer to six months now."

His brows lifted. "The fact that you're counting suggests that you agree it's an excessive amount of time."

"Speaking of time," she said, desperate to change the topic before she gave anything else away, "I really do need to get to the office."

"Then I guess we'll have to finish this conversation another time," he said.

She nodded, grateful for the reprieve and eager to escape.

Because despite her growing attraction to Deacon Parrish, she knew that nothing could ever come of it. For the next six and a half months, her focus needed to be on taking care of the baby in her womb.

And the absolute last thing she needed was to give her heart to another man who was likely to break it.

CHAPTER TEN

OVER THE NEXT WEEK, Sierra saw Deacon only in passing. And though he'd lift a hand to wave or offer a smile from across the room, he didn't seek her out for conversation. He'd obviously moved on, and she knew it was for the best. There was no point in nurturing the seeds of romantic fantasies that could never come to fruition.

The strange thing was that she kind of missed him. Aside from her ill-advised attraction, she'd actually started to like him. He was smart and interesting; he listened to her and challenged her; he made her feel seen and heard and valued in a way she hadn't experienced in a very long time.

Unfortunately it seemed that her first instincts about him had been right—he was a player and she wasn't interested in being played. Not again.

Anyway, she was keeping herself busy enough, getting to know her colleagues at the DA's office and meeting other people, not just at the courthouse but through interactions at the grocery store and the library and even the pizzeria. But Sky had claimed that they were going to be best friends, and Sierra was happy that their biweekly not-coffee dates seemed to be moving them in that direction.

"I gave notice to Duke that I'm quitting my job at Diggers',"

Sky said, when she sat down across from Sierra at their usual table at Sweet Caroline's.

"Whatever will you do with all your free time now that you'll only have two jobs?" Sierra wondered.

Her friend grinned. "Well, as Jake pointed out, in about four more months we'll have a baby to fill some of that time. And while I love hearing the personal confessions that seem to be part and parcel of tending bar, I don't love being on my feet until the wee hours of morning."

"Duke's going to be sorry to lose you."

"He offered to give me a stool. Or a raise. Then a stool and a raise." Sky rifled through her enormous purse, obviously looking for something. She pulled out a stainless steel water bottle decorated with numerous and various stickers and set it on the table as she continued to examine the contents of her bag. "Here it is," she said, triumphantly holding up her phone. "I'm waiting to hear from the high school about a meeting with a student, and I don't want to miss the call."

Sierra nodded, but her attention was on the water bottle—more specifically, one of the stickers on it.

"Are you a fan of the Cowboy Poets?" she asked.

"A huge fan," Sky said. "Jake and I got to see their show in Battle Mountain on Valentine's Day. But I'm kind of surprised that you know their music—I didn't think they had much of a following outside of this part of the state."

"I don't know their music," Sierra admitted. "But I was invited to that Valentine's Day show."

"Why am I only hearing about this now?" her friend demanded.

"Because I didn't think it was important, especially since I declined the invitation."

"Who... It was Deacon!" Sky said, answering her own question before she finished asking it. "Deacon invited you to the show, didn't he?"

"Yeah."

"And you turned him down...why?"

"Because I'm only going to be in town for another few

months, and I have no interest in getting involved with anyone while I'm here."

"I'm going to ignore the first part of that statement," Sky said.

"Now who's in denial?" Sierra couldn't resist teasing.

"And focus on the second," her friend continued. "Because while I understand all the reasons that you might be reluctant to open up your heart again, I wouldn't be a very good friend if I didn't tell you that Deacon is a really great guy and you might be sorry if you let him slip through your fingers."

"Too late."

"What do you mean?"

"He asked me to go to the show, I said no and he took someone else."

Sky frowned. "I don't think he did. I mean, The Vicar's Vice was pretty packed but it's not very big, so I'm sure I would have seen him if he was there."

"Maybe he gave the tickets away," Sierra allowed. "But he definitely celebrated Valentine's Day with someone else because I ran into both of them at The Daily Grind the next day."

"Hmm."

"You don't believe me?"

"I believe he was there—and with a woman, but I suspect you might have misinterpreted what you saw."

"I also heard her say, 'Thanks again for last night.'"

"That sounds pretty damning," Sky acknowledged. "But I still think there might be another explanation."

"It doesn't matter," Sierra said. "Because he's moved on and, considering how often we find ourselves on opposite sides of a courtroom, that's a good thing."

"Keep telling yourself that—because I don't think you quite believe it just yet."

"Anyway..." She let her words trail off when her friend's phone chimed.

"That's the school," Sky said. "I'm sorry, but I have to run."

"No worries," Sierra said. "I've got an appointment to get to, too."

* * *

Deacon had a rare, unscheduled afternoon on Tuesday, so when his brother texted to ask a favor, he was able to agree. Fifteen minutes later, he was in the parking lot of Blake Mining.

"Thank you for this," Regan said, as she buckled her seatbelt.

Deacon waited for the click before shifting into Reverse to back out of the parking spot. "You know I'm always happy to help," he told his sister-in-law. "Mostly because I'm keeping a tally of all the favors that I do for you so that you can reciprocate someday."

"I'm pretty sure you're joking, but I don't even care if you're not, because there's no way Connor and I could ever repay you for everything you do."

"Well, you did let me live with you all those holidays and summers when I came home from college."

"It was your home, too," Regan said.

"But it's lucky for all of us that I've got a place of my own now, because you're going to need that extra room for the new baby."

"Are we crazy?" she asked.

"That's probably a question you should have asked before you decided to have unprotected sex," Deacon told her.

She laughed. "I really hope Connor can get there in time for the ultrasound today—our first chance to see the baby."

"He'll be there," Deacon said confidently.

The deputy sheriff had been scheduled to testify in court that morning, but the lawyers had wasted so much time bickering over other matters that the judge had postponed his testimony until after lunch.

"How can you be so sure?"

Of course, he wasn't really sure, but he knew that what his sister-in-law needed right now was reassurance. "He didn't miss any of your appointments when you were pregnant with Piper and Poppy, did he?"

"No," she admitted, a smile curving her lips at the memory. "In fact, he was right there, holding my hand, when we found out I was carrying twins."

"And he'll be there this time when you get the same news."

"That's not funny," Regan told him.

"Actually, it is kind of funny," he said. "Could you imagine—*Double* Double Trouble?"

She shook her head. "I'd rather not."

Sierra had been hesitant to find a new doctor when she moved to Haven, albeit temporarily. She had a wonderful ob-gyn in Vegas, and she couldn't imagine sharing the same kind of rapport with a stranger. Or maybe she was worried that another doctor might not be as supportive of what she was doing as Dr. Shah had been from the beginning.

But the truth was, she hadn't really had a choice. Unless she wanted to make the long trip back to Vegas every four weeks for a checkup—which she definitely did not—she had to find a local doctor. Dr. Shah had recommended Dr. Camila Amaro.

At her first appointment, she'd spent almost an hour with the physician, going over not just her medical but familial history and talking about the unique circumstances of her pregnancy. And though the doctor's office in Battle Mountain was barely a twenty-minute drive from Haven, Sierra didn't worry about running into anyone she knew at the prenatal clinic, because the only other person she knew who was pregnant was Sky, and her friend's appointments were always on Fridays.

She certainly didn't anticipate that she might cross paths with Deacon Parrish there, but that's exactly what happened Tuesday afternoon. She was walking out of the clinic as he was walking in—with the same blonde woman he'd been with at the coffee shop.

Regan, he'd called her.

And she's a lot more than a friend.

Sierra halted in mid-stride, desperately looking around for an escape. But there was one door—and he was holding it open for her. Or maybe just holding it open, as his attention was on his companion and whatever she was saying.

So Sierra drew in a deep breath and walked right past him, murmuring a quick, "Thanks."

But she made the mistake of glancing up and their eyes met.

His widened in surprise, but she hurried away before he could say anything.

She punched the button to summon the elevator, silently chastising herself for believing that going to an out-of-town clinic would allow her to be anonymous. Not that she planned to keep her pregnancy a secret forever—an impossibility in any event. But she had hoped to keep it to herself a while longer, and if she was going to confide in anyone about the baby she carried, her first choice certainly would not have been Mr. Columbia Law.

Connor rushed into the waiting room of the clinic just as his wife's name was called, allowing Deacon to breathe a sigh of relief that his brother would be there to hold Regan's hand while they got a first peek at their baby. Of course, it also meant that Deacon had to rush back to Haven to pick up the twins from day care, but that was a task for which he was much better suited.

Piper and Poppy chattered the whole way home, regaling him with the most minute details of their day. As he listened to them talk, he secretly marveled over the fact that, just about four and a half years ago, his brother and sister-in-law had been looking at their tiny images on a screen.

Actually, Regan hadn't been his sister-in-law then, but she and Connor had married a few weeks later. Though Deacon didn't believe that getting married was necessarily the right thing for every couple having a baby together, it had certainly been the right thing for his brother and sister-in-law.

Even if, at the time, Deacon had been certain that Connor had taken leave of his senses. Because the rarefied world of mansions and manicured lawns in which Regan grew up couldn't have been further away from the rundown neighborhood where Connor and Deacon had occasionally kicked a battered soccer ball around the patchy grass of their postage-stamp-sized backyard.

But there was no denying that Regan loved his brother and the family they'd made together, and Deacon was sincerely pleased that their family would be expanding.

When they got home, he sat Piper and Poppy at the table with a snack—veggie sticks and dip. Baxter, their faithful canine companion, took up position under the table, ready to snatch up any bits of food that might fall off the table.

While the girls were eating, he rummaged through the refrigerator to see what he could find for dinner and wondered what Sierra had been doing at the medical clinic in Battle Mountain. He wouldn't have given her presence there a second thought if not for the fact that she'd seemed determined to avoid eye contact with him.

Or maybe he was reading something into nothing.

He pulled out a tray marked Chicken Broccoli Casserole with neatly printed heating instructions on the label. Apparently the Channings' long-time housekeeper was still feeding her employers' kids—despite the fact they all now had kids of their own.

"Whatcha doin', Unca Dunca?" Piper asked, deliberately dropping a cucumber round onto the floor for the dog. Baxter snatched it up happily.

"I'm getting dinner started so your mom and dad don't have to worry about it when they get home—and so that they'll invite me to stay."

Poppy wrinkled her nose as she examined the contents of the tray. "I don' wike bwok-wee."

"I'll tell you a secret," Deacon said, programming the recommended oven temperature. "I'm not a big fan, either, but I do like Celeste's chicken broccoli casserole."

Poppy, having finished what she wanted of her snack—and fed the rest to the dog—hopped down from her seat. "Can we do T-shirts now?"

"I don't know what that means," he admitted.

The little girl giggled and lifted the hem of her sweater to show him what she was wearing underneath. "Dis is a T-shirt."

"I know what a T-shirt is," he said. "But I don't know how to make one."

"Wif paint an' spah-kohs."

"You want to decorate T-shirts?"

She nodded.

He glanced at Piper.

She shrugged.

"Mommy's got ev'rythin' set up," Poppy said, taking his hand and leading him to the dining room where, sure enough, the table was covered with newspaper and craft supplies, with two pink child-sized T-shirts laid out.

Baxter, who'd been watching over the twins since the first day Connor and Regan brought them home from the hospital, followed.

"I think I'd better check with Mommy," he said, and sent a quick text message to his sister-in-law.

Regan immediately replied:

Make sure they wear their smocks and keep an eye on them—that stuff can be messy.

"Mommy says okay, but you have to wear your smocks."

Poppy immediately handed him hers—designated as such by her name printed across the bottom of it—so that he could help her into it. When she was ready, he picked up Piper's smock.

She folded her arms over her chest.

"Don't you want to decorate a T-shirt?"

"I wanna dec'rate my shoes, but Mommy said *no*."

"I can't imagine anyone not wanting—" he looked more closely at the supplies on the table "—puffy paint and glittery glue on their shoes," he said. "But if Mommy said you should decorate a T-shirt, then you should decorate a T-shirt."

With a heavy sigh, she unfolded her arms and let him help her with the smock.

While they were occupied with their craft, he decided to check his email, in case he'd missed anything important while he was out of the office. He filtered out the junk, drafted a couple of quick replies and flagged other messages that required more detailed responses to be dealt with later, periodically poking his head into the dining room to see how the twins were making out.

The paint was messy, but they were giggling and obviously having a good time—even Piper—so he let them be.

Connor and Regan returned home a short while later.

"How did it go?" Deacon asked. "Was the doctor able to tell you what you're having?"

The expectant parents looked at one another, as if not quite sure how to answer the question.

"Twins," Connor finally responded. "We're having twins."

"Again," Regan added.

Deacon couldn't help but chuckle at the stunned expressions mirrored on their faces.

"This is your fault," Regan accused.

He held up his hands in a gesture of surrender. "I bear absolutely no responsibility for your condition."

"You *joked* about me having twins again on the way to the clinic."

"I'm pretty sure there were already two little zygotes when I made the remark," he felt compelled to point out in his defense.

"The babies are well past the zygote stage," his brother told him.

"Not the point," Regan told her husband.

"What are the odds of having a second set of twins?" Deacon wondered aloud.

"Apparently pretty good when a woman is a hyperovulator. Of course, Regan's always been an overachiever," Connor said, with an affectionate glance toward his wife.

"So it's *your* fault," Deacon couldn't resist teasing his sister-in-law.

"Laugh all you want," she said, as the oven timer buzzed. "Because I promise you, I'll be the one laughing when it's your turn."

Deacon's name was on the docket as counsel for one of the defendants at First Appearance Court the following morning. Though Sierra trusted that he wouldn't comment on her doctor's appointment in the middle of the courtroom, she was nevertheless a little apprehensive. But when he approached the prosecutor's table, she found herself fighting to hold back the smile that wanted to curve her lips.

"Nice shoes," she remarked.

"Thanks," he said. "They're designer originals."

"Double Trouble?" she guessed.

He nodded. "And yet their mother wonders why I call them that."

"They look like they were new shoes."

"Cole Haan loafers that I wore for the first time yesterday."

"It could have been worse," she said, giving in to the smile now. "They could have decorated your cowboy boots."

"That would have been worse," he acknowledged.

CHAPTER ELEVEN

SIERRA PAUSED IN the entranceway of Diggers', surprised by the crowd that was already gathered at six o'clock on a Friday. Though there weren't any signs indicating that the bar was closed for a private event, the brightly colored streamers and balloons decorating a trio of booths against the far wall suggested that a celebration of some kind was going on, giving her pause.

"Grab a table wherever you can find one," a server said, as she made her way past with a tray of drinks.

"Okay," Sierra agreed, though she'd already decided that she wasn't going to stay.

Her decision to stop at the local bar and grill had been an impulsive one, and though her stomach was seriously rumbling for some of Diggers' infamous wings, she didn't feel up to battling with a crowd tonight.

Or maybe what she didn't want was to be alone in the crowd.

She'd stop at The Trading Post and pick up some chicken wings to cook in her air fryer at home instead, she decided.

And turning to leave, she walked right into Deacon Parrish.

"Whoa," he said, catching her arms when she stumbled back, reeling from the accidental bump and, even more, the awareness that sparked as a result of the physical contact. "Where are you rushing off to in such a hurry?"

She ignored the heat pulsing through her veins and pulled herself together to respond to his question. "The grocery store."

He grinned. "Are you having another Frosted Flakes emergency?"

"It's chicken wings this time."

His brows lifted. "Did the kitchen run out?"

"No. I mean, I don't think so. I didn't get any farther than this because it looks like there's some kind of big party happening."

"It's not a party—it's the last Friday of the month, which is when a bunch of us get together for a few drinks and some of those wings you're in the mood for. Come and join us."

"The streamers and balloons indicate it's a party," she told him.

He glanced over her shoulder and winced when he spotted the decorations. "Well, it wasn't supposed to be a party."

Following his gaze, she realized now that she recognized several people—including Katelyn Davidson, Deacon's boss, Brenna Flaherty, another associate from Katelyn's office, and the deputy sheriff, who she'd recently learned was Deacon's brother.

"It's your party," Sierra said, feeling foolish that it had taken her so long to put the pieces together.

"It's not a party," he said again.

The slight pique in his tone made her realize that Mr. Columbia Law didn't like people making a fuss over him—or at least over his birthday.

Just then, the exterior door opened and a couple more people walked in, bringing a blast of wintry air with them.

"Helluva night for a party, Dekes," the taller man with curly dark hair said, stomping the snow off his boots.

Deacon just sighed.

"There better be cake," the shorter guy with reddish hair and an unshaven jaw grumbled.

"It's a birthday party. Of course there's going to be cake," Curly told him. "The question is—will a half-naked chick jump out of it?"

Deacon shook his head. "You're such a Neanderthal, Luke."

"I'll take that as a no," Curly—Luke—said, in a disappointed tone.

"Who's your special guest?" Red asked. Though the question was obviously directed at Deacon, he was looking at Sierra.

"Sierra Hart, the new ADA," he said, sending her an apologetic glance. "Sierra, meet Ben Powell and Luke Ross."

"A pleasure," Ben said, touching the brim of his cowboy hat.

"Why don't you go charm the bartender into pouring you a couple of beers?" Deacon suggested, literally nudging his friends along.

"I can do that," his friend agreed. "And what can I get for you, Sierra?"

"Lost," Deacon said firmly.

Ben finally took the hint and followed Luke into the bar.

"Sorry about that," Deacon said.

"I'm the one who should apologize—I didn't mean to crash your party."

"You haven't crashed anything," he assured her. "Come on in and have some wings."

"Is it a milestone birthday?" she wondered. "Or do you always celebrate like this?"

"Not always," he denied. "But…well, the last few years have been like this. My sister-in-law's doing."

"She's big on parties?" Sierra guessed.

"Something like that," he hedged.

"Which means there's more to the story."

"Not one you're likely to be interested in," he said.

"What if I am?"

"Then come on in and I'll tell you about it."

She was wavering.

Then another server walked by carrying a platter of wings covered in sweet, sticky sauce and Sierra's stomach rumbled.

"What kind of wings did you order?" she asked.

"Every kind," he promised.

"Honey garlic?"

"Of course," he said. "Because those are my favorite."

"Then I guess you're going to have a chance to tell me that story."

* * *

Of course, it was too loud and crowded in the bar to be able to have much of a conversation, especially when there was a steady stream of people coming up to the booth where they were sitting to wish Deacon a happy birthday.

But there were wings, as he'd promised. Platters heaping with wings of every flavor, served with celery and carrot sticks and blue cheese dip. There were also mozzarella sticks and onion rings and potato skins and garlic bread.

Sierra filled half her plate with the fresh veggies before she allowed herself to take a little bit of everything else. Unfortunately, by the time the platter of honey garlic wings made its way around to her, there was nothing left on it but smears of sticky sauce.

Deacon left the table for a minute to greet some more friends who came in, and Brenna Flaherty and her husband, Gerard, slid into the seat that he'd vacated. Sierra didn't mind—she'd gotten to know Brenna a little during the few weeks that she'd been in town, and she found out now that both Brenna and Gerard had known the birthday boy since elementary school.

When Deacon returned to the booth, taking the seat beside Sierra, he had another platter of wings in-hand.

"Honey garlic," he said, adding a wink as he set the platter between them.

She smiled her appreciation and transferred several of the wings to her plate as a trio of Deacon's friends made their way over, each carrying two shot glasses.

"Happy birthday." Ben set one of his shots on the table.

"Happy birthday." Luke set another shot next to the first.

"Happy birthday." A third man, whom Sierra had not yet been introduced to, added a third.

"Thanks, guys," Deacon said. "But you know I don't do shots."

"We know," Ben confirmed. "But we bought them for you, because it's your birthday. And now, being the good friends that we are, we're going to drink them for you."

And they proceeded to do exactly that.

Katelyn and her husband approached the booth as the three men tossed back the first round of shots, then the second.

"You guys better not be driving," Katelyn cautioned.

"It's okay," Luke said with an exaggerated wink. "We know a good defense attorney."

"They're not driving," Deacon hastened to assure his boss as his friends wandered off. "My brother's playing taxi tonight."

"Good thinking," the sheriff said. "You don't want to have to wake a judge up on a Saturday morning to attempt to get your idiot friends out of jail."

"Or maybe he does," Gerard said, winking at Deacon. "If he could guarantee that the new ADA got the call."

"Why would you say that?" Sierra asked curiously.

"Because he's been hot for her since day one."

"Shut up, Gerard." This was a whispered plea from his wife. "Shut up *now*."

"Why? Is it supposed to be some kind of secret?"

Brenna dropped her head to thunk it against the table.

Katelyn pressed her lips together, obviously trying to hold back a smile.

"Well, this isn't awkward at all," Deacon remarked dryly.

"What?" Gerard said.

His wife finally lifted her head, her cheeks as red as the single hot wing left on the platter in the middle of the table. "Sierra *is* the new ADA."

"Oh. Crap." He glanced first at Sierra, then Deacon. "Sorry, man."

"Anyway," Reid said, his hazel eyes dancing with amusement. "We just wanted to stop by to wish you a happy birthday again before we head out."

"You can't leave before we have cake," Deacon protested.

"We have to," Katelyn said. "We promised the babysitter that we'd be home by nine."

Sierra glanced at her watch as Deacon rose from his seat to hug his boss and shake hands with her husband. "I didn't realize that it was so late."

"When did nine o'clock become late?" Gerard wondered.

"When we started adulting," Brenna said, nudging him with her elbow. "We should be on our way, too."

"But we haven't had cake," her husband protested.

"Deacon and Sierra need to talk about the elephant you brought into the room."

"No," Sierra said. "We don't."

"Stay," Deacon chimed in, returning to his seat.

"Hey, there's another one of your...friends," Sierra said, grateful to be able to change the topic of conversation.

Brenna twisted her head to follow the direction of Sierra's gaze. "Looks like the newlyweds are back from their honeymoon."

"We should have gotten married in February," Gerard said. "A Caribbean vacation in February makes more sense than one in June."

"Maybe," his wife acknowledged. "But I didn't want to be trudging through snow in my wedding dress and then swapping my shoes for warm slippers at the reception, like Liberty did."

"You were there?" Deacon sounded surprised by this revelation. "I heard it was going to be a small wedding, mostly just family."

"Liberty probably told you that because Travis refused to let her invite anyone who'd seen her naked," Gerard said, then winced. "And I just did it again, didn't I?"

"That wasn't exactly a revelation," Sierra assured him. "Liberty was happy to walk down memory lane with Deacon when they crossed paths at Jo's a few weeks back."

"We all have a history," Gerard said. "Travis Bell, Luke Powell, Chase Hampton, Dekes and me have known one another since kindergarten."

"Wait a minute," Sierra said, holding up a hand. "Are you telling me that Liberty's husband's name is Travis *Bell*?"

Three heads nodded confirmation.

"So now her name is... *Liberty Bell*?"

More nods, smirks.

Sierra pressed her lips together, trying to hold back the laugh that bubbled up inside her.

"I suggested that she should keep her maiden name," Brenna told them. "She asked me why."

"It's probably not so bad, being Liberty Bell from Haven, Nevada," Deacon said.

"But she better hope they never move to Philadelphia," Gerard added.

They all lost the battle against laughter then.

A cheer went up from the crowd when the cake arrived, a huge slab brought in on a wheeled cart being pushed by the "a lot more than a friend" Regan.

"Hey—no outside food or drink," the bartender called out.

"A big corner piece of this cake has your name on it, Duke," Regan called back, with a smile and a wink.

"Carry on, then," he said, with a wave of his hand.

She wheeled the cart closer to Deacon and everyone—even the patrons on the other side of the bar—began singing "Happy Birthday."

Sierra had been having a good time with Deacon's friends. Now she wished she'd never accepted his invitation to join the party.

Did he know the other woman was going to be here?

He certainly didn't seem surprised to see her—or the least bit uncomfortable about her presence.

The deputy sheriff made his way to the front of the crowd. "Why aren't there any candles on the cake?"

"Because no one wants to eat cake that someone has spit all over," Regan told him.

"I would hope my brother would spit a lot less than the twins, and you let them have candles on their birthday."

"They each had one candle in their own cupcakes."

The deputy sheriff and the blonde continued to bicker good-naturedly as they cut and served the cake—moist lemon sponge, layered with white chocolate mousse and strawberry *pâté de fruit* jelly, with an Italian buttercream icing—and the pieces finally clicked together in Sierra's mind.

"So Regan's your sister-in-law," Sierra said to Deacon when Brenna and Gerard had gone, leaving them alone at the table.

"Uh-huh," he agreed.

"Why didn't you tell me that when I saw you with her at the coffee shop, the morning after Valentine's Day?"

He shrugged. "It seemed to me you'd already made up your mind about who she was—at least in relation to me."

"Because I heard her say, 'Thanks for last night.'"

"She was thanking me for giving them my Cowboy Poets tickets—and babysitting their kids—so that they could have a night out."

"Oh," she said, feeling foolish.

"Although now I kind of understand why you were annoyed that morning," he said. "You assumed I was flirting with you after spending the night with another woman."

"You could have just told me who she was."

"I could have," he acknowledged. "But green is a good color on you."

"You think I was jealous?"

"Weren't you?"

"No," she denied. *Lied.*

"So how long are you going to pretend there isn't something between us?" he challenged.

"I'm not pretending anything."

He shifted on the bench seat, moving a little closer so that his thigh was pressing against hers, his arm touching hers.

She swallowed.

"There's definitely something," he said.

"A basic physiological attraction, perhaps," she said dismissively.

He rephrased. "Chemistry."

"Equally irrelevant," she assured him.

He lifted a hand to tuck a strand of hair behind her ear, letting his fingertip trace the outer shell, making her shiver.

His lips curved. "Do you really think so?"

"I know so," she insisted.

"So if I kissed you now, you wouldn't kiss me back?"

Her breath hitched; her heart raced. "If you kissed me now, in front of all these people, I'd introduce you to my right hook."

His smile widened. "What I'm hearing you say is that it's the location rather than the kiss that you'd object to."

Her cheeks burned. "It's both."

He held her gaze. "Is it really?"

She bumped her hip against his, signaling that she wanted out of the booth. "Good night, Deacon."

He rose to his feet. "I'll walk you out."

"That really isn't necessary."

"Haven may be a friendly town, but it's late and it's dark," he said, helping her with her coat before donning his own and following her to the door.

"It's snowing," she said, smiling as she tipped her head back to watch the flakes falling from the sky.

"Doesn't it snow in Vegas?"

"Hardly ever. And while I'm not a huge fan of snow on the ground, especially when I have to shovel it, snow falling from the sky is different," she said. "Almost magical."

"Except in a blizzard—then it's dangerous," he told her.

"This isn't a blizzard. Is it?"

He chuckled. "No. Definitely not a blizzard."

A fat snowflake landed on her cheek, then melted against the warmth of her skin. He lifted a hand to brush the trace of moisture away with his thumb.

Her whole body went still.

Even her breath stalled in her lungs.

His hand fell away.

She exhaled slowly. Unsteadily.

"Do you miss Las Vegas?" he asked her now.

She was grateful for the question—the return to neutral ground. "Not as much as I thought I would."

"I didn't think I'd ever come back here after college," Deacon confided. "But there's a sense of community here that I've never felt anywhere else."

"I can see that." She started to walk again, away from the restaurant, and paused after taking about a dozen steps to stand beside the green Kia. "This is my car."

"Hard to miss," he noted with a smile.

"And now you know why I said it was unnecessary for you to walk me to my car."

"But it was necessary," he said. "Because you wouldn't let me kiss you in front of all those people."

"And I'm not going to let you kiss me now."

"Aren't you as curious as I am to know if the chemistry between us will flare or fizzle?"

"Curiosity aside, I don't think it's a good idea," she told him.

But she didn't move away.

Not even when he took a step closer.

Their gazes held for one heartbeat. Two.

"Yet one more thing about which we obviously disagree," he said, just before his mouth covered hers.

CHAPTER TWELVE

SIERRA WOULD BE lying if she said she hadn't thought about kissing Deacon, but she'd never thought it would actually happen. And while the rational part of her brain was shouting at her to end this madness—because it had to be madness—the desire rushing through her veins drowned out the shouting. And that was before his tongue dipped between her lips to tease and tangle with hers.

It was only a kiss, but it felt like so much more.

Made her want so much more.

She clutched at his jacket, holding on to him as she kissed him back.

It was a long time later, and only when they were both desperate for air, that he eased his mouth from hers.

"Tell me again that there's nothing between us," he said, whispering the words against her lips.

"Apparently there is some chemistry," she acknowledged breathlessly. "But I'm still not going to sleep with you."

She felt rather than saw his lips curve.

"I don't want to sleep with you," he said. "I want to strip you naked and spend hours exploring every inch of your body with my hands and my lips and—"

"I'm not going to have sex with you, either."

But her voice wavered, *dammit*.

Because she wanted all the same things he did, so much so that her body was practically quivering. And if circumstances had been different, she might have taken what he was offering and had no regrets afterward.

But circumstances weren't different, and she couldn't let herself succumb to the desire thrumming in her blood.

"I got a baseball glove for my tenth birthday," he said, surprising her with the abrupt change of topic. "Brand new. That in and of itself had been a big thing, as money was always tight in our house. Gifts were more often secondhand or homemade, and I can still remember the scent and suppleness of the leather."

She was surprised by this revelation—and even more so to realize that Mr. Columbia Law hadn't led the charmed life that she'd imagined.

"It was the very best birthday present I ever got," Deacon continued. "Until now."

"It was a pretty great kiss," she allowed. "But it's not going to lead to anything else. It can't."

"You keep saying that, but you haven't told me why."

"The why doesn't matter."

"It matters to—"

"Shh!"

His brows lifted. "Did you really just *shush* me? We were in the middle of—"

She touched a hand to his lips.

Deacon heard it then, a plaintive whimper in the distance. "Is it...a dog?"

Sierra squinted into the darkness as another whimper sounded. "It sounds like it might be, but I can't see anything."

Though streetlights illuminated the sidewalk and nearby storefronts, the narrow alley between the restaurant and adjacent office building was in shadow.

He turned on the torch app on his phone and directed the light at the ground before venturing into the alley, Sierra right behind him.

There was a trash can against the building, and a tiny creature cowering behind it.

"It *is* a dog," she said softly.

He caught her arm when she would have moved forward. "I'm pretty sure it's a rat."

She shook off his hold. "It's not a rat—it's a Chihuahua."

"It looks like a rat to me," he insisted, though he could see now that its legs were too long and its ears too big to be a rat. Not to mention that a rodent would likely have scampered away when they approached. Unless... "It could be a rabid rat."

Sierra dropped to her haunches, a respectful distance from the obviously wary creature. "Hey, little guy. What are you doing out here?"

The dog—if it was a dog—was shivering.

With fear?

Or cold?

Probably both, Deacon acknowledged. The animal was obviously lost or abandoned, and its short hair didn't look like it provided much—if any—protection against the elements.

Whatever the cause, the critter was trembling so much that its whole body shook, and Deacon knew there was no way they were walking away from it.

"Maybe he's waiting for a rendezvous with a female rat," he suggested.

Sierra glared at him over her shoulder, but when she turned back to the animal, her voice was soft and coaxing.

"I don't see a collar," she crooned softly. "But I can see your ribs. Are you hungry?"

The dog, mesmerized by her voice, took a couple of tentative steps forward.

"Be careful," Deacon felt compelled to warn her. "He might be vicious."

"Yeah, he looks really vicious," she said dryly.

She reached into her purse and pulled out...a pepperoni stick?

She peeled back the wrapper and broke off a piece of the sausage, then held it toward the dog.

His nose twitched and his tongue fell out of his mouth.

"Why do you carry pepperoni sticks in your purse?" Deacon asked.

"In case of a zombie apocalypse."

"I'm not sure if you're joking," he admitted.

She laughed softly. "I have them in case I'm stuck in court and get hungry—or find a lost dog in an alley."

"While you're coaxing him out, I'll give animal control a call—"

"Don't you dare."

Her outburst sent the dog scrambling back behind the trash can, earning him another glare.

"Shelters exist for situations just like this," he said, trying to reason with her even as he tucked his phone back in his pocket. "He'll be taken care of there. It's what they do."

"C'mon, sweetie," she said, talking to the dog again. "Don't let the big bad man's talk about shelters scare you."

"I would think he'd be happy to have shelter—it's got to be preferable to freezing."

The dog cautiously ventured forward again, his beady-eyed gaze darting from the sausage to Sierra to Deacon and back to the sausage again.

"I know it probably isn't what you should be eating," Sierra acknowledged, as the dog snatched the meat from her hand, "but beggars can't be choosers, right?"

Apparently the animal agreed, because he gobbled up the pepperoni and looked to her for more.

"One more little piece," she said, breaking off another bit. As he took the meat, she carefully lifted the dog off of the ground, tucking him into the crook of her arm.

"Oh, he is freezing," she said. "Poor little guy."

"Which is why he should go to a shelter," Deacon said again, feeling inexplicably envious of the dog as Sierra cuddled it close to her chest.

"But if he was abandoned here, and then he gets taken to a shelter and left there, he'll feel as if he's being abandoned all over again."

He unhooked the scarf draped around his neck and gently wrapped it around the shivering animal. "And then someone will come and adopt him, and he'll go to a new home and live happily ever after with a family that always wanted a pet rat."

"Stop calling him a rat," Sierra said, but the admonition was without heat this time.

Perhaps the sacrifice of his scarf had lessened her annoyance with him.

"And while you're painting a pretty picture, I don't think anyone—even a dog—would easily forget the trauma of being abandoned."

"Maybe he wasn't abandoned," Deacon suggested. "Maybe he ran away because his home life sucked and he wanted to find something better."

He felt the weight of Sierra's gaze on him and knew that she knew he was no longer talking about the dog. Or not exclusively, anyway.

The dog whimpered quietly.

"I'll take him to the shelter tomorrow," she decided.

"And what are you going to do with him tonight?" he asked, though he was certain he already knew the answer to that question.

"I'll take him home with me."

"You don't know anything about his history or his health," Deacon protested. "He could be sick or ill-tempered or covered in fleas."

"He doesn't look sick or ill-tempered," she pointed out.

The dog tipped his head back and looked at her adoringly, and Deacon knew he was in the middle of an argument that he couldn't win.

Still, he felt compelled to make one final point. "At least give him a bath before you let him onto your bed."

"That's a rule I enforce with all my overnight guests," she said, then ducked her head, no doubt to hide the color that filled her cheeks. "Please forget that completely inappropriate comment."

"Why would I want to do that?" he asked mildly.

"Because I've been trying really hard not to lead you on."

"Because you're adamant that nothing is going to happen between us?"

"Yes."

"Too late," he told her.

"Go back to your party, Deacon."

"I'm going," he said, because he could hardly abandon the friends who'd shown up to celebrate with him, even if he'd rather be with Sierra. Despite the fact that her attention was focused now on the scrawny dog in her arms. "But you've got my number, if you need anything."

"I've got your number," she confirmed, then surprised him by touching her lips to his cheek. "Happy birthday."

Sierra woke up Saturday morning with doggy breath in her face.

"We should have brushed your teeth after your bath."

A tiny pink tongue swiped at the end of her nose, making her laugh even as her heart squeezed inside her chest.

"Or maybe I should have let Deacon call animal control to have you taken to the shelter."

Her miniature canine companion let out a soft whine.

"Do you know that word?" she wondered aloud. "Have you been to the animal shelter before?"

Another whine and a reproachful look from big dark eyes.

She sighed. "What am I going to do with you, Dog?"

He wriggled closer.

"I can't keep you." She'd come to that realization the night before and had abandoned her efforts to find a suitable name for him, knowing it would only be much more difficult to say goodbye if she'd given him a name.

Dog just looked at her with his big dark eyes.

"I never even thought about getting a dog," she continued her explanation—well, her excuse, really—to the poor little pup. "Before I came to Haven, I didn't have time to care for a pet. I probably would have forgotten to even feed a goldfish."

This time his tongue swept over her chin.

She sighed. "Deacon was right. Not that I would admit it to him," she confided. "But I should have let you go to the s-h-e-l-t-e-r last night, because now I don't think that I can." She gently stroked the dog's head with a fingertip. "But what other choice do I have?

"I can't keep you," she said again, needing to convince herself as much as Dog. "You probably don't understand why, because it no doubt looks like a pretty good setup here. But it can't be your forever home because I'm only here temporarily—because I needed a short-term job to see me through most of my pregnancy. And I'm already near the end of the second month of a six-month contract with the DA's office. After that... I don't know.

"I mean, I'm going back to Vegas, obviously. But I don't have a place of my own there. Nick and Whitney said that I can stay with them for as long as I want, but they won't really want me underfoot when the baby comes. And I know you're really cute and don't take up much room, but Whitney's allergic to dogs, so I really don't think there's any other option."

But the thought of taking him to a shelter—of handing him off to a stranger and waving goodbye to him through a pane of glass...

She swallowed around the lump in her throat.

"On the other hand, I might be completely misreading your situation. Maybe you weren't abandoned but somehow got separated from your family and then got lost trying to find your way home.

"Maybe, right now, someone is posting flyers around town with your photo on them. Maybe you even have a microchip." She rubbed the dog's ears gently, feeling for evidence of such a device. "And maybe, instead of speculating, I should take you to the vet to find out for sure."

"I brought leftover birthday cake," Deacon said, when Sierra opened the door in response to his knock Saturday afternoon.

"You should keep the cake—it was your birthday."

"There was a lot of it left over," he told her.

"In that case." She accepted the plate with a smile.

Looking past her, he saw a tiny head peeking around the half wall that separated the entranceway from the living area.

"I brought some things for your pet rat, too."

"He's not a rat," she said indignantly. "And he's not mine."

"And yet, you obviously didn't take him to the shelter this morning." He reached down for the dog carrier that she hadn't noticed was on the porch beside him.

She stepped away from the door so that he could bring it inside.

"No," she admitted. "But I did take Dog to the vet, to see if he was microchipped."

"Dog?" he echoed.

As if responding to a summons, the Chihuahua took a few tentative steps closer.

Sierra shrugged as she carried the plate of cake into the kitchen. "He needed a name."

"Dog isn't a name, it's a classification," Deacon said, following behind with the crate.

"Anyway, Dr. Stafford said he's not microchipped," she said. "And no one had called the clinic—or the shelter—looking for a lost pet."

"How do you know no one called the shelter?"

"The receptionist checked while we were there."

"So you're keeping him?" he guessed.

She shook her head regretfully. "I can't."

"And yet, he's still here."

"Not for long."

He smiled at that as he unlatched the door of the crate to retrieve the bags he'd placed inside.

"Where did you get all that stuff?"

"Fur, Feathers and Fins," he said, naming the local pet store.

She watched as he unpacked a memory foam pillow bed, two stainless steel bowls decorated with paw prints, a bag of small dog kibble, a box of treats, an assortment of toys, a collar and a leash and waste bags to clean up after him on walks. There was even a puffy jacket with matching boots with Velcro fasteners.

"I think you went a little overboard," she said.

"Maybe," he acknowledged. "If there's anything you don't want or don't need, it can be taken back to the store."

"You should probably take it all back," she said. "Because I really can't keep him."

"Why not? It's not as if you don't have room for him. You've even got a doggy door."

A doggy door clearly intended for a much larger breed, Deacon acknowledged. Sierra's little dog probably couldn't even push it open—and was likely to hurt himself if he even tried.

"I've got room for him *here*," she agreed. "But it wouldn't be fair to keep him for a few months and then leave him at a shelter when I go back to Vegas."

"That's true," he acknowledged, not wanting to think about her going back to Vegas. But as much as she seemed to enjoy her job in the DA's office—and was obviously good at it—she never missed an opportunity to remind him that it was only a temporary position. A six-month contract with a little more than four months left.

She sighed.

And then, as if another thought had just occurred to her, her expression brightened. "But *you* could keep him."

"Oh, no." Deacon shook his head.

"Why not? You like dogs."

"Yes, I like dogs." He picked the Chihuahua up with one hand, because it was that small, and tucked it into the crook of his arm. "But if I was going to get a dog, I'd get one that looked like a dog."

The Chihuahua snuggled into his elbow, yawned once, then closed his eyes and promptly fell asleep. As if he instinctively trusted that he was somewhere safe.

Deacon muttered a soft curse under his breath.

Sierra didn't even try to hold back the smug smile that curved her lips. "Admit it—you've fallen just as hard for Dog as I have."

"If you're going to keep him, he's going to need a better name than Dog," Deacon said.

"I'm not going to keep him—*you* are."

"Why don't you let him stay here for the next few months and I'll take him when you leave?"

"Or we could share custody," she said. "So that he gets to be comfortable at your place, too, and won't feel as if he's been completely uprooted when I leave."

"Shared custody of a Chihuahua," he mused. "Should we get Judge Wilkerson to sign off on our agreement?"

"I don't think that will be necessary."

"Well, even if we're not going to write up the paperwork, he still needs a name."

"Tiny?" she suggested.

He made a face.

"Bitsy?"

"You're not very good at this, are you?"

"I don't hear you offering up any suggestions."

"Remy," he said.

"Remy," she echoed, surprised that he hadn't suggested something like "Ratface" or "Mouse," and even more surprised to realize that she liked it.

CHAPTER THIRTEEN

"WHAT DO YOU say to taking Remy for a walk so that he can sniff out his new neighborhood?" Deacon suggested.

"I say *yes*," Sierra agreed.

All joking about shared custody aside, the dog was as high-maintenance as a child. Before they could go out, they had to size his collar and put it on him. Remy didn't object to that—it was almost as if he knew that the collar was a symbol that he belonged to someone, that he had a home. The coat he balked at initially, but once Sierra had wrestled it on to him, he seemed to tolerate it well enough. The boots were a different story. He did not appreciate their efforts in that regard—and yes, it was a two-person job, especially with the dog twisting and squirming and even nipping at them when they tried to put the boots over his paws.

"One thing I forgot to get was a muzzle," Deacon grumbled.

"I guess we'll have to take him without the boots," Sierra decided.

"Or we could take the ungrateful rat to the shelter."

"Stop that," she admonished.

"He bit me," Deacon reminded her.

"He didn't even break the skin."

"He still bit me."

And as if it wasn't enough that he had to shorten his stride to accommodate the tiny dog, Remy stopped every ten feet or so to lift his leg by a tree or a bush or a blade of grass sticking out of the snow.

"At this rate, it's going to take him six months to explore the neighborhood," Deacon remarked, when they finally made it to the end of the street and decided to turn back again.

Sierra didn't comment on that, and Deacon remembered that she wouldn't be around in six months. She only had a six-month contract and seven weeks were already gone.

"Did you want to come in?" she invited when they finally arrived back at her house.

"I should probably head home," he said. "It must be getting close to dinnertime."

"It is," she confirmed. "But you could stay and have dinner with me."

The lift of his brows indicated that he was surprised by the invitation.

"As a thank-you for the stuff you brought for Remy—and your help with him," she explained.

"In that case," he said, and followed her into the house.

"Do you like pasta?" Sierra asked, when they'd shed their outerwear and were headed to the kitchen.

"Moltissimo."

"Should I be impressed? Or is that the only word you know in Italian?"

"Posso dire qualche parola."

"Sono impressionato."

He grinned. *"Anchi'io."*

"You shouldn't be impressed," she told him, reaching into the drawer beneath the stove and pulling out a deep frying pan. "My knowledge of the Italian language dates back to Northwest High School. It's very limited and very rusty."

"You didn't sound rusty to me. Although I might be rusty, too."

She set the pan on the stove and dumped a package of ground beef in it. "Where did you learn Italian?"

"Francesca Moretti—an Italian exchange student."

"Pretty?" she guessed, retrieving a jar of spaghetti sauce from the cupboard.

"Very." He picked up the spatula she'd set on the counter and used it to break apart the lump of meat in the frying pan.

"I invited you to stay for dinner, not help make it."

"Am I doing something wrong?"

"I don't think there's a wrong way to brown ground beef."

"Then let me do it."

So she did.

And since he was taking care of the meat, she decided to put together a salad to serve with the pasta.

"You mentioned that you went to Northwest High School," he noted. "But I just realized that I don't know where you went to law school."

"Nowhere near as lofty as Columbia," she told him.

"I've never heard of that one," he deadpanned.

She rolled her eyes. "UNLV."

"A good school," he said. "I got my undergrad degree in poli sci there."

"Me, too," she admitted.

"It's interesting that we both did our undergrads in the same program at the same school but our paths never crossed on campus," he mused. "Almost as if destiny was waiting for the right time for us to meet."

"Or maybe it's because the student population at UNLV is approximately twice that of Haven," she countered. "Also, I was probably a couple years ahead of you."

"Why would you assume that?"

"Because it was your twenty-eighth birthday last night and I'm...older than that."

"How old are you?"

She chopped celery to add to the salad. "Didn't anyone ever tell you that it's rude to ask a woman her age?"

"You brought up the subject," he pointed out.

Because it was true, she relented and answered his question. "I celebrated the big three-oh on my last birthday."

"Wow, you are an old lady," he teased.

She reached past him to retrieve a pair of tongs from the

utensil holder on the counter, not-quite-accidentally elbowing him in the ribs.

He chuckled.

They chatted some more about mostly inconsequential topics while they finished preparing the meal.

And it was nice to have company, Sierra admitted. Even if it was male company that made her achingly aware of specific female needs.

"I've got a couple of beers in the fridge from when my brother was here," Sierra said, as she scooped the pasta into bowls. "Do you want one?"

Deacon hesitated for a second. "Yeah, I guess I could have one."

While he plated the garlic bread she'd warmed in the oven, she retrieved a bottle from the fridge, twisted the cap and set it on the table.

"I expected that Remy would be ready for his dinner, too," she remarked, taking a seat across from Deacon at the table. "But apparently he's more tired than hungry right now."

"I guess half a block is a long walk when your legs are that short."

"Speaking of Remy," she said, selecting a piece of garlic bread. "We should draw up a schedule to establish who has him and when."

"Or we could not worry about a schedule," he said.

"You're not reneging on our agreement, are you?"

"No, I'm not reneging," he assured her. "I'm just suggesting that you should have primary custody and I'll exercise visitation."

"Does that include exercising him when you visit?" she asked.

"Whatever you want."

"I want him to become as familiar with you as I'm hoping he'll become with me, so that when I leave, he'll still feel that he has a home."

"I could come by to take him out after work on Mondays, Wednesdays and Fridays."

"That would be great," she agreed. "But I have...a class on

Wednesdays at six, so I'll give you a key that you can use if I'm not here."

His brows lifted. "You won't go out for dinner with me but you'll give me a key to your house?"

"Because going out for dinner implies a date. Exchanging keys for access to the dog is a sign of friendship—not that I'm asking for a key to your house," she hastened to assure him, rising from the table to carry their empty dishes to the sink.

Deacon followed with the salad bowl. "It would be strange for me to have a key to your place and you not have one to mine."

"But if Remy's going to be living here full-time, there's no reason that I'd need a key to your place."

"Unless you had a shower emergency."

"A shower emergency?" she echoed dubiously.

"Such as your water tank going on the fritz," he said. "If that happened, you could come over to my place, strip out of your clothes—music optional—"

"Let me assure you, that is *not* going to happen."

"Water tanks can be finicky," he warned.

"I was referring to the stripping part."

"It's much more efficient to take your clothes off before you shower."

She shook her head, a smile tugging at the corners of her mouth. "You're enjoying this, aren't you?"

"Picturing you naked in my shower?" He grinned. "Absolutely."

She swatted at him with a tea towel.

Remy finally woke up from his nap then and wandered into the kitchen. Sierra measured kibble into his bowl and gave him fresh water while Deacon finished loading the dishwasher.

"Did you want another beer?" she asked, removing the empty bottle from the table.

"No, thanks," he said. "One's my limit."

She'd noticed the night before that he wasn't a heavy drinker. Though he'd had a beer in his hand most of the night, it hadn't taken her long to realize it was always the same bottle—almost a prop more than a beverage.

"Alcoholic parent?" she guessed.

He seemed taken aback by her question, but after a brief moment's hesitation, he nodded. "My dad was a drunk and a bully."

"I'm sorry."

He shrugged. "We all have our demons."

No doubt there was a lot more to the story, but he obviously didn't want to talk about it, and she felt she should respect his secrets if she wanted to keep her own.

"It's getting late," Deacon said. "I should probably be going."

She glanced at the illuminated display on the stove.

6:42.

"I'm sorry—which one of us did you say was old?" she asked, unable to resist teasing him.

"Okay, it's not actually late," he acknowledged. "But I've taken up a lot of your time today."

"I'm not sure I should admit this, but I enjoyed your company."

"See? I'm not such a bad guy when you get to know me."

"I never thought you were a bad guy."

"Am I a bad kisser?"

She narrowed her gaze. "I think you know the answer to that question."

"Maybe I want to hear you say it."

"We are not going to talk about that kiss," she said firmly.

"Why not?" he challenged.

"Because it never should have happened."

And because she hadn't stopped thinking about it since it happened. And because, even now, her lips were tingling in anticipation of touching his again.

"Okay, let's talk about our second kiss," he suggested.

She shook her head, dismissing the temptation that urged her to press her body to his. "There's not going to be a second kiss."

"Why are you so opposed to giving us a chance?"

"You're not going to let this go, are you?"

"I wish I could," he said. "But I can't think of any reason for us not to explore the obvious attraction between us."

"There is a reason," she insisted.

"Did you do one of those ancestry DNA tests and discover

that we're fourth cousins or something?" he asked, when she failed to expand on her response.

"Nothing quite that scandalous," she assured him.

"Then what is it?"

She took a deep breath and said, "I'm pregnant."

CHAPTER FOURTEEN

"PREGNANT?" DEACON ECHOED, stunned.

"You really didn't know?" Sierra asked skeptically.

He shook his head slowly. "How could I have known?"

"Because you saw me at the prenatal clinic."

He remembered seeing her in Battle Mountain when he took his sister-in-law to her appointment, but... "I didn't realize it was a prenatal clinic."

"What did you think it was?"

"A woman's health clinic. For all I knew, you were having an annual exam or renewing a prescription for birth control."

"I was there for a four-month prenatal checkup," she said. "The baby's due in August."

Baby. She was going to have a baby.

This wasn't just another brush-off—this was real.

"And the baby's father?"

"I'm not sure what you're asking," she hedged.

"Where is he?" It was probably none of his business, but he wanted to know.

"Las Vegas."

"Is that why you left?"

She shook her head. "I left because I wanted to make a career change—and to put some distance between me and my ex."

"Does he know about the baby?"

"No. And there's no reason for him to know. He's not the baby's father."

His brows lifted at that. "Rebound relationship?"

"No."

"One-night stand?"

"No," she said again.

"I'm not sure what options are left," he admitted.

"Does it really matter how this baby came to be? The fact is, I'm pregnant. But I haven't told anyone else yet, so I'd appreciate if this stayed between us for now."

He nodded.

"I'll probably share the news with my boss and my coworkers in the next week or so."

The news being that she was going to have a baby.

And while she was talking matter-of-factly about her next steps, he was trying to stop his head from spinning.

"And Sky, of course," she said. "I don't want her to hear about it from anyone else."

"You and Sky seem to be pretty chummy," he noted, latching on to a topic that was completely unrelated to pregnancies and babies. "Did you know her before you came to Haven?"

"No." Sierra shook her head again. "In fact, I met her the same day I met you. And the same place—the cereal aisle of the grocery store." Now she smiled. "But she didn't steal my Frosted Flakes."

"You're never going to let me forget that, are you?"

"Probably not."

But thinking back to that day now... "I guess you wanted the cereal to satisfy a pregnancy craving?"

Now she nodded.

"And that's why you don't drink coffee," he realized.

She nodded again.

"And also why that kiss should never have happened," she told him.

"Maybe," he acknowledged regretfully. "But I'm not sorry that it did."

The hint of pink that colored her cheeks told him that she

wasn't sorry, either. That in that moment, she'd wanted his kiss—maybe even wanted him.

But, of course, her pregnancy changed everything.

As her next question proved.

"Do you think... Can we be friends?"

The tentativeness of the request tugged at his heart.

"As long as being friends doesn't require me to abandon my shower emergency fantasy."

She laughed then, as he'd hoped she would.

"Trust me, in a few more weeks—maybe less—you won't want to picture me naked."

"I guess time will tell. And speaking of time, I really should be going."

She walked him to the door. "Thanks again, for all your help with Remy. And all the stuff you brought for him."

"It was my pleasure."

He donned his boots and coat, then paused at the door. "I guess I'll see you Monday. If not at court, when I come over to walk Remy."

"That reminds me—" She dashed off and came back half a minute later with a key.

He slid it onto his ring, then took off his own house key and gave it to her.

"Don't you need this to get into your house?"

"There's a spare in my garage."

She tucked the key into the front pocket of her jeans.

Slim-fitting dark denim that hugged her feminine form.

On top of the jeans she wore a soft knit sweater the color of ripe plums.

She certainly didn't look like a woman who was going to have a baby in five months.

She looked hot. Sexy. Desirable.

But she was going to have a baby, and that changed everything for Deacon.

Everything except how much he wanted her.

Having a dog waiting for her at home was giving Sierra a taste of what it meant to be a working mom. True, she didn't have to worry about day care for her canine dependent, but she did worry about other things. Such as if he was hungry or thirsty (despite the fact that she fed him in the morning and made sure his water bowl was full before she left the house) or scared or lonely (even though she left the television on so that the house wouldn't be too quiet) or getting into mischief. (The vet had recommended crate training to avoid this potential problem, but Sierra hadn't seen any hints of destructive behavior that made her think confinement was necessary. She had, however, blocked off the stairs to the upper level so that he wouldn't hurt himself trying to climb them when he was alone.)

But by the end of the first week, she was starting to feel more comfortable with their routines and confident that when she said goodbye to Remy in the morning, he didn't spend the rest of the day stressing about whether she would come back again. But he was always at the door when she walked in, and he'd bark happily when he saw her, not just his tail but his whole back end wagging. And it was kind of nice to have someone make a fuss over her, so she made a fuss over him in return.

He was just as excited to see Deacon, too, when the other lawyer showed up to take him for his evening walks on Monday, Wednesday and Friday. And it was a relief to Sierra to know that Remy would be not just taken care of but happy when she went back to Las Vegas and left him with Deacon.

Sky texted while Deacon was out with the dog Friday night, and Sierra exchanged a few messages with her friend while she cooked chicken and vegetables for her dinner. She was fluffing the brown rice when they returned.

"I made stir-fry," Sierra told him. "And there's enough for two, if you wanted to stay for dinner."

"That sounds a lot more appealing than what I had planned," he admitted.

"A microwaveable meal?" she guessed.

"Yeah."

"I've eaten my share of those," she confided. "But yes, this should be better."

He washed his hands at the sink while she dished up the meal.

They chatted mostly about work while they ate. In general

terms, of course, not discussing any details of any particular case that might breach confidentiality or disclosure rules.

"You're tiptoeing around something," Deacon remarked, as he set his fork and knife on top of his now empty plate.

She didn't deny it. "I want to ask a favor."

"Because it's not enough that I'm already walking your dog three days a week?" he teased.

"*Our* dog," she reminded him. "And I was hoping you might be able to dog-sit tomorrow."

"You do know it's okay to go out and leave the dog alone?"

"I know. But he's been alone every day this week when I've been at work, and I hate the idea of leaving him alone again tomorrow just so that I can go shopping with Sky."

"I'm surprised you don't want to take him with you."

"I guess I could," she said. "But a crowded mall might be too much stimulation for him."

"Or good socialization," he countered.

"If you don't want to look after him—"

"I didn't say I didn't want to look after him," Deacon interjected. "I said I didn't think he needed looking after. But I'm happy to have him over to my place for a few hours—or however long you're going to be gone."

"Thank you. I'll drop him off on my way out."

So that's what Sierra did, and then she drove to Battle Mountain to meet her new friend at a store called Baby Bump. Sky had recently been lamenting the fact that none of her clothes fit comfortably anymore. Of course, the other woman was nearing the end of her second trimester now and happy to show off her growing belly, while Sierra was doing everything in her power to hide hers.

She wasn't ashamed of her pregnancy, but she also wasn't ready to be the subject of any more local gossip. It had been a hot enough topic that the DA had hired an attorney from Las Vegas, and while she felt confident that she'd proven herself capable of doing the job, she was still an outsider and, therefore, a more likely target of scrutiny.

"So what's going on with you and Deacon?" Sky asked, as she rifled through a rack of tops.

"Nothing," Sierra said quickly.

Maybe too quickly, she realized, as her friend's gaze narrowed thoughtfully.

And then she compounded the error by asking, "Why? What did you hear?"

Sky smiled as she selected a dark blue peasant-style blouse. "What do you think I might have heard?"

"Nothing," Sierra said again, though she suspected that the heat filling her cheeks belied her words.

"So it's not true that you went to his birthday party last Friday night?"

"I didn't go to his party," she denied. "I went to Diggers' not knowing that there was a party."

"But then you stayed and hung out with him all night."

"I left before ten o'clock, so I'm not sure it's accurate to say *all night*," she hedged, handing a pretty paisley top to her friend to consider. "And how do you know any of this? You weren't there."

"No." Sky added the paisley top to the growing pile of clothes she intended to try on. "But my sister was."

Sierra had forgotten for a minute that everyone in Haven knew everyone else—and that Katelyn Davidson, formerly Katelyn Gilmore, was Sky's sister.

A salesperson took Sky's selections to a dressing room while she continued to browse.

"I also heard that you and Deacon are sharing custody of a dog," her friend continued.

"Did you hear that from Katelyn, too? Because I know you didn't hear it from Deacon, who refuses to admit that Remy is a dog."

Sky made a face as she considered—and rejected—a pair of stirrup pants. "What does he think Remy is?"

"A rat," Sierra admitted.

Sky chuckled. "I'm guessing he named the dog?"

"He did," Sierra confirmed. "But how did you guess that?"

"Because it's the name of the main character in *Ratatouille*."

"What's *Ratatouille*?"

"An animated movie about a rat who dreams of being a chef."

"I'm going to kill him," Sierra muttered under her breath.

"Don't tell me," her friend cautioned. "I'm not a lawyer, so our conversation isn't protected by attorney-client privilege."

"A threat to do harm isn't protected, anyway," Sierra informed her.

"I'll keep that in mind," Sky promised, dragging her friend into the changing room with her so their conversation wouldn't be put on hold while she tried on clothes. "But tell me how you and Deacon found this dog—and was it before or after the kiss?"

Sierra felt her cheeks burn. "How did you know about *that*?"

Her friend grinned as she quickly shed her clothes, showing no hint of self-consciousness. "Jake and I stopped by to pick up food for my cousin MG and saw your lips locked together. And you cannot know how much I've been dying to ask you about it."

She wanted to ask about MG, curious to know if Sky's cousin was the same man she'd heard the whispers about in the coffee shop several weeks earlier, but she felt compelled to respond to her friend's comment about the lip lock first. Because she knew if Sky had seen them kissing, anyone could have. And that Haven rumor mill might be running out of control if she didn't do some damage control. Fast.

"It was just a kiss," she said, because she knew she couldn't let it be more than that.

"A kiss that practically steamed our windows." Sky wiggled into a pair of maternity jeans.

"I'm sure you're exaggerating."

"Only a little." She donned the paisley top, studied her reflection in the mirror and made a face.

"It's a cute top," Sierra said.

"More your style than mine," her friend said. "So I guess you were mistaken when you said that he'd lost interest in you." Sky somehow managed to sound smug even with a shirt over her head.

"I was mistaken then," Sierra acknowledged. "But I'm sure of it now."

"Why? What happened after the kiss?"

"I told him...that I'm pregnant."

Sky hesitated a beat, then offered the paisley shirt to Sierra. "You should try this one on."

Deacon had just slid the pan of pork chops, potatoes and carrots into the oven when Sierra texted to let him know that she was on her way back from Battle Mountain—which meant that she should arrive just about the same time that dinner would be ready.

"How was your shopping trip?" he asked, when she showed up at the door.

"You wouldn't need to ask if you saw the mountain of packages in the back of my car."

"A success, then," he guessed.

"It was." She crouched down to pet the dog who, upon hearing her voice, raced to the foyer to greet her.

"I bought a few things for you, too," she said, opening the bag she carried to show Remy a buffalo plaid hooded pullover, a soft gray cable-knit sweater, a fuzzy blue sweater and a dark green faux suede coat.

"That's quite the wardrobe for a tiny dog," he remarked.

"I'm glad to hear you say that he's a dog," she said. "Because you named him after a *rat*."

Busted.

Deacon tried to keep his expression neutral, his tone casual. "You said you liked the name Remy."

"Because I didn't know it was the name of a rat in a kids' movie," she retorted.

"*Ratatouille* is a family movie," he felt compelled to point out. "Have you honestly never seen it?"

"I've honestly never seen it."

"We should watch it. If you saw the movie, you'd understand that naming our dog Remy isn't the insult you apparently think it is."

"I have no interest in a movie about a rat."

The oven timer buzzed, drawing him back to the kitchen.

"We'll watch it after dinner," he decided, ignoring her protest.

"Dinner?" she echoed, her attention momentarily diverted from the indignity of Remy's name.

"It's nothing fancy—just sheet pan pork chops, potatoes and carrots."

She breathed in the scent of the meat and veggies when he took the pan out of the oven. "Fancy or not, it sure smells good."

He retrieved a couple of plates from the cupboard and began to dish up the meal.

She found the cutlery drawer and got forks and knives.

"This is a really nice surprise," she said. "Thanks."

"You've cooked for me twice—it seemed that I had some catching up to do."

After dinner was done and the kitchen cleaned, Sierra suggested that it was time to be taking Remy home.

"Not just yet," he protested. "We've got a movie to watch."

"You were serious about that?"

"Of course."

"How are we going to watch it? Do you have Disney+?"

"I have twin almost-four-year-old nieces," he reminded her. "Of course I have Disney+."

"Do you have popcorn?"

He grinned. "And I have popcorn."

Over the next few weeks, Sierra spent a lot of time with Deacon—and Remy. They had interesting conversations about all manner of topics, and though he never hesitated to challenge her opinions, he always listened to her. But the more time they spent together, the more she found her thoughts wandering down paths it had no distance wandering.

Such as when he warned her against letting Remy sleep in her bed, because there was no way he would share his with the dog when she went back to Vegas. It had been a casual comment that somehow got Sierra thinking about Deacon in his bed... wondering if he wore pajamas or boxers...or nothing at all.

But she knew it would be foolish to get romantically involved when she was only going to be in town a few more months. And while Deacon had once flippantly suggested that they could skip the romance and go straight to the sex, that had been before he knew about the baby.

The revelation of her condition might have effectively quashed his attraction to her, but the actual condition seemed to have the effect of amplifying her own desire. She'd read that pregnancy hormones could increase a woman's libido, but she'd been certain it wouldn't be a problem for her. After Eric's betrayal, she'd vowed to take a break from men and dating. She hadn't anticipated meeting Deacon Parrish—or that their interactions, no matter how brief, would stir her up inside.

And while her hormones were in favor of stripping him naked and having her way with him—if he was still amenable to the idea, and that was a big if—the rational side of her brain kept reminding her that her body wasn't currently her own.

In addition to the conflict between her hormones and her head, there was another battle happening inside her heart. Because being with Deacon, and seeing him interact with others—especially his adorable nieces—only served to escalate her attraction to him.

So she tried to focus her attention on other things—doing her job, exploring the town, meeting new people and making sure Remy knew he was loved. She walked the dog every morning and every night after work—except the days that Deacon came by to take him out, per their agreement.

They generally exchanged only quick hellos and goodbyes in the early part of the week, but he usually hung around a little longer on Fridays. Occasionally to share a meal and sometimes long enough to watch the hockey game together if the Golden Knights were playing.

After a few weeks, Sierra realized the extended Friday night visits were more regular than occasional—and often the highlight of her week. Especially when he sat close to her, so that she could tip her head against his shoulder when she started to feel sleepy.

"You don't have to come every Friday," she told him, as they tidied up the kitchen after dinner. "I know that was the original deal, but this must be putting a kink in your social life."

"You seem to have all kinds of ideas about my social life, most of which bear little resemblance to the reality," he told her.

"I'm just saying, if you wanted to make plans that didn't include walking the dog, we can manage without you."

"Since subtlety doesn't seem to work very well with you, I'm going to be blunt," Deacon decided. "I don't want to make plans with anyone else. I want to make plans with you.

"And yes, I know why you don't want to get involved. But respecting your decision doesn't miraculously stop me from wanting you."

She was stunned. "You still want me?"

"Every minute of every day," he said, with an intensity that made everything inside her quiver.

And yearn.

Oh, how she yearned for him.

Was it the pregnancy hormones?

Or was it Deacon?

She couldn't be sure. But she knew that after only one kiss, she craved more.

More kisses. More touches.

So much more.

Not that she could admit any of that to Deacon, so instead she said, "Perhaps this shared custody thing was a bad idea."

"You don't have to worry about me jumping your bones, Sierra. I can control my urges."

"Maybe I'm worried that I can't control mine."

Okay, apparently she *could* admit it to Deacon—though the flare of heat in his eyes warned her it might not have been wise to do so.

"I promise not to fight you off," he told her.

"I'm sorry. I shouldn't have said that."

"Because you don't want me?" he asked, almost challenging her to backtrack now. To lie.

"Because nothing can happen between us," she said, sincerely regretful. "Because... I've been advised to abstain from sex until after the baby is born."

His gaze immediately sharpened. "Is everything okay—with you and your pregnancy?"

"I'm fine. The baby's fine. It's just…complicated."
He considered her response for a moment before he nodded. "Then I guess we'll have to suffer together."

CHAPTER FIFTEEN

"Isn't that the new ADA at the table by the window?" Regan asked, when Deacon lowered himself into the empty seat across from her at The Daily Grind.

He glanced in the direction she'd indicated, as if he hadn't seen Sierra the minute he walked through the door. As if he hadn't noticed that she was wearing the cranberry jacket again—this time over a black turtleneck sweater with black pants, having adjusted her wardrobe to the northern winter. Or that she'd done something a little bit different with her hair today, so it had that sexy, slightly tousled look, as if she'd just rolled out of bed—inspiring a man to fantasize about taking her back there again.

"Deacon?"

His sister-in-law's prompt drew his attention back to her table. "Yeah, that's Sierra."

"I didn't get an introduction at your birthday party, but I can see why you're smitten," Regan said. "She's gorgeous."

He frowned. "Who said I was smitten?"

"Your brother."

"I don't know why he'd say something like that."

"Because he saw the two of you facing off in court last week."

"When? I didn't see him."

Her smile was smug. "Exactly. So why did you bring your coffee over here to sit with me instead of taking it over there?"

"Because I didn't want to hurt your feelings."

"Nice try," she said. "Now try the truth."

"It's complicated," he hedged.

"Isn't it always?" Regan said, not unsympathetically.

He intended to leave it at that. But his brother's wife was also his friend—and one he'd found himself confiding in frequently over the years.

"Do you remember the day that I drove you to your doctor's appointment?" he asked her now.

"As if I could ever forget it." She sipped her latte. "It was the day we found out I was pregnant with twins—again."

"Well, as we were entering the clinic, another woman was exiting."

"I'd guess a fair number of women are in and out of that clinic on any given day," she remarked dryly.

"I'm sure you're right," he agreed. "But this particular woman was Sierra."

"Oh." Then, *"Oh."*

He nodded.

"I'm beginning to understand the complication," Regan said.

He nodded again.

"Where does the baby's father fit into the picture?"

Deacon wasn't entirely sure. It seemed to him that Sierra had been deliberately cryptic about the details of her pregnancy, but there had been one point about which she was clear. "She assured me that they don't have any kind of romantic relationship."

"Okay, then—what's the problem? Is it that you don't want to be a dad to another man's kid?"

"I don't want to be a dad—period."

The blunt assessment made his sister-in-law frown. "Why not?"

"Isn't it obvious?" he challenged.

"Not to me."

"Maybe because you never knew my dad."

"You're right. I didn't know him," she said. "But I know

that he was an abusive alcoholic, and I'm sorry that you had to grow up with that.

"I also know that the absence of a positive role model can make parenting a challenge. But your brother was raised in the same house, and I can't imagine a better father to our daughters than him."

"He is an amazing dad. But Connor is only my half brother," he reminded her. "He doesn't carry the burden of Dwayne Parrish's DNA."

Regan seemed to consider this as she took another sip of her drink. "That's true," she finally acknowledged. "Instead, he carries the burden of never having known his father. Of not even knowing who his father is. Half of your brother's DNA is a question mark. His dad could be a schoolteacher or a serial killer—he doesn't know and he has to live with the not knowing."

"I never looked at it from that perspective," Deacon admitted, duly chastened by his sister-in-law's words.

"I'm not trying to make you feel bad," Regan said, in a gentler tone. "I'm trying to make you see that biology is only a small part of the equation. What matters more—a lot more—is how you feel about both the mother and her child.

"If you really like Sierra, and it seems obvious that you do, then you shouldn't let the fact that she's going to have a baby scare you away."

"You don't think I should be concerned about the possibility that I might turn out like him?"

"Your past isn't nearly as important as your present," she insisted.

"Do you really believe that?"

"Absolutely."

"You never had any qualms about me babysitting your girls?"

"Never," she replied without hesitation. "Because you are the best—and their undisputed favorite—uncle."

"I'm not sure I deserve that kind of praise."

"You didn't even raise your voice when they painted your shoes."

"My new Cole Haan loafers," Deacon clarified. "And I think I was too stunned to speak."

"But when you did, you commented on their creative use of color."

He sighed. "They were so proud of their handiwork. I knew that if I got mad, they'd be crushed."

Regan smiled and touched a hand to his arm. "And that is why I have no doubt you'll be an amazing dad when the time comes."

It was Friday night, and though dinner wasn't long past, Sierra was rummaging through her cupboards.

"What are you looking for?" Deacon asked her.

"Salt and vinegar potato chips." She closed one door, opened another. "I'm sure I bought some when I was shopping last weekend."

"I saw an empty bag in the trash can in the garage when I dropped Remy's evening deposit in there."

She sighed. "I guess I finished them."

"Do you want me to pop over to the convenience store to pick up another bag?" he offered.

She hesitated, just long enough to let him know that she wanted to say *yes*, before she shook her head *no*. "I've got some fruit in the fridge. I can have an apple or a pear.

"I've got grapes, too," she discovered, when she opened the refrigerator to examine the contents. "Do you want some grapes?"

"Grapes are an after-school snack for a ten-year-old, not a game-watching snack for grown-ups," he protested.

"I could make popcorn," she said.

"In an air popper with no added butter?" he guessed.

"It's healthy."

"I think I'd rather have the grapes."

"I'll make a fruit tray," she decided.

He glanced at the time displayed on the stove. "There's at least twenty minutes until puck drop—I'm going to go out to get some real snacks."

She should have objected—not to the snacks but to his plan

to come back to watch the game. She felt a little guilty that he'd been spending so much of his time with her, but she didn't say anything, because that tiny bit of guilt was greatly outweighed by the pleasure of his company.

He returned from the store with the coveted salt and vinegar potato chips, a bag of white cheddar popcorn and a veggie tray.

"You dissed my suggestion of fruit, but you came back with veggies," she noted.

"The veggies aren't for me—they're for the baby," he told her.

"And the popcorn?" she prompted.

"You want some popcorn?"

"If you don't mind sharing."

He emptied the bag into a big bowl, and they sat close together on the sofa, watching the game and sharing the snack. But when there was a stoppage in play, she found herself asking, "Wouldn't you rather be watching the game at Diggers', where you could flirt with the pretty servers?"

"If I wanted to be at Diggers', I'd be at Diggers'," he told her, turning his attention back to the screen when the puck dropped again.

"You should want to be at Diggers'," she said. "It isn't normal for a young, single guy to spend his Friday nights hanging out with a pregnant friend."

Deacon slid her a look. "Are you going to talk through the whole game?"

"Maybe." She considered for a brief moment then revised her response. "Probably."

"Well, I guess that's proof we've come a long way from the early days when I could barely get you to say two words to me."

"I didn't like you at first," she admitted.

"Yeah, you did." He winked. "But you didn't want to like me."

She rolled her eyes. "And that's one of the reasons—because you're entirely too cocky for your own good."

"And yet here we are."

"Seriously, you're wasting your time with me," she told him, even as she leaned back against his shoulder.

Remy, not wanting to miss out on the cuddles, put his front paws up on the edge of the sofa cushion. Deacon scooped the little dog up with one hand and deposited him in Sierra's lap.

"That's not how I see it," he said, giving the Chihuahua a gentle scratch beneath his chin. "But even if I am, it's my time to waste."

A body check against the boards sent both players crashing to the ice.

Sierra turned her face into Deacon's shirt, her hormones stirring anew as she breathed in his familiar, masculine scent. She tamped down on her hormones and reminded herself that she was trying to be as good a friend to Deacon as he'd been to her.

"Do you know Madison Russell?" she asked, forcing herself to stop sniffing him and resume their conversation.

"Judge Wilkerson's clerk?" he guessed.

Sierra nodded as she stroked Remy's soft fur. "Who apparently has a major crush on you."

Deacon frowned. "She's barely twenty years old."

"Twenty-two," she told him.

"Still."

"I was in the judge's chambers to get an order signed and overheard Madison talking about going to Sparkle—that new dance club in Elko—with some friends tonight."

"And you're telling me this...why?" he asked, sounding genuinely baffled.

"Because I thought you might want to go."

"Are you saying that *you* want to go?"

She huffed out a breath. Obviously she was going to have to spell it out for him. "No, I thought you might want to go *because Madison is going to be there*."

He shook his head. "I've outgrown the club scene."

"You're twenty-eight years old," she pointed out.

"My mother always said that I was an old soul."

It was an offhand remark that served the dual purposes of distracting her from the original topic and also providing an opportunity to learn a little about the family he was usually reluctant to discuss.

"You don't talk about your mom very much," she noted, her tone deliberately casual.

"No," he agreed.

She waited for him to expand on that single word, but he remained tight-lipped, focused on the game.

"Can you tell me about her?" she prompted, after another minute had passed, the silence broken only by the play-by-play on the television.

"My mom was a good person who made some bad choices, and the people in this town never let her forget it," he finally said.

"Does she still live in Haven?"

He shook his head. "She died ten days after my high school graduation. Brain tumor."

She touched a hand to his arm. "I'm sorry."

"Yeah, it sucked," he agreed. "But it was a long time ago."

Still, it was obvious the loss had left a mark, as she knew only too well the loss of a parent could do.

It was something else they had in common.

"You don't talk about your dad much, either," she remarked.

A muscle in his jaw flexed, the only hint of any kind of emotional reaction, before he deliberately relaxed it.

"He was one of my mom's particularly regrettable choices," Deacon said, his tone flat. "He took off when I was eight. I haven't seen or heard from him since, and I definitely don't miss him."

"I lost both of my parents, too," Sierra told him, shifting the focus of their conversation away from his family in an effort to ease some of his obvious tension.

He turned so that he was sitting almost sideways, facing her. "I didn't know that."

She shrugged. "It's not something I like to talk about—mostly because…it was my fault."

She felt the unexpected burn of tears behind her eyes.

After more than fifteen years, she should have been able to talk about her mom and dad without being flooded by the emotions that had overwhelmed her fourteen-year-old self, but apparently not. Or maybe it was that this was serious confession time. Because she'd never told anyone about the guilt that she'd carried in her heart since that day—not even Nick.

But she suspected that her brother knew. Because he knew the details of the tragic accident that had taken their parents' lives. And yet, he'd never blamed her—even though she knew that he should.

"Why would you think it was your fault?" Deacon asked.

"Because they were on their way to watch me play basketball." Remy, as if sensing her distress, nudged at the hands folded in her lap. She untwisted her fingers to stroke his soft fur. "My parents were both lawyers. Both very busy and very successful, and while I appreciated that their work gave us a comfortable lifestyle, I sometimes resented their preoccupation with their careers.

"Anyway, I was playing in a big tournament hosted by one of the local high schools—a showcase of future varsity talent. Our team was playing well, and I'd scored double-digit points in each of the three previous games. But my parents were working a big case and hadn't managed to make it to any of them, so I had a bit of a hissy fit, and they promised to be there for the championship.

"They never showed, but I was more angry than worried, certain they'd just decided my game wasn't as important as whatever work they were doing. It was only after, when we were getting onto the bus to go back to school, that one of the tournament officials tracked down my coach to tell her the news—that their car had been hit head-on by a stolen vehicle being chased by police. They were both killed."

According to the police report, her mom had died instantly. Her dad had been rushed to the hospital with life-threatening injuries that he'd succumbed to three days later.

"A horrible accident," Deacon murmured sympathetically. "But an accident. You're not responsible for what happened, Sierra."

"I'm the reason they were on that road at that time. If I hadn't asked them to come to my game, they would have been safe at the courthouse, miles away."

"Or maybe the police chase would have happened on a different route at a different time...but with the same result."

"You're suggesting destiny killed my parents?"

"I'm saying you can't know. And you need to stop blaming yourself."

"I miss them." Her confession was an anguished whisper.

He pulled her into his arms. She didn't resist.

"It's okay to miss them," he told her gently. "And it's important to hold on to all the good memories. But you've got to let go of all the other stuff so that you can live your own life."

"Is that what you've done?"

He hesitated before saying, "I'm working on it."

She snuggled into him then, wanting to give back some of the comfort he'd given to her, and drifted off to sleep listening to the beat of his heart.

CHAPTER SIXTEEN

SIERRA HAD ALWAYS been an avid reader, and though her chosen profession required almost constant reviewing of reports and briefs and case law, she still enjoyed disengaging from work and losing herself in a good story when she could get her hands on one. Boxes of books had gone into storage when she'd moved out of the apartment she'd shared with Eric, but she hadn't seen any point in carting them to Haven when she would only be here for a few months. And since she didn't want to add to the quantity already in storage, she decided to put her name on the waiting list at the local library to get her hands on a copy of the latest Quinn Ellison title.

Her pickup notification came on Friday, so after Remy's morning walk on Saturday, she decided to pop over to the library. She'd visited the community center a few weeks earlier to get a library card and sign up for her prenatal yoga class, and the parking lot had been mostly empty then. Of course, it had been the middle of the day in the middle of the week, and today was Saturday—apparently a popular day for residents to visit the community center, as the parking lot was nearly full.

A sign on the library door advertised a reading of *The Intergalactic Adventures of Cosmic Cat—Vol. 29* by renowned children's author Anderson Hawley. No doubt the reason the library was so busy today.

She picked up her book from the Holds shelf, then followed the chorus of giggles to the back of the room where a group of about twenty kids, ranging in age from two to ten, were sitting in a semicircle facing the author.

There seemed to be a pretty even split between girls and boys in the audience, though most of the adults were moms with only a couple of dads—and Deacon Parrish.

Well, wasn't that a surprise?

She ducked back into the stacks to peer out between the rows of books so she wouldn't be caught staring. He was cross-legged on the floor, with one little girl on his lap and a second beside him.

Apparently Uncle Deacon had been recruited to take his nieces to story time. And maybe the sexy lawyer, with his broad shoulders and seductive smile, should have looked out of place there, but he didn't. In fact, he appeared to be completely at ease surrounded by kids and every bit as absorbed by the story as they were.

She didn't know if it was Anderson Hawley's voice or the silly antics of the titular character, but she was quickly mesmerized—and remembered, with a touch of melancholy, attending story time at the local library with her mom during the happy years of her childhood.

A brief question and answer period followed the reading, and Sierra found herself lingering for that, too. It was only when the crowd began to disperse that she realized she'd missed her window to escape undetected, because suddenly Deacon was standing in front of her.

He glanced at the cover of the book she held against her chest.

"That's a good one," he told her.

"You've read it already?"

He nodded. "I preordered it for my Kindle, so it downloaded automatically at midnight the day of release."

"I have a Kindle," she admitted. "But I prefer to hold a book in my hands."

"I've heard that's common for people over thirty," he said.

She narrowed her gaze on him.

He grinned, unrepentant.

"I wike to read, too," the little girl in the pink sweater chimed in.

"Me, too," her purple-clad sister said, nodding her head with so much enthusiasm her pigtails bounced up and down.

"'Cept we can't get books today cuz we fo-got our library cards."

"So we're gonna get ice cweam instead."

"I wanna donut!"

"Can we have ice cweam an' a donut?"

"No," Deacon said firmly.

His denial was met with identical twin pouts and pleading eyes.

"Piper," he told Sierra, gesturing to the twin in pink. "And Poppy," he said, identifying her sister.

They were cute names for cute kids who looked close to starting a mutiny.

"I should let you be on your way," Sierra said. "You've obviously got your hands full."

"And that's without the sugar high that will inevitably follow the ice cream I already promised them," he acknowledged.

"So how did you end up at story time today?"

"My brother had to work and my sister-in-law wasn't feeling well."

"Mommy was thwowin' up," Piper interjected.

"It was gwoss," Poppy said gleefully.

"She's not really sick," Deacon said. "Just pregnant."

"Ah, the joys of morning sickness."

"'Cept it wasn' mo'nin'," Poppy said.

Her sister's gaze narrowed on Sierra. "You're the wady who wiked our snowman."

"I am," she confirmed. "My name's Sierra."

"Are you Unca Dunca's goo-fwend?" Poppy asked.

"No," Sierra responded, refusing to look at the man in question. "Just his friend."

"But if you're a goo and his fwend, that means you're his goo-fwend."

Deacon smirked. "You can't argue with the logic of an almost-four-year-old."

"Unca Dunca's got a goo-fwend," Piper chanted in a singsong voice.

"Unca Dunca's got a goo-fwend," Poppy echoed.

"Unca Dunca?" Sierra said, her brows raised.

His smile faded. "They struggled to say Deacon when they first started to talk, and Unca Dunca seems to have stuck."

"It's cute," she decided.

"I'm sorry." He cupped a hand around his ear. "Did you just say that I'm cute?"

She rolled her eyes. "I said *the name* was cute."

"So you don't think *I'm* cute?" he pressed.

"That's not the first word that comes to mind when I think of you," she said.

"But you do think of me?"

Way more often than she should. Not that she would give him the satisfaction of acknowledging that truth.

"Annoying is probably the first," she said, ignoring his question. "Or maybe arrogant."

He just grinned. "I'm waiting to see where *charming* and *sexy* fall on the list."

"Did I mention *cocky*?"

"I think that falls under the same umbrella as *arrogant*," he told her.

"I think it warrants its own mention," she countered.

"How about generous?" he suggested. "Which I'll prove by buying you a cone if you want to come across the street for ice cream with us."

"One scoop or two?"

"As many as you want," he said.

"I want two," Piper said.

"Fwee," Poppy said, holding up three fingers.

"You guys get kiddie cones," Deacon told them.

Sierra had to fight the smile that tugged at her lips in response to their immediately crestfallen expressions.

"What do you say?" Deacon prompted.

"As much as I'd love a double scoop of rocky road, I need to get home to Remy."

"Never let it be said that I don't know how to take a hint," Deacon said, offering the pint-size container to Sierra when she opened the door for him a few hours later.

"It wasn't a hint," she protested, though her gaze seemed to be transfixed by the Scoops logo.

"Then you don't want this?" He started to draw the container back.

"Of course I want it," she said, practically snatching the ice cream out of his hand. "Thank you."

"Note to self—do not get between Sierra Hart and rocky road."

"It's my all-time favorite," she told him.

"I didn't forget you," he said, offering a treat to the dog, who was looking up at him expectantly.

Remy scampered off with his dog biscuit.

"You told me a long time ago that dogs like you," she noted. "You didn't tell me it was because you carried treats in your pocket."

"I only started carrying the treats for Remy."

"So you say," she retorted teasingly.

He followed her into the kitchen, where she put her ice cream in the freezer.

"You should know that Piper and Poppy ran into the house announcing to their mom that Uncle Deacon has a girlfriend," he told her.

"Don't you mean 'Unca Dunca has a goo-fwen'?"

"Either way, I just wanted you to be prepared for the rumors to start flying around town."

"I'm not worried that courthouse staff might overhear a couple of almost-four-year-olds chanting on the day care playground," she said. "As long as you understand that we're friends and why we can't be anything more than that."

"Actually, I'm not sure I do," he admitted.

"Have you forgotten that I'm pregnant?"

"Of course not," he assured her. "I also haven't forgotten your assurance that you don't have any lingering romantic feelings for the baby's father."

"Trust me—I *never* had any romantic feelings for him."

"And yet," he said, with a pointed glance at the very slight curve of her belly.

"A long story," Sierra said. "And not one I'm ready to share."

"How about popcorn?" he said. "Would you share some of that?"

"You always complain when I make popcorn because I don't put butter on it."

"I was thinking about real movie theater popcorn. At the movies. Have you been to Mann's Theater yet?"

She shook her head.

"*Thor: Love and Thunder* is showing in half an hour."

"I saw that in Las Vegas. Last summer."

"I've seen it, too," he told her. "Not in town, obviously, because Mann's is a second-run theater, but I enjoyed it enough to want to see it on the big screen again."

"It was a good movie." She felt her lips curve as she recalled one scene in particular where Thor was literally unrobed by Zeus.

"You're thinking about Chris Hemsworth's naked butt, aren't you?" Deacon's tone was accusing.

She felt heat climb into her cheeks. "I am not."

"You are, too."

"I was thinking about *Thor's* naked butt."

He shook his head despairingly. "Is that a *yes* or *no* on the movie?"

"It's a *yes*, as long as we're clear that this is just a movie and not a date."

"Just a movie," he confirmed.

Yet despite their mutual agreement that it wasn't a date, it felt an awful lot like a date. Especially when the lights went down in the theater and her fingers brushed against his when they both reached into the popcorn bucket at the same time. And when he drove her home afterward and walked her to the door, excited butterflies danced in her stomach in anticipation of the possibility that he might kiss her.

But he didn't.

Instead, she went inside alone, secretly wishing for something that she knew could never be.

The last time Deacon had overnight guests had been when Piper and Poppy stayed with him.

This weekend, instead of almost-four-year-old twins, he was hanging out with an almost-four-pound dog. All because Sierra had read some article about how moving was a traumatic experience for a dog, and she wanted Remy to get used to not only spending time with Deacon but also at his house.

Sierra had opted out of their usual Friday night dinner, ostensibly so that he could maximize his time with Remy. But when he picked up the dog, he couldn't help but notice that she looked a little pale, and she admitted that she'd been battling a headache all day.

So Deacon had picked up a pizza and watched TV with Remy beside him. And ignored Sierra's warning against giving the dog "people food"—to his own detriment. About thirty minutes after he'd peeled a couple of slices of sausage off the pizza for the dog, he suffered the consequences of the animal's shockingly pungent flatulence.

Saturday, having learned his lesson the hard way, he gave Remy only his own food and approved treats.

Sunday, Deacon was looking over the schedule for the upcoming week when there was a knock on the door.

"I brought my tools," Connor said, holding up the metal box he carried.

"Thank you?" Deacon said cautiously.

"You said you wanted a hand installing the new cabinet in your powder room."

"I didn't say I wanted to do it today."

"I know," his brother admitted. "But Regan was taking the twins to her parents' house for a visit this afternoon and staying for dinner—and I needed an excuse to beg off."

"You lied to your wife to get out of spending time with her family?"

"It's true that I promised to help you," Connor pointed out in his defense.

"And when Regan comes over to see the new cabinet?"

"Damn," his brother muttered. "She will, too, won't she?"

"Of course she will."

"So I'll tell her that you decided you didn't want to do it today."

"And that's why you were able to make it to Miners' Pass for dinner after all," Deacon said, naming the street where Haven's wealthiest families all lived.

"Alright," Connor agreed reluctantly. "I'll go for dinner because Celeste's cooking is almost good enough to make me forget that Regan's mother will never believe I am."

"Regan doesn't care what she thinks, so why should you?"

"You're right, I shouldn't."

But Deacon suspected that growing up the way they'd grown up meant they'd always be trying to prove themselves.

"Anyway." Connor glanced at his watch. "I've still got a few hours before dinner."

Deacon opened the door to let his brother in.

"Do you have coffee on?"

"No, but I can remedy that in about two minutes."

Connor followed him to the kitchen.

"When did you get a dog?" he asked, eyeing the tiny creature snoring on his pillow in the corner. "Assuming that is a dog."

"He is," Deacon said. "But he's not mine."

Connor looked pointedly from the dog to the personalized mat with the bowls for food and water and then the bin of toys, his brows raised.

"Okay, he's mine this weekend," Deacon admitted.

"You're dog-sitting?"

"Actually, it's more like a joint custody arrangement."

"Really?" Connor sounded amused.

"He'll go back to Sierra tomorrow."

"You're sharing custody of a dog with the new ADA?"

"Temporary ADA," Deacon felt compelled to remind his

brother—as Sierra was always quick to remind him. "Which is the reason for this arrangement."

"I'm going to need you to fill in some more blanks," Connor said.

"I was with Sierra when she found the dog outside of Diggers' one night. I wanted to take him to the shelter, but she—against my advice—decided to take him home. Then she realized that she was getting attached to a dog that she couldn't take back to Vegas with her because she's going to be staying with her brother and sister-in-law, who's allergic to dogs, so she asked me if I'd take him when she left."

"And instead of reminding her that the shelter would find him a permanent home, you decided that she'd provided you with the perfect opportunity to spend more time hanging out with her."

It was an uncannily accurate assessment of his thought processes.

"Anyway, he's with Sierra most of the time, but she wants him to spend a few nights here every now and then, to ensure it's a familiar place to him when he comes to live here."

"You're not going to take him to the shelter when she goes back to Vegas?"

"Of course not," he immediately replied, insulted that his brother would even suggest such a thing.

"Because you've fallen as hard for this ridiculous little dog as you have for Sierra," Connor noted with a grin.

Deacon didn't respond, because he wasn't ready to acknowledge that his brother was absolutely right.

CHAPTER SEVENTEEN

AFTER CONNOR HAD GONE, Deacon filled Remy's water bowl and measured out his dinner.

The dog was happily chowing down when Deacon's cell phone chimed with a text message.

He glanced at the screen.

Any chance you can keep Remy another day or two?

He immediately replied to Sierra's request:

Of course. What's up?

I think I've got a touch of the flu.

He knew it was making the rounds. In the past week alone, the trial coordinator, a court reporter and two judges had been out with it. While each had apparently bounced back from the bug within a couple of days, none of them was (as far as he knew) pregnant. And he couldn't help but worry that Sierra was on her own and obviously feeling unwell.

What do you need? Ginger ale? Chicken soup?

Just to stay in bed and not have to worry about the dog.

Then that's what you should do. Remy and I were planning a Marvel movie marathon tonight, anyway.

She responded to that with a smiley face.

Seriously, how long have you been sick?

It started in the middle of the night Friday.

Fever? Nausea? Vomiting?

Yes.

Have you eaten anything?

I'm not hungry.

While he didn't get sick often, Deacon had some experience with the flu, so he could understand that food wasn't appealing when battling nausea. Rest, which Sierra seemed to be getting, was crucial, and so was staying hydrated.
Was she drinking plenty of fluids?
Instead of sending another text message to ask that question, he called to the dog.
"Come on, Remy."
The Chihuahua lifted his head but, obviously tuckered out after chasing the ball Connor had kept tossing for him, made no move to get off his pillow.
"We're going to see Sierra."
Remy responded to her name with a happy yip and scrambled to his feet.
At any other time, Deacon would have walked over to her house. But he wanted to make a couple of stops first, so he put Remy's harness on him and buckled him into the passenger seat of his truck. Half an hour later, he texted from her driveway to let Sierra know he was using his key to let himself in.

She didn't reply to the message.

Once inside, he unclipped the dog's leash. Remy immediately went searching for Sierra—checking the living room, then the dining room and kitchen before making his way to the stairs. He sat there at the bottom and looked at Deacon expectantly, obviously waiting for him to carry him up to the bedroom, as Sierra always did.

Deacon hadn't considered that she might be in bed. Yeah, she'd said she wanted to sleep, but he'd assumed she'd be flaked out on the sofa in the living room with the TV on—as he tended to do when he wasn't feeling well.

Walking into her house with a key that she'd given him was one thing, venturing into her bedroom was another. But he set the bags he carried on the counter in the kitchen, then picked up the dog and made his way up the stairs.

"Sierra? Are you up here?"

She didn't respond, so he followed the sound of a television down the hall, pausing in the doorway of a room dimly lit by the screen. She was huddled under a mountain of blankets, and he tapped his knuckles on the open door before crossing the threshold.

"Sierra?" he said again.

"Mmm."

He approached cautiously, noting the half-full glass of water on her bedside table and bottle of Tylenol beside it.

The covers were tucked right up under her chin, and her hair was tangled around her face. He gently brushed the hair aside and touched the back of his hand to her forehead.

He wasn't really sure what he was checking for, but his mom had always done the same thing when he said he wasn't feeling well. If Sierra had been a little warm, he probably wouldn't have known it, but her skin was noticeably hot and clammy.

Her eyelashes fluttered, then parted.

"Deacon? What are you doing here?"

"I brought you soup," he said.

"Oh." She tried to smile, but the effort wasn't very successful. "That was sweet, but I'm really not hungry."

"You need to eat something."

Her eyes drifted shut again.

"When do you last take Tylenol?"

"Five o'clock."

The display on the clock on her bedside table read 6:10 p.m., so just over an hour ago.

He found a facecloth in the linen tower in the bathroom adjacent to her bedroom, moistened it with cold water and returned to the bedroom to lay it across her forehead.

"Mmm...that feels good."

"I've imagined you saying those exact words when I had you in bed, but not under these circumstances."

She managed a weak smile.

"Do you want to come downstairs to eat or do you want me to bring the soup up to you?"

"I'm really not hungry."

"Not eating wasn't one of the options."

She exhaled a weary sigh. "You can bring it up, please."

He couldn't find a serving tray, so he improvised, arranging the bowl of soup, napkin, spoon, a sleeve of saltine crackers and a glass of ginger ale on a baking sheet.

By the time he returned to her bedroom with the food, she'd managed to sit up in bed, the pillows propped up behind her back.

"I should have gone downstairs so you didn't have to come back into my germ-filled room," she protested weakly. "Now you're going to get sick."

"Doubtful. But if I do, you can return the favor and play nurse to me. Short skirt optional."

"Pretend I'm rolling my eyes at you," she said. "Because I'm too tired to actually exert the effort."

"Rolling eyes noted," he assured her.

She nibbled on a couple of crackers and managed half a dozen spoonfuls of soup before she decided that she was done.

He took the baking sheet/tray from her and set it on the dresser, leaving her with the glass of ginger ale.

"What are you doing?" she asked, when he began opening and closing drawers.

"Looking for some clothes for you."

"I don't need to get dressed—I'm not going anywhere."

"You're going to the hospital."

"It's the flu, Deacon. If everyone who got the flu ran to the hospital, it would be overflowing with sick people."

"If you don't think you need to see a doctor—"

"I don't," she interjected.

"—then think about the baby."

Her hand immediately went to the barely noticeable curve of her belly and her brow furrowed.

"Okay," she finally relented. "I'll go to the hospital."

He pulled out a sweater he was sure he'd seen her wear before and a pair of stretchy leggings, holding them up for her perusal. "Do these work?"

"Sure."

He deposited them on the foot of the bed.

"I'm going to need more than that," she told him. "I'm not in the habit of leaving the house commando."

Right. She needed underwear.

"Top drawer of the other dresser," she told him.

He pulled open the drawer and found himself staring at a colorful selection of bras and panties. He gritted his teeth and plunged a hand into the sea of lace and silk, grabbing the first items he touched and tossing them onto the bed with the other garments.

"Ordinarily I'd protest that those don't match, but right now I don't really care," she admitted.

"The doctor won't care, either," he told her, shoving the drawer closed.

And right now, he was trying really hard not to picture his (pregnant and sick) friend in sexy underwear—a not entirely successful effort.

"Do you need a hand getting dressed?"

He held his breath, torn between wanting her to say *yes* and hoping she'd say *no*.

"I think I can manage."

"How about undressed? I'm pretty good at that part."

"I have no doubt, but no, thank you."

He took it as a good sign that she'd been able to respond to his teasing and carried the remains of her meal downstairs so that she would have some privacy to dress.

When they got to the hospital, he pulled into a drop-off zone and left his hazards flashing while he ran inside to get a wheelchair, then he wheeled Sierra into the ER before going to park his vehicle. By the time he got back, she'd checked in at the desk and was in triage.

"What brings you in today?" the nurse asked in a bored voice.

"I think I have the flu."

"You and a lot of other people," the nurse responded.

"How many of those other people are pregnant?" Deacon asked.

That question seemed to generate at least a modicum of concern from the health-care worker. "How far along?"

"Eighteen weeks," the expectant mother said.

The nurse input that information. "Your doctor's name?"

"Camila Amaro."

"Lucky for you, she's on call tonight."

"I'd feel a lot luckier if I hadn't got the flu," Sierra joked weakly.

A few minutes later, they were ushered into an exam room by a nurse who checked the patient's vitals, drew some blood and sent her into the bathroom with a specimen cup. And a few more minutes after that, when she'd transferred from the wheelchair to the bed, the doctor came in.

"Couldn't wait until your next appointment to see me?" the white-coated specialist teased.

"I was willing to wait," Sierra told her. "Deacon didn't give me a choice."

The doctor shifted her gaze to him. "You're Deacon?"

He nodded.

"Friend or family?"

"Friend."

"I'm Camila Amaro," she said, introducing herself before turning her attention to the chart on which the nurse had recorded Sierra's vitals.

"We're going to get you hooked up to an IV, and then we'll

take you down to perform a quick scan to check on the baby, okay?" Dr. Amaro said, speaking to Sierra now.

"Okay," she agreed.

"I don't think there's any reason to be concerned about the little guy, but an ultrasound will let us be sure."

The doctor had barely finished speaking when the nurse returned with the IV drip. Dr. Amaro went ahead to get set up for the ultrasound and told Sierra an orderly would be there in a few minutes to transport her to diagnostic imaging.

"They run an efficient operation here," Deacon noted.

"We do our best," the nurse told him. Then to Sierra she said, "Your friend can go with you to your ultrasound, if you want."

Sierra looked at Deacon. "What do you think?"

"Whatever you want."

"I want you to come...unless this is weird for you."

It definitely felt weird, but his discomfort was greatly outweighed by his desire to be there for her.

"Then I'll go with you," he said.

So he followed along as the orderly steered the bed through the halls and into an elevator, delivering her promptly to the diagnostic imaging department where Dr. Amaro was waiting.

Sierra didn't have to change into a gown. Instead, she was instructed to push her leggings down to her hips and lift her sweater. The doctor then squirted gel on her belly and used some kind of wand to spread it around. As she did, an image appeared on the computer screen.

Sierra smiled. "There he is."

"He?" Deacon echoed.

She nodded. "It's a boy."

He squinted at the screen. "How can you tell?"

She managed a soft chuckle. "I can't tell, but Dr. Amaro identified all the relevant parts during my last scan."

"It's a boy," the doctor confirmed.

Deacon remembered seeing an ultrasound picture of Piper and Poppy at about eight weeks, which had looked like nothing more to him than a couple of whitish blobs on a dark background. At eighteen weeks, Sierra's baby actually looked like a baby. And it was fascinating to him to not only see the baby moving but also hear the rhythmic beat of his heart.

"Heart rate is 144 beats per minute," Dr. Amaro said.

"That seems fast," Deacon said, and immediately wished he'd kept his mouth shut.

"For you or I it would be," the doctor agreed, obviously unconcerned. "For an eighteen-week fetus, it's right in the middle of the normal range."

"That's good then, right?" Sierra asked.

"Very good," Dr. Amaro said. "More good news—your placenta is healthy and right where it should be, and your amniotic fluid level is good."

Sierra exhaled a quiet sigh of relief.

"All in all, the baby's doing just fine."

Sierra looked at Deacon. "I told you I didn't need to come to the hospital," she said, sounding tired and just a little bit smug.

"The baby's doing just fine," Dr. Amaro said again. "But your heart rate is a little high and your blood pressure is a little low, both signs of dehydration."

"Which is why I've got the IV, right?"

"Yes, but it's not an instant fix, so I'm going to keep you here overnight for observation."

"But—"

A pointed look from the doctor had Sierra cutting off her own protest.

"Instead of enumerating all the reasons you don't want to spend the night in the hospital—because none of those reasons is as important as your well-being and that of the baby—why don't you thank your friend for bringing you in?"

It wasn't really a request but a directive.

"Thank you, Deacon," Sierra dutifully intoned.

"You're welcome," he said, lest he be chastised by the doctor for not following her script.

"You can wait here while I finish the paperwork to get you admitted to a room," Dr. Amaro told her patient.

"Thank you," Sierra said again.

"Do you need me to bring anything back for you?" Deacon

asked. "Pajamas? Toothbrush? An actual book because you don't like to read on a Kindle?"

"I'll be fine," she told him. Then to the doctor she said, "It's just one night, right?"

"At this point, I'm optimistic about your chances of going home in the morning, but I'm not making any promises."

"If Sierra can go home tomorrow, what time should I be here to pick her up?" Deacon asked the doctor.

"You can't pick me up," Sierra protested. "You have a trial starting tomorrow."

"Jury selection is tomorrow," he said. "And I have complete faith in Brenna to handle that on her own."

"I start my rounds early," Dr. Amaro said. "If the IV does the trick, I should be signing Sierra's discharge papers by eight a.m."

"You don't need to come back tomorrow," Sierra said to him, continuing her protest when the doctor had gone. "I can get a cab or—"

"I'll be here at eight," he said, in a tone that brooked no argument.

"I appreciate everything you did today, but I'm not your responsibility, Deacon."

"Maybe not," he acknowledged, giving her hand a gentle squeeze. "But you are my friend."

She managed a wobbly smile. "Thank you for being my friend."

"Always," he said, and meant it.

Even if he suddenly found himself longing to be so much more.

CHAPTER EIGHTEEN

THE DOCTOR DID, indeed, start her rounds early. And by 8:00 a.m., Sierra was sitting in the passenger seat of Deacon's truck, on her way home.

She felt a little bit guilty that he'd driven all the way from Haven to Battle Mountain only to turn around and immediately drive her all the way back again, but he'd refused to even consider letting her make other arrangements. And when he pulled into her driveway, he didn't just walk her to the door but insisted on seeing her inside, settling her on the sofa where he'd already set up a pillow and blanket. Then he made her tea and toast, handed her the remote control for the television and kissed her on the top of the head before heading off to the courthouse with a pointed reminder that she was to call him if she needed anything.

She sat on the sofa, cradling the mug of tea in her hands, her heart overflowing with gratitude for everything he'd done.

Had anyone else ever taken care of her like this?

Her mom, obviously, when she'd been little. And maybe Nick. She remembered her brother blending frozen fruit into smoothies for her when she'd had her wisdom teeth removed—and having to spoon the thick liquid into her mouth, because the dentist had forbidden sucking through a straw, which he told her would put too much strain on the stitches.

But she couldn't recall anyone who wasn't related to her ever going to such lengths. Apparently Mr. Columbia Law was a lot more than a hotshot lawyer with a handsome face and sexy body, and she was immensely grateful that they'd found their way to being friends.

After she ate her toast (or at least half of it) and drank her tea, she decided to close her eyes and have a quick nap. When she woke up, three hours later, she was feeling much more rested and even strong enough to venture upstairs to change the sheets on her bed—only to discover that Deacon had taken care of that, too. He'd even put clean towels in the bathroom.

It was going to be a very lucky woman who managed to snag that man someday, she acknowledged. His willingness to take care of menial chores around the house was the least of it, and if she felt just a twinge of regret that she couldn't be that lucky woman, she was still grateful for his friendship.

She made her way back downstairs, ate the rest of her (now cold and hard) toast with another cup of tea, then fell asleep rewatching *Bridgerton* for the third time.

At the end of the day, Deacon stopped by to see how she was doing and to bring her some more soup. Minestrone. The day after that, he brought Remy to visit. And harvest vegetable soup. On the third day, she was standing at the stove when he arrived.

"What are you doing?" he asked.

"Making dinner."

"But... I brought you soup."

"Thank you," she said, not wanting to seem ungrateful. "But I'm sick of soup. I want real food."

"You should have told me that. I would have been happy to pick up whatever you wanted."

"I am capable of putting a meal together."

He came into the kitchen then and peered into the pan.

"Grilled cheese is real food?" he asked, sounding amused.

"Apparently I need to make a trip to the grocery store."

"Make a list," he said. "I'll pick up what you need."

"I need to take care of myself."

"You're just getting over the flu," he reminded her. "You need to be careful not to overdo it."

"I'm over the flu," she said. "In fact, I'm going back to the office tomorrow and would like to pick up my dog to bring him home after work, if that's okay."

"Our dog," he reminded her.

"Our dog," she agreed. "And I'm more grateful than I can express for everything you've done, but I'm really fine now."

"Okay," he agreed. Then, "Any chance one of those sandwiches is for me?"

"That's why there are two plates on the counter."

He got out two bowls to divvy up the chicken and rice soup he'd brought, and they ate it along with the sandwiches.

After they'd finished the meal—Sierra managed half a sandwich and most of her soup—they tidied up the kitchen together. Deacon wanted Sierra to sit and rest, but she reminded him that she'd been resting for nearly five days already.

When she straightened up after bending to close the dishwasher door, she sucked in a breath and pressed a hand to the side of her belly.

Deacon was immediately there. "Are you okay?"

"Yeah." She smiled to reassure him. "I think... I felt the baby move."

The worry on his face immediately eased.

"First time?" he guessed.

She nodded. "I've had these weird little flutters that I thought might be the baby, but this was different. This was a more distinct—oh." She smiled again. "A definite kick."

Then she took his hand and guided it to the same spot.

His eyes went wide, and she knew that he'd felt it, too.

"I guess you really do have a tiny human being in there."

"Seeing him on the ultrasound didn't convince you?"

"He looked like a baby, but that was still just an image on a screen. This is..."

She lifted her gaze when his words trailed off and suddenly realized that they were standing close, her hand on his hand on her belly.

Sierra knew that she should take a step back; put some distance between them. Instead, she stayed right where she was, her eyes locked with his.

"This is?" she prompted softly.

His response was barely more than a whisper, "Real."

It certainly felt real to Sierra.

Not just real but right.

She leaned in, breaching the scant distance that separated them, and tipped her head back to touch her lips to his.

She was kissing him.

Deacon's head was reeling over the fact even as her lips—so soft and sweet—moved against his. And while she might have taken him by surprise, he had no intention of letting this opportunity slip through his fingers. Though he knew there was at least one not-so-little reason that kissing Sierra was a bad idea—that being the slight (but growing) swell of her belly pressed against him—he didn't ever want to stop.

His tongue touched the seam of her lips, then slipped between when they parted for him. A soft hum of approval sounded low in her throat and she lifted her hands to his shoulders, holding on to him as the kiss went on and on.

As she'd been the one to start it, he let her be the one to end it. She did so far too soon for his liking, pulling her mouth away from his and dropping her head against his chest.

She exhaled a regretful sigh. "We can't do this."

"It seems to me that we can—and were."

She pulled out of his arms then and took a deliberate step back. "I'm sorry. I know I've been giving you mixed signals."

"You have," he agreed. "But I'm happy to forget all the earlier signals and get back to the kissing."

"Except that kissing is a slippery slope. And I'm not in any position to get involved in a personal relationship right now," she continued her explanation.

"It seems to me that we already have a personal relationship."

"And I'm grateful to you for your friendship."

"Friendship is always a good starting point," he agreed.

Sierra's boss wanted her to ease back into work, so he didn't assign her any court duty until a full week after she returned to the office following her bout with the flu. And her first assignment was First Appearance Court with Judge Graves. The overwhelming majority of cases were put over at First Appearance, which allowed the court to get through the docket quickly. Still, a two-page docket usually meant a mid-morning recess, but Judge Graves insisted on pushing through rather than take a break, and by the time court was finally adjourned, she was starving.

She'd lost three pounds when she was sick with the flu, but she'd gained them back fairly quickly—plus two more. Because now that her appetite had returned, she was eating regular healthy meals again—supplemented by more-than-occasional treats from Sweet Caroline's (the salted caramel brownie was her new favorite) and ice cream from Scoops (always rocky road).

As her colleagues filtered toward the exit at the back of the courtroom, Sierra found an emergency granola bar in the side pocket of her briefcase, tore off the wrapper and took a big bite.

"Sierra?"

She froze, a strange feeling—almost like dread—washing over her.

Could it be...

No, she couldn't imagine any circumstances that would have brought Eric Stikeman to Haven, Nevada.

But though she hadn't heard his voice in more than seven months and he'd only spoken a single word—her name—she knew it was him.

She chewed quickly and swallowed before glancing over her shoulder to confirm that it was, indeed, her ex walking toward her.

He approached the prosecutor's table, a half smile on his lips. "Of all the courtrooms in all the towns," he mused.

"That's exactly what I was thinking," she said, discreetly brushing a crumb off her lapel. "What are you doing here?"

"A careless driving trial, if you can believe it."

"You came all the way from Las Vegas to argue a case in traffic court?"

"The defendant is the daughter of one of my biggest clients. I couldn't say *no*."

"I guess not," she agreed.

"What are you doing here?"

She tucked the remainder of her granola bar into her jacket pocket. "Working for the Haven district attorney."

"Do you prosecute traffic violations?"

"Not usually," she said. "Ron Harding handles most of those." She gathered up her files and stuffed them into her briefcase. "Well, good luck with your trial."

Eric took a step closer, ignoring the obvious cue that she was ready for this conversation to be over.

More than ready.

"I should have reached out to you, when I got back from—" he cleared his throat "—when I got back."

"What would have been the point?" she wondered aloud. "We'd both said everything we needed to say."

"Did I say I was sorry?"

"I think what you said was that you were sorry I didn't tell you that I'd decided to meet you in San Francisco after all."

"I know you were upset about what happened—and you have every reason to be," he hastened to assure her. "But it was a mistake—an error in judgment—and I am sorry."

"So noted." She pushed her chair back from the table and rose to her feet.

Eric sucked in a breath. "You're...pregnant?"

"Yep."

His Adam's apple bobbed a few times before he managed to speak again. "Jesus, Sierra—why didn't you tell me?"

At another time, she might have enjoyed seeing the unflappable attorney so obviously and completely flapped. But that time had passed seven months earlier when she'd caught Eric with his pants down and Aubrey on her knees.

"I didn't tell you, because it has nothing to do with you," she said coolly.

"Are you saying...the baby's not mine?"

"The baby is definitely not yours."

He exhaled an audible sigh. "Thank God."

"Don't hold back," she said dryly. "Tell me how you really feel."

He had the grace to look chagrined. "It's just that we never talked about having kids. And then, to see you now...pregnant... was a bit of a shock."

"Instead of thanking God, you should probably thank the condom manufacturer."

"Oh. Right." He attempted a smile, but it was gone before it had fully formed. "Well, if you're sure..."

"One hundred percent."

"Then I guess the only thing left to do is wish you luck."

"I don't need luck," she told him. "I'm going to be just fine."

"I have no doubt," he agreed. "And for what it's worth... I'm sorry that I screwed everything up."

She accepted his olive branch and offered one of her own. "I don't know how long your trial is expected to last, but if you have time while you're in town, you should try Jo's Pizza."

"Is it half as good as Grimaldi's?" he asked, naming what had been their favorite pizza place in Vegas.

"No," she told him. "It's better."

"Then I'm definitely going to have to check it out. Or maybe you and I could..." The question trailed off as she shook her head.

"No," she said again. "There's no way we're going to share a pizza and conversation as if you didn't screw around on me with one of my friends."

His cheeks flushed. "You have to know it didn't mean anything."

"That only makes it worse," she told him.

Turning toward the exit and discovering that Deacon was standing there, waiting for her, further compounded her humiliation.

"I thought you'd gone," she said.

He studied her carefully neutral expression for a minute before responding. "I was going to head back to the office, then I realized it was past lunchtime, so I thought I'd see if you wanted to grab a bite to eat."

"I definitely do," she agreed. "I'm starving."

"Jo's?" he suggested.

She narrowed her gaze.

"You mentioned last night that you'd been craving it," he reminded her.

He was right—she had mentioned it. Because she had been craving Jo's Pizza, and she wasn't going to let Eric's unexpected appearance in town deprive her of it.

Deacon did her the courtesy of waiting until the server had taken their order before broaching the subject she knew had to be at the forefront of his mind.

"So...that was your ex?"

She nodded.

"Obviously he's a lawyer, too."

"We both worked at Bane & Associates," she said. "I was in the criminal law division, Eric specialized in civil litigation."

Deacon smiled his thanks to the server when she delivered their drinks, then turned his attention back to Sierra, obviously waiting for her to continue.

"You really want to hear the whole sordid story?"

"I think you need to tell someone," he said. "I got the impression, during your brief exchange in the courtroom, that you'd been keeping some pretty intense emotions bottled up for a while."

"I guess I have," she admitted. "So I'll tell you—but please cut me off at any point if you get bored."

"You worked together at the same firm," he said, prompting her to pick up where she left off.

She nodded again. "Practicing law in a big-city firm can be a cutthroat business, and I didn't have a lot of close friends at Bane. Except for Aubrey. We worked a lot of cases together, which meant that we spent a lot of time together, and she was one of very few people who I confided in when I started dating Eric.

"Bane didn't have an explicit nonfraternization policy, but they discouraged professional colleagues from getting personally involved. And while my relationship with Eric wasn't a big secret, we were discreet.

"Anyway, after six months of dating, we moved in together. Actually, I gave up my apartment and moved in with him, which meant that when we broke up, I was the one who had to move out.

"But that was at the end. In the beginning, things were really good. We enjoyed spending time together—whether out with colleagues or friends or alone at home."

She paused when the server delivered their pizza to the table. Deacon transferred a slice from the tray to her plate before taking one for himself. Between bites of pizza, she continued to fill in the details for him.

"We'd been living together for almost a year when Eric was invited to present at a law conference in San Francisco. It was a huge honor, but he hesitated to accept because he didn't want to be away on our eighteen-month anniversary. He did ask me to go with him, but I already had a two-week trial on the books that conflicted with the conference dates.

"So I convinced him it was too great an opportunity to pass up, and he promised to put my name on the room registration in the hope that my trial would finish early and I could join him in San Francisco for a few days, at least.

"There were half a dozen associates from Bane who were at the conference, including Aubrey. She checked in with me every day, asking me about the trial, sharing information about the conference. And when my trial did, indeed, finish early, she encouraged me to book a flight to surprise Eric.

"'Think about how romantic it will be, to celebrate your anniversary in San Francisco,' she'd said. It did sound romantic, and I figured, after my big trial win, I deserved to steal a few days away."

She lifted her glass to her lips and swallowed a mouthful of icy water, hoping it would cool the heat of embarrassment that she could feel spreading through her body.

"I think I can guess what happened next," he said.

"I'm sure you can," she agreed. "The worst part of the whole thing is that I actually apologized. I interrupted my boyfriend in bed with my friend, and *I* said *sorry*."

It still stung to realize that not only had her supposed friend cheated with her boyfriend, but Aubrey had obviously set Sierra up to find them.

"Then I retreated to the lobby, determined to book an immediate flight back home, but I was shaking so much, I could hardly hold on to my phone. A few minutes later, Eric found me there, still shaking and crying, and tried to convince me to go back to his room so that we could talk. He actually thought I would go back to the room where I saw him...them..."

She blew out a breath. "Obviously I declined. And not very politely. Apparently I said a few words that you don't often hear in the lobby of a Fairmont hotel, and so Eric went to reception to get another room."

She managed a wry smile then. "All they had available was a deluxe balcony suite, but he handed over his credit card, and we went up to the suite to talk. Actually, he tried to convince me to understand that the scene I'd walked in on was really one of my own making, because I hadn't given him a heads-up that I was coming to San Francisco."

Deacon looked horrified. "He honestly said that?"

She nodded. "And expected me to take at least some responsibility for the situation so that we could forgive one another and move past the unfortunate indiscretion—all his words."

"Please tell me that you told him to go back to his own room and screw himself."

"Oh, I did. Several times."

Deacon wiped his fingers on a paper napkin, then folded it on top of his empty plate. "And he's really not the baby's father?"

"The San Francisco fiasco was last September. The baby is due August twenty-second. Obviously this baby isn't his."

"I guess that's good then," he said.

"It's very good," she agreed.

He handed his credit card to the server, who brought a takeout box for the leftover pizza. A few minutes later, they walked out of the restaurant together.

Sierra blinked at the bright sunshine that greeted them, her mood instantly lifted.

"I think I love northern Nevada in the spring," she said.

"There's something to appreciate about every season here," Deacon told her.

"Well, I'll still be here for the beginning of summer," she noted. "And maybe I'll come back to visit in the fall."

"Or...you could stay."

She looked at him then, her heart filled with regret. "Haven't we had this discussion already?"

"I know you think there isn't any reason to stay after your contract is up," he said, "but what if you had a reason? What if we got married?"

"There's no point in asking *what if*, because I'm not going to marry you. I sincerely appreciate the white knight routine," she said, because she did. "But I'm not a damsel in distress who needs to be rescued."

"I know you're not," he agreed. "In fact, you are one of the most amazingly capable women I've ever known. But I grew up with a single mom, and I know the kind of struggles that she—"

"I'm not going to be a single mother, Deacon," she interjected.

"I don't understand," he admitted.

"My responsibilities with respect to the baby will be over as soon as he's born."

Deacon's brows drew together as he attempted to decipher the meaning of her words. "Are you telling me...are you giving your baby up for adoption?"

Sierra shook her head. "I'm telling you that he's not my baby."

CHAPTER NINETEEN

"I DON'T UNDERSTAND," Deacon said again, still trying—unsuccessfully—to wrap his head around what she was saying.

"I'm not the baby's mom," Sierra told him. "I'm a gestational carrier."

Gestational carrier?

"Is that like...a surrogate?" he asked.

"Some people use the terms interchangeably," she acknowledged. "But a surrogate might allow her own egg to be fertilized while a gestational carrier does not."

"So you don't have any biological connection to the baby you're carrying?"

"Actually, this little guy—" she smiled as she laid her hands on the slight curve of her belly "—is my nephew. My brother and sister-in-law's baby."

"But...why?" he asked, equal parts baffled by the revelation and stunned by her selfless generosity.

"Because I can't imagine any couple who would be better parents than my brother and sister-in-law. Because it totally sucks that Whitney had the option of carrying a baby taken away from her. And..."

"And?" he prompted.

"Because I owe my brother everything. Because he dropped out of college when our parents were killed to come home and take care of me. Because he put his life on hold so that I didn't end up in foster care."

"I don't know your brother," he admitted. "But I'm sure he would say that you don't owe him anything—that he did what he did because you're his sister."

"You're right," she agreed. "But he gave me so much, and I was glad to be able to do this one thing for him and his wife."

"It isn't just one thing," he pointed out. "It's nine months of your life."

"A short period of time to fulfill one of their lifelong dreams."

His mind was still spinning, but one thing was clear. "You really are an incredible woman, Sierra."

"They're going to be incredible parents," she said. "Which you'd know if you ever met them."

"I hope I have the chance someday."

She smiled then. "As it turns out, they're coming to visit next weekend. Why don't you join us for a barbecue?"

"I think you might have a touch of OCD," Deacon remarked, as he watched Sierra move through the house, inspecting each room from top to bottom, straightening towels in the guest bath, wiping a fingerprint off a picture frame, fluffing the decorative pillows on the sofa, running the vacuum around *one last time* to ensure there wasn't a stray dog hair to be found. (In deference to her sister-in-law's allergies, Remy and all of his belongings had already been packed up and moved to Deacon's house for the weekend.)

"I just want everything to be perfect," she said.

"Your brother and sister-in-law are coming to see you—they're not going to care if you forgot to dust the overhead light in the dining room."

"It's called a chandelier," she told him. "And *damn*—I did forget to dust it."

He caught her hand as she started to hurry past—no doubt to retrieve her cleaning supplies. "Relax, Sierra. Nobody cares about the chandelier."

She seemed about to protest, then slowly nodded. "You're probably right."

"So why don't you tell me what's really going on?"

"I guess I'm a little bit nervous about them meeting you—and you meeting them."

"This was your idea," he reminded her. "But I can go, if you've changed your mind."

"I haven't," she insisted. "I want you to meet them. It's just that this is new territory in our relationship."

"*Our* meaning *yours and mine* or *yours and theirs*?"

"Both."

"Because you've never introduced them to a...friend...before?"

He paused to emphasize the word, as she insisted on doing whenever he hinted that their relationship might be something more. But despite her repeated reminders, and the lack of physical intimacy in their relationship, he was already more than halfway in love with her. Unfortunately, he knew she wasn't ready to hear him say it—and even less willing to acknowledge her own feelings.

So for now, he was trying to be satisfied with her friendship. Because as much as he chafed at the restrictions imposed by the label, at least he was part of her life.

"I've introduced them to plenty of friends," she assured him.

"But maybe I'm a little bit more than a friend?" he suggested hopefully.

Before Sierra could respond to that, Nick and Whitney arrived—right on schedule.

Deacon watched from the porch as Sierra embraced her brother and sister-in-law.

Now that he knew Nick was her brother, Deacon could see a little bit of a family resemblance—mostly in the color of their eyes and the way they smiled. They were both smiling now, obviously happy to see one another for the first time in more than three months.

Whitney gave them a moment, then elbowed her husband aside to hug her sister-in-law. She was tall and slender with long reddish hair and dark brown eyes. As she made her way toward Deacon, he noticed that she had a sprinkling of freckles on her nose—and absolutely no reservations about throwing her arms around a man she was meeting for the first time.

"I'm so glad to finally meet you," she said.

"Glad to finally meet the guy Sierra told us about two days ago?" Nick said dryly, no doubt to ensure Deacon didn't get the impression he mattered enough to Sierra to have come up in earlier conversation with her family.

"Sierra has always been fiercely guarded about her private life," Whitney noted.

"But happy to introduce my family to my friends," Sierra interjected, ushering them all through the house and out to the back deck.

Now that the warmer weather had arrived, she was apparently determined to make full use of the deck—and the patio furniture that she'd found in the shed. Which was why she planned to barbecue burgers and dine alfresco (which meant that no one was even going to be eating in the dining room under the chandelier she'd forgotten to dust).

"Can I help you with anything?" Whitney offered, when Sierra remarked that it was getting close to dinnertime.

"Nope. I've got everything under control," she promised. "The macaroni salad is made, potato wedges are in the oven. I just have to get out the... Oh, no."

"What did you forget?" Deacon asked.

"Buns." She groaned in frustration. "We're having hamburgers, and I don't have any hamburger buns."

"Is the grocery store very far?" Whitney asked.

"Nothing in Haven is very far," Sierra said, rising from her seat.

"I can go," Deacon said.

"Thanks, but I'd rather you stayed here and started the grill."

"Or I could do that," he agreed.

Whitney nudged her husband. "Why don't you go with your sister?"

"Because I don't think picking up a package of buns is a two-person job," Nick replied.

His wife gave him a look that communicated without the need for words.

Nick got to his feet. "But this is my second visit to Haven, and I have yet to visit the grocery store," he noted. "It might be fun."

"Only if you know a different definition for *fun*," Sierra said, as they walked out together.

"Are you going to grill me like I'm a burger?" Deacon asked Whitney when they were alone.

She laughed. "No, but I did want a few minutes to chat with you alone."

"I kind of got that impression," he admitted.

"I don't want to freak you out, but Sierra introducing you to her family is kind of a big deal. In fact, in the ten years that I've known her, she's never introduced us to a boyfriend. Well, except for the last one," she allowed, "but he doesn't really count, because Nick already knew Eric from when they served together on the board of a not-for-profit housing corporation. But mostly he doesn't count because he's a dick."

Deacon had to laugh at that. "That seems to be the consensus. But getting back to Sierra's introduction of me, I'm sure you noticed that she put me—firmly and definitively—in the friend zone."

"I noticed," Whitney admitted. "But the fact that she introduced you at all proves that you mean a lot to her. And I hope she means a lot to you, too."

"More than she wants to know," he confided.

"So...how did you feel when she told you that she was having her brother and sister-in-law's baby?"

"A little bit like I was in the middle of a nineties sitcom."

"*Friends*." Whitney grinned. "One of my all-time favorite shows."

"My mom was a big fan of it, too," he confided.

And then, in what seemed an abrupt conversational shift, she asked, "Do you believe in love at first sight?"

"If you'd asked me that question five months ago, I would have said no."

She smiled again. "I've always believed that we instinctively know when we meet someone who is going to play an important part in our lives. That's how it was for me and Nick. We met in law school—our first class together on our first day—and that was it for me. I was head over heels in love.

"Nick was a little bit slower to acknowledge his feelings, but he proposed at the end of our second year, and we immediately started making plans to get married after graduation. Three weeks before we were scheduled to exchange vows, I was diagnosed with cervical cancer. Nick wouldn't let me call off the wedding."

"Why did you think he would?" Deacon wondered.

"Because he hadn't signed up for that. In all our conversations about the future, we never talked about the possibility of him having to hold my hand during chemo treatments.

"But one thing we had talked about—one thing I knew Nick really wanted—was children—and my diagnosis threatened all of our plans to have a family.

"Still, Nick never wavered in his commitment to me and our future. Yes, he wanted a family, he said, but only if he could have a family with me.

"So we talked to the doctors about our options. A hysterectomy was the best choice for a positive outcome, but the result would be that I'd never be able to carry a child, so the doctors reluctantly agreed to let me postpone the surgery long enough to harvest some eggs."

She paused then to look at Deacon and ask, "Is this too much information?"

He shook his head. "No, though I am wondering why you're telling me all of this."

"Because I want you to understand what a huge deal this is—what Sierra's doing for us, against the doctors' advice."

"Why did the doctors advise against it?" he asked, immediately concerned.

"Gestational carriers are usually women who have already had at least one successful pregnancy, who have proven their ability to carry a baby to term for mothers who can't do so," Whitney explained. "This is a first for Sierra. In addition, there was some concern that the close family connection would put a lot of pressure on her. It's one of the reasons—maybe the only reason—that Nick didn't protest more vehemently when she decided to take the ADA position here."

"So why did you choose Sierra to be your gestational carrier?" he asked.

"Because I was uncomfortable with the idea of a stranger carrying our baby, even one screened and approved by the clinic for precisely that purpose. It just seemed unnatural to me to involve someone we didn't know in such an intimate part of our lives. And because Sierra understood my concerns and she offered. And because I didn't imagine—and I'm sure she didn't, either—that in the nine months she'd be carrying our baby, she would finally meet the man she was meant to be with."

Before Deacon could figure out how to respond to that, Whitney spoke again.

"Now you better get that barbecue started and get the burgers on before Sierra and Nick get back with the buns."

"Have you given any thought to what you want to do when you come back to Vegas?" Nick asked, pushing his empty plate aside.

"Actually I have," Sierra said. "I'm thinking of applying to the DA's office."

"Proof that you've officially gone over to the dark side," her brother lamented.

She rolled her eyes. "I hardly think that's the dark side."

Deacon and Whitney had been equal contributors to the earlier dinner conversation, but they both sat back now and let the siblings carry this topic.

"Well, if you change your mind, my firm is looking to hire," Nick told his sister.

"Um, no."

Nick scowled at her immediate response. "You could at least take some time to think about it."

"No," she said again. "I'm not taking a job from my brother."

"Why not?"

"Aside from the fact that it would reek of nepotism, you mean?"

"The whole law profession reeks of nepotism," he pointed

out. "The directory in my building advertises Whitfield and Whitfield, Callendar and Associates—three of whom are also named Callendar—and Rowlands and Sons, and those are only the ones I remember off the top of my head."

"There's also Beringer and Beringer," Whitney chimed in.

Sierra nodded her head in acknowledgment of the point. "Nepotism aside, I need to live my own life."

"Says the sister carrying my baby," Nick noted dryly.

"For which we will be forever grateful and not interfere with the choices she makes with respect to her own life," his wife said pointedly.

"Right," Nick agreed, chastened.

"Speaking of choices," Sierra said. "We've got rocky road, chocolate chip cookie dough and cherry chocolate chunk ice cream for dessert."

"I'd suggest you opt for the cookie dough or cherry chocolate," Deacon said.

Nick chuckled in response to the warning. "Don't worry," he said. "I learned long ago not to get between my sister and her rocky road."

CHAPTER TWENTY

SIERRA ENJOYED THE weekend with her brother and sister-in-law, and she'd been happy to introduce Deacon to her family. Though Nick had obviously been reserving judgment when he shook hands with her friend and canine co-parent, Deacon had soon won him over. Or maybe her brother had taken his cues from his wife, who had taken an immediate liking to "Sierra's new man," as Whitney referred to him.

In any event, they all had a good time, and when Sierra waved goodbye to them after brunch Sunday afternoon, she knew that she would be seeing them again in only seven weeks, when she went back to Las Vegas.

Which meant that she only had seven weeks left in Haven.

Seven weeks left with Deacon.

Funny how six months had seemed like so much time when she'd been moving into her temporary home, but now she suspected the last seven weeks would pass in the blink of an eye.

On her way back to the office after court Tuesday morning, she made a quick stop to grab a cranberry apple tea from The Daily Grind and spotted Deacon's sister-in-law waving to her.

"Do you have a minute?" Regan asked.

She glanced at her watch. "Sure," she decided, taking a chair on the opposite side of the table. "How can I help you?"

"I'm aware that I'm overstepping here, but I wanted to talk

to you about Deacon," his sister-in-law said. "More specifically, about his feelings for you."

"Deacon and I have become good friends over the past several months," Sierra acknowledged, at the same time silently chastising herself for accepting the other woman's invitation to join her without question. "But it's not anything more than that, and he knows that I'm not looking for anything more than that."

"Does he?" Regan sounded dubious.

"He does," she confirmed. "I've also been very clear that I'm leaving Haven when my six-month contract with the DA's office is up."

"Or maybe you're just waiting for him to step up and ask you to stay."

"Step up?" Sierra echoed. Then the pieces clicked into place. "You mean because I'm pregnant?"

She was grateful that she no longer had to whisper the word. When she returned to work after recovering from the flu, she'd told her boss, and then her coworkers, about her pregnancy. It hadn't taken long for word to spread after that, and anyone who hadn't heard the gossip would be able to guess her status now that she was sporting an obvious baby bump.

Regan nodded.

"You think I'm looking for someone to be a father to my baby?" she guessed.

"I've been there," the other woman confided. "I was pregnant when Connor and I got married, so I understand that the prospect of being a single mom is daunting, and I know all the reasons that an expectant mother would want a father for her child."

"The baby I'm carrying will have a mother and a father," Sierra assured her.

Deacon's sister-in-law seemed taken aback by this response. "You're still in a relationship with the father?"

"Yes, but not in the way you're thinking."

"Can you clarify?"

"I thought Deacon would have told you," she admitted.

"Told me *what*?"

Now she did lower her voice, to tell Regan what she'd only

confided to Deacon and Sky. "The baby I'm carrying isn't mine."

Regan had to close the jaw that had fallen open before she could respond. "Are you saying...you're a surrogate?"

"A gestational carrier, actually, for my brother and sister-in-law."

"I did not see *that* coming," the other woman admitted.

"It's a rather unusual situation," Sierra acknowledged.

"I can't believe Deacon didn't tell me. Actually, I can believe it," Regan quickly amended. "He's nothing if not discreet, and if you asked him not to say anything, he wouldn't. Not to anyone."

"I'm relieved to hear that," she said. "Because I'm sure people have enough to say about my situation without adding that to the mix."

She'd heard some of the whispers and even speculation about the identity of the baby's father. Deacon's name had popped up in that conversation, notwithstanding the fact that she'd obviously been pregnant before she came to Haven. But gossips were rarely concerned about facts and, thankfully, Deacon didn't seem bothered by the rumors.

"Now I have another question," Regan said. "Since you're obviously not in a romantic relationship with anyone, why are you trying so hard to keep Deacon at arm's length?"

"Because the complication of my pregnancy aside, I'm only going to be in Haven a few more weeks."

"Because that's when your contract runs out? Or because you don't want to stay?"

"There's no reason for me to stay if I don't have a job," Sierra pointed out.

"I can understand why you might feel that way," the other woman said. "It wasn't so long ago that my career was the focus of my life. And I still love my job, but I love my family more."

"The best of both worlds," she acknowledged.

Regan smiled. "It is, indeed. Now I need to apologize for being rude, jumping to conclusions and taking up too much of your time."

"You don't have to apologize to me," Sierra said. "Not for looking out for your family."

"Deacon is family—whether he wants to accept it or not."

Sierra smiled. "He's lucky to have you."

"You really do care about him, don't you?"

"Of course I care about him. And if circumstances were different—" She cut herself off with a shake of her head. "But there's no point in speculating, because circumstances aren't different."

The Friday before Memorial Day, Deacon rushed back to the office after court in the hope that he could finish the sentencing memo he'd been working on and escape from the office a little earlier than usual. He and Sierra hadn't made any big plans for the holiday weekend, but they did plan to spend it together.

He'd suggested packing a picnic on Saturday and taking Remy to Cutthroat Lake to hike some of the easier trails. He knew he'd likely end up carrying the dog after about twenty minutes, but he didn't mind.

Today, though, the weather was perfect for a barbecue, so he wanted to stop at The Trading Post on his way home to pick up some steaks for dinner with Sierra. And salad stuff, because she insisted on balancing her meal with healthy vegetables, and apparently a fully loaded baked potato didn't count.

He'd just clicked save on the document when there was a knock on his door. He glanced up to see his brother standing there, attired in his deputy sheriff uniform.

"Is this official business?" Deacon asked.

"No," Connor said. "It's personal."

His brother's serious expression immediately set off alarms. "Is everything okay? Regan? The girls? The babies?"

"They're all fine," his brother hastened to assure him.

"Are you okay?" he pressed, wondering if Connor had received some bad news from his doctor about his health.

"I'm fine, too."

Another thought—even more chilling. *"Sierra?"*

Deacon had seen her in court earlier that morning, but several hours had passed since then.

"As far as I know, there's no reason to worry there, either."

He exhaled a quiet sigh of relief. Now that he knew everyone he cared about was okay, he had no reason to be anxious about whatever his brother wanted to discuss. "Then what is it?"

The deputy sheriff sat on the edge of one of the visitors' chairs. "There was a fight in the parking lot behind Diggers' last night," he began. "Did you hear about it?"

"I got my coffee from The Daily Grind this morning, like I always do," Deacon told him. "Of course I heard about it."

Apparently several men from out of town had stopped in for a drink, but they were already more than halfway to being drunk—and belligerent—so Duke kicked them out of the bar. Instead of going away quietly, they started fighting amongst themselves in the back parking lot. Tempers flared, fists flew—and then one of the guys pulled out a knife.

"That about sums it up," Connor agreed, after Deacon recounted what he'd heard. "But they weren't all out-of-towners. One of them—the one who was stabbed—was Dwayne Parrish. Your father."

Deacon felt as if he'd been sucker punched and had all the air knocked out of his lungs.

Just when he was finally moving forward with his life...

"I know who Dwayne Parrish is," he said, when he'd managed to catch his breath and could speak again. "And while he might have contributed half of my DNA, he was never much of a father."

Connor nodded slowly. "I'm not going to disagree with that. I just thought you should know, and I didn't want you to hear the news from anyone else."

"I appreciate it," Deacon said.

"He's in ICU at NNRH in Elko, if you wanted to see him."

"I don't." His response was blunt and firm.

"His prognosis is pretty bleak," his brother warned.

"And maybe you think I'm unfeeling, but the honest truth is, I figured he was already dead—or maybe in jail somewhere."

"Neither of those things would have surprised me, either," Connor admitted. "But he's here. And after more than twenty years, don't you want to know why he came back?"

"No," Deacon said fiercely. Because he'd stopped wondering about his so-called father years ago. Relegated him and the unhappy memories to the past. And silently cursed him now for not staying there. "I only wish he hadn't."

He sat at his desk after his brother had gone, thinking about the man he hadn't given more than a passing thought to in a very long time.

He'd meant what he'd said to his brother about wishing Dwayne had never come back. When his dad left, after that horrible fight with Connor that Deacon would never forget, he'd felt nothing but relief. Gratitude that the man was out of all their lives. That he wouldn't ever again have to hear him yelling at his mother or see him hitting his brother.

Dwayne's absence had allowed Deacon to believe that he could, if not forget about his past, at least put it behind him and move forward with his life. Recently, he'd even been foolish enough to hope that he might do so with Sierra.

But now Deacon's past had caught up with him, and he knew that did not bode well for his future.

Sierra heard the whispers around town. She usually didn't pay much attention to gossip, but when the name Dwayne Parrish caught her attention, she found herself straining to pick up the details.

Of course, there were several variations of a similar story circulating, the gist of which was that Deacon's dad had shown up in town and gotten in a fight in the parking lot behind Diggers'. According to the reports, he'd either been beaten up, stabbed or shot, and when the sheriff arrived on scene, he'd possibly skipped town, been taken to hospital or shipped to the morgue.

Back at the office, she got the official report—Dwayne Parrish had been stabbed three times and was in the hospital with serious injuries.

She wondered if Deacon had heard the same rumors and how he was handling the news. Though she felt certain that the deputy sheriff would have apprised his brother of recent events, she still felt compelled to reach out.

Heard about your dad. Just wanted to let you know that I'm here if you want to talk.

A few minutes later came a brief reply:

Not necessary, but thanks.

And that was the last she heard from him until two hours later.

I'm not going to be able to walk Remy tonight—and I have to bail on our plans for the lake tomorrow, too. Sorry.

Their planned visit to Cutthroat Lake (named for the fish that inhabited the water, he'd assured her) had been his idea. Since the warmer weather had arrived in northern Nevada, they'd been taking Remy to explore some of the local hiking trails. She'd enjoyed their outings and was looking forward to the picnic he'd promised her.

She responded:

Remy's going to be disappointed.

Because it was easier to blame the dog than admit that *she* was disappointed.

But even more than she was disappointed, she was worried about Deacon. Worried that this sudden change of plans was somehow linked to the news about his dad.

Maybe we can do it another time?

She held her breath, waiting for his reply to her suggestion. For his assurance that, of course, they would do it another time.

Or you could take Remy on your own. The trails are clearly marked.

As if she needed his permission or approval to take the dog hiking.

But she didn't want to take Remy on her own.

And she wanted to know why the man who'd been making

up all kinds of excuses to spend time with her over the past several months was suddenly bailing on her.

Why the change of plans?

It took him a while to respond to that one. So long, in fact, that she thought he might call rather than text, taking the opening she'd given him to talk.

In the five months she'd known him, he hadn't told her much about his family aside from the facts that his dad was an abusive alcoholic and his mom never should have married him. Still, she was sure he must have conflicted feelings about the man's return—and his injury—and she wanted him to trust her enough to open up to her.

Finally three little dots appeared, indicating that he was responding to her question. But his answer, when it came, wasn't anything she would have anticipated.

I ran into Madison Russell this afternoon and she invited me to a party at Spring Creek.

A party?
He was blowing her off to go to *a party*?
Maybe she shouldn't have been surprised. After all, she'd been pushing him to get out and do things with other people. She'd even specifically mentioned Madison—and he'd claimed to not be interested, that the judge's clerk was too young.

But maybe after hanging out with Sierra, who really wasn't that much older but whose activities were somewhat restricted by her pregnancy, he'd decided that he wanted to be with someone more fun and spontaneous. Someone with whom he could enjoy physical intimacy.

Because he'd been spending a lot of time with Sierra. Days out and about with Remy and quiet nights in front of the TV. And while they occasionally held hands—Deacon always took hers to help her navigate a narrow part of a trail—and cuddled on the sofa—there was no kissing (at least, not since the day she'd kissed him in her kitchen) and definitely nothing more.

And the thought of Deacon with Madison...doing *more* with Madison—

No. She couldn't go there.

Instead, she stared at his message on the screen, the letters blurred by the tears in her eyes, and wondered if he was waiting for her response.

Or maybe a reaction.

She swiped impatiently at the solitary tear that spilled onto her cheek before composing a reply.

Sounds like fun. Have a great time.

Her thumb hovered over the arrow that would send the message, a sick feeling churning in her belly.

Why should she send him off with her best wishes when he'd just ditched her and their weekend plans?

She knew it wasn't the same as saying *sorry* to Eric and Aubrey after catching them in bed together, but it felt a little bit similar. And she was *not* going to apologize for being wronged again.

Instead, she pressed the backspace key until every last letter of her reply was deleted from her screen.

CHAPTER TWENTY-ONE

SATURDAY AFTERNOON, Sierra took Remy to the lake.

She refused to sit at home alone and mope because Deacon had decided he'd have more fun at Spring Creek with another woman.

Even worse than moping was speculating about the kind of fun they might be having. And scrolling through Madison Russell's Instagram.

After she'd tortured herself with the pictures Madison had posted—of the five-bedroom house on the water that had been rented for the weekend (#funwithfriends), the refrigerator stocked with beer and coolers (#drinkingwithfriends), the volleyball net on the beach (#gettingphysicalwithfriends), and a photo of Madison herself in a teeny bikini top and skimpy shorts, ready to serve the ball (#tanned #toned #gigisgym)—Sierra had been desperate to get out of the house.

Because yes, she was jealous that Madison had abs.

And she was jealous that the other woman was with Deacon.

And she had no right to be jealous—because she and Deacon were *friends*.

She didn't bother to pack a picnic for her outing with Remy, but she did throw a water bottle and some snacks in her backpack, along with a collapsible water bowl she'd bought for the dog when she and Deacon had started taking him hiking.

But she wasn't going to think about those other outings today, she reminded herself firmly. She was going to focus on enjoying the weather and Remy's company.

There were a lot of trails around the lake, color coded to help hikers stay on their chosen path. Sierra opted for the purple trail—one of the shorter and easier routes. Though she prided herself on being in pretty good shape, she was carrying an extra fifteen pounds in front and didn't want to risk steep or uneven terrain on her own with Remy.

But they weren't really on their own, as Cutthroat Lake proved to be a popular destination on a sunny Saturday afternoon of a long weekend. By the halfway point, Remy was completely tuckered out, so Sierra picked him up to carry him the rest of the way. They were almost at the end of their route when she spotted Deacon's brother walking a tan-colored dog with a slightly squished face, a dark muzzle and a curled tail.

The dog barked and tugged on his leash, trying to get closer to Sierra and the Chihuahua in the crook of her arm.

"This is Baxter," the deputy sheriff said. "He's just excited because he wants to make friends, but I promise he's more pussycat than puggle."

"Puggle?"

"Part pug, part beagle."

She cautiously set Remy down so the dogs could sniff one another.

"Cutthroat Lake's a popular destination with the locals," Connor said. "But not a lot of visitors know it's here."

Though she didn't consider herself to be a visitor, she agreed that living in the town five months wasn't long enough to qualify as a local.

"Deacon told me about it," she admitted.

"I should have guessed. We used to come out here sometimes when we were kids."

"That's what he said."

"Speaking of my brother—have you seen him recently?"

"I saw him in court yesterday morning."

He frowned. "But not since then?"

She shook her head. "We exchanged a couple of text messages later in the day, though, so I know he was going to Spring Creek for the weekend."

"Oh." Connor didn't sound too pleased to hear it, and she wondered if he knew about the big house party happening on the beach. "I was hoping he would have talked to you."

"About his dad?" she guessed.

"Yeah."

"I hoped so, too," she admitted.

Remy and Baxter had apparently decided they were going to be friends and were wrestling on the ground and tangling up their leashes.

"I don't know what—if anything—he's told you about Dwayne, but I know it was a shock to him to hear that his dad came back, and that might have something to do with why he's acting like an idiot, if he is."

He definitely was, but Sierra had no intention of getting into that with the deputy sheriff.

Instead, she bent to untangle Remy's leash. "We need to be heading back to town."

"Actually, Regan and the girls are setting up a picnic over by the playground," he said. "Why don't you join us?"

"I appreciate the invitation, but Remy's more than ready for a nap."

"Are you sure? We've got three kinds of sandwiches—peanut butter, jelly and peanut butter, *and* jelly." Connor ticked off the options on his fingers.

"I'm sure," she said, and even managed to smile. "But thanks."

It turned out his brother was right.

Deacon did want to know why, after more than twenty years, his poor excuse for a father had decided to wander back into town. And since he was already in Spring Creek, Northeastern Nevada Regional Hospital wasn't much of a detour on his way home.

By the time he arrived Saturday afternoon, Dwayne's condition had been upgraded from "critical" to "serious" and he was sitting up in bed. Deacon paused in the doorway, a jolt of shock reverberating through him at the realization that the old man in the bed was his father.

Of course, more than two decades had passed since he'd last seen the man, and Deacon had only been a child then. A child afraid of the big man with the booming voice and quick fists.

But he was no longer a child, and the figure in the bed bore little resemblance to the one he remembered. His dark hair had gone gray and his formerly broad shoulders were noticeably less broad.

Everything about him just seemed...a little less.

And so, Deacon realized with no small sense of relief, was his power over his son.

"Did too many years of hard drinking catch up to you and you came back to Haven because you need a liver?" he asked, from his post inside the door.

The old man in the bed cackled as he turned his head to look at his visitor. "I wouldn't be surprised," he finally responded. "But no, that's not why I came back."

"So why did you?" Deacon asked the question he'd promised himself he wouldn't.

"Come in, boy, and let me take a look at you."

"I'm not a boy," he said, even as he stepped forward.

"I can see that," Dwayne acknowledged.

"Why are you here?" Deacon asked again.

"I heard your mom passed."

"Yeah. More than ten years ago," he said bluntly.

His father didn't look the least bit chastened by the pointed response but followed up by asking, "She leave you any money?"

"Are you kidding?" Deacon was stunned. And furious. "Is *that* why you came back? Because you thought there might be a few bucks for you?"

"She was still my wife," Dwayne said gruffly. "Anythin' she had when she died should've come to me."

"You mean like the pile of medical bills, courtesy of the cancer that killed her?"

"There must've been somethin' left," Dwayne insisted. "How else did you pay for that fancy law school diploma?"

"She had no money," Deacon said, needing to make it perfectly clear. "I had scholarships that paid for college and law school."

"No shit?"

"No shit," Deacon echoed dryly.

Dwayne scratched the stubble on his jaw. "I didn't think you were that smart."

"I was eight when you left home. And before that, the only time you thought about me at all was when you told me to bring you another beer."

The old man almost looked regretful for a minute—or maybe it was only wishful thinking on Deacon's part.

"I did my best," Dwayne said.

"Yeah, well, your best was pretty damn lousy."

"Some men just don't have what it takes to be a dad."

"Isn't that the truth?" Deacon agreed, and walked out the door.

Sky was sitting up in bed, holding her newborn swaddled in a pink blanket with a matching cap on her head, when Sierra walked into her hospital room in Battle Mountain on the first Friday in June.

"Jake was right," Sierra said. "Your baby girl is every bit as beautiful as her mama."

"When did you see Jake?"

"Two minutes ago—in the lobby downstairs."

"He's on his way home to feed Molly and take her for a run. The poor animal's been horribly neglected for the past couple of days."

Sierra set the vase of flowers she'd brought on the windowsill alongside several other arrangements, one of which she noticed bore a card signed by Paige and MG.

"The gerberas are gorgeous, thank you," her friend said. "But honestly—there are so many flowers in here, it's starting to look like the window display of Blossom's Flower Shop."

"Probably because everyone got their flowers at Blossom's," she noted.

"And I'm grateful to everyone," Sky said. "I just wish someone had thought to bring me cherry chocolate chunk ice cream."

Sierra pulled a container with the Scoops logo out of her purse.

The new mom's eyes went wide.

"Don't tease me," she warned.

"I'm not teasing you," Sierra promised, setting the ice cream and a plastic-wrapped spoon on the table beside her friend's bed. "But if you want the ice cream, you're going to have to put down the baby—or give her to me."

"I think that might have been your plan all along," Sky mused.

Sierra just grinned as she took the sleeping baby from her friend's arms.

Sky reached for the ice cream. "And now your status as my friend has been restored," she said, prying the lid off the container to dig into the contents.

"I didn't realize it had been revoked."

"It was in jeopardy," Sky told her. "Because Maya was born a full nineteen hours ago and you're only showing up here now."

"Not because I wasn't eager to get a look at your gorgeous baby, but because I knew your room would be overflowing with family and friends, and I didn't want to get in the way."

"You're one of my friends, too," Sky reminded her, as she dipped her spoon into the container. "My best friend again now," she added, with her mouth full of ice cream.

"I still think I got the sweetest part of the deal," Sierra said, cuddling the baby.

"She is pretty great—but trust me when I say that I now understand why they call it labor."

"I don't want to hear any details." Carrying her brother and sister-in-law's baby was one thing, bringing him into the world was another—and she was admittedly a little apprehensive about that part of the process. But right now, holding her friend's newborn in her arms, she was filled with awe and wonder.

"I promise not to share the details," Sky said, "except to say that every minute of the sixteen hours was worth it."

"Well, that's obvious," Sierra said, smiling at the sleeping baby.

"And while I'm thrilled that you're finally here, I'm a little surprised that Deacon didn't come with you."

"He was out with Remy when I left."

"Did something happen between you two?"

"Nothing except that he's suddenly decided that we've been spending too much time together."

Her friend frowned. "That doesn't sound like the man who's been chasing you for months."

"There was no chasing," Sierra denied.

"Well, whatever's going on with him, I'm sure he'll come around."

"Maybe it's better if he doesn't."

"Why would you say that?" Sky demanded.

"Because I'm only going to be in town another three weeks."

"No," her friend said. "If we're not talking about my childbirth experience, we're not talking about that, either."

"I'm going to miss you, too," Sierra told her.

"Not talking about it," Sky said again.

And for the next half hour, they talked about everything except the fact that the clock was ticking down on Sierra's time in Haven.

CHAPTER TWENTY-TWO

EARLY THE FOLLOWING Saturday morning, Sierra dragged herself out of bed because someone was pounding on her door. Not knocking, pounding. Remy wasn't happy about the early morning interruption, either. His hackles were up and he was growling deep in his throat as she carried him down the stairs.

Scowling with annoyance, she peered through the sidelight to see Deacon standing there before unlocking the door and yanking it open.

"Do you know what time it is?" she demanded.

"Eight thirty... Almost."

"It's eight twenty-two on a Saturday morning."

"You were still in bed," he realized.

"What do you want, Deacon?"

He held up the tray of drinks and bakery box from Sweet Caroline's.

"Not even a salted caramel brownie can make up for you showing up at my door before nine o'clock on a Saturday morning."

"How about a salted caramel brownie and a heartfelt apology?"

"Maybe," she allowed, after a moment of hesitation.

"Can I come in? Or are you going to make me grovel on your porch?"

She looked at the dog in her arms. "What do you think?"

Remy let out a sigh and rested his chin on her arm.

"I guess you can come in." She opened the door wider. "Actually, I'm a little surprised you didn't let yourself in. Did you lose your key?"

"I didn't think it was an appropriate time to use it."

"But you thought it was an appropriate time to bang on my door?"

"Only when you didn't respond to my knock."

She put the dog on the floor, and he immediately headed to the kitchen for his breakfast.

Deacon set the drinks and pastries on the counter while Sierra filled Remy's bowl.

Then she took a seat at the island and removed the lid from the to-go cup Deacon handed to her.

"Let's try this again," she suggested. "Why are you here?"

"Because I can't pretend anymore that I don't want to be with you."

Her heart bumped against her ribs. "Were you pretending?"

"I was pretending. I was an ass."

"Actually, I'd argue that you really were an ass."

His lips curved a little, but his expression remained contrite. "And I'm sorry."

She opened the bakery box to peer inside, waiting for him to continue.

He cradled his cup in two hands. "You asked me once about my mom, and I gave you a flippant response," he said.

"I remember."

"I don't like to talk about my childhood—or even think about it most of the time. It's easier to believe that I've moved on and left my past in the past. But I want to tell you some of that history now, so that maybe you'll understand why I acted like an ass."

"Okay," she said.

"My mom, by her own admission, was a little wild in her younger days. She was barely seventeen when she got pregnant the first time, and when she told the baby's father he was going to be a father, he drifted out of town again as aimlessly as he'd drifted into it, leaving her on her own.

"Despite her age and lack of a high school diploma, she insisted on keeping her baby. But she struggled to make ends meet as a single mom and occasionally found herself in…unhealthy relationships, because she was desperate for help to pay her bills and looking for a father figure for her son.

"Connor was five when she met Dwayne Parrish, six when she got pregnant again and seven when they got married—a few months before I was born. Of course, plenty of people had things to say about the fact that she'd been six months pregnant when they exchanged vows, but the consensus was that at least this one did the right thing and put a ring on her finger, because Connor's dad never did.

"Of course, it's easy for people to pass judgment based on what they can see from the outside, without ever knowing—and probably not caring about—the rest of the picture. Because marrying Dwayne wasn't the right thing for my mom, who didn't know he was an abusive alcoholic until it was too late. And it wasn't the right thing for my brother, who was frequently knocked around by Dwayne when our mom was out.

"And she was out a lot, because Dwayne was injured on a construction site job shortly after they were married and wasn't able to work after that. So my mom got a job—sometimes she had two or three jobs—to pay the rent and utilities and put food on the table and—far more important to Dwayne—beer in his belly."

Sierra's heart ached for the boy he'd been, living a life that no child should have to live. And it ached for the man he'd become, still living with the scars of his childhood.

She wanted to reach out to him now, to offer him comfort—or at least support—but she knew it couldn't be easy for him to talk about any of this, and she was reluctant to interrupt. So she held on to her cup with both hands and didn't let them tremble.

"That was my life. My family," he continued. "So you can maybe understand why I didn't grow up thinking that I'd ever want a wife and kids. The atmosphere in the rented, rundown bungalow on Second Street wasn't anything I'd ever aspire to emulate. All I ever wanted was to get out of that house, that neighborhood, the whole damn town.

"I was determined to make something of myself. To prove that I was better than who and where I came from. Going to college was the first step. Being accepted into law school was the second. When I got that letter from Columbia... I was blown away.

"Not that I actually had any plans to attend. I'd applied just to see if I was good enough, and I figured I'd hold on to the letter for the rest of my life, because it proved that I was. But there was no way I could afford to go to an Ivy League school.

"Connor was beyond proud—he was insistent that the opportunity was too big to pass up. I pointed out that I had other options—the William S. Boyd School of Law at UNLV, the University of Idaho College of Law or S.J. Quinney College of Law in Utah."

None of which was ranked number four of all law schools in the country, as she knew Columbia was.

"So I decided to go to New York—and tried not to freak out about what it would cost and how I would pay for it.

"Connor came through for me again, taking out a second mortgage on his house to pay for my tuition. Then I got a scholarship from Blake Mining, which coincidentally came through around the same time that Connor and Regan got married, so I suspect my sister-in-law had a hand in that."

"I didn't realize Regan was a Blake," she said, her surprise momentarily eclipsing her determination to stay mum.

"A Channing, actually," he clarified. "But her mom was a Blake."

"The Blakes and Gilmores really do have connections to everyone in this town, don't they?"

"It certainly seems that way," he agreed.

"So you went to law school in New York," she said, prompting him to pick up the thread of his story again.

He nodded. "And when I left, I was certain that I'd never want to come back. But the time away gave me perspective—and made me realize how much I'd miss Connor and Regan—

and later Piper and Poppy, too—if I decided to live and work anywhere else.

"When I came home that first summer, I thought I'd have to get a job bagging groceries or cutting grass—both jobs that I'd done in the past. Because despite the fact that I already had one college degree and a year of law school under my belt, I knew no one in town would be eager to hire Dwayne Parrish's kid. Because even though he'd been gone a long time by then, the shadow of his reputation remained.

"But the sheriff told my brother that I should send my résumé to Katelyn, and I did, not really expecting anything to come of it. I was thrilled to score an interview, but my cautious hope was trampled when I learned that she'd also interviewed Isabelle Graves."

"Judge Graves's daughter?"

He nodded.

"I was certain Katelyn would give the job to the candidate with the pedigree. Instead, she hired me. And now people who once looked down on me because of where I came from seek my counsel and representation. Because Katelyn gave me a chance when I didn't think anyone would."

"Which proves that she's a very smart woman."

"Anyway, the point of all of that was to show you that Mr. Columbia Law, as you like to call me, is really just a poor kid from the wrong side of the tracks, albeit grown up now and wearing a suit—and occasionally 'designer original' Cole Haan loafers."

She smiled at that, then her expression turned serious again. "Or maybe that poor kid was always a Columbia-educated lawyer just waiting to prove to the world what he was capable of."

"That's an interesting spin," he said. "But the fact remains, the earliest years of my childhood aren't something I like to revisit, and my fear of turning out like my...like Dwayne... made me reluctant to even consider getting married and having a family. Until I met you.

"And just when I was starting to think that I could have everything I never knew I wanted, Dwayne showed up in town again.

"That's why, when I saw Madison later that day, after hearing about his return, I jumped at her invitation to go to Spring Creek for the weekend. Because she didn't tempt me to want anything more than what I already had, whereas every time I'm with you, I find myself wanting to believe that I can be the man you deserve."

It was an effort to hold back the tears that burned the backs of her eyes. "You're making it really hard for me to stay mad at you."

"I'm...sorry?"

She managed a chuckle. "I'm grateful to you for telling me all of that, but none of it changes what I already knew—that you're a good man, Deacon Parrish. One of the best I know."

"Does that mean I'm forgiven?" he asked.

"You're forgiven," she said, and gave him a quick hug.

"There's one more thing I want you to know."

"What's that?"

"I didn't spend the entire weekend at Spring Creek."

A fact of which she was already aware, as she'd spotted his truck in his driveway when she returned from her trip to the lake with Remy on the Saturday afternoon. And because she'd later overheard one of the court admins whispering to another that Madison was annoyed "Dekes" hadn't stuck around.

"Also, I didn't sleep with Madison," he told her now.

"Your personal life isn't any of my business," she said, dropping her gaze to stare into the bottom of her now empty cup.

"The reason I didn't sleep with Madison," he said, continuing as if she hadn't spoken, "is that the whole time I was with her, I couldn't stop thinking about you. Because I don't want to be with anyone but you."

The sincerity in his tone tugged at her heart—a heart that she suspected might already be his.

But she was almost seven months pregnant and couldn't be sure if her feelings were real or a by-product of all the baby hormones in her system, so she kept them buried deep inside.

Or at least tried to.

But his words had touched her deeply, and the single tear that slid down her cheek felt as if it had been squeezed out of her heart.

Twenty-three weeks down, one to go, Sierra noted, as she walked into the DA's office early on the last Monday of June.

She anticipated a busy week, tying up lots of loose ends. But aside from writing case summaries for Jade on current cases, a few hours in First Appearance Court and a couple of bail hearings, Brett kept her close to the office. And anything new that came in went to one of the other ADAs, since Sierra wouldn't be there to see the charges through to trial.

It was understandable, and yet the restrictions on her duties were yet another reminder that her time in Haven was rapidly counting down.

Tuesday night, she started to pack. An hour later, she texted Deacon and asked him to come over to get Remy. He was there in five minutes.

"What's going on?" he asked, lowering himself onto the floor near where she sat, cuddling the little dog.

Judging by the sympathy in his tone, he could tell that she'd been crying.

"I'm trying to pack and he keeps climbing in to whatever box or suitcase I'm trying to fill."

"Obviously he wants to go with you."

"I can't take him," she said. "And we all knew that from the beginning."

"I'm not sure that he did," Deacon countered gently. "Aside from sit and stay, I'd guess the rest of our words are gibberish to him."

"He also knows t-r-e-a-t, w-a-l-k and s-h-e-l-t-e-r," Sierra noted, opting to spell the words that were likely to get an excited reaction from the dog.

"Do you want me to take him for a w-a-l-k now, while you finish up in here?"

"It would have to be a really long w-a-l-k. I've still got a fair amount of packing to do."

"Should I take him home with me tonight?"

Her eyes filled again as she nodded. "That's probably for the best."

"C'mon, Remy," he said, lifting the dog from her lap. "Let's give Mommy some space."

"I'm not his mommy," she protested. "I'm not anybody's mommy."

And, inexplicably, she began to cry.

Or maybe her roller coaster emotions weren't so inexplicable. After all, she was seven months pregnant with all kinds of baby hormones running rampant through a body that didn't seem to understand the baby she carried wasn't her own. And while her mind understood that basic truth, the knowledge did little to help control her emotions.

She wouldn't have blamed Deacon if he'd taken the dog and ran. Instead, he placed Remy in her lap again and put his arms around her, holding her while she cried.

His wordless support and understanding only made her cry harder as she realized how much this man had come to mean to her in such a short time—and how much she was starting to wish that she could hold on to him forever. But right now, she wasn't feeling strong enough or brave enough to risk her heart on a future filled with so many uncertainties.

"I'm sorry for the meltdown," she said, when she'd finally pulled herself together enough to be able to speak.

"You don't have to apologize to me," he assured her.

She brushed her hands over her tear-stained cheeks. "I'm such a mess."

"You're beautiful," he said.

She managed a laugh. "You really do need to get out and spend time with other people."

"I tried that," he reminded her. "It didn't go so well, because I only want to be with you."

"I'm leaving, Deacon."

He held her gaze for a long minute before he replied, "I know."

She wished he would ask her to stay, even though she knew that she couldn't and that his asking wouldn't change that fact.

And apparently he knew it, too, because, in an abrupt change of topic, he asked, "Do you have any plans for Friday night?"

"Just hanging with Remy, like I do most Friday nights. And almost every other night." Except this Friday would be her last Friday night with the little dog that had stolen her heart.

Her last night in this town.

The realization made her throat tighten again, but this time she managed—barely—to keep the tears at bay.

"Do you think Remy would mind if I took you out to dinner Friday night?"

They'd shared several meals together but, aside from that long ago Valentine's Day invitation, this was the first time Deacon had formally asked her to go out with him, which almost made it seem like a date...

"Not a date," he hastened to assure her, as if privy to her innermost thoughts. "Just an informal meal at Diggers'."

"I don't think he'd mind," Sierra said. "And I'd like that very much."

CHAPTER TWENTY-THREE

THE JOB WAS supposed to be something to tide her over—and provide much needed medical insurance—until Sierra had the baby and could get serious about looking for a more permanent position. And when she first came to Haven, she never would have imagined that she might someday envision a future here.

But the six months that she'd spent in the northern Nevada town had both challenged and fulfilled her in ways she hadn't anticipated. She'd enjoyed her work and made friends. She'd become part of the community. And she knew that she was going to miss this place and its people when she was gone.

She could promise to keep in touch with friends and plan to come back to visit, but she wasn't sure it was realistic that she'd be able to do so if she went back to working sixty-plus hours a week in Las Vegas. Because that was what was expected of an associate who wanted to make partner in the big firms—and didn't every attorney want to someday be a partner in a big firm?

Certainly it had been her goal when she first started at Bane & Associates. But now... Now she knew she was going to miss working in the Haven DA's office—and especially all the people she'd met through her job there.

When Deacon picked her up Friday night, she was feeling a little out of sorts that everyone at the office had gone about their business as usual, with only the occasional mention of the fact that it was her last day. And then, when they walked into Diggers', she paused in the doorway, an odd sense of déjà vu stealing over her as she took in the colorful streamers and balloons. But instead of a generic *Happy Birthday* banner there was one that read *Farewell Sierra.*

"This time it's your party," Deacon said with a smile.

"You said an informal meal at Diggers'," Sierra reminded him.

He shrugged. "I had to get you here somehow."

"I didn't expect anything like this." She wasn't just surprised, she was overwhelmed—and very much afraid that she was going to melt down in front of him again.

"Good, because if you'd expected it, it wouldn't have been much of a surprise," he pointed out.

Then, as if sensing that she needed to be rescued from her own emotions, he nudged her farther into the room. And suddenly she was surrounded by friends and colleagues. Even her boss was there, and her prenatal yoga instructor and Harvey—the courthouse security guard that she'd been certain didn't like her because he only ever responded to her good morning wishes with a grunt.

"I guess everyone likes a party," she mused. "Or at least cake."

"Cake?" Deacon's eyes went wide. "Was I supposed to get cake?"

It was a good time—with a lot of laughter and more than a few tears—and over the course of the evening, it seemed as if everyone she'd ever met in Haven had stopped by for at least a minute or two. Including Sky with Jake and their now three-week-old baby. They didn't stay long, and Sky refused to say goodbye, but Sierra was okay with that, because she didn't think she would be able to say the word to her friend, either. Deacon's brother and sister-in-law showed up, too. And Regan hugged Sierra and told her that she sincerely hoped she'd find her way back to Haven someday.

When there was nothing but crumbs remaining of the cake—because of course Deacon had arranged for a cake (delicious red velvet, layered with chocolate mousse and cherry *pâté de fruit* jelly)—he took her home. After he walked her to the door, he kissed her—a kiss so achingly sweet, it made her want to cry all over again.

When he eased his lips from hers, he lifted his hands to cradle her face and said, "I love you, Sierra."

They were the words she'd both longed for and dreaded. Words that simultaneously filled her heart and made it ache.

"Did you really think that now, only hours before I'm leaving town, was a good time to tell me?" she asked, her voice wavering more than a little.

"I'll admit the timing isn't ideal, but I didn't think you were ready to hear it before." He held her gaze as his thumbs gently brushed away the tears that spilled onto her cheeks. "I'm not entirely sure you're ready to accept the truth of my feelings now, but I couldn't let you leave without telling you.

"I understand why you have to go," he said. "But I hope, after the baby's born, you'll consider coming back."

She'd thought about it, of course. In recent weeks, she'd found herself thinking about it a lot. But her emotions were a tangled mess, and she didn't know how much of that was a result of her growing feelings for Deacon and how much was pregnancy hormones or even how much of her feelings for him could be attributed to those same hormones.

"I can't make a decision about this right now," she said.

"I'm not asking you to make a decision right now," he told her. "I'm asking you to think about it."

"I can do that," she agreed.

The drive to Vegas seemed to take a lot longer than any other time that Sierra had made the journey.

Maybe it was because she had to stop four times to use a restroom, as the baby had recently taken up position on her bladder.

Or maybe it was that she wasn't as eager to return to Sin City as she'd been on previous trips, because she knew this might be the last time she'd ever travel this route.

Because whatever else might have drawn her and Deacon

to one another, proximity had undoubtedly been a significant factor. And now that proximity would no longer factor into the equation, he might soon forget about her.

Out of sight, out of mind.

Besides, Vegas was her home. It had been her home her entire life. It was also where her brother and sister-in-law lived. Where her soon-to-be-born nephew would live with his parents.

She'd never imagined living anywhere else. Had never—except for a few days immediately following her trip to San Francisco and her breakup with Eric—wanted to live anywhere else.

Had Eric broken her heart?

She'd thought so, at the time.

He'd certainly wounded her pride and made her question her judgment.

She'd been duped—not just by the man she'd loved but also by a woman she'd considered a friend.

Still, she hadn't actually planned to leave Las Vegas. But when the job posting for a six-month position with the Haven District Attorney's Office appeared the same day she'd given her notice at Bane & Associates, she'd decided it was fortuitous timing. (Deacon probably would have said it was destiny.)

In any event, when she'd packed up her car and headed to Haven, she'd vowed to never succumb to the yearnings of her heart again.

And then she'd met Deacon Parrish.

Was it foolish to let herself believe that her feelings for him could be real?

She didn't know, and the pregnancy hormones running rampant through her system, messing with her brain and her heart, gave her reason to be cautious.

Which was why she couldn't make any decisions about her future right now. Why she needed some time and distance to think about her life and future more clearly. Because when she was with Deacon, she didn't want anything else.

Time and distance would give them both some necessary perspective, she decided.

If, after she had the baby, she still had feelings for him, maybe she'd reach out.

But she probably wouldn't.

Two months was a long time, and by then, he was certain to have moved on without her.

It was the third week of August—seven weeks after he'd said goodbye to Sierra, and Deacon had missed her every single day. Despite his best efforts to keep himself busy, she was always his first thought in the morning and his last thought at night.

He'd planned—and canceled—several visits to Sin City, because as much as he wanted to see her, he knew that he had to respect her request for space. She was reluctant to believe that her feelings for him were real, concerned that her emotions were amplified by her pregnancy. And he knew that any effort to insert himself back into her life while she was still pregnant would not serve any purpose.

But *damn*, he missed her.

"Deacon?"

He dragged his attention back to his sister-in-law. "Did you say something?"

"Your mind is a million miles away today, isn't it? Or would four hundred and fifty be a more accurate number?"

"Does it matter?" he said. "The babies' room is getting painted, isn't it?"

"It is," she agreed. "And I'm happy to say I love that color even more on the wall than on the paint chip."

He stood back to examine his handiwork. "It does look good," he agreed. "But are you sure it's blue? It almost looks purple to me."

"It's periwinkle."

"Sounds like a girl color."

"I don't believe in boy colors and girl colors," she said.

"So why is Double Trouble's room the color of Double Bubble?"

"Don't call them that," his sister-in-law admonished.

"They don't mind it," he pointed out.

"Well, I do. And don't think I don't see what you're doing."

"I'm painting your walls."

"You're sidetracking the conversation because you don't want to talk about Sierra."

"There's nothing to talk about."

"You miss her," Regan guessed.

"Yeah," he said, because there was no point in denying it.

He'd missed her every minute of every day since he'd watched her drive away. He'd thought he would get used to her absence over time, but he still looked for her car in the driveway when he drove down Larkspur Lane and Remy still wanted to run up to the door when their walk took them past her former house.

"You do realize that missing her is silly, don't you?"

"Gee, why wouldn't I want to talk to you about my feelings when you're so quick to dismiss them?" he said dryly.

"I'm not dismissing your feelings," she denied. "I'm saying that it's silly to be moping around here because you miss her when you could be in Vegas with her."

"Then who would be painting your walls?"

"The walls could wait another week or two."

He continued to paint.

Regan sighed. "Have you talked to her since she went back?"

"Almost every day." He also texted her when they didn't talk—and even sometimes when they did. "She's applied for a few jobs and even had an interview last week."

"How did it go?" she asked cautiously.

"She said they sounded really excited about her qualifications when they called to set up the interview—and a lot less enthused after she showed up for the interview."

"Because she's pregnant?" Regan guessed.

"Probably," he agreed. "Not that they were foolish enough to say anything that might open them up to a discrimination suit, but even after Sierra explained her unique situation, the interview ended pretty quickly."

"You keeping your ear to the ground so you can let her know if any jobs open up here?"

"I am," he confirmed. "I've also been looking at potential employment opportunities in Las Vegas—for me."

* * *

Sierra couldn't sleep.

It was hard to get comfortable when her belly was approximately the size of a beach ball.

She didn't know if it was the bed in her brother and sister-in-law's guest room that was responsible for her backache—or the fact that she was hauling an extra twenty-five pounds around with every step every day.

Not that she'd been hauling it too far.

She still walked every morning, but since her return to Vegas, she hadn't had to do much of anything else. She did have a doctor's appointment scheduled the following day, and Nick and Whitney were both planning to go with her. It would be her thirty-nine-week checkup—due date *finally* just around the corner!—and while Sierra absolutely understood that she was carrying their baby, she was also starting to realize that moving in with her brother and sister-in-law for the last two months of her pregnancy had not been the best idea.

Maybe it was because she'd had so much space in Haven—not just an apartment of her own but an actual house—and now she was essentially living in a bedroom. A spacious and beautifully decorated bedroom, but still only a single room.

Of course Nick and Whitney encouraged her to make herself at home, but it was their home—she was only a guest. The room she slept in wasn't her own, just like her body wasn't her own right now.

It wasn't just that the baby had stretched her out of shape and was making her get up to pee three times in the night and giving her heartburn when she ate anything spicy. It was that she rarely had five minutes to herself without her brother and sister-in-law hovering over her, which was another reason that she got up early to walk every morning.

She enjoyed the fresh air and the exercise, but she missed walking with Remy. And while the heat of a Las Vegas summer was more familiar to her than the cold of a Haven winter, she found herself missing the cooler temperatures of northern Nevada—among other things.

On her way back to Nick and Whitney's, she passed the same

little convenience store that she passed every day. Today she stopped in to pick up a snack.

Whitney was in the kitchen, refilling her coffee mug when Sierra walked in. Her sister-in-law had greeted her with a smile that quickly slipped when she saw the bag of salt and vinegar potato chips in Sierra's hand. It was only a snack-sized bag—just enough to satisfy her craving.

"There's a fruit plate in the fridge," Whitney told her.

"Thanks," Sierra said. "I'll have some later."

Whitney's gaze dropped to the bag of chips again, and she opened her mouth as if to say something, then snapped it shut.

Sierra tossed the chips into the trash can and retreated to her room, where she cried for no particular reason, as she seemed to be doing a lot in recent days.

She knuckled away a tear as a phone chimed with a text message.

Bail court with Judge Longo this morning.

The message was followed by a face screaming in fear emoji, making her smile.

Hope your client has a comfy cell.

She spent the rest of the morning thinking about Deacon. She wanted to blame his text message, but the truth was, he was never far from her thoughts.

Earlier, when she'd caught Whitney's disapproving look toward the bag of chips, she couldn't help but remember how Deacon had gone out of his way to get some for her, just because she'd had a craving.

Because that was the kind of man he was—and she missed him so much more than she could ever have imagined.

Whitney came home with a bag of chips.

A family-sized bag that she set on the end table beside the sofa, where Sierra was sitting reading a book.

"A peace offering," she said.

"Not necessary," Sierra told her.

"I think it is," her sister-in-law insisted. "And so is an apology. The closer we get to the baby's due date, the more I realize how ill-equipped I am to be a mom, and I think I've been trying to micromanage you because it gives me something to focus on rather than admitting my own fears."

She closed her book and set it aside to give Whitney her full attention, silently chastising herself for not considering that the baby's mom was dealing with a plethora of emotions, too.

"You better not be saying that you changed your mind," she said lightly. "Because this baby is yours, for better or for worse."

Her sister-in-law managed a watery chuckle. "I haven't changed my mind. I'm just scared that I'm not going to have a clue about what I'm doing."

"I'd bet that most first-time parents don't have a clue about what they're doing."

"Maybe not," Whitney agreed. "But sometimes I wonder…"

Sierra waited.

"I wonder if maybe God took my womb because I wasn't meant to be a mom."

Religion had always been boggy ground for Sierra. Though she'd been baptized in the Catholic Church, her parents had encouraged kindness and generosity over attendance at weekly mass. Her sister-in-law, on the other hand, had been born into a devout family, and Sierra knew that she needed to respect her beliefs as much as reassure her.

"God didn't take your womb," Sierra said gently. "The doctors did. And not because you did anything wrong but because cancer is a horrible, insidious and indiscriminate disease.

"But if you want to look for God's hand in some part of this process, perhaps you could trust that he gave the doctors the skills they needed to not only save your life but allow your eggs to be harvested so that the children you deserve to have could be born someday."

"Do you really think so?" Whitney asked hopefully.

"I really do," she said sincerely.

"You're giving us the greatest gift, and I know there's no possible way we'll ever be able to repay you."

"I was glad to do it and would happily do it again for you and Nick. In fact, I *want* to do it again," Sierra told her. "So that this little guy can have a brother or sister to grow up with."

"Really? Even after all my hovering and nagging, you'd be willing to do it again?"

"Well, maybe I shouldn't make any promises before I've been through the experience of childbirth, but I figure you'll be so busy with this little guy, you won't be able to hover or nag half as much."

Whitney brushed away the tears that spilled onto her cheeks. "The day I met Nick was the best day of my life—not only because I met the man I love more than I ever thought possible but also because I gained a sister that I couldn't love any more if she was my own."

"It was a good day for all of us," Sierra said. "But I think today's going to be a good day, too."

And it was, because just before midnight, Jameson Nicholas Hart was born.

CHAPTER TWENTY-FOUR

SIERRA SCROLLED THROUGH job posting after job posting, inexplicably irritated to discover that most of the positions weren't anywhere nearby. Because what was the point of setting the parameters of her search to the Las Vegas area if Carson City was still going to pop up?

And if she was willing to go that far, she might as well go back to Haven.

It was a far-too-tempting idea—and apparently a feasible option. Because after only six weeks back in the DA's office, Jade Scott had decided to take a job as a victim services advocate.

Deacon had texted Sierra as soon as the first whispers started circulating around the courthouse, and even Sky—preoccupied as she was with her new baby—reached out when the news made its way to her. Sierra didn't reveal to either of them that she'd already been contacted by her former boss, who'd assured her that the DA's office would be thrilled to have her back, if she was interested.

At that time, she'd still been two weeks away from her due date and told Brett she wasn't ready to make any decisions about her future. He'd assured her that he understood and promised not to post the position until he heard back from her.

Now, though, Sierra was tempted to leap at the opportunity to return to her former job. Haven was admittedly farther away from Nick and Whitney and three-week-old Jameson than she wanted to be, but she needed to move on with her life. And maybe doing so with a little distance from the baby she'd carried would be better for all of them.

Another factor in favor of accepting Brett's offer was that she'd made friends in Haven. Skylar, of course, but also Julie and Brenna and Lucy and Erin.

But the biggest factor was Deacon.

Because even after two and a half months apart and with four hundred and fifty miles between them, he still texted her every morning, just to say good morning, and again every night.

Those brief communications were always the highlight of her day. And their less frequent FaceTime calls put a smile on her face that lasted for days afterward.

But was this love?

After weeks—maybe months—of pondering that exact question, she was finally starting to believe that it was.

A seven-hour drive was a lot of time to have second thoughts, and Sierra had plenty of them as she drove the now-familiar route from Las Vegas to Haven.

She should have called to tell Deacon that she was coming, but she'd wanted to surprise him. And that impulse was the cause of most of those second thoughts, because the last time she'd traveled out of town to surprise someone, she'd caught him with his pants down. Literally.

Of course, Deacon wasn't anything like Eric.

He would never break a promise he'd made.

But he'd never made her any promises, and she wouldn't have let him if he'd tried.

And now she was both incredibly nervous and ridiculously excited about the prospect of seeing him again. So much so that she could hardly sit still in one of the two Adirondack chairs that flanked his front door as she waited for him to return home from work.

Finally, his vehicle pulled into the driveway. Her hands gripped the arms of the chair more tightly.

He got out of his truck, a grin spreading across his face as he made his way toward her.

She rose to her feet as he approached, a kaleidoscope of butterflies taking flight in her tummy.

"Well, this is the very best kind of surprise," he said.

"I should have called—"

"No," he interjected, cutting off her apology before dipping his head to brush his lips over hers.

The casual kiss quickly became something more, and when they finally drew apart, they were both breathless.

"You haven't even asked why I'm here," she noted.

"Because I don't care why," he told her. "I only care that you are. Although I am curious to know why you're sitting outside. Don't you still have the key that I gave you?"

"I do," she confirmed. "But I learned the hard way that you can't know what you might be interrupting when you walk into a room unannounced."

"The only thing you'd be interrupting here is Remy's all-day nap."

She smiled at that. "Life is exhausting when you're a four-pound dog carrying forty pounds of anxiety."

"He's got some baggage," Deacon acknowledged. "Which you, apparently, do not."

"My suitcase is in the car."

"Well, let's go get it," he said. "Then we can go inside so you can fuss over Remy while I figure out something for dinner."

"Actually, I didn't want to presume that you'd want to cook, so I brought Jo's pizza."

"Even better," he said, walking beside her to her vehicle to help with her things.

"I picked it up about an hour ago, so it will probably need to be reheated, but I figured we could do that…after."

His brows winged up. "After?"

She smiled.

He unlocked the door and ushered her inside.

Remy danced around her feet in excited circles, and while Deacon took the pizza into the kitchen, Sierra set her small suitcase on the floor to scoop up the little dog. The happy Chihuahua proceeded to lick her face all over, making her laugh—which resulted in a tongue in her mouth.

"I appreciate your enthusiasm, but you really need to work on your technique," she told the Chihuahua, as she set him on the floor again.

"And right now, you need to get lost," Deacon said, returning to offer the dog a treat that he knew would occupy him for quite some time.

Once Remy had wandered off, he took both of Sierra's hands in his. "Are you sure about this?"

She nodded.

"It's not too soon? After the baby, I mean."

Now she shook her head. "My doctor gave me the go-ahead. Though I feel I should warn you that it's been a while for me."

"I'm guessing at least nine months, since you were adamantly opposed to having sex while you were carrying your brother and sister-in-law's baby."

"And Eric and I broke up a few months before that, so it's actually been more than a year."

"It hasn't been quite as long for me," he confided. "But there's been nobody else since the first time I saw you."

"Really?" she asked, sounding equal parts surprised and dubious.

"Really," he confirmed. "I haven't wanted anyone but you since I saw you standing beside the last box of Frosted Flakes in the grocery store."

"Of course, that was before you knew I was pregnant—and before I got fat."

"You were never fat," he chided. "And you're even more gorgeous now than you were then."

"It's my breasts," she said. "They're up a whole cup size, but they should go back to normal when my milk supply dries up, so don't get too attached to them."

"I'm sorry," he said. "I didn't hear anything you said after *breasts*."

She laughed softly. "You're such a guy."

"Thank you for noticing."

"Believe me, I've noticed."

He kissed her again.

She parted her lips, allowing him to deepen the kiss. The sensual flick of his tongue against hers sent flames of heat licking through her veins, making every part of her burn.

She wanted him with a desperation that was both scary and unfamiliar. Had wanted him from the first moment she saw him. She'd tried to blame the instantaneous and intense attraction on pregnancy hormones, except that he wasn't the only man to have crossed her path, but he was the only one to have elicited such a reaction.

That first moment had been a long time ago. They'd waited so long for this moment now, and she didn't want to wait any longer.

She eased her lips from his to say, "Take me to bed, Deacon."

He lifted her into his arms and carried her upstairs to his bedroom.

She only had a brief moment to register her surroundings—pale gray walls, dark furniture, a wide bed covered with a sage green comforter—before he stripped away her T-shirt and jeans and deposited her on top of that cover. His shirt and tie and pants joined the pile of clothes on the floor, then he stretched out beside her.

"I've dreamed of you here, just like this, more times than I could count," he confided.

"If this is a dream, don't wake me up."

"It's not a dream." His fingertip traced the lacy edge of her bra, skimming over the swell of her breast, the slow sensual touch making her shiver. "It's a dream come true."

He opened the front fastening of her bra and peeled back the cups, exposing her breasts to his gaze. Her nipples immediately tightened, and his eyes darkened with desire before he lowered his head to swirl his tongue around one turgid peak. Sensations ricocheted through her system, like sparks dancing along a live wire, intensifying the ache between her thighs.

"You might not want to spend too much time up there," she warned, when he shifted to give the same attention to her other breast. "There's a very real possibility that I might start leaking."

"I don't care," he said. "After waiting so long to have you in my bed, dreaming of touching and tasting every inch of your body, I'm not willing to skip any parts."

"There are other parts—a little further south—that wouldn't mind some attention."

"I'll get there," he promised.

"Soon?" she asked hopefully.

He chuckled at that.

"It's been more than a year," she reminded him. "At least thirteen months since I've had a man-made orgasm."

"But not more than thirteen months since you've had an orgasm," he mused thoughtfully.

She felt her cheeks burn. "I'm going to shut up now."

"Don't." He brushed his lips over hers again. "In fact, I'd like to hear more about the ways you pleasure yourself. There's nothing sexier than a woman who goes after what she wants."

"That's why I'm here," she reminded him. "Because you're what I want."

"You're changing the subject," he protested.

"On the contrary," she said, reaching between their bodies to slip a hand into his briefs and wrap her fingers around him, making him groan. "I'm going after what I want."

"I know what else you want," he said.

He hooked his fingers in the sides of her panties and tugged them over her hips, dragged them down her legs and tossed them aside.

When she was finally, completely naked, he took a moment to strip away his boxer briefs before returning to the bed.

She sighed when his body came down on hers, relishing the feel of his skin against hers, the weight of his hard body pressing her into the mattress.

She lifted her hands to explore the taut muscles of his shoulders…arms…chest. She paused with her hand splayed over his heart, smiled to discover that it was pounding as fast and hard as her own.

At the same time, he was engaged in his own exploration. His hands were strong and sure as they moved over her, seeming to know just where and how to touch her. Apparently he was every bit as confident in the bedroom as he was in the courtroom, and she felt grateful to be the recipient of his careful and thorough attention as sparks flew through her body, igniting new wants, new desires.

She pressed her thighs together, as if that action might ease the desperate ache between them, but she already knew that relief—and satisfaction—would only be found when he was inside her.

His hands skimmed down her torso, touching, testing. His mouth followed, tasting, teasing. He nudged her legs farther apart and settled between them. His thumbs parted the slick folds of skin at the apex of her thighs, exposing her most sensitive core first to his avid gaze...then the gentle brush of his thumb...and the stroke of his tongue.

Her head fell back against the pillow and her hands fisted in the comforter as he continued to do wicked and wonderful things to her with his mouth. She bit down on her lip to hold back her cries of pleasure as he drove her ever closer to the edge of oblivion...and finally...over.

Delicious shudders continued to wrack her body as he made his way up her body again, dropping leisurely kisses along the way—on her abdomen, her navel, the valley between her breasts. He kissed her throat, then the underside of her jaw, then her lips. Lingering there for a long, breathless moment.

"I'm happy to reciprocate," she said. "Just as soon as I get feeling back in my body."

"No reciprocation required," he assured her, reaching into the drawer of his bedside table for a condom.

Required or not, she wanted to do for him what he'd done for her. To make him feel as good as he'd made her feel.

After he'd taken care of protection, he shifted so that his body was poised over hers, his weight braced on his forearms.

Later, she promised herself, as his erection nudged at the soft, swollen flesh between her thighs, and she drew her knees up, digging her heels into the mattress and tilting her pelvis to facilitate his entry.

In one deep stroke, he pushed inside her. Not just filling but fulfilling her.

She moaned her pleasure as he began to move, the glorious friction causing a whole new avalanche of sensations to crash over her, leaving her battered and breathless, flailing to hold on to something…someone.

He caught her hands and linked their fingers together, then let the storm take them both.

Deacon brushed a strand of hair off her cheek, tucked it behind her ear. "Can I tell you now?"

Sierra tipped her head back as she snuggled closer. "Tell me what?"

"That I love you."

He was obviously referring to the first time he'd spoken those words to her—and her subsequent admonishment about the timing. And though she was more amenable to believing him now, she felt compelled to protest again.

"No," she said. "Postcoital declarations of affection are inherently untrustworthy, more likely a response to dopamine lingering in one's system than an expression of genuine emotion."

"Sometimes you sound just like a lawyer," he mused.

"Imagine that."

"And if we were arguing this case in a court of law, I would suggest that declarations of affection, at any time, increase feelings of intimacy and provide an opportunity to communicate hopes and dreams of a future together."

"And I would have to object," she told him.

"On what grounds?" he asked, sounding more amused than offended.

"That counsel needs a recess—and food."

"Objection overruled."

"You can't be both advocate and adjudicator," she protested.

"Sure I can." He grinned. "It's my bed."

Her stomach growled.

Loudly.

"Perhaps court can adjourn for a brief recess," he allowed, rolling to the edge of the mattress. "I'll go put the oven on."

He scooped up his pants from the floor and stepped into them but didn't bother with anything else.

Sierra didn't mind watching him walk around half-naked. In fact, she wouldn't have minded watching him walk around completely naked. Unfortunately, she didn't get to watch him for long, as he exited the bedroom to deal with her dinner.

So she found his abandoned shirt and slipped her arms into the sleeves. Fastening only two of the middle buttons, she made her way downstairs.

He glanced over when he heard her enter the kitchen, then did a double take.

"That's my shirt you're wearing."

"Is it?"

"You know it is."

"Do you want it back?" She reached for one of the two buttons that held it closed, slid it through the opening.

He swallowed. "Maybe you should keep it until after we eat."

She glanced at the timer on the stove as she took a step closer. "We've got almost twelve minutes."

"I don't know whether to be flattered or insulted that you think..." His words trailed off when she unfastened the second button.

"You were saying?" she prompted.

"I have no idea," he admitted.

Her lips curved as she reached now for the button at the top of his pants.

"Tell me, Deacon, in all of those dreams you had of the two of us together, did any of them take place in the kitchen?"

"My fantasies of you encompassed every room of the house—and several other places," he confided. "But I never thought those fantasies might someday become a reality, or I would have prepared."

She pulled a condom out of the pocket of his shirt.

"You are full of surprises today, aren't you?" he mused.

And they forgot about the pizza and everything else for more than twelve minutes.

"Even slightly overcooked, this really is the best pizza," Sierra remarked, licking a smear of sauce from her thumb.

Deacon's lips twitched as he lifted the piece he was holding to peer at the very dark crust on the bottom. "I think this is a little more than *slightly* overcooked."

"Should I apologize for distracting you?"

"No. In fact, feel free to distract me like that any time you want."

She smiled as she rose from the table, then nudged his chair back so that she could straddle his lap and draw his mouth to hers for a kiss.

"I love you, Deacon."

He drew back to look at her.

"Did you just break your own rule against postcoital declarations of affection?"

"It seems that I did," she admitted. "Throughout the whole drive from Las Vegas, I've been thinking about how and when to tell you, and I didn't want to wait a minute longer."

He gently brushed her hair from her face and smiled. "I love you, too, Sierra."

"I know we've still got some logistics to figure out, but I'd really like to see if we could make this work."

"Me, too," he told her. "In fact, I've been looking at job postings in Las Vegas. I wanted to talk to Katelyn before I actually sent any applications, but I think she'd give me a favorable reference."

"It means a lot to me that you'd be willing to uproot your life and your career here—"

"I would do anything for you."

"—but I don't think that's going to be necessary."

"Why not?"

"Because I sent my application to Brett yesterday, and he said the job is mine."

"And you waited until now to tell me?"

She shrugged, a smile tugging at the corners of her mouth. "It didn't seem quite as important as the other things we were doing earlier."

"I can't disagree with that," he said, lifting her with him as he rose and carried her back to bed.

EPILOGUE

Fifteen months later

"THIS ONE'S A GIRL," Sierra announced when she and Deacon returned to the house on Sherwood Park Drive after her three-month appointment with Dr. Amaro.

Nick and Whitney, who'd brought their now fifteen-month-old son, Jameson, to Haven for a weekend visit, beamed happily in response to the news.

"Did you hear that?" Nick asked his son. "You're going to have a little sister."

"Cah!" Jameson said.

His mom laughed. "No, you can't trade your sister for a car."

"Cah!" he said again.

"Everything's good?" Whitney asked Sierra.

She nodded. "The doctor said there's no reason to believe that this pregnancy won't be every bit as uneventful as the last one."

"She also said there's no need to restrict your physical activities," Deacon said, with a wink.

"What does that mean?" Nick asked his sister. "You're not planning on taking up rock climbing or something like that, are you?"

Whitney looked at her husband with amusement. "It means that they can have sex."

"Please." Nick put his hands over his ears. "I don't want to hear that kind of stuff about my little sister." Then he removed his hands from his own ears to cover his son's. "And Jameson definitely doesn't need to hear it about his aunt."

"I doubt that you guys are abstaining because you're expecting another baby," Sierra pointed out.

"No. We're abstaining because we have a toddler who ends up in our bed almost every night," Nick grumbled.

"And since that's more information than I need to know, I'm going to go start the grill," Deacon decided.

Nick grabbed a couple of bottles of beer out of the fridge and followed him onto the back deck.

"Thanks," Deacon said, accepting the proffered beverage.

"Actually, I wanted to thank you," Nick said. "Whitney and I really appreciate you supporting Sierra's decision to be our gestational carrier again."

"It was always her choice," Deacon said.

"She'd certainly argue that point, but the first time she offered to do this for us, there wasn't anyone else to factor into her decision. This time, she obviously talked to you about it, and we're grateful that you didn't have any objections."

"No objections," he confirmed. "But I will confess to hoping that the next baby she carries will be ours."

"Are you going to put a ring on her finger before then?" Nick wanted to know.

Deacon grinned at his hopefully future brother-in-law. "That's the plan."

And six months after that...

Six weeks after Everleigh Sierra Hart was born, Deacon's plan was proving a little more difficult to implement than he'd anticipated, forcing him to improvise.

"What happened to the raisin bran?" Sierra asked, staring into the almost empty cereal cupboard Friday morning.

"It must be all gone."

"But I just opened the box on Tuesday."

He shrugged, playing it casual. "I guess I ate a lot of raisin bran this week."

She turned to look at him, a slight frown marring her brow. "You don't even like raisin bran."

"Just have something else today," he suggested, a hint of impatience leaking into his voice.

"Apparently all we've got is Frosted Flakes." But she took the box out of the cupboard, opened the flaps and tipped it over her bowl.

He sipped his coffee, pretending that his heart wasn't pounding wildly in his chest.

"What the—" Her breath caught, and she reached into the bowl to fish out the diamond solitaire engagement ring.

She stared at it for a long moment—an *endlessly* long moment from where he was standing—before she shifted her attention to him and said, "When I was a kid, I felt lucky to get a plastic ring in a box of cereal."

"How are you feeling now?" he asked cautiously.

The smile that curved her lips was reflected in her gaze. "Very lucky."

The vise that had tightened around his chest loosened, allowing him to release the white-knuckled grip on his mug.

"Are you going to try it on?" he prompted.

"Are you going to ask me the question?" she countered.

"Should I get down on one knee?"

She shook her head. "No. I don't want you on your knee but beside me, every day for the rest of our lives."

"You're kind of infringing on my territory now," he cautioned.

"Sorry," she said, but the sparkle in her eyes told him she wasn't sorry at all.

He set his coffee down and took her hands. "I love you, Sierra. The day that I met you was the best day of my life—until the next day and the day after that, because with each passing day I fell more in love with you. And though I can't imagine loving you any more than I do right now, I look forward to being proven wrong every day of the rest of our lives together and hope you will do me the honor of being my wife."

She was sniffling just a little as she offered her hand to him.

"I'm going to need a verbal answer to my question," he said, holding the ring poised by her third finger.

"Yes," she said. "I will marry you and prove you wrong every day of the rest of our lives together."

"I guess that's what I get for falling in love with a lawyer," he said, chuckling as he slid the ring into place.

"I can empathize with that," she said, drawing his mouth down to hers for a kiss. "Happily and forever."

* * * * *

Rachel's Bundle Of Joy

Christine Rimmer

Believe in love. Overcome obstacles. Find happiness.

CHAPTER ONE

RACHEL STOCKHAM WAS certain she had to be the only six-months-pregnant woman in the state of Oregon who spent the majority of her non-working hours fantasizing about sex.

Why me? Rachel found herself wondering on a daily basis.

As a medical professional she knew what she needed to know about pregnancy and childbirth. And beyond being a nurse, as a mother-to-be, she'd made it her business to read all the best and most current books on the subject.

She knew very well what her top preoccupations should be at six months along and none of them were sex. Uh-uh. Leading the list should be heartburn and swelling ankles—those and the bigger questions: Will my baby be healthy? And, in her case, How will I cope with single motherhood, a seriously bipolar mother of my own *and* my extremely satisfying but also demanding and emotionally draining career?

And, yes, Rachel did know it was perfectly normal for a pregnant woman to still enjoy sex, even *lots* of sex. But if lots of sex is what any given pregnant woman wants, it's helpful to have a man around to have sex *with*.

Rachel had no man. She planned to be a single mother in the truest sense of the word. Her baby's father was donor 1067 at OCS—Oregon Cryogenic Services. She knew his blood type, his ethnic extraction, his height, weight and interests. And that was all she knew. It was all and it was plenty. She did not dream of finding out more, nor did she hope that some gorgeous, perfect hero of a guy would appear in her life out of nowhere and adore her on sight—puffy ankles, bulging belly and all.

Uh-uh. Rachel Stockham was a realist. She didn't expect to be rescued by a man. She wasn't sitting around waiting for some fabulous guy to fall crazy in love with her.

She would like just one wild night of jungle sex, please. Before she was too huge to manage it, before she got all wrapped up in juggling motherhood, family problems and her career and had neither the time nor the opportunity—not to mention the energy—for a glorious, mad night of sexual abandon.

But was she considering finding a way to act on this burning desire for a single, memorable, all-night, one night stand?

Not a chance. The last—and only—time she had gone out and had a wild, monkey-sex night with a stranger, she'd discovered later that the stranger was her best friend's fiancé. It was a disaster. Never, ever again was she going *there*. And seriously. How many men would go there with her in her condition anyway, even if she *were* out hunting them down?

So. What do you do when you want it bad and you've reconciled yourself to the fact that you're not going to get it?

Maybe you fantasize.

Rachel did. A lot.

About Brad Pitt, shirtless. About Ben Affleck, buck-naked and giving her hungry looks...

But don't get the wrong idea here. Rachel didn't let herself get hot and bothered over just any handsome guy. No, no. She made a point of maintaining certain standards when it came to choosing imaginary partners for starring roles in her forbidden fantasies.

The rules went like this: Movie stars were okay. But no one in her real life. Not the muscular guy who lived down the street and mowed his tiny square of front lawn bare-chested, his baggy cargo shorts riding low on his lean, hard hips. And no one at Portland General—no handsome doctors, no hunky radiation techs. At the Cancer Care Center, she kept her mind firmly on what mattered.

And no innocent bystanders, either. Somehow, it seemed to her just one step beyond awful that she might get caught staring dreamily at some good-looking guy whose only mistake was that he happened to wander into a sex-obsessed pregnant lady's line of sight. Strangers were definitely out.

Or at least, they were until that April day at Becky & Huck's...

It was a Friday, the first day of a three-day weekend for Rachel. When you're in nursing, a three-day weekend is something to savor. A precious, uninterrupted span of time all to herself. Her plans for that Friday included running errands, a little shopping and then a movie...starring Brad or Ben, of course. In the evening, she would sink into a scented bath with a smile on her face and naughty fantasies in her head.

Rachel took care of her errands early and arrived at Portland's biggest mall, Lloyd Center, at a little after ten. By noon, she'd bought herself a couple of new pregnant-lady outfits—on sale at Motherhood Maternity—and wandered through Gymboree, Gap Kids and the Children's Place.

Becky & Huck's was her last stop—before she took a break at the food court and made a decision about which movie to see. The store was brand-new and sold seriously upscale kids' clothes. Out of her price range, really. But no harm in browsing....

Beyond the store entrance, bright banners hung from the ceiling and the cheery décor was in pink, yellow and apple-green. The clerks were right there, asking if they could help her.

"Just looking..." She smiled her most beatific expectant-mother smile and headed for the banner that announced, Baby Girls: Birth to 3 Months.

The clothes were so darling: infant capri sets of organic eyelet cotton; ruffled creations accented in the softest, prettiest lace; tiny dresses with patchwork tops; a downy-soft baby cardigan embroidered with flowers and trimmed in bright ribbons...

And wasn't there just something about baby clothes? Especially baby clothes like these, so sweet and unique and beautifully made. They were the kind of clothes a loving grandmother or doting aunt might create and they spoke to Rachel of hope—for the future in general and for her unborn child, specifically.

Okay, she was doing this solo with no man to lean on. And true, her mother was not going to be the kind of grandma who knits darling sweater sets and begs for a chance to baby-sit. The future didn't look perfect by any means. But still, Rachel and her little one were going to do just fine.

Setting her Motherhood Maternity bag between her feet, she picked up one of the embroidered, beribboned sweaters. It was fluffy as a kitten's belly, downy as a baby chick. She shook it out and held it high—and saw that a man was watching her.

He was right across the display stand from her, directly in her line of sight as she admired the tiny sweater—and he was gorgeous! A tender mouth, thick blond hair. He wore a light-weight cobalt-colored sweater that clung to his broad shoulders and made his blue eyes look deep enough to drown in.

Before she could remind herself that this was real life and he qualified as an innocent bystander—which made him *not* someone she ought to be drooling over—he winked at her.

Seriously. Actually.

That incredible guy winked at her. And she let herself smile at him.

At that point, she caught herself. She cleared her throat, dropped her gaze and—with slow, exacting care—refolded the sweater and laid it gently back in place on the display table.

Was he still looking at her?

Oh, of course not. She sternly applied herself to the task of admiring a pair of sea-green snap-on pajamas. Really, this was so silly. She must have imagined that wink. Or maybe he had something in his eye.

Since she was studiously looking down, she had a clear view of his pricey-looking, elegantly casual brushed-leather shoes. He hadn't moved.

Well, so what? A man can buy baby clothes, can't he? He was probably a new father, here to pick out something special for his darling baby girl. Yes. That had to be it: a very yummy loving dad.

"I think I need an expert." The hunk—whose voice was as smoothly masculine as the rest of him—had spoken.

Surely not to *her*.

She dared to look up—and right into those waiting laser-blues. He smiled. It was the perfect fantasy-man smile: a sexy hitch at one corner of that achingly sensual mouth.

That did it. She was throwing all her principles to the wind. Innocent bystander or no, he'd get the leading role in her dreams tonight.

He said, "I think you're it."

What did *that* mean? Her pulse suddenly racing, she made a vague noise in her throat and slid a glance at his ring finger. Bare. And no telltale pale crescent where a ring *should* have been. So. Not a dad, then, after all? Or at least not a *married* dad.

"An expert?" she asked warily.

"That's right. An expert. On baby clothes..."

The faster her heart beat, the slower her mind seemed to be working. It took her a moment to put it together. "Ah..." She brushed a hand over her rounded stomach as a self-conscious laugh escaped her. "Well, I'm not an expert, really. This is my first."

"Your first..." He said it softly, as if the fact that she was having her first child was the most wondrous thing in the world. And it was, to Rachel. What she couldn't figure out was why this heartbreaker-handsome stranger seemed to think so, too.

They stared into each other's eyes, neither speaking. Bizarre. If she didn't know better, she could almost start to think he was coming on to her....

"Congratulations," he said at last.

"Uh, thanks. I'm...excited about it."

"I'll bet. So. Your opinion..." He had a tiny outfit in each hand. He held them up: a sweet yellow romper and the cutest pair of pink corduroy overalls appliquèd with butterflies. "Which one do you like the best?"

Rachel ordered her heart to slow down and her cheeks to stop flaming and set her mind on applying her supposed expertise.

After a moment, she shrugged. "I'm not much help, I'm afraid. They're both so cute. Either one would be just right."

He glanced at the romper and then the overalls—and then at her. "Can't choose, huh?"

"Nope. Better go with your instincts."

"I will," he said, still looking right at her. "I do."

There. That. Definitely.

The man was coming on to her.

And so what? Get a grip, girl, she commanded herself. It's called flirting and he's clearly a master at it. He probably flirts with every woman he meets. "Well. Uh. And how old is your daughter?"

"No daughter. A niece. She's two months old. The most beautiful, brilliant little girl in the universe."

A niece. Not a dad, after all, but a doting uncle. And judging by that bare ring finger, an *unmarried* uncle...

"Mine's a girl, too," she heard herself saying. "The ultrasound was just last week. I watched her suck her thumb...." Rachel cut herself off. Really, was that more information than the poor man needed, or what?

Apparently not, because he said, "You've actually seen her?"

She nodded.

"Is she gorgeous?"

"Of course. And healthy, from all indications. She has all her fingers and toes. And she's active." She felt a tiny flutter of movement beneath her rib cage on the right side. She put her hand to the spot. "Very active."

He shook his head, a musing look on that wonderful face. "Modern medicine. Amazing. And I'll bet your husband is thrilled."

She gulped. "No. No husband."

"Boyfriend, then..."

"Uh, no."

There was another silence—distinctly dreamy—as they gazed at each other some more. And then it came to her: this guy was about to ask for her number.

No, she thought. Better not go there. A blue-eyed hunk like this one could break her heart without even breathing hard. And wasn't it odd, him trying to pick up a pregnant lady? Men in real life never hit on a pregnant lady. And even if her stomach had been flat, she was not at her most alluring. Not by a long shot. She wore stretch jeans with a preggie-panel and a loose white cotton shirt. Her short mousy brown hair was scraped back with a headband. Her makeup? A smudge of lipstick and a few dabs of mascara. She just knew her nose was shiny...

Uh-uh. There was absolutely no logic to this fabulous-looking man putting a move on her.

She picked up her shopping bag and grabbed a tiny wool hat from the stack near her free hand. "You know, I love this hat." She waved it at him.

"Cute." He gave her a nod.

"And I just realized, I really have to go."

He saluted her with the romper, looking friendly and relaxed—and totally unfazed by the fact that she was suddenly waving a baby bonnet at him and backing away. "Thanks," he said easily. "For the advice."

"Really. No problem..." Clutching the little hat in one hand and her shopping bag in the other, she made her escape by zipping around a floor-to-ceiling divider into the toddlers section.

As soon as she got away from him, she wished she'd stayed. What could it have hurt to have stood and chatted with him for a few minutes more? What had he done *wrong*?

The answer, on both counts, was nothing.

It was being pregnant, she decided. Being obviously pregnant and him *still* seeming attracted. Since she'd started to show, men in general displayed less and less interest. Not that men in general had been beating down her door *before* she got pregnant. But at least they had, on occasion, looked twice.

Nowadays they looked *three* times: first at her face, then at her stomach—and then right past her.

Except for this guy. *He* was different.

Point for him, right?

And the truth was, she did have a shy streak, one she'd battled all her life. So that was part of it, too—why she'd hurried off like that.

Now, looking back, she could see that it was so not a big

deal—having a friendly conversation with a handsome man she'd just met. If she had it to do over again, she'd have handled it differently. Been more relaxed, more *natural*...

As she wandered on up the toddler aisle and back down, headed for the check-out counters, she promised herself, grinning a little at the unlikelihood, that the next time some gorgeous hunk flirted with her, he was going to get better treatment.

A moment later, she realized her chance to keep her promise was upon her already. *He* was waiting in the check-out line. She stepped in behind him.

He turned, smiled—this time full-out, both sides of that sexy mouth lifting. "Hey." He held up the romper *and* the overalls. "Decided to get them both."

"Good idea." She stuck the bonnet under her arm and held out her hand. "I'm Rachel. Rachel Stockham."

"Bryce Armstrong." His warm, strong fingers closed over hers. They shook.

She let go reluctantly as the clerk said, "Sir? May I help you?"

He handed over a credit card and his purchases and then he turned back to Rachel. They chatted about the weather—rainy—and the Trailblazers—headed for the finals this year, no doubt about it—as the clerk rang up first his sale and then hers.

It just seemed the most natural thing, to stroll on out into the mall together. They started toward Nordstrom for no particular reason that Rachel could think of—she certainly hadn't planned to go there that day. She glanced at him beside her and knew she had to say goodbye—at the same time as she wished they could just stroll along side-by-side forever.

She was so focused on Bryce that she didn't move out of the way fast enough when a woman loaded down with shopping bags came right at her.

"Whoa, careful..." Bryce took her arm to pull her out of the way before she got bopped by one of the bags. A thrill shivered through her at the contact and she beamed him a grateful smile as the woman paused to apologize.

"No harm done," Rachel told her.

The woman lurched on, bags bouncing, and Rachel turned back to Bryce. They stared into each other's eyes. Again. She could smell his aftershave. It was a green kind scent. Fresh. Subtle. She liked it.

Endless seconds passed before she realized she was leaning in close, gripping his strong arm as if it—and he—belonged to her. "Ahem. Well..." She extricated her arm from his and stepped back—gesturing rather wildly over her shoulder, toward the ice rink and the escalators at the center of the mall. "I seem to be going the wrong direction for some reason."

"No problem. We'll just turn around and go back."

"No. Really..."

He shrugged then, looking rueful. "Back to work, huh?"

"Well," she confessed. "It's my day off, actually."

"From..."

"I'm a nurse. Oncology."

"That would be cancer care, right?"

She nodded and volunteered, "Radiation Oncology at Portland General. We have one of the best cancer care centers in the state." Busy shoppers milled around them. Mall music and the tempting aromas from Starbuck's drifted on the air. Maybe, instead of strolling the mall forever, they could just stand right here and chat until the end of time...

He said, "You love your work. I can see it in those big brown eyes."

She smiled a little at his flattering tone, but when she spoke her smile had faded to a somber line. "It's tough sometimes. I'm right there while people are dealing with something that could—and too often does—take their life."

"Sounds very rough."

"Yeah. But there is a certain...reward, I guess, in helping make it better for people going through a hard time, as painful as it can be to watch some of them slip away."

"You're brave," he said quietly.

"No. My patients. *They're* the brave ones." She shook herself. "And I have got to get going."

He just stood there, looking scrumptious. "One more thing..." She knew what it would be. "I wonder..." He looked charmingly hesitant.

She couldn't help prompting, "What?"

"Well, I was thinking, maybe coffee—latte, espresso, your choice. Sometime when you're not so rushed..."

She felt warm all over. A *good* kind of warm. She dared to tease him, "Coffee and pregnant ladies don't mix. Caffeine's not good for the baby."

He leaned a little closer, bringing with him another faint hint of that tempting aftershave. "Tea, then. Fruit juice. Whatever. I'm flexible when it comes to beverages."

She looked down, innate shyness surging to the fore. "Oh..."

"So..." He waited until she dared to look up at him again. "Will you let me have your number?"

Oh, what was the harm, really? Not only was he perfect fodder for her fantasies, he was so easy to talk to. And she *wanted* to see him again. "Tell you what. Why don't *you* give me *your* number?"

Frowning a little, he studied her face. "I don't know. I think you have a shy side."

She winced. "That obvious, huh?"

"Not obvious at all. It's very...charming, to tell you the truth."

She laughed, her cheeks warming. "Yeah, right."

"No. Seriously. It is. But I'm afraid it just might keep you from picking up the phone and dialing my number. Or maybe you just don't want to see me again—for whatever reason. If that's what's up here, I'd appreciate it if you went ahead and laid it on me right now."

"No. No, really. I *will* call you."

He gave her a sideways look, then agreed, "Fair enough."

The business card he handed her was on thick gray vellum stock. She ran her thumb over the embossed lettering. Armstrong Industries, it read. "Hmm," she said. "Bryce Armstrong, CEO. Very impressive."

He gave her a look—indulgent, good-humored. "What can I tell you? I'm a spoiled only son and also the boss."

Armstrong, she thought as she glanced at the card again. Bryce Armstrong. The name was vaguely familiar....

She almost asked him where she might have heard his name before. But no. She *had* promised she'd call him. If they ended up seeing each other again, she'd learn more about him.

Shifting her purchases to one arm, she stuck the card in a side pocket of her shoulder bag. The purse slid down her arm. She backed away from him, grinning, hands out, dangling her purse and her purchases from either hand. She felt kind of magical, right at that moment—graceful and pretty in spite of her big tummy and scraped-back hair. The world, all of a sudden, seemed chock-full of possibilities.

Truly, just when she'd given up hope that she'd ever meet a really great, handsome, fun and easy-to-be-with guy...there he was.

Across the display counter from her at Becky & Huck's.

Whatever happened next, he had made her week—heck. He'd made her *month*.

"Call me," he said again.

"I will," she promised, still backing away. "I will, I'll call..." She raised her hand to wave, though her purse was dangling from her arm and it made the gesture awkward and jerky. She didn't care how awkward she looked. She didn't *feel* awkward. She felt like a swan. "You'll be hearing from me."

He gave her a wave in response and turned to go.

And right then, as her purse dangled free from her arm, someone grabbed it.

"Wha—?" Somehow, she managed to catch the strap before it slipped past her fingers. "Hey!" She whirled as the snatcher—a skinny guy in baggy jeans—gave it a hard yank. She yanked right back, "Don't!"

The guy didn't listen. He stepped toward her. She shrank away, sudden terror shivering an icy trail down her spine. "No..." It came out a whisper of fear and frustration.

His bony hand came toward her. He shoved her—square in the chest. The breath flew from her body. She sucked in air, and somehow managed one sharp, helpless cry as her feet flew out from under her and she went down.

CHAPTER TWO

WITH A YELP of shock and pain, she landed hard on her tailbone.

"Omigod!" someone cried.

"Did you see that?" a man shouted.

"Somebody get that SOB!"

Furious, Rachel scrambled to get up. She was going to catch that skinny little rat if it was the last thing she did. She flailed, groaning a little.

And by then, a ring of people had pressed in close around her. She gaped up at all those concerned faces.

"Is she okay?"

"Oh, God. She's pregnant..."

"Are you all right?" Two women helped her to her feet, one on either arm.

Once upright, she tried to bat their clutching hands away. "I'm fine, really. But my purse—"

"Take it easy," said one of her rescuers, a big woman with hard red hair and kind brown eyes. She patted Rachel on the back. "Breathe deep..."

Her breathing wasn't the problem—it was her aching butt. *And* her missing purse. "That guy...he took my purse. I have to—"

"Honey, it's handled," said the woman on her other side, a shapely platinum blonde with a lived-in face.

"No, I have to—"

"Sweetie, they got him. Look."

She looked where the long flame-red fingernail pointed—at Bryce, about twenty feet away, by the entrance to Starbuck's.

He had caught the bad guy! He held the skinny little creep in a neck lock and he appeared to be handing him over to a couple of husky biker types. "Hold this guy, will you?" Rachel heard him say.

"Don't let the bastard go."

"Wow, man. Sure." One of the bikers—the bigger one, with a bald head, a black T-shirt with the sleeves torn off and an intricate skull-and-barbed-wire tattoo on his beefy right arm—grabbed the purse-snatcher by the scruff of the neck and shook him. Hard. "We ain't havin' no difficulties with you, now, are we?"

The would-be thief hung his head and mumbled something under his breath.

The biker shook him again. "What'd you say, scumbag?"

"Ow, man, you're hurting me!"

"I'll hurt you more," the biker growled. "Unless you plan to behave yourself."

"All right, all right," the snatcher grumbled, "I won't make any trouble."

The helpful redhead suggested, "Somebody better go find Security."

"I will." A tall balding guy in a jogging suit headed off toward the ice rink in search of a mall cop.

The worried shoppers pressing in on her fell back a little as Bryce approached with her purse in hand. "I believe this is yours."

She took it and hooked it in place on her shoulder. Right then, she felt as though she'd known him forever, as though he were a dear old friend who'd shown up just when she needed him most. "Oh, Bryce..." She reached out instinctively.

He gathered her in. "Okay," he whispered, bending his head down a little to breathe the word against her temple. "It's okay..." He stroked her hair, rubbed her back. "Thanks," she heard him say to the people surrounding them. "I'll look after her."

Oh, didn't she just wish...

She pulled away from Bryce's embrace—but only to tell the redhead and the blonde and the others, too, "Thank you. Thank you so much."

"It's okay, sweetie."

The redhead held out Rachel's shopping bags—rescued at some point during the excitement. "You want us to stick with you?"

She took the bags. "No. I'm all right. Honestly."

Another woman handed Bryce his bag of baby clothes. "I think you dropped this."

"Thanks." He touched Rachel's chin, a brush of a touch, so that she would look at him. "How badly are you hurt?"

She didn't know whether she was going to laugh or cry. "Just my tailbone," she confessed in a whisper. "And my pride."

He looked down between them, at the rounded shape of her stomach. "The baby?"

She rested her hand on the firm bulge. "We're fine, really." He still looked worried. She reassured him, "Bryce. Pregnant women and their babies are tougher than people give them credit for."

"Still, just to be on the safe side, I think we should get you to an emergency room."

"No, really. I'm fine. And so's my baby."

"You're shaking."

"Just...after-effects of a major adrenaline surge."

"Come on." He guided her to a nearby bench. "Sit down here..."

She eyed the hard bench. "Ugh. Easier said than done."

He frowned. "You *are* hurt."

"Yeah, a little," she confessed. "But I promise it's nothing permanent..." She lowered herself carefully to the seat, wincing when she got there. "See? I'm sitting on my injury." She held out her hands, palms down. "And the shaking is almost gone. Really, since you caught the guy and got my purse back, this is just not that big a deal."

He sent a hot glance toward the bony purse snatcher, who was flanked by the two helpful bikers and sulkily studying the off-white tiles of the mall floor. "The guy ought to be shot."

She reached up, took his hand and gave a tug. "Sit by me."

Obediently, he dropped to her side, turning his hand in her grip so that he could lace his fingers with hers. She started to lower her head to his broad shoulder—and stopped herself just in time.

She was being altogether too clingy. Gently, she pulled her hand from his. He let go—but with enough reluctance that she found herself wishing she'd gone ahead and held on.

They waited, with the bikers and the skinny thief. It wasn't long before the mall security guy appeared. He took brief statements from them and then put a call in to the city police. They waited some more.

When the police showed up, they gave their statements all over again. Unless her attacker got the bright idea to plead not guilty, the detective told her, she shouldn't even have to go to court to testify against him—given that she didn't want to sue.

She eyed her attacker, who was looking pretty pitiful by then. "As long as he doesn't try to say he didn't do it, I'm fine with letting a judge handle this."

After they led the purse-snatcher away, Rachel thanked the bikers.

"S'all right, no problem," they told her, and moved along.

That left her and Bryce side-by-side on the bench. She dared, again, to touch him, putting her hand over his. A warm little thrill zipped through her at the contact. "Thank you. For catching that guy. For *being* here..."

His other hand closed over hers, capturing it, so tenderly, between both of his. He gave a squeeze. Her face felt warm and her heart beat faster. Honestly, did a guy have a right to look this good? His skin was smooth and golden-tan. And he had just the faintest manly-looking shadow of beard on that square jaw. And what about those eyelashes? Thick and long and sable-brown. Men shouldn't be allowed to have eyelashes like that. He leaned in closer. She breathed in the tempting scent of him and felt her eyes drifting closed....

Stop. No. Bad idea. She jerked back and pasted on a bright smile. "Really. I am so grateful."

"And why do I get the distinct feeling you're about to say goodbye again?"

She glanced down at their joined hands and then up into his waiting eyes. "Well. I do think it's time that I—"

"Do me one favor."

As if she could refuse him anything now. "Name it."

"There's a halfway decent steakhouse just outside the mall. Have lunch with me."

"Oh, Bryce. I don't think—"

"Humor me. Please. Just stick around for a while, until I can be one-hundred percent certain you're really okay."

"But I *am* okay."

"Just for a while." He was looking very determined—as if he wasn't going to back down easily on this one.

And in the end, after all he'd done, how could she refuse him? Plus, there was the fact that she didn't even *want* to refuse him.

"I'm buying," she warned.

Two hours later they were still sitting in a corner booth in the cozy, dim restaurant. Their empty plates had been cleared away. They lingered over coffee—well, in Rachel's case, a tall glass of ice water in which the ice had melted long ago.

How had the time gone by so fast? They'd talked and talked—a lot about her work, a little about his. He said he was thirty-five, had a business management degree from Stanford and described his job as, "Mostly amounting to delegating effectively." She figured there had to be a lot more to it than that, but she didn't press him. She teased him about spending his workday at the mall. And he tapped the shopping bag on the seat beside him and said he'd just slipped out to pick up something for Ariel. And then he'd met Rachel...

"And then found yourself stepping in to handle a purse-snatching in progress."

"My pleasure. All the way."

She teased, "And shouldn't you be back at work by now?"

"What's the point in being the boss if I can't give myself an afternoon off now and then?"

"So true," she agreed and they shared another in the by-then endless chain of long, mutually appreciative looks. She broke the lovely silence. "Ariel. It's such a pretty name."

He nodded. "After *The Little Mermaid*. Chelsea, my sister, always loved *The Little Mermaid*..."

And that led to the subject of favorite movies. They discovered that their tastes were astonishingly similar. They shared a fondness for the edgy and offbeat. They both like anything directed by Quentin Tarantino.

"And what about *There's Something About Mary?*" she suggested.

"Just about the funniest movie ever made." He looked at her sideways. *"Two Days in the Valley."*

"Saw it. Loved it." She challenged, *"Suicide Kings."*

"You're kidding. You *saw* that?"

She nodded, feeling inordinately smug. "I'll crawl over ground glass to see anything with Christopher Walken in it." And Brad and Ben, too, of course—at least lately. But she didn't tell him *that*. He might just ask why.

And what about TV shows?

They both enjoyed Sunday night on HBO.

From movies and TV, they went on to music, where their preferences went in different directions. Rachel liked a good country song. Bryce preferred either blues or hard rock.

It was all just surface stuff, just getting-to-know-you casually kind of talk. Rachel thoroughly enjoyed herself. She was ready when the check came and got her hand over it before he could grab it.

"Mine," she said. "And don't say I didn't warn you."

"All right," he conceded. "But next time is my turn."

Next time. He said it as if he meant it—but did she really believe him?

Oh, probably not. He was just so *smooth*...and sexy. And perfect. Too perfect for a harried and hard-working single mom-to-be. He had that look, a look that whispered *money*. From his brushed-leather shoes to his Rolex watch to his fine cashmere sweater. And then there was the subtle, oh-so-expensive scent of him. And that business card he'd given her...

CEO of Armstrong Industries.

She had a sneaking suspicion he was one of *the* Armstrongs.

If so, he was most likely very rich indeed. Even Rachel, who didn't pay a whole lot of attention to the movers and shakers in her community, had heard of the Armstrongs. The family had been around since forever, since the founding fathers flipped a coin and decided to name the city Portland instead of Boston. The Armstrongs were in shipping and land development. There was even an Armstrong High School....

More than once during lunch, she'd started to ask him if he was one of *the* Armstrongs. But he never volunteered the information. And somehow, she couldn't quite figure out how to pose the question without sounding just the wrong side of rude. She did say something about Armstrong being an important name in Portland.

But he only shrugged and they left it at that.

"This was great," she said, as they got up to go.

"Was." He shook his head. "You say that as if the afternoon's over."

A flush of pleasure crept up her cheeks. He didn't seem to want to say goodbye any more than she did. "Well, Bryce..."

"Come on. Let's go over to the theatre complex and see what's playing."

She laughed. He was really so charmingly insistent about this. "I don't know. A wild afternoon at the movies may be too much for this particular pregnant lady. I think I should probably go home and...relax, you know? Rest a little, put my feet up..."

"So how about my place? We can watch a movie there. I offer free popcorn—and a good reclining chair, perfect for propping up a pair of tired feet."

"Oh, I couldn't..."

"Yeah, you could."

"But..." She felt so flustered, suddenly. The thing was, she *wanted* to go with him. But was it wise? "Bryce. I just...well, I have to keep reminding myself that I hardly know you..."

"Come to my place. Get to know me better."

"Well, I... I mean, it seems a little sudden, don't you think?"

"Yeah, it does. But sudden's okay with me. In fact, sudden is just great."

She heard herself asking, "Where do you live?"

"Portland Heights. Ten minutes away, max."

Portland Heights. One of *the* nicest neighborhoods, in West Hills. She wasn't surprised.

But where he lived really wasn't the question. The question was, should she go there with him? Remember Michael Carson, a warning voice whispered somewhere in the wiser part of her mind.

The thing with Michael Carson had happened really fast. She'd asked none of the usual questions, hadn't gotten to know him at all, just thought he was gorgeous and ended up in bed with him. Her one mad indiscretion.

And he'd turned out to be her dear friend Lily's two-timing fiancé. She was never letting anything like that happen again.

They were still standing by their booth. The busboy kept eyeing them, no doubt waiting for them to go so he could clear the table.

She took Bryce's hand. "Come on."

They left the restaurant. Outside, the rain that had been falling for most of the day had turned to a misty drizzle. They rushed across the wet walkway to the mall entrance, Rachel in the lead. Once inside, he slowed. She felt the tug on her hand and turned to him.

"Just wondering." He grinned.

"Wondering what?"

"Where we're going."

"This way." She marched on, dragging him along—to the bench where they'd waited for the mall cop. A pair of elderly ladies had claimed it. The ladies sat with their silver heads close together, shopping bags in a bright spill around their feet. The bench across from them was unoccupied.

Rachel hauled Bryce over to it, commanding, "Sit down." He sat. She perched beside him, sliding her shopping bags between her feet and setting her purse in what was left of her lap. "Are you married?"

His brows drew together. "Rachel, what's—?"

Before he could finish, she demanded, "Well, are you?"

"No."

"Engaged?"

He moved back a little. "No."

"Separated?"

"Rachel. I've never *been* married."

"Is there *anyone?* Some...special woman you're seeing who's not going to be happy when she hears you took a strange pregnant lady home for the afternoon?"

"A *strange* pregnant lady?"

Was he teasing her? She scowled at him. "You know what I mean. A stranger. A woman you don't even know. Forget the fact that I'm pregnant. It wasn't the point."

He was frowning now. "Rachel. What's going on? Why are you so damned angry? What did I do?"

She opened her mouth to tell him...what? She sighed. "It's not you."

"Well. That's *something*."

"Just answer my question. Do you have a special woman friend? You know what I mean. An exclusive relationship. Are you *committed* to anyone?"

The silver-haired ladies were watching them. Rachel turned her scowl on them and they quickly looked away.

"Rachel."

"What?"

"No."

She forgot about the silver-haired ladies—for the moment, anyway. "No?"

"There's no one...special. There's honestly not."

"Oh." She twisted her purse strap. Now what? "Listen..." She paused to swallow. "I...well, it's not that I think something's going to *happen* between us. I mean, I just, well, I don't want some innocent woman hurt because I didn't have the sense to ask you—"

"Rachel," he said softly.

"What?"

"It's okay. I understand."

"You do?" He nodded. She couldn't help asking again, "You *really* do?"

"Yeah. It's a question you have every right to ask, and, as I said before, the answer is no. There's no one. I am one-hundred-percent unequivocally single. And while we're on this subject, what about you?"

Her throat kept clutching. She swallowed some more. "Me?"

Now he looked very patient. "Yes, Rachel. You."

"Well, but I told you, back there in Becky & Huck's. I'm single. Completely, totally, utterly single."

"And what about your baby's father?"

Her baby's father...

Oh, she could not explain that one, especially not here in the mall, with shoppers strolling by and the silver-haired ladies very likely listening in. "He's...not involved. I promise you."

"How 'not involved?'"

"Bryce."

"Yeah?"

She leaned close and whispered, so that only he would hear. "For now, you're just going to have to trust me on that one. The father of my baby is not a factor. That's all I can say, at this point." She hitched her purse back over her shoulder and reached for her shopping bags. "And you know, maybe we should just—"

He caught her arm before she could stand, warm strong fingers digging in just a little. "Don't run away."

She sank back to the bench. "Oh, I don't know..."

He let go of her arm and he shrugged. That shrug told her everything. She should come to a decision. He was through pushing her.

"All right," she said, feeling just a little bit foolish that she'd made such a big deal about all this—but then again, not *that* foolish. She really had needed the answer to the question she'd asked him. "Yes, let's go to your house."

He started to smile.

"But I get to pick the movie," she teased.

"Your choice. All the way."

CHAPTER THREE

RACHEL AGREED TO follow him to his place in her own car. But first she got his home address and phone number and took a minute to call a friend, so someone would know where she was going. Michael Carson had not only almost cost her her two best friends, he'd also made her more than a little careful when it came to hooking up with a new guy.

She'd learned the sad truth that a dream man can very easily turn into a girl's worst nightmare.

"I think someone should know where I am," she explained to Bryce, "since I did only just meet you…"

He seemed to have no problem with her emphasis on caution. "Makes sense to me."

She got out her phone and auto-dialed Lily Tyler—correction: Lily Stone. Lily had been married for months now, to Jake Stone, a longtime friend who had turned out to be the hero—and the husband—Michael Carson could never be.

"Rachel." She could hear the smile in her friend's voice.

There was whimpering in the background. "Is that Samantha I hear?" Lily's baby was three weeks old.

"We are very fussy today."

"Give her a big kiss for me."

"Will do. So what's up?"

Bryce had wandered over to the Nordstrom entrance and appeared to be studying a display of camping gear—giving her space to make her call. He seemed to sense she was looking his way. He met her eyes. Warmth flooded through her.

"Rachel?" Lily prompted.

"I'm right here." Rachel ordered her mind back on the business at hand—at which point it occurred to her that she hardly knew where to start. "You're not going to believe this... I, well, I met someone. I mean, it's nothing serious. I only *just* met him. But I like him. A lot. He invited me to his house. And I want to go."

"Where are you now?"

"Lloyd Center."

"You met him at the *mall?*"

Rachel stiffened. "Something wrong with that?"

"Don't get cranky. Please. I've got Sam if I'm looking for someone to fuss at me. I'm just trying to understand what's going on."

Rachel muttered a contrite, "Sorry—and it's a long story. I'll fill you in later. The deal is, I like him and I'm going to his house for the afternoon and I want you to have his phone number and address—you know, just so somebody knows where I am."

The fussing baby on the other end whimpered more insistently. "Rachel..." Lily sounded doubtful. And distracted.

"Look. Got a pen and paper?"

"Hold on..." Rachel waited. She could hear Sam whining and her friend making those cooing, soothing noises a mother will make to a crying baby. Lily came back on the line. "Okay. I'm ready."

"His name's Bryce Armstrong." She repeated the information Bryce had given her. "Got it?"

"Just a minute...yeah." About then, Sam let out a long, unhappy wail.

"I'll let you go," said Rachel.

"Just a sec. This guy..." Lily's voice trailed off. Rachel could hear her talking to Sam. "Just a minute, honey. Give mommy just a minute... Rachel, can you hear me?"

"I'm here."

"This guy. Bryce Armstrong, you said his name was?" Rachel made a noise in the affirmative. "The name's familiar..."

"I know. I kind of thought so, too. But it's probably just the last name. You can't live in Portland and not have heard the name Armstrong."

"No, I mean his whole name. *Bryce* Armstrong. I'm sure I've heard of..." Sam's wail turned to something very much like an angry scream. "Rachel. Sorry. I have to go. We still on for Monday?" They were meeting for lunch.

"Wouldn't miss it."

"Great. Jenna?"

"Oh, yeah. I'll call her."

"Good." Sam wailed all the louder. "Jake volunteered to watch Sam."

"The man is a saint."

"He does have his uses—and plus, he adores her. Rachel..."

"I'm here."

"Please take care."

"I will. Promise." Sam wailed again, louder than ever, and Rachel heard the click as her friend hung up. She put away her phone and started toward Bryce.

He turned when she was almost to him and when her eyes met his, her breath got all tangled up in her chest. What a truly gorgeous guy...

He arched a brow. "Ready?"

Rachel nodded and held out her hand.

Bryce's house—on one of the highest hills in Portland Heights—was huge, Tudor in style and surrounded by trees. A long, curving drive led up to it.

"All I have to do is stay on the yard guys to keep the greenery trimmed," Bryce told her as they waited for the corn to pop, "and I've got views all around. Mountains in the daytime. Both St. Helens and Mount Hood..."

She stared out the kitchen's rain-jeweled bay window. Through the gaps in the lush maples and stately oaks, she could see the wide white cap of Mount Hood. "I *am* impressed."

"...and city views at night."

"What more could a bachelor ask for?"

"If I answered that honestly, you'd only say I was putting a move on you."

"Are you?"

"Absolutely—but hey. No pressure." The microwave beeped. He took out the bag of popcorn, tore it open and tumbled the fat, fragrant kernels into the bowl that waited on the black marble counter. "Soda?"

"Do you have something without caffeine?"

"Sure." He went to the stainless steel refrigerator—along with the Viking stove, it made the kitchen look like something straight out of a spread in *Gourmet* magazine—and got two cans of soda. "Grab the bowl and follow me."

He led her past a living room the size of a baseball diamond and down a wide hallway to a room with eight padded lounge chairs, all facing the biggest television she'd ever seen.

"This wouldn't be the media room, now would it?" In her mind's eye she could see her own cozy living room, complete with her trusty 27-inch Panasonic.

He sent her a grin and gestured at a chair, taking the one next to it, so they could share the popcorn on the table between them.

"The lever on the left side of the chair will put your feet up for you."

She pulled the lever and she was in lounge mode. "I think I'm in heaven."

The technical aspects of the setup amazed her. He explained, "As a normal, red-blooded American male, I have a weakness for electronic toys." He picked up a silver remote, pushed a button and the lights went down. Then he pointed the device at the screen. "I have over five hundred movies stored in the system." Titles began scrolling down the screen. "Here." He handed her the remote.

"I don't believe this. No man lets a woman hold the remote—at least not on the first date."

"Enjoy the feeling. It probably won't last—push that button to move down the list." It took several minutes to scroll through the choices and make a decision. "Hit Enter," he instructed approvingly when she chose the Coen brothers' latest release. "Good. Then hit Enter again."

The movie began and two hours flew by.

When Bryce brought the lights up, she started to tell him she had to be on her way.

"Just stay a little longer...."

She didn't need a whole lot of convincing. She was having a great time. Somehow, the drive home alone through the rain, a long, hot bath and naughty dreams of Brad or Ben didn't stack up to staying right there with Bryce.

Just for a little while...

Bryce led her back to the living room and lit the gas fire beneath the wide stone mantel. They shared the long sofa facing the cheery blaze.

And they talked. About the movie, at first.

He was just so easy to talk to. After just this one day with him, she felt as if she'd known him forever. And it was nothing short of a fantasy-come-true to have this incredible guy treating her like a queen, hanging on her every word.

She found herself telling him the most private things. About how her mother's emotional problems really got to her sometimes, though bipolar disorder *was* an illness. "It's not my mom's fault," Rachel said. "If only she would just be consistent about her meds..."

"You resent her." He said it frankly, and she knew he saw nothing wrong with her feeling that way.

She admitted that sometimes she did. "She wasn't the most attentive mother. I guess, deep down, I still have issues about that. I know now that she was battling her illness even back then, when I was a kid and nobody knew what bipolar was. They called her 'moody' and 'overly sensitive.' Until the condition became acute, ten years ago, she never would get professional help. My father couldn't deal with her. He left when I was five. And then, really quickly, he married again, had another family. I haven't seen him in years. It's as if... I don't even have a dad." She slanted him an ironic look. "Stop me when you're so depressed you'll slit your wrists if I go on."

He didn't stop her. And she just kept talking. Eventually

they went into the kitchen to raid the refrigerator. He had Ben & Jerry's Rum Raisin.

They sat at the table by the bay window and enjoyed the cold, delicious treat. The rain had intensified. It drummed against the window and cascaded down in rivulets, glittering as it went.

By the time they settled near the fire again, she was into the stuff about Lily and Jenna and their three-way pact to try artificial insemination if they got to the age of thirty-four without husbands—or at least serious relationships. "And we did it. Lily's had her baby. Jenna's about four months along..."

"And *you* meant what you said about your baby's father not being an issue."

She nodded. "He's twenty-eight, five feet eleven inches tall, has brown hair and blue eyes and no health problems. Oh, and he loves mountain biking and has a degree in biology. And that's the sum total of what I know about him, which is plenty as far as I'm concerned."

He listened as she talked, his gaze on her face. He seemed so *interested*. So she went on.

Into the whole fiasco with Michael Carson.

"I was a fool," she told him. "I didn't ask the right questions. I didn't ask *any* questions. I met him in a club. My mom had been driving me up the wall. I needed a break, decided to treat myself, to do something crazy and fun. To have my very own wild night on the town. There he was, sitting down the bar from me. He was incredibly charming. We had a few drinks. The truth is, I pretty much fell into bed with him, you know? A one-night stand is what it was. And then he never called and, well, what do you do?"

"Forget him."

"Yeah. After I got over the whole thing not going anywhere, I told myself I'd had a good time, kind of busted out a little for once and there was nothing wrong with that. Then he turns up with Lily on his arm. And I put it together. He was *her* Michael, the one she'd been talking about for months. He was *her* Michael and he'd spent the night with *me* while he was supposed to be her guy...and by the time I met him with her, he was a lot more than her boyfriend. By then, he'd asked her to marry him. He was her fiancé, can you believe it?"

His eyes shone with a knowing light. "So that's why the third degree before you'd come to my house with me."

"That's right. I learned my lesson. If you want to hang with me, I need to know upfront if there's a woman out there who trusts you and is waiting for you to come home."

He looked at her levelly. "There's not."

"I believe you."

"And back to your friend Lily and her slimeball fiancé. What did she say when you told her what had happened?"

Rachel shook her head. "That's the problem. I couldn't figure out how, exactly, to tell her. When I saw them together, I felt like something you scrape off the bottom of your shoe. I kept my mouth shut."

"Bad decision."

She couldn't have agreed more. "Very bad."

"But when you spent the night with him, you didn't have a clue he was your friend's guy, right?"

"Of course I didn't."

"So you really did nothing wrong."

"I kept trying to tell myself that. But somehow, I still felt like a creep. And then, when I didn't tell her right away, it got worse. I felt all the time that I *should* tell her, but the longer I didn't tell her, somehow, the harder it got to get the words out. And then, the day of their wedding, the lowlife dumped her. She was devastated. I did what a friend does. I comforted her. And while I was agreeing what an SOB the guy was, it just kind of...slipped out."

Bryce was shaking his head. "That's what I call bad timing."

"Yeah. You're right on both counts. It was a bad decision to start with, to keep my mouth shut—and then, when I did finally tell her...could I have chosen a worse time to do it? Doubtful. She was so hurt. I was *so* guilty. It drove a major wedge between us. And we put our other friend, Jenna, in the middle of it, until Jenna decided she couldn't deal with either of us.

"For a while there, I thought I'd lost the two best friends I'd ever had. And the real irony was, one of the lottery tickets we were always buying together paid off for five-hundred-thousand dollars a few days after everything went so wrong. The three of us were hardly speaking, but we split the money as we'd agreed. And we each went ahead—on our own—with our plans to have babies without the benefit of husbands." It caused a sharp ache in the vicinity of her heart to remember it. "We'd always talked about how, if the guy thing never worked out for us, we'd at least have each other when we became single moms…"

"But I take it that now things are improving, between you?"

"Yeah. Lily made the first move a few months ago, to repair the breach. And Jenna and I were both there the day Lily's baby was born."

"So…a rotten mess. But it ends well."

"Mmm, hmm…" She fell silent, looking at him. She'd kicked her shoes off long before and turned toward him on the couch, drawing her legs up to the side. She looked down at her white shirt where it curved over the growing bulge of her tummy and then back up at him. And she couldn't help laughing.

He wore a musing smile. "What?"

She rested her elbow on the back of the couch and braced her head in her hand. "Oh, I don't know. You're clearly the most eligible of bachelors. And yet here you are, by the fire on Friday night, listening for hours on end to an incessantly chattering pregnant person. Tell me. Do you know more about me than you ever wanted to know, or what?"

He lifted his hand and ran his index finger, a touch like a breath, down her cheek. The caress shimmered through her, leaving a trail of tender heat. "A woman who talks about what really matters to her is a fascinating woman. And then there's also the fact that vulnerability and honesty make a woman damn near irresistible."

"What a kind thing to say." She was whispering, a very husky whisper, though there was no one but him to hear. She had that fluttery, heated feeling down inside—a yearning feeling, frankly sexual.

"This is not about kindness…" His voice was husky, too. He

touched her again, cupping his warm hand around her neck, his fingers brushing up into her hair.

She made a small sound in her throat—of surprise, of longing. He answered that wordless question by covering her mouth with his.

They were kissing! Oh, boy, were they kissing. She sighed and let her lips part a little and his teasing tongue came inside. She moaned low and arched toward him. He pulled her in.

And her stomach touched him!

She let out a small, embarrassed cry and jerked back. "Oh, God. Sorry..."

"What for?" His lips were soft from kissing her, his eyes low-lidded, dreamy...

She glanced at her watch. "Uh, well. You know, I should probably—"

He was shaking his head. "Don't go."

"But it's after eleven. I really have to—"

"Just stay. You can have your choice of guest rooms. I have too many of them."

"Bryce..."

He gestured toward the French doors several feet away. The rain was still coming down hard. "It's pouring out there. You don't need to be out in that at this time of night."

She put her hand on her stomach, smoothed the wrinkled shirt a little, and then, slanting him a self-conscious glance, she dared to say what was on her mind. "It really doesn't...bother you? Kissing a seriously pregnant woman, having my stomach get in the way?"

Her face was flaming. He touched her cheek again, as if to cool the burning heat of it. The caress was so tender, it just about broke her heart.

"No, it doesn't bother me. I like kissing you. A lot. And I've only known you pregnant, so that's kind of part of the package, isn't it?"

"You've only known me pregnant—and that's been for less than a day."

"I thought I told you, sudden is okay with me."

"But I just...well, I'm not sure it's okay with me."

"I noticed." His eyes had rueful gleam in them. "And from all you've told me tonight, I can understand why you feel that way."

"You've just been so...terrific."

"And this is a problem?"

She reached out and touched his face, felt the warmth of his skin, the slight roughness of beard-stubble...

Oh, he was so perfect. *Too* perfect. She looked in his eyes and she felt beautiful. Beautiful and more than a little bit drunk, even though she'd had nothing with alcohol in it.

But still, she definitely felt high. High on this great guy who hung on her every word and seemed to love kissing her, who touched her with tenderness, who said that she was honest and vulnerable and that he found her fascinating and that her big stomach was part of the package.

Could this be real?

Oh, probably not. It wasn't something that was likely to last. It was just...one of those things that happens. A little bit of magic in her otherwise strictly ordinary, way too demanding life.

There was Brad and there was Ben.

And now... Bryce.

Oh, yes. It fit. It definitely fit.

She said, her voice gone husky again, "If I stayed, could I sleep in your room?" The words were out almost before she realized she would say them. She made a sound halfway between a bark of laughter and a sob and she put her hand over her mouth. "I can't believe I just asked you that."

He didn't look the least bit fazed. "But the real question is, did you mean it?"

She couldn't quite meet his eyes. "I, um..." Oh, how to explain herself. "It's just that lately my libido seems to be way out of control. I have a lot of...fantasies. I would just really like, one time before I get big as a house, for my fantasies to come true."

Oh, beautiful, she thought, staring bleakly down at her growing waistline. Way to go, Rachel. Was she going to tell him every last embarrassing secret she'd ever had?

She could hear the rain spattering the windows, and also the friendly hiss of the fire in the grate. He wasn't saying anything.

Not that she blamed him. What was he thinking? She just could not look at him...

He whispered, so softly, "Rachel..." She made herself raise her head. What she saw in his eyes sent heat in a flash fire blazing all through her. "Spend the night in my bed," he said. "Please."

She blinked. "Tell me you didn't just say what I thought you said..."

"But I did say it."

"You're serious?"

He was nodding.

"You and me...tonight...right now?"

"Yeah."

"Oh. Oh, well..."

"You're so charming when you're blushing."

"So, you mean, you *would*? With me?"

"In a heartbeat."

"Oh." She put her hand against her throat where she could feel her pulse frantically beating. "This is so unreal. And I am incredibly nervous."

"That's okay."

"Oh, I don't know. In my fantasies..." She didn't quite know how to finish that thought.

He whispered, "Go on. Tell me. Say it."

"Well, I mean, in my fantasies, I'm not six months pregnant, you know? But now... Well, in reality, I'm thinking it could be kind of...awkward."

"Awkward is fine with me."

"Oh, Bryce..."

He took her hand and pried open her suddenly-stiff fingers and brushed a kiss right there in the heart of her palm. Her senses were humming, she felt warm and shaky—but in a good way.

A very, very good way.

He guided her hand to his shoulder, a coaxing gesture. It was all the encouragement she needed. She went for it, sliding her hand up, wrapping her fingers around his nape, leaning in as he leaned toward her.

Their lips met for the second time. His strong arms came around her and he gathered her close. And that time, when her stomach pushed against him, she had no urge to pull away.

CHAPTER FOUR

THEY WENT UP the wide staircase hand-in-hand. The door to his room stood open. He led her through, into the shadows, toward the wide shape of the bed.

When he reached for the lamp, she caught his hand. "Could we...leave it off?"

"Sure."

She sought his eyes through the dimness—and then she laughed.

"What?" His white teeth flashed with his questioning smile.

"Oh, just...all my wild fantasies. I was so brave and so bold in them. And in the end, now it's really happening, here I am, asking you to leave the light off."

He touched her cheek, so lightly. "I already told you I think you're brave. But bold...? You know, maybe you'd better describe these fantasies of yours."

"I'll tell you this much...." And she lost her nerve. She slanted him a look. "On second thought, not tonight."

If he was disappointed that she wouldn't tell him all the naughty details, he wasn't showing it. "It's your call—and don't knock the dark. The dark has plenty to offer. A sense of mystery, of secrets that you have to find the answer to by feel."

"If you say so."

He studied her. "Nervous?"

"Extremely."

"Come here." He pulled her close for another long, bone-melting kiss and when he lifted his head, he slid the band from her hair. "There." He dropped the headband to the nightstand and ran his fingers through her short, dark curls. "Pretty. Soft..." He kissed her again, easing her nervousness, soothing her fears.

He began to undress her—and himself—pausing for tender kisses between each undone button, each loosened sleeve. He unwrapped her like a precious gift—with such reverent care, his eyes gleaming through the darkness, his hands brushing so lightly against her skin as he whisked away the barriers between them.

The rain drummed in a hollow, haunting rhythm against the windows and the wind made faint, sweet crying sounds. Rachel cried, too—small, hungry little cries. Of yearning. And wonder.

He laid her back on the bed and kissed his way down her body, pausing for a number of erotic detours: to take each nipple in his mouth, to lay his golden head against the swell of her belly, as if listening for whispered secrets from the little one inside. He pressed his palms against the roundness, long fingers spread, on either side of her navel. And then he waited...

"There," he whispered. "Did she just kick me?"

"A kick or a punch. Pretty hard to tell the difference most of the time."

His hands moved. She sighed. He caressed his way downward, over the slopes and the hollows. He stroked her thighs, following the long caresses with brushing kisses.

When he found her, when his fingers gently parted her, she whimpered, in need...in hunger. In stunned delight. He lifted his head and he looked at her, as she writhed and moaned at the touch of his hand.

"Rachel," he said, as if the mere sound of her name excited him. "Rachel..." He slid up beside her as his hand continued its shattering play below. He kissed her as he stroked her. She pushed herself hungrily against his pleasuring hand and gave him her lips and her tongue to do with as he pleased.

When she hit the crest, his kiss only deepened. She cried her delight against his mouth as she went over the brink and into that floating state of pleasure on the other side.

"I can feel you," he whispered, his hand still cupping her. "Feel the pulsing. Feel you coming..."

She moaned. He kissed her again, with such slow, delicious care.

And when the pulsing finally stopped, he rolled away from her and pulled open a drawer in the little table by the side of the bed.

"Bryce...?"

He came back to her. He had a condom in his hand. She watched him through the shadows as he rolled it down over himself. He did it smoothly, expertly. She lay there, dazed with delight, and wondered at him. At all she didn't know about him...

But then he was sliding a hard knee between her thighs, raising up over her, lowering his mouth to take her lips.

He kissed her—teasingly this time—his lean, hard body braced on his arms, holding himself above the swell of her stomach. And then he whispered, "I'm afraid to put my weight on you."

"It should be all right..." Though the truth was that, in the past few weeks, pressure on her swelling midsection felt odd and uncomfortable.

He must have heard the doubt in her voice. "I think maybe we're going to have to slide you over to the side of the bed."

It was a fairly high bed, with a thick, firm mattress. If he stood at the edge of it...

She reached up, ran her fingers lightly through the silky hair at his temple. "That would work better."

He was watching her probingly. "You're sure about this?"

She nodded, gave another low laugh. "But are you?"

He lowered his head and glanced down between them at the proof that he was still very interested in continuing this activity. He looked up at her again. And he winked. A smile trembled across her mouth as she remembered that first moment she'd become aware of him—was it really only hours ago?—across the display counter at Becky & Huck's.

Never in a hundred thousand years would she have guessed she would get here, from there—and in such a short time, too. Oh, my, she thought, I am such a wild, wicked mother-to-be.

"Come on, scoot this way..." He guided her hips to the edge of the bed and slid off to stand before her, with her thighs on either side of his.

In a slow, smooth stroke, he was inside.

Inside, and careful—at first. He moved cautiously in and slowly out—or almost out. But not quite.

She moaned and he came back to her. And that time, when she felt him go deep, she rested back on her elbows and let her eyelids droop shut.

He bent closer, slid his hands under her hips and lifted her.

"Oh!" she cried.

"Wrap your legs around me."

She did as he instructed. And then he stood taller. Her hips were off the bed and he supported her lower body in his arms. He began to move more swiftly.

And it was...

Just heavenly. She moaned and rolled her head from side to side as they found a mutually pleasing rhythm, as he held her tight and she pushed her hips against him, as he filled her and retreated and then filled her again.

In the end, he held so still, gripping her hips, pressing deep into her. She could feel his release, feel him pulsing within her. And, oh, that did thrill her. It was just so...erotic, so beautiful and right.

Her own release began. She felt the tightening, the gathering deep inside...

They were so still, locked together hard at the point of joining. So still on the outside, while within there was that rising magic flowing out along every nerve.

He held her hard against him, supporting most of her weight, until the pulsing faded down to a glorious, soft glow. Then, at last, he bent his legs—they were shaking, she could feel them—until her hips met the bed. And then he slipped from her. She let out a long sigh at the loss. "Come back..."

He sent her a tender look over his shoulder. "I will." He got rid of the condom and returned to her. Together, they scooted fully onto the bed again.

As if they'd always slept together, she turned on her side and he wrapped himself around her, pulling the covers over them. His thighs were a cradle for hers, his breath stirred her hair. She reached back for his hand, guided that muscular arm to rest on the cove of her thickened waist. His chest was warm and solid against her back.

Strange, she thought drowsily, how natural it felt to be here with him. How perfectly right.

He cuddled her closer. She sighed. For a while, they whispered together in the darkness. He stroked her hair, brushed a kiss now and then against her shoulder. Finally, with a small, contented smile curving her lips, she dropped off to sleep.

CHAPTER FIVE

IN THE MORNING Rachel discovered that Bryce had a live-in housekeeper and a cook. The housekeeper greeted them when they came down the stairs. Now, *that* was an interesting experience. Bryce said, "Rachel, this is Mrs. Davenbrook. Mrs. D. takes excellent care of me."

Rachel murmured "Nice to meet you," and Mrs. Davenbrook nodded crisply in response, a bland smile on her pleasant face. Rachel didn't even let herself wonder what the housekeeper was thinking. She did, however, kind of wish she'd taken a moment to comb her hair.

The cook served them breakfast at the table by the bay window. Outside, the day was bright and clear, the snow cap on Mount Hood seeming to twinkle at them through the lush branches of the trees.

"Stay," Bryce said as they inhaled their eggs Benedict. "We'll watch another movie. Or drive over to the Pearl District, if you'd like that. We can wander through the galleries, do some serious window-shopping, have lunch at a great new place I know..."

She was just about to say yes when her purse, on the chair in the corner where she'd abandoned it the night before, began playing the theme from "The Addams Family."

"My phone..." She got up and answered it.

"Rachel. Rachel, where *are* you? I've been calling all night..."

The frantic edge to her mother's voice sent a quiver of alarm racing through her. The gorgeous, sunny day seemed suddenly not quite so bright.

She spoke gently. "I'm sorry, Mom, I wasn't near my—"

Ellen Stockham was beyond the point of letting Rachel get out a whole sentence. "I can't... I can't *do* this. And don't you accuse me."

"Mom, I'm not—"

"Those pills... I just, well, I thought I would try it for a while, you know? Without them? And I... I felt fine. I really did. Well, a little bit down, you know? And then, last night, well, I was thinking about washing the curtains. You know how I am, I do like things *clean*. And then, I couldn't seem to get the rod loose from the wall-hook thingy and then I... Oh, Rachel... I..."

"Mom. Listen."

"Oh, what? What *is* it?"

"Did you call Doctor—?"

"The *curtains*, Rachel. They are impossible. I had to *cut* them off. And now, this morning, the sun came out. It's too bright in here. I just can't... I can't..."

As her mother rambled on, Rachel accepted the fact that this was not something she could handle over the phone. "Mom. Just sit tight."

"Oh, I don't... I just... I... Rachel..."

"I'll be right over."

"But Rachel—"

"Mom. Just wait. I won't be long."

"Let me take you," Bryce said, when she told him her mother was seriously down-cycling and she had to go, *now*.

"Thanks, but I'll handle it." She spoke as calmly as she could while racing for the door.

He followed her out and held the door for her as she got in the car. "I'll call you later, make sure you're all right."

"Yeah, okay. Thanks." She started up the car.

"Rachel."

"I have to go, Bryce."

"Your number?" She must have looked as frantic to get moving as she felt, because he added, "Just tell me. I'll remember."

So she rattled off her home number and he shut the door and she tore off down the drive.

Somehow, Rachel managed to make it to her mother's across the river a few blocks from her own place without getting a ticket or causing a wreck. She ran up the flight of steps to the second-floor apartment, noting as she got there that the curtains that usually hung on the window by the door weren't there anymore.

Just as she was collecting herself to knock, the door opened.

Her mother stood on the other side, wearing a pink chenille robe and a pair of black sneakers, the frayed laces untied. Blood oozed from a cut on her right cheek and dripped from another shallow gash on her hand. Behind her, on the living-room rug, what looked like every curtain in the apartment lay in a tangled mound.

Rachel whispered despairingly, "Mom..."

"Oh, Rachel," her mother cried. "Oh, Rachel, what will I do?" The dark eyes, sunken and haunted, but otherwise the same eyes Rachel saw when she looked in the mirror, pleaded for answers that Rachel didn't have. Yesterday's mascara ran in tracks down her too-thin face.

Rachel stepped over the threshold and carefully pried the bloody scissors from her mother's shaking hand. "It's all right, Mom. I'm here, now. I'm here..."

CHAPTER SIX

FOUR HOURS LATER, Rachel sat in the main waiting room in Portland General's psychiatric wing. She wasn't really *waiting* for anything—except maybe for the moment when she'd find the energy to get up and leave. Everything that needed doing for the day had been done. She could go home, draw a hot bath, pour in the scented bath salts...

Double doors to the main hall swung open—and there was Jenna Cooper, four months along now, her stomach gently rounded under her scrubs. Frowning, she scanned the waiting area.

Rachel dragged her tired body upright. "Jenna..."

Jenna spotted her and smiled. She hurried over and they shared a quick hug. "I heard a rumor you were here," she whispered in Rachel's ear. They stepped back from each other and Jenna took her by the shoulders to look in her eyes. "How are you holding up?"

"I've been better."

"Your mom?"

"They're keeping her here for a few days, until the crisis is past."

"How bad is it?"

"Bad enough. But she'll be okay once they get the meds back on track—are you on duty?"

Jenna nodded. "How can I help? What can I do?"

"Nothing. Honest. It's done. But thanks for checking on me..."

"You look beat."

"Yeah. I'm wrung out."

"You need someone to take you home. I can—"

"No. Really. I have my car. I'll manage. I'll just drive *really* slowly."

"You're sure?"

Rachel nodded, firmly—and then she remembered about Monday. "Wait. There is one thing..."

"Name it."

"Lunch. One o'clock Monday, the usual place. You, me and Lily. Jake's watching Sam, so it'll be just like old times."

Jenna's comforting hands dropped away. "Oh, I don't know. You should see my schedule..."

Sometimes Rachel wondered if Jenna was still a little wary, if she hadn't completely put the Michael Carson fiasco behind her. She patted her friend's arm. "No pressure. Just, you know, if you can..."

"I'll try..."

The phone was ringing as Rachel let herself in the door. It was Lily. "At last. I called your cell, but it was only taking messages."

"Sorry. I turned it off while I was at the hospital."

"Jenna called me and told me about your mom. She said things were...well, handled, anyway."

"Yeah. She'll be okay. Till the next time..."

"Listen. Jake's here." A firefighter, Jake would work round-the-clock and then get several days off in a row. "I can leave Sam with him and be right over."

"Thanks, but no. I just want to sink into a hot bath...for about a year." Rachel knew what her friend's next question would be. She was right.

"So...how was last night?"

From the perspective of a day spent having her mother temporarily committed, the magic of last night seemed so long ago...

"Rachel?"

"Sorry. Last night was wonderful. I... I do really like him."

"Ah."

Rachel knew when her friend had something on her mind. "When you say 'Ah' like that, I know there's more coming."

"Well, I told Jake you'd met a guy named Bryce Armstrong. We both felt sure we'd heard the name before. And then Jake remembered that a Bryce Armstrong showed up at the last Logan Burn Center fundraising drive. He delivered a huge check courtesy of Armstrong Industries. You think maybe this could be the same guy?"

"He's the CEO, actually."

"Ah."

"Lily. Say it. My bathtub is calling me."

"He's one of *the* Armstrongs."

"Figured that one out."

"Rich as they come."

"You only have to look at him to know that. But if I had any doubts, well, I followed him in his Mercedes to his mansion in Portland Heights. That he's got money is just not news."

"You sound defensive. I'm not telling you this so you'll get your guard up. This is only...information, you know?"

"I know. So go ahead. Tell me the rest."

"Okay. The guy's not only *an* Armstrong, he's the major heir. I think there's a sister, but you don't hear a lot about her."

"There is a sister. Her name's Chelsea. She has a baby named Ariel that Bryce adores. So what else?"

"Well, don't you remember him? He even made *People* magazine once. That issue on sexy CEOs. He got a whole quarter page. They wrote about how he had a different gorgeous woman on his arm every night..."

"Oh." Rachel sank to a chair. "Well. That's news... I mean, I kind of remember that article now you mention it." She'd read the brief piece and mused a little over how the other half lives. Oh, and she'd thought he was gorgeous, too. Unbelievable. Really, how *could* she have forgotten that article until now? She pulled at a loose thread on the chair seat. "Well, I guess that's me. Just another in an endless chain of stunning, willing women."

"Oh, come on. I only told you because we had an agreement, remember? No more secrets when it comes to men."

"I know. And I'm glad you told me."

"And it's not a huge issue that he's dated a lot of women, is it?"

"Well, no. No, of course not."

"Rachel. Wait a minute. You didn't happen to…?"

"Oh, you're just so tactful this afternoon."

"Well. *Did* you?"

"Yes. I slept with him." She stopped tugging on that thread and sat up a little taller. "And it was great. Believe it or not, lovely, passionate sex *is* possible even when you're six months along."

"Don't I know it."

Rachel actually giggled as she realized that Lily had been there, too. "And before I would go home with him, I at least made sure there was no special woman in his life."

"Good for you. And you know, if *he's* unattached and *you're* unattached and you treated each other with understanding and mutual respect, well then, is there really a problem?"

She let out a long sigh. "Oh, probably not. Other than the fact that's he's way out of my league."

"Stop that. There is no one—*no one*—who is out of your league."

"You are the very best friend a girl could have—and I have to stop falling into bed with every charming, handsome guy I meet."

"Oh, puh-lease. Two guys. It's hardly a pattern."

"Maybe not. It's just that, after this morning, it's a challenge to have a positive attitude about anything."

Lily made an understanding noise low in her throat. "Sure you don't want me to come over?"

Rachel demurred again, with many thanks, and told her friend she had to go. Once she hung up, she headed straight for the tub, shedding her clothes as she went. She took the phone in there with her, just in case the hospital called. It rang as she was settling back in the fragrant, soothing hot water.

"I'm guessing you just got home and don't want to deal with some guy who won't let you have a minute to yourself."

The world was suddenly a better place. "Bryce. Hello."

"How's your mother?"

She hesitated over what to say, then settled on a bare-bones version of the facts. "Not good. I took her to the hospital. Just got home a few minutes ago."

"Want some company?" Her first reaction was a delighted, *yes*. But she hesitated a fraction too long before she said it and he gently suggested, "Tired?"

She sank deeper into the lovely warm water. "Mmm, hmm."

"Then maybe later…"

She smiled at the thought. "Yeah. I'll hold you to it." She said the words and then wondered if she really meant them.

After all, he was Bryce Armstrong, sexy CEO—just ask anyone who read *People* magazine. With him, there was a different glamorous woman for every day of the week. Their brief time together had been perfect. But she didn't really fit the profile, now did she?

They talked about nothing in particular for a few minutes more and then he said goodbye.

On Monday, one of her favorite patients lost the fight for his life. He was only a kid, just twelve years old, as sweet and gutsy as they come. He'd been battling leukemia for over a year.

While the boy's father made the necessary arrangements, Rachel sat with the mother for a while. They whispered together of the twelve-year-old's goodness and bravery, how he greeted each day with a smile, how even at the end, he saw life as a great adventure. Rachel reassured his mother that he would never be forgotten, that years from now, people would remember him and speak of him with fondness and admiration.

But no matter what uplifting things she said—and meant—he was still gone. She looked in his mother's eyes and saw that awful, gaping hole of loss and felt her own inability to make things any better as a blow straight to the heart.

Yes, she was trained to help cope with the death of a patient. But coping seemed a paltry thing, so pitiful and small and useless when stacked against the agony in a grieving mother's eyes.

She met Lily for lunch at their favorite place. Jenna didn't show.

Rachel told her friend about the loss of her patient and for a while they sat there, looking at all the food they'd ordered, neither of them really feeling much like eating.

Eventually, they started talking about Jenna. Jenna worked in the E.R. She saw death close-up and far too often, and somehow she'd kept her plucky, ready-for-anything attitude intact.

At one point, Rachel dared to suggest, "Do you think, maybe, she's still kind of... I don't know...*guarded* with us?"

Lily was shaking her head. "She just works too hard." And then they started talking baby showers. Rachel had had hers the month before.

"But Jenna hasn't." Lily was looking very pleased with herself.

Rachel asked, "Should we go for it, you think?" It was a purely rhetorical question. Of course, they would go for it.

Before they left the restaurant, they had Jenna's shower halfway planned and Rachel's spirits had lifted, at least a little.

After her shift, she stopped in to see her mother. Ellen Stockham turned her face to the wall and whispered, "Go away."

The bright spark of optimism kindled during Rachel's lunch with Lily seemed to wink and go out.

When she got home, the guy down the street was mowing his postage-stamp of lawn—bare-chested in baggy cargos as always. He had an impressive six pack and shoulders for days. And she didn't even have to remind herself that he was out of bounds as an object for her fantasies.

Really, how could she lose herself in fantasy when her mother was in the hospital suffering from acute depression and a fine, bright young boy had just died?

She dragged herself inside, where the message light was blinking on her answering machine. It was Bryce. The sound of his voice, of the simple words, "How are you? Call me," sent a shiver of pleasure running under her skin.

So. The sight of the half-naked guy down the street didn't tempt her anymore, but she had shivers to spare if Bryce Armstrong was calling.

Was this good news?

She couldn't decide. She didn't *want* to decide. She didn't want to do anything much. Maybe brew a pot of tea and watch the news, broil a lamb chop, turn in early...

Somehow, she never got around to calling Bryce back.

The week dragged by. She went to her patient's funeral on Thursday. The little chapel was packed. She listened to the minister talking about fearing no evil and the hope of the righteous and the innocent in death and didn't feel particularly comforted.

That night, she lay in her bed with her hand on the firm mound of her stomach and cried.

Friday, her mother didn't turn away when Rachel entered the room. Ellen Stockham even managed a quivery smile. Rachel sat with her for a while, holding her thin hand.

Before she left, she spoke with her mother's doctor. She learned that if her mother continued to improve, she would be discharged in a week or so. The doctor said what her mother's doctors always said. "You're a nurse, Rachel. You have to know that, with proper medication, almost all bipolar patients can lead normal, productive lives. But then, the patient must be willing to stick with the course of treatment."

Rachel nodded and promised—as she always promised—that she would encourage her mother to take her meds.

Bryce called again that night. She was there when the phone rang. She listened in as he left his message. "Rachel. Just trying again. Call me back when you get a moment." His voice was flat. She almost picked up before he disconnected.

But she didn't.

Okay, she felt a little like a jerk. But her life was too complicated as it was. She just didn't have it in her to add a man to the mix. Especially not a guy like Bryce, who would probably get tired of her in no time flat. She just couldn't deal with it, with anything casual—or with letting herself start to feel too much for him and then having him walk away.

She wasn't regretting their one night or anything. She could never regret something so beautiful.

But if there was going to be more than one night, well, she wanted it all: a guy who would love her *and* her baby. A guy who could put up with her mother's scary, often overwhelming emotional disorder. A guy who was going to *be* there, just like in the marriage vows: For better or for worse.

It was a lot to ask of a man. And especially of a man like Bryce, who had money to burn and a high-powered job and status and good looks and women falling all over him.

Really, that was the biggest fantasy, now wasn't it? That of all the gorgeous, willing, glamorous women he might have had, Bryce Armstrong had somehow decided he wanted *her*.

Only in her dreams.

So she didn't pick up—and she never called him back.

Lily asked about him three days later, on Monday night, during a phone conversation when they were *supposed* to be talking about Jenna's upcoming shower.

"So, what happened with the sexy CEO?" Lily asked—way too casually, Rachel thought. "You haven't mentioned him in days."

Rachel tried to be casual right back. "Oh, he called a couple of times," she said airily. "But you know how it is. I don't really think he's the guy for me."

"Why not?"

So okay. The airy approach wasn't working. Rachel moved on to huffing a little. "Well. Isn't it obvious?"

"No, not particularly."

So she let out a big sigh and ran down the list: the money, the Armstrong name, all the women...

Lily said, "Give a rich, powerful, hunk of a guy a chance, why don't you? And hey, so what if there have been lots of women, as long as he's ready to settle down now?"

"Lily, I only spent that one night with him. There was absolutely no talk of settling down."

"So maybe you should bring it up to him."

"Oh, I don't even imagine Bryce Armstrong is going to be interested in settling down."

"See. There. That's a conclusion and you're totally jumping to it. You don't know what the man's interested in. You don't know what he's willing to do. Because you haven't asked him."

"Well, but, I mean, he's not going to appreciate—"

"How do you know what he'll appreciate? Have you asked?"

Rachel huffed out another exasperated breath. "Why is it married people suddenly think they know it all when it comes to how to relate to a guy?" Lily, not only a true friend, but a smart one, knew when to say nothing. And that's what she did. Finally, Rachel grumbled, "Well, okay. Fine. Just what do you want me to do?"

"Oh, something simple. Maybe give the guy a chance?"

"What do you mean, give him a chance? We weren't...well, you know. It wasn't anything...serious, between us."

"Maybe it wasn't. And just maybe that's because you wouldn't let it be."

"Why does this all have to be my fault? You're my friend. Why can't you just do the usual and be blindly loyal?"

"This isn't about whose fault it is. And I *am* loyal. But sorry, I'm not blind."

There was a smudge on the counter. Rachel got the sponge and scrubbed at it—hard. "Well. He probably won't even call again."

"So call *him*."

Rachel tossed the sponge into the sink. "I think we should get back to the subject of Jenna's baby shower."

But Rachel did take her friend's urgings to heart. She called him—or at least, she *started* to call him. Repeatedly. She would pick up the phone and begin dialing. Sometimes she'd even dial his whole number. But she could never bring herself to stay on the line until it actually rang.

On Thursday night, six days since the last time he'd called and she hadn't answered, she *started* to call him again. But—surprise, surprise—she lost her nerve.

Thoroughly disgusted with herself, she went ahead and called Sears to order the curtains that she and her mother had picked out from the catalog that day. She disconnected the call—and the phone instantly rang again.

Without stopping to think that it might be the very man she didn't have the courage to call, she hit the talk button. "Hello?"

"Rachel," Bryce said. "At last."

CHAPTER SEVEN

RACHEL CLUTCHED THE phone in a death grip. It was the only way she could keep herself from hanging up out of sheer nervous tension.

"Rachel. Are you there?"

"I...uh..."

"Rachel, please don't hang up."

She cleared her throat. "No. No, I won't. I'm here. I really am."

"You sound so strange. What's the matter? Is it the baby?"

"No. She's fine."

"Your mother, then?"

Her pulse was slowing a little, the feeling of blind panic passing. "She's better. She's, um, going home in a few days. I was just ordering her some curtains, as a matter of fact."

"Curtains..." He sounded puzzled.

Rachel told him the part she'd left out before. "She took a pair of scissors and really went after every curtain in her apartment. Sliced them to shreds. They were unsalvageable, so we're getting some new ones."

For a moment, there was silence. Then he asked hopefully, "But she *is* better?"

"Yeah. She is. And whether she stays better is a lot about the choices she makes. I can go on and on to her about sticking with her medication, taking care of herself, but if she won't do it..."

"Rachel."

"Yeah?"

"There are just some things you can't control."

"Tell me about it. And the good news is she does have decent insurance, which these days, is a miracle in itself. When she needs the care, she *can* get it."

There was a pause. Then he asked, "And what about you?" His voice was so soft. Can you wrap the sound of a man's voice around yourself?

Rachel longed to do just that. "Oh, I'm..." The words trailed off. She swallowed convulsively and forced herself to say what needed saying. "I'm so sorry I never called. It's just been...a bad time. And I don't really...well, I just didn't expect..."

"What? Tell me. You didn't expect..."

"You. I didn't expect *you*. You're just so..." Words failed her. They seemed to keep doing that. But he waited so patiently until she finally said, "I told myself it was just that one beautiful night. I was...ready for that. I could...deal with that..."

"Rachel?"

"Umm?"

"That one night?"

"Yeah?"

"It *was* beautiful."

"Oh. Oh, yes. But..." Again, he waited until she found the words. "I, well, I told myself you couldn't possibly want more than that and at the same time, deep down I've been thinking that maybe you do. And, well, I don't seem to know how to handle that...how to just...let it happen."

"I know," he said. And she realized she believed him, believed that he accepted her just as she was—imperfect and confused at times, and way too much on her guard. "And Rachel?" She made a small, questioning noise. It was the best she could do with her throat closing up and tears pushing behind her eyes. He said, "I do want more. A lot more."

"Oh," she whispered, clutching the phone so hard she was vaguely surprised it didn't shatter in her hands. "Oh, God..."

"Rachel, let me come over. I won't stay long. I just need to see you."

She glanced from her aging refrigerator to the cracked tile on the counter by the coffeepot—and then up at that faint watermark on the ceiling where the roof had leaked last spring. She'd gotten the leak patched, but never quite found the time to repaint the kitchen.

A small, tight laugh escaped her. "Bryce. I have to warn you. It's hardly Portland Heights around here. No gourmet stove, you know? And the furniture in my living room cries out for reupholstering."

"I'm not coming to see the furniture. I want to see *you*."

"You...sound so sure."

"I *am* sure."

"But...well, you've been in *People* magazine. You're one of *the* Armstrongs. Gorgeous women fall all over you."

"There's only one gorgeous woman who interests me. I mean it, Rachel. Only one woman. And that woman is you. Give me your address."

She did—really fast, before her nerve got a chance to desert her again.

"I'm on my way."

They sat on her slightly threadbare sofa and kicked off their shoes and she told him about her twelve-year-old patient, the one who hadn't made it, about how death was hardest to take when they were so young, when there should be a future shining out in front of them—middle school and football and science projects and that first special girl...

Bryce listened as she poured it all out. When her voice trailed off, he held out his arms. She went into them eagerly, with a long, grateful sigh.

He brushed a kiss against her hair and didn't say anything— not that he was sorry, not what she should do, not how he was going to somehow make everything right.

She hugged him close and listened to the steady beat of his heart and then whispered, "Thanks."

He kissed her hair again. "For what?"

"For just listening and holding me. For not offering one single word of advice."

He chuckled, the sound a low, lovely rumble against her ear. "I see you've noticed I'm a man."

She grinned against his chest. "Hard to miss." He hugged her closer. "And men give advice."

He tipped her chin up with a finger. "I think I read somewhere that it's genetically programmed."

She stared into those wonderful, warm blue eyes. "But you didn't give me any advice just now."

"I didn't think you needed any. Your patient died. It's a hard thing to deal with, but you're doing it. I can't see any quick fix. If I could, I promise you, I'd be laying it on you." She sat up straight again. He let her go with obvious reluctance.

"As usual, I've been yammering on and on."

"Fine with me."

"So nice of you to say that. And obviously, I could yammer away at you all night—but if I did, I wouldn't learn anything I didn't already know. And there's so much you haven't told me..."

"Such as?"

"Well, your life story, for starters."

"Oh, that." His expression was deadpan, but there was no mistaking the smile in his voice.

"Please. I want to hear it all."

He chuckled. "You say that now."

"Honestly. I do want to know about you. You can start with your childhood..."

"Got a week?"

"Quit stalling."

"Okay, okay. My childhood was..." He thought for a moment, then finished, "Busy."

It seemed an odd word to choose. "You were a busy little kid?"

"I was an Armstrong. I was brought up to excel. There was always pressure to do well—at sports and especially in my studies. I look back on being a kid and what I remember is that I never really felt like one. There was too much I had to do and not enough time to do it in. It was understood from the first that I'd take over the business from my grandfather someday."

"But what about your dad? Wasn't he the next in line?"

"My dad had no interest in working. Didn't have the drive for it, he'd always say. It was one of the few things he and my grandfather were in complete agreement on. My grandfather didn't believe my dad had it in him to run a major corporation and my dad was perfectly willing to live off the income from his massive trust and support my grandfather in his dream to make *me* the next head of the company."

"And where was your mother in all this?"

"Good question. One I'm still not sure I have the answer to. I remember my mother as beautiful and unavailable. Like some rare bird or an exotic butterfly. She seemed to be always flitting into rooms and then flitting out again. If I tried to get near her, she'd just...fly away."

"You didn't feel close to her?"

"*Close* is not a word I would use in conjunction with either of my parents. They weren't close to their children. And they never seemed particularly close to each other. They made their perpetual mutual estrangement official when I was fifteen."

"Meaning they divorced?"

He nodded. "My mother promptly moved to Tuscany to be with some Italian guy she'd met at a wine-tasting. My father moved to L.A. She's been married twice since and he's been married three times."

"What about you? And Chelsea? Did you go with one of them?"

"No. We stayed here—under the care of our grandparents. I lived with them when I wasn't at school. Chelsea had special needs. She was at school most of the time."

"Special needs..."

"My sister's developmentally disabled." He grinned when he saw her surprise. "Your mouth's hanging open, Rachel—and yes, as ideal as the life of an Armstrong might seem to the casual observer, there has been a challenge or two."

"Chelsea..." She said the name and then didn't know what to say next.

But Bryce did. "She's a fighter, my sister. She's as brave and strong as they come. She's fortunate that she's what they call 'high-functioning.' She does have the capacity to live on her own, after painstaking training in the basic stuff: personal care, cooking and all the other daily living skills. Thanks to the family money, she's always had the best care and the best teachers, people who not only knew how to help her become more self-sufficient, but also gave her the love, support and encouragement our parents never provided."

"And...now she's married?"

"That's right. His name is Thad Grover. He's also DD and high-functioning. They both went to the same special-needs school. Their marriage caused a major uproar in the family—at least with the grandparents. Our parents weren't here and didn't care."

"Oh, Bryce..."

But he wasn't looking the least upset. "And when I say uproar, I mean *strictly* within the family, of course. Nothing was allowed to leak to the press. My grandmother likes to think of herself as open-minded, but she's way old-school. She saw Chelsea as someone to be hidden away. God forbid my little sister should want a real life."

"That's terrible."

Bryce didn't seem to think so. "You don't know Chelsea. She never gives up. She finally broke even our grandmother down. And now, since Ariel was born..."

Rachel saw his point. "A great-grandchild. What grandmother could resist?"

"Exactly. Especially a great-grandchild like Ariel. I swear to you Rachel, she is so special."

"Spoken like a doting uncle."

"I don't deny it," he said and she turned to lean back against him, hoisting her feet up onto the couch in front of her. He wrapped his arms around her and kissed the top of her head. "Anyway, so now, both the grandparents are busy rewriting history. To hear them tell it these days, it was their idea that Chelsea and Thad should get married in the first place."

"So. It all...worked out, then?"

"Yeah. Well, as long as you don't count my parents. They're both still more or less wandering in the wilderness. Last I heard, my dad checked himself into rehab. Again. And my mother's got a new boyfriend, though there's no rumor of a wedding. Yet."

He felt so warm and solid at her back. Really, he was a great guy for leaning on. He'd laid one arm along the top of the couch. The other he rested, lightly, on the swell of her stomach. "There," he said and felt for her hand so he could press it against the right spot. "Feel that..."

She smiled her secret mother's smile and didn't remind him that the movements were happening inside her and of course she felt them—whether she had her hand at the spot or not. "Umm..."

He brushed his lips over her ear. "It's getting late...and I said I wouldn't stay too long."

With a happy sigh, she snuggled in closer. "Let's sit right here, forever."

He smoothed her hair aside and kissed the pulse at her temple. "Don't you have to work tomorrow?"

"Yeah, so?"

"You need your sleep."

She sighed again. "You may have a point."

He nuzzled her hair. "But how about tomorrow evening?"

"Hmm. I could be available...to the right guy."

"It's only fair to warn you, I'm talking about a big step here. A major step. A very scary step..."

Her mouth felt dry enough that she had to swallow. And then she elbowed him in the ribs.

"Hey! Watch it." He chuckled in her ear.

"Stop teasing. What are you getting at?"

"Dinner with the family...and relax. I only mean Chelsea and Thad and Ariel. My grandparents are out of town until next week. You can meet them then."

"Dinner with the family?" she gulped again. "Already?"

He whispered in her ear, "Please don't start talking about how we should take things slow..."

"But I...well, isn't this all just happening really fast?"

"And didn't I tell you that first day that fast was fine with me?"

"Yeah, but—"

"And we can stop by for a quick visit with your mom on the way."

"My mom? But—"

"Come on." He guided her to sit up and reached for his shoes. "Walk me to the door."

She went out on her tiny square of porch with him and he pulled her close for one last kiss. She concentrated on the strength in his arms around her, on the sweetness of his mouth playing over hers.

"Tomorrow," he said, as he turned to go. "Six o'clock. Be ready."

CHAPTER EIGHT

RACHEL SLEPT POORLY. Second thoughts kept her awake.

Bryce said he was just fine with things happening fast. Good for him.

She wasn't fine with it. She simply didn't have his guts, his go-for-it attitude—at least not when it came to giving her heart.

Her heart was a tender thing, thank you. And she just wasn't up for having it broken again.

Oh, and what about the baby? Could he really be ready for that?

As she lay there, curled around her burgeoning stomach, staring at the shadowed wall a few feet from the bed, she found herself thinking of her father, remembering the times he was supposed to come for her and didn't show up. How she'd sit on the creaky front porch step and wait.

And wait some more…

Until the door behind her would open and her mother, standing inside the screen, would coax, "Come in now, Rachel. Just come on inside."

And Rachel would argue, "But I can't. I have to be here when he gets here."

The screen door would screech open and her mother would step outside. Arms wrapped tight around her middle, she'd loom over Rachel, scowling down. "If he was coming, he'd be here by now." Her mother's lips were always a thin, pressed-together line at those times, as if she was barely holding in a lot of very mean words.

"Mommy, I can't go in. What if he comes and sees I'm not here and thinks I didn't wait?"

"Rachel. For crying out loud. If he was coming, he'd have been here three hours ago. He's *not* coming for you. Get that through your thick little head..."

Rachel squirmed in the bed, flipped to her other side, then flopped right back to where she'd started.

Oh, she was just a classic case, wasn't she? A manic-depressive mother and an absentee father had made her into someone who was really bad at giving her trust.

And now she was a grown-up. Thirty-four years old. Wasn't it about time she stopped living by the emotional limitations so painfully acquired in her childhood?

She thought back on the two serious relationships she'd had—one with a guy she'd met at a party while she was still in nursing school, the other, more recently, with a pharmaceuticals salesman. Both men had broken up with her in the end. But if she were honest, she'd have to admit that she'd never let either of those guys get too close. Danny Davison, the salesman, had even bought her a ring and asked her to marry him. She'd put him off, said she needed more time....

Danny had grown tired of waiting. And so had Tate Connor, the guy she'd dated while she was in nursing school. In both cases, she'd blamed the men for leaving her.

But now, lying here wide awake in the middle of the night, terrified to go ahead and take a chance on Bryce, she was seeing things in a different light.

She'd made Danny and Tate *wait*, hadn't she? Just like her dad had made *her* wait all those years before.

And now, here she was, three months away from having a daughter of her own. What lessons—consciously or otherwise—would she teach her child? Would her little girl grow up as afraid of trusting a man as she seemed to be?

Rachel pressed a hand protectively over her belly and the new life inside her. "I'm going to do better," she whispered to her little one. "I'm going to...put myself out there, put my heart on the line. Sweetheart, I want to be able to show you what love really is. I want to be ready, to be the best mom I can be."

At five-thirty the next afternoon, Rachel was all dressed up in a heather-gray twinset and black A-line skirt, ready to go to dinner at Chelsea and Thad's—following a delightful detour to the psychiatric ward, of course. She paced back and forth in the living room for a few minutes, ordering those old demons to get out of her head when they kept trying to whisper in her ear, *He's not coming.*

After ten minutes or so of walking back and forth and fighting off her ingrained fears, she decided she couldn't stay in that room one minute longer. She grabbed her purse and went out the door.

She sat on the step, just as she had done so long ago, when she waited for her father, who never came. It seemed appropriate, somehow, to defy all her own inner terrors so boldly.

Appropriate, and awful. Her heart pounded as if she'd run a long race. And her palms were sweating. And those old demons in her head?

They seemed to be chanting in glee: He's not coming, not coming, not coming...

She wanted to leap up and run back inside, lock the door, shut the curtains, turn off all the lights. She wanted, above all, *not* to be waiting if he didn't show up. But somehow she made herself sit there, made herself take slow, even breaths.

And silently, she talked back to those demons in her head: He *is* coming. I can trust him. He *wants* to be with me...and with my baby.

By the time Bryce's Mercedes eased up to the curb—two minutes early—she was sweating up her twinset and trembling a little, but she was still sitting right there on the step.

She rose on shaky legs and started down the walk as he got out and came around the front of the car.

They met on the sidewalk.

Frowning, he scanned her face. "You're white as a sheet. What's happened?"

She let out a tight laugh. "Oh, nothing. I was just sitting on the step. I was just...waiting..."

He touched her face. "You're sweating."

"Yeah..." She swayed against him and his strong arms were waiting to pull her close.

"You're shaking. Are you sick?" He held her so gently, so cherishingly, stroking her hair, rubbing her back.

She laid her head against his shoulder, breathed in the heavenly scent of him. "I'm okay. I'll be okay..."

He lifted her chin and made her look at him. "You're sure?"

She nodded. "Really. I'm okay." She stepped out of the shelter of his arms and pulled her shoulders back. "I have...some things to tell you. Later. But for now, let's go. Let's get this done."

His silky brows were still drawn together. "You're nervous? About my meeting your mom? About dinner at Chelsea's?"

"Right on both counts. Now, let's go."

CHAPTER NINE

HER MOTHER WAS sitting in the chair by one of the room's two narrow windows when Rachel led Bryce in. It was a double room, a drawn curtain down the center of it, masking off a second window and the other bed on the far side.

"Rachel." Her mother's smile was genuine. Then the big dark eyes found the man who filled up the doorway. Her thin hand went to her uncombed hair and fluttered quickly down to her lap. "I...wasn't expecting company..."

Rachel reached behind her, felt for Bryce's hand. It was right there, his fingers automatically slipping between hers, sending a message of warmth and support. He moved forward to stand beside her. "Mom. It's okay. We won't stay long. I just... I want you to meet Bryce Armstrong."

Her mother stared at him for a moment, her expression unsure. And then her smile returned. "Well. Hello, Bryce. I'm Ellen. So nice to meet a friend of my daughter's."

"Hello, Ellen."

So, okay. They'd gotten through the introductions. Bryce was smiling. Her mother was smiling.

What next?

Sit, she thought. They should sit down for a minute or two. She pulled her hand from Bryce's—well, yanked it free, really. "Uh. Chairs. We need—"

"Right here." He'd already picked up the one by the door. He carried it over and set it down next to her mother.

There wasn't another one. "I'll ask the orderly." Rachel started for the hallway.

"Wait," said her mother. "Linda?" she called. "May we use your chair?"

"Oh, all right," a voice from behind the curtain grumbled.

At Rachel's questioning glance, her mother mouthed, "Suicide attempt" with a philosophical shrug. Then, in a whisper, "They put her in here this morning." And finally, at full volume, "Thanks, Linda!"

"Yeah, whatever," Linda called back grudgingly.

Bryce went behind the curtain. She heard his words of polite greeting.

Linda mumbled something and Bryce emerged with another chair. They sat. Her mother looked from Rachel to Bryce and back again. Rachel slid a glance at Bryce. He looked so at ease, so completely relaxed. How did he do it?

Her mom cleared her throat. "So, this is something...special going on here?"

As Rachel agonized over her answer, Bryce said, "Yes, it is." He said it so simply, without the slightest hesitation. Rachel wanted to grab him and hug him—and never let go.

Her mother's smile widened. "Well." Ellen shot a pointed glance at Rachel's round stomach. "How nice..." She'd made no secret of the fact that she thought Rachel should have found a husband first and *then* started thinking about having a baby. It was an attitude that Rachel had found supremely irritating. After all, when you got right down to it, a fat lot of good it had done her mother to find a husband first.

Bryce asked how her mother was doing and Ellen launched into a blow-by-blow of her most recent stay at Portland General's psychiatric ward: which nurses were angels, which ones she couldn't stand. How the food here was pretty good. She especially enjoyed the rice pudding, which she could get on Tuesdays and Fridays. And she was making a point to take *all* her medications. And she *was* doing better. She sent Rachel a defiant look.

Oh, yes.

Better every day...

Every time Rachel dared to hope she might be winding down, Bryce would ask another question and off she'd go again.

Rachel almost interrupted more than once to say they ought to get going. But clearly, Bryce could take care of himself. If he'd had enough of her mother's never-ending answers, he could stop asking questions.

She watched her mother chattering away about the minutia of her days and a certain tenderness welled up inside her. Tenderness and gratitude.

Ellen Stockham might not have been the best mother in the world, but she *had* always been there, she'd stuck with it. As poorly suited as her illness had made her for mothering, she'd never walked away from the job.

There was much Rachel would have to learn for herself about raising a child. But when it came to loyalty and commitment and sticking around...

Thanks to her mother, she had those qualities.

When they got up to go, Bryce bent to kiss her mother's dry cheek. "I'll see you again, Ellen. Soon."

Her mother beamed up at him. "That would be so nice..."

Chelsea and Thad and Ariel lived in a three-bedroom cottage nestled in the oaks on Bryce's property.

"This way they have their privacy," he explained. "And I'm right here if they need me. There's a driver to take them wherever they need to go. And Mrs. Davenbrook, who's worked for our family for over thirty years, is devoted to Chelsea. She looks in on her several times a day."

Bryce rang the bell. When the door flew back, a tall, stunning blonde in a sweet-looking floral-print dress stood on the other side. Childlike pleasure flooded her angel's face. "Bryce! You're here!"

He held out his arms and his sister, long, silky hair flying, flung herself into them. She clasped her slim hands around his waist, squeezing hard. "Hug, hug," she crowed and laughed in delight.

Behind her, a man stood holding a wooden bowl full of pretzels. He was six or seven inches shorter than Chelsea, with brown hair and dark eyes and a slightly befuddled expression. "Hello, Bryce," he said shyly and then he looked at Rachel. "Hello," he said carefully, as if not quite sure of the word.

"Hello," Rachel replied.

Bryce managed to pry his sister's hugging hands away and made the introductions.

"Rachel!" Chelsea repeated when Bryce said her name. "Hello!" She reached right out and patted Rachel's tummy. "A baby. How nice."

"Sleeping," Chelsea announced when Bryce asked about his niece. "But you can see her..."

So they all tiptoed into the nursery and stood over the crib and Chelsea pantomimed "Shh..." with great enthusiasm as they admired the dreaming darling in the pink fleece footie pajamas.

They trooped back out into the living room. "Please have a pretzel," offered Thad solemnly.

So they sat and munched a few pretzels and chatted for a while. Rachel explained that she was a nurse and Thad spoke of his own job. He worked full-time at a local Burger King.

"He is the best worker there," Chelsea piped up proudly and patted her husband's leg. "And sometimes he brings me home a Whopper."

Eventually they moved into the kitchen for the meat loaf and mashed potatoes Chelsea had prepared.

"But Charles helped," Thad announced. Charles, Rachel remembered, was Bryce's cook.

Chelsea took that extra few seconds both she and her husband seemed to require to digest whatever was said to them and then nodded. "Charles is always helping. I *like* Charles."

Thad considered. "Me, too," he said.

Chelsea turned to Rachel. "And I like *you*." She beamed and Rachel's heart just went to mush. "You can come see us any time. You and your baby, too, when your baby comes. Ariel will like that. She will want to have friends."

Rachel promised she would come again and a little later,

when Thad and Chelsea walked them to the door, Chelsea made the offer a second time. "Please come back. Come back soon."

"I will. I promise..."

Rachel and Bryce walked out into the brisk early-May evening, Thad and Chelsea moving into the open doorway behind them. Bryce took Rachel's hand and they started down the walk to the garages behind the main house.

"Goodbye, come again!" Chelsea called from behind them. Rachel glanced back and saw Bryce's sister and her husband standing in the doorway, the flood of light from inside pouring out around them.

"I will!" Rachel called back.

At Rachel's house, Bryce came around and opened the car door for her. He took her hand to help her out. The cracked concrete walkway was too narrow for them to approach the house side-by-side, but she held tightly to his hand anyway, leading him along.

Inside, she turned on the lamps and they sat on the sofa, shucking out of their shoes, shifting around so they were facing each other.

"You were so great with my mother," she said. "Thank you. And your sister and Thad...they're really happy together, aren't they?"

He nodded. "They have what matters most. In fact, I'd say the two of them showed me what life—and love—could be."

"I can see how they could do that."

He looked so solemn suddenly, as solemn as Thad. "I've... been with a lot of women, Rachel."

She felt her mouth twisting wryly. "So I've heard."

Now he looked earnest. He leaned in a little closer. "But in the last couple of years, I *have* been seriously looking for the *right* woman. The one who'd not only have me wanting to make passionate, wild love to her—but the one I'd want to talk with for hours, the one I'd want to hold so close while we're sleeping. The one who, when the day's over, I wouldn't be able to wait to come home to."

"Tall order," she whispered.

"That day," he said. "That first day, that first moment I saw you, all dewy-eyed over that little sweater with the ribbons all over it, a voice in my head said, There. That's the one. Too damn bad she's already taken... I almost turned and walked away. Fast. But then I couldn't stop myself from getting you talking, couldn't fight the need to hear your voice. And when you looked up at me with those big brown eyes...*pow*. I was done for. I was gone for good. And then you told me that you *weren't* taken. From that moment on, my fate was sealed..."

Rachel knew she should say something. But what do you say when a guy you almost didn't dare dream of tells you he knew the moment he saw you that you were the woman for him? There were no words, just a warm pressure at the back of her throat, a lifting feeling in her chest.

He asked, so gently, "What happened to you, tonight, before I picked you up? Can you tell me now?"

She nodded.

He waited, then gave her his crooked grin. "Well?"

Oh, where to start? She didn't know how to explain. But then she just opened her mouth and said, "When I was little..." and it was okay. She was talking about it, all of it, from the father who abandoned her to the men she had kept waiting who'd finally given up and left her, too. She said, "So I was making myself sit on the porch and wait for you. I was...proving to myself that I could trust you, that you would come through, you wouldn't let me down."

"I won't let you down, Rachel. I swear to you. I'll be here, for you and the baby. If you'll have me."

"Oh," she said, her heart light as air. "Oh, yes. I'll have you. I..." Her nerve kind of wavered. She cleared her throat. "But what about your grandparents? How are they going to react when you tell them you're marrying an ordinary, everyday woman who's six months pregnant by a man she's never met?"

"They'll be shocked. At first. And then they'll get to know you and everything will work out fine."

"I don't know..."

"Rachel. They *will* accept you. And if they were really stupid and didn't, well, it would be their loss—but it's not going to happen that way. Don't forget, in the end, they accepted Thad."

She was shaking her head. "You're a brave, brave man."

"I'm a smart man. I know what I want. And Rachel, what I want is you. And your daughter. I want her to be *my* daughter, too. And I want to be your husband for the rest of our lives." He leaned closer, whispered, "I love you...and do not start telling me how this is so sudden."

"Well, but it—"

He put a finger to her lips. "There you go again."

"Oh, Bryce..."

"Sudden," he whispered, "is fine with me. Sudden is just great."

"Oh, Bryce..."

"I love you," he said again, the words so simple, direct. Honest.

With a glad cry, she reached for him. His arms were there to take her in. "Oh, Bryce..."

"I love you," he said one more time.

And she bravely whispered, "I...love you, too," just as his lips met hers.

* * * * *

Keep reading for an excerpt of
Dead Ringer
by B.J. Daniels.
Find it in the
Montana Legacy anthology,
out now!

Chapter One

Abby Pierce opened her eyes and quickly closed them against the bright sunlight. She hurt all over. As she tried to sit up, a hand gently pushed on her shoulder to keep her flat on the bed.

"Don't sit up too fast," her husband said. "You're okay. You're in the hospital. You took a nasty fall."

Fall? Hospital? Her mouth felt dry as dust. She licked her lips. "Can you close the drapes?"

"Sure," Wade said and hurried over to the window.

She listened as he drew the drapes together and felt the room darken before she opened her eyes all the way.

The first thing she saw was her husband silhouetted against the curtains. He was a big imposing man with a boyish face and a blond crew cut. He was wearing his sheriff's deputy uniform, she noted as he moved back to the bed to take her hand.

She'd known Wade for years. She'd married him three years ago. That was why when she saw the sheepish look in his brown eyes, she knew at once that he was hiding something.

Abby frowned. "What was I doing that I fell?"

"You don't remember?" He cleared his throat, shifting on his feet. "You asked me to bring up some canning jars from the garage? I'm so sorry I didn't. If I had you wouldn't have been on that ladder..." He looked at her as if expecting... Expecting what?

"Canning jars?" she repeated and touched her bandaged temple. "I hit my head?"

He nodded, and taking her hand, he squeezed it a little too hard. "I'm so sorry, Abby." He sounded close to tears.

"It's not your fault," she said automatically, but couldn't help but wonder if there was more to the story. There often was with Wade and his family. She frowned, trying to understand why she would have wanted canning jars and saying as much.

"You said something about putting up peach jam."

"Really? I wonder where I planned to get peaches this time of year."

He said nothing, avoiding her gaze. All the other times she'd seen him like this it had been after he'd hurt her. It had started a year into their marriage and begun with angry accusations that led to him grabbing her, shaking her, pushing her and even slapping her.

Each time he'd stopped before it had gone too far. Each time he'd been horrified by what he'd done. He'd cried in her arms, begging her to forgive him, telling her that he couldn't live without her, saying he would kill himself if she ever left him. And then promising he'd never do it again.

She touched her bandaged head with her free hand. The movement brought a groan out of her as she realized her ribs were either bruised or maybe even broken. Looking down, she saw the bruises on her wrists and knew he was lying. Had he pushed her this time?

"Why can't I remember what happened?" she asked.

"You can't remember *anything*?" He sounded hopeful, fueling her worst fears that one of these days he would go too far and kill her. Wasn't that what her former boyfriend kept telling her? She pushed the thought of Ledger McGraw away as she often had to do. He didn't understand that she'd promised to love, honor and obey when she'd married Wade—even through the rough spots. And this she feared was one of them.

At the sound of someone entering the room, they both turned to see the doctor come in.

"How are we doing?" he asked as he moved to the foot of her bed to look at her chart. He glanced at Wade, then quickly looked away. Wade let go of her hand and moved to the window to part the drapes and peer out.

Abby closed her eyes at the shaft of sunlight he let in. "My head hurts," she told the doctor.

"I would imagine it does. When your husband brought you in, you were in and out of consciousness."

Wade had brought her in? He didn't call an ambulance?

"Also I can't seem to remember what happened," she added and, out of the corner of her eye, saw her husband glance back at her.

The doctor nodded. "Very common in your type of head injury."

"Will she get her memory back?" Wade asked from the window, sounding worried that she would.

"Possibly. Often not. I'm going to prescribe something for your headache. Your ribs are badly bruised and you have some other abrasions. I'd like to keep you overnight."

Dead Ringer

"Is that really necessary?" Wade asked, letting the drapes drop back into place.

"With a concussion, it's best," the doctor said without looking at him. "Don't worry. We'll take good care of her."

"We can talk about it," Wade said. "But I think she'd be more comfortable in her own home. Isn't that right, Abby?"

"On this, I think I know best," the doctor interrupted.

But she could see that Wade *was* worried. He apparently wanted to get her out of here and quickly. What was he worried about? That she would remember what happened?

If only she could. Unfortunately, the harder she tried, the more she couldn't. The past twenty-four hours were blank, leaving her with the terrifying feeling that her life depended on her remembering.

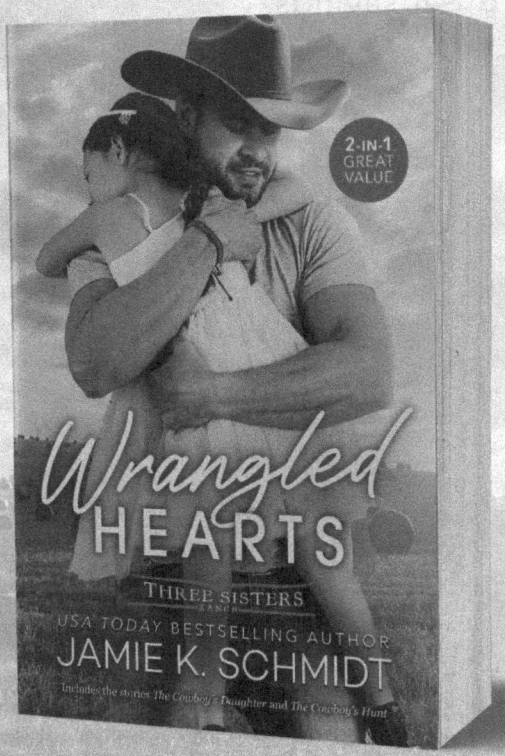

Subscribe and fall in love with a Mills & Boon series today!

You'll be among the first to read stories delivered to your door monthly and enjoy great savings.

MILLS & BOON SUBSCRIPTIONS

HOW TO JOIN

1

Visit our website
millsandboon.
com.au/pages/
print-subscriptions

2

Select your favourite series
Choose how many books. We offer monthly as well as pre-paid payment options.

3

Sit back and relax
Your books will be delivered directly to your door.

MILLS & BOON

JOIN US

Sign up to our newsletter to stay up to date with...

- Exclusive member discount codes
- Competitions
- New release book information
- All the latest news on your favourite authors

Plus...
get $10 off your first order.
What's not to love?

Sign up at **millsandboon.com.au/newsletter**

@millsandboonaustralia   @millsandboonaus